Musique Fantastique

A Survey of Film Music in the Fantastic Cinema

By
RANDALL D. LARSON

The Scarecrow Press, Inc.
Metuchen, N.J., & London 1985

Frontispiece by Allen Koszowski

Library of Congress Cataloging in Publication Data

Larson, Randall D., 1954–
  Musique fantastique.

  Includes index.
  1. Moving-picture music--History and criticism.
I. Title.
ML2075.L35 1985   782.8'5   84-13954
ISBN 0-8108-1728-4

<u>For My Parents</u>

To my mother, who provided continual support
for my pursuits in fields macabre and fantastic in
spite of her own distaste for the subject.

And especially, now, to the memory of my father, who first guided me to pen and paper, typewriter and Ko Rec Type, imagination and creativity.

Their support and encouragement through the
completion of this book has been invaluable and
unrepayable.

CONTENTS

ACKNOWLEDGEMENTS

The author wishes to acknowledge with thanks the invaluable assistance rendered over the years and in many ways by the following individuals:

Albert K. Bender/Max Steiner Music Society
Ronald L. Bohn
Monica Ciafardini/Columbia Pictures Music
Frederick S. Clarke/Cinefantastique
Jim Doherty
Gary D. Dorst
Douglass Fake
Ernest D. Farino
Jordon R. Fox
Jeffrey S. Frentzen
Ed Godziszewski
G. Roger Hammonds
David Hirsch
Scot W. Holton/Varese Sarabande
Preston Neal Jones
Richard E. Klemensen
David L. Kraft
Dr. Jiri Levy (Czecholslovakia Film Archives)
Bill Littman
Clifford McCarty
Fred Patten
William H. Rosar
Olga Rychlikova (Mrs. Jan Rychlik)
Greg Shoemaker
Rodney L. Sims
Bernard Soll
Fred Steiner
Tony Thomas
Luc Van De Ven
Mark Verheiden
Marc Weilage
Chuck Wilson
Jim Wnoroski
Roberto Zamori

And, of course, the many composers (besides Dr. Steiner) who generously allowed me the opportunity to interview them and otherwise occupy their time during the preparation of this book. I'd also like to acknowledge the many small press journals and fanzines, in whose pages I found a wealth of material and film music coverage often neglected by mass media publications, which has proven valuable in rounding out my survey and filling in gaps about films I've missed. Some of these are listed elsewhere in this book for readers desiring more material on motion picture music.

Finally, I want to acknowledge, with thanks, permission to quote at length from the following publications:

Bazelon, Irwin, Knowing the Score: Notes on Film Music (New York: Arco Publishing, Inc., 1981). Segments quoted with permission of Arco Publishing, Inc.

Hammonds, G. Roger, Recorded Music for the Science Fiction, Fantasy and Horror Film (Quarryville, Pa.: Sound Track Album Retailers, 1983). Discography and format used with permission of G. Roger Hammonds.

Jones, Preston Neal, "The Ghost of Hans J. Salter," Cinefantastique Vol. 7 #2, 1978. Segments quoted with permission of Preston Neal Jones and Cinefantastique.

Littman, Bill, "Music for the Bride," Gore Creatures (now Midnight Marquee) #25, 1976. Segments quoted with permission of Bill Littman.

Steiner, Fred, liner notes to King Kong soundtrack recording, Entr'acte Records, 1976. Segments copyright © 1975 by Entr'acte Recording Society Inc. Used by permission of John Steven Lasher & Southern Cross Records Inc. and Fred Steiner.

Thomas, Tony, Music for the Movies (La Jolla: A. S. Barnes & Co., 1973 edition). Segments quoted with permission of Oak Tree Publications, Inc., and Tony Thomas.

Thomas, Tony, Film Score: The View from the Podium (La Jolla: A. S. Barnes & Co., 1979 edition). Segments quoted with permission of Oak Tree Publications, Inc., and Tony Thomas.

For a complete bibliography of reference sources used in this book, please refer to the footnotes adjacent to each chapter. I am indebted to many of these books for supplying valuable details to my overall research which I have found useful in addition to the direct quotes referred to in the notes.

PRELUDE
An Introduction

Music for science fiction, fantasy and horror films (collective-
ly referred to as the "fantastic cinema") has always been a particularly unique area of film scoring due to the imaginative nature of
the subject matter. Just as fantasy has allowed the minds of writers and filmmakers to flow into new and unexplored regions, so has
it allowed the imaginations of film composers to create much of the
finest music composed for motion pictures. From the exotic and wonderful musical strains that accompanied KING KONG, THE BRIDE OF
FRANKENSTEIN and THINGS TO COME in the 30's to the full-blown
symphonic romances of STAR WARS and the imaginative orchestral
textures from PLANET OF THE APES, music has always seemed to
be at its best in fantastic films.

And at its most experimental. According to veteran genre
composer, Les Baxter, horror films present fewer restrictions to a
composer than a drama, because of the orchestral colors available.
"With a horror score," Baxter said, "the melodies can go much
farther out, the notes can be extremely strange. That gives you
a lot of leeway. You can be as far-out or as weird as you want to,
musically. The orchestration and the colors have to be more unusual and that of course is a pleasure for any composer."[1] Some of
the most innovative types of film scoring have been for fantastic
films, from the eerie use of the theremin in Miklos Rozsa's SPELL-
BOUND to the unique "electronic tonalities" heard in FORBIDDEN
PLANET and on to the powerful synthesizer scores created for THE
ANDROMEDA STRAIN, HALLOWEEN and TRON.

Clearly, the use of music within fantastic films has practically emerged as a musical genre all its own, at least in the minds and
hearts of the enthusiastic fans and students of the genre--both from
a cinematic as well as a musical standpoint. While genre film music
shares the same basic approach that is present in the scores for
most other types of films--the need to support the visual and achieve
the proper cinematic effect--the role of music in fantastic films has
taken on an almost greater responsibility in such films.

Science fiction author Ray Bradbury has said of the music for
KING KONG, one of the earliest and best-loved fantasy film scores:
"If you lopped Steiner's music from the film and substituted the usu-
al early Thirties thin-skinned one drum, two flutes and four violins

1

treatment you might well end up with the comedy of the century!"[2]
Perhaps an overstatement, yet it does illustrate the importance and
intrinsic contribution of music in fantasy cinema. Besides the classic KING KONG, afficionados can imagine what films such as THE
7TH VOYAGE OF SINBAD, HORROR OF DRACULA, THE CREATURE
FROM THE BLACK LAGOON or STAR WARS might have been like
without the exceptional music scores that added so much to their impact.

Composer Bernard Herrmann once described film music as "the
connecting link between celluloid and audience, reaching out and
enveloping all into one single experience."[3]

"Music is the art that begins where words and images leave
off," composer Elmer Bernstein wrote, "music can stimulate the
greatest possible range of moods, shades and fantasies." Bernstein
adds that, unlike the written word or visual image, there is no need
to intellectualize its existence. "That its source is unseen and that
it can enter and leave at almost imperceptible levels makes music an
invaluable tool with which the skilled film composer can practice emotional seductions upon the viewer."[4]

Noted film music historian Tony Thomas has provided perhaps
the definitive analysis of what film music is all about: "Film is a
kind of discourse among its component parts ... music comes to
bear in helping to realize the meaning of the film, in stimulating
and guiding the emotional response to the visuals ... music may also prepare the emotional climate of the other film components."[5]

The purpose of film music, then, would be to complement the
visual action and aid in setting the mood of a particular sequence,
thereby merging the musical sound with the visual elements in order
to create an emotional involvement between the viewer and the characters and story presented in the film. In fantastic films, this music also serves (if done correctly) to aid that all-important suspension of disbelief necessary for the audience to accept and relate to
the fantastic worlds and incredible events presented on the screen.
As author Robert Fiedel wrote, "The prime factor in determining
the effectiveness of a fantasy is its ability, and the degree of this
ability, to suspend the disbelief of the audience in regard to the
incredibility of its subject matter. The musical score thus gains
added importance in the fantasy film because it is one of the most
powerful forces in the suspension of disbelief."[6]

Orchestrator and writer Christopher Palmer has similarly commented that "way back at the time of KING KONG in 1933, it was
realized that the giant gorilla was far more effective at striking
terror into the hearts of the audience with musical support than
without--and not only terror but other species of emotion as well."
Palmer explains how music is "able to establish a direct relationship between screen and audience in a way denied all the other

component parts of a film." He has also described the responsibility of music in fantastic films: "music as a go-between, a telegraph wire which can bring us into direct contact with the remotest
provinces of the imaginative mind."[7]

Quite often, an exceptionally effective musical score breaks
through the background and becomes memorable for its "foreground"
quality. In other words, the score is capable of standing on its
own, apart from the visual elements of the film, as a noteworthy
composition of musical art. Music is one of the few elements of a
motion picture, other than the story itself, that can actually stand
alone and make sense in both its functional (as film music) and its
artistic aspects. This is one of the most enjoyed aspects of motion
picture music, and the recent plethora of sound-track recordings
featuring music from fantastic films is notable evidence that genre
film music is equally adept at standing on its own as creative and
respectable music.

Film music, therefore, is at its best a combination of the
functional and the aesthetic. On one hand, it should sound worthwhile and appeal either pleasantly or dramatically to the ears of the
audience; undoubtedly most composers desire that their efforts ultimately be regarded as "good music" and not simply "background
business." On the other hand, film music must be functionally
manipulative to bring out specific emotions in the audience, and to
lend more force to the visual elements presented on the screen.
"Film music is utilitarian, but so are a lot of things and some of
them are quite beautiful in their own right," said composer David
Raksin, in defense of these functional aspects of film music. "A
teapot is made for a purpose, but it can also be a work of art."[8]
Again, these qualities are especially apparent within the fantastic
genre.

It is the purpose of this volume to provide an historical and
analytical survey of the music that has been written for fantastic
films, with regard to both its functional and aesthetic value, and
with particular emphasis upon the composers of this genre, including many that have been neglected or only briefly discussed in other books and journals. This work concentrates on the fantastic
film genre and in most cases represents only a portion of the creative and technical output of the composers mentioned. It should be
noted, however, that there are virtually no composers who have
written exclusively for fantastic films, much as the enthusiastic fan
of the genre would like to believe. While there are those who have
become so adept at this type of scoring that such work has far
eclipsed their other efforts in the minds of many, most composers
refrain from specializing.

Additionally, most of the composers who have scored fantastic films do not approach the genre in any uniquely special or rev-
erent way, much as enthusiastic fans would sometimes like to pre-

sume. Professional film composers approach a science fiction or horror film in the same manner they approach any other type of film, intending to provide the right kind of music that will fit the scene and contribute to the effectiveness of the film. Composer Ernest Gold, who scored a few fantastic films in the 50's, may have summed it up when he said "You don't categorize. You simply take the picture for what it is at its own level, and you try to deal with it the best way you know how."[9] Jerry Goldsmith, one of the most popular contemporary film composers with many fine genre films to his credit, agrees that there are no exclusive techniques used in these kinds of pictures. "The dramatic content dictates the nature of the music," he said.[10] From there, the composer writes what he or she feels is appropriate for that particular film. It is important to keep this in mind when studying a specialized area of film music such as this, so that the work of the composers in question is kept in the proper perspective.

What the fantastic film genre may provide in terms of uniqueness to a composer is a great freedom in the type of music he or she is able to write. As Les Baxter has said, "The composer can use any notes that he wishes without staying in the realm of something that is pretty. Also the sounds you can get ... instead of a well-balanced orchestra where everyone has to play something that sounds good, the instruments can play where they do not usually play. You have a wider range at your command."[11] Basil Poledouris, who wrote the stirring music for CONAN THE BARBARIAN, added that fantastic films "give a composer a chance to try to create environments rather than match them."[12]

And so we see that fantastic film music has elements of uniqueness, creativity and imagination that are not always found in other types of music, or at least not as profoundly. In this Survey, I will attempt to explore these elements, analyzing in detail the various kinds of music written for fantastic films, its technique, use and development. This analysis shall be more in dramatic terms than in strictly musical terms. I have made use of three primary sources in the compilation of the material that follows. First are my own comments and hopefully objective analyses of the music discussed. Secondly are quotes from other sources providing either a composer's viewpoint or the analysis of another reviewer--specific comments or clarifications which I felt were important enough to include verbatim. Finally, I've included much original interview material with nearly two dozen composers that I've gathered myself during the preparation of this book, to provide the composer's specific intentions for a given work. All this will hopefully provide an overview of music in the fantastic genre from two basic viewpoints: the intention of the composer who wrote it, and the interpretation of the listener and film critic who heard it in a cinematic context. I also hope to provide a descriptive record of what the composers have done to musically embellish the films of the fantastic.

Notes

1. Les Baxter, interview with the author, January 9, 1982

2. Ray Bradbury, liner notes for King Kong original score record album (United Artists Records, 1975)

3. Bernard Herrmann quoted by Christopher Palmer in liner notes for The Mysterious Film World of Bernard Herrmann (London Phase-4 Records, 1975)

4. Elmer Bernstein, "Whatever Happened to Good Movie Music?," High Fidelity, July 1972, p. 55.

5. Tony Thomas, Music for the Movies (La Jolla: A. S. Barnes, 1973), p. 16.

6. Robert Fiedel, "KING KONG: Music by Max Steiner," in The Girl in the Hairy Paw, Ronald Gottesman and Harry Geduld, eds. (New York: Avon Books, 1976), p. 191.

7. Christopher Palmer, loc. cit.

8. David Raksin quoted by Tony Thomas, op. cit. p. 167

9. Ernest Gold, interview with the author, December 1981

10. Jerry Goldsmith, interview with the author, July 15, 1982

11. Les Baxter, loc. cit.

12. Basil Poledouris, interview with the author, May 28, 1982

Film music, surprisingly enough, was not entirely a product of the sound era of motion pictures, though it had its most important development during that period. The roots of motion picture music are actually found in silent films.

Music, initially represented by a pit piano, was first played during the showing of silent movies in order to drown out the racket of the projectors. But once the noisy machines had been enclosed by soundproof booths, music continued to be an important accompaniment to the action on the screen.

In the early days of motion pictures, the music consisted of, for the most part, standard classical motifs, familiar enough to piano players to be incorporated into appropriate scenes on the screen. Special effects, such as gunfire and thunder, were often provided by a percussionist. Eventually, music publishers saw the opportunity to aid (and make money), so books like Motion Picture Moods were published. These were collections of simple, easy-to-play classical and popular pieces, grouped under headings like "Children at Play," "Storm at Sea," "Awakening Love," and so on.

During these years, however, musical accompaniment was mostly an arbitrary matter, left up to the piano players at the individual theaters to work out or ad lib during their own screenings. Most theaters had their own music libraries, maintained by music directors whose capabilities often determined how effectively the music was synchronized with the picture. Eventually producers began to have original scores composed and the sheet music distributed to theaters along with the prints of the film, listing instructions as to when the music was to be played. One of the first films to have a musical score composed especially for it was George Méliès' A TRIP TO THE MOON, which was also one of the earliest fantastic films, made in France in 1902. Some films, such as LITTLE TICH AND HIS BIG BOOTS, a British film released in 1900, distributed a special phonograph record of musical accompaniment.

Cecil B. DeMille's THE TEN COMMANDMENTS (1923) was distributed with sheet music containing various cues of appropriate length assembled by Paramount's musical director, Irwin Talbott. The classic German horror film, NOSFERATU (1922) was scored by

6

Hans Erdmann. The 1924 version of THE THIEF OF BAGDAD had an original score written by Mortimer Wilson. Fritz Lang's classic silent films, DIE NIBELUNGEN (1924) and METROPOLIS (1926) included original scores written by Gottfried Huppertz. Lang's earlier DER MUDE TOD (1921) was scored by Giuseppe Becce, a composer who had pioneered Italian film music and whose penchant for lyrical melodies and wordless orchestral arias served him well in the film medium. Later releases of these silent films were often accompanied by new scores, as with Konrad Elfers' jazz music for the version of METROPOLIS distributed by Janus Films in recent years. A 1984 wide-screen rerelease of this film was dubiously scored by electronic pop composer Giorgio Moroder (MIDNIGHT EXPRESS, CAT PEOPLE).

Some of the more ambitious silent films were scored for full orchestra, although only the large city theaters were capable of providing a proper performance for the screenings. Smaller theaters were given similar scores orchestrated for smaller pit ensembles or keyboard solos. Lon Chaney's THE PHANTOM OF THE OPERA (1925) was accompanied by a score composed by Gustav Hinrichs, then a 75-year-old German-born conductor who had formerly been associated with the Metropolitan Opera. Hinrichs arranged a composition for a 45-piece orchestra for the large theater play dates, adapting most of the music from Gounod's Faust, which was performed on stage during much of the film.[1] A 1929 rerelease of Chaney's PHANTOM had music and sound effects added to the original silent footage. A number of new scenes were also added to bring dialogue into the film (these mercifully removed after the initial rerelease). David Broekman, a young conductor from Holland, was hired to adapt the Gounod Faust score for this edition. He also composed new music and added themes by as many as 24 American and European composers.[2] A 1931 rerelease of Chaney's 1923 HUNCHBACK OF NOTRE DAME included a partially original score by Heinz Roemheld and Sam Perry.

In a sense, music for silent films played more of a foreground role than it did in the sound era, simply because the music was the only sound that accompanied the movie, and therefore had a much greater responsibility to serve. Such composition, however, was still at the mercy of the individual theater owners and their musical inclinations and capabilities. When the sound era blossomed in the early 30's, the filmmakers regained control of the music which then became an irrevocable part of the release print.

With the coming of sound, however, film music nearly died out. Music was rarely used as underscoring unless there was a visible source--a radio, piano, restaurant band--appearing on the screen. Producers felt that unless there was such a source shown on the screen, people would become confused and uncomfortable, wondering where the music was coming from. Whereas music in silent films had been used to eliminate the complete absence of sound, it was felt that with dialogue and sound effects in the talkies, music was no longer needed to bridge this gap. (An intriguing contrast to the prevailing source-music-only attitude was initiated in 1931 by Paramount, whose idea it was to score their films completely, from beginning to end, with music--thinking that occasional music was distracting but continuous music was not. Other studios followed suit, and many early 30's films either had no music, or full-length scores.)

Max Steiner, the reputable "Dean of Film Music," paved the way for original music in films more than any other composer, recognizing the need and opportunity for a new kind of composition. His first major original score was a test reel done for SYMPHONY OF SIX MILLION (1932) upon the suggestion of producer David O. Selznick, which was so successful that the studio executives immediately put him to work composing an entire score.

SYMPHONY OF SIX MILLION was quite a success upon its release. It proved that underscoring was an invaluable aid in contributing to the effectiveness of motion pictures, and was readily accepted by audiences despite the absence of a "source."

It took a while for original scoring to catch on, though. Many films continued to utilize classical music until the desire for, and quality of, original composition won over. Many of the early horror films of the 30's featured no music at all, except for an opening fanfare over the main titles. DRACULA (1931), for example, utilized only an arrangement of the opening scene from Tchaikovsky's Swan Lake accompanying its main titles.

Perhaps the first original music written for a major sound horror film was for Universal's FRANKENSTEIN (1931), which featured a short cue by Bernhard Kaun (conducted by David Broekman) during the opening credits. Several other early Universal horror films dabbled with music, but it wasn't until 1933 that one of the very first full-blown symphonic scores graced a fantasy film, providing it with a remarkable life and pathos, and contributing vastly to its subsequent stature as one of the most enduring and beloved of all cinematic fantasies. The film was KING KONG, and the composer was the pioneering innovator, Max Steiner.

Steiner was born in Vienna, Austria in 1888 and grew up in a musical and theatrical environment. A musical prodigy, Steiner graduated from Vienna's Imperial Academy of Music at the age of 13, after completing the four-year course in only one year. The following year he wrote a musical that played Vienna for two years, and, studying under Mahler, Steiner became a professional conductor at age 16. In 1914 he came to New York, working as an orchestrator for various musical theaters, including shows for George White, Florenz Ziegfeld and Victor Herbert. Moving to Hollywood in 1929, he began arranging and conducting music for

films. Steiner went on to score more than 300 films over the next
35 years, being nominated 15 times for an Academy Award and winning three. His magnum opus, GONE WITH THE WIND, failed to
win the Oscar in 1939, but it has since become one of the most popular film themes ever written.

Prior to KING KONG, Steiner, who was the head of RKO
Studios' music department until 1936, had worked as music director
for three RKO fantasy/horror films in 1932, all for producer David
O. Selznick; THE MONKEY'S PAW, SECRETS OF THE FRENCH PO-
LICE and THE MOST DANGEROUS GAME. This last-named thriller
was produced by Merian C. Cooper and Ernest B. Schoedsack, who
produced KING KONG the following year. It was undoubtedly the
success of this collaboration that led to Steiner's assignment on
KONG.

Surprisingly enough, when Steiner was first assigned to the
picture, he was told not to compose any original music. In a characteristic lack of insight, the studio executives were very skeptical
about the film, and doubted that the public would take to it. They
thought the giant ape looked unreal and too mechanical and didn't
want to spend any more money on it. Steiner was told to use old
tracks from previous movies. Merian C. Cooper disagreed with
them, and asked Steiner to score the film as he saw fit, and that
he would pay the cost of the orchestra himself.

Steiner went ahead, writing the score in just two weeks,
bringing in a then unheard of 80-piece orchestra and running up
a bill for 50,000 dollars. Cooper's investment was well worth it,
though, for Steiner's music not only embellished the film extraor-
dinarily well, but it became a milestone in the developing art of
film music. "Never before had the full potential of an original
musical score for a film been so brilliantly realized," wrote Robert
Fiedel. "Consequently, Steiner's KING KONG music marks the
first major aesthetic step in the development of scoring for the
sound film."[3] The authors of The Making of KING KONG agree,
"No wedding of music, sound effects and pictures has ever produced a more stunning offspring."[4]

Cooper gave Steiner a bonus for his work, saying that 25
percent of the film's effectiveness could be credited to his music.
Movie music historian Tony Thomas attributes Max Steiner's score
with "literally making the film work. The score accents all the
strangeness and mystery and horror in the story, it limns the
frightful giant gorilla, but it also does something else--it speaks
for the tenderness in the monster, the fascination and the compassion he feels for the terrified girl he picks up in his huge paw--
the music is the voice of the doomed brute."[5]

Steiner once described himself as belonging to what he called
the "leitmotif school" of film composers, referring to his penchant

Max Steiner. Photograph courtesy Albert K. Bender, Max Steiner Music Society.

for creating specific leitmotifs (or themes) which were assigned to
individual characters, locales, abstract ideas and emotions of the
story. They served as musical identification tags, easily percept-
ible to the ears of an audience. Almost all of Steiner's film scores
have been built from this approach--many of them being quite complex in their development of and intermingling with the many diverse thematic elements. KING KONG is certainly no exception.

In addition to the leitmotifs given to the characters and loca-
tions, Steiner also included much "mickey mousing" in the score--
a term referring to a cartoon-like approach in providing musical
counterparts synchronized precisely to visual actions on the
screen. The speed of the native Chieftain, for example, is mimicked by the tempo of the music as he walks toward Denham and
his crew. Kong's climbing the Empire State Building is matched
with the rising and falling of the music, in step with Kong's ascending progress.

Steiner thoroughly enjoyed composing KING KONG: "It was
made for music," he recalled many years later. "It was the kind
of film that allowed you to do anything and everything, from weird
chords and dissonances to pretty melodies."[6]

The KONG score is built around three principal leitmotifs
representing the main protagonists, orchestrated amongst a number
of secondary motifs for subsidiary characters, locales and dramatic
situations. Musicologist Fred Steiner (no relation to Max), who recorded the KONG score in 1976, has described these three basic
motifs: "First--the Kong Motive, a group of three descending
chromatic notes, suggesting the overwhelming bulk and awesome
might of the giant ape; next in importance is the theme of the
heroine, Ann Darrow, which can also be construed as the love
theme; it is a pretty waltz melody which Steiner entitled 'Stolen
Love'.... In moments of fear and stress when Ann is in peril or
mortal danger, this theme usually appears in another, more chromatic guise, in which the first three notes ... match the three
notes of the Kong Motive. The third major leitmotif is the four-
note Courage Motive. This appears in several contexts during the
film ... first associated with the bravery and daring of the small
band of adventurers and the uncertainty of the outcome [and]
later with Jack Driscoll's efforts to rescue Ann from the clutches
of Kong. In certain scenes it is developed in such a way that it depicts the jeopardy and defenselessness of the puny humans when
Kong is on the rampage."[7] Fred Steiner goes on to explain how
the themes for Ann and Kong are often juxtaposed with one another
throughout the film, reinforcing the underlying beauty-and-the-
beast symbolism of the story.

Many writers have spoken at length on the KONG score. Bill
Littman describes "the 'march through the jungle' music--a con-

stantly repeated two-note rhythm counterpointed by an adventurous-sounding, two-note, 'push 'em forward' construction. Another is the use of blaring, staccato trumpets each time Kong is pursuing a helpless human being."[8] Reviewer Steve Vertlieb writes: "The slow, gradually building tension of the first hint of arrival on Skull Island is masterfully conveyed as Steiner subtly integrates the deceptive sounds of breakers near the shore with the warning drums of unseen natives from somewhere on the beach." Vertlieb goes on to describe one of the score's most frenzied moments as being the sacrificial dance performed by the natives. "Steiner captures the fury and vengeful fanaticism of the island's populace in an intoxicated rage.... It throbs and builds to a fever pitch, exuding an excitement from the screen that cannot fail to touch anyone in the viewing audience, and concludes sharply, abruptly at its very peak, leaving the helpless spectator literally gasping for breath."[9]

Another writer describes the music as "a masterpiece of broodingly ominous mood,"[10] and another points out how the music during Kong's first appearance to the captive Ann "seems to become the gargantuan heartbeat of the approaching Kong."[11] Furthermore, Fred Steiner has commented that the composer "was able to accomplish the seemingly impossible, viz., to portray on one hand the menace and danger of the savage monstrous ape, and, on the other, his love--if one can call it that--for the beautiful Ann Darrow, and thus, in certain instances, actually influence the audience's sympathy toward Kong himself, even provoke a pang or two of real regret during the moments of his final destruction."[12]

Oscar Levant, a pianist and actor who worked for RKO during the time KING KONG was made, said that its score was one of "the most enthusiastically written scores ever to be composed in Hollywood. Indeed, it was always my feeling that it should have been advertised as a concert of Steiner's music with accompanying pictures on the screen."[13] While Levant's statement might be unevenly balanced concerning the other elements that comprised KONG's whole, it demonstrates the invaluable contribution of Steiner's score to the success and sense of wonder that has made the film a timeless classic. The authors of The Making of KING KONG sum it up nicely when they write, "It would be difficult to overestimate Steiner's share in creating a classic tragic figure from what could have been just another monster."[14]

The music for KING KONG, incidentally, proved to be as durable as it was effective, and portions of the score were reused by Steiner in A STOLEN LIFE (the introductory cue, "A Boat in the Fog" is used as a suspense-building motif for Bette Davis), and by his successors at RKO. Among the films containing bits and pieces of the KONG score; THE LAST OF THE MOHICANS, MUSS 'EM UP, WE'RE ONLY HUMAN, THE LAST DAYS OF POMPEII, BACK TO BATAAN, MICHAEL STROGOFF, and many others.

Max Steiner went on to score the lesser sequel, SON OF KONG, with early touches of a style he would use a decade later in CASABLANCA (which film composers have referred to as "The Casablanca Technique"). Many of the dramatic moments of the score are derived from the melody of a simple song called "Runaway Blues," which is sung early in the film by heroine Helen Mack, and its use during the murder/fire scene and the giant bear scene are fine examples of how a skilled composer can develop highly dramatic moods from a simple thematic piece. Steiner also utilized a three-note theme for Little Kong, as well as weaving key themes from KING KONG into certain scenes. Steiner's score was effective, although without the pathos of the first film. SON OF KONG was, basically, a humorous story about a cute baby ape, forsaking the passion and excitement of its predecessor for a purely surface-level, Disney-esque charm. Steiner's music complies with this emphasis, containing many humorous touches and mickey mousings, such as a quotation from the Hebrew Mazeltof at one point when Kong Jr. makes a gesture suggestive of traditional Jewry. Fantastic-film historian Donald C. Willis has said that "Steiner's enchanting score actually makes the movie's amiable tackiness seem substantial at times."[15]

Prior to scoring the KONG films, Steiner had written the music for THE MOST DANGEROUS GAME (1932), which was produced by the same crew that went on to make KING KONG. Steiner composed the piano music, played by Zaroff, the film's villain, which pianist Norma Boleslawski performed for the sound track. Much of Steiner's score was founded on that piano theme—in the manner of the later SON OF KONG and CASABLANCA—which becomes identified with Zaroff. One reviewer observed that "the score is one of the most elaborate of the Thirties, containing eighty-three musical cues involving fourteen compositions. The prolonged chase contains some of the most exciting film music extant."[16]

Steiner's other fantastic film scores include the original SHE (1935), a quiet, moody piece reflecting the otherworldly nature of the lost kingdom; Frank Capra's 1944 black comedy, ARSENIC AND OLD LACE; THE BEAST WITH FIVE FINGERS (1946) (for which he built a score around Bach's Chaconne, the musical piece performed by the severed hand of the film's villain); as well as his last score, TWO ON A GUILLOTINE (1965), a weak, forgettable picture involving an heiress who must spend a night in a haunted house in order to receive her inheritance. It was an unmemorable conclusion to a mighty career which earned the composer a well-deserved reputation as "the Granddaddy of Picture Scoring."

Steiner's death in 1971 closed the door on a kind of film scoring that, while enormously popular in the 30's and 40's, had been gradually eased out during the 60's by a tendency toward pop music and commercially exploitable rhythms, and didn't regain its stature until the STAR WARS era of symphonic scoring in the late

Franz Waxman. Photograph courtesy Tony Thomas.

70's. As Steiner himself recalled in the late 1960's, "Most of my films were entertainments--soap operas, storybook adventures, fantasies. If those films were made today, they would be made differently, and I would score them differently."[17] While moviemaking techniques have indeed changed over the years, as have approaches to scoring, the influence of the early filmmakers--and especially of Max Steiner in the realm of film music--is undeniable. Steiner's pioneering work on KING KONG laid the groundwork for almost all fantastic adventure music that was to follow.

Another important fantastic film score of this early period was for the 1935 film, THE BRIDE OF FRANKENSTEIN, composed by Franz Waxman, which was similarly innovative in the field of horror.

Waxman was born in Upper Silesia (now part of Poland) in 1906. His family was not musically inclined, but the young Franz's fascination with the piano resulted in his studying music on his own. When he was seventeen he was convinced that music was what he wanted to do, and so enrolled in the Dresden Music Academy. He soon progressed to the Berlin Conservatory, supporting himself by playing piano in nightclubs. In 1930 he found the opportunity to arrange, conduct and compose music for a number of German films, including Fritz Lang's LILIOM, until emigrating to the United States in 1935. Film producer James Whale was then preparing to film his sequel to FRANKENSTEIN, and, being familiar with Waxman's music for LILIOM, felt that the composer could give the film the "something better than the average 'squeal and groan' horror score" that he was seeking. Waxman's resulting score set a new standard in the music of horror films, and was one of the first Hollywood movie scores to use the symphony orchestra in an impressionistic way, depicting musically the bizarre sounds of laboratory equipment, and so forth. Waxman himself said "it was a 'super horror' movie and demanded hauntingly eerie, weird and different music."[18]

The BRIDE OF FRANKENSTEIN score is basically dependent upon three themes. The first is the leitmotif for the Monster--a harsh, five-note theme written and played to resemble the Monster's growl; it suggests the creature's massive strength and uncontrollable nature. Various musical bridges are used to accompany the softer emotions of the Monster, such as the use of Schubert's Ave Maria during the hermit's cabin sequence, and the light suggestiveness when the Monster feebly tries to communicate with its would-be mate.

The second motif is that for the Bride. "This sardonically beautiful little three-note motif (with its major key, four-note coda) is Waxman's elegant miniature musical joke," explains Bill Littman in a lengthy analysis of the score. "Here we have this serene, smooth and lovely compact musical phrase representing this spastic, resurrected human corpse.... On the one hand she is, visually, an excellent example of the heights of grotesquerie, while musically, Waxman performs the amazing feat of mocking her appearance. Waxman's constant adding on and varying of this musical application throughout her creation and single, brief appearance (plus two early references in the picture to the possibility of creating a female monster) give 'the Mate' a dimension which would otherwise be sorely lacking. This theme, one could say, subconsciously forces the audience to relate to the grotesquely beautiful idea of the Bride's presence."[19]

The final major theme is that for Dr. Praetorius, and is the most complex and flexible of the three. It also represents the only human being of the trio. This motif is a sinister, four-note descending theme played throughout the film on a variety of instruments. While the Monster's theme is earthy and solid, and the Bride's is ethereal and buoyant, Praetorius' music is vaporous, wrapping itself about the former themes, sometimes eclipsing them, sometimes standing stolidly on its own. The theme is alternately dour (as when Praetorius discusses life and death with Dr. Frankenstein), foreboding (when he meets Minnie the Maid at the castle door) and mocking (when giving the Monster a sedative), although always it is a perfect reflection of Praetorius' deceitful character.

The highlight of Waxman's score is the thrilling music for the creation of the female monster, "in which a thumping timpani suggests the beating of the Bride's heart and a cacophony of wedding bells heralds her unveiling."[20] (Portions of this sequence bear a remarkable resemblance to the "Bali Ha'i" song from Rodgers & Hammerstein's 1949 musical, SOUTH PACIFIC.) The sequence is a marvelous example of complexity and thematic interplay that goes virtually unnoticed by most moviegoers, opening with a dark, agitated phrase for strings and then French horns, suggesting perhaps the approaching electrical storm. The theme illustrates the excitement of the participants without losing the sense of morbid complication that underlies the situation. The Monster's theme appears as the creature impatiently urges Frankenstein on. While elsewhere in the film there are no leitmotifs written especially for Dr. Frankenstein or his bride, Elizabeth, here Waxman uses a direct reversal of the Monster Bride motif for Elizabeth. The rising-falling, three-note, major key motif for the Bride is reversed into a falling-rising three-note minor key theme for Elizabeth. "Both ends of the thematic spectrum are placed before us: 'beautiful' monster bride and forlorn, tragic human bride," writes Bill Littman in his analysis of the score. He continues to describe Waxman's music for this sequence: "Praetorius' action in giving the Monster a drug to keep him quiet is backed up by a mocking rendition of the Praetorius theme, followed by a dismayed sounding Monster theme. The Praetorius motif appears immediately after, eminently satisfied. The music briefly loses its dark mood for just a few seconds as Praetorius, in answer to Henry's demand that he prove Elizabeth alive and well, allows Frankenstein to talk to her over an 'electrical device.' The music suddenly pitches forward, fortissimo, a great yearning, full orchestral piece as Henry hears her voice. We're back to the former mood immediately however as the approaching storm music reappears, cracklingly, on muted trumpets. The first full rendition, variation and resolution of the Bride theme in this sequence now appears, is repeated and then is coupled alternately with the storm music now played on the bassoons. As the music builds throughout the remainder of the scene, the Bride's theme loses its shape a bit, becomes vaulting as the lightning storm builds in intensity. Chimes appear as the kites sway in the wind. The Monster theme enters the picture as the creature, awakened from his drugged sleep, attacks Karl and tosses him from the roof of the castle. At the same time, lightning strikes the kites, the Bride's theme pours forth with full force as the creation's body is lowered to the lab floor."[21]

THE BRIDE OF FRANKENSTEIN remains a classic example of screen horror, a superbly crafted film whose many components combine perfectly to create a film which "in terms of style, visual design, literate scripting, performance, music and just about every other individual ingredient ... is virtually unsurpassed."[22] Waxman's music is most certainly a major contribution to the film's enduring success, and, as already stated, set a new standard in horror scoring.

The music was so effective that it became a stock item for the Universal music library, and was later reused in serials such as FLASH GORDON, BUCK ROGERS and RADIO PATROL. The score also earned Waxman an offer to head the music department at Universal Studios, a post he held for the next two years, supervising the scoring of more than 50 Universal films. Eventually Waxman gained recognition as one of the most gifted composers of American film music, considered at his best with suspenseful and psychological cinematic themes.

The year after BRIDE, Waxman contributed a fine score for the Karloff-Lugosi thriller, THE INVISIBLE RAY (1936). This music balances an ascending, heroic main theme heard from the brass (representative of the human aspect of Dr. Rukh) with a harsher, monstorus motif emphasizing Rukh's murderous state after being infected with "Radium X." A pair of minor themes include a pretty melody for Diane as well as a love theme for her and Ronald.

Waxman also included some effective incidental cues, such as: the eerie motif for high, shimmering organ and xylophone heard as the laboratory guests view the ray travelling through space (this music is the same as the "heaven music" used by Waxman in his LILIOM score in 1930); a pretty Parisian melody for strings and accordion heard as Rukh roams the streets in search of a decoy to kill; and an effective viola piece which overtakes the wedding music as Rukh gazes at Diane and Drake, supplemented by brass when he sees a vision of the six expedition members he will kill in the cathedral statues. In addition to the LILIOM music, Waxman had reworked a cue from W. Franke Harling's score for Universal's DESTINATION UNKNOWN (1933) in the opening scene at Rukh's Carpathian castle, as well as using a few cues from BRIDE OF FRANKENSTEIN near the end where Rukh tries to kill Diane and her new husband.

Another notable fantastic film score was that of the 1941 version of DR. JEKYLL AND MR. HYDE, starring Spencer Tracy. Waxman was struck by a deep religious significance in the story and felt the author had meant it as a moral lesson--the triumph of goodness over evil. As a result, he composed an especially majestic score which emphasized the spiritual implications of the story, rather than the horrific elements, even to the point of incorporating a choir over the opening and closing credits. Waxman, again demonstrating his penchant for the effective use of leitmotifs, and recalling Max Steiner's "Casablanca technique," skillfully wrought the song that Ingrid Bergman sings early on ("You Should See Me Dance the Polka") in a number of later variations that underline her growing fear.

Waxman continued to score an occasional borderline fantasy such as THE BRIGHTON STRANGLER and ALIAS NICK BEAL through the 40's. His romantic approach served him well in a trio of films for Alfred Hitchcock, including SUSPICION (1941), wherein he used an electric violin to create an element of fear in a manner similar to Miklos Rozsa's later use of theremin in SPELLBOUND. In the late 50's and 60's, Waxman lent his hand to television scoring, including episodes of THE TWILIGHT ZONE (see Chapter XI), TIME TUNNEL and BATMAN, until his untimely death in 1968. While not an especially noteworthy conclusion to Waxman's career, the composer retained a consistent musical craftsmanship in everything he wrote. While Max Steiner pioneered the scoring of fantasy/adventure films with KING KONG, Franz Waxman created a breakthrough in the development of music for horror films with the score to THE BRIDE OF FRANKENSTEIN.

The third area of fantastic cinema is the science fiction film, and the earliest important score for this type of movie was for the 1936 classic, THINGS TO COME, scored by the British composer, Sir Arthur Bliss. Bliss, who was best known for his concert works, consented to write an occasional film score, and his music for the prophetic H. G. Wells story is generally regarded as the best of his film compositions.

The score is also considered by many to have been a "major achievement in the synchronization of musical and visual ideas ..."[23] which was of vast importance in the development of British film music. H. G. Wells, who wrote the film script based upon his book, became involved in all aspects of the production, including Bliss' music, although to what extent is difficult to say. Director William Cameron Menzies also collaborated on the score in such a way that entire sequences could be planned in advance to make maximum use of the full orchestra. "This collaboration produced one of the first major British films in which a composer played an inherent role in the development of the film itself," wrote one reviewer. "Wells later praised both Bliss and his work, observing that the score was not intended to be merely attached to the film, but was rather an integral part of the creative design."[24]

The composer employed a symphony orchestra with an extra percussion section as well as a large choir, and the score required 14 recording sessions to complete. The music is dramatic, yet subtle, its melody subdued. It opens with a somber prologue for violins and oboe; an ominous and shadowy piece suggesting unfavorable events forthcoming. A brassy, energetic march (a theme which later became popular on English radio) accompanies the war sequence, and an extended musical montage is heard over the scenes of reconstruction. For the sequence where the sculptor rouses a mob to storm the Moon-Gun, Bliss created a rhythmic motif which Christopher Palmer has described as being "familiar from the opening of Beethoven's Fifth Symphony" which forms a "steady crescendo of tension." Palmer sums up Bliss' effective score when he writes that "in the end, Bliss' art, essentially one of gesture and action, always at its best when responding to some extra-musical stimulus, added a new dimension of spectacle and vision to Wells' and Korda's conception."[25] Bliss also employed subtle changes in orchestration to underline key visual elements that might otherwise have gone unnoticed, as one writer described: "In a scene where children play with toys, happy melodies for harp, strings and winds sound appropriately innocent; when a close-up reveals war toys, the music suddenly turns menacing."[26]

The final sequence of the film, where Cabal and Passworthy gaze into the heavens at the satellite they have shot out into space, incorporated a moving musical epilog that reflected "the visionary grandeur and nobility of Cabal's final speech in what Wells termed 'a heroic finale amidst the stars.'"[27] John Baxter, writing in Science Fiction in the Cinema, described the music of this sequence saying that Bliss "imposes a soft but powerful melody, building with the intensity of Cabal's speech until the full orchestra and choir surge up at the end with an echo of his final question." Baxter is not uncritical of the music, however: "Despite its many qualities it seems often coarse and shrill, and [screenwriter H. G. Wells'] claim that 'the music is part of the constructive scheme of the film' is seldom borne out. The final scene, however, is a triumph of music and image."[28]

THINGS TO COME is also noted for being the first British film music to have been issued commercially in the United States,

and appeared on three 12" 78-rpm Decca Records. Bliss' other
dabblings in fantasy have included the 1937 film, THE CONQUEST
OF THE AIR.

With these three pioneering films demonstrating the power
and effectiveness of original musical composition, the use of music
in fantastic films came to be recognized--at least within the indus-
try--as an important element of a film's success. The further development of fantastic film music in the 30's and 40's continued to
reinforce its effectiveness and to open the doors for continued experimentation in the years to come.

Notes

1. George Turner, "The Phantom Set," American Cinematograph-
    er, July 1982, p. 677

2. Ibid., p. 734

3. Robert Fiedel, "KING KONG: Music by Max Steiner" in The
    Girl in the Hairy Paw, Ronald Gottesman and Harry Ge-
    duld, eds. (New York: Avon Books, 1976), p. 192

4. Orville Goldner and George Turner, The Making of KING KONG
    (La Jolla: A. S. Barnes, 1975), p. 190

5. Tony Thomas, Music for the Movies (La Jolla: A. S. Barnes,
    1973), p. 115

6. Max Steiner quoted by Tony Thomas, ibid.

7. Fred Steiner, liner notes to King Kong record album (Entr'Acte
    Records, 1976)

8. Bill Littman, "The KING KONG Score--Primitive Rhythms on
    Skull Island," Gore Creatures #23, 1975, p. 10.

9. Steve Vertlieb, "The Men Who Saved KING KONG," The Mon-
    ster Times #1, 1972, p. 15.

10. Doug Moench, "KING KONG: Monarch of Monsters," Monsters
    of the Movies #1, 1974, p. 10

11. Carlos Clarens, An Illustrated History of Horror Films (New
    York: G. P. Putnam's Sons, 1967), p. 93

12. Fred Steiner, loc. cit.

13. Oscar Levant quoted by Goldner & Turner, op. cit., p. 191

14. Goldner & Turner, ibid.

15. Donald C. Willis, Horror and Science Fiction Films II (Metuchen, N.J.: Scarecrow Press, 1982) p. 363

16. Goldner & Turner, op. cit., p. 73

17. Max Steiner quoted by Tony Thomas, op. cit., p. 121

18. Franz Waxman quoted by John Waxman, liner notes to Classic Film Scores of Franz Waxman (RCA Records, 1974)

19. Bill Littman, "Music for the Bride," Gore Creatures #25, 1976, p. 53

20. Gregory William Mank, It's Alive! The Classic Cinema Saga of Frankenstein (La Jolla: A. S. Barnes, 1981), p. 60

21. Bill Littman, loc. cit.

22. William K. Everson, Classics of the Horror Film (Secaucus, N.J.: Citadel Press, 1974), p. 43

23. Mark Evans, Soundtrack--The Music of the Movies (New York: Da Capo Press, 1979), p. 42

24. Ibid.

25. Christopher Palmer, liner notes to Bernard Herrmann Conducts Great British Film Scores (London Phase-4 Records, 1976)

26. Mark Evans, loc. cit.

27. Christopher Palmer, loc. cit.

28. John Baxter, Science Fiction in the Cinema (New York: Paperback Library, 1976), pp. 61-62

III

UNIVERSAL'S MONSTERS AND OTHER OLD FRIENDS
The 30's and 40's

With the popularity of DRACULA, FRANKENSTEIN, THE MUM-
MY and other films, Universal Pictures launched what may be regarded as the first Golden Age of fantastic films. From the early
30's through the mid-40's, many innovative films and screen monsters were first brought to life--or death--and along with them, a
great deal of noteworthy music. Scoring for fantastic films encountered a lot of growth during this period, although there were still
occasions in which classical music, anonymous library cues, and
segments of previous scores were used due to the rushed pressure
of the B-movie treadmill. While KING KONG, THE BRIDE OF
FRANKENSTEIN and THINGS TO COME may be regarded as the
blockbuster scores in the infancy of fantastic film music, at the
same time there were many other important developments of less
eminence which played a significant part in the evolution of music
for fantasy and horror films.

During these years most composers worked under contract to
one studio or another, supervised by a music director, who was in
charge of the studio's music department. Thus, composers scored
many different kinds of films in rather quick succession as assignments were handed down from the music director. However, as
William H. Rosar[1] revealed in an important retrospective on their
horror music, Universal had dismissed all of its music staff by 1931,
deciding instead to contract composers on an individual basis under the supervision of Gilbert Kurland, who headed up their sound
department--an arrangement that lasted several years. Many of the
same composers were recruited from film to film, though, so it
might be said that Kurland in fact organized an unofficial staff of
composers who were prominent in the early days of the Universal
horror cycle.

Before its disbanding, the head of Universal's music department in 1930 had been Heinz Roemheld, who succeeded David Broekman as general music director. Roemheld, born in Milwaukee in
1901, had studied in Berlin to become a concert pianist. He worked
as a theatrical music director during the 20's, conducting the pit
orchestra for silent movies at Milwaukee's Alhambra Theater. Carl
Laemmle, the theater's owner as well as the founder and president
of Universal Pictures, heard Roemheld's musical accompaniment for

Heinz Roemheld. Photograph by Jack Freulich, Universal, Courte-
    sy William H. Rosar.

a showing of THE PHANTOM OF THE OPERA in 1925, and was so
impressed that he contracted Roemheld to work in a number of his
other theaters as musical director. In 1929, Roemheld became a
staff composer at Universal, and when he was appointed head of the
music department the following year, it became his responsibility to
oversee all aspects of music in the Universal films, one of which
was the early horror picture, THE CAT CREEPS (a remake of the
1927 silent film, THE CAT AND THE CANARY). As Rosar noted,
Roemheld composed original title music instead of a dramatic score
for this film. Roemheld also handled the music for the first major
sound horror film, DRACULA, released in 1931.

DRACULA contained no score per se, utilizing just the music
from the opening scene of Tchaikovsky's Swan Lake under the main
titles, a piece which had been frequently used in silent films as a
brooding and mysterious cue. The only other music in DRACULA
are excerpts from Wagner's Die Meistersinger and Schubert's Un-
finished Symphony heard as source music during the concert hall
sequence (a scene, incidentally, which was originally to have taken
place in a living room--but was switched to the concert hall in order to allow for the use of background music). It is interesting
to note, as did William H. Rosar, that these classical excerpts actually seem to follow the action. "The illogical order in which the
excerpts are heard in this concert hall context suggests that they
were chosen and arranged in this sequence for dramatic effect,"
wrote Rosar.

While Roemheld's efforts in DRACULA consisted of selecting
these excerpts, and undoubtedly manipulating them slightly to cor-
respond with the actions, he composed original music for a number
of Universal films until the music staff was eliminated in late 1931.
He returned, however, two years later as a contract composer and
became an important force in the music of these early horror films.

Roemheld scored ten minutes of music for THE INVISIBLE
MAN (1933), heard during the opening and closing sequences.
Both scenes occur during a heavy snowfall and Rosar has pointed
out how the music heightens the drama of these important scenes.
The first introduces the invisible man while the second depicts his
demise when the falling snow betrays his invisibility. Roemheld's
music effectively captures an atmosphere of flurrying snow, and
seems to retain a somewhat mock-serious satirical character in keeping with these subtle elements of the film itself. The music is
actually based on two contrasting motifs, one stark and ominous,
and the other slightly whimsical. The two motifs are ingeniously
developed in these two cues, while a syncopated rhythm predomi-
nates the music throughout (the main title almost has the sense of
a tango, as the invisible man stealthily makes his way through the
snow towards the lighted inn).

Roemheld scored Universal's THE BLACK CAT the following

year, although in this case director Edgar G. Ulmer requested that
he score it with classical motifs, corresponding to the refined taste
of the villain, Poelzig. THE BLACK CAT, a devil-worship thriller
teaming Boris Karloff and Bela Lugosi for the first time, also contained the most amount of music during the Universal horror cycle,
according to Rosar--of the film's 65 minutes, 55 contain music.
Roemheld chose appropriate classical pieces to employ as leitmotifs
for the characters: the first theme from Liszt's Piano Sonata in B
Minor is the motif for the satanic Poelzig (the composition is nick-
named "The Devil Sonata"); the opening of Liszt's symphonic poem,
Tasso, represents the melancholy, vengeful Dr. Weredegast; and a
modification of Tchaikovsky's Romeo and Juliet love theme is used
for the honeymooners. Other excerpts of Liszt, Schubert, Chopin,
Bach, Beethoven, Schumann and paraphrased Tchaikovsky were
used as underscorings to augment the drama of various scenes.

A particularly effective excerpt from Beethoven's Seventh
Symphony--a hymn-like arrangement of the second movement (alle-
gretto)--is heard during Poelzig's reflective monologue while escort-
ing Weredegast through the chambers of his mansion. "Rakoczy
March," from Liszt's Hungarian Rhapsody #15 reflects the Hungarian locale during the first long shot of Poelzig's monolithic home,
and reinforces its unsavory military history. This same march is
later adapted for a humorous scene with visiting local gendarmes.

The selection and arrangement of the classical motifs worked
well in THE BLACK CAT, heightening the drama in the manner of
an original score, as one reviewer noted: "Though Hollywood musical scoring was still in its early stages and used haphazardly,
it plays a vital part in elevating BLACK CAT to its classical level,
at times endowing the principal players' movements with a lyrical
opera-ballet rhythm underscored by variations from Brahms, Liszt,
Tchaikovsky and others."[2]

Roemheld composed an extensive score for DRACULA'S
DAUGHTER (1936), a film which Rosar noted was initially to have
been scored by Franz Waxman until he accepted a contract at MGM
and became unavailable. Roemheld's score was a predominantly
subdued one, melodic in approach and enveloping the film in an
overall mood of eeriness, punctuated by occasional musical excitement, as in the furious agitato heard during the telegraph montage and Garth's later flight from Croydon Airport. But the somber, almost dreary mood prevailed, and Roemheld captured a passionate, intimate feeling through the use of many cues scored for
solo woodwinds and strings--avoiding a stereotypical horror approach in preference of an underlying emotional resonance; almost
scoring against the action (a musical approach which would become
popular during the 70's, especially in European films).

Roemheld's principal theme for DRACULA'S DAUGHTER is a
baleful, tragic leitmotif for Countess Zaleska, female progeny of

the dreaded vampire. As Harry Robinson would do 36 years later
in a very similar film, COUNTESS DRACULA (1972), Roemheld underlines the tragic poignancy of the woman afflicted with the everlasting curse of vampirism. As the film portrayed its leading character with more sympathy than was done in Lugosi's DRACULA,
this approach was appropriate. The unseen Dracula himself, and
the ancestral curse he embodied, is suggested through an ominous
motif heard during the main titles.

In 1938 Roemheld began a lengthy association with Warner
Brothers which lasted through 1945, after which he freelanced for
a variety of studios. He worked on several insignificant fantasies
during the 40's and early 50's, occasionally returning to Universal
to contribute to the scores of later horror pictures such as THE
MUMMY'S TOMB (1942) and THE MOLE PEOPLE (1956). While these
later horror efforts were notable, Roemheld's most important (and
unrecognized) significance in the fantastic cinema remains in his
contributions to the moody horror films of Carl Laemmle during the
early pioneering days of both the horror film and its music.

While Roemheld assembled an effective few pieces for DRA-
CULA, the first original music heard in a major Universal horror
film was in FRANKENSTEIN (1931). As Rosar reports, David
Broekman, who had worked as Universal's music director in 1929-
30, was engaged as conductor, hiring Bernhard Kaun to compose
a short cue under the opening titles. Kaun had been born in 1899,
the son of Hugo Kaun, a rival of Richard Strauss with whom Heinz
Roemheld had studied in Berlin. Under the tutelage of his father,
Bernhard began music studies at an early age. He came to the
United States in 1924, working as an arranger for various theaters
and assisting Roemheld at the Alhambra. After spending two years
in Germany, Kaun was brought to the Universal music department
in 1931 by Roemheld, where Kaun worked on a number of films.
After the dissolution of the music staff, Kaun was hired by David
Broekman to compose the music for FRANKENSTEIN and an earlier
film, HEAVEN ON EARTH (which has the distinction of being the
first Universal sound film with a complete background score), which
Broekman was responsible for supplying. Kaun later orchestrated
Max Steiner's monumental KING KONG score in 1933.

Rosar notes that Kaun's main title music for FRANKENSTEIN
bears many of the marks of traditional horror film music, especially as it came to be stereotyped in the ensuing years. Opening
with a repeated modal figure invoking a thick, Teutonic feeling
over a churning, chromatic bass line and punctuated by frightful
brass trills, the latter half of the theme consists of a more mysterious, subdued woodwind meandering, culminating in an abrupt
piano glissando that sweeps away the music, ending with a mood of
bleak mystery. The end title music for FRANKENSTEIN was a piece
of existing music by Giuseppe Becce, "Grand Appassionato," written
for use in silent films.

MURDERS IN THE RUE MORGUE (1932) likewise utilized dramatic music only over the main and end titles. In this case, though, Gilbert Kurland assembled stock library tracks for the titles, using the Swan Lake excerpt heard in DRACULA under the opening titles (after a brief, anonymous misterioso) and for the end titles, a march written by Heinz Roemheld for a 1930 German silent film, distributed here by Universal, called THE WHITE HELL OF PITZ PALU. Incidental scoring in the body of the picture was nonexistent, as was THE DARK OLD HOUSE (1932), although in this case the main title was an original composition by David Broekman.

Broekman, born in Holland in 1902, received his musical education there, eventually conducting orchestras for opera houses in France before emigrating to America in 1924. After working as a violinist and as musical advisor for a research firm, Broekman became the musical director for Universal in 1929, succeeding Josef Cherniavsky. While actually composing music on a few occasions, Broekman was, according to Rosar, primarily only a music supervisor and conductor, although he frequently claimed credit for scores actually composed by others--a claim contributed to by the fact that Broekman was the only one to receive any screen credit for music during his tenure at Universal (a typical practice at many studios during the 30's and 40's).

While Roemheld's PITZ PALU music again served as the end title cue for THE OLD DARK HOUSE (this time the finale was used), Broekman's original main title was a rather atonal conglomeration of musical effects augmented by a repeated figure which briefly characterizes the grotesque humor of the film.

While these earlier Universal films only housed music over their titles, THE MUMMY (1932) was the first picture in Universal's horror cycle to contain a significant amount of music as underscoring, an approach dictated by the film's director, Karl Freund (who had been cinematographer on DRACULA and MURDERS IN THE RUE MORGUE). As Rosar reports, Freund worked closely with composer James Dietrich in suggesting specific scenes in which he wanted music, such as where Im-Ho-Tep casts spells by the magical pool, and the final sequences.

Dietrich was born in Missouri in 1894, receiving a bachelor's degree in music from its University. He also studied at the Schola Cantorum in France before gaining employment as composer, arranger and conductor in New York, which eventually resulted in his becoming involved in films. After exploiting his affinity for cartoon music in Universal's Walter Lantz animated shorts, Dietrich began to score feature films, one of his earliest being THE MUMMY.

While he wrote a number of pieces as Freund had requested, Dietrich's own idea, as he explained to Rosar, was to work the vari-

ous themes into a recapitulation at the finale, but this wasn't what
Freund had in mind. The director rejected a couple of Dietrich's
cues, and supplemented the score with library music (such as the
familiar Swan Lake piece which comprises the main title, prefaced
by the same misterioso heard in MURDERS IN THE RUE MORGUE).
As it wound up, about half of the movie's 20-odd minutes of music
consists of original composition by Dietrich.

Dietrich wrote five cues for the film, all of which (except
one) are heard more than once in the film. According to Rosar,
Dietrich originally composed a tragic waltz for the flashback to ancient Egypt, but this piece was not used and was replaced with a
montage of library cues including excerpts by Heinz Roemheld and
Belgian composer Michel Brusselmans. Dietrich's haunting ostinato
for Im-Ho-Tep's casting of magic spells becomes something of a
leitmotif for the supernatural powers of the living Mummy. In fact,
Dietrich had originally wanted to use this motif during the early
scene where Im-Ho-Tep first comes to life, a scene which was
eventually played silent.

By 1933, film music was emerging as an important attribute
of filmmaking, so well demonstrated that year in KING KONG.
Universal's horror films gradually began to utilize scoring to a
greater extent. Heinz Roemheld provided lengthy scores for THE
BLACK CAT (1934) and DRACULA'S DAUGHTER (1936); likewise
Karl Hajos composed a fine score for THE WEREWOLF OF LONDON
(1935), which featured about 15 minutes of original Hajos music
and about 13 minutes of tracked material originally used by Roemheld in THE INVISIBLE MAN and THE BLACK CAT.

Hajos was born in Budapest, Hungary, in 1889, and was educated there in its Academy of Music. Rosar notes that he claimed
to have studied composition and orchestration with Richard Strauss.
Hajos began his association with films in 1928 as a staff composer
at Paramount, a post he held until 1934. Hajos composed a
straightforward and compelling score for THE WEREWOLF OF LON-
DON, and both his original work and the stock material provided a
rich musical backdrop for this classic werewolf movie. The film is
thick with music, containing a number of lengthy musical cues
built around two primary themes. The first is the werewolf theme,
comprised of three strong brass notes echoed by four alternate
notes ("DIT-da-duh...DIT-DIT-da-duh"), which is balanced by a
wistful, descending minor-keyed melody which seems to be associated with the exotic mariphasa flower, the blossoms of which offer
a cure for Glendon's lycanthropy as well as indirectly instigating
it.

The main title introduces the werewolf theme in a loud brass-
and-string overture emerging from mysterious cymbal-and-string
swirls, which alternates with the mariphasa theme. A moody string-
and-woodwind cue is heard as Glendon climbs the Tibetan mountain

and is attacked by the werewolf (this music is tracked from Roemheld's INVISIBLE MAN finale). Wounded, Glendon reaches out and
clutches the rare mariphasa, and the music carries us into a visual
segue to Glendon tending the flower in his London laboratory.
The music here is a variation of the mariphasa theme, which returns as Glendon meets Dr. Yogami and discusses the flower's rare
cure for lycanthropy. The werewolf theme emerges subtly as Yogami reveals that Glendon is now a werewolf.

The werewolf motif is heard fully as Glendon later watches in
shock as his hand sprouts hair, alternating with the mariphasa
theme as he is transformed into the snarling beast. An elegiac
version of the werewolf theme, for tender strings, is heard as
Glendon reads of lycanthropy in an old book, and as a mournful
dirge when Yogami (himself a werewolf) reads of Glendon's first
murder in the morning newspaper. The two themes are combined
throughout the film's development, resolving with Glendon's death,
where the werewolf theme is played as a funeral march, transform-
ing into a swelling, majestic finale with obvious inspirational overtones as the dying Glendon likewise reassumes the appearance of a
man.

The pair of themes effectively convey the dual nature of
Glendon's lycanthropy, representing not only the two sides of his
nature--calm, rational man one moment (the wistful mariphasa theme)
and savage, howling werewolf the next (the agitato werewolf theme),
but it also emphasizes, in the interplay between the two motifs,
those occasionally shared characteristics as well. Other motifs include a long, impending cue (tracked material) as Glendon, sitting
alone in his study, is hissed at by a cat, and then runs through
the house turning into a werewolf; and a tender, meditative ballad
for solo cello as Glendon prays in his rented room just before
another transformation.

Clifford Vaughan was engaged to compose the music for THE
RAVEN (1935), an effective chiller teaming Karloff and Lugosi for
the second time. Vaughan was born in New Jersey in 1893, initially studying to be a concert pianist. Vaughan earned a Bachelor's degree in music from the Philadelphia Conservatory, and
worked as a choral director, piano accompanist, arranger and conductor before coming to Hollywood in late 1933. The following year,
he replaced Edward Ward's orchestrator at Universal, one of his earliest assignments being the orchestration of Ward's THE MYSTERY
OF EDWIN DROOD, a score which he partly ghost-wrote. Vaughan
was also the orchestrator of Franz Waxman's monumental BRIDE OF
FRANKENSTEIN score. Vaughan later composed the title music for
Universal's FLASH GORDON serial (1936), which was supplemented
by library music from Roemheld, Hajos and W. Franke Harling. The
shortened feature version utilized Waxman's BRIDE OF FRANKEN-
STEIN as a score.

Like Hajos, Vaughan composed about 15 minutes of original music for THE RAVEN, which was supplemented with about 20 minutes worth of tracked material from W. Franke Harling's DESTINATION UNKNOWN (a 1933 mystery) and Roemheld's BLACK CAT. As Rosar explained, Vaughan's score is comprised of two themes, the first being the "Raven Theme," which is a sinister motif for Dr. Vollin, the deranged Poe fanatic. The second motif is a brooding piece for Edmund Bateman, the criminal who goes to Vollin for a surgical face change. Vaughan's use of the Raven theme is especially clever when it is first heard under Vollin's recital of the Poe poem, wherein a xylophone suggests the sound of the Raven's pecking and bass clarinets augment the lower strings to create a brooding atmosphere. Vaughan also makes fine use of flutter-tongue brass which creates a weird, braying dissonance at climactic moments.

Like Waxman in THE BRIDE OF FRANKENSTEIN, the interplay between these two themes is adroitly executed to underline the developments between Vollin and Bateman; a prominent example is the scene in which Vollin unveils Bateman's new face. Rosar has described how Vaughan provided a gradual crescendo built upon the Bateman theme, which reaches its peak as we see his disfigured face. Here the Bateman theme is given a grotesque dissonance, followed by a mocking statement of Vollin's theme from muted brass as Bateman, unaware of his true appearance, asks the doctor if he looks different. The Bateman theme then repeats another gradual crescendo as Vollin draws the curtains on a series of wall mirrors, each reflecting Bateman's new, monstrous image, giving way to silence as Bateman, enraged, methodically shatters each pane. The two themes are similarly contrasted and developed at the dramatic conclusion, in which Bateman accomplishes a narrow justice upon Vollin.

These early Universal horror films shared a similarity in musical approach, both stylistically (most favored a romantic, leitmotif style) and with regard to a repetition of the same library tracks and classical material (such as Swan Lake). But more importantly --even though they achieved none of the musical acclaim that has surrounded KING KONG and THE BRIDE OF FRANKENSTEIN, and their musical compositions have been, for the most part, unrecognized and uncredited--they all made noteworthy contributions to the development of film music as an integral part of horror films (and, therefore, to film music in general).

William H. Rosar concludes his essay on the subject with an intriguing comparison of the use of music in these early Universal films with that of the horror cinema as it stood in the 80's. "It is perhaps ... important to point out that unlike many of today's horror films which present the viewer with unrelenting horror both visually and on the sound track, reflected in the music with a continuous stream of weird musical sounds, the scores to Universal's films also contain music of considerable beauty and pathos reflecting these elements in the films, such elements forming a strong dramatic contrast to the horror, and creating sympathy for the characters. There are examples of this in nearly every score: Dietrich's theme, 'The Mummy,' clearly seeks to express the solemn beauty and romance of the pyramids in the Valley of the Kings in Egypt; the soulful little ballade Roemheld wrote to accompany the death of the invisible man as he bids farewell to his girl; Roemheld's Tchaikovskian 'Cat Love Theme,' 'Morgue' and 'Cat Threat' in THE BLACK CAT; the enchanting 'Female Monster Music' in THE BRIDE OF FRANKENSTEIN; the soulful variations of the 'Werewolf Theme' in Hajos' WEREWOLF OF LONDON score; the heroic theme associated with Karloff in THE INVISIBLE RAY; and lastly, the tragic main title theme of DRACULA'S DAUGHTER. The musical depiction of these more sympathetic elements added to the 'human' side of these stories, a side often missing in today's horror films."[3]

Outside of Universal, the majority of the fantastic films of the early 30's were produced by small, independent studios in the form of low-budget, action-packed B-movies and serials churned out by the likes of Monogram, Mascot, Halperin, Majestic, Republic and other production companies. Few of these films contained original music, most relying on previously recorded library music or published material assembled by a music director.

One of the most active of these music directors in the 30's was Abe Meyer, who operated his own music studio, Meyer Synchronizing Service, providing suitable music from a vast repertoire of music compiled from various sources. Meyer, who gained considerable experience as a theatrical music director in the silent days, had been unable to attain a supervisory position with the major studios, and so he began to supply music on his own for the independents.

One of Meyer's most memorable jobs was for WHITE ZOMBIE (1932), which combined stock music tracks with original source music by Guy Bevier Williams (who composed the native drumming and chants) and Xavier Cugat (who was commissioned by Meyer to write a Spanish jota, a fast dance, for the film). As one retrospective said of the scoring for WHITE ZOMBIE: "Fine use is made of long silences punctuated with sudden noises and occasional bursts of music. In this respect, WHITE ZOMBIE proves an ancestor of the unusual handling of sound in the Val Lewton productions THE CAT PEOPLE (1942) and I WALKED WITH A ZOMBIE (1943).... An unusually weird effect is produced by the tragic spiritual, 'Listen to the Lamb,' as hummed by alternating male and female choruses. Some action is underscored by appropriate agitatos from silent films."[4]

Meyer also supplied the melodramatic opening music for THE VAMPIRE BAT (1933), which he assembled from a widely used misterioso composed by Charles Dunworth "and" Jean de la Roche (de la Roche was not actually a composer, but a French agent given credit in order to collect foreign royalties, a common practice). The theme, entitled "Stealthy Footsteps," was a popular mystery theme Meyer had used before and would use again, as in the 1935 vampire movie, CONDEMNED TO LIVE, which also sported original main and end title music composed by Universal alumnus David Broekman.

Meyer's library provided the score to the 1933 serial, TAR- ZAN THE FEARLESS. A main theme, reportedly by Sam K. Wine- land (also a music supervisor) was built around Tarzan's three- note war cry, arranging it as an interlude for occasional romantic scenes; the action sequences were scored with silent film agitatos from Meyer's vast library. Meyer also provided effective stock chase music for THE MINE WITH THE IRON DOOR (1936), culled from Joseph Carl Briel's venerable accompaniment to the 1915 BIRTH OF A NATION.

Arthur Kay was another music director who circulated be- tween Republic, Mascot and other small studios. Kay was a Ger- man-trained composer and conductor who headed the music depart- ment at Fox Film Company in the early 30's. Kay composed much original music for Republic's fantasy serial, DARKEST AFRICA (1936), which was used in addition to stock tracks selected by mu- sic director Harry Grey. These stock themes included material by Heinz Roemheld, Milan Roder, Jean Beghon, plus Abe Meyer staples Charles Dunworth and Jean de la Roche. The wild chant of the Tiger Men was the composition of the picture's codirector, B. Reeves Eason. DARKEST AFRICA was one of the first serials to use musical scoring to notable effect, as one retrospective noted: "One great step forward from previous serials is the use of elaborate musical scoring, which became a hallmark of Republic's product. This quality set an industrial standard; in fact, one of the greatest improvements in serial production that may be credited to Republic is the utilization in heroic proportions of exciting, mood-building music."[5]

Kay was also the music director for the Mascot serial of the previous year, THE PHANTOM EMPIRE (1935), which also featured songs by Gene Autry and Smiley Burnette. Kay supplied the in- cidental scoring from classical music, such as Herold's Zampa Over- ture, in addition to original material such as Henry Hadley's stir- ring chase music and Hugo Riesenfeld's theme for the underground kingdom.

Republic's 1937 film, RIDERS OF THE WHISTLING SKULL,

made use of stock music by Kay as well as that of Karl Hajos, Hugo Riesenfeld, Leon Rosebrook, J. S. Zamecnik, and Sidney Cutner, compiled by music director Harry Grey. Grey also compiled a similar array of previously published work by Kay, Hajos, Riesenfeld, Beghon and William Frederick Peters for Republic's 1937 serial, DICK TRACY. The library music was augmented by original scoring by Alberto Colombo, who also scored Republic's THE FIGHTING DEVIL DOGS (1938).

Another prolific music director for the serials was Val Burton, a British-born composer who had written musical revues and hit songs in England before relocating in Hollywood. He later wrote and produced radio dramas and movies. Burton acted as musical director on a number of low-budget action thrillers of the early 30's, and composed the score for THE DELUGE (1933), collaborating with Dr. Edward Kilenyi, an eminent Hungarian-born composer who had been George Gershwin's piano teacher. Kilenyi had also led the famous old Waldorf-Astoria orchestra before associating with Hollywood, where he scored several important silent films. The DELUGE score was performed by a 30-piece orchestra supplemented by a large cathedral pipe organ which massively sounded the doom cry heralding the catastrophic worldwide disasters.

Edward Kay was a music director for Monogram Pictures during the 40's, working on such dubious horrors as KING OF THE ZOMBIES (1941) and THE VOODOO MAN (1944). Kay, born in Brooklyn in 1898, had studied music privately while training in dentistry. He began professionally as a conductor of vaudeville shows, musicals and operettas, later working as an arranger and conductor in radio before starting in films in the 40's.

The score Kay assembled for THE APE MAN (1941) seems fairly representative, providing a rousing arrangement of rapidly ascending brass chords, lacking in any cohesive pattern. Monotonous, low, brooding woodwind tones are heard as Bela Lugosi is revealed to his parents as an ape-man locked in a cage--the music here is poorly suited and undoubtedly ill-chosen library tracks. It lacks any emotional involvement at all, simply droning on, eventually adding a noncommittal harp and brass as Lugosi shambles out of the cage, remaining somber and dreary throughout the scene and, indeed, throughout most of the picture.

Similar uninspired activities were assembled by music director David Chudnow, who worked for various small studios. Chudnow's compilation of presumably library tracks for THE DEVIL BAT (1941) included typically loud, brassy terror motifs, but often made an overabundant use of what sounds like saxophone, suggesting an out-of-place hint of jazz to the score. As a liaison between studio and composers, Chudnow also gave Albert Glasser and Bert

A. Shefter their first assignments as film composers. Both went
on to score many horror films in the 50's.

R. Dale Butts also worked on many Republic "B" actioners
during the late 40's and on into the 50's. Butts, who got his start
as an orchestrator for radio shows (including the famous Edgar
Bergen & Charlie McCarthy show) began at Republic in 1945.
Among his many scores there was the interesting lycanthropy
thriller, THE CATMAN OF PARIS. Butts later scored Republic's
1955 serial, PANTHER GIRL OF THE KONGO. When Republic sold
its studios to CBS television later that same year, Butts went with
it and worked on a number of TV episodes including ALFRED
HITCHCOCK PRESENTS.

Lee Zahler acted as both composer and music director for
many classic serials of the 30's and 40's, providing effective music for films such as CAPTAIN MIDNIGHT (1942) and THE BAT-
MAN (1943). Zahler also composed a theme song and synchronized
score for one of the first sound serials, Mascot's KING OF THE
KONGO (1929), which was released in both silent and sound ver-
sions. Zahler's old-fashioned but often effective music highlighted
this and many other serials throughout the 30's and 40's, working
mostly for Columbia and Producers' Releasing Corporation in the
latter decade.

While mostly forgotten by all but dedicated enthusiasts, the
low-budget features and serials of the early 30's contained their
own brand of adventurous music which--like its better-known counterparts in Erich Wolfgang Korngold's big-budgeted swashbucklers,
and the more recent but no-less unrelated RAIDERS OF THE LOST
ARK from John Williams--kept the aciton flowing and the audiences
cheering.

The trends in the Universal horror films of the 30's continued
to be developed throughout the 40's. By this time, film music had
emerged as a full-fledged cinematic art form, and the 1940's were
the heyday of many fine scores from mainstream cinema from GONE
WITH THE WIND (1939) through THE TREASURE OF THE SIERRA
MADRE (1948). Free from the executive skepticism of the early
30's, music was used prominently as a major attribute of the fantastic films of the late 30's and 40's, and this was aptly demonstrated at Universal, which continued to be the dominant producer
of horror cinema throughout most of the decade.

By the 40's, however, Universal had once again gathered together a powerful music department, and all of its films were
scored by staff composers under the direction of a head music
supervisor, with an occasional outside composer called in when
necessary. The two staff composers at Universal in the 40's who
were the most consistent at scoring their horror films were Frank
Skinner and Hans J. Salter.

Frank Skinner.   Photograph courtesy Preston Neal Jones.

Frank Skinner, born in Illinois in 1897, had studied music privately and at the Chicago Musical College before moving to New York, where he found employment arranging stock orchestrations for music publishing houses. He also gained experience playing in a dance band. Skinner came to Hollywood in 1935, where he arranged THE GREAT ZIEGFELD and soon began to work for Universal, eventually becoming their top orchestrator. Skinner's first score as composer was for SON OF FRANKENSTEIN in 1939, a score which was orchestrated by Hans J. Salter, a Viennese composer with whom Skinner would collaborate frequently.

The music for SON OF FRANKENSTEIN might be considered characteristic for the monster movies of the 40's, in that the primary horror theme is derived around a slow, plodding, footstep-like motif, in this case for deep brassy chords with echoed percussion and cymbal, a gradually ascending motif driving the creature ever onward. (The piece is used especially well as the revived Monster creeps up on the Baron in the laboratory.) This was a motif that Salter used himself very satisfactorily when he scored subsequent Frankenstein pictures, and is a device used repeatedly by other composers in the genre. Skinner also used rapid, downward harp glissandos during climactic moments, as in the Baron's first view of the ailing Monster. A romantic string motif is used to support the film's quieter moments, such as when Ygor talks with the Baron in the family crypt.

The music also exemplifies much of the Monster's pathos, as in his mourning for the dead Ygor, after which the music erupts into a frenzy as the enraged monster destroys the lab. Film historian Donald F. Glut described the SON OF FRANKENSTEIN score thusly: "Frank Skinner, as had Franz Waxman, wrote a superb musical score which inevitably found its way into many later features and serials. The music actually seemed to say 'Frank-en-stein' with its ascending notes of three written in 4/4 time."[6]

Skinner and his orchestrator were given a hectic two weeks in which to compose, orchestrate and record the score. As Salter later said, "I recall one stretch in scoring SON OF FRANKENSTEIN in which we didn't leave the studio for two solid days. Frank would sit at the piano, compose a sequence, and then hand it to me, and I would orchestrate it. While I was doing that, he would take a nap. Then I would wake him up so he could write some more, and I would take a nap. This went on for forty-eight hours."[7] Imminent deadlines and preset recording dates were fairly standard in those days, according to Salter, a situation aggravated by Universal's enthusiastic music director, Charles Previn, who pressured them for speedy results.

Skinner next scored TOWER OF LONDON (1939), which was also orchestrated by Salter. Much of what was written, however, including the clever use of period English music to create an underlying mood, was later discarded by the studio and replaced with previously used material, including cues from SON OF FRANKEN-STEIN. The main title (which in many cases is an overture of the score's main thematic elements) starts the film out creepily enough, though, featuring harsh chords segueing into a slow-moving, march-like rhythm for brass and strings, increasing in tempo and dissolving into a frenzy of violin notes.

Salter continued to orchestrate Skinner's work even after he had begun to compose his own scores; in fact such were the conditions at the studio that quite often a single score would be created by an entire cadre of composers, each one taking a hand in the composition, orchestration and what-not in order to get it done in time. Skinner scored a few bars at the end of THE INVISIBLE MAN RETURNS (1940) and collaborated with Salter and Charles Previn on THE WOLF MAN (1941--considered by many to be a breakthrough score), elements of which were later used in further sequels. In THE WOLF MAN, Skinner and his colleagues contrasted a series of frenzied string horrifics, punctuated by a repeatedly climactic, three-note brass phrase, with a poignant string melody. The music, like Karl Hajos' earlier WEREWOLF OF LONDON, conveyed both the horror and the pathos embodied in Larry Talbot's dual nature. Skinner later had an opportunity to provide some exciting music and take a poke of fun at his ominous cues for SON when he scored ABBOTT AND COSTELLO MEET FRANKENSTEIN (1948), mingling a horror theme with humorous musical mickey mousings.

Skinner, along with Salter, Herman Stein and Henry Mancini, were the main contract composers working under music supervisor Joseph Gershenson at Universal in the 50's, where they worked on dozens of pictures, often collaborating on cues and frequently receiving no screen credit.

While Skinner's work in the genre has been eclipsed by the more pervasive role of Hans J. Salter, he distinguished himself as a talented composer whose solo efforts such as SON OF FRANKEN-STEIN and ABBOTT AND COSTELLO MEET FRANKENSTEIN, while not among the composer's favorites, nevertheless demonstrated a keen insight into music for horror films.

Born in Vienna in 1896, Hans J. Salter was educated at its Academy of Music and later became music director for the Volks-opera there. He conducted music in small theaters throughout Vienna and neighboring towns, supplying music for many kinds of theatrical presentations. When he was 23 he was hired by a film company to conduct the musical accompaniment to filmed operettas, and eventually went to Berlin where he worked for the prestigious UFA film company on a number of musical pictures. The threat of Hitler led to Salter's return to Vienna, and, in turn, his emmigration to the United States in 1937, where he began scoring films for

Hans J. Salter. Photograph by Bob Burns. Courtesy Tony
      Thomas

Universal the following year. Salter spared no time in providing
his wide range of abilities, and ended up becoming one of the
studio's mainstays for the next 30 years. He was handed assignments in almost every conceivable genre, including dramas, comedies, Westerns, mysteries, swashbucklers, as well as popular Dean-
na Durbin musicals.

        When he joined Universal, the busy studio was churning out
an average of 70 pictures a year, mostly inexpensive productions
but all requiring music. This kept Salter and his colleagues such
as Frank Skinner and Paul Dessau very busy. Salter recalls that
during his first few years with Universal he barely had a week off,
and in 1942, for example, he worked in various capacities on the
scores of some 30 films. Somewhat to his own surprise, Salter became a specialist in the scoring of horror films, and even at the
time he was quickly recognized as "The Master of Terror and Suspense." Most of the Universal Frankenstein, Dracula, Mummy and
Wolf Man pictures were held together by his expertise.

        Salter's first contribution to the fantastic cinema was in or-
chestrating portions of the scores for SON OF FRANKENSTEIN and
TOWER OF LONDON in 1939, which Frank Skinner had scored under music director Charles Previn's supervision. The latter film
also reused portions of Skinner's earlier SON OF FRANKENSTEIN

music to replace period cues arranged and recorded by Salter which were later deemed improper.

This practice of reusing parts of previous scores was commonplace during the 40's, as it had been during the 30's, usually as a matter of necessity due to lack of time. Salter often found himself having to use bits and pieces of scores written by himself or his colleagues when he ran out of time. Charles Previn affectionately called the process "Salterizing." Hans Salter explains: "I would try to create something that would be on an equal footing with a complete new score, and I'm sure that ninety percent of the people didn't notice the difference."[8] As Universal owned all the rights to the music Salter and others had written for them, they were within their rights to shuffle the music about in this manner.

It was also common in the 40's and 50's for a variety of studio composers to collaborate on a single score, each providing specific themes which were then linked to form a cohesive whole. Each composer tried to write in a style that was not too far apart from the other, remaining within the same boundaries of tonality. Salter's most frequent collaborator was Frank Skinner, and the two worked very closely together to provide between the two of them a cohesive score. The success of these collaborations was due in a large part to their thinking along the same musical lines, although Salter was a little ahead of Skinner in certain respects, such as harmony and melodic development. Salter and Skinner were also close friends, and their work together contributed greatly to some of the best horror scores of the 40's.

Charles Previn, as Universal's music director in the 40's, was responsible for assigning projects to composers like Salter and Skinner, as well as occasionally taking a hand in composition. Previn was born in Brooklyn in 1888 and was educated at the New York College of Music, Cornell University and the Ithaca Conservatory, where he was awarded an honorary music doctorate. Previn also studied with Joseph Schillinger, eventually becoming employed as a conductor for vaudeville, Broadway, the St. Louis Opera, and film theaters. Previn spent seven and a half years as the head of Universal's music department in the 40's, and contributed to many of the horror films of this period.

Other prominent composers who collaborated with Salter, Skinner and Previn at Universal include Paul Dessau and Charles Henderson. Dessau, born in Germany in 1894, had studied in Berlin and Hamburg, and gained acclaim as a concert hall composer. He came to the United States during the Nazi era at which time he was associated with Universal. Among the scores he contributed to were HOUSE OF FRANKENSTEIN (1944) and its sequel, HOUSE OF DRACULA (1945). After the War, Dessau returned to Europe, settling in East Germany and continuing his career as a film and concert composer. Charles Henderson was born in Boston in 1907 and received a bachelor's degree from Harvard. Studying with Ernst Toch and others, Henderson first worked as a pianist and arranger for orchestras, musicals and radio. He became involved with Universal in the 40's, later working in television and for Las Vegas nightclub acts. Henderson contributed to segments of BLACK FRIDAY (1940), THE MAD GHOUL (1943), HOUSE OF DRACULA (1945) and others.

Hans Salter and Frank Skinner, however, remained the primary force behind the Universal horror film music. They both scored THE INVISIBLE MAN RETURNS (1940), providing an effective thematic motif which is given many varied treatments, reaching its loveliest variation in the conclusion when Radcliffe regains visibility and is reunited with his beloved. While Skinner worked on the score with Salter to some extent, almost all of the music was actually composed by Salter, who recalls that only the last three or four bars, where it goes into an apotheosis at the end, were written by Skinner. Later Salter added a violin filigree to this reunion music and used it in the last scene of SON OF DRACULA (1943), lending it a bittersweet quality which carries the quiet denouement on its own, without dialog. (This is a good example of the ability of orchestration to transform the same basic material from a happy, joyful mood--as in THE INVISIBLE MAN RETURNS --to a sad, bittersweet feeling in SON OF DRACULA.)

Other films, while often constructed from similar musical modes, contained equally effective moments. For THE MUMMY'S HAND (1940), Salter wrote an Egyptian-sounding funeral chant, but had to get an extra provision in the film's music budget in order to hire the eight vocalists he needed for that cue. "I always like to dress up certain scores," Salter said, "with unexpected ingredients like the human voice."[9] MAN-MADE MONSTER (1941) utilized, in addition to the horrific themes, a clever scherzo, heard as Lon Chaney Jr. played with his dog, worked as a delightful set piece unrelated to the score's thematic elements. The music for THE MAD GHOUL (1943) has many leitmotifs intertwined with a variety of "incidental" suspense and action passages, including a driving brass-and-string motif, a mournful theme for two or three violins, and a piece of solo horn.

Another noteworthy score, and the only one that can really be said to be 100 percent Salter, was THE GHOST OF FRANKEN-STEIN (1942), and it was the music for this film that firmly registered him as a master in the genre. The score has been described as "complex and richly descriptive, to say nothing of essential. Of the film's sixty-seven minutes, forty-seven are supported by Salter's pulsating music."[10]

Opening with a harsh musical explosion, Salter's music is heavy on brass with swirling string underscoring, building an appropriately dramatic and "monstrous" mood as the main titles appear. While Salter provides leitmotifs for various characters, the primary essence of this score can be broken down into three components. Firstly, strings are used to represent the moods of the human characters, as in the love theme for Elsa and Erik; in the slowly brooding passages that underly Ludwig Frankenstein's discovery of his father's diary; and scenes of the villagers' preparation to storm the castle.

Secondly, woodwinds represent the evil, cunning Ygor, characterized by the strange sound of the horn played by the character. Frank Skinner had used a similar device in his score for GHOST's predecessor, SON OF FRANKENSTEIN, utilizing a woodwind instrument called a blute. Salter similarly felt it logical to devise a strange-sounding theme for Ygor's horn which he could enlarge in various disguises and fashions throughout the rest of the score. Salter used an English horn for this sound, giving it a peculiar flavor through the use of a repeated lowered fifth in the melodic line.

Finally, the Monster is represented by the brass section, typically enough. This is the dominant theme of the film, admirably suggesting the Monster's uncertain, plodding footsteps. The motif starts out furtively with several loud, brassy punches. There are three notes and a pause; two notes and a pause; and so on, until emerging completely as the notes strike faster and higher in pitch, effectively complementing the often aimless prowling of the Monster. As one music reviewer recently commented of the scene when the Monster breaks his straps and lunges for Dr. Frankenstein, "Salter's orchestral descension down the tonal scale evokes a brutal inevitability which seems to propel the Monster's attack."[11] Ygor's horn theme is often intermingled with the Monster theme, illustrating the demented shepherd's control of the unfortunate creature. Salter also makes use of eerie shimmering percussion sounds and low piping woodwind in some scenes in the castle. An interesting variation on the Monster's theme, punctuated with xylophone, is heard as the Monster's new brain is implanted.

Salter went on to score the next two Universal Frankenstein films, FRANKENSTEIN MEETS THE WOLF MAN (1943) and THE HOUSE OF FRANKENSTEIN (1944), providing a pair of wonderfully effective scores. The former reprises some of the themes that he, along with Skinner and Previn, had created for THE WOLF MAN. A particularly moody theme is heard in the opening sequence as grave robbers approach the Talbot crypt. The eerie melody was played on a novachord, which sounds chords based upon fourths, giving them a strange quality. "Usually, chords are based on thirds," Salter explained, "but these are based on fourths--there's a fourth interval between each voice. When you move these chords back and forth it gives a special, eerie and mysterious feeling. And then, if you put on top of it an eerie-sounding melody line with the novachord, it really adds up to something very strong."[12]

Salter also provides a touching funeral march as the villagers carry the dead girl through the street, an effect similar in style to an earlier dirge composed for Chaney's final walk in MAN-MADE MONSTER. A particularly notable moment in FRANKENSTEIN MEETS THE WOLF MAN occurs when the moonlight shines through the hospital window, creeping slowly toward Larry Talbot's bed. A mysterious theme for strings, woodwind and celesta stirs moodily, mingling with the three-note Wolf Man motif, evoking the dark significance the moonlight has for Talbot. When he sees the glowing rays, he turns his face away, his torment suggested powerfully by the soulful strings. As Talbot's transformation into the werewolf ensues, the music builds forcefully into the unhindered Wolf Man theme. The score also features a song, "Faro-La, Faro-Li" (with lyrics by screenwriter Curt Siodmak), which is first sung at the Festival of the New Wine in the film.

The score for THE HOUSE OF FRANKENSTEIN was dominated by gypsy themes, in addition to characteristic loud, brass passages amid swirling strings and piping woodwinds, driven by a powerful bass line from the brasses. This harsh flavor is nicely balanced by a tender solo violin theme for the gypsy girl. The score paints a melancholy picture of tragedy, with low horns and strings undulating as, one by one, the various characters enter into their doom. The influence of Paul Dessau, one of the collaborators on this score, seemed especially prevalent in the use of modern dissonances and the like.

Salter contributed to the music of the sequel, HOUSE OF DRACULA (1945), along with no less than seven other composers whose music found its way into the film. The score was assembled by music director Edgar Fairchild from library tracks originally composed for previous films, although most of the cues were re-recorded for this film--as in Frank Skinner's SON OF FRANKENSTEIN theme which was used over the main titles here.[13] There was some original material composed by Salter for HOUSE OF DRACULA, however, most notably a sequence in which the heroine is playing Moonlight Sonata on a piano when Dracula enters the room and begins to mesmerize her. Subtly, the piano melody segues to a moody piece based on the Dracula theme which takes over until the girl grabs a crucifix, thwarting Dracula's influence. Moonlight Sonata returns as he flees from the room.

HOUSE OF FRANKENSTEIN was, in effect, the Swan Song of Universal's Golden Age of horror films. HOUSE OF DRACULA was merely an unsuccessful low-budget attempt to rekindle the flame; ABBOTT AND COSTELLO MEET FRANKENSTEIN, while an amusing vehicle for the comedy team, in actuality only served to ridicule the venerable movie monsters. Likewise, Salter's output shifted into

unmemorable fantastic films like HOUSE OF HORRORS (1946) and
THE STRANGE DOOR (1951), until the science ficiton boom of the
1950's rekindled a second Golden Age of fantastic filmmaking, of
which Salter became an important part (as we shall see in Chapter
V).

"In scoring horror pictures," Salter recalled, "the main element is that of creating atmosphere--the apprehensive mood, which
keeps the viewer on the edge of his seat." For example, in the
opening scenes of FRANKENSTEIN MEETS THE WOLF MAN where
the ghouls approach the Talbot crypt, it was necessary to give the
scene a sense of impending dreadfulness. This is the scene in
which Salter used the novachord to great effect. "In the same
sequence, after the robbers open the Talbot coffin and the moonlight filters into the crypt, I placed the theme which accompanies
every instance of Talbot turning into the Wolf Man. There is a
celesta in that theme, with high strings and high woodwinds, and
it is the interplay between those elements that creates the scary
effect. The music in all these horrific moments must, of course,
be chilling. When strange, ugly hands reach out, the music is
usually low-pitched and builds on slow chords."[14]

Despite the respect and longevity his horror scores have
maintained, Salter and his collaborators had no special feeling for
it at the time. "I don't think anybody who created the basic material for a film like this, not even the writers or directors, had
that feeling at the time," Salter said. "I, personally, think the
horror films of that period will survive everything else. It's such
a valid piece of Americana that it'll overshadow, not the westerns,
but all the romantic comedies, the adventure stories, and so on
... it was such a good wedding between music and story and direction. I think film music, per se, is an art form, and the horror picture, per se, is an art form, and the wedding of these two
elements created something unique."[15]

While some of the scores he wrote were fairly routine assignments, other times the music affected Salter deeply, giving him an
exhilerating thrill that he couldn't find in any other endeavor.
"The laws that govern the flow of a scene, visually, and the laws
that govern music, aurally, are diametrically opposed, and to bring
these two disciplines into unison is not easy," he said. "Sometimes it made me cry, to see how well the music fitted the scene,
how much it did for the scene or lifted the picture to some new
heights that it didn't have before. I just couldn't believe it."[16]

In view of the graphic realism of today's pictures, most of
the Universal horrors that Salter scored seem very tame and almost
amusing rather than frightening--yet they retain a charm and a
nostalgic flavor that is truly timeless. When released, however,
they were regarded as strictly routine by their creators; and the
subsequent popularity of the pictures is a tribute to the craftsman-

ship of those who brought them to life. For Hans J. Salter, specializing in the horror genre was not something he intended to do.
"It was just a matter of being in the right place at the right time
and finding that I had the right musical devices at my command to
do the job," he said. "I remember people at that time, and since,
expressed surprise that a nice, mild-mannered fellow from Vienna
could develop such a sense of horror and mayhem. The only way
I can explain it is to say that these so-called horror pictures were
a great challenge, because when I looked at them before scoring
they didn't seem to have much fright about them or much cohesion,
either. The challenge was in creating the sense of terror and suspense, and that is something that music can do."[17]

     Salter's style is somewhat characteristic of film scoring during
the 40's, what with its utilization of a variety of leitmotifs orchestrated in many variations and heard amid various musical bridges
and incidental passages. Whereas film scores of the 70's and 80's,
after having overcome the pop-tune mania of the 60's, seemed characterized by fewer themes that tended to dominate the score more
pervasively, Salter's music (and that of his colleagues) was more
complex, shifting forms more often, changing unexpectedly into
something else--like the transformed creatures portrayed on the
screen. Salter didn't reach the plateaus of acclaim that some of his
fellows did--men like Max Steiner, Franz Waxman, Bernard Herrmann and others--probably due to the simple fact that most of
Salter's work was on second-feature studio programmers rather than
on the big-budgeted A-pictures that Steiner and crew got. Regardless of his place on the roster, though, Salter's music is
constantly effective, lending a distinctive and very evocative flavor
to the horror films which have, in many ways, surpassed in endur-
ance even those A-pictures scored by his contemporaries.

     RKO Radio Pictures was another major producer of horror
and fantasy cinema during the 30's and 40's (they released KING
KONG in 1933), and by the 40's their foremost composer was Roy
Webb, whose music embellished many of their atmospheric films--
most notably those of Val Lewton. Webb was born in New York
City in 1888, but was not initially inclined to music until he volun-
teered to write background music for plays put on by New York's
Art Students' League, where he was studying. Discovering a
knack for music, Webb enrolled at Columbia University, where he
wrote music for variety shows and composed the University's fight
song. A songwriting career ensued, and Webb was one of the co-
founders of ASCAP in 1914. When sound came to motion pictures
in 1929, Webb embarked for Hollywood, eventually gaining work as
a music director for RKO, a post he held until 1952. Webb received his first composing credit in 1935, and went on to have a
prolific career in music direction and scoring until his death in
1982.

     Webb's scoring is very much in a symphonic style, somewhat

akin to that of Max Steiner, with whom he worked during his first two years at RKO. Webb was also a pioneer in the use of the click-track, a metronome device used by the conductor to coordinate the timings and pace of a cinematic musical cue. Webb also advocated the use of precise timing-and-action relationships, much the same way that Stiener did--in which certain actions on the screen are precisely accompanied by their own musical counterparts. While such mickey mousing has been effective at times, it has also been criticized for being too distracting and redundant. Steiner and Webb utilized this style to a great degree in the 30's and 40's, although since then its practice in feature films has diminished considerably. Webb also frequently practiced Steiner's "Casablanca technique"--using a set-piece song as a leitmotif throughout the film.

Webb scored dozens of Westerns, detective thrillers, dramas and the like during the 30's, including marginally fantastic pictures such as THE NITWITS (1935) and MUMMY'S BOYS (1936), but his most notable work in the genre began in the 40's with the score for CAT PEOPLE (1942).

CAT PEOPLE marked the first collaboration between Webb and producer Val Lewton. The teaming was so successful that Webb went on to score all but one of Lewton's subsequent RKO horror films. Webb, and music director Constantin Bakaleinikoff, were brought into the picture long before even the screenplay was underway, an unusual practice as most composers are normally consulted only during post-production, after the photography and basic editing have been completed. Lewton, however, did not want to settle for the pastiche scores often assembled for low-budget pictures, and Webb was involved even in the story sessions, where he contributed ideas for linking visuals with music. Webb later said that by being involved in the planning he was able to provide a more effective score.

Lewton wanted a lullaby theme that was suited to a story about cats, one that had a haunting quality to it. A traditional French lullaby, "Do, Do, Baby Do," appealed to Lewton and Webb agreed that it would make an ideal leitmotif for the picture. The lyrics were translated into Russian and sung by the Irena character at one point ... the melody reinforced throughout the score as the piece is reprised. This lullaby theme is balanced by a subtle, dramatic theme which acts as an effective counterpoint to the childish song. As one reviewer described it, "Roy Webb's music conveys an undercurrent of menace without becoming obtrusive, adding immeasurably to the gathering atmosphere of dread."[18] A notable aspect of this and other scores for Lewton films was the contrast between extended periods of silence and sudden surges of music, which contributed much to the moody, haunting atmosphere of these films.

The following year, Webb scored Lewton's THE LEOPARD
MAN (1943), to which he lent an appropriate Spanish flavor, in
keeping with the Latin locale of the picture. Actually a murder
mystery given a suggestive, supernatural atmosphere through
Jacques Tourneur's masterful direction, Webb's music added a
subtle dimension of uncertainty and eerieness to the mystery. A
particularly effective string motif is heard as the young girl is
locked in the walled cemetery. Webb provides a meandering melody which urgently accentuates the girl's panic as she runs to
seek an exit and ends--as she is pounced upon silently by the
unseen "leopard"--with a long, sustained organ note that fades almost imperceptibly out. Elsewhere, the film's mood of eerie terror
is achieved through silence--as when the first victim sees the
panther beneath the railroad trestle.

Also in 1943, Webb scored Lewton's I WALKED WITH A
ZOMBIE, a moody and well-told tale of Haitian voodoo. Webb's
music conveyed "intimations of melancholy and evil," according to
fantastic-film historian Donald C. Willis.[19] Webb composed a variety of motifs, with few recurring themes, such as a cue for
strings, harp and woodwind, heard as the nurse spots a white-
gowned figure strolling across the yard at night. A low woodwind
moan commences as the nurse is later awakened by a distant, sob-
bing voice. A woodwind and string melody, tinged with a slight
romance, is heard as the nurse and doctor discuss the ailing Mrs.
Holland in the bedroom. A mourning, passionate cue for strings
and harp echoed the mixture of emotions as Wes stabs Jessica,
and the zombie guard shambles up.

The same year, Webb scored two more pictures for Lewton,
GHOST SHIP and THE 7TH VICTIM, maintaining throughout a
characteristically subtle, dreamlike undercurrent of mood. In 1944,
Webb adapted his CAT PEOPLE score for Lewton's sequel, THE
CURSE OF THE CAT PEOPLE, laying out the original themes
against new music. Irena's lullaby is used effectively, as when
it is heard in counterpoint to the Christmas carols sung by Aimee's
family as the little girl secretly leaves the house to meet her.
The score is characterized by low-key string and woodwind moods,
an eerie, shimmering violin motif for the mysterious Mrs. Farren
and her bitter and menacing daughter; a tender woodwind theme
(drawn from Irena's lullaby) signifies Aimee's friendship with the
ghostly Irena. The score becomes more urgent and pronounced as
Aimee runs off into the woods, melting into the mysterious theme
as she finds strange solace at the Farren house, and reuniting at
last with the friendship theme as Irena rescues her and Aimee is
restored to her now-understanding father.

Lewton's next film, ISLE OF THE DEAD, was scored by
Leigh Harline, but Webb returned in 1945 with the music for THE
BODY SNATCHER. The main theme for this film emphasized
strings over a brass and drum rhythm something like a funeral

dirge. THE BODY SNATCHER also makes use of a song, heard at
one point by a street singer and reprised orchestrally at various
points in the film. Much of the score reflects the sound of old
Scottish ballads, and mixes the use of source music (that of the
street singer, the group of townsfolk at the Pennycook Inn, etc.)
with the main theme.

Webb scored Lewton's last, and most expensive, RKO horror
film, BEDLAM, in 1946. A characteristically conservative score
dominated by strings, the music revolved around a romantic
string theme associated with Quaker Hanney and Lady Bowen and
their sympathetic involvement in reforming the poor treatment of
the asylum inmates. This was counterpointed against a variety of
darker, more somber motifs associated with Master Sims and the
cruelty perpetrated by him within Bedlam's walls; with brasses
moaning and erupting during moments of shock and angry resolution, as when Lady Bowen is unwillingly committed to the asylum
by Sims in order to quiet her protests. The Sympathy Theme remains the most dominant, though, especially in the final scenes as
Lady Bowen learns to demonstrate active mercy during her incar-
ceration. The Sympathy Theme and the dangerous motifs play off
each other, underlining her initial fear of the sometimes dangerous
lunatics and the contrasting kindness of her heart; the music always
segues darkly as the glowering form of Sims strides in, but the
lower strains are always overcome by the higher melody of the
Sympathy Theme. Behind its spooky atmosphere, BEDLAM was a
very moralistic film, making a strong statement for mercy and compassion in the midst of cruelty and corruption; Webb's music reinforces this theme with its primary leitmotif constantly reassociating
the score with the attitude of kindness advocated by Hanney and
personified by Lady Bowen.

Webb's last major fantasy score was also one of his most
lively; that of MIGHTY JOE YOUNG (1949). Webb's approach to
scoring this lighthearted, giant-ape movie was very much along
the lines of its predecessor, KING KONG, although Webb again
makes strong use of a source song as a major leitmotif. "Beautiful
Dreamer" is the tune whistled by Jill to calm the oversized ape,
and is also the theatrical piece played during Joe's performance
at the nightclub. Webb expands the song into a leitmotif for the
ape's pathos, and his relationship with Jill. Balancing it is an effective, slow-moving brassy motif, built around a three-note
phrase, which becomes a gargantuan theme representing the extraordinary aspects of the huge ape, while "Beautiful Dreamer"
represents his spirit and feelings.

While his incorporation of songs as leitmotifs and his penchant for mickey mousing have been described as obtrusive by some,
Webb tried to maintain an artistic balance. "I think you can hurt
a motion picture a great deal by making audiences conscious of the
music," he said, "unless you want them to be aware of it for a

particular reason. If someone is singing a song, you should hear
that and be conscious of it. But if it's what you call mood music,
that's another thing entirely."[20] Webb contributed in various ways
to more than 200 pictures in the nearly 20 years he worked for
RKO. While most of the films were routine programmers, several
of them have since attained prominent status as classics of the fantastic film, and Webb's consistent expertise in providing the right
kind of score earns him a memorable place in the music of the fantastic cinema.

A number of other composers lent themselves notably to the
music of the fantastic films of the 40's, although they did not
achieve the kind of status as dependable "masters" of the medium
in the way that Salter, Webb and Skinner did.

A Viennese composer who, like Max Steiner, had a great influence on the early development of film music was Erich Wolfgang
Korngold, who wrote music for dramatic and adventure films such
as THE SEA HAWK and THE ADVENTURES OF ROBIN HOOD (and
who was a major influence upon the work of John Williams, who has
done much to reintroduce the lavish symphonic score into film music of the 70's and 80's). Korngold's single fantastic film was BE-
TWEEN TWO WORLDS, a 1944 remake of OUTWARD BOUND, which
told the story of people killed in a London blitz, finding themselves on an ocean voyage waiting to be judged "between two
worlds." The film's psychological story especially appealed to
Korngold, and it is said that this was his favorite score. His
mystical music creates ominous moods even in the main title, and
Korngold emphasized those moods through a slow, lyrical and often
sad melody played by high strings and low brasses. Korngold had
also composed a few instrumental cues, without credit, for the religious fantasy, THE GREEN PASTURES (1936).

Alfred Newman was one of Hollywood's most prolific, versatile and inspired film composers. A concert pianist at age seven,
he went on to conduct symphony orchestras and Broadway musicals
before going to Hollywood in 1930. Associated with more than 200
films, Newman won nine Academy Awards and was nominated 46
times. He scored very few fantastic films, however, the most important being the Charles Laughton remake of THE HUNCHBACK
OF NOTRE DAME (1939), for which he received his seventh Academy Award nomination.

This score is a rich, full-blooded adventure score with a
variety of themes and a powerful use of large cathedral choir over
the titles, emphasizing the Notre Dame Cathedral. The motif for
the cathedral is a dominant one, a proud, hymnlike theme for
strings which underscores the power of the church and its sanctuary, which figures prominently in the story. Newman also provides a melancholy, dirgelike theme for Quasimodo, the hunchback, which is used especially well after Quasimodo's torture on

the pillary and his subsequent, staggered walk back to the cathedral. A love theme, a sweeping, high string motif, is given for Esmeralda, which is heard during her tender scenes with Gringoire as well as over the mutual compassion shown between her and Quasimodo. In addition, a rousing, swashbuckling theme is given to Phoebus, Captain of the Guards, and is nicely heard from strings and brass in the early scene where Phoebus rescues Esmeralda from the menacing hunchback.

In addition, several minor motifs are used to great effect, such as the ominous, low shivering string passage heard as Gringoire enters the Court of Miracles, home of the beggars; and a particularly stunning choral cue, heard first for low, chanting choir as Esmeralda is escorted to the gallows; thundering forth with brass and victoriously shouting choir as Quasimodo swings down from the Bell Tower and carries her to safety, shouting "Sanctuary! Sanctuary!"

Newman accomplishes a great bit of mickey mousing at the climax where the various groups of Parisians converge upon Notre Dame to "rescue" Esmeralda; great, monstrous brass chords erupt as Quasimodo hurls the wooden beam down upon them; the Notre Dame theme is heard as the crowd picks up the beam and uses it as a battering ram upon the cathedral's great doors, the music gradually getting more frenzied as the crowd anticipates entry, culminating in a slow, triumphant cue as Quasimodo pours the vat of molten metal over them. Newman also included an effective "smashing" cue as Quasimodo throws the evil Frollo from the tower, which musically conjures up the grisly effect of his landing! This segues to the Notre Dame motif as the camera cuts away to a Christ statue, suggesting the divine justice accomplished in Frollo's death; the love theme is heard as Gringoire and Esmeralda are reunited, which then segues to Quasimodo's sad theme as the final shot moves from him sitting alone on the parapet to a vast, distant long shot of the entire cathedral. The choir motif returns, ending with the love theme for the final titles. THE HUNCHBACK OF NOTRE DAME is Newman's strongest entry among his few genre scores, and remains a superior composition, effectively underscoring the film's romance, adventure and tragedy.

Newman also wrote the music for THE BLUE BIRD (1940), a charming if neglected fairy tale concerning two children's search for happiness in a fantasy world. Newman's music was comprised primarily of fairy-tale jingles, utilizing familiar instruments of the Tyrolean region during the real-world sequences and full symphonic orchestration in the fantasy scenes. Newman also reportedly made use of new electrical instruments, constructed by the studio sound crew, to gain new effects of musical fantasy.

The film music of Victor Young is characterized by sweet, warm melodic themes. Born in Chicago but trained in Europe,

Young became an extremely prolific songwriter whose sense of lyricism prevailed in his approach to film scoring. Young's catchy tunes became popular both on and off screen, and films such as SHANE and AROUND THE WORLD IN 80 DAYS benefitted from his light romantic touch. Similarly, Young lent his sentimental romanticism to the fantastic films he scored. Young's first work in the genre was as the musical director for Max Fleischer's animated feature, GULLIVER'S TRAVELS (1939). The film featured songs by Ralph Rainer and Leo Robin; Young provided the incidental music. The film was scored, cartoonlike, with wall-to-wall music and endless mickey mousing which heightened Fleischer's zaniness. Young also came up with several recurring motifs, such as a seafaring Voyage Theme, and a deep, heavy brass motif reminiscent of later colossal-man pictures as Gulliver awakens in the land of the Lilliputians. While the scores for thrillers such as THE MAD DOCTOR (1949), THE UNINVITED (1944) and NIGHT HAS A THOUSAND EYES (1948) had their more sinister moments, Young's opulent love themes dominated. Some critics regarded Young's approach as overly sentimental, but his style ultimately became the prototype of "Hollywood music."

David Raksin came to Hollywood in 1935 with the definite idea of becoming a film composer. He had studied music in Philadelphia, and in his teens had organized his own dance band, and worked as a musician and arranger for various bands in New York, including Benny Goodman's. Through the assistance of Alfred Newman, Raksin was brought to Hollywood to arrange Charlie Chaplin's music for MODERN TIMES. Raksin continued to work as an arranger, adapter and collaborating composer on many features, documentaries, and shorts until 1943, when he had the opportunity to compose original scores for films.

Among the features on which Raksin collaborated during the early 40's was THE UNDYING MONSTER (1942), a small but effective werewolf chiller cocomposed with Cyril Mockridge and Arthur Lange, supervised by Emil Newman at Twentieth Century-Fox. One reviewer commented on their score thusly: "Dominating the ominous scenes was an utterly eerie six-note leitmotif on the flute and underscored by the ghostly wail of distant voices.... More prevalent were shocking atonal organ passages that grew in intensity.... When the monster jumps from the balcony, he is accompanied by a blast of trombones, and when Curtis enters the doctor's lab and starts up a centrifuge, the leitmotif is heard over a tingling cacophony on the celesta."[21]

The score included an interesting effect from the piano, which Raksin, in a sense, invented. "People had found that by cutting off the impact of a piano chord," Raksin explained, "they could get a certain kind of odd sound. The problem with that was, however, that you would still get a noise when the sound came in, and if you tried to ease the sound in by using the dials

in the mixing controls you would have too short a chord. I was
doing the score to a picture called THE UNDYING MONSTER, and
I needed some low chords of a certain kind, and I hit upon a simple expedient: after first placing the microphones the way the
sound engineer and I wanted them, I would sit at the piano and I
would start counting. On three the sound engineer would 'close'
the microphone completely, on four I would strike the chord on the
piano, and on five he would start bringing up the level, and continue bringing up the level until he got system noise. From that
we could make an actual sound loop and duplicate it. We could
turn one the other way around and equalize them so we got the
chord we needed."[22] The effect created an unusual sound which
added to the eerie tension of the picture.

Raksin continued to score low-budget horror films for Fox,
and other studios, throughout the early 40's. It was an experience he found limiting, but nevertheless of value, as he later recalled: "I was not considered sufficiently domesticated to be
trusted with anything that didn't have mystery or violence. Those
pictures were enjoyable because nobody ever urged me to write
anything pretty, which is the bugbear of film composers."[23] In
1944, Raksin gained widespread acclaim for his romantic score for
LAURA, which he found as a welcome relief after "all those horror
films," and his theme song has gone on to become one of the most
recorded pieces of popular music. Raksin developed the piano effect he had used for UNDYING MONSTER in this score as well.

In the later 40's, Raksin scored a few light fantasies, such
as THE SECRET LIFE OF WALTER MITTY and THE NEXT VOICE
YOU HEAR, but his music for the 1953 whimsical animated short,
THE UNICORN IN THE GARDEN, was a particularly notable one.
Raksin wrote the music for a number of UPA shorts, of which this
was the fourth, and he found the experience very enjoyable, despite the limitations of small orchestras (UNICORN used only six
musicians). "The theme for the unicorn was scored for recorder,"
Raksin recalled, "perhaps the first time that instrument was used
in a film. Unicorns make you think of tapestries, where you saw
the beast for the first time. And that leads to the Renaissance
and to the sound of the recorder."[24] James Thurber, from whose
story the film was adapted, was quite pleased with Raksin's music
as well, and wrote to the composer to say how much he enjoyed
the unicorn theme. Interviewed in the early 70's, Raksin was happy to say that "the music doesn't sound terribly far out two decades later. That's because of a process of counter-validation going
on between music and film. While an audience, upon hearing in
concert some of the dissonances we employ in film, would run
screaming from the theater, they accept it when experienced con-
jointly with the image. The music validates the image."[25]

While Raksin has scored many films since then in the 50's
and 60's, very few of them contained elements of fantasy, until

1971 when he provided a fine score for the low-budget chiller, WHAT'S THE MATTER WITH HELEN?, which may be something of a return to Raksin's cinematic roots. Raksin has also composed many concert works, and for many years conducted a course in film music at the University of Southern California. While only a small portion of his musical output has been for genre films, and these mostly unremarkable pictures, his scoring retains a large degree of musical substance, characterized by his penchant for subtle sonorities instead of melody, and was quite effective for the small chillers he scored in the 40's.

Dimitri Tiomkin became most popular as a composer of catchy tunes for Westerns such as HIGH NOON in the 50's, although he began scoring for pictures in the early 30's and produced some fine fantasy scores during this period.

Born in the Ukraine, Tiomkin was taught to play the piano by his mother. He studied at the St. Petersburg Conservatory, emigrating to Berlin in 1919, where he eventually performed as solo pianist with the Berlin Philharmonic before moving to Paris where he performed with a former St. Petersburg colleague. The pair did well enough to get an offer to tour America in 1925, which eventually resulted in Tiomkin's composing for motion pictures.

Tiomkin's film career began in earnest in 1933 with his music for the lavish but vapid ALICE IN WONDERLAND. He also composed the music for the Peter Lorre film, MAD LOVE (1935), but the film that was Tiomkin's milestone during this period was Frank Capra's LOST HORIZON in 1937. Capra had hired Tiomkin despite objections from the studio executives who felt Tiomkin's relative inexperience would be a disadvantage to what was a highly ambitious project, although as a safeguard Capra also hired Max Steiner to conduct Tiomkin's score, admitting later that "I knew that if wise old Steiner thought the score inadequate, he himself would step in to rewrite it--fast."[26] According to Hugo Friedhofer, though, who was one of Tiomkin's orchestrators on the score, Tiomkin himself asked for Steiner in preference over Columbia's music director, Morris Stoloff.[27]

Tiomkin, in his autobiography, described his working relationship with Steiner: "LOST HORIZON spoiled me completely. The conductor was Max Steiner, who was also a first-rate composer. Composers are usually jealous of each other, like rival tenors in an opera company; but Steiner had only one idea--to get the best out of the score. If I made a suggestion, he wanted to find out what was in my mind and do it that way. He was responsible for much of the musical success of the film."[28]

"During the scoring of this picture," Steiner later recalled in his unpublished autobiography, "we had to do quite a lot of re-

vising. Capra kept on changing the picture, and the timing, which
Tiomkin had obtained from someone, wasn't quite exact. So I used
to orchestrate and copy or revise whatever was required during
the daytime. Then we would start to record about 8 o'clock at
night and seldom finished until about 6 or 7 in the morning."[29]

No less than nine orchestrators were recruited for the task
of orchestrating Tiomkin's music. "Since he was a pianist," recalled one of them, Bernhard Kaun, "one had to re-think his ideas
in an orchestral way. I did this in the few numbers that I did
for him. He would give his pianistic sketches to a good arranger
who would make the best of it. But it was still Tiomkin's music."[30]
The score was then recorded by a large orchestra, ranging from
45 to 65 pieces, utilizing a large number of percussion instruments,
including a Tibetan Rata drum, various other drums, gongs, cymbals and bells, as well as several kinds of keyboard instruments.
At the time, this was the largest orchestra ever assembled at Columbia Studios. Tiomkin also used the Hall Johnson Choir, a popular group of black singers, in certain sequences. A number of authentic Tibetan instruments were also borrowed for appearance
within the picture, although they were not actually heard in the
score.

Tiomkin's music was suitably romantic and exotic, with a
dominant use of the choir and bells to establish a mystical flavor
in the primary Shangri-La Theme. The score is lavish and expressive, and was enthusiastically received by Capra, who later remarked that "Tiomkin's music not only captured the mood, but it
darned near captured the film."[31] A dissenting opinion, however,
was voiced by one recent reviewer: "The heavenly choir, serving
as an allegorical narrative, only intensified an already overroman-
ticized screen imagery. A puerile, laughable musical convention,
the angel voices were dated years before LOST HORIZON. The action takes place, for the most part, in Tibet, an exotic land filled
with sounds strange to the Western ear, and yet not one single
note of Tibetan musical language appears on the sound track."[32]

The appropriateness of Tiomkin's music, however, may have
been more subtle, as was noted by another recent reviewer:
"...strong and weak beats, metric definition, conventional Western
phrase structure that involves one phrase ending and another be-
ginning--all are absent.... Rather there is an affinity with Oriental or medieval monody in which tune is never-ending; it just flows
on and on, perpetually regenerating itself--the 'continuous continuation' of the Orient as opposed to the Western conception of 'moment in time.' There is no 'stress' here (in the technical, musical
sense) just as there is no 'stress' (in the wider, general sense)
in the Valley of the Blue Moon; we have in fact the ageless beauty
and serenity of Shangri-La."[33]

Tiomkin continued to score films for Frank Capra through

1946, their last collaboration being the sentimental fantasy, IT'S
A WONDERFUL LIFE. While this alliance came to an end, Tiomkin
was establishing notable associations with Alfred Hitchcock, Howard
Hawks and Carl Foreman, which resulted in many of the composer's
best scores. Tiomkin's last genre scores of the 40's included the
unmemorable TARZAN AND THE MERMAIDS (1948) and David O.
Selznick's delicate ghost story of the same year, PORTRAIT OF
JENNIE. This picture contained Tiomkin's remarkable assimilation
and orchestration of four compositions by Debussy (Nocturnes,
Afternoon of the Faun, The Maid with the Flaxen Hair and Ara-
besque), for which Selznick had spent thousands of dollars to use.

Initially, Bernard Herrmann had been selected to arrange
these pieces for the film as well as composing original music. As
the production became delayed, however, Herrmann had to leave
the project, and he was replaced by Tiomkin. The only piece of
Herrmann's music left in the film (uncredited), is the haunting
song sung early in the film by Jennie and later reprised in the
score. Jennie is the young girl who lived and died years before
the man who, despairing and hopeless, has met and fallen in love
with her ghost, and the simple melody of "Jennie's Theme" lends
an effective flavor of nostalgia and simplicity to her scenes. "The
sharp contrast," wrote one reviewer, "between [Tiomkin's] alternately commonplace and grandiose arrangements and the haunting,
atmospheric Herrmann music is quite obvious."[34]

While the Debussy music acts as complementary underscoring,
Jennie's sad song and its lyrics are used as a means to suggest
her otherworldliness, as another reviewer described: "When Eben
meets her unexpectedly the second time, ... Jennie's theme pre-
cedes his finding her among the crowd. And here too she
emerges out of the glare of the sun on ice and snow. In moments
of solitude, the melody of the song haunts Eben and suggests his
longing for her. The phrase 'the wind blows, the sea flows' becomes the clue that leads Eben to their final encounter in the autumn storm."[35]

During the 30's and 40's, Tiomkin's style had grown and developed, but it wasn't until the 50's that it actually crystalized
with the many fine scores, quite a few of them for Westerns, that
he wrote during this period. Tiomkin was also noteworthy in establishing the use of a theme song, as he did in HIGH NOON, as
a thematic element of the score--a practice which has unfortunately
since evolved into mindless commercialism of potentially marketable
songs usually unrelated musically to the film itself. It was in the
50's, as well, that Tiomkin scored his greatest fantastic film, THE
THING, which will be discussed at length in Chapter V.

George Duning began his film career in the 40's, and in the
early days encountered a number of semi-fantasies and psychological dramas. Duning's background was in both jazz and symphonic

music, having been a trumpet player in Cincinnati before becoming music director for a number of radio and television orchestras, in addition to the Armed Forces Radio Service during World War II. After the war, Duning began to work as an orchestrator for Columbia Pictures, eventually gaining the opportunity to score films as well. During the next 40 years, Duning achieved a notable reputation as a composer for dramas such as PICNIC and FROM HERE TO ETERNITY, being nominated for an Academy Award five times in the process.

Among Duning's early scores in the late 40's were semifantasy films such as THE RETURN OF OCTOBER (1948), for which he provided a light, romantic score, and THE GUILT OF JANET AMES (1947), which conversely suggested to the composer a more dramatic approach. "That, to me, called for a very dramatic, heavy theme," Duning recalled. "I had a very long theme, about forty-six bars, which I used almost entirely throughout the picture; and then where she went into the dream sequence I would use sounds, mixtures of high strings, vibraphones, different types of cymbals, shimmers, and things like that to convey the feeling that the mind was in another strata." [36]

Duning's most overt fantasy score of this period was his popular BELL, BOOK AND CANDLE (1950), one of his favorite scores. A romantic comedy involving an urban witch, Duning scored the film with a characteristically light touch and an effective use of jazz. "I felt it needed a good, strong theme," Duning said, "and then I had shorter themes; a cockey little theme for Jack Lemmon, a gimmick for the cat sequences with Kim Novak, and then where Jack would flick his hand and the street lights would go on and off, I worked out what I guess you'd call an electronic device, by recording certain sounds on tape and then speeding up the tape, doubling or tripling the speed, and using a variable mixer which would raise the pitch. That was one of the early ones that I tried with experiments of that type." The music for BELL, BOOK AND CANDLE was primarily recorded in Munich, conducted by Kurt Graunke, with Duning supervising. The jazz sequences, however, were recorded at Columbia's Hollywood studio, where Duning was able to employ some of the top Los Angeles jazz musicians, as well as pianist John Williams (who would later gain fame as a top film composer in the 70's and 80's).

In the later 50's Duning scored the animated Mr. Magoo feature, 1001 ARABIAN NIGHTS (1959), investing into the film an exotic, Oriental score tinged with an occasional touch of jazz (as in the incorporation of the Mr. Magoo theme in the main title) and easy-listening choral songs. The majority of the score, though, is atmospheric orchestral music--Duning avoided scoring the film in mickey-mouse fashion, instead underlining situations and locales with suitable musical motifs. Duning also used a number of little-known instruments to achieve an authentic Oriental sound, including boo bams, crotales, rhythm logs and Oriental ceremonial bells.

Morris W. Stoloff was the head of Columbia's music department during the 40's, contributing composition and conducting for
hundreds of their films until his retirement in the late 60's. Born
in Philadelphia in 1898, Stoloff was a child-prodigy violinist who
played with the Los Angeles Philharmonic before joining Paramount
as a concert master in 1928. He joined Columbia in 1936 as a music director, and was eventually promoted to the head of the music
department. Stoloff won three Academy Awards for film music, and
was nominated in that category 18 times. While most of his work
was for nongenre films, Stoloff did contribute in varying degrees
(mostly in a supervisory capacity) to films such as THE DEVIL
COMMANDS (1941), RETURN OF THE VAMPIRE (1943) and others.

Herbert Stothart scored a majority of MGM's "prestige pictures" of the 30's and 40's. Born in Milwaukee in 1885, Stothart
taught music at the University of Wisconsin from 1910 to 1915 before becoming involved in the New York theater scene in the 20's,
where he composed, orchestrated and conducted various operettas
and musicals. One of these operettas was adapted by United Artists into the 1930 film, LOTTERY BRIDE, and as a result Stothart
became established in Hollywood as MGM's chief staff composer and
conductor, working most notably on the Nelson Eddy/Jeanette
MacDonald musicals. The MGM films of these years were lavish,
full of romance, charm and sentiment, and Stothart provided music
for them that was refined and pleasant, mostly written for small
ensembles. "Tender, lucid melodies, played by soft, glamorously-
crooning strings, became his trademark," wrote a biographer, "in-
tensifying emotion, clarifying motives and intuitively underlining
the essential qualities of a film's characters.... His more luxuriant
orchestral sounds effectively built tension and atmosphere, added
continuity to the action, colored exotic locales and authentically
evoked the pomp and circumstance of bygone days."[37]

Undoubtedly, Stothart's most popular film was THE WIZARD
OF OZ (1939), on which he worked as musical director, and for
which he won an Oscar for best score. There is little original
scoring in the film, however, as Stothart's work mostly involved
arranging the Harold Arlen songs. In the 40's Stothart turned
more toward the composition of original scores for dramatic films,
and one of the best scores credited to Stothart during this period
was for THE PICTURE OF DORIAN GRAY in 1945. Miklos Rozsa
points out in his autobiography, however, that the score is actually almost entirely the uncredited work of Mario Castelnuovo-
Tedesco.[38]

Stothart had frequently borrowed from classical composers in
his scores, usually due to time pressures. Rather than simply in-
serting the classical motifs routinely, however, Stothart used them
creatively. THE PICTURE OF DORIAN GRAY is no exception, taking as a major leitmotif an orchestral setting of Chopin's Prelude
for Piano No. 24 in D Minor. This piece becomes, in effect, Dori-

an's theme. It is heard several times in its original form, although most often it is orchestrated for woodwinds and strings to provide an underlying orchestral flavor. While the Prelude is identified with Dorian, his love interest, Sibyl, is identified with a song she sings early in the picture, "Goodbye, Little Yellow Bird." In the manner of Max Steiner and Roy Webb, this tune becomes her leitmotif and recurs throughout the score to reinforce her relationship with Dorian and its tragedy. As David Balsom noted in a lengthy retrospective on this film: "By creative design or luck, the seven-note title phrase of the song resembles the fundamental nine-note motif of the Prelude."[39]

A third motif is an ascending five-note phrase suggestive of a hymn, which might be considered the Fate Theme. First heard in the sequence where Dorian plays the Chopin Prelude for Sibyl on the piano prior to seducing her; the orchestra begins to accompany the piano notes, and the Fate motif is played by muted horns against the melody of the Prelude. A more powerful statement of the motif is heard from the brass over the final piano chords. "In later scenes this theme takes on connotations of redemption," Balsom wrote. "In the final sequence of the film, after Dorian's prayer, the restoration of the portrait begins with a swirling passage in the strings, which then take up the fate theme. Transferred to the brass after Dorian's corpse is found, it develops into a triumphal march involving tympani and snare drum. With the final title, the theme resolves in a crashing chord from the full orchestra."

In addition to these three major leitmotifs, a number of incidental passages contribute to the powerful effect of the score. David Balsom describes the music of the scene where Dorian writes his first, cruel letter to Sibyl, which dissolves to a scene of Sibyl reading it in her dressing room: "In the background can be heard the jaunty xylophone and bass drum music for an onstage puppet show and the music slows down while the drum amplifies, briefly reflecting her own staggered heartbeat."

While Stothart, who died in 1949 after scoring BIG JACK (a borderline horror-thriller concerning grave-robbing), is best remembered for his work on THE WIZARD OF OZ and other lavish MGM musicals, the carefully crafted score attributed him for DORIAN GRAY remains a poignant and memorable fantasy score. As for the highly respected Castelnuovo-Tedesco (who did receive credit for his earlier music for RETURN OF THE VAMPIRE [1945]), his involvement with the score undoubtedly contributed much to its strength; more so, in fact, than Stothart himself, whose credit may have stemmed more from his staff position at MGM than any extensive compositional involvement in DORIAN GRAY.

German-born Werner Heymann started out working for the Vienna and Berlin Philharmonics, until gaining employment as the

assistant to the musical director at UFA, the German film company,
in 1925. Heyman later became the company's musical director, until emigrating to the USA in 1933, where he scored numerous Hollywood films for a variety of studios until returning to Germany
in the early 50's. While most of Heymann's scores were for lighthearted romances, he demonstrated an effective penchant for the
dramatic and horrific with his music for ONE MILLION B.C. (1940).
Since this prehistoric adventure/fantasy had no intelligible dialog,
it depended entirely upon the visual action and Heymann's driving,
dramatically punctuated score to carry it along. The score is
heavy on brass, laying the music on thickly to accompany what was
more of a prehistoric soap opera with occasional lizards-cum-dino-
sauers than a bona fide fantasy tale. Heymann's only other genre
offering was TOPPER RETURNS (1941), a sequel to the successful
farcical ghost story of 1937, in which he provided a lighthearted
score along the lines of his non-genre work.

Leigh Harline studied at the University of Utah and after-
wards became a member of the Utah Radio Orchestra. In 1938 he
moved to Hollywood, where he became affiliated with the Disney
Studios, providing the background music for SNOW WHITE AND
THE SEVEN DWARFS (1939) and the entire score for PINOCCHIO
(1940), including the famous song, "When You Wish Upon a Star"
(which was, incidentally, interpolated in a few passages of John
Williams' score for CLOSE ENCOUNTERS OF THE THIRD KIND in
1977, and at one time was even to be used in its original form at
the film's conclusion). Harline worked for a variety of studios but
spent the majority of his time at RKO, although he continued to
score a number of Silly Symphony cartoons for Disney, providing
some of the most memorable musical accompaniment for these short
films which, however simple in appearance, required painstaking
care to produce and score.

Harline scored most of the Blondie pictures for Columbia, including one with minor fantasy overtones (a haunted house),
BLONDIE HAS SERVANT TROUBLE (1940). His first true horror
film, however, was Val Lewton's ISLE OF THE DEAD in 1945, for
which he provided a "moody, minimal, unclichéd setting for a rather
muddled exercise in backlot Gothicism," as one reviewer had it. [40]
Harline established a mood of melancholy and dread with a sustained
passage for muted trumpet-calls in the early scenes of Karloff pick-
ing his way through a littered battlefield on the way to the secret
isle. Another writer described the music as "autumnally-toned,"
working against the cynical stance apparently evoked by the film's
story. [41]

Harline provided an "off-beat, oddly idyllic" score for THE
BOY WITH GREEN HAIR (1948), which used as a leitmotif the song
"Nature Boy," extending its lyrical mood into the film's fantastic
symbolism. In 1952 Harline scored Howard Hawks's lighthearted
comedy, MONKEY BUSINESS, in which an absent-minded professor

concocts a rejuvenating formula which makes him grow gradually
younger. Harline's music was fairly typical, light-comedy scoring,
characterized by lush strings, but the inclusion of high saxophone
and xylophone in the fantasy sequences where we see the results
of the formula is quite evocative of the theremin, and lends an
eerie, "twilight-zonish" undertone to the primarily zany proceedings. Harline also composed the orchestrations and incidental music for George Pal's THE WONDERFUL WORLD OF THE BROTHERS
GRIMM (1962), which more dominantly featured Bob Merrill's vocal
score. Harline's last score before his death in 1967 was for Pal's
SEVEN FACES OF DR. LAO (1964), which we will discuss at length
in Chapter IX.

Mischa Bakaleinikoff was born in Russia and came to the
United States in 1926, joining the Columbia music department in
1931. During the 40's and 50's, Bakaleinikoff worked as a music
director on hundreds of films, one of his earliest assignments being the supervisor for Franz Waxman's BRIDE OF FRANKENSTEIN
score in 1935. Bakaleinikoff also received credit for the music of
a number of films, including most of Columbia's serials such as
SUPERMAN (1948), BATMAN AND ROBIN (1949) and CAPTAIN
VIDEO (1951), although these were presumably compiled from library tracks, as Bakaleinikoff was primarily a conductor. He
served as musical director on these films, as he did on many of the
"jungle" films and serials of the 50's, including JUNGLE JIM IN
THE FORBIDDEN LAND (1951) and KING OF THE CONGO (1952).
In the later 50's, he worked on many of the science fiction B-
movies including several of Ray Harryhausen's early pictures, until his death in 1960. Bakaleinikoff's scores have always been adequate if unremarkable; one reviewer described them as having "a
tendency to sound alike, heavy with blaring horns and mock-
urban rhythms."[42]

Mischa's brother, Constantin Bakaleinikoff, was also a musical director in Hollywood. Born in Moscow in 1896, Constantin began studies at the Moscow Conservatory when he was nine years
old, graduating in 1916 as a cellist and composer. After experience with a chamber ensemble touring Siberia and the Orient,
Bakaleinikoff came to the United States and began his musical career as a member of the Los Angeles Philharmonic. A year later
he was engaged as a conductor for Grauman's theater until 1928,
when he worked as a music director for Paramount and Columbia.
In 1933 he joined MGM, where he stayed for eight years, after
which Bakaleinikoff became the head of RKO's music department in
1941, supervising many of the fantasy scores of Paul Sawtell and
Roy Webb.

Edward Ward wrote the music for the lavish, colorful PHAN-
TOM OF THE OPERA (1943). Ward began his career as a piano
soloist in New York, eventually gaining acclaim as an arranger.
He also headed his own orchestra in Detroit before coming to Hol-

lywood in 1929. Initially at Universal, Ward joined MGM in 1935, scoring more than 60 films until moving to United Artists and then back to Universal in 1942, where he scored PHANTOM OF THE OPERA. For this extravagant picture, Ward adapted excerpts from Von Flotow's Martha (Acts III and IV), themes from Tchaikovsky and Chopin, and composed the haunting "Lullaby of the Bells," which is the film's main theme. The Lullaby figures heavily in the film both as source music (it is the concerto Erique Claudin composed--and believed stolen--prior to his becoming the Phantom) and as the running love theme representing Claudin's feelings toward Christine. Ward also provides an amusing woodwind scherzo mixed with lush romantic strings for the two rivals vying for Christine's hand. A variety of horrific motifs are also in evidence, such as the monotonous, high organ tones that accompany the mysterious appearances of the Phantom, and the use of organ and dreamy harp glissandos as Claudin leads Christine into the catacombs beneath the opera house.

Ward later adapted the music of Schubert and Chopin for THE CLIMAX (1944), a similar horror story set in opera surroundings. In this case, Ward reportedly collaborated on the musical adaptation with the film's producer, George Waggner.

The 1940's have been called the Golden Age of Film Music, an appropriate appellation in view of the many great and memorable film scores produced during this decade. While each composer maintained an individual approach to the films he was assigned, some trends can be discerned. Most films of the period were scored in the romantic tradition, embraced by composers such as Newman, Salter, Skinner, Rozsa, Waxman and others; although there was also a tendency by other composers, such as David Raksin, Hugo Friedhofer and others to go into a more dissonant and modern harmonic direction. Both styles are equally suited to the fantastic genre, with the latter perhaps achieving the greatest experimentation simply due to the bizarre and fantastic subject matter which was much more conducive to musical experimentation.

Notes

1. William H. Rosar, "Music for the Monsters" Library of Congress Quarterly, Fall 1983. (My gratitude to Mr. Rosar for supplying in advance the invaluable background material contained in this important work of scholarship; all the background facts of Universal's horror music from 1930-1936 are derived with permission from his research.)

2. Calvin Thomas Beck, Heroes of the Horrors (New York: Macmillan Publishing Co., 1975) p. 128-129

3. William H. Rosar, loc. cit. #1

4. George E. Turner and Michael H. Price, Forgotten Horrors (La Jolla: A. S. Barnes & Co., 1979) p. 58. (Many details which have been specified on the music for these Republic and Mascot serials come from this fine book.)

5. Ibid., p. 182

6. Donald F. Glut, The Frankenstein Legend (Metuchen, N.J.: Scarecrow Press, 1973) p. 138

7. Hans J. Salter quoted by Tony Thomas from an interview by Preston Neal Jones, Film Score--The View from the Podium (La Jolla: A. S. Barnes & Co., 1979) p. 110

8. Hans J. Salter quoted by Preston Neal Jones, "The Ghost of Hans J. Salter," Cinefantastique Vol. 7, #2 (1978) p. 14

9. Ibid., p. 19

10. Tony Thomas, liner notes to The Ghost of Frankenstein soundtrack record album (Tony Thomas Prods., 1980)

11. Preston Neal Jones, op. cit., p. 10

12. Hans J. Salter, op. cit., p. 19

13. Gregory William Mank, It's Alive! (La Jolla: A. S. Barnes & Co., 1981) p. 15

14. Hans J. Salter quoted by Tony Thomas, op. cit., p. 111

15. Hans J. Salter, op. cit., p. 15

16. Ibid.

17. Hans J. Salter quoted by Tony Thomas, liner notes to The Film Music of Hans J. Salter record album (Tony Thomas Prods., 1979)

18. George Turner, "Val Lewton's CAT PEOPLE," Cinefantastique Vol. 12, #4 (May-June 1982) p. 27

19. Donald C. Willis, Horror and Science Fiction Films II (Metuchen, N.J.: Scarecrow Press, 1982) p. 186

20. Roy Webb quoted by Mark Evans, Soundtrack--The Music of the Movies (New York: Da Capo Press, 1979) p. 196

21. Paul Mandell, "THE UNDYING MONSTER--In Retrospect," Photon #24 (1974) p. 36

22. David Raksin quoted by Roy M. Prendergast, Film Music: A
     Neglected Art (New York: W. W. Norton & Co., 1977) p.
     66

23. David Raksin quoted by Allan Ulrich, The Art of Film Music--
     A Tribute to California's Film Composers (Oakland, CA.:
     The Oakland Museum, 1976) p. 26.

24. Ibid.

25. Ibid.

26. Frank Capra, The Name Above the Title (New York: The
     MacMillan Co., 1971) p. 198

27. William H. Rosar, "LOST HORIZON--An Account of the Com-
     position of the Score," Filmusic Notebook Vol. 4, #2 (1978)
     p. 42

28. Dimitri Tiomkin with Prosper Buranelli, Please Don't Hate Me
     (New York: Doubleday & Co., 1979) p. 204

29. Max Steiner quoted by William H. Rosar, loc. cit., p. 45

30. Bernhard Kaun quoted by William H. Rosar, ibid., p. 43

31. Frank Capra, loc. cit.

32. Irwin Bazelon, Knowing the Score (New York: Arco Publish-
     ing, Inc., 1981), p. 26

33. Christopher Palmer, liner notes to LOST HORIZON--The Clas-
     sic Film Scores of Dimitri Tiomkin record album (RCA Rec-
     ords, 1976)

34. Jim Doherty, "The Overlooked Bernard Herrmann," Soundtrack!
     The Collector's Quarterly #25 (Spring 1981) p. 25

35. Dennis S. Johnson, "PORTRAIT OF JENNIE--A Retrospect,"
     Cinefantastique Vol. 1, #3 (1971) p. 16

36. George Duning, interview with the author, January 8, 1983
     (and following quotes)

37. Philip J. S. Hammond, "The Career of Herbert Stothart,"
     The Max Steiner Annual #7 (Max Steiner Music Society,
     1973) p. 10-11

38. Miklos Rozsa, Double Life (New York: Hippocrene Books,
     1982) p. 193

39. David Balsom, "An Evil Enchantment: THE PICTURE OF DOR-
    IAN GRAY," Midnight Marquee #29 (October 1980) p. 16
    (and following)

40. Ross Care, "The Film Music of Leigh Harline," Filmusic Note-
    book Vol. 3, #2 (1977) p. 39

41. Donald C. Willis, op. cit., p. 199

42. David J. Hogan, Who's Who of the Horrors and Other Fantasy
    Films (La Jolla: A. S. Barnes & Co., 1981) p. 19

<u>Miklos Rozsa.</u> Photograph courtesy Tony Thomas.

IV

THE MUSIC OF MIKLOS ROZSA

Perhaps the most enduring composer in Hollywood is Miklos Rozsa, whose work in cinema started in the late 1930's and continued on through the early 80's, when Rosza--in his 70's--still maintained an energetic career scoring for films and the concert stage. "No other serious composer has retained the impressive consistency of excellence," wrote one admirer, "in countless film after film for over forty years that Rozsa has admirably maintained. The symphonic score has not been more ably served or more hauntingly expressed than when composed by Miklos Rozsa."[1]

Rozsa was born in Budapest, Hungary, in 1907, and received his education in Leipzig, Paris and London. A violin player at the age of five, Rozsa wrote a ballet while in his 20's and later composed a number of chamber and symphonic works. He became involved with films in 1936, scoring a number of pictures for producer Alexander Korda, the greatest of which is undoubtedly the music he composed for Korda's extravagant Oriental fantasy, THE THIEF OF BAGDAD, in 1940. Christopher Palmer, Rozsa's orchestrator during the 80's, has said of this score: "It has a wonderful freshness and agelessness about it, despite occasional traces of influences which in later years would either be more perfectly assimilated or filtered out."[2] Palmer goes on to describe the "certain elusive magic" inherent in his early scores for Korda, a magic "which is never quite recaptured in the music of his maturity, nor could it be, for it is essentially the magic of youth."

Rozsa's score for THE THIEF OF BAGDAD is certainly full of magical music. "The score is a plethora of melodic bounties," Palmer continues, "a cornucopia of spectacular set pieces one after the other, all arrayed orchestrally in the brightest primary colors." The music is sweeping, exotic, and lavishly orchestrated for full orchestra and choir. Palmer has elsewhere noted that, "after the opening fanfares, Rozsa's music expresses not only the exhilaration of Abu's ride across the heavens, but also the might and magnificence" of the scenery. Palmer concludes: "A true childlike spirit of enchantment and wonder is enshrined in the soft luminosity of Rozsa's music."[3]

Rozsa almost didn't have the chance to write the music for THE THIEF OF BAGDAD. One of the movie's three directors, Lud-

wig Berger, had insisted that Oscar Straus (with whom he had
worked previously) compose the film's score even though Korda had
assigned the task to Rozsa. Straus sent his music via air mail from
Paris, which was described as "some quite charming late 19th Century Viennese operetta material." Muir Mathieson, who was Korda's
music director on the film, felt this was inappropriate for an Oriental fantasy. Korda had Rozsa prepare several themes and play
them, over and over, day after day, on the piano in the office
next to Ludwig Berger's. Finally, the director came in and asked
Rozsa what he was playing. "Oh, just some ideas for THE THIEF
OF BAGDAD," the composer replied. Berger was soon sold on
Rozsa's music!

    The movie began production in England, until the outbreak
of World War II forced Korda and crew to move to Hollywood, where
the film was completed. Director Berger had initially wanted Rozsa
to write many sequences before they wre filmed, in the manner of
a musical, so that the action could be choreographed perfectly to
the music. However, after attempts to synchronize the actors with
Rozsa's recorded music resulted in chaos, the director changed his
mind, and the majority of the score was written after filming. "In
the end the only sequences shot to pre-composed music," Rozsa
explained, "were those involving the special effects--the gallop of
the flying horse and the Silvermaid's dance which begins à la Rim-
sky but turns into something quite different at the climax when she
stabs the old Sultan."[4] Berger also wanted a number of songs to
be included in the score, and Sir Robert Vansittart, a distinguished
diplomat who was also a spare-time poet, was hired to write the lyrics to Rozsa's tunes.

    In the importance afforded the music by Berger, Rozsa's ef-
forts for THE THIEF OF BAGDAD are elevated to foreground music
rather than background music, as most scores seem to be considered. "It literally sweeps the film along," wrote one reviewer.
"Leitmotifs abound, and exotic atmosphere is omnipresent in the
richly textured conceptions, but most important is Rozsa's vibrant,
singing lyricism."[5] Another described the film as a "marvelous
blend of magic, action and music."[6]

    Rozsa himself particularly enjoyed working on the film. "I
loved it," he said. "I lived with it day in, day out for well over
a year, and it became part of me. It had so many fine qualities....
Visually the production was so sheerly beautiful that it was bound
to prompt a composer to try to give his best to match. I like to
think that the love I bore THE THIEF OF BAGDAD is in some way
reflected in the music I composed for it."[7]

    Rozsa lent a similar magical aspect to Korda's next fantasy,
THE JUNGLE BOOK (1942). "Rozsa composed in the manner of authentic Indian ragas for the Hindu scenes," Rudy Behlmer explained, "and wrote characteristic and diatonic music for the main

part of the film. The approach is operatic; each of the principle
characters, whether animals or human, has an individual motif. The
main theme is that of the jungle--depicting the eternity and vastness
of nature."[8] Like THE THIEF OF BAGDAD, Rozsa's score for THE
JUNGLE BOOK is very much in the foreground. Tony Thomas has
noted that "the scoring of the various animals is particularly deft
and tuneful: the elephants are characterized by roaring trombones
and tubas, wolves by glissando horns, Baloo the Bear by a chuck-
ling contra-bassoon, Bagheera the Black Panther by slithering
strings, the hyenas by gurgling alto saxophones, the monkeys by
high, perky piccolos, and Shere Khan the Tiger by muted, low
brass."[9] THE JUNGLE BOOK allowed Rozsa to compose a tour-de-
force in delightful instrumentation.

The two Korda fantasies partially comprised what Rozsa has
described as his first musical period. His success at scoring these
Oriental pictures led to a number of similar assignments almost to
the point of typecasting him. In 1945, Rozsa scored Hitchcock's
mysterious psychological thriller, SPELLBOUND, which was so
unique and evocative that it quickly typecast Rozsa as a composer
of psychological films, and many similar assignments followed.
Then Rozsa scored THE KILLERS, a brutal gangster film in 1946,
and soon found himself besieged by nearly a dozen similar films to
score. In the 50's, Rozsa scored QUO VADIS and BEN-HUR and
became a specialist for epic historical and biblical films. "They
say that Beethoven had only three periods in his lifetime," Rozsa
quipped. "I had, in the movies, four. This is known as one-
upmanship!"[10]

The psychological pictures of the 40's were particularly prone
to having moody, mysterious and often horrifying scores. The
most notable element in the music of SPELLBOUND was Rozsa's
use of the theremin, an electronic instrument which produces sound
oscillations (similar to a high-pitched female voice). The instrument has an electrical rod which produces a continuous sound, the
pitch determined by how close the player held his hand over the
rod. Rozsa was fond of the theremin as well as a similar instrument, called the ondes martenot. It, too, produced eerie sound
oscillations, except the pitch was more controllable through the use
of a keyboard attachment. On the theremin, Rozsa explained,
"when you said 'F natural' you couldn't just say it was here, here,
or here--you had to more or less slide into it to find the note.
With the martenot, you could have staccatos and interrupt the
color of the continuous tone. It was exact."[11]

Rozsa originally wanted to use the martenot in THE THIEF
OF BAGDAD for the scene where the genie first emerges from the
bottle, but was unable to get the instrument from its French inventor during the war. The following year, Rozsa tried to use it
for an African picture called SUNDOWN, but the producers felt it
was too unusual for their tastes. When Rozsa was assigned to score

SPELLBOUND for director Alfred Hitchcock and producer David O. Selznick, he asked to use the theremin. The reluctant producer allowed him to test-score one scene (where the amnesiac Gregory Peck carries a razor downstairs with sinister purpose) using the theremin and the full orchestra. The resultant recording so amazed the filmmakers that they decided to have the theremin in almost every scene highlighting Peck's paranoia.

While Rozsa actually used the theremin for the first time in SPELLBOUND, it was first heard in THE LOST WEEKEND, another psychological film scored by Rozsa which, although filmed and scored after SPELLBOUND, was released some months earlier. The instrument effectively expressed, in THE LOST WEEKEND, Ray Milland's paranoia and amnesia, and the craving and despair of his alcoholism. Rozsa has always strongly believed that music should complete a film's psychological effect, and his haunting use of the theremin was superbly realized in these films.

There's an interesting story about how David O. Selznick was upset by the fact that Rozsa had used the instrument for someone else's film, having wanted its unique sound to be exclusive to SPELLBOUND. Selznick's secretary called Rozsa to ask if he had, in fact, used the theremin in THE LOST WEEKEND. Rozsa calmly advised the caller to inform Mr. Selznick that he had indeed used the theremin. "And I used the violin, the oboe and the clarinet as well. Goodbye!"[12]

Whatever reservations David Selznick may have had, Rozsa's music for SPELLBOUND had become a landmark film score which won the composer his first Academy Award. The eerie sound of the instrument was effectively integrated with the orchestra, and the resultant sound intensified the film's theme of potential madness. The use of the theremin has also influenced subsequent fantastic film scores, and was used prominently in science fiction film scores such as Ferde Grofé's ROCKETSHIP X-M (1950), Bernard Herrmann's DAY THE EARTH STOOD STILL (1951), Herman Stein's IT CAME FROM OUTER SPACE (1953), Herschel Burke Gilbert's PROJECT MOONBASE (1953), Ronald Stein's THE DAY THE WORLD ENDED (1956) and many others including numerous television scores for THE TWILIGHT ZONE. The unique tonalities achieved with the theremin were perfect for films about outer space or weird, unearthly occurrences and found a welcome home in the genre-- eventually evolving into a purely electronic medium with the advent of the synthesizer scores of the 70's and 80's.

After featuring the theremin in SPELLBOUND, THE LOST WEEKEND and THE RED HOUSE, Rozsa abandoned it, fearing that it might otherwise become too much of a trademark. Instead, he went on in the 50's to score the numerous biblical epics which trademarked him in that milieu! Most of Rozsa's fantastic film scores during the 50's were basically borderline--well-scored but unremarkable as genre film music. THE SECRET BEYOND THE DOOR (1948), was a psychological thriller directed by Fritz Lang, whose collaboration with Rozsa on this film was noteworthy. The two analyzed each scene together, and the director provided Rozsa with many valuable ideas for heightening a dramatic moment through music. Since Rozsa no longer wanted to use the theremin, Lang suggested, in view of the film's psychological aspects, that the composer write the music backward--the musicians would play the music backwards which would be recorded and then played in the proper musical direction; the result would be normal music, yet with a strange and different sound.

THE STORY OF THREE LOVES (1953) was a three-part anthology film, one story of which ("Mademoiselle") is a charming fantasy involving a witch who transforms a recalcitrant schoolboy into a handsome young man in order to teach him an important lesson. Rozsa's music for this segment is primarily an impressionistic nocturne for solo violin and cello, shimmering strings, harp, celesta and vibraphone. The film's minor fantasy aspect was toned down considerably in favor of its romantic qualities, and the music aptly follows suit.

Rozsa provided a dramatic score for the apocalyptic THE WORLD, THE FLESH AND THE DEVIL (1958), after which his musical output in the 60's included only seven films, the majority of his time spent with concert work. Of these seven, only one was a fantasy effort, and Rozsa provided a rousing score for George Pal's 1968 science fiction venture, THE POWER. The main theme is quite dramatic, its melodic style characteristic of Rozsa's work of this late period: a series of rapidly progressing notes ascend to abruptly halt for a beat, followed by one or more sustained notes. This motif was very effective in developing a sense of drama and cinematic motion, and can be heard in moments of subsequent films such as THE GOLDEN VOYAGE OF SINBAD, EYE OF THE NEEDLE and DEAD MEN DON'T WEAR PLAID. One reviewer noted that THE POWER is "bound tightly together by Miklos Rozsa's clever music score, with its echoes of Dvorak's chamber music and recurring motif of the zimbalom."[13] The zimbalom is a Hungarian variant of the medieval dulcimer, and provides a distinctive sound which becomes an ominous leitmotif suggestive of the evil telekinetic supermind which seeks to destroy the film's protagonists. At one point, the zimbalom interplays with a solo violin in a gypsy motif, which captures a flavor quite reminiscent of Hans J. Salter's violin themes from THE HOUSE OF FRANKENSTEIN.

THE PRIVATE LIFE OF SHERLOCK HOLMES (1970) featured a score derived largely from Rozsa's earlier Violin Concerto, as requested by director Billy Wilder, having associated the introspective melancholy of Rozsa's Concerto with Holmes' "private life." As Christopher Palmer wrote: "The music of the Concerto is adroitly integrated in the fabric of the film score, nowhere more so than in the Scottish safari or the 'bicycle-made-for-three' sequence. The theme of this distinctive and memorable episode evolves quite naturally from the love theme of the Concerto but is developed in a rhythmic and textural setting quite different from that in which it was originally conceived."[14]

Rozsa's next fantasy score, THE GOLDEN VOYAGE OF SINBAD (1974), marked a return to the exoticism of THE THIEF OF BAGDAD. This Ray Harryhausen film was something of a follow-up to his previous classic, THE 7TH VOYAGE OF SINBAD (1958), which featured one of Bernard Herrmann's finest scores, and Rozsa aptly met the challenge of providing a richly expressive and "foreground" score. The composer himself described this score as being in his "finest Oriental mood," and while not quite as extravagant as his earlier work for Korda, GOLDEN VOYAGE is one of Rozsa's most sweeping scores of this period.

"Few composers," wrote reviewer Royal S. Brown, "could write a title theme with quite the exotic romance and sweep that hits you immediately in the prelude, which sounds ever so much like a theme from Rozsa's SODOM AND GOMORRAH score. The theme itself is good enough; but what really gives it movement and life are the various instrumental overlappings and filigrees that pervade every Rozsa score. Similarly, he proves masterful in creating diverse moods of suspense, excitement and grotesquerie."[15]

The score is ripe with deep brassy chords, adventuresome motifs, passionately melodic phrases, as well as an eerie theme for, presumably, an ondes martenot, during the scenes involving the Homonculus. The effect of the latter is quite similar to Rozsa's use of the theremin in the 40's.

Rozsa was not entirely pleased with the final sound track of the film, as much of his music became buried beneath other sounds during the dubbing stage. "The main things were the sound effects," Rozsa complained. "Why did I have to write a score then? I remember that at the end of the picture a mythical animal--a centaur--came in and I needed two tubas, because one wasn't enough for me. It was very difficult to get them in August because of the holidays, so we got one from Naples. It was a tremendous sound, but you don't hear it at all in the film. All you hear is the howling of the creature; that was what counted, you see. To the producer the fantasy was much more important than the music."[16]

In 1977, French director Alain Resnais commissioned Rozsa to compose the music for his first English language film, PROVIDENCE, a rather bizarre story exploring the uncertain boundaries between reality and delusion. The score's central motif captures the passion of the film's tortured protagonist, and concentrates on augmenting musically the lighter side of the character through the use of rhythmic violas, punctuated brass, resonant oboe and clarinet solos,

and an effective elegy for solo piano. The dark side of the character played by John Gielgud is suggested only through an occasional raggedly rhythmic pursuit motif for honking woodwinds and
repetitive strings. There is also a nostalgic theme for Gielgud's
son and daughter-in-law which is quite romantic in nature.

Rozsa worked closely with director Resnais in scoring, as he
recalled in a recent interview: "Resnais told me there would be 42
minutes of music in it. He knew exactly. He said, 'Here I want to
express this...' and I quickly wrote it down. He came to my place
every week and actually he didn't object to anything, he liked it.
I followed not his instructions, but his ideas, which were very
sound."[17]

"The movie seems to have struck a personal response within
Miklos Rozsa," wrote one reviewer of the PROVIDENCE score, "for
he conducts a score full of the yearning and vascillating emotions
that marked his most worthy music of the past."[18] Another wrote:
"Rozsa's score beautifully provided a much needed sense of cohesion
musically which the picture lacked visually. His melodies ... were
instrumental in injecting enlightenment into an otherwise melancholy
film."[19]

Rozsa's music for THE LAST EMBRACE (1979), a Hitchcockian
thriller, was likewise "tender, haunting and evocative, a triumph
of sensual splendor that dreamily transports the viewer out of his
seat at the film's completion and continues to surface as an exquisite
recolleciton of a memorable film."[20]

The next Rozsa score was for the entertaining time travel
story pitting a youthful H. G. Wells against a sinister Jack the Ripper in modern-day San Francisco: TIME AFTER TIME (1979). The
film features a "fully symphonic score, rich in texture and executed
in the grand Rozsa tradition of pomp and fanfare."[21] As with
PROVIDENCE, Rozsa's approach to the score reflects the energy and
romanticism of his peak period of the 40's, and is invested with a
variety of leitmotifs.

There is a powerful time-machine theme for brass and strings,
punctuated by trilling flutes, which becomes the dominant theme for
the film as the machine itself is the central means around which the
action of the story unfolds. An urgent motif is provided for Wells,
built around a single bass note with occasional ascending and descending modulations pivoting around it. A sinister Jack the Ripper
theme is scored for quivering violins, basses and cellos, which effectively emphasize the film's schizoid portrayal of the Ripper by
utilizing this menacing theme only when his murderous inclinations
are evident, thus allowing the audience to be somewhat swayed by
his charm at other times.

The Love Theme for Wells and Amy is one of Rozsa's finest

romantic compositions, and is especially effective during the scene
in which Wells tells Amy the truth about his origin. Amy becomes
skeptical, hurt, and angry, but agrees to Wells' attempts to prove
his sincerity by taking her on a short trip in his time machine.
Amy is still unconvinced, as the trip has only taken a moment, and
even though they have traveled several days into the future there
are no physical differences to see. Amy begins to leave. Their
once-tender Love Theme is played mournfully, underscoring her
dejection, until she happens to find a newspaper and reads its
date, realizing that they have indeed traveled into the future.
The theme sweeps upward in a moving swell of renewed happiness,
but abruptly falls short as she sees a picture of herself on the
front page, identified as the Ripper's latest victim.

Another motif that pervades the score is the Utopia theme.
As Jim Doherty explains in a lengthy analysis of the TIME AFTER
TIME score,[22] this piece is drawn from a variant on the Wells
Theme, and is first heard during an early scene in Wells' Victorian
home. It is associated with Wells' prediction of a Utopian society
coming in the future. When Wells actually arrives in the future and
sees that the world is far from Utopian, the theme keeps turning
up, mockingly, just when some modern problem confronts him: after eating at a McDonald's, Wells glances at an indigestion commercial on a store window television, as the Utopian Theme is intoned
queasily by a saxophone. Elsewhere, the theme is played cheerfully as bright, sunny morning dawns over the city, until we see
Wells lying on a park bench, where he wound up spending the
night. The theme is used with subtle satire in scenes such as
these.

The film's finale highlights the preceding thematic elements
of the score. As the Ripper is about to escape in Wells' time machine, H. G. yanks the safety device from the vehicle, which
causes the villain to vaporize into nothingness, and the orchestra
plunges into an agonized yell of the Ripper's Theme, emphasizing
blaring horns and bristling triangles. The music fades out and a
tense silence underscores Wells' and Amy's painful parting as he
prepares to return to his own time. As Amy suddenly realizes she
doesn't want to remain without him, she rushes to the machine.
The Love Theme returns, at first somewhat distraught and urgent
until Wells delays his return trip to allow her to join him, at which
point it resounds joyfully. It is fleetingly interrupted by the
Utopia motif for a last satirical moment, as Amy asserts her own
20th-Century personality before the machine whisks them into the
past. "Maybe it is a musical farewell to 1980," wrote Jim Doherty
in his score analysis, "or perhaps a foreshadowing of the strange
new world in store for Amy. Whichever it is does not seem to
weigh too heavily on their minds, for their love theme reemerges
for their final screen embrace. It segues into the time machine
theme as the invention sparkles and vanishes. The Wells' theme
returns for just a moment to accompany a short on-screen capsule

summary of the remainder of Wells' life, but it is their love theme
which surges up in full unrestrained orchestral splendor to escort
the ending credits to what must rank as one of Rozsa's most triumphant finales, replete with tympani, bass drum and cymbals."[23]

The music for TIME AFTER TIME, while emphasizing character and relationship more than fantasy or spectacle, remains a powerful and brilliantly portrayed film score. "TIME AFTER TIME
elicits the full range of Miklos Rozsa's kaleidoscopic powers of
mood painting, scene setting and narrative pacing," wrote one reviewer. "It is his strongest, most vibrant and multidimensional
score in more than fifteen years."[24] Another wrote: "In TIME
AFTER TIME, Rozsa has written a filmscore that is the measure of
all that is great in him, and though it be modest in its dimensions
it does what it should do as well as or better than anything Rozsa
has ever written."[25]

With his music for TIME AFTER TIME, Rozsa recalls his timeless music for the fantasies of his early days in Hollywood, THE
THIEF OF BAGDAD and THE JUNGLE BOOK, although without their
exotic aura. While Rozsa has grown, developed and matured over
his 40 years of film composing, the genius he displayed in his earliest scores has not diminished. In a day when the advent of pop
music threatens to overrun film music to suit the whims of commercial-minded film and record moguls, Miklos Rozsa's music remains a
proud example of a musical heritage embodying the best of fine
cinema. "I write music which tries to bring the happenings and
characters close to the listener," he said. "No tricks, no gimmicks."[26] That is perhaps the essence of Rozsa's music--rather
than relying on gimmicry or musical effects, he straightforwardly
wrote music suggestive of relationships and events. (Even his use
of the theremin was more than a mere gimmick, creating a profound
and frightening musical coloration unique to the genre.) The apparent simplicity of this method is contrasted by the complexity
with which Rozsa organizes his themes and integrates them into the
score. While only a small portion of Rozsa's film music has graced
fantastic films, the few times he has lent his talent to the genre
have resulted in exceptional film scores.

Notes

1. Steve Vertlieb, "Soundtrack," Cinemacabre #1 (Winter-Spring,
    1978-79) p. 51

2. Christopher Palmer, liner notes to The Thief of Bagdad record
    album (Warner Bros. Records, 1978)

3. _____, liner notes to Miklos Rozsa Conducts His Great Film
    Music record album (British Polydor Records, 1975)

4. Mikos Rozsa quoted by Christopher Palmer, "Miklos Rozsa on THE THIEF OF BAGDAD," Filmusic Notebook Vol. 2, #4 (1976), p. 26

5. Rudy Behlmer, liner notes to SPELLBOUND: The Classic Film Scores of Miklos Rozsa record album (RCA Records, 1975)

6. Leslie Halliwell, Halliwell's Film Guide, 2nd Edition (New York: Charles Scribner's Sons, 1979) p. 871

7. Miklos Rozsa, op. cit., p. 28

8. Rudy Behlmer, loc. cit.

9. Tony Thomas, Music for the Movies (La Jolla: A. S. Barnes & Co., 1973) p. 94

10. Miklos Rozsa: "The Rozsa Transcript," CinemaScore (pending)

11. Ibid.

12. Miklos Rozsa quoted by Rudy Behlmer, loc. cit.

13. John Baxter, Science Fiction in the Cinema (New York: Paperback Library, 1970) p. 173

14. Christopher Palmer, liner notes to Rozsa Conducts Rozsa record album (British Polydor Records, 1977)

15. Royal S. Brown, "Recording Review," High Fidelity, November 1974, p. 138

16. Miklos Rozsa interviewed by David and Richard Kraft, Soundtrack! The Collector's Quarterly Vol. 1, #3 (September 1982) p. 15

17. Ibid.

18. John Caps, "Record Review," Soundtrack Collector's Newsletter #11 (August 1977) p. 12

19. Bradley W. Cowden, "Rozsa Tryptych," Soundtrack Collector's Newsletter #21 (April 1980) p. 10

20. Steve Vertlieb, "Film Review," Cinemacabre #2 (Fall 1979) p. 41

21. Lawson Hill, "Record Review," CinemaScore #5 (January-February 1980) p. 6

22. Jim Doherty, "Music for Worlds to Come," Midnight Marquee #29 (October 1980) p. 24

23. Ibid., p. 25

24. Paul A. Snook, "Record Review," High Fidelity, March 1980, p.
     91

25. Frank De Wald, "TIME AFTER TIME: An Analysis," Pro Musica
     Sana #32 (Fall 1980) p. 19

26. Miklos Rozsa quoted by John Caps, "A Correspondence with
     Miklos Rozsa," Filmusic Notebook Vol. 2, #1 (1974) p. 4

V

BIG BUGS AND OUTER SPACE

As the distinctive science fiction films of the 50's brought to life a new breed of monster--one characterized by atomic mutation or invasion from outer space as opposed to the supernatural vampire, the lycanthropic werewolf or the man-made creature of the 30's and 40's--the music that accompanied them shifted slightly as well. While primarily drawn from the same styles and traditions dominating in the 40's (which tended mostly to concentrate around either the romantic tradition or the more dissonant, modern style favored by some composers), the 50's brought a great deal more experimentation with musical styles and forms. Jazz began to find its way into the film scores of several composers, as did a variation on the dissonant style of the 40's, that of the atonal or linear score, in which the music is not characterized so much by melody as by ambience and orchestral texture.

Perhaps the film that started the whole science fiction trend of the 50's was George Pal's DESTINATION MOON (1950). This slow-moving story of the space race featured an effective score by Leith Stevens, who had scored Pal's previous film, THE GREAT RUPERT (1950). Stevens, a child prodigy born in Missouri in 1909, began his professional music career at the age of 11 as an accompanist in Kansas City. When he was 16 he made his debut as a conductor there. In 1930 Stevens joined CBS radio as an arranger and eventually began to conduct and compose. In the 40's he began scoring films for RKO and Universal, until he served as a radio director during World War II. Stevens' association with producer George Pal began in 1949 during the filming of THE GREAT RUPERT, a low-budget, whimsical comedy about a vaudeville performer and a trained squirrel. Stevens' score was somewhat inconsequential; it was his atmospheric score for DESTINATION MOON that helped to establish him as a composer of merit.

While not the first film concerning outer space, DESTINATION MOON was the first motion picture to seriously deal with the subject of a lunar landing. Stevens carefully crafted his score to enhance the atmosphere of space travel and exploration on the moon, reportedly consulting with several scientists to get an idea of what space was like in order to suggest it musically. The score is a subdued one, mostly quiet with only occasional "action." Stevens

Leith Stevens. Photograph courtesy William H. Rosar.

subtly accents the stillness of space and of the moon, underlining the film's characters and their conflicts with thin brasses and hollow woodwinds. The main theme is a fine example of muted grandeur, comprising in its slow pace a sense of restrained jubilance, heroic exploration and the awe of entering untouched territory. What John Williams was later to accomplish in STAR WARS with rousing crescendos and plenty of pomp and fanfare, Stevens managed to provide in DESTINATION MOON with a tranquil mood of solitude and stillness.

Irwin Bazelon wrote of Stevens' score: "Consisting of soft, high, long-held, sustained tones, his music hangs like icicles over the bleak moon landscape and gives an ethereal feeling to the panorama. Even though his overall interpretation is basically romantic--almost Tristanlike in thematic content--the unfamiliarity and coldness of the terrain lend a strange aura of suspense."[1] Stevens' portrayal of the weightlessness of outer space is especially interesting. As one writer described it, Stevens "created a sound picture of infinity, a sense of no bottom and no gravity. The violins perform a shimmering figure to indicate the silence and the clear, far-away stars, the moon coming nearer. The woodwinds enter to tell of the curious mental aberrations that effect the crew in a world of no gravity."[2] Stevens also uses an interesting technique--apparently scraping the strings of a violin with a metal object--to achieve the eerie sounds heard in the early sequences on the moon's surface.

Pal was so impressed with Stevens' work on DESTINATION MOON that he brought him back for his next two pictures, WHEN WORLDS COLLIDE (1951) and WAR OF THE WORLDS (1953). The former film score was discussed in great detail in James C. Hamilton's doctoral analysis on the music of Leith Stevens. Hamilton describes four main themes which run throughout the film, the most striking being a melodic female vocal passage, or wordless melisma, which creates an eerie mood for scenes associated with space (first heard behind a space mural, later behind the quasi-religious narration as cities are evacuated in the middle of the film, and finally at the end after the ship has landed safely on the new planet). As Hamilton wrote, the use of this theme at the beginning, middle and end created a sense of continuity to both score and film. "At no other time in the film does Stevens use vocal background. He reserves this effect for mysterious space music. By providing more traditional, nonmysterious music for the bulk of the film he is able to make the story more believable.... It is a situation in which Stevens uses a realistic approach to capture the audience's trust and then, from the point of departure, subtly transports them into the realm of science fiction."[3]

The second theme is identified by Hamilton as a Danger Theme, which underscores moments of uncertainty and apprehension, especially near the beginning when the approaching planets

are first sighted and studied, their impending collision with Earth
confirmed. As the scientists commence building a rocket ship to
save selected members of the human race from the cataclysm,
Stevens introduces a Progress Theme, for brass and woodwind,
which is associated with the building of the spaceship. Both the
Danger Theme and the Progress Theme, as well as other musical
structures, are combined into an extended cue for the calendar
montage, a concise visual documentary of the work being done on
the space ship, interspersed with calendar pages that announce the
approaching deadline.

The fourth and final recurring theme is a Love Theme, underscoring the relationship between Dave Randall and Joyce, which
by the latter half of the film has become the central romantic theme
of the story; the Love Theme comes to the foreground as their
love blooms. Another romantic motif, resembling this main Love
Theme, is provided for Eddie and Julie, emphasizing their dilemma
when only one of them is selected for the rescue flight.

Each of the themes is used sparingly and inobtrusively, subtly embellishing the themes of danger, progress, expedition, love
and sacrifice that are portrayed in the film. As the picture ends,
Stevens accompanies the triumphal denouement with a glorious and
majestic cue signifying the exuberant joy of the passengers disem-
barking onto the new world. Instead of recapitulating the earlier
themes in a final, concluding suite, Stevens simply offers this jubilant crescendo, embellished by the female chorus intoning the Space
Theme. He ends the film, therefore, not with a backward glance
at what has gone before, but with a positive exultation of hope for
the future.

As James C. Hamilton writes in his dissertation, the music
for WHEN WORLDS COLLIDE can be divided into two categories, the
first being what he calls "practical music": "This type encompasses
all the standard film music clichés, such as violins playing ascending chromatic figures to signify the space ship's ascent, the orchestra playing descending scales to signal the falling of the crane,
and the providing of a locomotive theme for travel music.... The
music in this category is representative of a film composer's craftsmanship. It tells little of the composer's musicality or philosophical insight; it relates only to a composer's ability to reproduce pre-
learned forms.

"The second type of music ... is the non-duplicating mood
music and its only limits are the limits of the composer's imagination.
With this type of music a composer is able to be creative and to
demonstrate not only a command of his compositional tools but also
his perception and sensitivity. By Stevens's expert use of the
leitmotiv technique we are able to witness his grasp of the psychological innuendo and his ability to weave a patchwork of background music through a utilization of the principal themes, which
adds immeasurably to the impact of the screen action." [4]

WAR OF THE WORLDS likewise featured an effective musical backdrop for the catastrophes and characters depicted on the screen. Built around a progression of brooding woodwind and string atmospheres subtly meandering through the various investigative sequences, the score often erupts into a flurry of brass and strings in the battle scenes. During the evacuation of Los Angeles, Stevens composed nicely loud and dramatic music, with a dirgelike quality reminiscent of the main title music from WHEN WORLDS COLLIDE, also scored for strings and brass over a pounding drum beat.

Stevens continued to be quite prolific in the 50's, although with only a few subsequent genre films such as WORLD WITHOUT END (1956). He contributed to television's TWILIGHT ZONE, LOST IN SPACE and THE IMMORTAL in the 60's, eventually becoming head of Paramount's television music department until his death in 1970. While best remembered in the mainstream for his innovative jazz score for THE WILD ONE (1954), Stevens' contributions to George Pal's classic science fiction films of the 50's were major elements of their success.

A film that attempted to emulate much of the mood of DESTINATION MOON was ROCKETSHIP X-M (1950). While released a few weeks before George Pal's picture, ROCKETSHIP X-M had actually started production later; it was, in fact, a hurried attempt by Lippert studios to cash in on the publicity surrounding Pal's venture. Lippert wanted a "name" composer to provide the film's score, and commissioned famous concert composer Ferde Grofé to write it. Grofé, noted as a remarkably "visual" composer best known for his famous Grand Canyon Suite, first became involved with film music through Walt Disney studios, whose short scenic film, GRAND CANYON, had been synchronized to Grofé's suite. Grofé scored a handful of other films, but spent most of his time composing for the concert stage. He possessed a disdain for film music composition, considering it a "step down," and perhaps this is why most of his film scores lack the vigor he gave to his concert works. However cynical Grofé was toward film scoring, he did an admirable job with ROCKETSHIP X-M, which is undoubtedly his best work for the movies--possibly due to the imaginative subject matter.

Grofé, however, was unfamiliar with the technical timings required for motion picture music. He also refused to provide orchestrations for the music he composed. At the time, Lippert's head composer was Albert Glasser, a thoroughgoing craftsman in the field of film music who had started in the mid-40's. Glasser was called upon to orchestrate Grofé's compositions and conduct the orchestra. During the course of postproduction, Grofé delivered a few musical lines each week, which Glasser would then flesh out for a 35-piece orchestra. It was also Glasser's idea to use a theremin during the Martian scenes, which brought a notably weird quality to those sequences. Grofé's music was quite atmospheric and appropriate, achieving many heroic and haunting melodies and in some cases evoking moods quite similar to those created by Bernard Herrmann in the later 50's.

Born in Chicago in 1916, Glasser was educated at the University of Southern California. He became associated with film music in the 30's as a copyist for Erich Wolfgang Korngold at Warner Brothers. Much of what Glasser learned and eventually incorporated into his own compositions came as a result of what he learned by copying Korngold's compositions onto music sheets for the various members of the orchestra. In 1944, Glasser got a chance to compose the music for THE MONSTER MAKER, providing an odd, plaintive musical score. In 1956, Glasser became associated with B-movie producer Bert I. Gordon, when he scored THE CYCLOPS. Gordon had been working down the hall from Glasser when he heard the sounds of Glasser's music for the big-budget war adventure, HUK. Gordon was impressed and hired Glasser to score his film of a man mutated by radiation into a horribly deformed 25-foot giant. Glasser went on to score seven additional films for Gordon in a collaboration that resulted in many fine scores, often surpassing in quality the films for which they were written.

Glasser preferred a melodramatic style of scoring, punctuating the action and underlining the drama in highly effective, if predictable, means. His primary approach to horror films can be broken down into very fundamental elements, centering around a dramatic, horrifying melodic line for the monster. In THE AMAZING COLOSSAL MAN (1957), Glasser's best horror score, the composer based the Monster Theme upon the giant's huge, ponderous footsteps. "I wanted a very heavy, deep monstrous sound from all the basses," Glasser explained. "Whoever I had on the bottom--string bass, the tuba, trombones, low French horns, and so on--all of them would play almost in harmony, following his footbeats, but changing notes--up and down, back and forth, slowly, always in tempo. You can't go too fast or you'll make him walk too fast, it'd feel funny; you can't go too slow or you'll fall asleep. You more or less try to follow his rhythm, his tempo. On top of that, if things were happening, if his hand comes out and he pushes a house down, you catch it with cues, and all the brass flies up in the air in a shrieking sound, with dissonance. Plus your simple crashes, your gongs, anything that would make a lot of noise and would augment what he's doing and make sense."[5]

Glasser's style of scoring for horror films followed the same tried-and-true technique he found so successful in other action films; having scored over 100 films by this time, it came almost as second nature to Glasser to provide just the right musical cues to enhance the action on screen. "If somebody gets hurt," he said, "if he's chasing a little baby who's screaming, you have all the violins, way up, tearing your heart out, so the message that the violins say to the audience is, 'look out! He's going to kill the baby!' You frighten them any way you can, as long as it makes sense and is also logical. If things are going to happen in a terrible way, you build up; the sound gets louder and louder and louder, heavier and heavier; you come up and up and up and it's about to burst; if nothing happens, you go down a little bit. You think of it in terms of physical, emotional, and what can be done with the music. You follow it right down the line."

THE AMAZING COLOSSAL MAN was something of a reversal of the same year's INCREDIBLE SHRINKING MAN, which had been scored by Hans J. Salter and others. Both films tried to give their main characters an aura of tragic sympathy. Salter accomplished this through the use of a rhythmic melody, while Glasser used a soft violin solo to provide a degree of pathos toward the film's unfortunate protagonist. As one reviewer explained: "Using a violin theme that cries from the heart, Glasser made the audience feel the sadness of the mutated man, his hopeless separation from the woman he loved, his bitter hatred of life for turning him into a nonhuman, and his tortured mental deterioration."[6] "I had this long violin solo," Glasser recalled, "very tender; not romantic but simply sad. Not too sad--after all, he's still alive. So you use some sad music, not too much, not too obvious, not tear-jerking, that'll be too saccharine."[7] The film was fairly successful and spawned a sequel, WAR OF THE COLOSSAL BEAST (1958), which Glasser scored using the same technique.

Albert Glasser scored a number of other horror pictures for Gordon, investing them with the strong dramatic motifs balanced with softer, more passionate melodies that had become almost routine for him. THE BEGINNING OF THE END (1957) was given a stabbing, driving beat, reminiscent somewhat in its pounding terror to James Bernard's later work in Hammer films. Glasser's first score for Gordon, THE CYCLOPS, builds slowly with short, detached phrases which gradually grow into a crazed frenzy with pounding drums and wild orchestra.

Glasser's most ambitious score was for Gordon's THE BOY AND THE PIRATES (1960), a light fantasy involving pirates and genies. This was the score to which Glasser best put what he had learned from Korngold. "I followed, more or less, his style of writing," Glasser said. "Not his lines, not his melodies, far from it. But the effect was there; that's what I wanted to get." The biggest limitation in providing the kind of sweeping, grand score Glasser envisioned was the budget restrictions inherent in Gordon's films. While Korngold was accustomed to writing for 80 to 100 musicians, Glasser was forced to produce similar results with an orchestra of 22! "You have to be real careful," Glasser said of the challenge. "If you write a violin line, you don't want it real lush and real thick--you're not going to get it, you only had four fiddles, one viola and two cellos! So I can't write a rich, thick,

luscious violin line; it's got to be a simple thing that four violins
can hold and handle. The writing changes the whole structure."

In the 60's Glasser retired from active film scoring, although
he has returned on occasion to help out fellow composers. Glasser's work for the low-budget films of the 40's and 50's demonstrates
his professionalism at his craft, and his work for fantastic films,
while restricted by the limitations of B-movies, provided some of
their most memorable qualities.

Dimitri Tiomkin, who had begun scoring for films in the 30's,
provided his finest genre score for Howard Hawks' 1951 classic,
THE THING (FROM ANOTHER WORLD). Tiomkin, who had been
hired early on and started scoring while the picture was still being
shot, provided a chilling score. Heavy on brass and percussion,
it featured the effective use of strings and the wailing of four
women's voices to underline the film's eerie atmosphere, lending a
quality similar to that of the theremin as used in Miklos Rozsa's
SPELLBOUND, this time accentuating early references to the alien.
While embodied with a variety of spooky motifs and variations, the
score is built around a single, chilling triad for ominously growling
brass, a powerful 3-stage progression of notes which remarkably
sets off the growing mood of tension which rises almost unbearably throughout the film. "The score is appropriately jaunty for the
scenes of cheerful camaraderie that open the film," wrote one reviewer, "and punctuates the action sequences with the same brash
rambunctiousness Tiomkin employed for the fights and shootouts in
RED RIVER (1948) and DUEL IN THE SUN (1946). Several pop
tunes are heard in the romantic scenes. The destruction of the
Thing is particularly well handled: a strong buildup to the moment
when the bolts of electricity are unleashed, followed by a gradual
'crumbling away' of the orchestra as the alien dies."[8]

Much of the best fantastic film music of the 50's, as it had
in the 40's, was coming from Universal Pictures, the leading
producer of genre film fare up until the end of the decade. Unlike the major solo efforts of Leith Stevens at Paramount, Universal
and many studios under the contract system maintained a regular
staff of composers who each contributed, in varying degrees, to
the B-movies of the period. Comprised of Hans J. Salter and
Frank Skinner, who continued their association begun in the 40's,
along with newcomers Henry Mancini and Herman Stein (as well as
a wide variety of occasional efforts from other composers), this
competent crew provided the majority of the music for the Universal
science fiction and horror films of this period, frequently collaborating together on a single film score--as had been the case in the
40's.

Herman Stein recalled the process: "Sometimes two or three
of us would work on a picture; I would do a reel or Hank Mancini
would do a reel, that sort of thing. Whoever would come up with

the main theme, the rest of us would use that theme in the cues
we'd do. We'd use each other's themes interchangeably, but we
would compose it in our own way." [9] Quite often, when two or more
composers scored a film in this manner, only the music director who
oversaw the project received screen credit.

As head of Universal's music department in the 50's, it was
Joseph Gershenson's responsibility to assign composers to score
various reels and films, and to maintain a musical continuity
throughout. Gershenson was born in Russia in 1904, and studied
music privately in New York. In the 20's, he worked as a conductor for a theatrical orchestra until becoming the assistant general music director for the RKO theaters in 1928. Gershenson
worked there until 1933 when he joined Universal as an associate
professor of features, under the name of "Joseph G. Sanford" in
the 40's, and eventually became the head of Universal's music department, working on nearly all of their films in the 50's and mid-
60's.

While many filmographies and film reviews give Gershenson
music credit, he was, in fact, not a composer but an executive,
and his involvement with film music was as a highly competent and
respected supervisor and conductor. When Gershenson received a
film project, he would assign either the entire film or various reels
thereof (as this was the simplest way to divide a film so each composer had something to work from on the moviola) to certain composers, usually depending upon availability and the requirements
of the film in question. On many occasions, Gershenson would as-
semble a score, completely or in part, from preexisting stock or library music--cues composed by the Universal staff for earlier films
and subsequently housed in a recorded music library meticulously
indexed by type and length--the same process as used in the 30's
and 40's. Gershenson also maintained a musical consistency throughout the film by assigning specific composers to provide the main and
subsidiary themes, and insured that the other contributing composers based their writing on those main themes.

Many of these scores are among the best genre film compositions of the 50's, although due to the collaborative method by which
they were scored it's difficult to assess the contributions of single
composers to these films. Plainly though, Hans Salter, Frank Skinner, Henry Mancini and Herman Stein were a powerful force, and
under the guidance of Joseph Gershenson they composed much important and evocative fantastic film music.

IT CAME FROM OUTER SPACE (1953) was director Jack Arnold's first science fiction feature and one of Universal's earliest
science fiction pictures of the decade. The film remains a highly-
regarded classic, due largely to an intelligent, literate script, atmospheric direction, and a moody score composed jointly by Herman
Stein, Irving Gertz and Henry Mancini. The main thematic material,

though, was by Stein, who provided a sustained mood of impending terror through the use of loud, plodding brass "footsteps" punctuated with rumbling percussion over a furtive woodwind melody, accented occasionally by the eerie tonalities of the theremin. Born in 1915 in Philadelphia, Stein was a self-taught musician who became a noted arranger for jazz orchestras and radio programs in New York in the 30's and 40's. In 1948 he moved to Los Angeles, where he studied formally with Mario Castelnuovo-Tedesco, joining the music staff at Universal in 1951. His first work on a genre score was in arranging a classical cue for THE STRANGE DOOR in 1951, and many of the best moments of Universal's subsequent horror and science fiction films of the 50's would be composed, at least in part, by Stein.

One of them was THE CREATURE FROM THE BLACK LAGOON (1954), which contained a highly dramatic and furious score comprising the talents of Stein along with Hans Salter and Henry Mancini, plus reused library cues by Milton Rosen and Robert Emmett Dolan. The score includes a variety of minor melodic passages, mostly suggestive of the tranquility and solitude of the lost lagoon (emphasizing woodwinds and gradually anticipating trombones) and the romantic interludes, but the most striking moments consisted of a discordant, blaring theme for trumpets, built around an ascending, three-note, shouting brass motif that is heard whenever the Creature attacks; a harsh and unexpected blare that literally jolts us out of our seats and provides an electrifying punch to the picture. This theme ("da-DA-DAA") was the composition of Herman Stein, and is somewhat similar to James Bernard's loud, descending "DRA-cu-la" motif from HORROR OF DRACULA (1958) in the use of a repeated, three-note crashing crescendo. The music builds rapidly to suddenly break off, almost prematurely; an effective means of lurching the audience along with the film's rising and falling moments of suspense and terror.

The first sequel, REVENGE OF THE CREATURE (1955) contained mostly library tracks by Stein, Mancini, Skinner, Salter and others; the only original material was a new main title by Stein and four new cues composed by William Lava. Stein's three-note Creature Theme, from the first film, was used heavily, although re-recorded with a slightly different orchestration that made it more ominous than suddenly shocking, until the scenes of the Creature attacking where it bursts forth loudly from the brass section out of an explosion of drums and cymbal. Stein was also among the contributors to the final film in the trilogy, THE CREATURE WALKS AMONG US (1956), along with Heinz Roemheld, Hans Salter, Irving Gertz and Henry Mancini (who wrote most of the music). The score maintained an appropriate air of foreboding tinged with a sense of compassion consistent with this film's more sympathetic portrayal of the Creature.

Stein composed most of THIS ISLAND EARTH (1956), assisted

by Salter and Mancini who scored the last reel. In this case, Stein avoided the leitmotif style which had comprised much of the earlier films, and strived to establish a sustained, brooding atmosphere, given an unearthly quality through the use of minor electronic effects. These included using vibraphone tremolos, flutes and high-register cellos in wide vibrato to achieve eerie, synthesizer-like tonalities.

Like most composers, Herman Stein recognizes the fact that music for science fiction and horror films such as these are composed with the same musical techniques as for any other type of film. "Music is music," Stein said, "and if you compose for a dramatic situation, which happens to be a film, you approach it fundamentally the same way. The fact that it's an outer space plot, or a supernatural one really doesn't matter to the composer. You're composing music for a film and you're fulfilling the function of a film composer which is to intensify what you see on the screen--not necessarily to describe it or to identify it, but to get an overall effect."[10]

Stein also recognizes the continual evolution of music for films over the years. "The nature of music, specifically for these films, will change through the years," he said recently. "It already has. They wouldn't make these rather naive outer space pictures, they would make them differently today, and therefore the music is different. Certain basic things, like the function of music in a film, will always be the same, but in 1953 films were different and the music was different. In IT CAME FROM OUTER SPACE I used the theremin, but today of course I wouldn't think of using a theremin, I'd use something else."

Hans J. Salter continued to play an important role as a major supplier of fantastic scores, as he had in the 40's. As the distinctive 50's-styled science fiction films brought to life a new breed of monster, Salter's music likewise shifted focus somewhat in bringing them to life. While his music for the Frankenstein and Wolf Man films of the 40's tended to be in a melodic, romantic idiom, Salter scored these films of the 50's with more dissonance and harsh musical frenzy. Salter recalls no intentional shift in style, however, explaining simply that "what is right for one picture is not necessarily right for another picture. I tried to write music that would be appropriate for those particular scenes."[11]

THE MOLE PEOPLE (1956) contained an effective score, composed jointly by Salter, Stein and Roemheld, which included a memorable slow, rhythmic march during the paleontological expedition's trek into the Asian mountains where they will discover the titular inhabitants. The motif, featuring a smooth string melody over a repeated, deep brass undulation, is brooding and subtly adventurous, and occasionally evocative of horrors to come.

A particularly notable score that provided quite a sympathetic undertone to the picture, was for Jack Arnold's classic, THE INCREDIBLE SHRINKING MAN (1957). The score, rich with anxious terror and subtle pathos, is built around a theme with a slow nightclub dance-band tempo, suggesting a nonchalant, bucolic calm interrupted often by stridently menacing trumpet blasts, effectively suggesting the idea that things are not so serene as they may seem. The music dramatically echoes the shattered world faced by Scott Carey as his secure life-style is driven more and more asunder as he decreases in size, finally providing us with chaotic battle music as Carey fights for his life against a now-gigantic garden spider. The music concludes with a sense of breathtaking religious spirituality, as Carey realizes that he needn't view his shrinking as something terrible, accepting it as a wonderful adventure into a new kind of world.

Herman Stein also composed a few cues for the film (including the End Title), as did Irving Gertz (whose contributions included the early scene in which the ocean mist envelops Scott Carey). The dance-band theme, which achieved some popularity, was the composition of Foster Carling and Earl E. Lawrence. Unfortunately, none of these people received any screen credit for their efforts, the sole title card crediting only music director Joseph Gershenson, who conducted the orchestra for the score.

Frank Skinner kept active during the 50's, although much more in the background than he was in the 40's. He composed portions for various Universal horror and science fiction pictures, including the comedies featuring Francis, the talking mule, and was represented in even more (as all the composers were) via the reuse of library tracks. Skinner's most notable work of the period was his solo score for THE MAN OF A THOUSAND FACES (1957), James Cagney's interesting quasi-documentary of Lon Chaney. Skinner's music remained highly romantic, emphasizing the characters dramatized in the film. The picture actually touched on fantasy elements only in its depiction of Chaney's portrayals and really is only peripherally fantastic. Skinner wisely chose to avoid overplaying these moments with horrific music. Instead, his tender violin strains and charming scherzos effectively underscore the humanity of the great actor. The score is drawn primarily from a main theme for woodwind over strings which represents Chaney's relationship with his family, its changes, conflicts and eventual restoration at the denouement. It was an emotional and moving score which did much to bring life to the film's essentially inaccurate but tasteful recreation of Chaney's life. Herman Stein had a small hand in the music, as well, improvising the organ music played by Cagney during the Phantom-of-the-Opera scene.

Of the regular staff composers at Universal during the 50's, only Henry Mancini has gone on to achieve a wide degree of fame in subsequent years. While Salter and Stein drifted away from the

film industry in the late 60's to write concert music, Mancini went
on to gain considerable recognition with his pop/jazz scores for
PETER GUNN (TV) and THE PINK PANTHER films, assuring him
of success both in film scoring as well as on record albums. Born
in Cleveland in 1924, Mancini claims to have been forced into music
by his father, although he later came to recognize his own affinity
for arranging and composing. In the 50's, Mancini became ac-
quainted with Joseph Gershenson, who offered the composer a temporary job at Universal that wound up as a six-year stint in the
studio music department. Mancini contributed to many of Universal's
horror and science fiction films during this period, although the
only screen credit he got was for TARANTULA (1955) and THE
CREATURE WALKS AMONG US (1956). The former picture had a
particularly good horror score, achieving a dramatic climate of tension and motion in its use of brass and trilling flute figures suggesting the menace of the oversized arachnid.

Despite the "cheap" nature of many of Mancini's early films,
the composer has fond memories of the assignments. "Those years
at Universal were like taking a doctorate in film scoring," he recollected. "It was six years of training in which I was required to
do just about everything a film composer comes across in the course
of his craft--arranging, adapting, orchestrating, using stock material, working fast, working against time and slim budgets, and
generally functioning. It prepared me to face just about any assignment that would come up in the years ahead."[12]

Heinz Roemheld, who had made some important contributions
to the early Universal horror films of the 30's, was occasionally reunited with the genre in the ensuing years, such as his collaboration with Universal's stable of composers on THE MUMMY'S TOMB
(1942), THE MOLE PEOPLE (1956) and THE CREATURE WALKS
AMONG US (1956). One of his most interesting collaborative efforts
was on Columbia's THE 5000 FINGERS OF DR. T (1952), with Hans
J. Salter and Frederick Hollander. The score opens with rapid,
descending string notes over plodding piano, moving into a con-
certo-like piano motif before shifting again into a romantic melody.
Elsewhere, a motif for harp and strings over toy piano leads into
the first fantasy scene, using deep, ominous horn chords as the
small boy is chased by unseen pursuers. The fairy-talelike fantasy
utilized music to a great degree, since the Dr. T of the title was a
music teacher, and played upon the fantasies of his young pupil in
the music (as with the use of the toy piano in the orchestra).

Irving Gertz also contributed greatly to the Universal science
fiction films of the 50's. Born in Providence, Rhode Island, in 1915,
Gertz was educated there at the College of Music. He became associated with the Providence Symphony and composed several chorus
works for the Catholic Choral Society. In 1939 he began working
at Columbia's music department until joining the army two years
later. After World War II, Gertz returned to motion pictures, scor-

ing and arranging for many companies. His first work in the genre at Universal was in collaborating with Herman Stein and Henry
Mancini on the score for IT CAME FROM OUTER SPACE (1953), all
of them composing about an equal third of the film, although the
main thematic approach was created by Stein. Gertz also contributed to the scores of THE CREATURE WALKS AMONG US (1956)
and THE INCREDIBLE SHRINKING MAN (1957), and composed
nearly all of the music for THE MONOLITH MONSTERS (1957).
It is this score that perhaps best exemplifies Gertz's science fiction scoring of the 50's, and stands out as a fine "B" score of the
period.

THE MONOLITH MONSTERS was a well-made programmer concerning crystalline rocks from outer space that react chemically to
the water on Earth, growing to monstrous, threatening proportions.
Gertz scored all of the film's nine reels except for reels six, eight,
and part of seven. Herman Stein scored reel six and the balance
of seven, while Henry Mancini scored reel eight; the main thematic
constructions being by Gertz. The music builds a strong brooding
mood of tension, providing a number of motifs for various sequences.
The main theme is a loud, three-note shouting phrase for brass
(something like Stein's theme for THE CREATURE FROM THE BLACK
LAGOON in its use of three rapidly ascending notes, the last one
held slightly), and a repeated four-note ascending piano motif (four
quick piano notes accompanied by simultaneous drum taps, ascending
in rapid succession and then stopping abruptly, repeating itself
amid string meandering). The former motif is an effective horror
theme, while the latter provides an ominous furtiveness to many of
the suspenseful sequences.

One memorable moment is achieved in the early scene in which
Miller discovers the petrified body of the scientist: vibrato strings
under woodwind mixed with the four-note piano motif grow and
build with warbling woodwinds and ultimately, pounding piano and
tympani, all of which culminates in rapid bursts from strings and
brass and a loud orchestral punch which segues into the laughter
of school-children in the next scene. As the children explore the
desert rocks, their teacher, Miss Barrett, begins a friendly chat
with Jennie, one of her pupils. Gertz introduces a tender theme
for string and woodwinds as their conversation turns toward Barrett's affection for Miller. This light mood is sustained until the
piano/drum motif barges in when Jennie finds a piece of the alien
crystal, signifying its ominous threat.

Gertz also scored Universal's THE LEECH WOMAN (1960) as
well as THE ALLIGATOR PEOPLE for Twentieth Century-Fox (1959),
before joining Stein and Salter on Irwin Allen's television series,
VOYAGE TO THE BOTTOM OF THE SEA and LAND OF THE GI-
ANTS, where he composed the music for several episodes.

A number of composers who later became quite successful

in the 60's and 70's had their cinematic beginnings in the 50's, and a great many of them had occasion to provide the music for more than one film in the fantastic genre.

Among them was Elmer Bernstein, a young composer who had studied in New York, preparing himself for a career as a concert pianist. He performed widely during the early 40's and during World War II he composed dramatic musical scores for the Armed Forces Radio Network. After the War, Bernstein returned to the concert stage for a few years, eventually becoming reacquainted with radio scoring in 1950, which led to assignments in motion pictures. Bernstein scored a number of low-budget films during the early 50's until he was given the task of scoring Cecil B. DeMille's lavish THE TEN COMMANDMENTS (1955), the score that elevated Bernstein to prominence. He has since become noted for his introduction of modern jazz into the foreground of a film score, in movies like THE MAN WITH THE GOLDEN ARM, and in the 60's became popular as a composer for Westerns such as THE MAGNIFICENT SEVEN.

Bernstein has scored few genre pictures, most of them being in the 70's and 80's, although there are a pair of notable science fiction films scored in his early days in 1953--notable mainly for being considered two of the worst genre films ever made: ROBOT MONSTER and CAT WOMEN OF THE MOON. However microscopic these films' budgets were, and however laughable they turned out to be, Bernstein's music remarkably shone through the squeaky, papier-mâché props and ludicrous nonacting to provide some rather exciting film music. As Bernstien recently recalled: "Those two pictures were written for rather similar orchestras and they were in their own way sort of oddly avant-garde scores. There was a leaning on electronics in both of those.... They were written for instruments like the Novachord and the electronic organ and things of that kind."[13]

The music for ROBOT MONSTER was particularly good, considering the film's ridiculous premise of a gorilla-suited extraterrestrial wearing a deep-sea diving helmet hobbling around a cave trying to decimate the world's few remaining survivors with a gurgling, bubble-spouting machine. The main motif is a plodding, five-note low brass motif which is heard whenever Ro-Man is on the screen. This is balanced with a jangly piano theme and a lower, repetitive piano motif something like Herrmann's Radar music in THE DAY THE EARTH STOOD STILL. As one reviewer wrote: "Bernstein offers a ... heroic theme repeated over and over again by a loud brass section, piano, xylophone and glockenspiel. These ruffles and flourishes seem more appropriate for some widescreen biblical spectacle than for the shabby antics in Bronson Canyon."[14]

The ruffles and flourishes that suggested a biblical epic to

that writer were put to good use two years later in Bernstein's
magnificent music for THE TEN COMMANDMENTS, which contains
elements of supernatural fantasy in its otherwise mainstream tale of
biblical history. Bernstein was initially hired to write only a single
dance for the film, but DeMille was so impressed that he retained
the composer to write other pieces of music, and eventually the entire score, which took more than a year and a half to write. The
score is rich and complex, brimming with leitmotifs for most of the
central characters and framed with a powerful and inspirational religious theme.

Ernest Gold likewise had his start in the B-movies of the
early 50's. Gold had been born in Vienna in 1921 to a very musical family. He studied at the State Academy of Music in Vienna,
later emigrating to the United States in 1938, where he worked as
a piano accompanist and as a popular songwriter. In 1945 he
moved to Hollywood and was put to work in motion pictures.
Among Gold's few genre scores are UNKNOWN WORLD (1951)
and THE SCREAMING SKULL (1958), for which he provided effective accompaniment. The latter film incorporated the traditional
Dies Irae, a medieval plainsong chant associated with the Catholic
mass for the dead, and an oft-quoted motif in horror films. The
ominous piece is heard from low, surging brass notes in the main
title, mixed with an effectively high, childlike female voice, and
the contrast between the two creates a notably spooky mood at the
outset.

Gold typified the feeling of many composers scoring low-
budget movies such as these when he explained his approach to
these types of films: "I approached them in exactly the same way
as any other picture. If the story in a B picture was a cheap kind
of story, then the picture needed a 'cheap' score, because, no
matter what the story, the score has to support it. You take each
picture and you try to do justice to what it is. The only differences are the budgets. For instance, on SCREAMING SKULL,
there was a very small budget for the orchestra, so I could not
have used a large one. I had to use a lot of imagination to get the
expression and the effects I wanted from the small group."[15]

Gold, who prefers writing music for "people-oriented" films
rather than action pictures, normally strove to emphasize in the
score the conflicts and relationships between the characters. One
genre film that gave him a good opportunity to do this, which was
also his first "big" film that elevated him above the B-movie as-
sembly line into respectable film scoring, was Stanley Kramer's
futuristic, post-holocaust drama, ON THE BEACH (1959). Gold
composed a number of leitmotifs for individual characters and their
relationships, as well as utilizing, at Kramer's request, the traditional Australian song, "Waltzing Mathilda," as a motif creating
local color.

Gerald Fried, later to become quite prolific at scoring TV-movies and miniseries such as the acclaimed ROOTS, similarly started in the 50's, scoring numerous B-movies and similar programmers. Fried was born in New York City in 1926 and studied composition at Juilliard, also majoring in the oboe. After graduating in 1948, Fried gained employment as first oboist with symphony orchestras in Pittsburgh, Dallas and New York. He scored his first film in 1951, a short for childhood friend Stanley Kubrick. Fried went on to score Kubrick's first three feature films, thereby embarking on a career in film music.

Among Fried's early B-movie scores were several low-budget horror pictures, and he became rather adept at scoring these kinds of films with his strong flair for melodrama. One of his most effective early horrors was THE RETURN OF DRACULA (1958), which featured a strong, driving theme for throbbing horns over strident string chords, the melodic line being that of the Dies Irae. Fried's music here provides a single primary theme used throughout the picture to suggest and accompany the presence of the diabolical Count Dracula. The score is a noteworthy example of the ability of music--and what it has come to suggest to an audience--to instill a sense of terror through the use of such a repeated phrase, as one reviewer noted: "This score begins with that rhythmic device now known universally as 'the JAWS motif,' though of course it was no more original in '58 than it was in '75. Nevertheless, the device is equally as fitting for vampires as for sharks, and Fried provides an elaborate orchestration for the main title, full as ever with the hallmarks of his spirited style and swelling to a furious climax as the camera closes in on the darkened eyes of 'The Count.' Throughout, Fried seems to try harder than anyone else involved to give the lack-lustre movie some vigour and excitement, and his intelligent style of 'squeal and groan' (sounds almost like electronics, but is actually just clever instrumentation) is commendably bold for this category of picture. So often a B-movie composer would write something nondescript that would, hopefully, pass unnoticed, but Fried believed from the beginning in stamping some sort of authority on the soundtrack to promote a definite atmosphere. The score ends as it began with the frenzied main theme finally disintegrating as Dracula falls down a mine shaft, landing conveniently on a wooden stake and thereby himself disintegrating into a skeleton."[16]

Fried feels that the most important thing a composer can instill into his score is a sense of believability in the characters and the situations they face. "I've done some pretty crummy pictures in my life as well as some good ones," Fried admitted recently. "I think what I do is believe that this is really a great picture and these are important people and their emotions are valuable and are pertinent and relevant, and, within the discretions of taste, I just try to elaborate on that. The fact that there's going to be a vampire or a monster coming out of the scenery soon is incidental to that premise. If there is dramatic reality, then it works whether or not the threat or the antagonist is psychological or another army, a jealous nephew or a monster."[17]

Fried's music for I BURY THE LIVING (1958) was likewise a carefully crafted score for a film which was otherwise unremembered. Fried found the film's unusual premise, about a caretaker who believes he has the power of life and death by shifting stickpins in his graveyard map, very much to his liking: "I tried to imply to the audience that something bigger was going on than just a Friday-night-scare-teenager-giggle-movie; that there was a philosophical content larger than what appeared, and I wrote in fugal form. I wanted a classical structure to imply to the audience that this was not your ordinary movie."

Both RETURN OF DRACULA and I BURY THE LIVING make effective use of traditional musical material, the Dies Irae in the former picture, and the latter quoting briefly from another traditional hymn/chant. Fried finds the incorporation of such pieces quite useful in a horror score: "It's useful to me because it conjures up in me many centuries of association. It gets me to dig deeper."

Fried's main title for CURSE OF THE FACELESS MAN (1958) made use of an evocative, whispering/squeaking string whine under low trombone notes and rapid trumpet trills, developing into a horrific dissonance broken by a slow, climactic descending group of chords from the brass, creating an uneasy atmosphere from the start which is maintained throughout the score. Fried scored a few other horror pictures in the 50's and 60's, becoming quite involved with television in the 60's, where he contributed episode scores for STAR TREK and other series, in addition to many made-for-TV movies.

Bronislau Kaper was one of MGM's leading composers from 1936 through the early 60's, providing the music for many of their period adventure films, his magnum opus being the full-blooded and lavishly symphonic score for MUTINY ON THE BOUNTY (1962). Kaper was born in Warsaw in 1902. Discovering his affinity for music through the piano, he studied at the Chopin Music School in Warsaw and in Berlin, where he became a popular songwriter. One of Kaper's songs was heard by Louis B. Mayer, who was impressed enough to sign the composer to an MGM contract, which started Kaper's career as a film composer. Among the one hundred films Kaper scored before his death in 1983, were a few borderline fantasies and psychological thrillers; his single attempt at a bona fide horror score was also one of the 50's best genre scores, for the 1954 classic, THEM!

The film, one of dozens concerning the fantastic results of atomic radiation, depicted an invasion of giant, mutated ants into the Los Angeles sewer system. While similar in concept to any num-

ber of Big-Bug movies of the 50's, THEM! was noteworthy for its
literate approach, and came across as a much more powerful and
durable picture. The film was essentially a horror picture of science gone wrong, but Kaper downplayed the scientific aspect. "I
treated it not like a science picture," the composer said. "I treated
it like a real menace. I was getting tired of the usual effects. I
treated it as an action movie, you know, 'Boom-Bang!' Oh, you
should have heard this music on the stage--it was really good.
And I wrote a 'fugue' which was out of the picture later ... it
was a 'Fugue for Ants.' Just for fun, I knew it was going to be
out of the picture, but I wrote it for kicks. Took me four days to
write it. Very chromatic too (mimics the patterns which sound like
groups of ants skittering along.)"[18]

Kaper's score for THEM! is built around a dramatic main theme
for strings over blaring horns. The theme is comprised of a 4-note
descending phrase; the first note held, the next two rapid and the
final note stopping abruptly ("DAAA-da-da-dap"), creating an effective atmosphere of drama and action. The music is used sparsely in the film, coming up only in a few places. The main theme is
reprised very effectively as the young girl found earlier in the
desert awakens from her coma, and screams "them" before becoming
hysterical. The few snatches of the main theme here reinforce the
menace that Kaper was trying to capture. The climactic scenes are
nicely scored as well, including an urgent Business motif for violins and brass, with a strong bass line, as the assault on the desert nest is prepared, while the actual attack upon the nest is accompanied by loud, crashing brass chords which are soon inundated by sound effects. The final assault on the L.A. storm drain
conduits features a similar action motif for driving brass punches
over a pounding drum beat.

While Bernstein, Gold, Fried and Kaper represented the newcomers to the film music field whose potential for success would become more prominent and recognized in the 60's, there were many
other composers who failed to achieve the same kind of acclaim,
and yet who contributed important scores to the fantastic films of
the 50's.

One of the most memorable and intriguing horror scores of
this period was that of INVADERS FROM MARS (1953), credited to
Raoul Kraushaar. Born in Paris in 1908, Kraushaar was educated
in the United States and became the assistant to composer Hugo
Riesenfeld on a number of silent films, including the original TEN
COMMANDMENTS. In 1928 he began working as musical assistant
at United Artists, RKO and Pathe; he later became an assistant music librarian at MGM and Warner Brothers, eventually working as
an assistant to music director Abe Meyer. Kraushaar also worked
as music director for a variety of studios during the 40's and 50's.
INVADERS FROM MARS has gone on to become something of a cult
classic, and the music is one of its most effective components, being

dominated by eerie choral arrangements performing in almost chant-
like acapella. As one reviewer put it, "Kraushaar's choral group
conjures up visions of a dying Martian landscape or the wailing of
frightened minds in hell."[19]

While Kraushaar has spoken frequently about his composition
of the score, there are a number of reliable sources contemporary
to the film which have revealed that Kraushaar was in reality only
the music director on the picture, and that the actual score was
ghostwritten for him (a frequent practice in the 40's and 50's on
low-budget movies) by Mort Glickman, another Republic composer
who worked on many of the serials in the 40's. Kraushaar conducted the score, which was recorded at Republic Studios. Glickman reportedly ghostwrote any number of the scores that Kraushaar,
as music director, got the credit for, including BRIDE OF THE
GORILLA (1951) and UNTAMED WOMEN (1952). After Glickman
died in 1953, Kraushaar reportedly got composer Dave Kahn to
ghostwrite for him.

The use of the choir is undoubtedly the score's strongest
point, especially accentuating the scenes where the people disap-
pear beneath the sand, and gives them an especially eerie quality.
The choral arrangements were recorded with 16 singers, eight men
and eight women; during the dubbing the sound was put through
an echo chamber to give it an additional weirdness.

Paul Sawtell was a notable figure in the fantastic film music
of the 50's, although his career in the genre actually harkens back
to the RKO Tarzan films of the 40's. Sawtell was born in Poland
in 1906, receiving his musical education in Munich before becoming
a violin soloist with various symphonies in Europe. He emigrated
to the United States in 1923, where he worked as a violinist and
conductor for theaters, radio and concert halls throughout the 20's,
arriving in Hollywood as an arranger in 1935 (his assignments including working for Universal alumnus David Broekman). In 1940,
Sawtell became associated with RKO as a music director. He also
worked at Universal, supervising Hans Salter's scores for films such
as WEIRD WOMAN and HOUSE OF DRACULA. During the 40's, Sawtell was noted for scoring RKO's Tarzan movies, and in the 50's
maintained a successful collaboration with colleague Bert A. Shefter.

Born in Russia in 1904, Shefter was educated in the United
States. He was a member of the piano team, Gould (Morton) and
Shefter, performing on radio and in theaters. He also conducted
music for silent film screenings during the 20's, as Sawtell had.
Shefter also gained notice as a concert pianist, performing frequently in concert halls. During the 50's, Shefter began to compose for films, while continuing to write songs and make many
records throughout his association with cinema.

Shefter's first collaboration with Sawtell was for THE BLACK

SCORPION (1957), which also contained electronic effects by Jack Cookerly. Only Sawtell received screen credit, since he was allowing Shefter to assist "on speculation," to see what kind of job he did. "I helped to conduct and orchestrate," Shefter said recently. "I also helped to compose, but would only compose after he had made some sketches. I would compose in the same style."[20]

The collaborative nature of their association allowed them to compose a full score very quickly, which naturally made them popular with producers of low-budget quickies. "The ordinary composer writes three minutes of music a day," said Shefter. "But both of us could write ten minutes a day and have a score in one week. That was the beauty of our relation."

Both Sawtell and Shefter came from different backgrounds of experience, Sawtell having gained a proficiency at scoring serials and action movies while Shefter had done a variety of period and contemporary dramas. Their musical ideas, however, were close enough that their relationship became a very compatible one. "If it was a two-minute sketch and I wrote a minute of it, Paul would take over and finish it according to what I had done with the development so far. I never felt that two people have to write differently for a picture; that wouldn't be appropriate. This way no one knows who wrote what." Thus, their styles were adapted together and fit their films more cohesively than a more self-asserting collaboration would. Shefter did most of the orchestrations as well, an area that Sawtell preferred to avoid.

One of their most successful collaborative efforts was for the FLY trilogy, begun in 1958. While the three films each contained distinctive scores, there was a similarity of style between each picture that linked them together. "They were all related," Shefter said. "We did not use the same themes, but we used the same style of musically accompanying a body transported from one part of the world to another. We didn't use electronic music but we did use the eerie type of music, plus the classical style of drama."

The first film in the trilogy was THE FLY (1958), scored by both of them, although due to a production error only Sawtell received screen credit. The primary element of the score is a tender love theme for the scientist André and his wife, Helene. The motif is comprised of strings and woodwinds over harp, and is often balanced with a louder string-and-brass motif, signifying the mixture of pathos and horror embodied in the film's treatment of the scientist whose head and arm have been molecularly "switched" with that of a housefly. The music is used sparingly, perhaps too much so, actually, since certain scenes seem to suffer from a lack of musical accompaniment--such as when Helene breaks down after failing to catch the "white-headed" fly needed to cure her monstrously altered husband, and later when François sits and sadly contemplates the circumstances after the fly's death. Both sequences are devoid of music and would seem to have benefited from some kind of warmth to underscore the emotions portrayed.

There are a number of fine musical moments, however, such as the brief brass-and-string crescendo, subtly laced with a phrase from the Love Theme, as André's fly hand slips from his coat pocket and is seen by Helene for the first time, who realizes the nature of his unusual accident. The same crescendo accompanies the scene where Helene yanks André's hood off to reveal his huge fly head; the music then segues to a variation of the Love Theme as André replaces the hood and comforts her. The music erupts into a frenzied string-and-brass motif as André, angered and frustrated by his circumstances, destroys the lab. This lengthy musical segment utilizes an effective mixture of the love theme and horror motif to illustrate dramatically both the passion and the horror of the fly/man. There is also a slight use of swirling high strings as Helene wakes up in the morning, suggesting the buzzing of a fly as her waking face recoils in shock as she recollects the awful events of the previous night.

Sawtell and Shefter collaborated again on the sequel, RETURN OF THE FLY (1959), which takes as its main theme a buzzing string motif, characterized by a high violin vibrato, echoing the haunting sound of the fly and the similar accident which has infected André's son. Numerous other motifs abound here and there, mostly slow and meandering incidental pieces, a brassy fight cue, and a routine Love Theme. Near the end, a low, rumbling woodwind figure is provided as a motif for the human fly, and at the conclusion the Love Theme segues into the buzzing Fly Theme for the film's final shot. Shefter returned by himself in 1965 for the final film in the trilogy, CURSE OF THE FLY, when an illness rendered Sawtell unavailable. Shefter made use of eerie, dreamlike harp reverberations behind a furtive woodwind melody, a pleasant trumpet theme and a concertolike piano Love Theme, again using a style similar to that in the previous FLY films.

An earlier score for KRONOS (1957) was provided with a dominating two-note Horror motif. A churning brass chord is heard on the first note, echoed by a high, warbling woodwind and piano chord on the second note. The repeated interplay between the high woodwind howls and the low brass groans comprise a strong and memorable Terror Theme, which is given various treatments throughout the score. IT! THE TERROR FROM BEYOND SPACE (1958) was given a harsh, monstrously claustrophobic score, while Irwin Allen's THE LOST WORLD (1960) contained a lighter approach evocative of the lush, primordial landscape discovered by the explorers.

Sawtell and Shefter continued to collaborate through the 60's, until Sawtell's death in 1970. One of their most memorable works of this period was for VOYAGE TO THE BOTTOM OF THE SEA

(1961), the original theme of which was resurrected by Sawtell for the TV series three years later. They also scored the "poor-man's Sinbad voyage," JACK THE GIANT KILLER (1962), investing it with a symphonic, promenadelike march for brass and strings with much pomp and fanfare.

While there were a number of lyrical, melodic themes in their fantasy and horror scores, the primary approach was dramatic and eerie, accentuating those elements of the films. "We'd use the high intensity of the string section, with harmonics for a certain effect," Shefter said. "We'd use the basses with the contrabassoon and bassoon for suspense, with cello and violas in a more melodic mode, although it remained in the horror vein. We used very little brass because we didn't like what we called 'stingers'--sudden musical shock effects. We never gave a surprise away before it happened, and when it did happen we didn't mickey mouse it with a brass stinger. We did use brass when there was a heroic moment, in the style of Wagner. We used the classical style."

William Lava, best known for his numerous Western scores for Warner Brothers in the 40's and 50's, provided effective music for several low-budget thrillers of the 50's. A self-taught composer, Lava was born in Minnesota in 1911 and was educated at Northwestern University. He studied conducting with Albert Coates, and worked as a band arranger in the 30's before arriving in Hollywood in 1936, where he began work in RKO's music department. The following year he was hired by Republic to write the music for their serial, THE PAINTED STALLION, and his resulting score impressed the studio enough for them to offer Lava a contract. The prolific composer worked for Republic until the mid-40's, when he moved to Warner Brothers. There Lava scored dozens of short films and Westerns, in addition to ghostwriting for a number of other composers. During the 40's and 50's, Lava collaborated with staff composers at Universal on horror films such as THE INVISIBLE MAN'S REVENGE (1944) and THE DEADLY MANTIS (1957). The latter film contained a rousing, dynamic, ever-ascending brass-and-string score, punctuated by tympani. He also wrote the amusing honky-tonk piano music for the "Once Upon a Time" episode of TV's THE TWILIGHT ZONE. Lava's final score before his death in 1970 was the low-low-budget DRACULA VS. FRANKENSTEIN (subsequently released as BLOOD OF FRANKENSTEIN in 1971).

Russell Garcia, a popular recording artist during the late 50's, composed a handful of film scores, including the memorable music for George Pal's THE TIME MACHINE (1960). The opening theme intersperses a sirenlike ascending electronic whistle with a romantic string melody, which characterizes the mixture of idyllic life (the Eloi) and harmful threat (the Morlocks) in the 800th millenium. (This theme later became the theme for the children's TV show, CAPTAIN SATELLITE.) In contrast, a soft woodwind ballad over

mandolin in classical style represents the year 1900, and recurs occasionally during the futuristic scenes to illustrate George's home-
sickness. Garcia also scored Pal's ATLANTIS, THE LOST CON-
TINENT (1961).

Herschel Burke Gilbert began as an orchestrator for Monogram and Columbia studios in the mid-40's before freelancing as a
composer in 1947. Gilbert wrote a fine score for PROJECT MOON-
BASE (1953), emphasizing the theremin to create a weird and scary
atmosphere. First heard in the main title, the theremin plays a
spooky, quivering melody over harp strings and xylophone, punctuated by brief brassy punches. A militaristic theme contrasts
nicely with the eeriness, representing the technological space station and lunar base while the theremin sounds accentuate the alien
setting. Gilbert later worked on various television scores in the
late 50's, returning to low-budget genre films like I DISMEMBER
MAMA (1974) in the 70's.

Marlin Skiles began as a pianist for several dance orchestras
near his hometown of Harrisburg, Pennsylvania. Born in 1906 and
educated at the Froehlich School of Music, Skiles studied with
Ernst Toch and eventually became an arranger, moving to Hollywood in 1933, where he orchestrated and scored many kinds of
films. Skiles' earliest fantastic score was for the Columbia "Aladdin's lamp" fantasy, A THOUSAND AND ONE NIGHTS, under the
direction of Morris Stoloff, in 1945. In the early 50's, Skiles
moved to Monogram, where he scored two fantasy films in 1951,
ALADDIN AND HIS LAMP and FLIGHT TO MARS, before joining Allied Artists for the duration of the decade. Skiles' scores for Allied consisted of many borderline fantasy-comedies as well as serious science fiction films such as THE MAZE (1953) and QUEEN OF
OUTER SPACE (1958). In the 60's Skiles went on to score films
for various companies, his only genre effort being a low-budget
quickie made in 1965, SPACE MONSTER, which was distributed
only to television by American International some years later.
Skiles was still scoring films in the early 70's, including the 1971
science fiction offering, THE RESURRECTION OF ZACHARY
WHEELER, until his death in 1980.

Michel Michelet was born in Kiev, Russia, where he eventually became a professor at conservatories in Kiev and Vienna.
Michelet scored more than a hundred films in France before coming
to the United States in 1941, where he continued to compose concert works and film scores, as well as arrange Russian period music for films like ANASTASIA. Michelet's fantasy scores include
THE END OF THE WORLD, made in France in 1930, the 1951 remake of M, and CAPTAIN SINBAD (1963).

David Buttolph was a musical director for Twentieth Century-
Fox from 1935 through 1941, where, as a member of the music department, he contributed to "patchwork" scores with colleagues

Cyril Mockridge and David Raksin. After leaving Fox, Buttolph
worked for several studios before moving to Warner Brothers in
1948, where he received more prestigious assignments such as
Hitchcock's ROPE and Bogart's THE ENFORCER. During this
period, Buttolph scored his best genre films, HOUSE OF WAX and
THE BEAST FROM 20,000 FATHOMS, both released in 1953. Characterized by a particularly dense orchestral sound, Buttolph's
score for BEAST is an especially evocative composition illustrating
the monolithic power of the prehistoric Rhedosaurus with a surging,
four-note theme for deep, booming brass chords over wildly flurrying strings. Quieter moments--such as the poetic musical soliloquy
for Professor Elson's reflective exploration of the murky depths in
a diving bell--stand out amid the chaos of the rampaging Beast
music. HOUSE OF WAX was likewise characterized by deep brass
chords, dissonances, and a typically thick orchestration, with instrument after instrument joining in the fray to depict the tortured
horrors of Vincent Price's corrupt wax museum. Although clichéd
nowadays, Buttolph's high-pitched, wailing string/flute motif was
effective in the 50's, acoustically imitating the theremin and other
electronic instruments then in vogue. The cues for the museum
fire (a crackling and blazing composition matching the conflagration
on screen) and the killer's pursuit of Sue through the foggy
streets (mingling a three-note theme for Price with flurrying violin and orchestra chase music) are other highlights of a notable
score. THE PHANTOM OF THE RUE MORGUE (1953) contrasted a
rapid string theme over staccato brass and percussion with a classical violin love theme.

Gordon Zahler was an independent music supervisor who, in
the manner of Abe Meyer and others of the 30's, operated a music
library with which he scored films like the infamous PLAN 9 FROM
OUTER SPACE (1956). Zahler himself was not a composer.

Darrell Calker also scored a number of fantastic films during
the 50's. Born in Washington D.C. in 1905, Calker was educated
at Maryland University and the Curtis Institute. He became associated with films in the early 40's, where he scored many Woody
Woodpecker cartoons. Among his horror scores of the 50's are
SUPERMAN AND THE MOLE MEN (1951) and VOODOO WOMAN
(1956). Calker died in 1964. Nicholas Carras, born in Pittsburgh
in 1922, was educated in Chicago and in Europe, eventually becoming an arranger for George Antheil and David Rose, with whom he
studied. He began to score films in the late 50's, among which were
low-budget horrors such as FRANKENSTEIN'S DAUGHTER (1958).
Carras also provided an interesting score for SHE DEMONS (1958),
which opens with pounding jungle drums under brassy blares and
violin swirls in a semi-jazzy motif; as the music moves into meandering mysteriousness for strings and woodwinds, the drum pounding lingers on. A pleasant horn theme accompanies the beach sequences, lending them significant music rather than the incidental
nonmusic often given to low-budget films like this. Alexander

Laszlo, born in Budapest in 1895 and establishing a successful career as a pianist and an inventor in the 20's, provided the music
for similarly forgotten efforts such as THE GIANT LEECHES (1959)
and THE ATOMIC SUBMARINE (1960).

Nathan Van Cleave composed much effective music for horror
films and later for television's THE TWILIGHT ZONE. Born in
1910, Van Cleave was a student of Schillinger, and began professionally as a jazz trumpet player, later becoming an acclaimed arranger for Andre Kostelanetz, and others. By the 40's Van
Cleave was working prolifically in radio, scoring and arranging
various programs. After shrugging off the offers of Robert Emmett Dolan, Paramount's head music director, Van Cleave finally re-
lented in 1945 and came to Hollywood, where he eventually scored
a number of science fiction films, characterized by rich orchestration, striking harmonic modulations, and a skillful blending of
electronic instruments and standard orchestra.

One of Van Cleave's most notable scores was that for THE
COLOSSUS OF NEW YORK (1958). This was an unusual score because it was conceived and composed entirely for piano. While Van
Cleave received sole credit for composing the score, in actuality he
collaborated with friend and colleague, composer Fred Steiner (no
relation to Max Steiner). Steiner and Van Cleave had been associated in New York, where Steiner orchestrated many of Van
Cleave's radio scores, and in fact, ghostwrote several radio episodes for him. Shortly after Van Cleave came to Hollywood, Steiner joined him, and their collaborative association continued.

Basically, Steiner's uncredited work for Van Cleave in films
such as ROBINSON CRUSOE ON MARS (1964) and on THE TWI-
LIGHT ZONE consisted of ghostwriting and orchestrating from thematic material that Van Cleave had already composed. Van Cleave
would then return the favor in due course on Steiner's own assignments. In the case of THE COLOSSUS OF NEW YORK, however, Steiner did in fact compose the main theme and much of the
score for Van Cleave, whose idea it was to score only for piano.
"It was done on three pianos of various types," Steiner recently
recalled. "We had three grand pianos and an old oak upright piano
for a slightly different timbre. One of the reasons that Van asked
me to help him on it was because he had a very indifferent technique as a pianist, and so he thought it would be good to bring
me in. I actually furnished the main theme, a kind of passacaglia."[21]

The music opens with this concertolike motif under the main
titles, the piano pounding with slowly ponderous, melancholy notes.
The score utilizes furtive keyboard tinkling during the early operation sequence, though elsewhere little more than nonmelodic piano
motifs, phrases and incidental dawdling are provided. As interesting as the instrumentation was, the simple piano does not always

completely accent the full emotional range of the film, though frequently it does provide an effective ominousness to the main theme.

Clifton Parker's music for CURSE OF THE DEMON (1956) is
built in the shape of a somewhat morbid tone poem, as Bill Littman
has described it: "Parker has eschewed the use of leitmotifs as a
basis for the score, giving us instead a group of gradually building mood pieces which reflect the main characters' growing anxi-
eties as the film proceeds. The music for the pre-credit narration
sequence and the main titles acts as a sort of miniature overture
for the total score, each section of the 'overture' containing the
musical building blocks that will shape the completed composition."[22]
Parker does a bit of musical experimentation within these boundaries as well, as in the use of violins sustaining their highest
register and, soon thereafter, tubas sustaining their lowest register, in the scenes illustrating the presence of demons. Strings
and massed flutes dominate in other demonic sequences. Parker
keeps the use of stereotypical "crash chords," so prevalent and
overused in horror scores, to a minimum, instead using the medium-
sized orchestra and piano to build the score gradually, underscoring its mood rather than titillating the audience with shock crescendos.

As Littman explains, the score's dominating theme is "the
nine-note, two-part 'devil theme' that appears at regular intervals
throughout. The theme, suspiciously enough, is composed for the
key of 'D' ('D' for Demon, what else?) and is sectioned into a four-
note (two ascending--two descending) opening which one might
characterize as illustrating the power of the 'Dark Forces' mainly
through its basic, forceful nature and the fact that it invariably
appears each time Holden's faith in the 'real and the touchable' is
shaken; and the less-often-heard five-note descending conclusion
to the theme, a despairing musical piece illustrating the eventual
end of the objects of the demon's attacks." A particularly remarkable piece of music accompanies the appearances of the demon itself, which utilizes basically the same music each time, beginning
with a "staccato squeaking noise indicating the sudden presence of
the demon" and the sustained low drone of the tubas, followed by
sustained notes from the flutes. A piano then emerges, playing
the "devil theme" punctuated by a cymbal crash, with the flutes
appearing here and there throughout, often joined by rhythmic
beats on the tympani. The sequence ends with a grotesque figure
for the brass. As Littman concludes: "...the final, overall effect
of the score is to show the almost utter helplessness of the human
being versus the forces of darkness. Not one musical piece can
be identified personally with any of the human characters involved.
From beginning to end, it's the demon."

Clifton Parker wrote little else in the genre, although he did
compose the scores for many action films from the mid-40's until
the early 60's, and CURSE OF THE DEMON remains a fine and com-

plex horror score. Another composer whose sole effort in the genre remains an outstanding example of leitmotif film scoring is Walter Schumann. Best known for his theme to the DRAGNET radio
and TV series, Schumann scored a small number of films during
the 50's, including several Abbott and Costello comedies for Universal (though some of these used tracked music originally composed
for earlier films). Schumann lost an important lawsuit--claiming
his DRAGNET theme was stolen from Miklos Rozsa's very similar
theme for THE KILLERS (1947) (though in view of Schumann's
talent elsewhere it is more than likely that the DRAGNET incident
was one of <u>unconscious</u> plagiarism)--probably resulted in his failure to become more widely known as a film composer. His last,
and most superlative score, was for the classic 1955 psychological
thriller, NIGHT OF THE HUNTER.

Schumann's very unified score makes use of a variety of leitmotifs. Preacher Harry Powell, the psychotic killer who charms
young women in order to gain their wealth, is denoted by a
strong, four-note ascending theme; while widow Rachel Cooper,
who protects the children of one of Powell's victims, is given a
jaunty scherzo. These are the only characters represented musically, the remaining leitmotifs signifying specific situations in the
story, as Jim Doherty described in an extensive analysis of the
score. A "frantic disarray of violin strokes" is used for the children's flight from the killer. "What first appears to be a theme
for Willa Harper ... later turns out to be a theme for all the wom-
en Powell charms. A simple child-like melody is used to express
safety and security. It appears throughout the film in conjunction
with the children: the safety of the river in their flight, or the
security of having Rachel Cooper protect them. The theme also
appears as a song sung by Pearl (one of the children) in the context of the story, the words of which are about her mother, Willa.
Another melody, appearing twice as a song in the film, is the
'Lullaby,' which is played when the children think they are far
enough ahead of their pursuer to rest from their flight. It is a
soothing melody which imparts a feeling that 'everything is all
right.'"[23]

The film's conclusion nicely wraps up all the themes as the
story is brought to a close, and illustrates Schumann's thematic
interplay. As Rachel and the children leave the town after the
trial, an arrangement of the Hunted Children's Theme is heard
from brass and violins; as the preacher is escorted to a police car,
a statement of the Hunter's Theme is played. The scene shifts to
Christmas at the Cooper orphanage, heralded with sleigh bells and
pizzicato strings, over which the lullaby melody is heard, reinforcing their safety from the hunter. All the themes are drawn together in a final symbolic contrast as the children open their
Christmas gifts. "When Ruby receives her gift from Miss Cooper,
the Willa/love theme is heard; a contrast between her childish in-
fatuation with Preacher Powell, and the present. When John opens

his present, the security theme is played showing that Miss Cooper has filled the emptiness left in his heart by his mother's death. The 'Lullaby' then smoothly arises out of the other theme, this time played with full force indicating that everything is now truly all right.   The score then ends with one final statement of the Hunter's Theme, to remind the viewer what the children have gone through, and are now free of."[24]

Schumann, writing about the score in the old magazine Film Music, described his musical approach as one based on director Charles Laughton's idea of dividing the musical sections into six segments, each of which would become an entity.   "Since no one scene in the picture lasted more than a minute and a half," Schumann wrote, "the purpose of the music was to form a continuity for each segment.   This simply meant that I would not play each scene but write an overall composition to cover the entire segment."

"The first segment consisted of the main title and establishing scenes.   I have always believed that a main title, as in the case of an overture, should establish the character of the main subject.   Since we were dealing with the symbolism of good vs. evil, I started the main title with Preacher's stark foreboding theme and then segued to the lullaby sung purely and simply by children's voices.   The second segment involved the transformation of Willa, the children's mother, from the time of courtship by Preacher, through the marriage to the murder scene.   My first thought for underscoring these highly dramatic moments was to use an emotional and tense musical treatment.   But in discussion with Mr. Laughton he used an expression I will always remember. He said, 'If the actors and I have stated it properly on the screen, then you don't have to restate it with music.'   Consequently, I devised a very simple waltz which, when used against the preacher theme, formed a dramatic background against which the actors seemed to be playing."[25]

The Preacher is also identified somewhat by the hymn "Everlasting Arms," which he sings on several occasions throughout the film.   Schumann, though, did not want to use the hymn as underscoring for the character, since he felt it would dignify and create sympathy for Preacher's psychopathic religious beliefs.   "Therefore," Schumann wrote, "for the Preacher's theme, I wrote what I considered a pagan motif, consisting of clashing fifths in the lower register."   Walter Schumann's exquisitely crafted score for THE NIGHT OF THE HUNTER remarkably demonstrates the symbolical use of leitmotifs to make a subtle exposition on the overall statement of the film.

Carmen Dragon, who scored a number of dramatic films in the mid 40's and 50's, composed the music for Don Siegel's classic INVASION OF THE BODY SNATCHERS (1956), lending it a strong musical backdrop for the story of "pod people" taking the place of real persons in a small, rural town. Dragon's main theme emerges from the drum rolls of the main title, consisting of long, drawn-out horn notes punctuated with cymbal crashes, pounding tympani, and harp glissandos. The score effectively heightens the romance and paranoia embodied by the film and lifts them into a lifelike importance.

Ted Astley's score for THE GIANT BEHEMOTH (1958) was adequate if unremarkable accompaniment for this standard prehistoric-monster-invades-major-city picture. As it was described by one reviewer, "Astley's music was scored military-style using trumpets, snares, kettledrums and flutes. More practical than provocative, the drum riffs added tension to the transitions between claustrophobic scenes of the torpedo-head being welded and those of the urban rampage. Uniquely, electronic sound effects were used to underscore the creature's electro-radiation discharge, or merely to zap the audience for an aural shock."[26]

Many remarkable fantastic film scores emerged from England during the 50's, and these will be discussed at length in Chapter VIII. One of the most unique scores of the decade was for the science fiction classic, FORBIDDEN PLANET (1956). Rather than an orchestral score, as previous outer space films like DESTINATION MOON and THIS ISLAND EARTH had used, the film was scored with the imaginative "electronic tonalities" of Louis and Bebe Barron. While this style of scoring failed to catch on in the 50's, it found greater acceptance and expansion in the decades to follow. The Barrons' score will be discussed at length in Chapter XII.

As we have seen, the fantastic films of the 50's retained much of the musical styles of the decade that preceded. But a great deal of experimentation took place, either in complete scores such as FORBIDDEN PLANET and INVADERS FROM MARS or in elements of other scores, such as the unusually dissonant approach taken in scores such as THE CREATURE FROM THE BLACK LAGOON, and the quotations from traditional music incorporated into THE SCREAMING SKULL and I BURY THE LIVING. By and large, the music remained primarily symphonic, although the influence of jazz in the later years of this decade was felt to a slight degree in the fantastic genre. However, it was during the following decade that the greatest upheaval in film scoring was felt--the invasion of pop music which suggested new ways of scoring but at the same time threatened to put an end to traditional symphonic film music, until the resurgence of the symphonic film orchestra in the 70's.

Notes

1. Irwin Bazelon, Knowing the Score (New York: Arco Publish-
    ing, Inc., 1981) p. 87

2. Scot W. Holton, liner notes to DESTINATION MOON sound-
    track recording (Varese Sarabande Records, 1980 rere-
    lease)

3. James C. Hamilton, Leith Stevens: A Critical Analysis of His
    Works, a doctoral dissertation for the University of Mis-
    souri, Kansas City (Ann Arbor: University Microfilms In-
    ternational, 1976) p. 92

4. Ibid., p. 114-115

5. Albert Glasser, interview with the author, December 16, 1981
    (and following quotes)

6. Kerry O'Quinn, liner notes to The Fantastic Film Music of Al-
    bert Glasser, Vol. 1 record album (Starlog Records, 1978)

7. Albert Glasser, loc. cit.

8. George Turner, "Howard Hawks' THE THING--A Retrospect,"
    Cinefantastique Vol. 12, #5/6 (1982) p. 84-85

9. Herman Stein, interview with the author, May 6, 1983.

10. Ibid. (and following quotes)

11. Hans J. Salter quoted by Preston Neal Jones, "The Ghost of
    Hans J. Salter," Cinefantastique, Vol. 7, #2 (1978) p. 20

12. Henry Mancini quoted by Tony Thomas, Film Score: The View
    from the Podium (La Jolla: A. S. Barnes & Co., 1979) p.
    168

13. Elmer Bernstein interviewed by John Caps, Soundtrack! The
    Collector's Quarterly Vol. 2, #6 (June 1983) p. 21

14. Harry Medved with Randy Dreyfuss, The Fifty Worst Films of
    All Time (New York: Popular Library, 1978) p. 198

15. Ernest Gold, interview with the author, December 22, 1981
    (and following quotes)

16. James Marshall and Ronald Bohn, "Gerald Fried," Soundtrack
    Collector's Newsletter #15 (1978) p. 4

17. Gerald Fried, interview with the author, November 29, 1982
    (and following quotes)

18. Bronislau Kaper interviewed by W. F. Krasnoborski, Motion
    Picture Music, ed. Luc Van De Ven (Mechelen, Belgium:
    Soundtrack, 1980) p. 130-131

19. Jim Wnoroski, "INVADERS FROM MARS--A Review," Photon
    #21 (1971) p. 23

20. Bert A. Shefter, interview with the author, June 5, 1983 (and
    following quotes)

21. Fred Steiner, interview with the author, February 27, 1983

22. Bill Littman, "CURSE OF THE DEMON--The Music," Photon
    #26 (1975) p. 40 (and following quotes)

23. Jim Doherty, "THE NIGHT OF THE HUNTER--A Musical Cri-
    tique," Midnight Marquee #26 (September 1977) p. 13

24. Ibid., p. 15

25. Walter Schumann, "Scoring THE NIGHT OF THE HUNTER,"
    Film Music, September-October 1955 (material courtesy Pres-
    ton Neal Jones)

26. Paul Mandell, "Of Beasts and Behemoths," Fantastic Films,
    March 1980, p. 62

Bernard Herrmann. Photograph by John Engstead. Courtesy Tony
Thomas.

VI

MYSTERIOUS WORLDS
<hr>
The Music of Bernard Herrmann

The name that almost invariably leaps to mind whenever one
considers music in fantasy films is undoubtedly that of Bernard
Herrmann, who, although he worked on many other kinds of motion
pictures, has made perhaps the most significant contributions to
fantastic film music. Herrmann's scores to fantasy, science fiction
and horror thrillers have provided some of the most gripping and
evocative music ever to grace these types of films.

It is to Herrmann's credit that he refused to give anything
less than his best to whatever film he was scoring, and he took his
craft with the utmost seriousness, no matter how far-fetched a film
may have been. Herrmann disliked being called a film composer,
aware that the title often brings with it a derogatory ring to con-
noisseurs of "serious music." He resented the idea that writing
for films was somehow of less value than writing for the opera
house or concert hall. He was infamously outspoken, despising
most film producers, whom he felt were tasteless and moronic in
their musical understanding. On at least one occasion, while being
shown a film by a producer desiring his services, Herrmann stormed
out of the screening room, shouting "Why do you show me this
trash?" Herrmann's eloquent contempt and ferocious manner gave
the composer an irascible reputation in Hollywood, matched only
by his genius as a composer. As difficult as Herrmann was to work
with, inevitably the work he produced was of the finest quality and
irretrievably a vital part of the completed motion picture.

Born in New York City in 1911, Herrmann studied music from
an early age, receiving much of his training at New York University and at the Juilliard School of Music. By the time he was 18,
Herrmann was earning a living as a musician, and had already
written a ballet for a Broadway show. In 1933, he began to work
for CBS, composing and conducting for radio programs, and a year
later he was made staff conductor. During this time he met Orson
Welles, and soon Herrmann was scoring Welles' CBS radio series,
The Mercury Theatre on the Air, beginning in 1936. The series
included the famous broadcast of H. G. Wells' War of the Worlds,
and Herrmann conducted the orchestra for that presentation. He
also composed two original cues heard briefly between the various
snatches of source music used in the dramatization. "The purpose

was to create the illusion of reality," Herrmann later recalled. "We played some dance music at the beginning of the show until Welles 'interrupted the program' to announce the discovery of the Martian spacecraft."[1] Herrmann did provide a considerable score for the Mercury Theatre's broadcast of Dracula, utilizing eerie strings and tolling bells, and the distinctive major-minor chord changes that would become a trademark in later years.

Herrmann's association with Welles resulted in the start of his motion picture career. In 1940, when Welles filmed his famous CITIZEN KANE, he offered Herrmann the chance to write the music. In his Herrmann biography, musicologist Fred Steiner remarked of this first score: "No motion picture career could possibly have had a more auspicious beginning--Herrmann's name became linked with a film which, though never a conspicuous commercial success, is acknowledged to be one of the all-time masterpieces of cinematic art."[2] Herrmann couldn't have started out on a better foot, and his subsequent scoring assignments included a great many all-time classic motion pictures.

Following the success of CITIZEN KANE, Herrmann wrote his first fantasy film score for THE DEVIL AND DANIEL WEBSTER (1940), although fantastic elements are not really present in the music. Instead, Herrmann opted for "some superlative Americana, dexterously employing a number of New England folk melodies. The score is full of charm and humor,"[3] very much in keeping with the film's treatment of its subject. The music won Herrmann an Oscar for best original score.

In 1944 Herrmann wrote the music for HANGOVER SQUARE, a moody psychological thriller. The film concerns a composer who suffers momentary fits of insanity, causing him to commit brutal murders. As the composer is in the process of writing a piano concerto during these attacks, his fluctuating state of mind drastically affects his composition. The piano concerto, therefore, becomes integral both as dramatic accompaniment and as a major element in the film itself. As one reviewer had it: "Herrmann had a unique opportunity to build a self-contained musical statement out of all the welded fragments, themes and episodes from the earlier part of the score"[4] by the time the completed concerto was heard at the film's climax.

Herrmann's score for THE GHOST AND MRS. MUIR (1947) was an intriguing blend of romance and fantasy as it told of the love between a young widow and the ghost of the sea captain who "haunts" the seaside cottage she comes to live in. The story obviously appealed greatly to the composer, and Herrmann considered it one of his best efforts in film music, as well as being his most romantic. Herrmann orchestrated the picture for an orchestra of 67 players, in certain places rearranging it, doubling certain instruments and leaving others out in order to achieve unusual

orchestral colors, a trait Herrmann became quite adept at. The
score for THE GHOST AND MRS. MUIR is especially heavy in the
woodwinds. In addition to being his most dramatic score, it is also one in which Herrmann relied greatly on leitmotifs, a style he
normally avoided in preference of musical textures and orchestral
progressions. Lucy Muir is represented with a charming, lyrical
theme; while Daniel, the ghost, is given a suitably haunted theme
for quivering strings and woodwind. While this theme is appropriately eerie, Herrmann noticeably refrains from the use of conventional Hollywood "ghost music," concentrating instead on the romantic and dreamlike qualities of the film.

The most dominant theme, and the one from which the others
are derived, is that for the sea; a slow, undulating motif, alternately turbulent and calm. As one reviewer wrote: "What is most
fascinating is that all the themes and decorations of Herrmann's
score add up to something considerably more than the sum of its
parts. One's most striking remembrance of the score is the sea,
which is appropriate because the cumulative effect is one of timelessness. The sea swells connote the methodical passage of time
and the gently inserted undertows eat away and change the face
of the earth--yet nothing really disappears. The restlessness of
the sea reaches toward an undefinable point at some undisclosed
future time, some culmination when the meaning of all will become
clear. That moment occurs when finally in death Lucy and Daniel
are united forever and the music for the first time rises with bra-
vado to celebrate their sturdy triumph over time."[5]

The blending of the themes for Lucy and Daniel suggest
their growing love, bridging their scenes together and voicing the
unspoken. "The mercurial music speaks of love and timelessness
with energy but the constantness of ebb and flow are also reas-
suring. Like Lucy, the music also seeks resolve--which is why
the ... 'Finale' is such a brilliant and natural touch. The fanfare
of resolution is the balm that seals the cycle of time and gnawing
love and I cannot think of another musical fadeout that is so important to any film. Like the theme of the story, it's part of the
whole great musical scheme for the film."[6] Tony Thomas aptly
summed it up when he wrote: "It is among the most delicate and
romantic scores ever written and moves a touching story into an almost sublime atmosphere."[7]

In 1951, Herrmann provided the music for his first science
fiction picture, providing quite an innovative score which accomplished much in influencing the style of scoring such pictures in
the 50's. THE DAY THE EARTH STOOD STILL represented one of
Hollywood's first serious attempts to treat science fiction as an
art form, and Herrmann's music was perfect in underscoring its
story of an alien peace emissary and his invulnerable robot guard
brought to Earth to warn against atomic warfare. Once again,
Herrmann provided just the right orchestral sound by rearranging

the orchestra, eliminating the woodwinds and balancing what remained of the conventional orchestra (in this case, piano, harps, brass and a large tympani section) with a sizeable electronic group (consisting of two theremins as well as electronic guitar, bass and violin).   As Herrmann described it, "my goal here was to characterize a man from another world, and the music had to reflect an unearthly feeling of outer space without relying on gimmicks."[8] While Miklos Rozsa introduced the theremin in the 40's as a superbly eerie sound for psychological thrillers, Herrmann proved its effectiveness in science fiction films with this score.   (Ferde Grofé had used a theremin the previous year in ROCKETSHIP X-M, but its use wasn't nearly as profound as Herrmann's treatment of it here.)

The dominant thematic element of THE DAY THE EARTH STOOD STILL was one that ran through almost all of Herrmann's fantasy scores, its origin going back even to parts of CITIZEN KANE: a multitude of variations upon a relatively simple two-note phrase, repeated in various shades and textures, growing and diminishing and providing a marvelously apprehensive atmosphere. While the motif was used in dozens of other scores by Herrmann, it really doesn't suffer from overuse, as one reviewer noted in an analysis of Herrmann's fantasy scores: "Certain chord structures were used in basic combinations throughout much of his music, and his singular 'sound' was, at times and to the uninitiated ear, tiringly repetitive. Yet, with attention, Herrmann's apparent flaws fade beside the very real, very exciting, very imaginative complexity his film compositions brought to the mass audience. And, as Alfred Hitchcock has said, self-plagiarism can also be defined as 'style.'"[9]

The music for THE DAY THE EARTH STOOD STILL is brimming in this imaginative complexity, its musical progression and orchestral texture adding a unique and, at times, electrifying quality to the picture. The main two-note motif is used first to signify outer space during the title sequence, and later as an ominously dangerous theme for Gort, the indestructible robot. There is also a very interesting piece for rapidly fingered piano, heard during the introductory radar-room sequence in which Klaatu's spaceship is first spotted. The motif, subtly heard beneath dialog in the film, effectively builds a sense of busyness and excitement through a single keyboard instrument.

In 1955, Herrmann began a lengthy and successful association with Alfred Hitchcock that resulted in some of his finest scores, one of the most impressive being VERTIGO (1958), which featured a very ominous and frightening theme, played by shivering, up-and-down violins and creeping horns. Hitchcock's psychological thriller concerned a detective with a fear of heights who becomes obsessed with a mysterious young woman who seems to have become dominated by a dead person. Hermann's swirling music perfectly underscores and reinforces these visual and psychological elements from the very first frame. As one reviewer explained: "The music for VERTIGO opens with a triadic figure, ascending and descending, punctuated by phrases and chords, all of which expertly capture the emotions of the title. The ... credit sequence, filled as it is with swirling spiral figures and kaleidoscopic images, is matched by Herrmann's inventions based on the polytonal chord that dominates the score and the triadic figure. As 'directed by Alfred Hitchcock' appears on the screen, a low note, D, is heard on the tuba (a fitting instrument for the rotund filmmaker and a characteristic bit of wit on the part of the composer.)"[10]

The repeated rising and falling triadic music of the opening dominates the score, although there are other motifs, such as a vibrant movement accompanying the night chase over the rooftops, culminating in reverberating drum beats as the detective falls to his death; a sharp discord derived from the triad augments the detective's acrophobia; Madeline, the mysterious woman, is denoted by an amorously slow motif for strings, which is developed throughout the film as we learn more about her. The use of castanets and Spanish rhythms is effective in representing the deceased Carlotta, who was of Spanish-Mexican descent, and the overall use of the key of D, and its consistent intonation, creates a musical obsession in tune with that of the detective. Likewise, his feelings of vertigo are imaginatively captured in the very contours of the music. While Herrmann's later score for Hitchcock's PSYCHO (1960) is more immediately chilling, the music for VERTIGO is certainly the finest overall score of their creative association.

While Herrmann's work for Alfred Hitchcock was blossoming, another successful collaboration began in 1958 when Herrmann scored THE 7TH VOYAGE OF SINBAD for producer Charles Schneer and visual effects creator Ray Harryhausen. The SINBAD score was the first of a series of exotic fantasies which Herrmann composed during the next five years. As Tony Thomas has written, "these films allowed Herrmann rich orchestral palettes and scope for musical imagination. These scores called for a kind of Rimsky-Korsakov texture, which Herrmann gave them along with wit and charm."[11] Another reviewer described the score as displaying Herrmann "at the height of his orchestral genius. Most of the composer's stylistic traits are evident: moving minor chords played by various choirs of the orchestra, a penchant for low woodwinds, repeated rhythmic and harmonic sequences, and a pulsating sense of orchestral dynamics. Rarely does Herrmann use the entire body of the orchestra for tutti passages: instead, he more often utilizes separate choirs, such as brass or woodwinds, playing specific segments in the form of short motives."[12]

Herrmann has described his approach to the score thusly: "For this exciting and colorful Arabian nights fairy tale, I worked with a conventional sized orchestra, augmented by a large percus-

sion section. The music I composed had to reflect a purity and
simplicity that could be easily assimilated to the nature of the fantasy being viewed. By characterizing the various creatures with
unusual instrumental combinations ... and by composing motifs for
all the major characters and actions, I feel I was able to envelop
the entire movie in a shroud of mystical innocence."[13]

The most unifying factor of the SINBAD score is the main
theme, first heard over the titles. This is a colorfully orchestrated, two-bar motif which captures an exotic Arabian flavor and
promises adventure and excitement. This theme, and a few specific set pieces (such as the evocative and highly rhythmic motif
heard during the introductory sequences in Bagdad) are in the
Arabian tradition, while the music that accompanies the visual effects sequences involving the Cyclops, dragon, Roc and other
mythological creatures were more abstractly approached. The theme
for the Cyclops is a variation upon the two-note fantasy motif heard
earlier in THE DAY THE EARTH STOOD STILL. Low, groaning
horns mingle with the cavernous roar of the horned beast, creating
an unforgettable sound accompaniment. The music for the Roc sequence is a clever mixture of horn fanfare and woodwind twitter-
ing, punctuated by rumbling tympani. The theme for the chained
dragon is an ominous, slow two-note motif for strong brass chords,
whispering cymbals and pounding drums, creating an audible aura
of danger as Sinbad furtively makes his way past the imprisoned
reptile. When the dragon is set free and attacks the Cyclops, the
music is loud, cacophonous, built upon the two-note phrase that
forms the foundation for both the Cyclops and the Dragon Themes.

The most intriguing music for THE 7TH VOYAGE OF SINBAD,
however, is the unique music accompanying Sinbad's duel with the
skeleton. Herrmann utilizes xylophones, castanets and wood block,
with melodic phrasing by tubas and trumpets, to augment the battle. The music marvelously suggests the idea of rattling bones and
scraping swords.

Herrmann next wrote the music for the Jules Verne fantasy,
A JOURNEY TO THE CENTER OF THE EARTH (1959), much of
which is again built around Herrmann's distinctive two-note motif
and makes profound use of a greatly rearranged orchestra. As
Herrmann described: "I decided to evoke the mood and feelings of
inner earth by using only instruments played in low registers.
Eliminating all strings, I utilized an orchestra of woodwinds and
brass, with a large percussion section and many harps."[14]

The orchestra's most powerfully felt factor was the presence
of no less than five organs--four electronic and one large cathedral organ--the music of which is used to suggest ascent and descent, as well as the mysteriousness of Atlantis. The overall effect is that of massiveness in the music, which superbly captures
the feeling of the massiveness of the earth's crust and the huge

caverns depicted in the film. Herrmann also resurrected an obsolete musical instrument called a serpent, used--appropriately enough--in the scene with the giant lizard, which had a bizarre, somewhat nasal sound quality and contributed highly to the otherworldliness of the scene.

Also in 1959, Herrmann began to provide music for a television series considered by many to be the pinnacle of televised fantasy, Rod Serling's THE TWILIGHT ZONE. Herrmann composed the series' original opening motif, an eerie melody for harp, flutes, strings and brass which gradually grew to a low-pitched crescendo. "Scored for a small orchestra," wrote Jim Doherty in his critique of Herrmann's TWILIGHT ZONE music, "it begins as soft, glowing, dissonant, horn chords sway amidst gentle harp arpeggios.... As Rod Serling's voice intoned the famous opening definition of the ambiguous grey region, ominous little fragments creep in and out of the music--a flute plaintively whispers two notes; a disturbing low tone hollowly emanates from the woodwinds--as the music begins to sound vaguely more foreboding. A group of strings subtly enter, weightlessly shifting back and forth with the horns. A deep chord in the woodwinds and basses accompanies the title THE TWILIGHT ZONE as it forms over a bizarre Dali-esque landscape. This music is the perfect essence of THE TWILIGHT ZONE. With its incessant swaying motion and dreamlike quality, it draws the viewer into that void, 'the middle ground between light and shadow.'"[15]

Herrmann's Title Theme didn't last very long, though, as it was soon replaced by the now-popular up-and-down "da-DI-da-duh" motif provided by French avant-garde composer Marius Constant. Herrmann composed original music for seven of the show's episodes, although more than 20 subsequent segments used his music from either previous TWILIGHT ZONE episodes or from other CBS programs.

Herrmann lent the same craftsmanship to the television shows that he did to major feature films, refusing to compose mere "program music." His TWILIGHT ZONE scores often produced in the viewer the inner feelings similar to those the characters felt in the stories, and acted more as important dramatic elements rather than simple background music. Herrmann scored the pilot episode, "Where Is Everybody" (originally broadcast October 12, 1959) with what is at first a fairly plain three-note theme, heard as amnesiac Air Force pilot Mike Ferris enters a deserted town and soon comes to feel he is being watched, even though he can't find any people. As Ferris desperately explores and discovers the town's strange emptiness, Herrmann's music becomes more dissonant and less assuring, reaching a frenzied climax before reverting back to the initial three-note theme as the mystery is solved and the episode closes in normalcy.

One of the most famous episodes was "Walking Distance" (shown October 30, 1959), which featured an all-string score dominated by a soft, gentle melody that neatly captures the nostalgic memories of a harried businessman who returns to his hometown to find it unexplainably just as it was in his youth. As in "Where Is Everybody?," the music grows stranger and more dissonant as the man discovers more oddities, eventually realizing that he has actually gone back in time to the era of his youth. The music regains its nostalgic and bittersweet mood when the man accepts what's happened and reluctantly agrees to return to the pressures of his proper time.

"The Lonely" (November 13, 1959) featured a score for vibraphone, organ, harp, bells and muted brass, initially suggesting the loneliness of a convict sentenced to solitary confinement on an uninhabited asteroid. The music opens up into a tender nocturne when a sympathetic supply ship captain leaves a female robot as a companion for the convict. The moribund chords of the opening are then transformed into a tranquil love theme until seguing back into a motif of loneliness as the convict realizes dramatically that his companion has been, indeed, only a machine.

Another memorable episode scored by Herrmann was "The Eye of the Beholder" (November 11, 1960), which utilized ethereal vibraphone-and-harp passages to suggest the otherworldliness of the story, punctuated in a climactic moment by "piercing trumpets and sharply struck chimes." The "Little Girl Lost" episode (March 16, 1962) is covered nearly wall-to-wall with music, enveloping the story with an air of wonder and mystery through the use of harp, woodwinds and viola. Low harp glissandos, somewhat akin to their use in JOURNEY TO THE CENTER OF THE EARTH, suggest the infiniteness of the fourth dimension into which the little girl has slipped, and the score relied primarily on sparse musical phrases rather than recognizable melodies.

Herrmann's score for the "Living Doll" episode (November 1, 1963), effectively rendered for a small ensemble of harp, bassoon and small bells, provides an unsettling progression for the unfolding story, beginning mildly and gradually growing more discordant. The introductory music suggests a child's world as a young girl receives an expensive doll as a gift. "As it becomes more apparent to the father that there is something a tad bizarre about the talking toy," wrote reviewer Jim Doherty, "the music slowly begins to change its tone. For instance, when Dad throws Tina [the doll] in the garbage only to discover her missing minutes later, the harp and bassoon return, but the harp plays in such a low register its frightening intent cannot be misinterpreted. Still, under its tone of dread lies that inkling of a child's world. The repetition of this kind of morbidly cute music after each unsuccessful attempt to destroy the doll acts as a perfect counterpart to the story, returning to prove that the nightmare is not over, returning to subliminally torment us in the same way the doll torments the father."[16]

The last episode for which Herrmann composed an original score was "Ninety Years Without Slumbering" (December 20, 1963). The music revolved around a variation on the melody of a children's song ("The Grandfather's Clock," sung earlier in the segment) for harp, woodwinds and flute. Perhaps the basic appeal of the TWI-LIGHT ZONE television series was in its taking a very ordinary, routine setting or situation, and injecting into it something out-of-place, something alien and fantastic. Herrmann's music perfectly captured this basic theme of the series, and the carefully crafted scores composed for these episodes are among the finest music written for television.

Herrmann took a similar approach to scoring several episodes of THE ALFRED HITCHCOCK HOUR in the early 60's. A number of these shows maintained a semblance of fantasy, as with Ray Brad-bury's "The Jar," for which Herrmann composed a distant-sounding calliope theme, in keeping with the side-show atmosphere of the early scenes. The opening bar of this segment also features an effective quotation from the Dies Irae. "Where the Woodbine Twineth" was one of Herrmann's best Hitchcock TV scores, as Jim Doherty has elsewhere noted: "For the very chilling story of people who don't believe a little girl's claims that her playmates are not imaginary, Herrmann provided a little waltz for flute and harp which perfectly offsets the real terror of the story."[17] Herrmann's other Hitchcock episodes were "The MacGregor Affair," for which he wrote music reminiscent of Scottish folktunes, and "The Life Work of Juan Diaz," which contained the same type of "unsettlingly dismal" Spanish-flavored themes he had used so evocatively in VERTIGO.

About the time that Herrmann began to score the TWILIGHT ZONE episodes, he wrote what has since become his most popular score during his association with Alfred Hitchcock. PSYCHO (1960) gave Herrmann his best opportunity thus far to create an absolutely terrifying film score. The composer himself termed the film Hitchcock's "supreme achievement in suspense" and for the score he used an orchestra consisting only of strings. He felt, in so doing, that he was able to complement the black-and-white photography of the film with a "black-and-white sound." The resultant orchestral texture and tone color created a unique effect, and the remarkable success of the score in accompanying the film is a credit to Herrmann's inventiveness and, in fact, his daring to attempt such a musical combination.

In a lengthy study on the music of PSYCHO, Fred Steiner noted the difficulty that Herrmann faced when he limited his orchestra purely to strings: "To begin with, such a choice imposes strict limits on the available range of tone colors. This means a commensurate increase of composing problems ... for one of the important secrets of successful writing for orchestra is the very ability to call upon the many resources of the symphonic ensemble

--strings, woodwinds, brass, percussion--for variety and contrast in the treatment of musical material.... In addition ... Herrmann's selection of a string orchestra deprived him of many tried-and-true musical formulas and effects which, until that time, had been considered essential for suspense-horror films: cymbal rolls, tympani throbs, muted horn stings, shrieking clarinets, ominous trombones, and dozens of other staples in Hollywood's bag of chilling, scary musical tricks."[18] Steiner also notes the fact that the strings are often called "the soul of the orchestra" and represent its most sentimental and expressive section, normally evocative of romance rather than horror. Thus, Herrmann's choice of such a "sweet-sounding ensemble" for Hitchcock's spine-chiller was doubly unique; and the fact that he succeeded in establishing such musical terror through these instruments is a strong testimony to his musical genius. As Tony Thomas wrote, Herrmann's PSYCHO score was "probably the first example in cinema history of music being able to chill an audience to the marrow."[19]

There are five primary thematic motifs in the score. The first portion of the film, that which concerns the ill-fated Marion Crane, is dominated by the music initially heard under the titles, an urgent, harshly accented, driving rhythm which powerfully underscores the fear/panic encountered by Marion during her long flight with the stolen money. In this particular driving sequence the music is matched to the slashing of the windshield wipers on Marion's car, the sound and the streaking visuals combining to create an unforgettable nightmarish quality, as one reviewer noted: "As the rain hammers against the windshield, one notices a barely-perceptible relationship between the movement of the windshield wipers and the 'back-and-forth' rhythm created by syncopated beats from the violas."[20] Another writer has aptly described the music of Marion's frantic drive in the rain as consisting of "an undertone of monotonous rocking phrases somewhat like the tuneless chant a frightened child might sing to reassure itself in the dark, but the very reverse of comforting."[21]

The secondary motif is first heard immediately following the main titles, in the long camera pan over the rooftops of Phoenix, Arizona. As Fred Steiner describes it, "this melancholy piece exemplifies another aspect of Herrmann's 'tuneless' approach to PSYCHO. There is no melody, no clearly stated motive--only atmosphere created by the slow descent and ascent of the divided strings."[22] The music is derived somewhat from Herrmann's distinctive two-note phrase, used frequently in his other scores, and takes on a notably pensive and restless mood. It reappears in several places throughout the score, mostly associated with the hopelessness of Marion's situation, particularly just before her murder.

The third motif is somewhat similar to the second, in that it is comprised of slowly descending and ascending string chords and

builds an uncomfortably apprehensive mood, although it is actually
derived from the first motif, slowing the rapid pace of the harsh
Flight music to a spooky, rhythmic series of phrases. This motif
is especially effective during Lila Crane's search of the Bates
House for clues concerning her sister's whereabouts. As another
reviewer explained, "an insistant rhythm climbs with her from the
cellos up through the violas to the second violin."[23]

Fourthly is a motif entitled "The Madhouse," and is as close
to a leitmotif as Herrmann comes in PSYCHO. In this piece, which
is associated with Norman Bates and his relationship with his mysterious mother: "The strings are twisted throughout," wrote Steiner. "An eerie, disturbing atmosphere is created by the twisted
configurations of the various forms of the leitmotif, the dissonance
of the counterpoint, and the constant use of crescendo-decrescendo
dynamics. This is quiet, unobtrusive, but unsettling music, and
as it progresses, we get the first feeling that all is not what it appears to be at the Bates motel."[24] The piece also recurs when detective Arbogast enters the house seeking Mrs. Bates, and at the
film's finale where it accompanies the final closeup of Norman's face
with his mother's mummified visage subtly superimposed over his.
For this denouement, the cellos and basses slowly and heavily pro-
nounce the leitmotif until the scene dissolves to the swamp, where
Marion's car is being lifted out. "The picture fades out on a low,
heavy, acidulous dissonance in the massed strings--a chord without resolution, a finale without an ending."[25]

The fifth and final motif of the PSYCHO score, and the most
famous, is the Murder music. The motif consists, simply, of shrill,
stabbing thrusts of the strings playing in their highest registers;
a brutal series of "reiterated, dissonant, sharp downward strokes
and ... wild glissandos" which accompanies the downward slashing
motions of the large kitchen knife thrust beyond the shower curtain
to savagely attack Marion. The motif has been erroneously described by several critics as being bird shrieks or distorted bird
cries, when no such sound effect is actually present, although the
shrieking string sounds do retain a birdlike quality (appropriate in
view of Norman's hobby of bird taxidermy and Hitchcock's recurring
bird-symbology throughout his films), while at the same time the
shrill sounds also suggest (and, in fact, take the place of) Marion's
terrified screams. This unforgettable (and most frequently imitated)
motif is heard in the murders of Marion and Arbogast, and again
in the film's climax where Lila is attacked after discovering "Mrs.
Bates."

It is interesting to note that when Herrmann first saw a
rough cut of PSYCHO in preparation for scoring it, Hitchcock told
him not to compose music for the stabbing scene. It wasn't until
later, when the director felt unsatisfied with the finished film, that
the stunning Murder music was added.

There are additional musical pieces used in various places, although they are not as easy to define as the preceding five. The scenes in which Norman argues with his mother and finally carries her to the fruit cellar for hiding are accompanied by slow-moving, near-static "pyramids of chord-clusters [which] seem to suggest Norman's mind becoming ever more clouded and confused as the threat of exposure looms closer."[26] When Lila, secretly exploring the Bates house, spies Norman approaching, trembling, muted strings accompany her flight to the cellar with an "extraordinary flesh-crawling effect." Fred Steiner describes five separate pieces of music which accompany the scenes where Norman grimly removes Marion's body from the bathtub, mops up the mess, and disposes of the corpse and her car in the swamp: "The music is a grim bit of tone painting whose basic color emanates from Hitchcock's close-up of the swirling, bloodstained water in the sink. Muttered accents and furtive tremolos serve to heighten the urgency with which Norman performs his grisly chores. Herrmann again uses his module technique, the basic elements being three: fast accented slides in the low register; rapid tremolo wisps in the violins; ... and crescendo-decrescendo trills in the mid-range, which bind the whole together."[27]

Film music reviewer Royal S. Brown pointed out that much of the score is shaped around a single seventh chord (which was also used in the prelude to VERTIGO) until the score's final chord, which expands to a multiflatted ninth: "Because of this essentially chordal orientation, Herrmann is able to avoid the aural relief of harmonic resolution, and the listener is no more able to latch onto a comfortable resting place in the music than he is in the film." Brown continues: "A tension is created between the indefiniteness of the harmonic language and the exaggerated definiteness of the rhythmic idiom, which in many places is so relentless, so heavily accentuated that the listener is aware not so much of temporal divisions as of a subliminal pulse suggesting primordial violence."[28]

Bernard Herrmann's music for PSYCHO is more than "merely a fine and suitable" film score, as Fred Steiner points out. "The music itself is actually very much in keeping with Hitchcock's 'out-of-the-ordinary' concept of PSYCHO, having certain features which set it apart from any other motion picture score which had been produced up to that time, even by Bernard Herrmann himself."[29] Another reviewer sums it up by saying: "Herrmann succeeded in conveying in his PSYCHO score a level of suspense and tension that is established in the opening bars, and continues to pervade the score from its title theme to its non-climactic finish. The sense of mounting tension, which is inherent throughout the film itself, is marked by numerous yet subtle changes in the tempo of the narrative."[30]

After completing PSYCHO, Herrmann returned to collaborate

with Schneer and Harryhausen on THE THREE WORLDS OF GULLI-
VER (1960). The resultant score is something of an oddity in
Herrmann's fantasy film scoring, in that it bears little resemblance
to any of his other works in the genre. Only in a few places are
the prowling chord progressions and ominous, lumbering musical
moods that characterized previous fantasy scores used. Instead,
the music is based upon light, airy eighteenth-century British music, blending the period orchestration with Herrmann's own contemporary style, but with the dominance clearly on the former.

The score does contain a varied number of leitmotifs, representing not only specific situations but orchestrated for appropriately specific instrumental groupings. The theme for the diminutive Lilliputians, for instance, is performed by a "miniature" orchestra dominated by piccolos, triangles, sleighbells, harps and
glockenspiels. In contrast to the smallness of the Lilliputians,
Herrmann includes a massive figure representing Gulliver's huge
size, in their perspective, as one writer noted: "But if they appear thus as pygmies to him, to them he appears enormous; hence
the fact that the opening clarinet theme later reappears on ponderous low strings, its character completely inverted." [31] A clever
and effective touch. Likewise, the world of the giants is given a
slow and lumbering theme for two tubas, and the relationship between Gulliver and Elizabeth is given a sweet and tender interlude
for strings.

But the dominant theme that runs the course of the score is
that for the Lilliputians, even when Gulliver has long journeyed
from their land. In the climactic scene where Gulliver and Elizabeth are pursued by the Brobdingnagians, "the music is essentially that of the Lilliputians, since the fears and imaginings which in
Gulliver's mind produce the one are essentially those which produce
the other. Here everyone in the orchestra is playing in his nether-
most region (including the full-fathom-five contrabass tuba) and all
the music's original charm is lost to nightmares.... But all traumas
are forgotten when Gulliver and his bride regain their familiar
workaday Wapping, and the music reverts to its rock-firm reliable
18th century" mood. [32] While a weak score in terms of retaining
an overall fantasy effect, Herrmann's GULLIVER music was appropriate for the juvenile fairy-tale nature of the Schneer/Harryhausen
adaptation.

Herrmann composed the music for Schneer/Harryhausen's next
fantasy offering, an adaptation of Jules Verne's MYSTERIOUS IS-
LAND (1961), and provided one of his best scores for this picture.
Here, the recurring two-note fantasy motif which appeared in many
of Herrmann's earlier genre scores was developed into a main theme,
first heard in the crashing brass and warbling woodwind of the
main title. For this film, Herrmann's orchestration duplicated the
gigantism of the Island's wildlife, utilizing four tubas, eight horns,
and much extra percussion and woodwind. The powerful and omi-

nous main theme marvelously portrays the grand mysteriousness of the island and its inhabitants. In addition, Herrmann provides unique themes for each of the giant animal encounters. The giant crab's onslaught is accompanied by the animated, rhythmic piping of the eight horns, climaxing in a series of high, frenzied glissandos. The giant bee buzzes on-screen to an arrangement of the main theme for <u>vibrato</u> strings, woodwind trills and brass flutter-tonguing. For the attack of the prehistoric bird, Herrmann adapted a lively baroque organ fugue, by J. L. Krebs, into a delightful comic grotesquerie for brass and woodwind. The centuries-old prehistoric bird, masterfully animated by Ray Harryhausen, immediately suggested centuries-old music to the composer, and the grotesqueness of the animated creature perhaps recalled to Herrmann that "one of the shades of meaning of the term 'baroque' is outlandish, extravagant, grotesque."[33] The use of the fugue, as well as being somewhat tongue-in-cheek, is remarkably complementary for a scene of an awkward, comical giant bird.

Herrmann next collaborated with Hitchcock again, on the director's only true excursion into science fiction, THE BIRDS (1963). This collaboration was an unusual one, in that the film contained no actual music, and the composer worked as "sound consultant." The sound track was created on a keyboard instrument called the Studio Trautonium (after its inventor, Dr. Frederick Trautwein), which was designed by Remi Gassman and Oscar Sala to create atonal sounds. The device was first used commercially by the New York City Ballet, and for THE BIRDS, it embellished natural bird sounds to give them greater resonance. These bird caws were then used to underscore screen action, achieving an effect similar to that of a violin crescendo, or introduced like musical cues to heighten the visual images. As Hitchcock commented, "Conventional music usually serves either as a counterpoint or a comment on whatever scene is being played. I decided to use a more abstract approach. After all, when you put music to film, it's really <u>sound</u>, it isn't music <u>per se</u>."[34] Herrmann's task was to supervise the final sound track, which was recorded in West Berlin, since at that time there was no electronic recording studio available in America. The unique sound track for THE BIRDS is an interesting example of pure sound taking on many of the dramatic functions of music, and yet not abused as it has often been since then.

Herrmann scored Hitchcock's next thriller, MARNIE (1964), and in fact composed the music for the director's following film, TORN CURTAIN (1966), before pressure from Hitchcock and from the studio resulted in Herrmann's score being discarded for a new one composed by John Addison which was hoped to be more commercially oriented. Thus ended the Herrmann-Hitchcock collaboration, and adding to Herrmann's growing bitterness with Hollywood which would some years later result in his moving to London.

Herrmann's association with Schneer and Harryhausen likewise

reached an end with his majestic score for JASON AND THE ARGO-
NAUTS (1964), although on less disagreeable terms. Herrmann
here used a huge ensemble of brass, woodwinds and percussion--
strings were eliminated from the orchestra. As Christopher Palmer
remarked, "the music has a certain edge and sheen as a result,
now of copper plating, now of beaten gold."[35]

The JASON score is dominated by three themes: the majestic, Roman-styled march of the main theme, which ties together the
scenes of the Argo at sea; the mystical Olympus Theme which accompanies the activities of the manipulating Greek gods; and a
Love Theme for flutes and mellow brass, heard during the romantic
scenes of Jason and Medea. As with MYSTERIOUS ISLAND, though,
each of the scenes featuring Harryhausen's monsters was given its
own musical interpretation, as were other individual fantasy sequences. Among these subordinate themes is a delightful figure
heard when Jason appears in a puff of smoke in the palm of the
god Hermes. "The music nimbly pokes fun at his diminutive size,"
wrote one reviewer, "while keeping the sequence light. The theme
is later used when Hercules loses his contest with Hylas and hoists
him aloft, the gods joining in the gaiety."[36]

The repulsive Harpies are given a theme for woodwinds mixed
with high trumpet harmonies: "Portentious, throbbing music anticipates the trapping of the creatures. Herrmann then adds exciting percussion and crazy glissandos up and down the scale on
xylophones as the Harpies resist capture, and cymbals smash as
the ropes on the net are severed. A whimsical passage in quick
tempo cheerfully mocks the [captured] Harpies as they fight over
a bone."[37] This music is later developed and varied, with urgent
undertones, as the journey continues.

While the Hydra sequence is mostly without music, the fight
against the skeletons is a frenzied woodwind-and-brass motif, punctuated by solo oboe, which is sometimes ominous, sometimes nearly
carnival-like, in its frenzied abandon. The music for Triton, the
sea god who rescues the Argo from the clashing rocks, is sturdy
and monolithic, consisting not of chords but of long, linear melodic
formations, dramatically accentuating the might of the undersea god.
The best sequence, musically, is perhaps that of Talos, the huge
bronze statue that comes to life when Jason's men foolishly loot
its treasure-chamber. "When Talos awakens ... Herrmann wisely
allows the echoing wind and creaking of the monster to evoke terror. Only when Talos makes his towering entrance around the cliff
does Herrmann begin his theme. It is a fine one, with four ascending notes played by the tympani, punctuated with crashing
brass and cymbals. The music is menacing and gigantic, like Talos, and creates just the proper tension. The theme continues
throughout the sequence, mixed climactically with agonized brass
as Talos 'dies.'"[38]

The same year, Herrmann's credits appeared on episodes of the television series, VOYAGE TO THE BOTTOM OF THE SEA and THE TIME TUNNEL, but these were not original compositions, only library music taken from the scores of JOURNEY TO THE CENTER OF THE EARTH and THE DAY THE EARTH STOOD STILL, respectively.

By the mid-60's, Herrmann was receiving fewer assignments in Hollywood. In fact, JASON AND THE ARGONAUTS was his last "big" Hollywood film, his following scores either for foreign films or low-budget thrillers. In 1966, he scored FAHRENHEIT 451 for French director François Truffaut, who told Herrmann the reason he chose him over his usual modern composers was "because they would give me the music of the twentieth century, you'll give me the music of the twenty-first."[39] Herrmann's score wasn't precisely what Truffaut had in mind, as he played down the hard, emotionally dry futuristic concept, instead underscoring the repressed emotions of the characters. As Herrmann described it: "Since the story took place in the distant future and involved a society that was politically oppressed from displaying any outward emotion or compassion, I felt that the music score should mirror the innermost thoughts and feelings of the leading characters.... Attempting to avoid the electronic clichés which are so much in vogue at present, I employed a large string orchestra, plus harps and a few percussion."[40] In addition to Herrmann's score, the sound track included electronic effects by British composer Barry Gray.

The following year, Herrmann scored Truffaut's mildly psychological thriller, THE BRIDE WORE BLACK, lending it a Hitchcockian score dominated by strings, woodwinds and harp. In 1968 Herrmann scored a made-for-TV thriller, COMPANIONS IN NIGHTMARE, which included a moody score, somewhat akin to the texture of his later SISTERS (1972). The highlight of the score is in the murder scene, where Herrmann utilized "shrill violins, staccato brasses, trilling woodwinds, and sharply struck chimes [which] blend to form an aural whirlpool to match the ghastly killing."[41] Another Hitchcockian thriller of the same year, TWISTED NERVE, featured an uncharacteristic use of jazz in its whistled main theme. The solo whistle begins to sound more Herrmannesque when it is backed with the more familiar use of strings, brass and xylophone. Later the theme is given a contemporary jazz arrangement, but the more subdued melancholy version dominates.

By this time, Herrmann had moved to London, and was scoring mostly British films. One of them, THE NIGHT DIGGER (1971) was another low-budget psychological thriller that benefited from the strength of Herrmann's music. The score here is reminiscent of PSYCHO in its use of an urgent, harshly accented violin theme. The score also incorporated a subtle harmonica theme which nicely captured the solitary and mysterious personality of the young handyman with the unusual hobby. Herrmann also composed the

music for ENDLESS NIGHT, an Agatha Christie murder-thriller, in
1971.

Two years later, he returned to Hollywood to score SISTERS,
a noteworthy Hitchcockian thriller directed in homage by Brian De
Palma, who has said that Herrmann's fee was the most expensive
single item on the film's minuscule budget. The score is one of
Herrmann's best during these later years, and comes closest to
equalling PSYCHO in the power of its music. The music "covers
an amazingly diversified spectrum of musical moods and ambiences,
most of which will chill you to your bone marrow," wrote Royal S.
Brown. "As is usual for the composer, many of the effects are
sustained by the use of strings and woodwinds modulating in
eerily restive harmonic patterns that rarely seem to resolve."[42]
The score achieves much of its power through the additional use of
bells, chimes, vibraphone and two synthesizers, which add a chillingly visceral touch to the music.

Initially, director De Palma did not want to use a title theme,
but Herrmann felt it important, dramatically, to establish a mood of
suspense from the outset, "so that the half hour preceding the
expected-unexpected murder would be colored not by an establishing shot but by establishing tones," according to Brown. "De Palma
saw it Herrmann's way, and the result is one of the most stark,
marrow-chilling openers the composer has ever produced. Against
an X-ray shot of a human embryo in the womb, the music immediately established an atmosphere of intense, even morbid, tragedy,
with chimes and a four-note marcato horn pattern played in typical
Herrmannesque thirds (alternating major-minor) serving not only as
a principal motive appearing at several points in the film but also
as an accompaniment for a theme played in the strings and on two
Moog Synthesizers, the latter representing Herrmann's flair for
mobilizing an incredible wide variety of instruments in his scores."[43]

The music is also very appropriate to the film's generally sardonic tone. The first, unexpected murder is preceded by an innocent, tinkling motif as the impending victim buys a birthday cake
for the psychopathic murderess. "The deceptively ingenuous
Birthday Cake Theme, played on the bells and vibraphone, manages to capture the sparkle and glitter of the occasion and then
casts it in a disquieting pallor through one of Herrmann's characteristic major-minor shifts. And the return of this theme to accompany the film's final shot must stand as a classic of music irony."[44]
The film ends with a view of the couch-bed, which contains the
body of the murdered man (the evidence everyone has been searching for throughout the film), placed in a lonely train station. The
irony is at first amusing--for here is the couch, unknown to all
but the suspicious detective who still maintains a vigilance over it,
unaware that his efforts are now useless, but when the Birthday
Cake Theme is reintroduced, the humor is darkened with "a border
of bitter poignancy. For the music resurrects, at the moment when

he was the most alive, the most warm, the most human, a man who is now a forgotten, hidden cadaver."[45]

The film, and its music, went over well with the critics (and launched De Palma on a successful career). Variety wrote that Herrmann's score was "a textbook example of film music ... the music lends dramatic viability to scenes" while The Chicago Daily News praised Herrmann's use of brittle, slashing chords, which, like knife strokes, gave the movie a breathless tension.

The following year Herrmann was approached by director William Friedkin to write the music for THE EXORCIST, but due to disagreements between the two it never came about. (Friedkin then signed Lalo Schifrin to score the picture, and he actually composed the music, but the director was unimpressed and discarded it in favor of creating his own questionable pastiche from record albums--see Chapter XV.)

Herrmann next scored IT'S ALIVE (1974), a low-budget horror thriller about a horribly mutated, killer infant. Herrmann's music was dominated by his dependable, two-note fantasy motif, emphasizing the film's contrast between loving parental emotions and grotesque horror. The score is dark and moody, sparked with sudden musical jolts and shocks.

The following year he scored a second film for De Palma, OBSESSION. The picture was De Palma's poignant reworking of Hitchcock's VERTIGO, which Herrmann had also scored, but the composer wisely refrained from imitating any of his musical approach to the earlier film. The score is comprised of three major elements. The first is a romantic waltz motif which swirls at the heart of the protagonist's "obsession" with the loss of his wife and daughter, representing his longing to resurrect the past. An organ theme relates to the church where he first met his wife and where he later meets her alter ego, which is the birthplace of both loves. Later, the organ represents the death of his wife and of his mounting despair. These two elements are united by a choral line which provides "subtle emotional variations and references throughout the picture ... [as in the] dazzling conclusion where De Palma's camera ... spins the embracing father and daughter around and around in a tearful reunion. Herrmann brings in his whirling waltz, lets it catch up to the once morose vocal and organ elements, and exorcises them all into a singular, joyful swirl of emotion."[46]

Herrmann was quite moved by this film, recalling in an interview: "I don't really remember writing it, I was so carried away with the picture. I don't know. I used to write at four o'clock in the morning--it just all came to me, I don't know where from. And I identified with the girl, you know, how she felt it. This I did in a month. It's a very strange picture, a very beautiful picture, very different for me. It's all about time. Has a Proustian, Henry Jamesian feeling to it."[47]

When the film was released some months after Herrmann's death in 1975, the score received mixed reactions from critics, though most were enthusiastically favorable and praiseworthy. Some, however, felt the score was overly derivative of earlier works, and several noted that De Palma had overemphasized the music in its placement and volume to the extent that it became distracting in the film.

OBSESSION was Herrmann's last original score in the fantastic genre--his last composition was the music to TAXI DRIVER, completed the day before he died--but the Herrmann filmography was rounded out to an even fifty when Laurie Johnson, a longtime friend of Herrmann, adapted his music from IT'S ALIVE for use in the sequel, IT'S ALIVE AGAIN (1978, also called IT'S ALIVE 2). Johnson, who composed a few additional cues himself, faithfully re-created the Herrmann sound for this sequel, which--like SISTERS--is given a pulsing, visceral chill through the use of electrifying synthesizer tones and zaps. "There are some impressive, heavily-scored passages," wrote one reviewer, "but they are brief and quickly subside into a moody, droning ... ostinato which sheathes the film in a dreamlike, partially synthesized haze of sound. The synthesizer ... is subtly woven into the chamber context of the score, and much more prominence is given to the harp, the special effects of which often create a droning sheen of sound behind solo clarinet, pizzicato cello and synthesizer. Herrmann's characteristic sound of massed regular and bass clarinets, muted horn and brass is also often in evidence and much of the score has the expectant sound of the Roc country music in 7TH VOYAGE."[48]

Bernard Herrmann has left an awesome legacy of film music, which is often difficult to analyze. He was by no means a composer one could pigeonhole. He disliked the leitmotif style and rarely employed real themes, in terms of a lengthy melodic line. Herrmann preferred to write short phrases, often no longer than a minute or two. "I think a short phrase has certain advantages," Herrmann once said. "I don't like the leitmotif system. The short phrase is easier to follow for audiences, who listen with only half an ear...."[49]

In addition to short cues (what musicologist Fred Steiner has termed Herrmann's "modal" technique), Herrmann employed outrageous orchestral ensembles, included bizarre instruments, and utilized it all to marvelous effect in creating some of the most expressive sonorities in film music. His approach was particularly suitable in the fantastic film, where his style of scoring achieved the greatest amount of orchestral freedom, and his work for the genre has resulted in many landmark film scores. He has been frequently copied and imitated by hosts of young composers, and his influence is far-reaching.

"His emphasis is on orchestral texture and colorings," wrote Jim Doherty, "and the creation of an overall atmosphere that plays directly on the emotions, and more often than not will not depend heavily on obvious melodies. Yet, the music is always clear in its meaning. It does not merely sound scary or joyful--the music is fear, it is happiness...."[50]

Notes

1. Bernard Herrmann interviewed by Leslie Zador and Greg Rose; quoted by Tony Thomas, Film Score--The View from the Podium (La Jolla: A. S. Barnes & Co., 1979) p. 149

2. Fred Steiner, "Bernard Herrmann--An Unauthorized Biographical Sketch," Filmmusic Notebook Vol. 3, #2 (1977) p. 7-8

3. Tony Thomas, Music for the Movies (La Jolla: A. S. Barnes & Co., 1973) p. 143

4. Christopher Palmer, liner notes to CITIZEN KANE: The Classic Film Scores of Bernard Herrmann record album (RCA Records, 1974)

5. W. F. Krasnoborski, "Mrs. Muir and Mr. Herrmann," Soundtrack Collector's Newsletter #5 (1976) p. 4

6. Ibid.

7. Tony Thomas, op. cit., p. 146

8. Bernard Herrmann, liner notes to The Fantasy Film World of Bernard Herrmann record album (London Phase-4 Records, 1974)

9. Paul M. Sammon, "Farewell to the Master," Photon #27 (1977) p. 14

10. Jay Alan Quantrill, liner notes to VERTIGO sound-track record album (Mercury Records, Netherlands reissue, 1978)

11. Tony Thomas, op. cit., p. 147

12. John W. Morgan, liner notes to THE 7TH VOYAGE OF SINBAD sound-track record album (Varese Sarabande Records reissue, 1980)

13. Bernard Herrmann, loc. cit.

14. Ibid.

15. Jim Doherty, "The Herrmann Zone," Midnight Marquee #31 (October 1982) p. 10

16. Ibid.

17. Jim Doherty, "The Overlooked Bernard Herrmann," Soundtrack! The Collector's Quarterly #25 (Spring 1981) p. 23

18. Fred Steiner, "Herrmann's 'Black-and-White' Music for Hitchcock's PSYCHO." Filmmusic Notebook (Autumn 1974) p. 31-32. Lengthy quotes included by permission of the author.

19. Tony Thomas, op. cit., p. 145

20. Lawson Hill, "The Fantasy Film Music of Bernard Herrmann," CineFan #2 (1980) p. 31

21. Ivan Butler, Horror in the Cinema (New York: Paperback Library, 1972) p. 192

22. Fred Steiner, "Herrmann's 'Black-and-White' Music for Hitchcock's PSYCHO, Part 2," Filmmusic Notebook (Winter 1974-75) p. 31

23. Christopher Palmer, liner notes to PSYCHO record album (Unicorn Records, U.K., 1975)

24. Fred Steiner, op. cit., p. 33

25. Ibid., p. 41

26. Christopher Palmer, loc. cit.

27. Fred Steiner, op. cit., p. 37-39

28. Royal S. Brown, "Bernard Herrmann and the Subliminal Pulse of Violence," High Fidelity, March 1976, p. 76

29. Fred Steiner, op. cit., p. 31

30. Lawson Hill, loc. cit.

31. Christopher Palmer, liner notes to The Mysterious Film World of Bernard Herrmann record album (London Phase-4 Records,1975)

32. Ibid.

33. Ibid.

34. Alfred Hitchcock quoted by Kyle B. Counts, "The Making of THE BIRDS," Cinefantastique Vol. 10, #2 (1980) p. 29

35. Christopher Palmer, loc. cit.

36. Craig Reardon, "Bernard Herrmann and the JASON Score,"
     FXRH #3 (Summer, 1972) p. 53

37. Ibid.

38. Ibid.

39. François Truffaut quoted by Tony Thomas, op. cit., p. 148

40. Bernard Herrmann, loc. cit.

41. Jim Doherty, op. cit., p. 25

42. Royal S. Brown, "Record Review," High Fidelity, May 1975,
     p. 104

43. Royal S. Brown, "Bernard Herrmann, Brian De Palma, and
     SISTERS," Main Title Vol. 1, #1 (Winter 1974-75) p. 15

44. Royal S. Brown, loc. cit.

45. Ibid.

46. William F. Krasnoborski, "Omens and Obsessions," Soundtrack
     Collector's Newsletter #9 (Jan. 1977) p. 18

47. Bernard Herrmann interviewed by Royal S. Brown, High
     Fidelity, September 1976, p. 66

48. Ross Care, "Record Review," Soundtrack Collector's Newslet-
     ter #20 (January 1980) p. 9

49. Bernard Herrmann, loc. cit.

50. Jim Doherty, op. cit., p. 13 (my emphasis)

VII

JAPANESE INVASIONS
From Godzilla to Yamato

The Japanese science fiction boom began in 1954 with the giant monster film, GODZILLA (released in America in 1956), and with
it came a distinctive style of fantasy film scoring that would lend a
unique sound to the multitude of films that would follow. While the
subsequent GODZILLA and other monster-invasion movies produced
by the Toho studios in the 70's have bordered on (and often
plunged headlong into) the ridiculous and inane, those original films
of the 50's and early 60's retained a style and craftsmanship that
resulted in a number of effective genre films.

Japan's leading composer for the fantastic film is without
doubt Akira Ifukube. Noted outside the genre for scores to
CHUSHINGURA, DAREDEVIL IN THE CASTLE, and a number of
Zato-Ichi samurai movies, Ifukube's first horror score was GOD-
ZILLA. His music characterized the sound of the Japanese monster
film for the next 20 years.

Ifukube studied at the University of Hokkaido where he met
Fumio Hayasaka, another composer who began to score films in
Tokyo in the late 40's. At Hokkaido, Ifukube and Hayasaka performed together, Ifukube on violin and Hayasaka accompanying on
the piano. After graduating, Ifukube became established as a concert composer. In the early 50's, Hayasaka asked Ifukube to join
him in Tokyo, and Ifukube began to compose for motion pictures.
At the same time, he started to teach music at the Gei-Dai University.

In 1954, Ifukube was hired to write the music for Toho's entry into the giant-monster cycle of the 50's. As the composer's
first foray into the genre, it was an assignment he enjoyed. "I'm
a country boy and a megalomaniac," Ifukube later recalled. "I get
happy when I see big things. Some musician advised me not to
work on GODZILLA saying that once an actor plays a part in a
ghost movie, he cannot go back to play an artistic role. But I
didn't mind it, because I felt I wouldn't be spoiled by writing more
direct music."[1]

Ifukube had the unusual experience of having to compose the
music for GODZILLA without seeing any of the film's footage. He

Akira Ifukube. Photograph courtesy Ed Godziszewski.

was told little about the title character, only that it would be "one
of the biggest things ever on the screen." As one Toho historian
explained: "With that in mind, Ifukube took his copy of the script
and authored a powerful composition for the picture. Audiences
seldom forget the ominous, pounding march heard during [Godzilla's]
rampage through Tokyo, conjuring up an atmosphere of death."[2]

   Ifukube's music for science fiction and horror films can essentially be broken down into three parts. Almost every genre
score he has composed contains these three elements, which remain
highly similar from film to film with only moderate variation. While
this may be overly derivative, the music remains quite effective in
most of the pictures and links the monster films with a similar musical atmosphere. GODZILLA launches these three motifs with a
bang.

   The first motif is the March (or Battle Theme), usually for
fast-moving brass or strings over militaristic drum beats, which
most often refers to the machinations of the humans as they either
try in vain to defend themselves against the giant beasts or launch
a triumphant victory. Secondly, there is the Horror Theme, often
played by low, rumbling growls from the woodwinds and brass with
much percussion added. This motif refers to the monstrous aspects
of the creatures, usually opening with three of four heavily ac-

cented, ascending notes, pausing and followed by a series of descending notes. Finally, there is the Requiem, an intensely sorrowful and beautiful motif, for strings, woodwind or piano, which refers to the emotions of either the human characters or the monsters themselves. The Requiem is characterized by a slow rhythm and a slight, ultrasad melody, the final note of which descends dramatically below the previous note, giving it a very powerful emotional grip.

The March is the primary theme for GODZILLA, first heard during the main title, a fast-moving motif for see-sawing strings punctuated with drums and cymbals. This is the music that accompanies the monster's onslaught against Tokyo. The Horror motif is mixed with the March as the two join for strings over cymbal rumbling and plodding horns. The Requiem is heard in the finale after Godzilla has been destroyed, which ends the film on a sad and somber note of pity for the immense creature, the scientist who killed himself in the process, and the Japanese people who now face the long reconstruction of their city. The Requiem is also used earlier, in a chanted vocal rendition for female choir, when the people offer prayers for those killed by Godzilla. In addition, Ifukube composed a "Chant of Daito Island," a high woodwind melody over repeated drum beats, cymbal crashes and drum taps, which is based more on traditional Japanese musical styles and provides an interesting counterpoint to the monster motifs.

Ifukube was also involved in creating the intense roar of Godzilla, which was achieved through a combination of musical instruments and acoustical sound effects. "I loosened the strings of a contrabass and pulled them with a resin-coated leather glove," Ifukube said. "We lowered the sound and tried other things. As for the sound of Godzilla's footsteps, we found that the echo machine ... turned out to be perfect."[3]

While the fast-moving March and low, rumbly Horror motif create a brisk and omnipresent atmosphere for Ifukube's horror scores, the Requiem really stands out as a unique and evocative piece of music, powerfully compelling the audience to an emotional involvement with the characters. "The reason my music sounds like a requiem is because of the scales," Ifukube said. "In Japanese music, the one above the ending tone is a half tone. One below is a full note. This cannot be classed as a major key nor a minor key ... I value our traditional sense of beauty. When Westerners hear my music, they think of church music of the MIddle Ages; when Japanese hear it, it sounds like Japanese but its tempo is slow and sounds like a requiem."[4] One reviewer has described Ifukube's requiem-styled music as "related to peace preceded by destruction or death followed by birth," as seen in GODZILLA.[5]

Most of Toho's major monster movies of the next ten years were scored by Ifukube, especially those featuring new adventures of Godzilla, and all of them were composed around the same three motifs.

The Horror motif became the main theme for RODAN, Ifukube's second monster epic (made in 1956 and released in the U.S. the following year). Creating a superb atmosphere of impending dread and alienness, the theme is first identified with the Meganurons, huge insectlike creatures that are discovered in a coal mine. The motif is in this case given a spooky variation for deep, rumbling woodwind under shimmering strings, trilling high flutes and distant, softly rhythmic piano pounds punctuated by occasional moans from the brasses. RODAN also made use of a brassy March and the soft Requiem.

Ifukube's score to RODAN "ranked among his most atmospheric," according to one reviewer. "With the use of muted horns, shrill woodwinds and quivering violins, Ifukube succeeded in creating an eerie, sub-strata impression ... [an] example of such effect occurred when Shigeru's amnesiac memory was jarred by witnessing the hatching of a bird's egg. A loud, harsh chord sounded as the egg cracked open, followed by a variation of the main theme as Shigeru relived the hatching of Rodan in his mind.... A unique aspect of Ifukube's original RODAN score was the unusually subdued volume at which it was played."[6]

Unfortunately, little of Ifukube's music was heard in the film's U.S. release, being replaced in the American dubbing by what was apparently anonymous library tracks. All that remained of Ifukube's original composition were the opening and closing themes, and a portion of the Meganuron Theme heard during the search for Goro in the mines. The replacement music was mostly ineffective; substituting a grating, saccharine Romance Theme as Shigeru comforts Kiyo, and leaving the film's highlight, Rodan's attack on Sasebo City and the subsequent jet chase, completely unscored where Ifukube had provided his thrilling, brassy march to whip the action along.

The March became the primary theme for THE MYSTERIANS (U.S. 1959). Ifukube provided a powerful and spirited score for this lavish science fiction spectacle. The score includes an eerie Outer Space Theme for violin mixed with electronics, which in one place is effectively counterpointed against the Requiem. BATTLE IN OUTER SPACE (U.S. 1960), a clone of THE MYSTERIANS, was scored along similar lines, with a three-note March figure arranged over prominent snare drum beats, heard at one point very rapidly from chanting trumpets over frenzied drums and urgent brass bleats. The primary theme, however, is the Horror motif, here put through a variety of arrangements including solo French horn over piano, and low, raspy brass over rumbling percussion. Another recurring motif consisted of quick, low viola and piano notes in a thrice-repeated, four-note pattern. KING KONG VS. GODZILLA

(1963) used the March, at one point having it orchestrated in the manner of the Horror motif, providing a notable mixture of the two musical elements. Earlier, the March is counterpointed against the frenzied chant of the Skull Islanders (a bizarre meeting of Steiner and Ifukube) as deep, throbbing horn chords behind the chanting create an effectively ominous mood. Ifukube's score for this film, however, was heard only in the Japanese release, as the American edition featured new music assembled by editor Peter Zinner.

A particularly fine version of the March surfaces in DOGORA, THE SPACE MONSTER (U.S. 1964), arranged for rapidly slashing string notes, matched by simultaneous piano notes, backed with sustained woodwinds that create a strong counterpoint. The cue builds as horns are added to the mixture, at which time the contrast between the rapid string notes and the brass chords is especially effective. In addition, Ifukube uses an instrument that sounds like a cross between a theremin and somebody shaking a big sheet of aluminum at specific pitches, which creates a very eerie, spacey sound. This same effect was reused later in WAR OF THE GARGANTUAS and MONSTER ZERO (both 1970).

Daiei Studio's samurai version of the golem legend, MAJIN, THE HIDEOUS IDOL (U.S. 1966) featured a heavy, omnipresent score derived from the Horror motif, as did its pair of sequels released the same year. Unlike many of Ifukube's other period films, the composer avoids referring to traditional Japanese musical styles and emphasizes the horrific aspects in his musical treatments. Heavy, plodding, footstep-like brass chords, characteristic of giant beings, resound over shimmering strings, while a repeated, four-note phrase for deep, groaning woodwinds dominates. Ifukube also composed an intriguing theme for solo timpani, later joined by other percussion in a frenzied drums-only variation of the Horror motif. The Requiem, arranged for muted horn over rhythmic piano and strings, is also used.

By the mid-60's, the Toho monster films were becoming more and more juvenile and silly, in terms of story and the painfully obvious actor-in-suit monsters, although the miniature and optical work, along with the music, remained for the most part of consistently high quality. The contrast between fine music and inane film was particularly evident in KING KONG ESCAPES (U.S. 1968), Toho's second--and relievedly last--foray into the sacred territory of Kong's Skull Island. The Horror Theme is used to a great extent, here arranged for horns over cymbal rustling and piano pounding, with two primary notes followed by three ascending notes that peak, and then descend for two final notes. The score varies the sequence somewhat, but the mood remains the same throughout. The dominant theme of the film, however, is the Requiem, which gives the film a remarkably moving, emotional feeling--all the more amazing considering the hilarity of the bouncing, cross-eyed, clown-in-suit Kong--and manages to signify the soul and free spirit of the captive ape.

While the repetitive monster films all used the same musical elements, Ifukube scored more exotic, period fantasies with a wider range of material. THE THREE TREASURES (1960), a samurai fantasy directed by Hiroshi Inagaki, was drawn from traditional Japanese musical styles. Ifukube used a chorus extensively, as in the opening where the voices sing a wordless chant over rhythmic drum pounds. Later the choir sings an interesting variant on Ifukube's Horror motif, in which a similar melody is given a unique effect by the singers.

One of Ifukube's biggest films was Kenji Misumi's BUDDHA (U.S. 1963), a religious film with mystical fantasy elements. Like his horror scores, Ifukube chose to emphasize the lower registers of his instruments. "I like a good foundation with contrabass in it," Ifukube said. "I like low sound. In the case of recording for movies, there is a limit in the number of musicians. My typical numbers are ... eight first violins, six second violins, four violas, three cellos, and two contrabasses. When we are short of money we eliminate the first violins. It is going to sound cheap and people will notice, so I tend to lower violins and raise cellos. This tends to lower the music." [7]

One of Ifukube's richest fantasy scores was for the animated fairy tale, THE LITTLE PRINCE AND THE 8-HEADED DRAGON (U.S. 1963). The rumbling Horror motif is present as a theme for the dragon, and the Requiem is pleasantly arranged for violin and woodwind over harp, taking on a more traditional Japanese style than in previous variations. Ifukube also composed a resonant, clear trumpet theme over punctuated brass rhythm and piano counterpoint, as well as a rhythmic brass March. Voices are also used to good effect, as in the finale which features a large wailing female choir over the rhythmic brass, accompanied by woodwind melody; a very poignant theme that closes the lighthearted film nicely.

During the 70's, when Ifukube's horror scores all seem to be continuous repetitions of one another, LATITUDE ZERO (U.S. 1970) stands out as a fine effort. In addition to utilizing the March (horns over snare drum here) and the Requiem (strings over faint piano beats and low woodwind moans), there are a number of unique touches, such as the elusive melody of paired woodwinds over rhythmic pounded drums during the main titles, and a mixture of the March and a shrill wailing vocal elsewhere in the film. In a lengthy retrospective on LATITUDE ZERO, one reviewer noted the appropriateness of Ifukube's score: "One particularly effective bit of scoring occurs when Malec has captured the Alpha in the magnetic field. Using a slowed-down Battle Theme [the March] set to the scene of [the] Alpha being slowly drawn towards and crunching into the cliffs of Bloodrock, Ifukube succeeds in evoking the mood of suspense and helplessness.... While the surface visitors are being shown about ... a very faint Baroque melody [for harpsichord] is played to convey the quaint and old-time atmosphere of Latitude Zero." [8]

In the later 70's Ifukube slowly withdrew from active film composing, scoring his last monster film, REVENGE OF MECHA-GODZILLA, in 1975 (U.S. release two years later). The 1976 U.S. release of GODZILLA ON MONSTER ISLAND (made in 1972 as GOD-ZILLA VS. GIGAN) contained Ifukube's stock Godzilla music, replacing Kunio Miyauchi's awkward rock music heard in the Japanese edition. Eventually, Ifukube retired completely from film composing in order to teach music full time. The timing may have been advantageous, since his genre scores of the later 70's became increasingly self-derivative with fewer new variations upon his standard themes. It is remarkable and not without criticism that Ifukube managed to score more than 20 genre films utilizing the same three thematic pieces in all of them, yet it is to his credit that despite this repetition, most of these scores worked quite well and achieved a distinctive effect for these pictures, unequalled by any other composer scoring horror films in Japan.

Ifukube's classmate and colleague, Fumio Hayasaka, managed to become quite well known as a composer for Japanese cinema, maintaining a successful association with director Akira Kurosawa until the composer's death in 1955, scoring such classics as SEVEN SAMURAI and IKIRU for the acclaimed director. The first of Kurosawa's films to be scored by Hayasaka was DRUNKEN ANGEL (1948), a poignant drama which contained a fantasy dream sequence. The two worked closely on establishing music that would accentuate--in one way or another--the overall impression Kurosawa wanted from a particular scene, as with the use of a vapid Cuckoo Waltz for the film's saddest sequence, and a Hopeful Theme something like Debussy's Clair de Lune.

In 1950 Hayasaka scored RASHOMON, Kurosawa's compelling study of human nature as varied accounts of a brutal rape-murder are told by the four people involved, including the ghost of the victim. The main theme is a rhythmic woodwind motif under softly beaten drums, written in answer to Kurosawa's request that Hayasaka "write something like Bolero." The piece established a pleasant mood for the proceedings, although Western critics found the familiar reference distracting. The score opens atmospherically, with a meandering motif for woodwind over strummed koto, with rumbling cymbals and horn passages entering in for a ponderous, bassy theme.

Hayasaka also scored Kenji Mizoguchi's classic ghost story, UGETSU, which won the Academy Award for best foreign film of 1953.

When Hayasaka died in 1955, Kurosawa turned to Masaru Sato to score his pictures. The new composer's first complete assignment (he finished the score for RECORD OF A LIVING BEING, which was left incomplete by Hayasaka's death) was for Kurosawa's ambitious samurai retelling of Macbeth, THRONE OF BLOOD (made in 1957 but not released in the U.S. until 1961).

Like Ifukube, Sato was born in Hokkaido, but he had been raised in Sapporo, where he was introduced to Fumio Hayasaka, a composer Sato had long admired. "When I was a teenager," Sato recalled in a Japanese interview, "I considered Fumio Hayasaka and Akira Ifukube gods. I think it was RASHOMON that made my mind up to study under Hayasaka. I thought he was THE person."[9] Through his eventual association with Hayasaka, Sato began to work with the acclaimed composer, assisting with the orchestration of such scores as SEVEN SAMURAI, eventually being given the opportunity to fill his shoes after the elder composer had died.

Sato's film music seems to be quite influenced by Western music, particularly jazz, and these styles are often mixed with Japanese musical traditions to achieve very unusual effects in his films. THRONE OF BLOOD balanced original Western music--including a theme appropriately based on Verdi's opera, Macbeth--with the abrupt three drums and flute sounds of traditional Japanese Noh theatre (the latter in keeping with Kurosawa's notable Noh characterization of many of this film's characters). The haunting Noh sounds accompany many scenes, especially those involving the Lady Asaji, and embody the film in a stark, memorable sound track. Even the Verdi theme has been described as being "very much like Noh, with its distinctly moralistic overtones."[10] The film's stunning climax, with its prominent, dramatic images and harsh sounds, becomes almost operatic, "where Macbeth becomes Verdi's rather than Shakespeare's,"[11] as another writer remarked, and the music takes on a very foreground presence. Sato went on to score many of Kurosawa's best films of the 60's, including the classic samurai films, YOJIMBO and SANJURO.

At the same time, Sato was scoring somewhat less-dignified horror films for Toho, providing an entirely different type of sound. Sato scored the first GODZILLA sequel, titled, for its 1959 U.S. release, GIGANTIS, THE FIRE MONSTER, and the same year composed a fine score for the moody and atmospheric Inoshiro Honda film, THE H-MAN. Honda was the director of GODZILLA (at least the original Japanese version; American releases featured distracting and ill-paced new footage directed by Terry Morse), and his use of Ifukube's music in the giant-monster film was notable. Likewise, Honda put Sato's semijazzy rhythms to good use in THE H-MAN. The main theme is a brassy rhythm for trumpet--an uncharacteritic Horror motif more akin to a theatrical prelude. Sato also provides a Suspense Theme for slightly jazzed saxophone over droning woodwinds and muted xylophone rolls.

Similar jazzy riffs were used in GODZILLA VS. THE SEA MONSTER (U.S. 1968), which opened to an electric guitar motif over prominent drumming. The main theme is a rhythmic brass melody over electric guitar strums and percussion, backed with woodwind and strings. It's a pleasant theme but hardly what one would expect after all the dismal, omnipresent rumblings of Ifukube!

Sato's approach is much more contemporary, drawn from Western
jazz and pop. SON OF GODZILLA (U.S. 1969) likewise featured a
rhythmic pop theme for woodwind and strings over drums, with repetitive two-note brass punctuation which sounded almost like a TV
series theme. Sato did provide an ominous motif for growling
woodwinds over jazzy drum and cymbal beats, but this is later arranged in a jazzier version for brass. GODZILLA VS. MECHA-
GODZILLA (U.S. 1976) made use of another pop brass riff under
a jazzy string melody, embellished by vibraphone and drums.

As to his preference for contemporary musical styles over traditional music, Sato was influenced by the tutelage of Fumio Hayasaka, who urged the young composer to write modern music. "It
was a time when music which sounded like a prelude to a popular
song was popular," Sato recalled. Hayasaka "said this was the
time to make modern music. He told me to make use of electric
media and orchestral music. Sometime later, when I became independent, I met Quincy Jones and he said the same thing."[12]

Sato's penchant for modern music was put to especially good
use in his fine score for THE SUBMERSION OF JAPAN (1973, released in the U.S. with new footage as TIDALWAVE). The score
opens impressively with loud, crashing brass chords embellished
with pronounced guitar strokes, as well as electronic and percussionistic effects under a higher trumpet melody. The early underwater scenes, as the mini-sub discovers the fissure in the ocean
floor, are accompanied by an awesome, low, groaning sound (made
by what sounds like either reprocessed strings or a low, hollow
gourd being blown into) which provides awesome, titanic, shifting
movements of sound ominously suggestive of gargantuan scraping
land masses. Sato also provides a love theme for Onoda and Reiko,
the characters whose romance parallels the cataclysmic disaster.
First heard from soft woodwind over acoustic guitar and harp, the
theme mingles with strains from the earlier underwater motif as
Onoda talks of the undersea mudslide, and which later grows into
a rich arrangement for violins and jazzy saxophone as the two are
alone on the beach. A variation on the love theme becomes a loud,
mournful theme for strings over growing brass which is heard first
as the Japanese population flees in helpless terror during the quak-
ing of Tokyo, and later during the eruption of Mt. Fuji and subsequent evacuation of Japan.

When the final earthquake occurs and the central fissure
opens up, splitting the island in two, deep, doom-sounding organ
tones emerge from the silence, building louder until overcome by
the sounds of destruction. Japan is overwhelmed by the waves,
and the musical mood shifts from tragedy to hope for the surviving
refugees: as shots alternate between Reiko and Onoda travelling
on separate trains anticipating their reunion, Sato brings up a
rousing, very Western-sounding, jazzy theme for trumpet and
strings over an electric guitar and cymbal riff, linking their ro-

mance--and suggesting the other survivors in the process--and
ending the film on a strong note of hope born out of tragedy.

Sato's mixture of pop-jazz and earthy symphonics provides an
intriguing sound to horror films, embellishing monstrous aspects
with low orchestrations and utilizing appropriately jaunty moods for
the cartoonlike visuals of the later Godzilla films.

Another composer who provided some memorable music for
early Toho fantasies was Ikuma Dan, perhaps best known for scoring Hiroshi Inagaki's award-winning SAMURAI TRILOGY (1954).
Dan's score for THE LEGEND OF THE WHITE SERPENT (1956),
based on a traditional Japanese fairy tale, opens with a grand
flourish from brass, cymbals and harp glissandos, seguing into a
wordless solo female vocal accompanied by what sounds like a
theremin wail. This motif recurs throughout the film, providing
a fine sense of grandeur. Elsewhere, Dan utilized a rhythmic
trumpet theme over loud drum beats echoed by string chords, as
well as traditional Japanese motifs on xylophone over strings. Dan
also scored the apocalyptic THE LAST WAR (U.S. 1961), which featured a harsh, brassy motif with percussion rattles and rolls creating a hopeless, plodding theme that is balanced by a soft violin
theme, playing a moving classical five-note melody repeated in de-
scents.

Daiei Studios' popular juvenile monster series, Gamera, made
use of a variety of composers. The first film, GAMMERA [sic] THE
INVINCIBLE (1966), was scored by Tadashi Yamaguchi[13] with an
effective James Bernardlike theme of crashing, plodding brass over
monotonous tympani beats, heard as Gamera attacks Tokyo. There
is also a military motif for plodding brass and strings over snare
drum as the army fights back with their "Z Plan." Yamaguchi's
music was heard only in the Japanese release, however, being replaced by Wes Farrell's music for the Americanized version.
Yamaguchi also scored the third film in the series, GAMERA VS.
GAOS (called RETURN OF THE GIANT MONSTERS for its 1967
American release), again mingling militaristic music with apprehensive strains for orchestra and synthesizer. Other Gamera films
made use of rather unexceptional brassy scores by Chuji Kinoshita
and Kenjiro Hirose, growing increasingly more pop-oriented with
the final three films scored by Shunsuke Kikuchi, who provided
catchy, rhythmic tunes for GAMERA VS. GUIRON (1969), GAMERA
VS. JIGER (1970), and GAMERA VS. ZIGRA (1971). Kikuchi had
earlier scored two horror films released (in the U.S.) in 1968,
GENOCIDE and GOKE: BODY SNATCHER FROM HELL, both of
which were more dissonant and less rhythmic than the Gamera pictures, demonstrating a greater sense of orchestral complexity in
the varied interplay of a thereminlike instrument, electric guitar
strums, harmonic organ chords and orchestral phrases.

Several other Japanese composers have contributed occasion-

ally to the genre. Yuki Koseki provided a pleasing score for
MOTHRA (U.S. 1962), providing a main theme, associated with the
monstrous size of the huge caterpillar, comprised of an eight-note
phrase (three primary notes followed by a five-note response) for
horn blares over rhythmic up-and-down string notes and rumbling
cymbals. This is balanced by the recurring chant sung by the
Aelinas, the diminutive twins kidnapped by ruthless profiteers who
are pursued by Mothra. The song is a very pretty tune, har-
moniously sung by the Japanese duo, The Peanuts, and becomes
an effective leitmotif summoning the awesome insect. Koseki also
provides an Island Theme for the natives on Mothra's island, consisting of massive drum pounding under a trilling woodwind motif
amid vocal chants of "Mosura!" (Mothra).

Hiraki Hayashi composed an effective score for ONIBABA
(1965), Kaneto Shindo's horror mystery, achieving a notably eerie,
dissonant mood at one point through the use of a percussionistic
motif, beginning with pounding drums broken by a regular human
yell, eventually combined with vibrato strings, soft woodwinds and
brass, while the alternating drums and yell continue monotonously.
The mixture creates a mysteriously weird mood which adds to the
unease of Shindo's moody film.

By the 1970's, most of the Japanese science fiction and
horror films had become insipidly juvenile in nature, more akin to
Saturday morning cartoons than serious genre excursions, and the
music frequently followed suit, perhaps reaching the pinnacle of
mediocrity in the loud, grating rock-and-roll noise and disjointed
pop rhythms spawned by Riichiro Manabe for GODZILLA VS. THE
SMOG MONSTER (U.S. 1972) and its sequel, GODZILLA VS. MEGA-
LON (1973). Manabe wrote a blaring Godzilla Theme used in both
films, as well as other themes that sounded more like parade music
than dramatic film scoring. Kunio Miyauchi scored GODZILLA VS.
GIGAN (made in 1972) along similar lines, with several awkward
vocal tunes which were mercifully deleted for the film's 1976 American release (then called GODZILLA ON MONSTER ISLAND) and replaced with stock cues by Akira Ifukube.

A notable exception to this pop-music trend was found in the
work of Yasushi Akutagawa, a Japanese symphonic composer during
the 50's, who scored several films in the 70's. Akutagawa provided
a fine, lyrical composition for the atmospheric samurai ghost story,
VILLAGE OF EIGHT GRAVESTONES (1977). The score is dominated
by rich strings in a variety of motifs, most being classical in nature. The score provided a fine sense of mood and legend as the
ancient curse of a dying warrior reaches through the centuries to
modern-day Japan.

After the phenomenon of STAR WARS in the late 70's, the
Japanese fantasy film turned to space opera, and a number of epic
outer space adventures were produced, eventually to become a multi-

tudinous array of animated science fiction which seemed almost endless. These films brought about a new kind of scoring, mixing
the symphonic grandeur of STAR WARS with contemporary pop
rhythms, an eclectic mixture which did not always congeal properly. One of the first of these films was the lavish and exotic
MESSAGE FROM SPACE (1978), nicely scored by Ken-Ichiro Morioka, a well-known composer of Japanese pop music. The main
theme is a lyrical, sweeping romance for strings and chorus, and
there is a fine theme for the space battle, scored for woodwind
punctuated by repeated piano, brass and percussion strikes, mixed
with incidental brass and percussion passages. Unfortunately,
much of the score is comprised of substandard, loud rock-and-roll
tunes, which are noticeably out of context here.

The same problem that detracted from Morioka's score seems
to be prominent in the rush of live-action and animated space adventures that followed. Toshiaki Tsushima's score for THE WAR
IN SPACE (1978) likewise sported an impressive, proud main theme
for brass over twangy electronic swirls which provide an intriguing
spacey sound under the heroic melody, but the theme is quickly
overcome by a pop/rock melody which is at odds with itself.

CATASTROPHE 1999 (1975), while making its appearance before the STAR WARS outburst, nevertheless was a forerunner of
the pop-rock style that followed. Scored by Isao Tomita, who has
become known outside of Japan for his classical synthesizer records,
the music was primarily endless repetitions of a single pop tune
with little variation. Hiroshi Miyagawa scored the successful
SPACE CRUISER YAMATO series (1977-80) with a fine adventurous
main theme, alternately arranged for brass over see-sawing strings
and for solo female voice, but the theme was rarely given a chance
to stand on its own without being overstaged by obnoxious pop ver-
sions. Miyagawa does provide a pretty Love Theme, very classical
in its use of strings, but again the pop arrangement soon barges
in and the piece becomes a nightclub-styled piece for guitar, piano
and string bass, which did little to accentuate dramatic situations.
There is also a loud and rumbling Disaster motif which is reminiscent of Akira Ifukube's Horror motif. Nozumi Aoki likewise provided a notable main theme for the animated space adventure,
GALAXY EXPRESS (1980), which is unfortunately watered down by
the saccharinelike, overly lush, "101 Strings" arrangements. The
main theme, which represents the external adventures occurring on
the interplanetary steam train, is balanced by a lyrical motif,
"Wanderling," which suggests the inner conflict of the questing
boy and his companions. The latter motif is first heard on nicely
arranged strings over plucked guitar, and then by solo female
voice, but finally succumbs to a pat-patting pop rhythm which ruins
the emotional quality built up by the piece earlier. Other composers who have frequented the Japanese fantastic film over the years
include Sei Ikeno, Kan Ishii, Chumei Watanabe and Seiichiro Uno.

The mixture of the symphonic and the popular seems to be the vogue for the current Japanese space opera product, although the pop elements in many of these scores tend to be overly obtrusive, detracting from the dramatic value of the symphonic elements. The evocative and powerful scoring of the early Toho horror films seems to have come to an unfortunate end, at least in the fantastic cinema. Mainstream Japanese films, such as Kurosawa's KAGE-MUSHA (1980), have avoided the pop sounds so prevalent in the juvenile-oriented space movies--and maybe that gives the answer right there. Most of these pictures seem specifically oriented towards children, and apparently it's felt that only a catchy tune and a tapping rhythm will appeal to their youthful ears. While this may be in keeping with the commerciality of this onslaught of space adventure, it may also result in a setback of real dramatic scoring in genre films from Japan. The true Golden Age of fantastic film music in Japanese cinema remains in the early efforts of the 50's, and the unique sounds created by Akira Ifukube.

Notes

1. Akira Ifukube interviewed by Tomohiro Kaiyama, "The World of Akira Ifukube," liner notes to Works of Akira Ifukube record album (Toho Records, Japan, 1978). Professional translation for the author

2. Ed Godziszewski, "The Making of GODZILLA," Japanese Fantasy Film Journal #13 (1981) p. 21

3. Akira Ifukube, loc. cit.

4. Ibid.

5. Tomohiro Kaiyama, ibid.

6. Ed Godziszewski and Peter Brothers, "RODAN--Commentary," Japanese Giants #6 (September 1980) p. 17

7. Akira Ifukube, loc. cit.

8. Ed Godziszewski, "Latitude Zero--Commentary," Japanese Giants #5 (not dated), p. 18

9. Masaru Sato interviewed by Tomohiro Kaiyama, liner notes to Works of Masaru Sato record album (Toho Records, Japan, 1978). Professional translation for the author

10. Marilyn D. Mintz, The Martial Arts Films (La Jolla: A. S. Barnes & Co., 1978) p. 199

11. Donald Ritchie, The Films of Akira Kurosawa (Berkeley: University of California Press, 1970) p. 121

12. Masaru Sato, loc. cit.

13. While most sources provide no credit to the music composer of GAMMERA THE INVINCIBLE, the excerpts included on the recent Gamera sound-track collection from Toho Records credit Yamaguchi with its composition.

VIII

HORRORS FROM HAMMER AND OTHERS
The British Cinema (1955-1980)

When Hammer Film Studios rose to popularity in the late 50's
as Britain's foremost producer of science fiction and horror films,
the genre took on a distinctive new look, characterized by the
richly colored, Gothic set designs and a daring emphasis on sensuality and violence. Likewise, Hammer, early on, achieved a very
distinctive sound for their films, as richly Gothic as the moody visuals and as sensual as the flowing, white-robed ladies who floated
with evil intent through the echoing catacombs of ancient castles.
Music for Hammer films conjured up ornate, shadowed visions and
strident, smooth action, brimming with crashing cymbals, attacking
trumpets, mellow French horn interludes, and frantic, pounding
drum beats.

Hammer's first music director was John Hollingsworth, who
supervised the composition of the film scores and conducted the
orchestra from 1954 until 1963. Hollingsworth, born in 1916, was
educated at the Bradfield College in Berkshire and trained at the
Guildhall School of Music. In 1937 he conducted the London Symphony Orchestra, joining the RAF in 1940 and eventually becoming
the first RAF sergeant to conduct the National Symphony Orchestra,
in 1943. He conducted various orchestras including the Royal
Opera House, Covent Garden, and held long-term positions as music director for various organizations until becoming Hammer's music director. Although Hollingsworth did not compose film music
himself, he oversaw all aspects of the film's scoring, supervising
Hammer's regular and occasional composers until his death in 1963,
while preparing the music for THE EVIL OF FRANKENSTEIN.

Philip Martell, a conductor who had worked for Hammer previously, was called in to take over as musical director. Martell had
been born in London's East End in 1915 and received his training
at the Guildhall School of Music, starting at the age of eleven.
Martell later studied with Benoit Hollander, a pupil of Camille Saint-
Saens, whose influence left a strong mark on the young student.
At the end of the 20's, Martell became involved with the film industry as an arranger--taking excerpts from classical music and fitting
them into appropriate sequences in the films.

When sound came to the movies, Martell drifted away from films

John Hollingsworth. Photograph courtesy Richard E. Klemensen.

Philip Martell. Photograph courtesy Richard E. Klemensen.

and began performing in concerts, first as a violinist and finally conducting musicals. Eventually, he formed his own orchestra and performed for the BBC (British Broadcasting Corporation), conducting music which appealed to his own particular taste. Much of this music was from British and American films, which rekindled Martell's interest in the motion picture industry. Director Val Guest enabled Martell to enter the film music field, conducting the music to one of his comedies. Martell's first association with Hammer began in 1955, as a conductor of another one of Guest's comedy films. He took over the musical direction of THE EVIL OF FRANKENSTEIN after the death of John Hollingsworth, and Martell continued in this capacity to the current day. In the late 70's, Martell also became musical director for Tyburn studios, supervising the music of their short-lived horror film output.

During John Hollingsworth's tenure, Hammer's film scoring tended to remain basically symphonic, with heavy romantic and Gothic overtones. During the later 60's, though, under Martell's direction, the Hammer sound tended to become more pop-oriented, and the film scores took on a more rhythmic beat; although this might have resulted from the style of new composers being commissioned and the overall shifting into pop music that occurred in film scoring in the mid-60's, rather than an intentional shift in musical style dictated by Martell.

While Hollingsworth and Martell were primarily responsible for supervising the scoring of Hammer films, they did not directly compose the music for any of the films. This task fell upon a variety of composers, some of whom worked frequently for Hammer, while others contributed only an occasional score or two. The composer whose music most often characterized the sound of Hammer films, and who scored more of them than any other composer, was James Bernard, who began composing for Hammer at the start of their horror cycle in 1954.

Born in 1925 and educated at Berkshire's Wellington College, Bernard was interested in both acting and music from an early age. Encouraged by composer Benjamin Britten's favorable response to a piece he had written for a school music competition, Bernard began to study music steadily. In 1943, he joined the RAF, where he met conductor John Hollingsworth. Later, after gaining a thorough musical training at the Royal College of Music, Bernard began to score plays for the BBC. There his friendship was renewed with Hollingsworth, who conducted many of Bernard's scores and eventually asked him to compose the music for Hammer's THE QUATERMASS XPERIMENT (1955; released in the U.S. the following year as THE CREEPING UNKNOWN). This launched for Bernard a successful career as a film composer, scoring Hammer films as well as those of other studios; although it has been through the Hammer horror pictures that Bernard has really found his niche.

The music for THE QUATERMASS XPERIMENT was an impressive debut for the composer not only in scoring for motion pictures, but for scoring horror films in particular. Written exclusively for strings and percussion, the music is built around a slow, plodding, two-note motif for low viola, culminating in higher violin and rustling cymbal. This motif is later balanced with a fast and vibrant high string passage which is put to good effect in characterizing the horror brought back from space--as in the scene when the recovering astronaut sees a plant in the hospital and is reminded of the horrors he encountered in space; a frenzied string motif accentuates his fears. An effective piece for ominous, swirling strings over drum beats is heard at the police station following the astronaut's rescue, and in the climactic scene at Westminster Abbey, Bernard provides a fine composition for sustained strings over percussion raps (a technique he later employed in the climax of HORROR OF DRACULA). Music was used sparingly in THE QUATERMASS XPERIMENT, retaining a discordant quality in the moments when it is used, and the strong, powerful sound of the pure strings did much to increase the film's tension.

Bernard used similar arrangements of strings and percussion for the sequel, QUATERMASS II (1956, released in the U.S. the following year as ENEMY FROM SPACE), as well as X THE UNKNOWN (1957). He emphasized the brass and woodwinds a little more in THE CURSE OF FRANKENSTEIN (1957), which featured a slow, melancholy theme, given a vibrant sense of power with high string flurries, large gong shimmers and tambourine ruffles.

The score that really brought Bernard to the forefront of genre composers was that for Terence Fisher's masterpiece, HORROR OF DRACULA (1958). Bernard's music is immensely powerful, dominated by a repeated, three-note brass and percussion motif (one sustained note followed by two repeated notes an octave lower). The score remarkably captured the power and dangerous presence of the savage vampire. Like the film, Bernard's score has come to be regarded as a classic of horror film music and demonstrated the composer's particular affinity at scoring these types of films. As one writer said, comparing Bernard's earlier "repetitive, skeletal string musings" with his dynamic HORROR OF DRACULA score: "It is not until DRACULA that Bernard produces a finely measured work possessing motifs which evoke logically, and are used in apt conjunction with the subject matter of the motion picture."[1]

Interestingly, Bernard derived his main theme for HORROR OF DRACULA from the three syllables of the word Dracula. "The name gave it to me just like that," Bernard explained in an interview many years later. "I've often used that way of taking the name of a film to suggest a sort of pattern or rhythm. But that was a very simple thing in DRACULA, that dropping of an octave. Sometimes it's the drop of an octave, sometimes it's the drop of an

augmented fourth or diminished fifth. It's more or less the same.
But it seems to have been very effective.... It was just a sort of
lucky chance that I hit on that, because it's terribly simple. And
I suppose that's its strength, really."[2]

Bernard balances the "DRAC-u-la" theme, which represents
vampiric evil, with an emotionally weaker motif representing Van
Helsing and the "good" people on which Dracula preys. This second motif, a five-note theme for strings, is given many more variations than the vampire's theme, which remains relatively unchanged
(as does the malevolent vampire) throughout most of the film.
The Good motif is alternately helpless, terrified, resolute and,
eventually at the film's climax, proudly self-assured. But it is
the overpowering Dracula Theme which dominates the film up to
that point.

The interplay between these two themes is used carefully
and purposefully throughout the score. The Dracula motif always
resolves itself, musically representing the strength of the vampiric
character. As Bill Littman wrote in a detailed analysis of the music, the motif "has to be literally broken up to lose this resolution."[3] (This, of course, happens only at Dracula's destruction at
the end.) In contrast, the Good Theme is only resolved twice during the film, elsewhere it lacks total definition, since, in the story,
the indomitable presence of Dracula is constantly overpowering the
group that has joined to stand against him. The only occasions
where the Good motif achieves a full musical resolution is after the
staking of Lucy, when the newborn vampiress is released from her
undead state, and finally at the dissolution of Dracula in the film's
climax.

The counterpoint between these two themes is especially effective in that climactic confrontation between Dracula and Van
Helsing, and demonstrates again the symbolic value of the leitmotif
style in underscoring various elements of the visuals with musical
suggestions of what they represent: "Here in this scene, the two
motifs are brought together in a veritable whirlwind clash of full
orchestral musical force," wrote Bill Littman. As Van Helsing and
Holmwood approach Dracula's castle, the vampire is seen digging a
temporary grave for the captured Mina. "The brass of Bernard's
orchestra rips out with an agitatedly repeated statement of the
Dracula motif," Littman continues. "Almost all of this frenzied sequence is percussively supplemented by tom-toms and snare drum,
alternately, adding still more drive to the music. A variation on
the Good motif suddenly begins repeating itself _agitato_ ... in juxtaposition with DRAC-u-la, and snare drums...." As Dracula and
Van Helsing tangle on screen, the music makes short, choppy brass
statements as Dracula overpowers his opponent until Van Helsing
manages to shove him away as the Good motif accompanies his action; as the two stare at each other worriedly, Van Helsing notices
the sun has risen. "Van Helsing leaps upon a ledge extension

leading towards the window (Good motif variation again) and tears away the curtains blocking the sunlight. The strings scream out an agonizing figure as the sun's rays hit Dracula. The string figure becomes a screeching, twisted variation of the Dracula motif as the process of disintegration begins. The orchestra now begins a long, downward spiral while Dracula turns to dust, and the Vampire's Theme is broken and dissipated. A single cymbal crash breaks the mood as the Good motif, now triumphant, alternates briefly with a shapeless Dracula motif, and finally ends the scene, and the picture, with its own forceful resolution."[4]

Bernard's score for this film remains a phenomenally powerful and unforgettable work, expertly underscoring the essential battle of good vs. evil comprising the story, and brutally portraying for the first time the real horror of Dracula. As Donald C. Willis wrote, HORROR OF DRACULA "is perhaps, properly speaking, less Hammer's most exciting horror movie than it is James Bernard's most exciting score. The latter seems, roughly, half the film. It's clearly that wildly surging music that makes Christopher Lee's presence as Dracula as imposing as it is: <u>because</u> Bernard's score is so overwhelming, all Lee need do is appear, or open his eyes, and it's a stunning moment."[5] While perhaps unfairly disposing of Lee's commanding performance as the vampire, Willis' statement does reflect the memorable strength of the film's music, and its important contribution to the film.

Bernard utilized the same musical premise when he scored subsequent Dracula films for Hammer, beginning with the first sequel, DRACULA, PRINCE OF DARKNESS in 1965. Here the DRAC-u-la motif is given a variety of arrangements (more in tempo than in orchestration), as in the quick, rapid bursts of horn and drums during the vampire attacks, and the slow and deliberate phrases during the vampire's destruction beneath the ice. Like the first film, Bernard's music is threatening, stalking, purposeful.

The next picture, DRACULA HAS RISEN FROM THE GRAVE (1968) balances a subtler DRAC-u-la Theme with a recurring religious motif for strings and tubular bells. TASTE THE BLOOD OF DRACULA (1970) balanced it with a tender Love Theme for high, inspirational strings mingling with low, dangerous horn intonations. SCARS OF DRACULA (1970) mixed the DRAC-u-la motif with a similarly pleasant string melody over synthesizer notes. After this film, Bernard left the vampire series to other composers. While the Dracula films scored by him are basically derived from similar musical themes, Bernard nevertheless approached each picture of the series individually. "Each film," Bernard explained, "whether part of a series or not, has its own musical problems, and I try hard ... not to repeat myself (except, of course, when themes need to be repeated.)"[6]

Bernard prefers to score films with a specific thematic ap-

proach, as he did in the Dracula movies. "I build each score
around two or three main themes, and perhaps one or two subsidiary themes," he said. "I do not give a theme to every character in the film--it would become much too complicated. Film music is, in my opinion, most effective when it is basically simple,
even if it sometimes demands elaborate orchestration. A single
melodic line played by a solo instrument ... can be immensely
telling in a cinema, whereas a lot of clever counterpoint, particularly if mixed with natural sounds or speech, will be totally ineffective. In horror films, I am always pleased when there is the
opportunity for a love theme, or at any rate something romantic,
as a contrast to the main Horror Theme. Unrelieved tension and
horror in the music can become a bore!"[7]

Bernard's score for THE GORGON (1964) is memorable for
its haunting use of reverberated female voice over organ, amid the
characteristic, brutal percussion and brass figures. SHE (1965)
was another score which Bernard invested with a number of leitmotifs. "SHE gave me great opportunities," the composer recalled,
"as it contained a splendid mixture of love, adventure, magic, horror, and even African and Arab music."[8] In a later interview,
Bernard elaborated: "I had the main romantic theme for 'She',
and the fanfare theme for when She was in a bad mood and when
She had to be obeyed as opposed to when She was falling in love
with Leo; and there was a theme for trekking across the desert;
there was a theme for the second romance. There was another
girl who he fell in love with and she was sacrificed in the end
... I had a little theme which was played on an oboe."[9]

Bernard hadn't scored the first two sequels to CURSE OF
FRANKENSTEIN, but he did write the music for a trio of series
efforts in the late 60's and early 70's. For FRANKENSTEIN
CREATED WOMAN (1967), he provided a score centered around a
simple theme, which became (as one reviewer described it) "increasingly more elaborate as the film unfolds until, during the
murders, it has become completely altered into a dissonant, morbid
dirge. All the characters' leitmotifs can be traced back to the
main theme, just as each of the subplots eventually find a place
within the total significance of the subject."[10]

As with most of the Frankenstein films, there was no recurring theme, such as in the Dracula movies, but each was characterized by a predominant sense of ominous resignation and danger
in the music, effectively capturing the inherent evil of the Frankenstein family--in this case by an effective string-and-brass motif,
ascending and descending, wavelike. FRANKENSTEIN MUST BE
DESTROYED (1970) featured a five-note brass theme that remained
central to the score, conjuring up a powerful Gothic atmosphere.
Bernard's final score in this series, FRANKENSTEIN AND THE
MONSTER FROM HELL (1974), was occupied with a similar five-
note theme for ascending strings, capped by brass on the final

note or two, which builds an inexorable atmosphere of dread. The
score balanced a lighter theme for solo violin that contrasted well
with the harsher Monster motifs.

Bernard also scored the Hammer-Shaw Bros. coproduction,
THE LEGEND OF THE 7 GOLDEN VAMPIRES (1973; released in the
U.S. in 1979 as THE 7 BROTHERS MEET DRACULA), giving it a
brassy, Oriental theme in addition to the more traditional Horror
motifs. Characteristically, Shaw Bros., the Chinese produciton
company that collaborated with Hammer on this unusual kung-fu
horror film, originally wanted to release it with a bunch of stock
scores housed in their musical libraries, as they had done in previous kung-fu movies. Hammer's production executive, Michael Carreras, insisted on an original score by Bernard, which turned out
to be, if unremarkable, a much better choice than simply ripping
off music from another source. Bernard was asked to score THE
GHOUL for the newly formed Tyburn Studios in 1975, but regrettably had to turn it down because the producers needed the music
in only three weeks; Bernard, exhausted from having scored 7
GOLDEN VAMPIRES in just that amount of time, simply couldn't
tackle another rush assignment. "I really couldn't go straight on,"
he recalled. "I get so exhausted doing a score."[11] He did score
a few episodes of Hammer's foray into television in 1980, THE
HAMMER HOUSE OF HORROR, but aside from that has been con-
spicuously absent from genre scoring for nearly a decade.

Bernard has seldom composed pop or contemporary-styled music, preferring a classical symphonic idiom--rare exceptions including a jazz theme for one episode of TORTURE GARDEN (1967), an
Amicus film he scored in collaboration with Don Banks; and a semipop song used in THESE ARE THE DAMNED (1965), with lyrics by
the film's director, Joseph Losey. Bernard gradually scored fewer
films for Hammer as their emphasis on pop increased and composers
from the recording field were brought in; Bernard's interest in
returning to stage musicals was also giving him less time for film
scoring.

The fact that James Bernard has been somewhat typecast as
a horror composer doesn't seem to bother him. He has always been
interested in fantasy, and enjoys scoring horror and supernatural
films. Bernard's only real irritation as a film composer is a common
one among his colleagues: "It's always slightly irritating when you
spend a great deal of time on the music for some big action sequence and the music has got to be terribly exciting, and it's got
to be fast--and [it's] always much more tiring writing that sort of
music, because there are so many more notes to get down on paper--
so you work like mad getting it scored, and then, when you get the
finished effect, the whole thing is completely drowned by the clash
of swords and shrieks of vampires and zombies and things."[12] Despite this frequent annoyance, Bernard's music has emerged as one
of the most powerful elements in the distinctive, richly endowed

Hammer horror pictures. Bernard's superior work for these films
has earned him a lasting place as an important composer of genre
film music. As Hammer's production executive, Michael Carreras,
has said of Bernard: "He's my favorite and he understands these
films, too. I think his score for our first DRACULA has never
been bettered and we still use that same motif on all our Dracula
appearances. He's a very fine composer in his own right."[13]

Various other composers, although less frequently, have
scored films for Hammer. While their first successful horror films
were supplied with music from James Bernard, the highly under-
rated 1957 film, THE ABOMINABLE SNOWMAN OF THE HIMALAYAS
was scored, without credit, by Humphrey Searle--only music director John Hollingsworth received screen mention. Searle, an
English composer trained in London and Vienna, was best known
as a composer of concert works, having written several symphonies,
operas and ballet. His only other effort in the genre is the music
for THE HAUNTING (1963). Searle composed a very moody, evocative score for the slow-moving yet intriguing ABOMINABLE SNOW-
MAN.

Leonard Salzedo scored THE REVENGE OF FRANKENSTEIN
(1958), their superior sequel to THE CURSE OF FRANKENSTEIN.
Salzedo, born in London in 1921, had studied at the Royal College
of Music, and worked primarily in composing ballets and concert
works. He became associated with Hammer in the early 50's, scoring various dramas. Salzedo's score for this low-key but effective
film grows out of the church bells that are heard in the opening
scene, developing into a slow, melancholy string motif. The theme
is given an effective counterpoint by broad horn notes, a piping
woodwind discord and the regular, chanting toll of the bells.

Franz Reizenstein scored only one film for Hammer (THE
MUMMY, 1959) but provided an excellent composition. Reizenstein
was born in Nuremberg in 1911 and died in London in 1968. Between that time he had become quite successful as a composer of
concert works, and was well respected as a concert pianist. Reizenstein's compositional style was influenced to a degree by Vaughan
Williams, with whom he studied. For THE MUMMY, Reizenstein
embodied the film in a basic and quite tragic Love Theme, for
large choir over brass and tympani, which recalls the 2,000-year-old
lost love of the Egyptian, Kharis. The theme passionately underscores not only the flashback sequences placed in ancient Egypt,
but also the feelings of Kharis, now a reawakened mummy, toward
a contemporary woman who resembles his beloved princess. As one
reviewer wrote: "The sheer magnitude of Reizenstein's work lends
a sort of TEN-COMMANDMENTS-style elegance to the Egyptian
flashbacks, and produces a tender, tragic beauty in the Kharis-
Princess Anaka sequences."[14] Reizenstein's only other effort in
the genre was CIRCUS OF HORRORS (1960), a score which unfortunately was marred by the use of an out-of-place theme song,

"Look for a Star." The horror music for this film, however, was characteristically Hammerlike, as in the shuddery string theme mixed with a circuslike fanfare heard in the main title.

Richard Rodney Bennett, best known for his classically styled music for dramatic films, scored Terence Fisher's unremarkable THE MAN WHO COULD CHEAT DEATH (1959) during his early days in the field. Bennett was born in Broadstairs, England, in 1936, and began to score films at the age of 20. The music for THE MAN WHO COULD CHEAT DEATH featured a main theme for electronic organ in shimmering reverb, over repeated tympani and mysterious piano, as well as a variety of xylophone, brass and percussion used as Suspense motifs throughout the score. Bennett's later work in the genre included Hammer's THE WITCHES (1966, called THE DEVIL'S OWN in the U.S.), for which he composed a nicely sinister theme for screeching woodwind over rhythmic piano, drum and xylophone, which is balanced with a triumphal theme for string and brass. For the TV movie SHERLOCK HOLMES IN NEW YORK (1975), Bennett composed a pleasing and energetic Victorian theme for a fast-moving string and woodwind melody over rapid violin chords.

Benjamin Frankel, born in London in 1906, gained a great deal of experience in classical music before becoming noted for his concert works. He provided a fine score for Fisher's CURSE OF THE WEREWOLF (1960), approaching the film in a very dissonant manner, emphasizing strings and percussion with few melodies and few repeated motifs other than the use of similar orchestration. Midway through the film, Leon, inflicted with the werewolf's curse, has been jailed for murder and begs his father to kill him with a silver bullet; the music here responds to his tortured mind, building to a violent crescendo of strings and xylophone as he attempts to resist the spell of lycanthropy. As one reviewer wrote, "the music conveys the uncontrollable feelings of Leon to combat the more powerful spirit within him."[15]

Near the end, as the villagers pursue Leon, now a werewolf, into the town square, dramatic percussion and strings express the villagers' enmity toward the creature. When Leon's stepfather ascends the church tower where the werewolf has taken refuge, Frankel injects motifs from the earlier scenes, reminding the viewer of the tragic circumstances surrounding Leon's birth and his tragic curse. After Leon has been shot and killed, the music bespeaks relief now that the werewolf's curse has been lifted. As another writer put it, Frankel's "gorgeous music [exhibits] tremendous power, particularly in the final sequence, when he works the ringing of the bells into the final pounding surges of music. Quite grand."[16] Frankel later scored Hammer's coproduction with William Castle, a dreary remake of THE OLD DARK HOUSE (1963), and a few earlier genre films, but none of them had as memorable a score as that for CURSE OF THE WEREWOLF. Frankel died in 1973.

A particularly unique sound was given to Hammer's prehistoric epics by Italian composer Mario Nascimbene, who lent them his characteristic blend of symphonics and unusual musical sound effects for films such as ONE MILLION YEARS B.C. (1966) and WHEN DINOSAURS RULED THE EARTH (1970). Nascimbene provided a mixture of bizarre noises like clacking bones, electronically reprocessed sounds and varied atonal instrumental motifs, linked by proud, brassy themes which underly the triumphal reign of mankind amid the chaotic prehistoric world. (Nascimbene's work will be covered in more detail in Chapter X.)

Malcolm Williamson's first Hammer score was BRIDES OF DRACULA (1960), an evocative and powerful followup to HORROR OF DRACULA. Williamson was born in Mosmon Bay, Australia, in 1931, and while still a teenager, his interest in films led him to scoring several Australian documentaries. He continued to compose for small films until contacted in 1960 by John Hollingsworth, who arranged for him to score BRIDES OF DRACULA. Before starting on the music, Williamson reportedly studied several of James Bernard's earlier Hammer scores, and found them "faultless." Bernard's influence is quite evident in Williamson's fine Gothic overtones for BRIDES OF DRACULA. Although lacking the thematic unity of the Bernard score, Williamson suffused the film with a variety of screaming brass, rapidly fingered piano and woodwind motifs, and a religious-sounding organ theme which contrasts effectively with the brassy Terror Theme. Williamson also scored Hammer's HORROR OF FRANKENSTEIN (1970) and others.

Monty Norman, best known for scoring the first James Bond film, DR. NO (1963--the score was reworked by John Barry after Norman was finished), had previously written the music for Hammer's THE TWO FACES OF DR. JEKYLL in collaboration with David Heneker. The music, however--like the film--was fairly unmemorable, dominated by a tuneful trumpet theme over a rapid piano-and-drum beat, which lent the film an awkward pop atmosphere.

Edwin (Ted) Astley, who scored British films during the early 50's, was called upon to provide the highly operatic music for Hammer's ambitious remake of THE PHANTOM OF THE OPERA (1962). Astley's music, besides the obvious operatic selections needed for theatrical scenes, included an unusual use of choir mixed with loud, dramatic Horror motifs from the brass section. Astley also provided a low, subdued and somber organ motif, along with the usual Hammer crescendos for brass punches and cymbal crashes. Astley later composed the lighthearted score for the Disneyesque, DIGBY, THE BIGGEST DOG IN THE WORLD (1974).

Don Banks began a fruitful association with Hammer in 1962 when he scored their adaptation of the Dr. Syn adventure, NIGHT CREATURE, lending it a heavy brass theme mixed with strident string figures. Born in Australia in 1923, Banks settled in Eng-

land during the 50's. Noted as a composer of many classical
works, Banks wrote the music for ten horror pictures, most of
which were for Hammer. He returned to Australia in 1980 to take
up a teaching position at Sydney University, a post he held briefly until his untimely death in 1981. One of Banks' best scores
was for THE EVIL OF FRANKENSTEIN (1964), which opens with a
slow, ominous prologue, building into swirling strings accented by
brass., The main theme is strong on brass and percussion; the
use of a sustained note followed by several descending notes creates a fine dramatic atmosphere. The melodic line is also taken by
the strings very effectively. Banks composed a marchlike theme
for choir and brass over tympani for THE MUMMY'S SHROUD (1967).
The same year he collaborated with James Bernard on Amicus' TOR-
TURE GARDEN, an anthology film which they were given only two
weeks to score. The two composers divided up the episodes in order to complete it in time.

Stanley Black, also a recording artist for various easy-
listening records, scored a handful of fantasy films and thrillers
during his association with the film industry since the late 40's,
including Hammer's psycho thriller, MANIAC (1963). Black was
born in London, and for ten years starting in 1944 he was the
resident conductor of the BBC Dance Orchestra. Under contract
to Decca Records since 1943, Black has conducted many recordings
including film theme albums for London Records. In 1958, Black
was appointed music director for Associated British Studios. He
scored various films of little note throughout the 50's and 60's,
including genre offerings such as Jimmy Sangster's THE CRAWL-
ING EYE (1958) and WAR GODS OF THE DEEP (1965).

Harry Robinson, who scored several films for Hammer, and
later Tyburn, in the 70's, is in reality producer Harry Robertson.
The name Robinson appeared on his first paycheck due to a clerical error early in his career, and not wishing to contest it and de-
lay his salary, Robertson continued to use that name on his musical
endeavors through the 70's, finally correcting the confusion in 1981
when he produced and composed HAWK THE SLAYER under his real
name. Robertson was born in Scotland and trained as a classical
musician. In 1958 he entered the television industry, and soon became musical director for EMI and Decca Records. He was an arranger for many British pop-music TV specials, as well as for the
SHINDIG series in the U.S. He has worked as a composer, arranger and conductor on numerous documentaries, children's films,
television commercials and features since the mid-60's. His first
fantastic film score came in 1966 with one of the Ansus Films series
of fantasy shorts, DANNY THE DRAGON, after which he started
working for Hammer, composing the theme and episode music for
their short-lived series, JOURNEY TO THE UNKNOWN (1968). The
producer of this show had wanted a Scottish flavor in the theme,
and selected Scotsman Robertson to score it after rejecting the efforts of several previous composers. Robertson came up with a

heavy pop Whistling Theme incorporating sound effects, such as a woman's scream, for the strange shapes and visuals used for the title sequence.

Robertson went on to provide the richly Gothic music for a number of memorable Hammer films, while continuing to score occasional films for the British Children's Film Foundation. One of the early Hammer scores was for their bold mixture of horror and sexuality, THE VAMPIRE LOVERS (1970). Robertson's music opens with almost weeping violins in a subtle flourish, which is soon interrupted by a throbbing bass note, over which the main theme is played on an oboe which, itself, quickly dissolves into an eerie, menacing atmosphere of apprehension which builds, slowly, through the use of strings and brasses, to a dramatic crescendo. The music is very Gothic in character, including a rich love theme, and underlines both the vampiric and romantic aspects of the film's sensuous characters.

Robertson also scored the sequel, LUST FOR A VAMPIRE (1971), which he considers his worst score because he was "forced to write an absolutely horrible pop song--'Strange Love'--to be played during a love scene." The song, said Robertson, "drew hoots and jeers from every audience that heard it."[17] Producer Harry Fine wanted Robertson to come up with a similar song for TWINS OF EVIL (1971), but the composer refused to oblige, instead composing a fine theme featuring a dominant, powerful trumpet melody over brass, piano and tympani, giving a dramatic strength to the film and its evil characters. (Fine later had words set to the film's theme music anyway, and had it released as an unsuccessful single.)

Robertson started to score DR. JEKYLL AND SISTER HYDE (1971), but disagreements between him and the producers resulted in his departure from the production. David Whitaker was called in to score the picture, although the music Robertson had managed to compose was partly included, uncredited. Robertson went on to score COUNTESS DRACULA (1972), which was a profoundly romantic composition for zimbalom and forceful, Gothic strings, effectively depicting the passion of the aging countess, her sincere love for her suitor and her inevitable tragedy in reverting to her true, aged state.

Robertson writes very quickly, and considers his music to be very sonorous and large, the type of music that lent itself to rapid scoring and conducting. This, naturally, resulted in some extremely short time-periods in which he had to score his films. "THE VAMPIRE LOVERS was a brutal score to write," Robertson recalled. "There were about seventy-five minutes of music in the movie, and I did it in ten days. The worst part was that I had to nearly do two pictures at one time. I had just barely finished THE VAMPIRE LOVERS when I had to start COUNTESS DRACULA...."

The fastest score I did was ... COUNTESS DRACULA. I think I
did it in a week. It was a very easy score to write. I didn't use
what I would call 'Hammer Chords'...."[18] For TWINS OF EVIL,
Robertson admits that he "always wanted to do a Western score.
So I saw all this bit about the Puritans and the Brotherhood, and
I said ... 'I'm going to do a big cowboy theme for the Brotherhood'.... The music comes on at a hell of a speed. There are
great chunks of it ... about ten minutes each."

In 1975, Robertson scored the pair of debut films from the
short-lived Tyburn Film Studios, THE GHOUL and LEGEND OF THE
WEREWOLF, both symphonic and Gothic in quality, before shifting
into a pleasant mixture of symphonic and rock orchestration for
HAWK, THE SLAYER (1981), an unusual combination that works
effectively in this sword-and-sorcery adventure film. Robertson
blends synthesizer and orchestra in a noteworthy manner, providing in the main theme a rock melody slightly reminiscent of Les
Baxter's theme for THE DUNWICH HORROR, utilizing a synthesized
woodwind sound, as well as an evocative zimbalom theme for Voltan,
a lyrical motif for piano, synthesizer and percussion associated
with the elf, and a pleasant Love Theme for woodwinds over subdued synthesizer. The synthesizer is also used to create bizarre,
swirling rumbles during some of the sorcerous scenes. While the
pop beat of some of the cues may seem at odds with the period adventure, it is to Robertson's credit that his imaginative orchestrations and effective blend of symphonic and synthesizer music
works well here.

David Whitaker first came to note when he composed the
cheerful, breezy music for RUN WILD, RUN FREE (1969), and subsequently scored Amicus' forgettable SCREAM AND SCREAM AGAIN
(1970). Whitaker's music for Hammer's stylish DR. JEKYLL AND
SISTER HYDE (1971) is outstanding, and often suggestive of a
lilting Victorian waltz. The score is built around a single five-
note theme (two primary ascending notes echoed by three up-and-
down notes), which is put to very good use in a variety of deft
arrangements, particularly in the climax where the theme's melody
is taken by a concerto-style piano, backed with awesome, building
horn notes, rising majestically out of the piano melody and growing
to a rousing crescendo which ends the film in a powerful resolution. Whitaker also utilizes a variety of suspense cues, mostly involving vibrato strings under brass chords or rapid, stalking piano
notes.

The following year, Whitaker scored Hammer's VAMPIRE CIR-
CUS, underlining the film's magical tone and tempo with a highly
romantic score which included a violin theme, best heard when
young Jenny marvels at the splendor of Mitterhouse's Castle, and
a pulse-pounding cathedral organ theme. Whitaker also scored OLD
DRACULA (1975), combining elements of humor and horror with a
contemporary tone; and in 1982 composed a pleasant mixture of sor-

cerous horror and lighthearted adventure for THE SWORD AND THE
SORCERER. The music here is dominated by a proud, Militaristic
Theme for string and brass over percussion, often embellished with
a prominent xylophone. The score also includes a lyrical Love Theme
for violin notes over weaving strings, and a number of eerie, atmospheric passages for low woodwinds, weird string rustlings, and
the like.

In 1972, when Warner Brothers, Hammer's American distributor, convinced the British studio to make a pair of contemporary
Dracula films geared to the rock-and-roll crowd, the moody Gothic
atmospheres of James Bernard were replaced with loud rock music
that, while in keeping with the film's milieu and theme, failed to
underscore the film's drama in any way. Michael Vickers, a former
member of the Manfred Mann rock group with no previous film experience, was called in to score DRACULA A.D. 1972, providing a
grating, pop-jazz score which was awkward, drastically out of
place, distracting in the fight scenes, and overall sounding more
like TV cop-show muzak. Vickers later provided similar musical
carpeting for Amicus' AT THE EARTH'S CORE (1976) and WARRI-
ORS OF ATLANTIS (1978).

The second modern-day vampire movie, THE SATANIC RITES
OF DRACULA (1974), which--due to the awful reception given the
first film--was not released in American until many years later, under a variety of other names, utilized a pop score for strings over
a rock drum and tambourine beat, by American composer John
Cacavas. Born in South Dakota, Cacavas had gained experience
as an arranger for several popular singers and groups, including
The 101 Strings and similar bands. One of Cacavas' first film
scores, composed while working in Europe, was HORROR EXPRESS,
for which he provided a pop theme and a numbr of suspenseful
passages employing electric guitar, percussion, and a soft, tender
theme for strings and woodwind.

Hammer's ambitious action adventure film, CAPTAIN KRONOS,
VAMPIRE HUNTER (1974) featured a rousing score by Laurie John-
son, a notable composer born in Hampstead, London, in 1927, who
had studied at the Royal College of Music, where he later taught.
After World War II, Johnson served in the Band of the Coldstream
Guards, and embarked on a professional career in the 50's, composing and arranging for a variety of big bands. In 1956, he began
scoring films and television, one of his earliest being the heavily
Herrmannesque score for Ray Harryhausen's THE FIRST MEN IN
THE MOON (1964). Herrmann's influence is not at all unusual in
this film, in view of the fact that he and Johnson had been close
friends since the early 60's, and that Herrmann's music had been
so profoundly effective in Harryhausen's previous four films.
Johnson's score was replete with a loud, brassy, pounding theme,
its Herrmannesque rolling waves driving the music along at a relentless pace, relieved only by occasional quiet, swirling tones

from harp and woodwinds. One reviewer described Johnson's music for this film as being a "grand audio experience with deep notes of a concert-hall organ added to an orchestra of woodwind, brass and percussion to create a powerful and ominous sounding theme."[19]

Johnson had also achieved much popularity earlier in composing for the television series THE AVENGERS. Johnson created the rousing, jazzy main theme with its thudding brass introduction and catchy strings over glockenspiel with pop drum beat, as well as similarly jazzy music for various episodes. Johnson scored episodes of THRILLER during the early 60's, as well as Kubrick's DR. STRANGELOVE (1963), matching the film's satire with cues such as a thunderous, militaristic rendition of "When Johnny Comes Marching Home" during the bomb-run sequence. His score for CAPTAIN KRONOS featured a main theme comprised of urgent string notes under cavalrylike trumpet calls emphasizing the crusading adventure of the Vampire Hunter. Johnson also adapted Bernard Herrmann's IT'S ALIVE music for the posthumous sequel, IT'S ALIVE AGAIN (1978).

Paul Glass composed an eerie score for TO THE DEVIL ... A DAUGHTER (1976), featuring droning, reprocessed orchestral tones, atonal choral motifs and bell tones to achieve a weird, unearthly mood. The sound is somewhat reminiscent of the Ligeti motifs used in 2001: A SPACE ODYSSEY. The choir is heard in more triumphant fashion, no longer weird and harsh but victorious, over strong brass and tympani, during the end titles. The score was used sparingly, heard only in about one-fourth of the film; the remainder is given a strange contrasting quality by the absence of music.

A variety of other composers, although with less regularity or less remarkable results, have touched upon Hammer's horror output over the years, including Gerard Schurmann, Tristram Cary, John McCabe, Carlos Martelli, and others. Their efforts have characterized much of the Hammer mystique and have made an important contribution to horror film music, similar in character to the distinctive sound of the Universal horror films of the 40's.

Just as Hammer Films achieved a reputation for producing notable horror pictures, in the mid-60's a second, smaller company began to make a name for itself through the production of horror films. The company was Amicus Productions, and, unlike Hammer, their films were not characterized by the richly Gothic atmospheres and sensual portrayals found in the films of the established company. Instead, through a variety of anthology films set in contemporary themes, Amicus began to establish a favorable reputation within the genre.

The most prominent composer for Amicus' terror films was Douglas Gamley, whose classically styled scores lent a pleasingly

somber and apprehensive atmosphere to the films. Gamley began to
score motion pictures in the late 50's, including a fantasy-comedy,
ONE WISH TOO MANY, in 1956. Two years later he teamed up
with fellow composer, Ken Jones, to provide the instrumental music for George Pal's TOM THUMB, an American film partially filmed
in England. The composers musically reinforced the whimsical mood
evoked by the film. Another collaboration with Jones resulted in
the score for HORROR HOTEL (U.S. 1963), which featured a variety of motifs, including a jazzy cue for serpentine-warbling saxophone and woodwind over tympani and electric guitar plucks as
the girl tries to flee from the hotel. The score also makes prominent use of a dirgelike, choral Chanting Motif, often accompanied
by a lonely, tolling bell, representing the witches' coven. A chorus
of heavenly voices overwhelms it as the power of Good is restored
at the film's finale; the concluding choir melody also contains a suggestion of the Dies Irae.

In the early 70's, Gamley began to work for Amicus, beginning with their hit, TALES FROM THE CRYPT (1971). After a
Gothic organ rendition of Bach's Toccata & Fugue in D Minor over
the main titles, Gamley draws on various musical styles for the individual episodes. His use of a muzak-type rendition of Christmas
carols heard over the family radio for the first segment, in which
the woman who has just murdered her husband is menaced by an
escaped lunatic in a Santa Claus outfit, was appropriate and frightening. As one reviewer wrote: "The music takes on a maddening
contrast as events take a distinctly unseasonal turn and achieved
a scary effectiveness."[20] Elsewhere, Gamley utilizes music ranging
from classical to jazz with satisfying results, including a sentimental theme during the "Poetic Justice" segment, which poignantly
underscores the heartache of the kind old man who is being unfairly persecuted by a mean businessman; even in the last half of this
episode, in which the old man, driven to suicide, returns from the
grave to wreak a hearty vengeance upon his tormentor, retains this
quiet, understated mood.

Gamley scored the film's sequel, THE VAULT OF HORROR
(1972), along similar lines. Likewise, Amicus' next anthology film,
ASYLUM (1972), was given separate treatments for each segment,
although much of the music was based on the classical works of
Mussorgsky. Often the score utilized rapidly swirling strings over
plucked violins capped with a brass punch, a slow-moving, plodding
theme that is mixed with a very classical motif bracketed with
chilling string swirls and loud brass crashes. The slow, lumbering motif is very foreboding--suggestive, like so many other horror
scores, of some vague monstrosity walking ever onward, ever nearer. ASYLUM had an exceptionally moody and memorable score.

Gamley's score for THE LAND THAT TIME FORGOT (1975),
Amicus' first foray into the prehistoric territory of Edgar Rice
Burroughs, is also comprised of a variety of motifs--characterized

by slow-moving, lethargic, undulating rhythms from the lower scale --without any dominating "theme" as such. A lighter motif for harp and woodwind is heard as the U-boat first sights the island of Caprona, while rhythmic, driving string chords opposite woodwind phrases mingle with dinosaur roars in the monster-attack scenes. Gamley's music evokes strong moods of somber anticipation from the very start, setting the stage for the terrors to come, and lends a powerful throb when they arrive. His music is particularly well-suited to the dark and macabre subjects filmed by Amicus.

Another composer who scored several of Amicus' earlier films, including their first horror anthology, DR. TERROR'S HOUSE OF HORRORS (1964), was Elisabeth Lutyens, who started into a music career in order "to be independent of family influences." Daughter of famous architect Sir Edwin Lutyens, Elisabeth entered the film industry in 1944 and went on to score numerous films, radio and television shows, as well as a variety of concert works. In 1964, she was awarded the CBE Medal (Companion of the British Empire). "She has constant energy," reports the British Film Archives, "and works with ceaseless activity and a perfectionist's insistence on accuracy of detail."

Lutyens said she enjoys writing music for horror films, explaining: "They're fun to do. What is difficult is having to write in an 18th-century style, when required, since this involves eight-bar phrases and, as one does not make a cut at a beginning or ending of such bars, it means writing more than wanted in order to 'cut it.'"[21] Lutyens' music embellished such early Amicus films as THE SKULL and THE PSYCHOPATH (both 1965), as well as Hammer's PARANOIAC (1963), for which she provided what has been described as "spidery music" of a very modern style.

Amicus' I, MONSTER (1970) was given a moody score by Carl Davis, a Brooklyn-born composer who started working in British films and television in the mid-60's, and has since become noted for his award-winning music from THE FRENCH LIEUTENANT'S WOMAN (1981). Davis also scored several semifantasy comedies in the early 70's, and in 1971 received an Emmy Award nomination for his score for the television movie THE SNOW GOOSE. Davis' I, MONSTER score embraces the film with a subtle musical backdrop, culminating in a slow, weaving violin-and-woodwind theme as Blake, the Mr. Hyde character, reverts back to Marlowe, casting the denouement in a quiet, bittersweet, quasi-melodic musical tone.

Amicus' second Edgar Rice Burroughs picture, AT THE EARTH'S CORE (1976), received a jangling electronic pop score by Michael Vickers, hardly appropriate for a film set in Victorian times, although the use of symphonic instruments in the main title disguises this somewhat. The third Burroughs film was more akin to the moods of Gamley's score for their first Burroughs epic, composed by John Scott: THE PEOPLE THAT TIME FORGOT (1977) was given a variety of distinctive themes, whereas Gamley, in the earlier picture, relied mostly on unrelated atmospheres and Vickers, in the second merely rolled out a bouncing rhythm. Scott provided an introductory theme for solo horn over strings, which leads into a slow-moving, ponderous but essentially melodic string theme. A slow motif for oboe with a subdued melody acts as a love theme, and the score also features an appealing horn theme over rhythmic, driving string chords and pounding tympani; a rousing motif for loud, piping brasses (which somewhat preludes Scott's later brassy theme for THE FINAL COUNTDOWN); and a graceful motif for strings heard as the amphibian soars out of Caprona at the film's conclusion.

This was Scott's only score for Amicus, although the composer has earned a reputation as a gifted genre composer in several other films both before and after his Amicus debut. Previously called Patrick John Scott in the late 60's, Scott was one of England's foremost jazz flute players. He began scoring films in 1965, and among his earliest assignments was the Sherlock Holmes/Jack the Ripper thriller, A STUDY IN TERROR, which was dominated by a twangy, electric guitar tune. The orchestration seemed somewhat weak in this early score, and as a result the music tended to bog down and failed to really move. The weaknesses of A STUDY IN TERROR were short-lasting, however, as Scott's magnificent score for THE FINAL COUNTDOWN (1980) infuses that film with a proud, brassy theme sustaining much of its excitement and drama. This theme opens with a swelling, jubilant brass fanfare and quickly grows into a massive, powerful horn melody. The theme is later given a superb arrangement over rhythmic string-and-percussion beats as the aircraft carrier, flung back in time, prepares to battle the Japanese fleet, giving it an excitement that bristles with anxious preparation.

This glorious main theme dominates the score, and Scott intended it to represent the huge nuclear aircraft itself. "I had to bring out in music the majesty of the ship," Scott said, "and the excitement of being on board this magnificent war machine. I had to paint a picture of it in music--the way that it stirs your imagination."[22]

Scott was initially brought in from England to score the film in New York, although at that time production had not been completed and he was forced to work to a large extent only from storyboards. The filmmakers wanted Scott to regard the bizarre storm that sends the U.S.S. <u>Nimitz</u> and its crew back in time as a major element which should be referred to in his score. They asked the composer to regard it in the same way as the shark in JAWS, "a presence that is not seen, just felt," Scott said. "That was extremely helpful in motivating my thinking."[23] Scott composed a haunting pan-pipe sounding theme, which he played himself on an ocarina, although the instrument is barely audible beneath the

strumming violin rhythm and brass/woodwind phrases. A Love
Theme, for the romance between crewmember Owens and 40's-era
Laurel, is first heard for woodwind over strings, and later given
an eerie, thereminlike arrangement (achieved through strings and
percussion effects) during the finale, combining the Romantic
Theme with an ethereal suggestion of the fantastic time-shift which
brought them together.

Scott's next genre score was quite a contrast to THE FINAL
COUNTDOWN. Whereas in that film he had concentrated solely on
symphonic instruments, occasionally to achieve electroniclike effects,
his music for INSEMINOID (1981) was created purely through an
array of synthesizers. The music for this quirky ALIEN-inspired
science fiction horror picture is a mixture of jazzy rock rhythms
and atonal, eerie synthesizer motifs.

Among Amicus' earliest efforts was DR. WHO AND THE
DALEKS (1965), a feature version of the popular BBC television
program. The film was scored by Malcolm Lockyer in a semipop
style in keeping with that of the TV series. In addition, electronic
music was provided by Barry Gray, a veteran of Gerry Anderson's
"marionation" TV shows such as FIREBALL XL-5. A similar arrangement occurred between Gray and Lockyer the following year
on ISLAND OF TERROR. The two did not actually collaborate--
Lockyer simply composed the symphonic music while Gray indepen-
dently supplied the necessary electronic cues on tape. While Gray
remained primarily in television (more details in Chapter XI), Lockyer went on to score several low-budget horror films, including
ISLAND OF THE BURNING DAMNED (1967), for which he provided
a loud and rhythmic, pop-styled theme for brass melody over harsh
drum beats, which seemed at odds with the dark moody horror of
the picture. Lockyer also scored episodes of the 1973 DR. WHO
series.

A variety of other composers have made significant contributions to genre film music in England outside of the memorable halls
of Hammer and Amicus. Although not essentially a composer, Muir
Mathieson was one of the most prominent music directors and con-
ductors in British films. Born in Scotland, Mathieson became a
music director for major British studios in 1931, and his name became synonymous with the development of film music in England.
Until his death in 1975, Mathieson conducted the scores of more
than 600 films, and was also known as a conductor of opera, ballet
and theater, conducting most of the great orchestras in England
and abroad. Mathieson also wrote and directed many educational
films about musical instruments, and was awarded the CBE Medal
for his services to music. Among the notable fantastic film scores
conducted by Mathieson are Bliss' THINGS TO COME (1936),
Rozsa's THIEF OF BAGDAD (1940), Parker's CURSE OF THE DEMON
(1956) and Salzedo's REVENGE OF FRANKENSTEIN (1958).

Malcolm Arnold was noted for his concert works, particularly symphonies, chamber music and ballets. Born in Northampton in 1921, Arnold was educated at the Royal College of Music and in Italy. He began his career as a trumpet soloist with the London Philharmonic, and composed the ballet "Homage to the Queen" for the 1953 coronation. Arnold began scoring films in 1949, and eventually won an Academy Award for his music for THE BRIDGE ON THE RIVER KWAI (1957), known primarily for its catchy, whistled "Colonel Bogey March." Arnold scored a few fantasy films, such as the quirky NIGHT MY NUMBER CAME UP (1955), a somewhat forgotten film about a man whose dreams start to come true; a film that was something along the lines of a TWILIGHT ZONE episode in concept, though not in execution, and in this sense one reviewer commented that "only Malcolm Arnold's score approximates the chilly tenor of the better TWILIGHT ZONEs."[24] Arnold's music for the prophetic 1984 (1955) is characterized by a rhythmic, pounding brass theme that surges forth, suggestive of Orwell's controlled and authoritarian futuristic environment.

Robert Elms wrote the music for a couple of English science fiction films, including THE MAN WITHOUT A BODY (1958), which featured an interesting, harsh three-note brass theme mixed with a five-note string and woodwind motif, to achieve its sense of terror.

Australian-born Ron Grainer has scored many British films and television series, including the popular theme for the DR. WHO series, THE PRISONER, and the more recent ROALD DAHL'S TALES OF THE UNEXPECTED. Grainer's score to THE OMEGA MAN (1971) relied primarily on a heavy rock tune as well as a variety of percussionistic sound effects, including the use of water bell plates, which produce the unusual sound of a tone dropping off at the end, achieved by striking one of the chimelike plates and immediately dipping it into water, a technique used previously to great effect by Michel Legrand in ICE STATION ZEBRA and by Michel Colombier in COLOSSUS, THE FORBIN PROJECT.

Paul Giovanni, a musician from New York with theatrical experience, was hired to score THE WICKER MAN (1973), providing a number of folk songs based on Scottish musical traditions. As the film concerns itself with the clash of stoic Christian beliefs and pagan ritualistic beliefs, the music underlines the pagan tradition of the Scottish islanders visited by Howie, the Christian investigator. As one reviewer noted: "...the potent blend of folk songs and traditional melodies ... became the Greek chorus for the drama that followed."[25] The songs have a particularly notable effect as they signify to the naive Howie the strangeness of their belief system, as he sees it, and they emphasize the sexuality inherent in their fertility rites.

Because of the importance of the film's music, Giovanni

was brought into the project early; he composed all of the music before the film even started shooting, after he had spent a great deal of time tediously researching traditional Scottish and English folk music. The songs were then recorded and played during filming, at which time the actors would lip-sync the songs as needed. British composer Marc Wilkinson (who's done an occasional horror picture himself, such as BLOOD ON SATAN'S CLAW, 1971), gave Giovanni some guidance on the technical aspects of film scoring.

Giovanni avoids the usual motion picture mood music on the assumption that traditional film scoring approaches would create artificial tension or would telegraph upcoming action. In THE WICKER MAN, the music does not play up to the drama of the visual action, but instead underlines the ritualistic paganism of the main characters with a variety of songs scored for authentic traditional instruments. Giovanni also composed an original May Day march, taking the melody of an old fourteenth-century song, "Willy of Winsbury," and forming it into a piece for the London Symphony's brass section. "I wanted a waltz, in three[-time]," Giovanni said, "so that it could be slower and stranger and that the whole procession could sort of sway. Just after that, the 'burning' music, also used over the anointing scenes, prominently uses the Celtic harp.... To give the film a bizarre ending, that they should be singing a happy song while Howie is dying, we worked the May Day procession tune in brass and fit it harmonically with the 'summer ich iccumin in' lyric so that the instruments and voices blend on the two different pieces."[26]

Giovanni's unique musical style for THE WICKER MAN provided a unique score and an intrinsic element in the film's effectiveness. As producer Peter Snell described the music, "it's haunting, and an unorthodox way to do it, but the music is probably alien to anything you have ever heard on film before."[27]

Paul Ferris provided a lovely theme for WITCHFINDER GENERAL (1967, released in America the following year as THE CONQUEROR WORM). The music is drawn from a medieval-sounding "Greensleeves"-type melody which was quite effective in this film concerning Puritanical witch hunts. Excerpts of the music were later reused in British TV commercials and series such as MINDER (1979). Ferris' music for THE CREEPING FLESH (1973) took a similar approach, as one reviewer noted: "The main theme ... was an eerie off-key waltz that drifted in and out to echo the madness that was the key to the entire plotline. Ferris' style was once more simple, direct and melodious, yet definitely macabre in its impact."[28]

Paris Rutherford, in his single genre score, provided in CRUCIBLE OF TERROR (1972) an impressive ominousness through the use of a furtive, two-note ascending woodwind figure, building

over pounding drums, growing in tempo and force into warbling
woodwind shrieks, which themselves give way to a solo brass melody over tympani, snare drums, cymbal and pounding keyboard.
A jazzy arrangement of the theme follows, which is less effective
with its steady beat.

From the Gothic imagery of James Bernard and Douglas Gamley, to the unique and diverse styles of Scott, Johnson, Giovanni
and others, British horror films have maintained a rich musical
heritage, providing much of the most evocative applications of film
music in the genre, and retaining the unique qualities of the distinctively British fantastic cinema.

Notes

1. Bill Littman, "DRACULA--His Music," Photon #27 (1977) p. 42

2. James Bernard interviewed by Bruce G. Hallenbeck and John
       McCarty, Little Shoppe of Horrors #6 (July 1981) p. 40

3. Bill Littman, loc. cit.

4. Ibid.

5. Donald C. Willis, Horror and Science Fiction Films II (Metuchen,
       N.J.: Scarecrow Press, 1982) p. 175

6. James Bernard interviewed by Ed Mumma and Neil Leadbeater,
       Fantasmagoria #2 (1972) p. 8

7. Ibid., p. 10

8. Ibid.

9. _____, op. cit. #2, p. 42

10. Robert E. Seletsky, "Double-Take," Photon #27 (1977) p. 21

11. James Bernard, op. cit., p. 42

12. Ibid., p. 40

13. Michael Carreras quoted by Richard Klemensen, "Hammer:
       Yesterday and Today--The Music," Little Shoppe of Horrors
       #4 (April 1978) p. 91

14. Uncredited writer, "Hammer's Mummy," Movie Monsters #1
       (1974), p. 67

15. Stephen R. Pickard, "The Music of Hammer," Little Shoppe of Horrors #3 (1974) p. 29

16. Richard Klemensen, "An Old Favorite Censored," Fandom's Film Gallery #3 (Hove, Belgium: Jan Van Genechten, 1978) p. 163

17. Harry Robertson paraphrased by Richard Klemensen, op. cit., p. 93

18. _____ interviewed by Bruce G. Hallenbeck, Little Shoppe of Horrors #7 (December 1982) p. 51-52 (and following quote)

19. Doug Raynes, "Record review," Soundtrack! The Collector's Quarterly #25 (Spring, 1981) p. 8

20. Allan Bryce, "The Music of the Macabre," Soundtrack! The Collector's Quarterly #22 (Summer 1980) p. 21

21. Elisabeth Lutyens interviewed in Sight and Sound, (Autumn 1974) (quoted by Chuck Wilson, letter to author, August 1, 1975)

22. John Scott quoted in, "An Added Dimension for THE FINAL COUNTDOWN," United Artists Corp. press release, June 26, 1980

23. Ibid.

24. Donald C. Willis, op. cit., p. 279

25. Allan Bryce, loc. cit.

26. Paul Giovanni quoted by David Bartholomew, "THE WICKER MAN," Cinefantastique Vol. 6, #3 (Winter 1977) p. 36

27. Peter Snell quoted by David Bartholomew, ibid., p. 34

28. Allan Bryce, op. cit., p. 11

IX

BAXTER, CORMAN & CO.

While Hammer was establishing itself as Britain's foremost producer of horror films, a small studio in Hollywood was gaining a
similar reputation through the frequent release of effective, if often
overly exploitative, horror pictures. Largely through the work of
producer Roger Corman and his series of macabre Edgar Allan Poe
films, American International Pictures (AIP) spawned a prolific run
of successful, low-budget genre offerings during the late 50's and
60's. The majority of these films were scored by Les Baxter, a
productive and highly versatile craftsman who composed the music
for dozens of films, of every type, for AIP during his stay at the
studio from 1959 until 1974.

Born in Texas in 1922, Baxter gained an interest in the piano
at an early age. He studied at the Detroit Conservatory of Music
and later at Los Angeles' Pepperdine College before working as an
arranger for famous bandleaders in the 40's, and ultimately in radio
and films. Baxter's career has been as varied as the films on which
he has worked. In addition to scoring motion pictures, Baxter recorded a series of exotic and easy-listening albums for Capitol
Records, as well as arranging the records of many other artists,
and has written show music for theme parks and sea worlds, all of
which has provided him with an arena for his penchant toward
experimentalism. This inclination was particularly suited to science
fiction and horror films, and it is with these films that Baxter's
reputation is linked the strongest.

Baxter feels that horror films present fewer restrictions to
a composer because of the variety of orchestral colors available.
"With a horror score," Baxter said, "the melodies can go much
farther out. The notes can be extremely strange, and that gives
you a lot of leeway. You can be as far out or as weird as you
want to, musically. The orchestration and the colors have to be
-more unusual and that of course is a pleasure for any composer."[1]

Baxter's first horror score was THE BLACK SLEEP, in 1956,
and was followed by several other since-forgotten genre pictures.
In 1959, when he moved to American International, the first score
he composed was for GOLIATH AND THE BARBARIANS, an apt
vehicle for his exotic talents which got his AIP career off to a

<u>Les Baxter</u>. Photograph courtesy BAX Music.

rousing start. The film, made in Italy during the surge of muscle-
man pictures, was imported by AIP and the original Italian musical
score was replaced with Baxter's composition. The score revolves
around a brassy theme which propels the action scenes with a
proud, victorious march. Baxter also provided an exotic Love
Theme for woodwind, harp and triangle, as well as a pair of sumptuous, archaic dance numbers. The score was highly successful--
so much so that AIP reused portions of it in subsequent imports,
GOLIATH AND THE DRAGON (1960) and GOLIATH AND THE VAM-
PIRES (1962).

In 1960, Baxter commenced his most acclaimed work for AIP
in the first of Roger Corman's Edgar Allan Poe films, THE FALL
OF THE HOUSE OF USHER. The Poe movies retained the same
primary crew throughout, and their talents combined to convey a
claustrophobic atmosphere appropriate to Poe's mysterious tales of
terror.

One reviewer has noted that, in the Corman Poe films, "Baxter liked to juxtapose brooding themes and sinister orchestrations
with sudden, sharp musical shock tactics for scenes such as where
a coffin is opened to reveal the owner was a cataleptic. For the
nightmare scene in USHER, we hear a wailing battery of ghost
choirs, a bold stroke on the part of the composer.... PIT AND
THE PENDULUM emerges as more startlingly effective musically
than USHER, with Baxter's exceptional flair for the macabre contrasting fleetingly with the haunting theme for Elizabeth (yet
another deceased character who won't lie down). The end-title,
perhaps a little controversial, takes the form of a lavish arrangement of Elizabeth's theme. Some may feel such an ending inappropriate for a Poe story, others may feel the 'contrast' of the
music a fair idea, inasmuch as the horrific happenings are over."[2]

Each of the Poe films was vastly different from the others,
although there was an overall brooding continuity between the films,
as Baxter described: "THE FALL OF THE HOUSE OF USHER was
full orchestra and choir. I used choir to represent the ancient
souls coming out of the castle, and so forth. It had a brooding-
and-then-going-into-flames kind of sound. In THE PIT AND THE
PENDULUM I used some stark atonal writing--which is, to simplify
somewhat, one or two or three lines, say in the manner of a fugue,
each playing very unmelodic and unrelated notes, one to the other,
which makes for very strange music. I also did something that
had been called very advanced, which was the assortment of instruments on the main titles striking in tape reverb. You had random,
sparse, different sounds hitting in tape reverb, rather than music.
At the end, I had the enormous, swinging pendulum sound done
with the orchestra, and for the huge walls I wanted to have a massive sound of metal or stone grating on stone; I did that with the
orchestra, a very slow, massive, undulating dissonance that seemed
to move slowly but massively."[3]

The third Poe film was a trilogy, TALES OF TERROR (1962), in which Baxter scored two somber tales and one comic interlude. This middle episode, "The Black Cat," demonstrated Baxter's flair for macabre comedy, utilizing some clever "mewing" arrangements for the diabolic feline of the title. This musical flair was put to better use in THE RAVEN (1963), in which Baxter composed a great variety of comic motifs and little scherzos that suitably embellished the comical approach to the film's story of duelling wizards. "THE RAVEN was greatly comic," Baxter said. "Vincent Price does some things that are very tongue-in-cheek. He sidestepped the telescope on his way to see why the raven was pecking on the window, and he did a little funny dance side step going around it, so I simply could not resist playing it cartoon style."

There is a lot of mickey mousing in the score, closely following the actions of the screen characters, moving with their footsteps, colliding into obstacles, rising into a frenzy of woodwind and percussion as Price knocks over equipment in his laboratory. Baxter's musical tour-de-force during the whimsical duel of the sorcerers was especially delightful, with all manner of musical references, gags, pastiches and what-have-you cleverly patched together to form an amusing and delightful backdrop to the screen antics.

The comic approach to THE RAVEN was followed with a similarly zany score for A COMEDY OF TERRORS (1964). This score is built around a tongue-in-cheek use of Chopin's Funeral March, which pops up--like a reanimated corpse--every so often, appropriately enough for the professional undertakings of morticians Trumbull and Gillie. As with THE RAVEN, a variety of motifs and pastiches appear throughout the score in a well-crafted composition of macabre humor.

Amid the Poe films, Baxter scored one of his best-remembered films, MASTER OF THE WORLD (1961), lending it "a magnificently soaring main theme, marvellously descriptive of the flights and raids of Price's flying fortress, the Albatross,"[4] as one biographer put it. "When the balloon was in flight," Baxter said, "I had soaring arpeggios, harp and woodwinds going up and down, but not just in a simple manner. I like to write them interestingly or complex, so that they are doing something important and at the same time they're doing a rather simple effect. The strings did the same thing; they are rustled and led up and down scales, but on interesting notes, for flight."

For PANIC IN THE YEAR ZERO (1962), Baxter provided a score comprised of big band swing music, which gave an interesting backdrop to the story of a family struggling against lawlessness in a post-holocaust America. THE MAN WITH THE X-RAY EYES (1963) featured a striking sequence for female voices to accompany Ray Milland's supernatural visions, followed by a series

of agonizing shock chords as Milland takes the advice of St. Matthew's Gospel: "If thine own eye offend thee, pluck it out!" The
finale was a suite of previous themes arranged to convey an omnipresent mood of loneliness.

Like TALES OF TERROR, Mario Bava's BLACK SABBATH
(1964) allowed Baxter the opportunity to score three stories in
one. Filmed the previous year in Italy and scored there by Roberto
Nicolosi, AIP scrapped its original music when dubbing it into English, and had Baxter score the film fresh, a practice he had been
doing for some years at the studio. Given two weeks to provide
the complex music for BLACK SABBATH's trio of tales, Baxter provided a noteworthy score which ranks among his best work.

For the first segment, "A Drop of Water," the music surges
with swift, aggressive passages, as one reviewer has described:
"Deep string sounds and a bold brass motif [convey] nurse Helen's
fearsome haunting after stealing from a corpse in her charge.
The main theme becomes gradually more relentless as Helen tries
to escape from a ubiquitous dripping noise, and climaxes in a
weird, swirling organ concerto as the avenging spirit tears back
her ring."[5] The second episode, "The Telephone," begins "at a
busy and brutal pace--tingling pizzicato against driving bass
rhythms--with call-girl Rosy fighting for her life as a mysterious
intruder tries to gain access to her apartment. There's a soothing
interlude in the form of a romantic piano concerto (adapted from
the love theme heard in all three segments), but this soon sub-
sides into Baxter's typical musical 'shock tactics' as Rosy discovers
her flat mate dead in her bed." The third and longest episode,
"The Wurdalak," is a period piece scored for a mixture of romantic
and sinister, atonal music. "Baxter throws in the full spectrum of
his considerable horror repertoire and maintains interest and anticipation throughout ... the romantic elements are virtually eliminated with Sdenka's death, an agonized electronic rendering of her
theme ending sadly and weirdly."[6] The film closes with a lush arrangement of the Love Theme over the end titles, surreptitiously
drawing the three stories together thematically and closing the film
with a peaceful tranquility.

In addition to horrors such as these, Baxter scored "lighter"
science fiction films such as THE INVISIBLE BOY (1959) and
BATTLE BEYOND THE SUN (1963), lending them a more emphasized electronic scoring with fewer melodies and themes. "In the
science fiction category I'm more linear," Baxter explained, "more
stark, more synthesizers, more echoplex, which is similar to tape
reverb. They are mechanical, spacey-sounding themes."

In the mid-60's, AIP began to experiment with teenage beach-
party movies, and the inevitable mixing of these with horror and
science fiction subjects wasn't too far behind. Baxter was called
upon to score such silly pictures as DR. GOLDFOOT AND THE

GIRL BOMBS and GHOST IN THE INVISIBLE BIKINI in 1966, lending them interesting pop/rock scores appropriate to the visuals, which Baxter had a lot of fun with, enjoying the composition of "science fiction rock." By this time the Poe cycle had ended and American International veered away from the atmospheric horrors of the previous decade and concentrated much more on typical exploitation fare, often calling on contemporary, but little-known, pop groups to lend a few songs to films such as the DR. GOLDFOOT pair and WILD IN THE STREETS, for which Baxter provided incidental music and continuity cues.

The beach movies soon gave way to stories of the supernatural, and one of the first was THE DUNWICH HORROR (1969), loosely based on the H. P. Lovecraft novelette. Baxter provided a catchy pop score with a powerful and memorable main theme, dominated by synthesizer, although the poppiness of the rhythm did not always seem entirely appropriate to Lovecraft's cosmic horror (but, then, neither did the filmic adaptation). CRY OF THE BANSHEE (1970) had much more depth to its score, which was a rich, colorful composition varying from catchy melody to tender romantic interludes, to the brash, horrific passages Baxter is so effective with. Dominated by strings and occasional electronic effects, BANSHEE's music conjures up a great many weird images all by itself. The main theme is a powerful one, with occasional hints of Bernard Herrmann in its back-and-forth swerving strings, which aptly sum up the romance and horror of the story.

A TV movie, AN EVENING WITH EDGAR ALLAN POE (1970), reunited Baxter with the period atmospheres of the earlier Roger Corman Poe films, as well as giving him another multistory format. The music is composed for a small chamber group of strings and percussion, with a few woodwinds and electronic instruments added. The first segment, "The Tell-Tale Heart" is quite effective in its brooding suspense, utilizing mysterious, sustained, high string passages and plucked harp. "The Sphinx" appropriately opens with an Egyptian-flavored crescendo, seguing into a soft, eerie motif for woodwind, harp and keyboard, culminating in a maelstrom of synthesizers swirling over a muted, pounding percussion. "The Cask of Amontillado" opens with a brief festive passage before it follows its characters--the jovial wine taster and his malevolent companion--down into the catacombs to the "wine cellar." A festive musical phrase for flute returns occasionally, countered by shimmering strings which suggest the companion's intentions. The segment is nicely wrapped up with a three-note phrase by strings, as if to suggest the evildoer's "washing his hands" of the affair and walking away, leaving the wine taster walled in behind him. The final segment, "The Pit and the Pendulum," avoids musical references to the earlier Corman film, and is dominated by slowly swinging strings, sharply emphasizing the pendulum and its never-ending arc as it slowly draws nearer the throat of the bound victim. The eventual rescue is accompanied by jubilant bells, strings and harp.

Baxter's score for FROGS (1972) is a highly unique composition, in that he composed and performed it single-handedly utilizing actual frog sounds. "We thought it would be a very interesting experiment," Baxter said, "to score the film entirely with synthesized sounds, in this case recorded frog sounds. I taped frog sounds, slowed them down and used them, I think, intelligently and effectively."[7] The resultant score is brimming with weird, atonal, slowly oozing frog noises, vibrating eerily and creating a bizarre and unforgettable audio accompaniment. Baxter faced another single-handed assignment with his next score, BARON BLOOD (1972), another Italian import which Baxter rescored for American release. The music retains a bleak atmosphere with slowly paced, footsteplike brass chords over distant, echoing harp glissandos, mixed with piano and synthesizer. The keyboard and horns play off each other darkly until the theme is eventually taken by the piano and synthesizer, culminating at the film's end with blaring horns and pounded piano, seguing into eerie, atonal, processed keyboard spasms, bringing the score's previous elements together in a frightfully eerie and disturbing conclusion. The same year Baxter also scored a horror film called BLOOD SAB-BATH, using a small orchestra dominated by flute and guitar, but just as the film was being sold for release as YGALAH a fire destroyed all the original prints--except for Baxter's music, as the audio tapes were stored elsewhere.

After these films, Baxter retired (or "was retired" by Hollywood, as he remarks) and moved to Hawaii until he began to get some television assignments in the late 70's and returned to Hollywood, scoring episodes of CLIFFHANGERS and the BUCK ROGERS series. "BUCK ROGERS was somewhat tongue-in-cheek and yet very spacey and fun," Baxter recalled. "I wrote futuristic melodies and did some of the effects I did on the CLIFFHANGER series, which had a futuristic episode that gave me a lot of freedom. That series also had 'Dracula,' so I could use brooding and expressive string passages there, and the final one was an adventure, James Bondish kind of thing which had a little jazz-suspense feel to it. They were all vastly different."[8]

The CLIFFHANGER series utilized three composers working on alternating weeks, composing about 40 or 50 minutes of music to be used each week. Baxter wrote a new score every other episode, although he was asked to score the final segment of the "Curse of Dracula" episode when the other composers fell sick. "In the last segment we got to kill off Dracula, and I must tell you the orchestra really loved playing that last score," Baxter recalled. "At the end of the recording session, the orchestra had stood up and applauded, which is exceptionally rare in TV-scoring, to say the least. What I did, I simply threw in everything from my 'bag of tricks' (including a little Tannhäuser!) into that last episode. I just pulled out all the stops and let the orchestra go."[9]

In 1982, Baxter returned to feature films with a remarkable score for THE BEAST WITHIN, creating a mixture of synthesizers, conventional orchestral instruments, and a variety of amazingly eerie and fantastic sounds. "It was a tremendously long score, highly developed, nonrepetitious," Baxter said. "Synthesizers would do things that sound like moans of dreaded animal spirits from another world. More variety of sound from synthesizers than I think have ever been used. I used a lot of electronic music as well as strings; but the strings don't play a straight melody as they must in a comedy or a straight dramatic film. The melody is much more elusive. The music is quite violent and I think interesting; I think it contributes some solid and new sounds to music."[10]

The score is dominated by an eerie, synthesizer motif suggestive of the "beast within" as it gradually emerges, cicadalike, from its human host. As the beast grows and becomes more and more defined until finally breaking free, so does Baxter's theme become more pronounced and dominant in the film, reaching its fullest variation during the prolonged transformation sequence. This music opens with a low synthesizer rumbling underneath deep up-and-down piano notes, all amid occasional two-note horn blares; it eventually rises to a pulse-pounding apprehensiveness before seguing into a variety of suspenseful arrangements as the scene continues. The theme is an effective, repeated three-note motif ("DAH duh dom"). A more lyrical arrangement of the theme, scored for the title sequence, unfortunately was not used in the finished film, repeated with the more dissonant music of the transformation sequence. Baxter also made effective use of deep cello chords that start low and then rise up quickly to abruptly stop (this during the scene where Michael enters the barn to confront the unseen "beast"); and during the final sequence where the beast pursues Amanda through the forest, there is a notable use of rolling percussion capped with piano chords.

THE BEAST WITHIN demonstrates that Baxter hasn't lost his touch after a ten-year absence from the genre. "There are tricks," he explained. "There are orchestral sounds that one gets to know, and after one hears them a lot then one can develop on these sounds that one had used before. In other words, after you do the tried-and-true once, then you say 'oh, it would be nice if I added a low harp and a flute to that' or some other such combination. Then you create your own diversions, and each time you do that it gives you a new idea to create another orchestral sound. Suspense or terror in terms of a creature attacking is one kind of terror, and for attack usually the instruments are more active, busier, more pounding, or the tempo might be faster or more important. For a monster not attacking, the movement would not be there; it would simply be ominous, without the pounding characteristic. And for simple suspense--the animal is not lurking or attacking, he's just suspected--then it would be quite sparse."

From these basic ideas, Baxter develops often complex scores, creating spooky moods of tension and suspense through his music, yet remaining highly versatile from film to film, despite similarities in subject. "I wouldn't want all the pictures to sound alike" Baxter said. "Let's say you do five horror films in a row, you don't want them all to have the same kind of music, and each of my scores is vastly different. In some cases I used percussion and voices; others, brass and strings or a legit orchestra, others synthesizers." Along the same lines, Baxter doesn't feel that he's done too many horror films or has become unreasonably stereotyped. "The more you do in one genre, the more opportunity you have to be different and experiment. Bach wrote a lot of fugues, but after he'd done a few people didn't ask if he was a spent force. No, he carried on and wrote lots of others, brilliantly ... horror films, in fact, present far less restrictions to a composer because of the extreme range of orchestral color at your disposal. The hardest films to score are those like BORN AGAIN where nobody turns into a monster or develops X-ray vision, where there are no ghostly houses sinking into the swamp, etcetera. Straight movies are more exacting, one cannot be too indulgent in the instrumetation, and the drama and the situation have to be scored very accurately."[11]

While demonstrating his effectiveness at dramas such as BORN AGAIN, Baxter remains at his best and most innovative in the horror genre, proving himself time and again a major craftsman in the field of horror film music.

Another notable composer prolific at scoring low-budget horror films in a minimum amount of time is Ronald Stein. Unrelated to Herman Stein, who scored for Universal in the 50's, Ronald began his musical career in St. Louis as the assistant director and soloist at the Municipal Opera. In 1954 he came to Hollywood to try to become a film composer, and after several unsuccessful attempts to gain entry into the studios, Stein was offered an assignment by Roger Corman.

Among Stein's earliest genre efforts was the score for IT CONQUERED THE WORLD (1956), which he composed for symphony orchestra supplemented with electronics--in the form of an oscillator, a wave-form generator with which Stein achieved eerie, high-pitched sounds. These were particularly evocative during a scene in which wild birds emerge from the cucumber-monster and attack helpless extras. "This particular scene," Stein recalled, "I scored with swirling flutes above the rest of the orchestra while these birds were attacking. Then I overdubbed that with piccolos played by the same three flutists an octave higher, and then I overdubbed that an octave higher with the oscillator, and since most of the music was trills, I could set the frequencies and just move my hand nervously on the oscillator at that frequency and then slide to the next frequency in time with the music. I used electronics that way, which I suppose is about the crudest way a person could ever do it...."[12]

Another early horror score was NOT OF THIS EARTH (1956), for which Stein composed a score based on a four-note motif resembling the theme of Beethoven's Fifth Symphony. "That was one of the few times I wrote a fugue," Stein said. "You don't very often get a chance to experiment with classic forms of music in films, and you shouldn't unless the scene gives you the opportunity."

Stein used a theremin in THE DAY THE WORLD ENDED (1956), which was played by Dr. Samuel Hoffman (who had played the instrument for Miklos Rozsa in SPELLBOUND and for Ferde Grofé in ROCKETSHIP X-M). In Stein's score, however, the theremin was used as a solo instrument playing the melody, rather than as a piece of orchestration or underscoring as in the manner of Rosza and others.

Stein used electric violin in THE SHE CREATURE (1956), in addition to seven gongs called "tam-tams," which created a uniquely unearthly sound for the monster's appearances: "I guess for me, as the She-Creature appeared from the ocean," Stein said, "she appeared with the sound of splashing Chinese gongs. At least that was my feeling, but the point is, I didn't just use one-- I used different pitches and combinations at different appropriate times." ATTACK OF THE CRAB MONSTERS (1957) supplemented a full orchestra with an organ, while in ATTACK OF THE 50-FOOT WOMAN (1958), Stein provided an exotic, classically romantic theme played in a slow, ponderously moving way, similar in concept to Albert Glasser's lumbering theme for the similar AMAZING COLOSSAL MAN (1957).

Stein enjoyed the opportunity to write a comic score for INVASION OF THE SAUCER MEN (1957): "I loved doing that," he recalled, "especially the main title theme, which was played on the xylophone--a kind of Flight of the Bumble Bee, except there's another tune going on in the orchestra. I had a chance to do some comedy there with the drunken farmer, the saucer men stabbing his cattle with alcohol, and various things like that. No matter what you imagine musically, the music has to enhance whatever is happening dramatically." Another score to use comedy was DINOSAURUS (1960), which had some effective mickey mousing when the caveman inspects the modern house. "I used four instruments for that treatment--that's almost like doing a TV comedy show. I wrote some nice heroic dinosaur music, but the theme was drowned out pretty much by the sound effects."

An effective score was composed by Stein for AIP's THE PREMATURE BURIAL (1962). (Some sources, incidentally, credit this as a collaboration with Les Baxter; but Stein, in fact, scored the entire picture, the only Baxter material being the reused AIP signature music, heard when their logo appears on the screen prior to the main titles.) For this movie, Stein combined his theme with the song, "Molly Malone," which is performed by a whistler and woven into the score in a variety of deft orchestrations. THE HAUNTED PALACE (1963) was given a "classic Frankenstein type of romantic theme with Tchaikovskian overtones," as Stein put it, used quite well during the scenes where Vincent Price strides the endless hallways of the mansion. The music was written primarily for the lower instruments, with trumpet figures counterpointed above them. THE TERROR (1963) was similarly scored for lower instruments, evoking an ominous, richly foreboding sound: "It's the only two times I've written the main theme in the bass," Stein said, "with other kinds of movement of music above it. It's a challenge to do that. You won't hear many themes in movies in which the harmony and other melodic lines are playing above the tune. It's not done too often." Stein also composed an effective score for Francis Ford Coppola's first film, an axe-murderer movie called DEMENTIA 13 (1963). Twenty years later Stein found the opportunity to return to the genre with a wild comic score for FRANKENSTEIN'S GREAT AUNT TILLIE (1984), a horror satire.

While equally prolific in Westerns and youth-oriented movies, Stein enjoyed the opportunity to write unusual music for horror films. "I was able to experiment," he said, "to write in styles that are perhaps more modern and strident and dissonant than many film scores that we hear. When everything is crumbling down or the monster is eating a person, I think that's a rather dissonant occasion! It calls for extreme treatments inside the music, as long as it all fits together. Science fiction music is a wonderfully exciting experience for a composer because, as science fiction is in the beyond and near the impossible, you can think in the beyond and practically the impossible, and you have the chance to achieve something new."

Fred Katz also provided some effective scores for small AIP movies of the 60's. Born in Brooklyn in 1919, Katz had gotten his start as a musician and arranger for various popular singers during the 50's, finally becoming involved with the Chico Hamilton Quintet in the later 50's. He moved into motion pictures when director Alexander Mackendrick selected the Quintet to perform the jazz music for THE SWEET SMELL OF SUCCESS (1957), which Katz had written, supplementing the Elmer Bernstein score. The jazz music impressed filmmaker Roger Corman, who subsequently hired Katz to write the music to his horror quickie, A BUCKET OF BLOOD (1959). Katz provided a fairly jazzy score, much of which was performed on saxophone by Paul Horn. Katz wrote in a suspenseful vein, appropriate to the visual action, but using a jazz idiom.

THE WASP WOMAN (1959) followed, and Katz provided an

effective "hook," comprised of a suspended series of atonal chords, used each time the girl turned into a wasp. Katz's music was also heard in Corman's memorable LITTLE SHOP OF HORRORS (1960), although in this case the economy-minded producer simply had a music editor piece the score together from the previous pictures Katz had done for Corman. A similar practice resulted in Katz's music being used in THE CREATURE FROM THE HAUNTED SEA (1961).

Katz did not especially enjoy scoring these horror pictures, looking at them primarily as a means to gain experience toward writing for the concert stage, which is what he does currently. "I hated every picture that Corman did," Katz recollected recently, "but you've got to be a professional about this. This is what you have to do, and you do it to the best of your ability. I wrote to the top of what I could write. You never write down. I don't care what job you get, you always write to the top, because that's what integrity's all about."[13] Katz, too, found these low-budget films advantageous in providing opportunities to experiment. "Some of the most experimental and avant-garde music came out of them," he said, "because you figured: 'you've got nothing to lose, let's try something different!' You weren't getting paid that much, of course; I did it for the experience. I did a film called WASP WOMAN and I said, 'let me experiment with this, let me try coming out with different musical ideas,' and that's what I did."

Paul Dunlap provided effective musical scores for a number of low-budget horror and science fiction films of the 50's and 60's. Dunlap had originally trained to be a classical composer, studying briefly under Toch and Boulanger. His film career started when he was recommended to director Sam Fuller, who eventually hired him to score a number of his films.

Dunlap's earliest notable fantasy score was for THE LOST CONTINENT (1951), Lippert studio's low-low prehistoric adventure. The music was especially good for this otherwise unremarkable picture, particularly during lengthy mountain-climbing scenes. Dunlap also had the advantage of a fairly good-sized orchestra, comprised of about 50 musicians. In 1957, he began a fruitful association with exploitation producer Herman Cohen when he scored I WAS A TEENAGE WEREWOLF. For this youth-oriented horror film, Dunlap tried to supply an original sound without the use of electronics, which at that time were not in prevalent use or development. "It's quite easy now to provide a film with the right atmosphere," Dunlap said recently, "because all the electronic gear is at hand. In those days, we had to do those sounds with a small orchestra. In the score for I WAS A TEENAGE WEREWOLF, with that twenty-man band or whatever it was, I was trying assiduously to create new sounds in the orchestra, and that's very difficult to do when you're limited that way."[14]

I WAS A TEENAGE WEREWOLF and the similar Cohen films that followed were geared towards a youthful audience, and the music to a degree reflected this in the use of, usually, at least one party scene with a rock band playing. Dunlap did not want the rock music to interfere with the symphonic approach he took elsewhere in the film, however, and took care to avoid any such conflicts. "You can't create any tension with that, you'd defeat the whole purpose," he said. "The minute you go to a foot-tapping rhythm you've destroyed the bizarre or odd or fascinating or horrifying aspect of the music." Dunlap's score accentuated the tension of these films quite appropriately with his symphonic approach.

A particularly effective score was composed by Dunlap for the 1966 undersea monster movie, DESTINATION: INNER SPACE. Opening with a pleasant theme for horn and strings over harp glissandos, the motif is vaguely reminiscent of the mood John Williams would later capture in THE TOWERING INFERNO (1974). The monster attack scenes are accompanied with a harsh drawn-out, low brass motif mixed with rapidly bowed strings. Dunlap also makes effective use of fast, monotonous brass notes capped with a single, lower note. An eerie apprehensiveness is conveyed through the use of reverberating electric guitar plucks for the underwater scenes.

"That was the beginning of electronic music for me," Dunlap recalled, speaking of this Underwater motif. Dunlap worked with electronic music specialist Jack Cookerly to achieve the effect. Cookerly had created his own instrument which housed a variety of tape loops used to obtain the reverberating pings and pongs heard in the music. The cues were recorded in the echo chambers beneath the Capitol Records studio in Los Angeles. "I think that's the first time we were ever able to use that," Dunlap said. "There were four french horns and this fantastic instrument of his, which was light years ahead."

Like most composers working on B-movies during the 50's and 60's, Dunlap ran the full gamut of action films, from horrors to Westerns to detectives to war movies. Though his preference has always been to write music that is more uplifting and positive, but he was infrequently given the chance in films such as I WAS A TEENAGE FRANKENSTEIN. "The horror pictures are tough to do," he said. "You've got to write ugly or threatening or fearful or suspenseful music ninety percent of the time. There's very little if anything that is beautiful, or, let's say, 'soft' in texture in such a film. It's difficult, at least for me, to maintain that kind of approach." It is to Dunlap's credit, however, that the music he did write for horror and science fiction films turned out to be among the superior efforts from the 60's, and DESTINATION: INNER SPACE remains a prime example.

Leigh Harline culminated a lengthy and notable career in 1964 with his excellent music for George Pal's THE SEVEN FACES OF

DR. LAO. While the film allowed star Tony Randall to portray the seven characters suggested in the title, it likewise gave Harline an opportunity to accompany musically these seven aspects of the Chinese wizard. Harline's orchestrations closely paralleled the diverse personalities played by Randall.

Harline chose to score the picture in a distinctive leitmotif format, a treatment he had shunned previously but felt was necessary for the fantastic and episodic nature of DR. LAO. The score seldom utilizes full orchestra, instead achieving a variety of musical textures through astute orchestration. In a lengthy analysis of Harline's score, Ross Care writes: "A variety of musical modes and means, as multifarious as Dr. Lao's attractions, are called upon to support the 'star-turns' by the circus's inhabitants and to deepen and clarify the reactions of the townspeople to each. For example, a theme for solo bassoon, moving because of its strangely 'vague' quality, is given to Appolonius, the blind fortune-teller who is destined to reveal to his clients the absolute truth no matter how unpleasant it may be. With its hollow timbres and spare, modal lines developed into a two-part contrapuntal duet for bassoon and English horn, this theme underscores the encounter between the prophet and a self-deluding matron who finds his blunt candor profoundly disturbing; it is briefly restated at the close of the sequence with sustained octave doublings in the strings and a touch of solo cello."[15]

Elsewhere, as Care explains, Harline provides a slow, dance-like melody for oboe, strings and harp during the Marlin sequence, and a "weirdly florid, cadenza-like theme for shrill soprano saxophone accompanied by two marimbas, two harps and cistrum" for the scene involving the serpent-haired Medusa. The liaison between the young widow and the seductive goat-god, Pan, is accompanied by a choreographic motif as Pan performs a sensuous dance. Harline scored this sequence with florid arpeggios for solo E-flat flute ("a little-used instrument midway between a piccolo and the ordinary C flute, and characterized by its somewhat archaic timbre"), accompanying Pan's initially playful piping, which is eventually joined by harps, bass and tambourine, and finally by three standard flutes as the dance climaxes and Pan is transformed into a young newspaperman whose advances the widow has rejected. The music becomes increasingly frenzied, with a solo french horn introduced to "provide splashes of vivid dissonance against the modality also suggested in the dance's harmonic structure." The sequence is brought to a wild and agitated climax with flutes and xylophone, accompanied by harp, horns and bass, with a flurry of simple cross-rhythms, as Care points out: "Though using only limited if exotic chamber scoring, ... Harline achieves remarkable effects of momentum, acceleration and coloration. The flute/harp passages are repeated later in the film to represent the widow's gradually reawakened sexuality."[16]

Harline also composed a catchy motif for the film's title sequence, a somewhat jazzy mixture of Hollywood-Western sound with
a touch of the Orient, an interesting blending of "small-town Americana and a mind-bending Chinaman's traveling roadshow of myth
and fantasy, simultaneously providing a motif for the dual comic/
serious nature of the doctor himself."[17] The score is rich in musical styles and flavors, with various textures of fantasy, symbolism
and turn-of-the-century realism interplaying against each other.
"A deft and frequent strategy of brief but vivid musical transitions,"
Care concludes, "along with an expressive spectrum of character
motifs, unite to lend coherence to the narrative's episodic structure,
particularly the circus sequences themselves, and to consistently
sharpen the film's crucial interplay between fantasy and reality."[18]

The late 50's and 60's have been noted as being significant in
establishing a trend toward theme-song mania, and a prevalent commercial attitude among many film studios, seeking pop scores (which
would sell records and thus become part of the film's promotional
package) over traditional dramatic scoring. Somewhat due to the
unexpected commercial success of early 50's theme songs such as
Tiomkin's HIGH NOON and jazz-oriented scores like Elmer Bernstein's MAN WITH THE GOLDEN ARM, in which these popular elements were used effectively in legitimate settings, exploitation-
minded producers, as Bernstein himself has put it, "quickly began
to transform film composing from a serious art into a pop art."[19]
Many film composers who established themselves in the 40's and 50's
were either unwilling or unable to produce the pop- and rock-
oriented scores desired by producers in the 60's, and so found
themselves out of work, despite their symphonic capabilities. However bleak the film music field may have seemed during the 60's, a
number of notable symphonic scores did emerge (as with Harline's
DR. LAO and much of the work of Baxter, Stein and Dunlap), although the pop-music orientation seemed to dominate.

This emphasis made itself felt in the fantastic film as well.
The rock-oriented "beach party" horror films from American International were perhaps the most flagrant rock-scored films, the rock
music being very much a part of the film's milieu and concept, but
pop-scoring also managed to find its way into films which, a decade
earlier, would have been satisfied with a traditional symphonic score.
While electronic scoring, and even rock music, has been effective in
films in some instances, by and large the trend toward pop tunes
and commercial appeal resulted in repetitious rhythms that rarely
emphasized the film's dramatic elements, instead simply providing a
droning beat. Many science fiction and horror scores of the 60's
featured pop scores, some with more effective results than others.
Ib Glindemann's music for JOURNEY TO THE 7TH PLANET (1961)
opened with a pleasing, slow theme for woodwind over shimmering
harp and percussion, with occasional deep tones adding an interesting color, but the motif quickly segued into an awkward pop tune
which hardly created a sense of drama for the low-budget activities
on Uranus.

Vic Mizzy, perhaps best known for his catchy finger-snap-ping theme for TV's THE ADDAMS FAMILY (1964), that same year provided an adequate pop score for the psychological thriller, THE NIGHT WALKER. Mizzy had been born in Brooklyn in 1922, and was educated at New York University, where he later taught the Schillinger System of musical composition. Mizzy was an arranger for radio in the 40's, and started writing for television and films in the late 50's. He was also a prolific songwriter. Mizzy's NIGHT WALKER score opened with a brass riff under an interesting rhythmic piano melody; a slow-moving, five-note pop theme emerges, with the same melody repeated in descending pitch over the bass riff, which eventually becomes a slowly meandering motif for strings and wood-wind, with rapid xylophone and harp accompanying the film's intro-ductory narration. The five-note main theme dominates much of the film, and its pop style seemed somehow appropriate to William Cas-tle's direction of this modest thriller. Mizzy's tuneful music later found its way into a variety of science fiction comedies and TV series.

Along with the trend for pop-oriented scores came the trend of having popular recording artists score the films themselves. Herein is perhaps the ultimate exploitation--for now producers could not only market a popular movie theme, but have it written by al-ready marketable recording artists. Fantastic films did not lose out on this trend, either, although it tended to dominate the more main-stream product. Frank Sinatra, Jr., wrote songs for THE BEACH GIRLS AND THE MONSTER (1965). Roger Vadim's BARBARELLA (1967) featured pop music written by Bob Crewe and Charles Fox, which was performed by Crewe's then-popular recording group, The Bob Crewe Generation Orchestra. Even after the dramatic symphonic film score had regained its rightful place in film music in the mid-70's, producers still often chose to have their films scored by popu-lar songwriters, often to the detriment of the films. The folk-rock duo of Paul Beaver and Bernard Krause wrote the music for New World's LAST DAYS OF MAN ON EARTH (1974). British rock star Harry Nilsson wrote the music for the English musical, SON OF DRACULA (1974). Former Manfred Mann rock musician Michael Vickers began to score British horror films like DRACULA A.D. 1972 (1972) and AT THE EARTH'S CORE (1976). New wave star David Bowie was to have written the score for THE MAN WHO FELL TO EARTH (1976), in which he starred, but instead a variety of big-band jazz music was used, in addition to the bizarre percussion effects of noted percussionist Stomu Yamash'ta. Heavy-metal rock group Queen wrote the music for Dino De Laurentiis' FLASH GOR-DON (1980), lending a variety of screaming vocalisms which were ludicrously out of place, although highly marketable. Pop artist Paul Williams wrote the songs for Brian De Palma's PHANTOM OF THE PARADISE (1974), which were appropriate for the film's rock concert setting, and were balanced by George Aliceson Tipton's orchestral score. Europe was especially prevalent with this trend of buckling up a film with a rock score written by a popular rock

artist, and these have included groups such as Goblin (SUSPIRIA),
Libra (BEYOND THE DOOR II), Popol Vuh (NOSFERATU) and solo
performers like Brian Eno (LAND OF THE MINOTAUR), Rick Wake-
man (THE BURNING), Keith Emerson (INFERNO), Mike Oldfield
(CHARLOTTE), Edgar Froese (KAMIKAZE 1989) and Japan's Isao
Tomita (CATASTROPHE 1999) and Kitaro (QUEEN MILLENIA).

One pop-oriented science fiction score of this period that
stood out for its effectiveness was for SILENT RUNNING (1971).
Peter Schickele, well known for his comic PDQ Bach recordings, was
hired by director/effectsman Douglas Trumbull to compose the film's
score, and maintained a noteworthy balance between the popular
theme song (given lyrics and sung by folksinger Joan Baez) and
more orchestrally oriented dramatic music. The two songs are un-
characteristically effective in the film, lending an emotional air of
melancholy, sorrow and joy, especially over the final scene. Initially, Joan Baez wanted to have the songs accompanied only by a
solo piano, but Schickele convinced her otherwise, and the strong
string-and-woodwind backing--added to the piano, Baez's powerful
vocal and the subtly embellishing triangle--achieves a rich and
memorable sound. The instrumental scoring was likewise highly effective, particularly Schickele's proud brass-and-drums march which
accompanies the spectacular camera pullback revealing for the first
time the spaceship Valley Forge and its companion freighters. The
music here superbly conveys the grandeur of space and the import
of the space fleet's mission. Elsewhere the music captures the inner feelings of the characters, both human and mechanical (as in
the sequence where the drone operates on Lowell's injured leg, and
the corresponding scene later in which Lowell undertakes emergency
repairs on the damaged drone Huey). Schickele's score, in its
dominant use of woodwind, strings, harp, xylophone and an occasional rock-styled drum beat and roll, remarkably captured the mood
of the film, emphasizing the seriousness of Lowell's beliefs, the
charm and poignancy of the drones, and the action inherent in the
plot. Of the pop orientation of the 60's and early 70's, Schickele's
music for SILENT RUNNING emerges as one of the best crossbreeds.

Notes

1. Les Baxter, interview with the author, January 9, 1982

2. James Marshall, "Les Baxter," Soundtrack Collector's Newsletter
    #20 (January 1980) p. 19

3. Les Baxter, loc. cit. (and following Baxter quotes)

4. James Marshall, op. cit., p. 20

5. _____, "Record Review," Soundtrack! The Collector's Quarterly #24 (Winter 1980-81) p. 8

6. Ibid.

7. Les Baxter interviewed by David Kraft and Ronald Bohn, Soundtrack! The Collector's Quarterly #26 (Summer 1981) p. 21

8. _____, loc. cit. #1

9. _____, op. cit. #7, p. 22

10. _____, loc. cit. #1 (and following unreferenced quote)

11. _____, op. cit. #7, p. 16

12. Ronald Stein, interview with the author, March 30, 1983 (and following quotes)

13. Fred Katz, interview with the author, February 22, 1983 (and following quotes)

14. Paul Dunlap, interview with the author, February 24, 1983 (and following quotes)

15. Ross Care, "The Film Music of Leigh Harline," Filmmusic Notebook Vol. 3, #2 (1977) p. 41-42

16. Ibid.

17. Ibid., p. 41

18. Ibid., p. 42

19. Elmer Bernstein, "Whatever Happened to Great Movie Music?" High Fidelity (July 1972) p. 58

X

EUROPEAN STYLISMS

European film music is predominantly associated with the prolific composers of France and Italy, although there have been notable efforts made by composers working in Germany, Spain, Czechoslovakia, Poland and other countries whose output in the fantastic
genre has been considerable, if normally unheard by mainstream
American audiences. While mostly drawn from the same European
roots that paved the way for traditional American film scoring, the
music--like the films themselves--often retains its own distinctive
qualities unique to its country of origin.

France

While it may be said that French filmmaking invented fantasy
films with Georges Méliès and A TRIP TO THE MOON (1902), subsequent progress in science fiction and fantasy films has been infrequent in France, as compared with the prolific offerings from
Germany, Italy and Spain. During the 40's and 50's, poet and filmmaker Jean Cocteau became noted for his use of fantasy in a number of surreal, lyrical and highly personal films. All of Cocteau's
films were scored by his friend Georges Auric, who debuted in
cinema with him in 1930 with THE BLOOD OF A POET. Born in
Lodeve, France, in 1899, Auric began to compose at the age of 15,
and later studied at the Paris Conservatoire and at the Schola Cantorum. He began to write prolifically for the concert hall, ballet,
stage and screen, and eventually became noted as France's ablest
creator of film music. Auric died in 1983.

Auric's music for BEAUTY AND THE BEAST (1946) was especially notable in capturing the delicate, haunting essence of Cocteau's exquisite fairy tale. Cocteau had been especially precise in
his instructions to Auric on the kind of music he wanted. The director told Auric to use normal orchestra and choir, and a "very
strange, small orchestra" for the Beast's castle. Auric was told to
avoid the close association of image and music, wishing the synchronization to be achieved spontaneously during the recording sessions. "The result," Cocteau wrote in his published diary on the
making of the film, "will be a counterpoint; that is, sound and
image will not run together both saying the same thing at the same
time, neutralizing each other. I shall give positive emphasis to

those creative syncopations which jolt and awaken the imagination, by suppressing the music in certain passages. Thus it will be even more noticeable when it is heard and the silent sequences will not form a void since they contain a music of their own."[1] Auric's score, with its dramatic use of choir, and weird orchestrations underlying the fantastic nature of the Beast's castle, satisfied Cocteau's feeling that "it is only the musical element which will permit the film to soar ... the music is wedded to the film; it impregnates it, exalts it, consummates it.... Sometimes a burst from the choir envelops a close-up, isolates it and thrusts it toward the spectator."

Auric's next fantasy for Cocteau, ORPHEUS (1949), was an equally lyrical score with a variety of themes and motifs. The first half of the film is dominated by a woodwind love theme that surrounds Orpheus and his obsession with the mysterious Princess of Death, heard as he returns from his stay at her "house," and later as they meet after the underworld tribunal; a secondary woodwind-over-strings Love Theme is provided for Eurydice and Heurtebise. Auric includes an effective, rhythmic motif for strings, brass and xylophone punctuated with string strokes backed by groaning brass, loudly repeated as Orpheus strides through town trying to keep up with the elusive princess. The pronounced motif carries the scene briskly, reminiscent, in effect, of Bernard Herrmann's music for the museum scene in VERTIGO and its look-alike sequence in DRESSED TO KILL, scored by Pino Donaggio. A low, somber rhythm for low strings and melancholy, muted brass accompanies Orpheus' journey into the underworld through the mirror, punctuated with plucked violin strokes.

The actual passing through the mirrors, which is the means by which the characters travel from one world to the other, utilizes high tones, almost like feedback or the sound made by rubbing the wet rim of a wine glass, an effectively eerie tonality. The music for the film's final scenes is comprised of loud drum rolls and jazzy beats, first heard as the crowd of angry poets attack Orpheus. The sound here is loud and disruptive, somewhat awkward and appropriately so; the booming drum motif remains as Orpheus is shot, taken away by the shrouded cyclists, and arrives again in the underworld, at which time low, sustained strings play a variation of the Love Theme as he is reunited with the Princess of Death, counterpointed by the rumbling drums as the film ends. Auric's score sounds sufficiently otherworldly throughout, remaining low key and melancholy even in the Love Theme, nicely capturing the poetic mood of Cocteau's fantasy.

Auric provided a similar musical mood for Cocteau's follow-up a decade later, TESTAMENT OF ORPHEUS (U.S., 1960), although in this case he also drew extensively from classical music of Bach, Wagner and others. Auric provided effective scores for other filmmakers, including the ominous music for DEAD OF NIGHT (1945).

For this five-part anthology, Auric composed five distinctive musical pieces for each segment, including an unstructured, rapid,
dirgelike motif for brass in "The Bus Conductor," a dramatic theme
for bass strings and groaning brass emphasizing the haunted mirror of the third story, growing louder and more forceful with each
successive scene; and a pleasant mixture of jaunty tunes and synchronized cues for the humorous "Inexperienced Ghost."

For Jack Clayton's THE INNOCENTS (1961), Auric's music
was based on a soft, simple five-note lullabylike tune ("O Willow
Waly") sung early in the film. The main theme is built upon this
childlike melody (in a manner recalling the "Casablanca technique"
of Max Steiner and Roy Webb), and is later heard from one-
fingered piano and elsewhere from a music box (identified with the
ghostly Miss Jessel). The music effectively underscores the "innocence" of the possessed children with its ascending melody, culminating in a bittersweet, descending final note; it aptly represents
the apparent evil manifested in the children, and the lullaby takes
on a haunting counterpoint in this sense, as one reviewer noted:
"In one of the film's most disquieting moments, Flora begins humming the same tune absently while she and the governess sit in a
gazebo overlooking a pond. When the governess looks across the
water, the apparition of Miss Jessel stares at her enigmatically.
Immediately, the orchestra plays a jangled, minor-key version of
the same tune, giving the scene additional frission."[2] Auric also
captures a superb eeriness through the use of harmonizing strings
and shimmering cymbals.

The composer's relationship with director Clayton, despite an
ongoing working relationship, was a stormy one. Clayton was not
satisfied with Auric's finished score and demanded numerous revi-
sions. Auric, however, was unable to comply due to ill health, so
Clayton commissioned Lambert Wilson to completely reorchestrate the
music. The final result, however, retains Auric's flair for lyricism
and understatement which contributes greatly to the haunting essence of the film.

If Auric was France's best-regarded composer of the 40's and
50's, perhaps Georges Delerue is his contemporary counterpart.
Delerue was born in 1925 and began his musical career at the age
of fourteen, gaining extensive training in piano and clarinet. He
studied with Darius Milhaud, a colleague of Auric's, at the Paris
Conservatoire, and soon after his graduation began to write original music for theatrical and radio productions, and eventually motion pictures. In the late 50's, as the "new wave" films dominated
French cinema, Delerue's music became associated with many of them.
It was here that his long-term collaboration with director François
Truffaut began, and their subsequent association brought Delerue
widespread recognition.

Delerue's musical style is distinctively light and melodic,

Georges Delerue. Photograph by Robert Bettens. Courtesy Luc
Van De Ven, Soundtrack!.

characterized by lyrical melodies and classical romanticism. As one
reviewer stated: "The music of Georges Delerue possesses a unique
and recognizable style. The structure itself is rooted deeply in the
stylisms of Vivaldi and other French composers of the Renaissance
period. There is a gentle folk-song quality to most of his work.
And while most contemporary film composers have added striking
(and often startling) modernisms to their scoring techniques, Delerue has remained delightfully constant." [3]

While being enormously prolific in films, television and the
concert hall, Delerue has written relatively few genre films. A
handful of borderline psychological fantasies and shorts were among
his assignments of the 60's, his first full-fledged genre project being Jack Clayton's film of Gothic psychological terror, OUR MOTH-
ER'S HOUSE (1967). Clayton's macabre film told of children who
choose to carry on as if nothing were changed after the death of
their mother, and, like Georges Auric emphasizing the childlike innocence of the children in Clayton's earlier THE INNOCENTS, Delerue likewise suggests the innocence of adolescents in OUR MOTH-
ER'S HOUSE with a lovely, lyrical melody. As one reviewer described, the music was "soft, strangely beautiful, innocent, with
an elusive underlay of haunting sadness. Like the children who
will not admit how hopeless is their lot, the music is never overly

melancholy; most of it, in fact, is so sprightly it seems to call for
dancing and laughter ... Delerue's music has that operatic quality
of furthering a story by the full cooperation of the melodic line.
Every theme in the picture has its own identifiable melody, yet
never does the music overpower the story."[4] The score, dominated
by violins, piano and harpsichord, underscores the film's darkly
macabre events with a light airiness.

In 1972, Delerue scored the surreal Belgian fantasy, MAL-
PERTUIS, lending it a balance between his remarkable lyricism and
a deep, bellowing awesomeness. The main theme is a lovely melody
for oboe over strings and xylophone, which represents the character Yann, a sailor who finds himself amid the lair of Olympian
gods; the latter milieu is represented by slow, plodding, deeply
ascending brass chords, evoking the grandeur and awe of such beings. There are a variety of other motifs, both lyrical and sus-
penseful/fantastic, and as Delerue's only true venture into sur-
realistic fantasy, it is a notable effort.

A similar mixture of lovely lyricism and deeper, mysterious
scoring was found in THE DAY OF THE DOLPHIN (1974). Delerue
conjured up a Love Theme between the scientist and the dolphin
with whom he learns to communicate, and the music superbly emo-
tionalizes this relationship and adds a great deal of empathy to the
conflicts of the final sequences. This theme is balanced with a
mysterious Underwater motif, achieved through the use of twangy
synthesizer tones over shivering strings, and elsewhere with the
metallic tapping of piano strings echoing over sustained string passages and wandering harp notes. The latter motif evokes the distorted sound of hearing noises underwater, and builds a remarkably claustrophobic and eerie mood into these scenes. The film was
one of the first American films Delerue had the opportunity to
score, and for it he was able to use a larger orchestra than he
was normally allowed in European pictures; the result was a beautifully lyrical, poignant musical score.

Since DAY OF THE DOLPHIN, Delerue has become increasingly more involved in American productions, eventually moving to
work in Hollywood full time in 1983. While most of the assignments
he received were for romantic and dramatic films, he was hired to
score Jack Clayton's adaptation of Ray Bradbury's SOMETHING
WICKED THIS WAY COMES in 1982. He composed and recorded a
fine, whimsical score, embodying his characteristic sense of poignant lyricism and light classical style in addition to a variety of
carnival motifs, but the score was dropped when Disney executives
decided to beef up the picture with new scenes, new editing and
a livelier score (by James Horner) after a lackluster preview.

While Delerue's music seems best suited to romantic films, because of his remarkable gift of melody and poignancy, his few efforts in the fantastic genre are notable not because he has sudden-

ly shifted in style and composed expected horror music, but because he has approached the subject with the same lyricism and delicate melody that he lends to romantic films. He underscores the emotions of characters and their relationships rather than emphasizing elements of horror or fantasy, and by thus playing "against" the expected mood manages to heighten the emotional impact of the picture. This style of playing against the film--providing light, lyrical melodies for dark and somber subjects--is something that has become quite effective in recent years, and seems to be especially prevalent in European films.

Another notable French composer was Joseph Kosma, who was born in Budapest in 1905 and became involved in motion pictures when he came to France in 1933, also composing popular songs, ballet and concert music. Kosma's film scoring tended to be highly melodic, often reflecting his penchant for popular songwriting, and this style has remained in his genre efforts, as one critic noted of his score for Jean Renoir's futuristic PICNIC ON THE GRASS (1959), writing of its "uneven Kosma score which (like the film) gets too cute at times."[5]

Georges Van Parys provided some fine thriller music for the title sequence of DIABOLIQUE (1955). While the body of the film contained no music, Van Parys lent an urgent, frenzied atmosphere at the very start with an anxious motif for harsh, plodding string chords, later accompanied by brass and woodwind, repeating a single, monotonous chord in rapid, footstep fashion. The sound becomes more and more dissonant as more instruments are added, until broken by a brief bridge of wailing children's choir and heavy cathedral organ (in keeping with the film's Boys Home milieu). Van Parys concludes the film with a slow-moving string variation of the opening theme, which segues into a climactic brass-and-organ resolution.

Jean Prodromides scored two notable French fantasy efforts of recent years: the "Metzengerstein" segment of the collaborative anthology, SPIRITS OF THE DEAD (1967), and Roger Vadim's earlier vampire movie, BLOOD AND ROSES (1960). Prodromides made particularly good use in the latter score of a variety of musical styles and ideas, which surround a classically styled main theme that recurs throughout the film in various arrangements. Prodromides also utilizes an effectively somber, foreboding motif during the scenes in the vampire's crypt. Other notable French film composers frequenting the fantasy genre, include René Cloerec, Paul Misraki, Bernard Parmeggiani, Michel Magne and Maurice Thiriet.

The pop vein has always been prominent in much contemporary French cinema, as it is in Italy, and popular tunes and melodies have pervaded many French fantastic films of recent vintage. Alain Goraguer scored the notable 1973 animated science fiction picture, FANTASTIC PLANET, with an effective pop-rock idiom,

emphasizing electric guitar, electric bass, strings, voices and a
light rock drum beat. While overly dependent upon its main theme,
the music does provide a sufficient backdrop for the unusual adventures of a newborn Om who seeks to escape the tyranny of the
Draggs and lead his diminutive people to freedom. Especially notable is a catchy waltz melody for woodwinds and strings over electric guitar, oom-pah brass and drums which is heard as the Om
discovers the secret of the planet Ygam. The bulk of the music,
however, is simple rhythmic matter which moves things along without really accentuating dramatic and emotional elements of the
story.

Michel Legrand and Francis Lai have both become successful
in America as well as Europe for their easy-listening, pop-styled
approach to film music; Legrand popular for his themes from
SUMMER OF '42 and the like, and Lai known for scoring A MAN
AND A WOMAN and LOVE STORY. While the themes from all these
films have become immensely popular on radio and record albums,
they have also been scorned by many due to the pop-tune approach
taken by the composers in the place of serious dramatic scoring.
While the matter is open to some debate, both have contributed occasionally to the fantasy genre, Legrand with the musical fairy tale,
DONKEY SKIN (1970) and the James Bond thriller, NEVER SAY
NEVER AGAIN (1983), as well as several borderline fantasies; and
Lai, with a French version of Tom Thumb, LE PETIT POUCET
(1972), among a handful of others; the musical styles remaining
primarily pop throughout.

Claude Bolling, who began scoring French films in the late
50's and became popular in America as a jazz recording artist during the 70's, managed to avoid an overemphasis of pop in his genre
film scores, which included the 1960 French remake of THE HANDS
OF ORLAC (released in America in 1964), and the 1980 horror film,
THE AWAKENING. The latter score is particularly good, providing
a rich symphonic work built around a stirring, romantic melody,
arranged predominantly for woodwind and strings, with various
other instruments used here and there to provide an Egyptian flavor.
The horror motifs are effective bits of growing tension and suspense, avoiding simple "shock" crescendos.

Another French composer who has recently become noted for
scoring American fantastic films is Philippe Sarde. Born in 1945,
Sarde enrolled in the Paris Conservatory at the age of ten. By
the time he was 13, he was sure of his vocation and spent a decade
studying harmony and composition. In 1970, Sarde burst upon the
French film world with his score for Claude Sautet's THE THINGS
OF LIFE, and has since scored many popular French films, including
all of Sautet's subsequent efforts. Sarde's first foray into the fantastic genre was for the Roman Polanski film, THE TENANT (1976),
in which he provided a melodic score described by one reviewer as
being "like a children's tune slowed to a dirge."[6] The score was

effective, but it wasn't until the early 80's that Sarde really came to the notice of American audiences when he scored in quick succession Polanski's TESS (1981), GHOST STORY (1981) and QUEST FOR FIRE (1982), the latter pair being significant genre film music.

GHOST STORY is wrapped in a haunting, romantic musical composition, balancing the attractive melodies with elegantly weird motifs. One reviewer described Sarde's score in detail as follows: "Through the dexterous deployment of four memorable, malleable and closely related ideas--the melancholic, mesmerically lyrical, stepwise 'ghost' theme; an alternating minor/major triadic motif, which gives rise to a telegraphic, xylophone-accented triplet 'terror motto' and an innocently vernal 'love theme' (almost a mirror image of the 'ghost' theme)--Sarde assembles a tight, fluid, and consistently fertile score, which maintains unity in diversity in several imaginative ways. By the telling but frugal use of organ pedal-points, female vocalise, and woodwinds in their low-to-middle registers, he achieved some truly fresh and unconventional tonal effects."[7] The main ghost theme is particularly haunting, both in its effect and its composition--the dominant four-note part of the theme rises on its first half and floatingly descends on the latter, leaving a sense of immateriality and incompleteness--a ghostly texture, especially when performed by solo female voice.

While GHOST STORY was heavily romantic, the prehistoric "drama," QUEST FOR FIRE, is given a marvelously orchestrated yet basically earthy score, built from three primary elements. There is the love theme, often performed by a solo pan-flute and later by strings, which evokes a spirit of humanity among the more primitive sounds. The second motif is an action motif, churning and driving the action relentlessly onward with bristling brass chords and a rolling, surging drum accompaniment. The third is a choral/chant motif, suggestive of the more primitive, beastlike aspects of the cavepeople, built from male chorus chants interplaying with female chorale wails, gradually becoming more frenzied, as in a climactic ritual. The music is occasionally reminiscent of the orchestration of Mario Nascimbene's prehistoric film music. As the film has no recognizable dialog, it is up to Sarde's expansive music to carry much of it along, and he accomplishes this admirably. As one reviewer noted: "Sarde mixes the Stone Age-evoking sounds of the pan flute and a battery of percussion instruments with symphonic passages of incredible magnitude, to produce one of the most 'serious' scores in recent years."[8]

Italy

Like France, Italian film music has become increasingly dominated by pop music in recent years, a style that is due in part to the predominance of the rock-styled Italian Western sound of the

60's, a style of film scoring which was notable for its dynamic mixture of rock-and-roll electronics with traditional symphonics and
playing a large role in introducing the child of rock and roll (such
as this author) to the expansive world of movie music. The sound
was unique, and appropriate for the larger-than-life characters
portrayed ultradramatically on the screen. The leading composer
in the Italian Western genre, and the man who virtually revolu-
tionized the sound of European Westerns, was Ennio Morricone, undoubtedly Italy's most prolific and popular composer. So prolific,
some say, that his music tends to lack consistent quality, some
scores being outstanding works and others appearing mediocre.
Whatever the case, Morricone has gained a large following and
has composed some stunning film music for a variety of motion pictures, including a small array of fantastic and semifantastic films.

Morricone was born in Rome in 1928, and was encouraged into music by his father, who was a musician. By the time he was
18, Morricone had gained a fine command of music and could play
many instruments. He studied music with Giofreddo Petrassi at
the University of Saint Cecelia, gaining honors in symphonic performance. Eventually he became involved in an orchestra which
played selections of film music, and he started to critically analyze
the medium. In the early 60's, producer Luciano Salce recognized

Ennio Morricone. Photograph courtesy Martin Van Wouw, Musica
Sul Velluto.

his talent and hired him. Morricone had been old friends with director Sergio Leone (they had gone to school together), and when Leone entered the film industry and eventually began to make the first important Italian Western, A FISTFUL OF DOLLARS, in 1964, he asked Morricone to write the music. As Leone went on to film subsequent Westerns including the noteworthy THE GOOD, THE BAD AND THE UGLY (1968) and ONCE UPON A TIME IN THE WEST (1969), he continued to commission Morricone to score them, and this collaboration has since resulted in a remarkable marriage of sound and image, the prototype of European Western music, which can almost be considered operatic.

Morricone went on to score nearly 300 films in just two decades, running the gamut of filmic and musical styles, writing very rapidly and basically following his own inclinations for the sound. Often, instead of synchronizing music directly to the film, Morricone writes a series of themes which he thinks will be fitting, and lets the director choose those he feels will be most appropriate. (Those left over often appear in wholly different films later on.) While many critics object to this approach, it remains apparent that Morricone's music has, nonetheless, contributed remarkably to the films in which it is used. As one reviewer has written: "The unpredictability of Morricone's music, through its large dynamic and rhythmic jumps and odd sound-sources is ideally suited to the violent films he is most noted for. He is able to create or hugely amplify the feeling of the unexpected looming just outside the frame.... Great classical and pop music has often been used in films to the detriment of the film itself: the music is either at cross-purposes emotionally with the film, or overwhelms it completely, distracting us from the picture on the screen. Herein lies Morricone's true genius: his music may not always stand up as great music on its own but, in the making of music that has the ability to create and sustain an emotional state in conjunction with moving pictures, he has few peers."[9]

The unusual sound sources referred to, in addition to Morricone's dramatic use of melody (particularly in suddenly rising or dropping an octave), are among the most striking elements in his music. As the reviewer notes, Morricone's penchant for bizarre instruments, ocarinas, electric guitars, tinny electric organs, "junk" percussion, out-of-tune brass instruments, bizarre vocal techniques, and other devices matched with his simple melodies and bold, incisive rhythms have resulted in some especially memorable film scores. "He created fascinating juxtapositions of these sounds with his 'big' orchestra sound," the reviewer goes on to say, "often in conjunction with human voices used as instrumental, lyric-less effects.... A real Morricone trademark rhythm device is to stop a large, fast-moving orchestral section dead in its tracks and insert a quiet, sometimes arhythmic, solo over silence, and then suddenly bring the full orchestra back at the end of a phrase. When combined with an unexpected jump cut or a sudden move in the film's action, the effect is like a hammer blow--it literally jolts you out of your seat."[10]

While Morricone's most melodic and exotic work has been for Westerns and dramas, his music for the fantastic genre has tended to remain more atonal and free in form--a style Morricone is said to prefer over the gorgeous, rich themes that have brought him his most fame. During the 60's and earlier 70's most of these genre films were psychological thrillers, only occasionally achieving a full-fledged departure into the fantastic, and Morricone's scoring techniques have been quite varied. From a pop-vocal theme song for the futuristic DANGER: DIABOLIK (1967) to bizarre, strangely orchestrated passages that defy description in Dario Argento's FOUR FLIES ON GREY VELVET (1972) and others; moody symphonic pieces for SPASM (1974) and BLUEBEARD (1972); free-form jazz for Argento's THE CAT O'NINE TAILS (1972), of which one reviewer has written: "...there is no pretense even at melodic phrasing; every instrument, voice and trumpet included, is concerned only with its own time";[11] classical parody as an element of LE TRIO INFERNEL (1974); wildly flailing violins and religious organ music used in ANTICHRIST (1974; a collaboration with Bruno Nicolai); and striking pop melodies combined with his own unique style of female voices singing cheerful melodies in the prehistoric comedy, WHEN WOMEN HAD TAILS (1973). Often each individual film contains a variety of musical styles, such as THE BIRD WITH THE CRYSTAL PLUMAGE (1970), which includes a breezy main title theme with voices, a bossa nova piece, several jangly free-form pieces for jazzy saxophone over percussion, and a bizarre use of quasi-orgasmic female gasps over a quickening solo heartbeat.

An early true horror score was for NIGHTMARE CASTLE (1965), which is given an easy-listening violin melody over a simplistic piano riff that is highly reminiscent of that used in his later pirate drama, L'AVVENTURIERO (1967). Later the same piano riff is used under suspenseful string wanderings and woodwind moans for a different effect, and there is a great deal of clerical organ used throughout the score.

In the 70's, as Morricone became more popular in America, he began to receive offers to score American films, many of which have been among his best works of the latest decade. He was contacted by Stanley Kubrick to write the music for A CLOCKWORK ORANGE (1971), but the composer regrettably had to turn it down due to another commitment.[12] In 1977 he scored EXORCIST II: THE HERETIC, composing the score with a series of bizarre, assaultingly loud atonal conjurings evocative of demonic affections. The main theme is in a rock style, using keyboards and a small choir chanting a wordless riff; much of the other suspense and terror music is of a free-form, loud, and almost unpleasant nature, consisting of voices, warbling woodwinds, strings and percussion. This is all balanced by a very pretty melodic piece for Regan, the demon-possessed child, which uses solo female voice over a gently plucked guitar and whispering strings. Used in the finale, Regan's Theme emphasizes the happy ending, neatly symbolizing the relieved ray of light amid the previous darkness.

The same year Morricone provided a beautifully moving score for the mammalian JAWS-facsimile, ORCA: THE KILLER WHALE. The film, on the surface level, seems silly and contrived as it tells of a bereaved Orca rampaging a coastal fishing village in its pursuit of the whaler who killed its mate, but Morricone's poignant music endowed the picture with a sense of profound sympathy, allowing it to transcend the pretentions of the plot and become a sadly beautiful tragedy of a whale. The main theme, which embodies the emotions and personalities of both its human and cetacean protagonists, is classical in style, with flowing strings, the composer's characteristic harpsichord underscoring and the haunting wordless female vocal. Through the music, we identify with the emotions of the whale--his idyllic love for his mate in earlier sequences, and his unaccountable sorrow at her needless and cruel loss in the beautifully filmed death procession. As the film moves on, the same music is later used to shift our emotions to sympathize with the fisherman as he is uncannily persecuted by the avenging Orca, finally realizing his misgivings over his earlier deed. At the conclusion, the theme again joins with the whale as, his vengeance achieved, he swims to a lonely death beneath the polar ice, still unsatisfied. The main theme is balanced by a Suspense-and-Attack motif, comprised of slow, deep strings coupled with weird, slashing percussion effects, and occasional additions of organ, quickly sputtering brass chords, chilling high-pitched spiralling strings, and plucked violins. It is to Morricone's credit that his score transcended the level of pretentious monster movie and created a profoundly moving story of two creatures caught up in the sad whims of fate. The beautiful theme draws us into the film and makes it live despite its inherent flaws, haunting us in its poignancy after the picture is over.

Similar mixtures of lyricism and atonal effects work well in Morricone's other genre efforts. The apocalyptic HOLOCAUST 2000 (1977, shown in America as THE CHOSEN), features a lovely main theme built around a simple, ascending two-note melody for woodwind and then choir over contrastingly rapid piano notes and a chanting "bom-bom-bom" choral underscoring, in addition to various dismal and atonal motifs. As one reviewer wrote of this score: "The holocaust computer is suggested by agitated strings that manage to create the buzz of a giant beehive ... the Holocaust Theme, a somewhat dreamy melody, contrasts vividly with the film's subject matter, a trick Morricone uses again when he typifies the holocaust itself. [Elsewhere] he takes the easy way out by means of the usual strident strings and dissonant sounds."[13] The American thrillers, BLOODLINE (1979) and THE ISLAND (1980) used similar contrasts between very lyrical, hauntingly pretty themes and unsettling suspense motifs; BLOODLINE being particularly unified, orchestrally. Even its suspenseful cues remain structured and progressive, unlike the often seemingly directionless freeform constructions provided for many of his other thriller scores.

While best known for his brilliance at melody and the grandeur of the full orchestra, it's Morricone's untamed diversity that makes his music so difficult to characterize. One of his most unique efforts was the quirky electronic score composed for THE HUMANOID (1978), a futuristic science fiction thriller. While the score's dominant rock beat emphasizes rhythm more than drama, the music remains effective due to Morricone's clever orchestration. The score includes a droning march for synthesized "brass" over a strong rock drum beat, a soft Love Theme for strings, synthesizers and drum, and an intriguingly twangy electronic motif for the robot dog.

Obviously, Morricone strives to avoid musical clichés in his scores--often to the extent of scoring a particular film in the opposite way one might expect it to be scored, as with the dominating use of romantic melodies in thrillers such as BLOODLINE, and elsewhere the use of lyrical, singing children's voices during a murder scene. This technique of scoring against the obvious mood of a picture is one Morricone has frequently employed to remarkable effect, as have a variety of other composers including Pino Donaggio in Italy, Georges Delerue in France, and Laurence Rosenthal in America. When asked if he was fond of drawing the audience's attention by using music that is opposed to the visual images, Morricone agreed that it was "definitely one of my motives. After all, it may follow that a contrasting treatment gets through to an audience's feelings more successfully than an appropriate one."[14]

An unusual film score, in this light, was for John Carpenter's THE THING (1982). This was the first film that director Carpenter hadn't scored himself, deciding instead to offer the assignment to Morricone, whom he had long admired. The resulting music, however, seemed to retain more of Carpenter's influence than Morricone's own imagination, as one reviewer noted succinctly: "Morricone ... strove to reproduce the electronic Carpenter ambience, instead of suffusing the score with his own personality."[15] A series of discussions between Morricone and Carpenter in Rome and Los Angeles resulted in the score's evolution into a dreary, bleak landscape of ominous, heavy orchestral textures. Carpenter wanted a "cold" score, yet one not totally without hope, and Morricone provided this with a mixture of cues comprised of straight symphonic instruments and others featuring synthesizer. Morricone described the principle characteristic of the score being one of static movement: "Nothing happens," Morricone said. "It seems to suggest that something is going to happen; however, nothing happens. It's starting to move, something happens--no,

<u>nothing</u> happens; but still it moves. That's the characteristic.
It's like a big question mark. That's how the film ends, with a
question: what will happen now? That moment is a mixture of
hope and despair. Hallucinated hope and despair, as expressed in
the music."[16]

While his score for THE THING lacks the vivid, sweeping
melodies of his best-loved film music, it is nevertheless in keeping
with his basic philosophy of composing for motion pictures: "Music in a film with certain artistic value should tell the things that
are not told in the film's dialogue, and therefore underline the psychological and sub-psychological aspects, the characters, the relationships between the characters, the choral relations between different situations and persons. You could say, the things which
one doesn't say with dialogue or that aren't explicit in the chrono-
logical story and the action. These things should draw out the
music."[17]

One of Morricone's countrymen who has developed a highly
similar musical style--to the point of his once even being considered
nothing but a pen-name for the prolific Morricone--is Bruno Nicolai. Like Morricone, Nicolai has shown a notable expertise in scoring a wide variety of films with a wide variety of musical styles,
sharing the same penchant towards experimental sounds and an
eclectic mixture of diverse styles. Nicolai was born in 1926 and
studied with Morricone under Gioffredo Petrassi at Santa Cecelia.
After graduating in 1950, Nicolai began to work in the theatre,
from which he received scoring assignments for television and ultimately motion pictures, starting with the Italian Western explosion
of 1964. Nicolai maintained a notable association with Morricone
until 1975, conducting many of his colleague's scores as well as
occasionally collaborating on the composition. This association,
many say, resulted in a tendency for much of Nicolai's own film
music to be virtually indistinguishable from Morricone's.

Nicolai has composed a fair number of admirable film scores,
and his work in the horror genre is notable. Although mostly for
low-budget Italian quickies, he has lent a passionate musical atmosphere that gave these films a remarkable presence. Nicolai's first
genre score, O.K. CONNERY, a 1967 spy movie in which he collaborated with Morricone, was primarily a jazzy pop score, while
his music for Jess Franco's film EUGENIE ... THE STORY OF
HER JOURNEY INTO PERVERSION (1969), was a highly atonal
and hysterial score that matched the sadism and insanity explored
in the film.

Nicolai's music for Franco's COUNT DRACULA (1971), however, provided a uniquely Italian sound for this attempt at filming
a "definitive" adaptation of the famous vampire. Nicolai's main
theme is a distinctive five-note motif for zimbalom: three rapidly
ascending notes, pausing, followed by two or more down-and-up

notes. The motif gives an effective eerieness to the terror scenes
with its repetitive notes and the unusual sound of the zimbalom.
Nicolai also utilized weird, slowly building string tones and faint,
roaming keyboard notes over bizarre, wolflike wails as Dracula
chastises his brides when they prowl upon the sleeping Jonathan
Harker, and in other vampire attack scenes. The alien wailing
sounds are unearthly, but seem a little too gimmicky here. The
main theme is also used prominently over see-sawing high woodwind
piping, with rhythmic string chords and sporadic drum pounds, in
addition to a number of suspenseful variations and the use of eerie,
slow-moving synthesizer notes over weaving strings. Another musical effect is achieved through the use of string chords echoed by
high-pitched woodwind notes. The end title is a memorable motif
for loud, slow-moving church organ notes over rapid, up-and-down
woodwind piping--a technique used previously by Morricone, and
to great effect here.

While Nicolai's music for COUNT DRACULA and earlier genre
efforts tended to take a dissonant, horrific approach, further
scores played against this mood with a number of pleasant, catchy
melodies. One of his most memorable works was for the poorly received NIGHT OF THE BLOOD MONSTER (1972; called THRONE OF
FIRE in Italy), for which he composed a beautiful, sad string theme
over faint choral backing which harkens back to his fine, moving
Western themes. THE NIGHT EVELYN CAME OUT OF THE GRAVE
(1973) sported a catchy trumpet theme over keyboard and percussion, later taken by the distinctive wordless female voice. The
tune adds a breezy counterpoint to this horror-mystery film. The
score also made use of various "wowing" electric guitar chords,
drum beats, sitar and a similar eclectic mixture of instruments for
the horror cues. THEY'RE COMING TO GET YOU (1976; made in
1972 as TUTTI I COLORI DEL BUIO) featured a lush woodwind,
string and vocal melody over xylophone and pat-patting drum beat,
balanced with a variety of atonal string and percussionistic effects
for the suspense sequences. A final collaboration with Morricone
in 1974 on ANTICHRIST resulted in an evocative contrast between
clerical organ and dizzy, chaotic string fiddling suggestive of the
adverse conditions between the forces of Light and Darkness portrayed in the film.

"The importance [of film music] is relative," said Nicolai.
"A film is a very precise object, like theatre. The music can be
useful, very useful, sometimes even quite superior to the film.
But it is clear that the music always should tell something and that
it should be the criterion of comment."[18]

Another Italian composer gaining a large degree of recognition
in America for scoring macabre and violent horror films with lyrical
melodies is Pino Donaggio, whose prominent work in the horror
genre has earned him repeated comparison with Bernard Herrmann,
although his approach is far more melodious, achieving a haunting

Pino Donaggio. Photograph courtesy Scot W. Holton, Varese Sara-
    bande Records.

effect through lush melody where Herrmann used omnipresent chord
repetitions. As one writer noted: "Donaggio's film music is in the
rich symphonic tradition of Bernard Herrmann's best scores, and
while they obviously exhibit the influence of Herrmann's orchestrations, the thematic constructions are uniquely his own. The scores
... are characterized by his use of the rich textures of the string
basses, jolting shifts in structure, textures and mood, and the use
of lyrical melody juxtaposed with nerve-snapping tension. Donaggio's orchestrations share with Herrmann a feel for unexpected
modulations and exotic orchestrations created by his additions of
harpsichord, glockenspiel, celeste, organ and voice used for its
inherent musical value."[19]

Born in the Venetian lagoon in 1941 as Giuseppe Donaggio,
the young musician emerged from a highly musical family, receiving
a great deal of training as a classical violinist at Milan's Giuseppe
Verdi Conservatory. In the early 60's, Donaggio started a successful career as a popular songwriter until hired by director
Nicholas Roeg to score the mystery thriller, DON'T LOOK NOW
(1974), which resulted in an impressive debut as a film composer.
While deeply entrenched in his pop music background, Donaggio
nevertheless began to demonstrate the classically oriented arrangements and atmospheric pieces which would later become his trade-

mark. The score's main theme is a pretty piano melody along pop lines, representing the protagonist, John. A second theme is composed for Laura, which is a soft string and woodwind melody over underlying piano, which is more classical in style (as in the dramatic variant heard during John's vision of Laura in widow's clothing). The score also makes prominent use of plodding, dramatically climbing string chords to emphasize tension, as well as rhythmic string motifs to spur sudden action or flight.

Donaggio's next genre score was for Brian De Palma's CARRIE (1976), for which he composed one of his best works, and one which established him as a notable film composer. De Palma had initially negotiated for Bernard Herrmann to score the picture, as he had done previously, but Herrmann's untimely death curtailed this arrangement, and on the strength of his music for DON'T LOOK NOW, Donaggio received the assignment. CARRIE opens with a fine, slow flute solo over slowly modulating string piano harmonies, somewhat reminiscent of Georges Delerue. The quality is almost of a slow motion sound, but properly pitched, appropriate for the slow-motion introductory sequence. A secondary theme is built around Carrie's fanatically religious mother, with the deeper string tones hinting at her mental instability, backed by occasional harp and bells and finally emerging into a rising and falling piano riff with strings sliding over them to evoke suspense. Later, a clerical organ is played over rapidly swirling piano and strings as her psychosis reaches its culmination. A highly effective and dominant Horror motif is comprised of quick, furtive violin and moaning brasses over a wailing string melody (particularly effective during the "bucket of blood" sequence with Carrie at the prom).

Discussing the music from CARRIE, Royal S. Brown remarked that "instead of suggesting catastrophe around every corner, the music often has a poignant simplicity that highlights the deep, and very sad, human dimension so skillfully built up by De Palma." Brown goes on to explain Donaggio's use of musical understatement in the climactic scene when Carrie returns home after wreaking destruction at the prom: "Rather than pulling out all the stops to accompany the violence that occurs, Donaggio uses a sad little ostinato (played principally on the piano) that de-emphasizes the violence and greatly enhances the viewer's involvement with the heroine. For part of this scene, in fact, Donaggio had originally composed something even more lyrical, following his tendency to go in just the opposite direction when there is a large amount of suspense or terror. De Palma got him to write music with 'more drive' without sacrificing the basic character, and the result quite simply drains the emotions."[20]

One of Donaggio's most interesting scores was for the imitative psycho thriller, TOURIST TRAP (1979), which featured a wide array of percussion effects including drums, bells and rattles, and a sparing use of synthesizer. An effective love theme is first heard

in tinkling, music-box form as the killer demonstrated the mannequin shrine created for his departed wife; the theme is later arranged for piano and strings, lending an awkward sense of humanity and loneliness to the otherwise deranged psychopath.   The
score also features excellent climactic "murder music" in a repetitive, six-note string motif backed by a ghostly moaning female
chorus, suggesting the voices of the deadly mannequins brought to
life by the telekinetic killer.

Another collaboration with De Palma resulted in Donaggio's
superb symphonic score for DRESSED TO KILL (1980).   The composer embodied this psychological thriller with a rich, symphonic
romance, effectively blending the romantic with the bizarre.   The
main theme is among Donaggio's prettiest, a grand melody for string
and woodwinds, backed with subtle choral touches.   Elsewhere,
rapid, striking string chords are nicely sustained by a flowing
classical theme resulting in a memorable suspense cue; the terror
motifs consist mainly of dizzying string swirlings, ascending higher
and higher; and there is an exceptionally effective, long cue for
Kate's curious pursuit of the man in the museum, a rich, classical
motif which, as the only sound heard in this scene, strongly carries the sequence and matches the sensuous fluidity of De Palma's
expert direction.   The one drawback to the score occurs during the
murder scene in the elevator, where Donaggio resorts to string
screeches annoyingly similar to the oft-copied PSYCHO murder music of Bernard Herrmann (with a touch of his SISTERS style added).

Another effective psychological thriller score was composed
for THE FAN (1981).   Donaggio's music here was particularly
Herrmannesque in its use of fervent, staccato string chords.   These
are first heard in the main title, where the strings deftly join with
celesta to match the rhythm of the typewriter heard on the sound
track, taking its clacking as a percussion beat complementing the
music.   The subsequent use of the string motifs constantly recalls
the staccato typewriter strokes and emphasizes the growing pos-
sessive psychosis of fan Douglas Breen, as initially revealed through
typewritten letters to actress Sally Ross.   The theme is later accompanied by throbbing synthesizer beats as Breen stalks Ross'
secretary.   There is also a gently rolling string-and-piano Love
Theme, a lush violin arrangement of which draws the film to a
pleasant resolution.

Less effective scores were heard in Joe Dante's PIRANHA
(1978) and THE HOWLING (1981).   While adequate for the horrific
proceedings, Donaggio's music here lacked the continuity of a
strong, central theme which gave a lot of power through its repetition in other films.   While containing some very effective moments,
both films are mainly comprised of disjointed Suspense motifs, characterized by Donaggio's rich, sustained string chords.   PIRANHA
includes a number of promenadelike marches (à la JAWS), as well as
electronic echoing effects and synthesizer warbles, the latter heard

interestingly during the fish attacks. One reason for the apparent
piecemeal fashion, at least in THE HOWLING, may be that Donaggio
reportedly had to write it while the film was still being shot, and
therefore did not have specifically timed scenes to work from.
"Donaggio didn't have the time to wait until it was done," one writer explained, "and did it hoping that things would work."[21]

Continuing his productive association with De Palma, Donaggio
composed a fine score to the Hitchcockian thriller, BLOW OUT (1981),
dominating it with a delicate, classical Love Theme emphasizing
strings and woodwind. The bulk of the score is reserved for the
final half of the film, where it unleashes a lush romanticism as the
preceding events lead to a suspenseful conclusion; Donaggio's
melodious theme symbolizes the relationship between Jack and Sally
and reinforces Jack's panicked drive to rescue her from the threat
he unwittingly led her into. As the killer forces Sally to the top
of a building during a gala parade celebration, the music alternates
between strong, emotional string chords punctuated by echoing keyboard as we see Sally and the killer, and high woodwinds over
weaving, ascending strings as Jack rushes after them, trying to
locate them in the crowd. Striking string and high-pitched piano
stabs accompany Sally as she breaks free and screams; an urgent,
emotive horn melody over strings is heard as Jack hears her and
runs, seen in slow-motion, up the stairs of the building. The
horn melody turns sour as Jack reaches the top and, too late,
comes upon the killer, who is stabbing Sally. As Jack races up
and deflects the final stab into the killer's own body, the music
segues to the main theme, and all other sounds fade out except for
the dull thud of exploding fireworks lighting the sky above them,
allowing Donaggio's heartbreaking theme to accompany the climactic
sequence as Jack clings to Sally's lifeless body and the camera pans
around them. The music has a profound and moving effect here,
sharing equally with the visual element in portraying the ironic
tragedy and shattered emotions brought into play at the climax.

After a series of moody horror scores, Donaggio demonstrated
an equal penchant toward a broader heroic vein when he scored
HERCULES (1983), replacing Ennio Morricone who had to bow out
of the project due to an untimely injury. Donaggio's score is
built around a classical string-and-horn theme which lends an appropriate period air to the proceedings, recalling the old Hercules
and Samson films of the 50's with its use of a brassy, marchlike
theme as a heroic leitmotif. (It's also somewhat in the vein of
Herrmann's JASON AND THE ARGONAUTS theme.) As was done
in old Hercules films, Donaggio has scored many passages for solo
tympani. In addition, Donaggio provides an effective action/sus-
pense cue for groaning low brass against repeated high violin
streaks.

Although a resident of Venice, Donaggio's most recognized film
music has been for American films. His style, however, retains

the highly melodic roots of contemporary European film scoring,
and his passionate scores for films of tension and horror have lent
a distinctive musical embellishment to the genre and earned Donaggio a prominent place as an important contemporary composer for
the fantastic genre.

Nino Rota, a highly respected Italian composer since the
40's, scored all of Fellini's films until the composer's death in 1979,
including an occasional dabble into the fantastic. Born in Milan in
1911, Rota studied at the Milan Conservatory, and during his
schooling he developed a lasting friendship with Stravinsky. He
began scoring films in 1933, but didn't become established as a major film composer until the 40's. During the 60's and 70's he became especially noted for his rich, moving scores to ROMEO AND
JULIET and THE GODFATHER. Rota's musical style was predominantly lyrical, characterized by poignant melodies tinged with an
air of sadness, although his music for the Fellini films tended to
be more varied, from the classically somber opening to FELLINI'S
ROMA to the tuneful dance melodies of LA DOLCE VITA and almost
carnival-like musical abstractions heard in many other Fellini pictures. Rota's music for fantasies of the 50's, such as Terence
Young's VALLEY OF THE EAGLES (1951) and the mythological
FACE THAT LAUNCHED A THOUSAND SHIPS (1954) were in keeping with Rota's classically symphonic vein, while Fellini's surreal-
istic JULIET OF THE SPIRITS (1965) was scored with an array of
bouncy, catchy melodies with the dominant use of organ, saxophone, voice and carnival orchestra. The vivid tunes and unusual
orchestrations nicely embellished the surreal atmosphere of Fellini's
unusual fantasy. A similar carnival-like musical tone was heard in
Fellini's earlier semifantasy trilogy, BOCCACCIO '70 (1962), while
Rota provided a quickly fingered piano theme for the Fellini-
directed "Toby Dammit" segment of SPIRITS OF THE DEAD (1967),
a motif which was later reused during a portion of THE GODFATH-
ER (1972).

Rota's musical style was notably symphonic in an era of electric guitars and pop music, and he did not compromise his musical
preferences with the contemporary vogue. In a sense, his style
harkens back to the romantic, almost operatic scoring styles of the
50's. The Italian fantastic cinema was particularly active during
this period--especially with the infamous eruption of semifantasy
muscle-man films involving Hercules, Samson and other heroic
figures, most of which were scored with grand, epic symphonic
music. Many Italian composers emerging during this period scored
an occasional such film, including Armando Trovajoli, Francesco De
Masi, Carlo Savina, Piero Umiliani, Carlo Franci and Angelo Francesco Lavagnino.

Lavagnino, in particular, has scored a large number of fantastic films, including many of the "sword and sandal" muscle-and-
myth epics, providing a wide variety of musical motifs, including

exotic dance music for GOLIATH AND THE VAMPIRES (1961) and
a number of trilling flamenco melodies for SAMSON AND THE SLAVE
QUEEN (1963). As was common for these films when picked up by
American International Pictures for stateside distribution, their
original scores were removed during redubbing and replaced with
new scores, usually by AIP's master craftsman, Les Baxter. Thus,
Lavagnino's original music for many of these heroic costume films
were heard only in Italy except in rare instances when portions
were retained, as with the dance and flamenco cues just mentioned.
Another effective musical style of these Italian Samson-type epics
scored by Lavagnino and others was a frequent use of lengthy
passages scored for nothing but solo tympani, which added an unusual musical texture to portions of the films.

Lavagnino, who was born in 1909 and studied at Milan's Giuseppe Verdi Conservatory, started out writing a prolific flow of
classical compositions before commencing a career in films in 1950,
including many documentaries. One of these latter pictures was
THE LOST CONTINENT (1957) which, in spite of its evocative title, was not a fantasy film but a documentary on the customs of
native Indonesian islanders.

One of Lavagnino's earliest horror scores was for the British
monster film, GORGO (1960), for which he provided a rich and
haunting musical score built around a pleasant ballad. This main
theme, scored for accordion with a slight sea-chanty flavor to it,
suggests the dedicated affection of the mother monster for the
young Gorgo who is captured and taken to a London circus. The
theme is later used to emphasize the boy Sean's affection toward
the lumbering, captive beast. Lavagnino's score also makes a very
effective use of deep, groaning chords from the string and woodwind
sections, and much obligatory brassy action music for the attack of
Mama Gorgo, which features large, crashing notes for bass drum
and low, growling brass. Lavagnino's score for this semiroutine
monster movie very effectively surpassed its monster formula and
underlines the sentimental approach of the filmmakers.

THE CASTLE OF THE LIVING DEAD (1964) had a good horror score in the Universal vein, characterized by a dissonant
string melody over a rapid piano counterpoint. SNOW DEVILS
(1965) featured a rousing, rhythmic action score, drawing much
of its musical style from that of the Italian Westerns, which were
then reaching their peak. The main theme for this science fiction
horror story was a brusque synthesizer melody played over a rock
drum beat and later taken very nicely by female voice. Lavagnino's
dynamic rock theme is a very catchy piece of music, far more memorable than the film in which it was used, and was quite a departure from the sumptuous symphonic music for the earlier muscle-
man pictures, but somehow appropriate for this quirky story of
invading spacemen.

Carlo Rustichelli is another highly respected Italian composer who scored a handful of such "routine" period assignments during his early career. Rustichelli, who was born in 1916 and, gaining an interest in music as a youth, studied at the Accademia Filarmonica in Bologna and later Rome, became particularly notable for a lasting association with director Pietro Germi, for which he scored all but one film. Rustichelli, whom one reviewer described as being the only Italian composer "whose music sounds characteristically Italian, giving his music ... a profound sense of smell of the land or of the sea, of the scorching sun or of the azure Italian sky,"[22] scored the 1960 Italian-French version of THIEF OF BAGDAD, in addition to films in the mythological cycle such as L'ATLANTIDE (1961) and SAMSON VS. THE GIANT KING (1963).

Mario Nascimbene also emerged during the 50's, scoring a few mythological fantasies such as LE BACCANTI (1960) and THE GOLDEN ARROW (1962), although his most notable efforts in the fantastic genre were for the prehistoric epics filmed by England's Hammer Films. Nascimbene, born in Milan in 1916, studied at the Giuseppi Verdi Conservatory there. After composing a variety of symphonic and chamber pieces, Nascimbene began to write film music in the 40's, and soon gained a reputation for utilizing strange instruments and effects in his scores. For example, he used a typewriter as the lead instrument in his score for the 1953 film ROME 11 O'CLOCK, and other film scores have made extensive use of clock-ticking, anvils, bicycle bells and the amplified sound of a heartbeat. Nascimbene's famous music for BARABBAS (1962), with its electronically enhanced sounds, clinched his controversial reputation as a film composer of unconventional methods. "My personal philosophy on film scoring," Nascimbene said, "has now become a fairly oft-repeated motto: 'No longer are we tied down by the inflexible rules of composition and instrumentation laid down by tradition. Now we can exploit to the full those musical possibilities offered by films, both in actual composition and the scoring of the visuals.'"[23] Nascimbene avoids electronic gimmicks, preferring to create his musical sounds through acoustics occasionally supplemented by electronic reprocessing: "I often use new recording techniques, but I don't like electronic music," he said. "I make a different use of electronic techniques; I use them only in a real orchestra in order to obtain new sounds, never heard before."[24]

In the mid-50's, Nascimbene found himself popular as a composer for epic films, such as SOLOMON AND SHEBA and THE VIKINGS, and during the 60's he was given several opportunities to explore his suoni nuovi (new sounds) with a variety of Italian fantasies and secret agent films, but his efforts for Hammer pictures provided his most memorable genre output. ONE MILLION YEARS B.C. (1966) contained such effective period sounds as rocks and shells being tapped together, and even the clacking jawbone of an ass, in unusual contrast to the rapturous Love Theme for orchestra and chorus. Another odd instrument used in this score was

called a "rastrophone," which was none other than the rake from
Nascimbene's garden! The music for the introductory scenes,
dramatizing the creation of the world, are also notable in their use
of electronically reprocessed sounds combined with atonal string
chords, which eventually segue to a strong, brassy main theme--
something like a Roman march--which proceeded sluggishly over
rhythmic, muted cymbal banging and other percussion effects.
The motif nicely suggests the immensity of the newly created world,
and retained a sense of tremendous primitivity through an orchestra consisting mostly of percussion and brass. Music director
Franco Ferrara conducted the musicians in double time, and the
recorded music was then reproduced at half speed--thus obtaining
music at the proper speed but with an unusual character to it.
The use of choir added a dramatic, profound sense of historical
importance, as well.

Nascimbene scored Hammer's THE VENGEANCE OF SHE the
following year, and returned to prehistoric music in 1970 with
WHEN DINOSAURS RULED THE EARTH, in which he utilized a triumphant main theme in addition to musical oddities similar to those
incorporated into the first picture. The theme appears in various
guises throughout the film, including a variation for large, mixed
choir, a more subdued and almost lullaby-sounding arrangement
used in some night scenes, and a comic version for the sequences
of mother and baby dinosaurs frolicking. A final visit to ancient
times occurred the following year in CREATURES THE WORLD FOR-
GOT, which was less interesting, described by one reviewer as
"somewhat behind its predecessors and Nascimbene finds himself
scraping the bottom of the Stone Age barrel. The disconcerting
main theme is only a couple of notes different from SOLOMON AND
SHEBA and the musical 'authenticity' sounds very much déjà vu."[25]
The winner of several Silver Ribbons (Italy's equivalent to the Oscar), Nascimbene's penchant for suoni nuovi has earned him much
respect in Europe, and his unusual and distinctive music for these
Stone Age films was uniquely suited to the subject, and has made
a valuable contribution to fantastic film music.

Piero Piccioni's highly romantic music for the Italian fairy
tale, MORE THAN A MIRACLE (1966), was comprised of a pleasant
theme for woodwinds and strings which dominated the score. The
film's vague fantasy elements are emphasized by choir and harp;
and there is a particularly moving variation on the theme, with fantasy elements added to it, for the first scene of Brother Joseph's
flight. The music also utilizes the distinctive Italian Western-
styled bass guitar, chimey keyboard and rock drum beat. The
U.S. release of the film included an ill-fitting song over the titles,
performed by the Roger Williams Chorale.

The current fantasy film in Italy seems to be dominated by
contemporary pop music, and many new composers have come to
prominence with a flair for catchy tunes and rhythms. Riz Orto-

lani is one of them, though he actually began to score films in the 60's, with a couple of early horror efforts such as HORROR CAS-TLE (1963). He scored the American release of the exorcism film, BEYOND THE DOOR (1975), replacing Franco Micalizzi's original melodic and pop-oriented score with a monotonous mixture of droning synthesizer and seemingly routine pop muzak.

Stelvio Cipriani shared a similar approach to horror films such as the Italian version of BARON BLOOD (1972; scored for AIP's stateside release by Les Baxter) and TWITCH OF THE DEATH NERVE (1973). Cipriani's music for TENTACLES (1977) was ba-sically an array of easy-listening, contemporary pop, hardly com-plementary for this film of a rampaging giant octopus, though he does provide an effective underwater suspense motif for piano, synthesizer and percussion effects. THE GREAT ALLIGATOR (1981) featured a pop theme with a bass disco riff and synthesizer melody over repetitive South Sea Island drum pounding; the result-ant sound, akin to the droning of native drumming, was evocative of some mood and had a catchy enough rhythm but remained dis-tractive to any dramatic feeling due to its overreliance on a toe-tapping rhythm.

The penchant for pop tunes in horror films has perhaps reached its peak with the rock group Goblin, led by Italian film-maker Dario Argento. The group, the members of which all take an active hand in composition, have scored each of Argento's films since 1975 (Argento had previously been associated with Ennio Morricone), lending them an oppressive, repetitious loud rock sound somehow in keeping with the grisly visual nature of such all-out shockers as Argento's SUSPIRIA (1977) and CONTAMINA-TION (1980). The SUSPIRIA score is loud, gaudy and baroque, like the movie itself, according to one reviewer: "The multitrack stereophonic soundtrack makes the music an integral part of the scariness of things. SUSPIRIA is set in a vast and foreboding dancing academy ... when two girls swim in a cavernous indoor swimming pool and Argento's camera drifts menacingly around them to take up a position high above the floating bodies, the music swells unbearably loud almost as if Jaws were in the vicinity. In this instance the music is a red herring and yet it makes the se-quence memorably frightening."[26]

Goblin also scored George Romero's DAWN OF THE DEAD (1979), a highly graphic sequel to the director's earlier NIGHT OF THE LIVING DEAD (which, incidentally, had been scored purely with stock music from the Capitol Records library, including many cues from 1950's horror films). Goblin's music for this grisly film of flesh-eating zombies inhabiting a shopping mall was harsh, brutal and often highly satirical, and was quite appropriate to the similarly jolting and burlesque visuals. The music features simple, pulsating motifs and textures of electric and acoustic elements dominated by guitar and drums, but includes effective motifs such as a light, catchy violin melody over bongos during a zombie shooting spree and a comical honky-tonk piano elsewhere. Goblin also scored the Italian release of the Australian thriller, PATRICK (1979), replacing Brian May's original, lightly symphonic score with a series of electronic rock rhythms, including a chilling background use of what sounds like a dentist's drill (a sound which is horrifying enough in and of itself!).

A living-dead movie similar in its graphic grotesquerie to the Romero pair is ZOMBIE (1980) which features a violent rock score by Fabio Frizzi and Giorgio Tucci, as in DAWN OF THE DEAD, in addition to some electronic effects. The use of the score, however, is highly inappropriate, accompanying dramatic and suspenseful scenes (such as the girl's underwater fight with the zombie and the zombie's subsequent evolution into sharkmeal) with a mellow pop motif which hardly accentuates the visuals, not even as interesting counterscoring in the vein of Donaggio or Morricone.

Not all recent Italian horror efforts have featured rock and pop in their sound tracks, however, and a notable example is Luciano Michelini's fine symphonic score for the repulsive SCREAMERS (1981). Michelini drew upon three basic themes: a main theme, which opens with a "screaming" chord from brass and strings over throbbing drums before moving into a rushing, frantic theme for horns; a poignant, melodic Love Theme for strings and woodwind; and a Morricone-esque action piece with slicing string chords over a driving keyboard and percussion rhythm, evoking a strong sense of urgency.

Germany

Whereas the film music of France and Italy has frequently made great use of pop and rock scoring, the film scores from German films, for the most part, have seemed to remain fairly symphonic in tradition. Germany motion pictures have an especially rich musical heritage, harkening back to the silent films of the 20's. In fact, much of the earliest composition for fantastic films was for German pictures, including the work of Gottfried Huppertz (Fritz Lang's DIE NIBELUNGEN and METROPOLIS) and Hans Erdmann (Murnau's NOSFERATU and Lang's TESTAMENT OF DR. MABUSE).

Erdmann's score for this latter 1932 film was quite a good one, embellishing the slight supernatural elements with eerie, shimmering tones that sound like high organ and vibraphone. An effective, dirgelike motif is heard from woodwind and brass as Mabuse exhorts Dr. Baum into masterminding his criminal empire. A slow-moving, vaguely melodic Love Theme for woodwind and strings escorts the relationship between Kent and Lilly. Erdmann also provides a lengthy cue for the destruction of the warehouses, opening with tympani under high string vibrato and brass chords as the structures are blown up, seguing to an adventurous Action Theme for brass and strings as the fire trucks arrive--the cue remains as Baum is spotted nearby and pursued by Inspector Lohman. Baum returns to his Asylum, where a soft, meandering woodwind theme is heard as the spectral Mabuse informs him of his failure. Low-key woodwind and brass join the eerie organ/vibraphone motif as Baum turns mad in Hofmeister's cell, and the music segues into a brassy resolution as the film ends. This was a notably expansive use of music for the early 30's, and in keeping with the strong use of music that was prominent in the German expressionist cinema of the 20's and 30's.

Another notable German composer from this period was Wolfgang Zeller, who began his career during the silent era and went on to provide music for films of the 30's, including Carl Dreyer's VAMPYR (1932) and the 1932 L'ATLANTIDE. Zeller scored a few other fantasy films during this decade, and continued to write music for nongenre films through to the early 60's. During this decade, Peter Thomas became recognized for scoring the sensationalistic documentary, CHARIOTS OF THE GODS (1969) and THE BLOOD DEMON (1967), a Poe adaptation. Peter Sandloff, Raimund Rosenberger and Martin Boettcher also scored a handful of German fantasies during the 60's. In the 70's, Jerry Van Rooyen scored several German horror thrillers, and the avant-garde rock group, Popol Vuh, provided the music for Werner Herzog's 1979 NOSFERATU, as they had for Herzog's other stylish and bizarre films. The music for NOSFERATU was quiet and droning, comprised of acoustical motifs for sitar, keyboard and voice (electric guitar is used in one cue), and has a mantralike chanting quality to it, rather uninteresting as music but in keeping with Herzog's infinitely slow pacing and quietly hypnotic approach to the story. One noteworthy motif is a languid, two-note moaning chant for male choir which evokes an ancient and tomblike atmosphere in scenes in the vampire's castle. The score also utilized excerpts from Wagner's Das Rheingold and Charles Gounod's Sanctus.

A contemporary German symphonic composer gaining a great deal of deserved notice lately is Rolf Wilhelm, who began scoring films in the 60's. His most notable work is for the two-part epic, DIE NIBELUNGEN (released in America in 1967 as SIEGFRIED), a mythic fantasy which called for a rousing, sweeping symphonic score, and one that Wilhelm delivers satisfactorily with a variety of leitmotifs, including a heroic march signifying the overall scope of the epic, a similarly heroic theme for Siegfried, a warblingly brassy motif for the fight with the dragon, and a tender violin Love Theme underlying Siegfried's love for Brunnhilde, which results in his heroic crusade to win her hand.

Mexico and South America

The prolific Mexican film industry has become somewhat infamous for producing a surging plethora of low-budget horror films, distinctive in their styles and basically unremembered by most American audiences, but they have been scored by a number of talented composers whose work, as so often is the case, frequently surpasses the quality of the films for which they were composed.

Gustave Cesar Carrion has written music for a number of the wrestling superhero and vampire films since the late 50's. His style is heavily influenced by the musical textures of the late 30's and early 40's Universal horror-film styles, and he has become so adept at scoring genre films such as THE WORLD OF THE VAMPIRES (1960), SANTO AGAINST THE DAUGHTER OF FRANKENSTEIN (1972) and many others that he has become something of a Mexican equivalent to Hans J. Salter. Some of his earlier scores show up in varied forms in other films scored by him at a later date. For example, the music passages in EL VAMPIRO (The Vampire, 1958) can be heard, slightly jazzed-up, in the Santo/Blue Demon films he scored in the early 70's. "Generally," one researcher wrote, "Carrion is a foremost spook picture musician in Mexico, and, although his talents are just adequate, the prolific nature of his talents are not to be ignored."[27] He is probably the best-known Mexican horror film composer, mainly through his work in EL VAMPIRO, subsequent "Nostradamus" films, and THE WITCH'S MIRROR (1961).

Antonio Diaz Conde has written the music for the infamous "Aztec Mummy" series and other horrors that shambled onto American television in the mid-60's. Conde's work is somewhat similar to that of the American serials of the 30's. His style is histrionic, unpalatable, and tinny (no fault of his, but it sometimes sounds as though the engineering on the "Aztec Mummy" series was purposefully mediocre in order to render the results suitably hackneyed). His score for THE CURSE OF THE DOLL PEOPLE (1961) is a slight deviation, relying upon the visual components to give his music some substance. Most of the time, though, it sounds as though someone bought a record composed by Conde and used it as a background for some of their movies; it is amusing, pseudo-library music.

Luis Hernandez Breton scored a handful of horror films during the 50's and 60's. He worked on the score for Buñuel's EL (1952), but since then has been little heard, at least on this side of the border. The only outstanding example of Breton's talent lies in the strange, melodramatic score for INVASION OF THE VAMPIRES (1963). The soft, melodic choir and the low, deep string accompaniment is a nice touch in an otherwise execrable film.

Sergio Guerrero has scored horror pictures since the mid-50's. His score for THE MUSEUM OF HORROR (1963) was used rather poorly in the film--dramatic highlights were scored with overly subtle cues, while the volume was raised during action scenes and subdued during the many pedestrian scenes; the entire experience was akin to listening to one long, uninterrupted song, with the volume raised and lowered at intervals. Raul Lavista scored INVASION OF THE ZOMBIES (1961) and SANTO VS. THE VAMPIRE WOMEN (1963) with a serial-like music score that seemed lifted straight out of FLASH GORDON, though the rest of his output seems devoid of this delightful postserial amusement. Other composers who have frequented Mexican horror films include Enrico Cabiati, Manuel Esperon, Fondo Jorge Perez, Rosalio Ramirez and Alice Uretta. Readers are referred to the Filmography for further details.

Horror films from South America have featured a wide array of musical styles, although most of them have not been heard outside of their native countries, and background information on them and their music is unfortunately elusive. Among the composers who have scored fantastic films in South America are Gabriel Migliori (Brazil), Roberto Duprat (Brazil), Kiril Dontchev (Brazil), Jorge Andreani (Chile), Rudolfo Arizaga (Argentina), Eduardo Armani (Argentina), Julian Bautista (Argentina), Leo Brower (Cuba) and Albert Levy (Colombia). The latter individual is credited with the music for a pair of "Jaguars" superhero films made in Colombia during the 70's and later sold to American TV, where they were heard with short excerpts from popular rock albums, such as a tune by the group Black Sabbath used in KARLA CONTRE LOS JAGUARES. This is a rather common practice on many foreign films, which may either be the fault of the composer/music director who scored it or the heavy-handed "improvements" of some economy-minded domestic distributor.

Spain

Spain's leading film composer is Anton Garcia Abril, who began scoring movies in the 60's and has written the music for a number of Spanish horror films since then, using a variety of impressive horror and melodic motifs, such as a romantic theme for THE LORELEI'S GRASP (1975, rereleased in 1980 as WHEN THE SCREAMING STOPS). This film also features a theme song, "Evil Eyes." Regrettably, further details on Abril's work is not available to this author, nor is it for other Spanish composers notable for their horror output, such as Angel Arteaga, Waldo de los Rios and Gregoria Segura.

Sweden

Sweden's most notable and versatile composer is Erik Nordgren, who is best known for his long association with filmmaker

Ingmar Bergman. Born in 1913, Nordgren studied at Stockholm's
Musical Academy, and began scoring films in 1945. His association
with Bergman commenced two years later and resulted in Nordgren's few scores in the fantasy genre, including Bergman's symbolic SEVENTH SEAL (1956) and WILD STRAWBERRIES (1958).
Lesser known Swedish composers working on more overtly fantastic
films include Harry Arnold, who scored INVASION OF THE ANIMAL
PEOPLE (1960) and Sven Gyldmark, who wrote the music for the
original REPTILICUS (1962) and who had the nonexclusive pleasure
of having it replaced with a new score (by Les Baxter) for the
film's American release.

Eastern Europe and Asia

Two Greek composers have become noted for their distinctively Greek musical style, which has been used effectively in American
films as well as in their own native countries. Mikis Theodorakis,
born in 1925, was educated at the Conservatory of Patras, and
later at Athens Conservatory, where he also gained unfavorable
notoriety for his political associations. In 1953 he studied at the
Paris Conservatoire and gained some recognition as a composer of
concert music, ballets and film scores, particularly for the political
thrillers of Greek director Costa-Gavras, and the acclaimed
ZORBA THE GREEK (1964). Theodorakis' distinctively Greek musical style was put to good use in such borderline science fiction
films as THE DAY THE FISH CAME OUT (1967). Manos Hadjidakis,
born in Athens in 1925, has become acclaimed as a leading Greek
composer of popular music and film scores; his music tends to be
more melodic and easy-listening in character than Theodorakis'.
Hadjidakis won an Academy Award for his popular theme from
NEVER ON SUNDAY (1960); his single effort in the fantasy field
being the 1957 film, BED OF GRASS, about a girl thought to be a
witch. While the music of both composers tends to be more tuneful
or rhythmic than dramatic, and is often characterized by Greek instruments such as balalaika rather than symphonic orchestra, they
have provided a unique musical accompaniment to many films, although their output for the fantastic genre is sparse and deserving
of only passing mention.

Christopher Komeda, known in his native Poland as T.
Krzysztof Komeda, gained some note in America for his interesting
score to ROSEMARY'S BABY (1968). As a leading jazz pianist and
composer, Komeda began to score films in 1958, and went on to enjoy a notable association with director Roman Polanski. Komeda's
music for ROSEMARY'S BABY is quite haunting, with its prominent
lullaby theme, sung by female voice, and eerie, satanic motifs.
Komeda's earlier music for THE FEARLESS VAMPIRE KILLERS (1967)
included an effective male chorus chanting a somber melody over a
rapid, up-and-down female chorus monotonously intoning a swirling,
whirlpool drone; under this was percussion, jangly keyboard and

electric bass guitar, all of which built an effective contemporary-sounding ominousness.

The leading Czech composer for fantasy films is undoubtedly Zdenek Liska, who lent his talents to a number of effective semi-animated films for director Karel Zeman. Liska's score for Zeman's THE FABULOUS WORLD OF JULES VERNE (1958) was a particularly notable work, featuring a music-box style harpsichord theme with a chamber ensemble of strings and woodwinds added, very much in keeping with the nostalgic visual style that suggested the old engravings illustrating Verne's original stories. Liska's score is similarly old-timey and contributes greatly to the film's quaint adventuresome quality. Liska provides a very nice cue when the submarine rams the merchant ship Camelle: a profound theme, full of brief pathos in sympathy for the doomed crew of the sinking vessel, erupts from the strings and woodwinds, seguing to a similarly styled action motif as the Camelle sinks to the bottom. In contrast, Liska's music remains too moody during the giant octopus battle, failing to build any excitement when a more dramatic orchestration is sorely needed. The blows struck against the octopus, however, are nicely punctuated with keyboard strikes. Liska also provided a pretty Love Theme for woodwinds over muted harpsichord, which seems to be based somewhat on Gilbert and Sullivan's "Tit-willow." The film ends with a happy string finale as the hero and his companion soar into a woodcut sunset on the captured balloon, which segues into a rendition of the Love Theme alternating with a footsteplike string motif for the end titles.

Jan Rychlik was a notable composer of concert works during the 40's and 50's who composed music for many popular short films in Czechoslovakia. Born in 1916 and educated in many different fields, Rychlik eventually found his niche in music. By the time of his death in 1964, Rychlik had scored 55 films, eight plays and many concert pieces. His film music was mostly for animated and puppet films, such as Jiri Trnka's ARIA OF THE PRAIRIE (which later became a feature film and a theatrical musical called LEMONADE JOE, both using Rychlik's original music). The composer's fantastic film scores include CREATION OF THE WORLD (1958) and BOMB MANIA (1959).

Lubos Fiser also provided scores for a variety of Czech fantasies. Like Rychlik, Fiser is a productive composer of concert and chamber music, his "Report" having been performed by the American Wind Symphony Orchestra in Pittsburgh. In 1966, Fiser won first prize at the UNESCO International Composer's Competition in Paris. His occupation, however, remains in film composition, and he has scored 300 television, feature and short films, including Karel Zeman's Jules Verne movie, NA KOMETA (1970), and THE DEADLY ODOR (1970), a uniquely animated horror spoof. Fiser's personal favorite is his score for Jaromil Jires' poetic fantasy, VALERIE AND THE WEEK OF WONDERS (1970). "This film

is a fantasy exploring reality and dreams," Fiser said. "It offers
the composer many possibilities of expression. To convey its extraordinary atmosphere I have used a lot of unusual orchestral
means, such as children's chorus, ancient instruments, viola da
gamba, violone, special flutes, historical cembalo and baroque organ."[28]

Other Czech composers contributing to the fantasy genre,
most often through the country's noteworthy animated shorts, include Julius Kalas, Evzen Illin, E. F. Burian and Petr Hapka.
Yugoslavian composers of similar repute include Tomislav Simovic,
who scored many fantasy shorts during the 60's, and Branimir
Sakak. Dimitru Capoianu is a Rumanian composer who wrote the
music to many animated cartoons with fantasy elements. Readers,
again, are referred to the Filmography for more details.

The prolific film industry of India has produced a significant
number of fantastic films in recent years, most of which seem to
be ghost stories of one kind or another. Indian film music is particularly characterized by the frequent use of the Indian film song,
but unlike the more commercial use of songs in Western cinema,
the Indian film song is deeply rooted in cultural tradition and
mythology. As Siddharth Kak wrote in his editorial introduction
to a special music issue of CinemaVision India, "The Indian film
song holds sway as a unique phenomenon, an inescapable part of
our everyday lives.... The one note, commonly struck [about] the
Indian film song is that it's trashy, vulgar and degrading....
Perhaps it has elements of great art--however unintentional. Perhaps it is the new folk music of India, which is possibly why 'Film
music has become more important than the films themselves'....
Is that because film music really 'bridged the gulf between classical and folk'?.... Is it because songs have acquired 'Greater
abandon, more tonal colour, variety and polish'?.... Or is film
music so popular because 'it is a legacy of India's rich 4,000 year-
old musical tradition'?"[29]

The importance of the film song to Indian cinema has of
course been felt in fantasy films, though few composers can actually be pigeonholed as frequenting the genre. One of India's most
respected composers, B. V. Karanth, scored THE FERTILITY GOD
(1976), a ghost film about demon possession. Karanth is particularly noted for his incorporation--like Mario Nascimbene--of sound
effects as part of his musical score, such as his use of such natural sounds as cycle bells, door bells and police sirens in the
music for EK DIN PRATI DIN. As Karanth said, "When I take up
a film, I do not confine myself to just the songs and the background music. I design the complete sound track."[30] Karanth's
view that there should be a detailed sound scenario along with the
screenplay, thereby blending sounds, music, and dialog for the
greatest effect, characterizes his approach to film music.

Other composers opt for a more traditional musical style;
Vanraj Bhatia has frequently used religious chants and ragas, as
in his music for KONDURA, a mythic fantasy. Bhatia's theme
song, based on raga Marwa, reflects the confusion in the hero's
mind when he is presented with a gift from Kondura, the sage of
the sea, a gift that may well be as much a curse. Bhatia weaves
into the song the weird wailing of women, to characterize the
siren-song of the sea. In NISHANT, Bhatia epitomizes the dark,
somber mood of the film through low, mournful music. "To the
composer it is the totality of the film that matters--its basic theme,
its narrative style, its pace, the period and the place in which it
is set."[31]

India's most famous filmmaker is Satyajit Ray, who, since the
60's, has composed his own music for his films, including fantasies
such as GUPI GYNE BAGHA BYNE (1969) and its sequel HIRAK
RAJAR DESHE (The Kingdom of Diamonds, 1980). In both of these
films, Ray made use of Indian classical music to achieve a humorous
effect: "I wanted to use parody, I wanted to have fun.... It
seems funny because of the contrast, because classical music was
being used in a funny situation. But the music evolved as an organic aspect of GUPI GYNE. I was not trying to consciously prove
that I was great at blending all kinds of music effortlessly."[32]
Ray, however, is quite outspoken on his view that music should
ultimately be unnecessary in films, and scorns the broad use of
romantic music in the Hollywood movies of the 40's. "My belief is
that a film should be able to dispense with music," Ray said, "but
half the time we are using music because we are not confident that
certain changes of mood will be understood by the audience. I
would like to do without music if such a thing is possible--but I
don't think I'll ever be able to do that. I have used very little
music in my contemporary films and as much natural sound as possible."[33] Other composers who have dabbled in a fantasy score or
two include M. Roy, Sathyam, Sonik-Omi, A. Banarjev, and S.
Jagmohan.

The film industry in Hong Kong, when it isn't cranking out
martial arts battle fests, has become quite prolific recently in science fiction and fantasy films of similar style. As in India, though,
few composers have yet to become noted for contributing excessive-
ly to the genre. Those who are credited with an occasional such
film include Wang Fu-Ling, Pan Chao, Chan Fun-Kay, Wong Tse
Yan and Chen Yung-Yu. Other composers in nearby countries
who have contributed in some way to fantastic film music include
Tito Arevalo in the Philippines, who scored a number of vampire
movies in the 60's and 70's, and Sabir Said, a Malayan composer
with a couple of vampire films under his baton.

Again, background information and commentary on many film
scores from these countries is sorely lacking. The previous pages
will hopefully serve to at least pinpoint those foreign composers

who have touched base, in some manner, with the fantastic cinema of their own countries.

Notes

1. Jean Cocteau, Beauty and the Beast: Diary of a Film (New York: Dover Publications, 1972) p. 128-129 (and following quotes)

2. Stephen Rebello, "Jack Clayton's THE INNOCENTS," Cinefantastique Vol. 13, #5 (June-July 1983) p. 54

3. Steve Harris, liner notes to A LITTLE ROMANCE sound-track album (Varese Sarabande Records, 1979)

4. Miriam Benedict, liner notes to OUR MOTHER'S HOUSE sound-track album (MGM Records--Polydor reissue, 1978)

5. Donald C. Willis, Horror and Science Fiction Films II (Metuchen, N.J.: Scarecrow Press, 1982) p. 305

6. David Bartholomew, "Film Review," Cinefantastique Vol. 5, #2 (1976) p. 29

7. Paul A. Snook, "Record Review," High Fidelity, June 1982, p. 69

8. Jim Doherty, "Record Review," Soundtrack! The Collector's Quarterly Vol. 1, #2 (June 1982) p. 26

9. Philip Perkins, "Ennio Morricone," OP: Independent Music, September-October 1982, p. 24

10. Ibid.

11. Simon Frith, "Sound and Vision," Collusion #1 (England, 1981) p. 9

12. Ennio Morricone interviewed by Massimo Cardinaletti, Soundtrack Collector's Newsletter #14 (June 1978) p. 21

13. Luc Van De Ven, "Record Review," Soundtrack Collector's Newsletter #14 (June 1978) p. 11

14. Ennio Morricone, op. cit., p. 18

15. Tim Lucas, "Film Review," Cinefantastique Vol. 13, #1 (September-October 1982) p. 49

16. Ennio Morricone interviewed for the author by Martin Van Wouw, September 8, 1982.

17. _____ interviewed by Martin Van Wouw, Musica Sul Velluto #9 (Holland: September 1981) p. 9

18. Bruno Nicolai interviewed by Martin Van Wouw, Musica Sul Velluto #9 (Holland: September 1981) p. 16

19. Scot W. Holton, liner notes to TOURIST TRAP sound-track album (Varese Sarabande Records, 1979)

20. Royal S. Brown, "A Poignant Backdrop for Cinematic Horrors," High Fidelity, May 1977, p. 80

21. Ford A. Thaxton, "Letter of Comment," CinemaScore #10 (Fall 1982) p. 34

22. Enzo Cocumarolo, "Carlo Rustichelli," Soundtrack Collector's Newsletter #11 (August 1977) p. 7

23. Mario Nascimbene interviewed by Ezio Reali and James Marshall, Soundtrack! The Collector's Quarterly #24 (1981) p. 4

24. _____ quoted by Roberto Zamori, "The Fantastic Universe of Mario Nascimbene," manuscript forthcoming in Cinema-Score.

25. James Marshall, "Mario Nascimbene, Part 2," Soundtrack Collector's Newsletter #13 (March 1978) p. 21

26. Allan Bryce, "The Music of the Macabre," Soundtrack! The Collector's Quarterly #22 (Summer 1980) p. 19

27. Jeffrey S. Frentzen, letter to the author, dated January 26, 1976. (My gratitude and appreciation to Mr. Frentzen for supplying much of the background commentary on Mexican horror film music for this section.)

28. Lubos Fiser, letter to the author, dated September 9, 1983.

29. Siddharth Kak, "Editorial," CinemaVision India, Vol. 1, #4, (1980), p. 3

30. B. V. Karanth interviewed by J. N. Kaushal, "There's More to Sound Than Music," CinemaVision India, Vol. 1, #4 (1980) p. 27

31. Vanraj Bhatia interviewed by Ram Mohan, "Stop the Action, Start the Song," CinemaVision India, Vol. 1, #4 (1980) p. 34

32. Satyajit Ray interviewed by Dhritiman Chatterjee, "Towards an Invisible Soundtrack?," CinemaVision India Vol. 1, #4 (1980) p. 19

33. Ibid., p. 21

TELEVISION SCORING

Writing music for television presents a whole different set of challenges to the composer, primarily from the highly commercial nature of the medium. Laurence Rosenthal, who has scored a number of TV movies and series episodes, put it succinctly when he commented that "television is like an enormous monster that keeps gobbling up all the material it needs to fill all those thousands of hours. Sometimes in television one gets to feel like one is in a sausage factory, just grinding out the stuff. There is rarely a chance to seriously consider an approach in as deep a way as in a feature film. It pretty much has to be rough and ready."[1]

The major limitations facing the composer on television are an extreme lack of time in which to compose, greater financial limitations not only in salary but also in the size of the orchestra one's budget will allow, and also the fact that one's music is going to be listened to primarily over a tiny television speaker instead of the multitrack sound systems available in some theaters. As Rosenthal goes on to point out, composers find that, in television, "small instrumental combinations really work better than huge, massed orchestral sounds. That doesn't necessarily have to be a limitation, it simply means that you have to conceive of it that way in the beginning, and then make the most of it."

During the earlier 50's, few fantasy shows were broadcast on television, and with the exception of Leon Klatzkin's heroic music for THE ADVENTURES OF SUPERMAN (1953), TV scoring tended to be fairly straightforward for the comedies and dramas produced regularly. ALFRED HITCHCOCK PRESENTS, a popular anthology series of mystery and occasionally semifantasy stories that debuted in 1955, often featured some noteworthy scores during the later seasons of the 60's, and particularly in its hour-long incarnation. Stanley Wilson, a music director for Republic Pictures during the 40's and 50's who worked on many of their science fiction serials, supervised the music for the series' first few years. Wilson was the music director at MCA Television, in charge of all musical operations, including HITCHCOCK PRESENTS. The familiar main theme was an arrangement of Charles Gounod's Funeral March of a Marionette, and lent a clever jauntiness to the title and Hitchcock's satirical opening monologue. The theme went through several arrangements during the course of the show. Likewise, the solo

two-note tympani phrases over low, droning strings, provided a
simple, but very evocative air of mystery to the episode titles and
commercial breaks. Dramatic scoring was uncredited during the initial HITCHCOCK PRESENTS series, although episodes of the hour
show featured notable scores by Bernard Herrmann, Jeff Alexander,
Frederick Herbert (who also acted as music director in the late
50's) and Lyn Murray.

In 1959 Rod Serling's phenomenal anthology series, THE
TWILIGHT ZONE, became the first series to really allow a variety
of impressive and often awe-inspiring stories to be aired. The
show's original main title and first few episodes were scored most
effectively by Bernard Herrmann, although Herrmann's theme was
later replaced by the more recognizable up-and-down guitar theme
composed by French avant-garde composer Marius Constant. Although Herrmann's theme was more subliminally weird and fantastic,
Constant's theme nicely set a mood of eeriness with its driving,
high-toned plucks from the electric guitar, broken by a short roll
on bongos and eventually brought to a swift conclusion with a
series of downward spinning brass-and-drum chords.

Much of the show's most atmospheric music was also provided
by Herrmann (as discussed in Chapter VI), either through original
scores or by anonymous reuse of his cues in later episodes. This
practice of assembling a score from previously composed material--
housed, after its initial use, in a studio library of stock music--
was a common one in television in those days and actually harkens
back to the 30's, and 40's, as we have already seen. The responsibility of maintaining this common stockpile of recorded library
music for TWILIGHT ZONE fell upon music supervisor Lud Gluskin.
Gluskin, who for many years headed CBS's music department on
the west coast, was in charge of hiring composers and supervising
the music for each episode. "The trick was for Gluskin to pick
out episodes which would not only need new music," recalled Fred
Steiner, one of the series' regular composers, "but would also be
useful for subsequent episodes when it was recorded for use that
following year."[2] During the season's summer break, Gluskin would
take original scores (composed for certain episodes the previous
year) over to Europe, where he recorded them in library format,
indexing each one meticulously by type and duration (for instance:
"tension music - 47 seconds"). He would then return with this
material on tape and select which episodes for the following season
would have original scores, and which would be scored with this
stock music. This is the reason only certain episodes give a music credit, and why certain musical cues recurred throughout the
series.

Bernard Herrmann, for example, only composed original
scores for seven episodes, although his music actually appears in
more than 30 subsequent episodes. Herrmann brought with him
his remarkable sense of musical atmosphere which, in its usually

nonmelodic use of chord progressions and broodingly ominous
phrases was highly appropriate to the mysteriousness and senti-
mentality of many TWILIGHT ZONE episodes, as one reviewer wrote
of the poignant episode, "Walking Distance": Herrmann's "string
writing in descending lines of affection and regret were barely
audible under the dialogue ... but it provided an effect that was
nonetheless deeply moving and memorable." [3]

In addition to Herrmann, the first few seasons of TWILIGHT
ZONE were aided by many fine scores written by a variety of composers including veterans as well as newcomers. Franz Waxman
provided an evocative score for the series' fourth episode, "The
Sixteen-Millimeter Shrine" which featured a sumptuous romantic
melody for strings emerging out of a jazzy waltz (for saxophone,
trumpet and brushed snare drum) to describe the aging actress'
sentiments for the past. This tender theme is contrasted with an
eerie motif for full orchestra over harp strums and ringing vibraphone which describes the actress' near-fanatical obsession to return to that past. The two themes play off each other nicely and
provide a fine musical representation of the character.

Leith Stevens wrote the music for the memorable "Time
Enough at Last," in which meek Henry Bemis survives an atomic
holocaust and finally has enough time to pursue his life's passion,
reading--until he breaks his glasses. Stevens' music is built around
a light theme for woodwind and brass over a plucked string rhythm,
which incorporates a number of slightly comic scherzos for scenes
such as Bemis clumsily trying to hide a book from his domineering
wife. But the music turns poignantly sour as she rips the book
to pieces in front of him. The cacophony of the atomic explosion
segues to rumbling, sliding string chords under pounded high percussion; the latter half of the film highlights the music more
and in a lower key, emphasizing Bemis' solitude in contrast to the
earlier portion which emphasized his lack of time through predominantly short cues. Stevens provides a nicely eerie descending
three-note pattern for woodwind and strings as Bemis awakens
from his first night in the post-holocaust world, seguing into the
semijaunty Bemis theme which again sours as he contemplates a
pistol in the wreckage of a sporting goods store. This extended
musical cue ends with a flourish as Bemis spies the public library
and realizes the opportunity to nourish his love for books. The
music ends with a final surge of monotonous tragedy as Bemis'
glasses break and he is left standing amid his piles of books, crying "it's not fair!"

Leonard Rosenman, a concert-hall composer from New York
who came to Hollywood in 1954 to score EAST OF EDEN, worked
extensively in television during the late 50's and early 60's while
also gaining exposure in feature films. Rosenman provided a highly effective score for the first-season TWILIGHT ZONE episode,
"And When the Sky Was Opened." The story, which told of three

astronauts, returned from an ill-fated space flight, who start to vanish unremembered by the survivors, was scored by Rosenman with emphasis upon trilling woodwind melodies, moody solo violin, and climactic brass passages. The primarily atonal score makes dominant use of repeated two-note, staccato piano chords over brass and woodwind, and the music is used very effectively to emphasize the strangeness of the events. It enters ominously as strange things happen or are referred to, such as the repeatedly changing newspaper headline, and the deeply rumbling cymbal sounds as Harrington looks in the cafe mirror and feels that he "shouldn't be here." Rosenman also utilizes repeated electronic tones mixed with the woodwind motif, as well as a fine use of wandering piano notes (its high and low ends matching each other harmonically) over woodwind, shimmering thereminlike electronics, and cymbal rumbles. The cymbals lend a very nice, doomsaying feeling along with the piano chords.

Nathan Van Cleave, whose composing career had started in New York, came to Hollywood in the late 40's and eventually became involved in films and television. During the course of the series' five seasons, Van Cleave composed 12 original scores which were highly effective. "Perchance to Dream," first broadcast in November, 1959, concerned Edward Hall, a man terrified of falling asleep lest his realistic nightmares kill him, and Van Cleave provided a fine mixture of symphony orchestra and electronics, as with the throbbing, echoed electronic tones and woodwind trills under weird, shimmering violins as Hall describes his dreams and later meets the mysterious girl at the carnival. This same two-note motif is later taken by low woodwinds as Hall describes the dreams' genesis when a child. The well-directed and highly suspenseful scene of Hall driving home and imagining a sinister figure in the back seat was accompanied with growing strings and surging brass chords under high, shimmering, ascending theremin and Novachord tones, a cue that was reused effectively in the climactic carnival sequence, building to a near-traumatic height of power and terror through the frightening, two-note echoed descending theremin wail, driven by a maelstrom of rapidly increasing staccato brass strokes, ascending like a slowly pulled roller-coaster car.

A more sentimental score was composed by Van Cleave the following month for "What You Need," which told of Fred Renard's attempt to profit from the aging Mr. Pedott's ability to tell the future. Van Cleave provided a slow, melancholy viola theme for Pedott (elsewhere taken by woodwind), with an eerie, descending organ glissando touched with xylophone representing his clairvoyance. The viola theme turns darker for low string tones under furtively piping woodwind notes as Renard confronts Pedott on the street corner, demanding he continue to aid him. Deep, ominous, descending brass chords enter as Renard rummages through Pedott's case, searching for "what he needs," in a nicely suspenseful arrangement of the main theme.

"A World of Difference," a remarkable episode telling of a
man who arrives at work one morning to find he's only an actor on
a movie set, was scored by Van Cleave with dominant use of an
eerie, high theremin wailing which describes the strange and nightmarish quality of the story. The first visual revelation of the fact
that Curtis is on a movie set is accompanied effectively by a low
cello chord with high, shivering strings and brass/woodwind piping, with the electronic wailing in the background. The constant,
buzzing wail, sounding deep and hollow, wavers throughout much
of the score and surrounds Curtis' confusion, rising higher and
higher as he runs in exasperation from the studio. An especially
frenzied wail, under frantically piping brass, is heard as Curtis
races back to the studio, trying to recapture his life in the movie
set before the stage is torn down.

Jerry Goldsmith, who later went on to gain much acclaim as
one of the finest contemporary film composers, scored seven episodes of TWILIGHT ZONE during his early days in Hollywood. His
first was for the episode, "The Four of Us Are Dying," an intriguing tale of a man with the ability to physically impersonate others
simply by "changing his face." The score is uncharacteristic in
that, rather than being comprised of brooding moods and eerie ac-
centuation, Goldsmith scored the episode with heavy, percussive
jazz, an approach which managed to work with the loud, nightclub
strip atmosphere of the show, as one reviewer noted: "Made up
of piano, drum, xylophone, trumpet and flute, it is all hard edges
and sharp movement, perfectly fitted to and enhancing the story."[4]

"Back There" utilized an evocative motif for two slowly ascending notes, performed by strings under a clanking celesta.
The impending two-note motif provided an awesome sense which
really suited more of a horror subject than the weak drama of a
man who finds himself transported in time to the eve of Lincoln's
assassination, and in fact, did find its way into the stock scores
of subsequent episodes such as "Death Ship" and "Nightmare at
20,000 Feet."

Goldsmith also scored what may be TWILIGHT ZONE's most
famous episode, "The Invaders," which told of an old woman tor-
mented by diminutive aliens who eventually turn out to be a crew
of Earthmen exploring a world of giants. Goldsmith scored the episode for successive waves of swirling strings mixed with piano,
organ and celesta, building up to a climax with low brass and
harp, repeating itself in variable arrangements through the course
of the narrative. The strings are embellished with sparse use of
atonal piano notes and bells accompanying eerie, wailing string
and woodwind chords. One especially shocking sequence, when
the woman reaches for the door latch and is stabbed through the
hole with a knife, is accented with chilling, heavy string chords,
and the episode concludes with a powerful use of sustained, low
synthesizer chords under bells for the final revelation of the

spaceship's origin. The music, like that of "Back There," was very spooky and scary, although in this case it worked much better with the excellent story and performance. "The fact that there was no spoken word made the impact of the music so much more important," Goldsmith later recalled. "The sounds had to convey all the feelings and emotions of the story. I'm very pleased with the results and feel that was one of my better efforts." [5]

Fred Steiner, who had started in radio with Nathan Van Cleave in New York, had come out to Hollywood in the late 40's and moved into television as many of the radio shows he had scored were translated into TV series. Steiner composed seven original TWILIGHT ZONE episodes, providing, as did most composers, a wide range of musical styles depending upon the requirements of the individual episodes. As Steiner pointed out, there was no real musical continuity between the episodes, other than the opening and closing themes, which were not used in the actual episodes. "In spite of the fact that it was a fantasy show," Steiner said, "it was an anthology format, and the shows were so different that there might be some that would demand a science fiction approach, with electronic or weird sounds, but then there might be another which had a lyric sound. Depending on the story, some of the music could be rather advanced, harmonically." [6]

The first TWILIGHT ZONE episode Steiner scored, "A Hundred Yards Over the Rim," broadcast near the end of the second season on April 7, 1961, featured an effective balance between a simple guitar-and-harmonica theme for the old Western wagon-train portion, and a heavy percussionistic motif for the modern-day scenes. Steiner describes his initial Western motif as being an almost banal, folksy tune. "I wanted it to be almost mindlessly simple," Steiner explained, "so that when you get to the highway and these big trucks are barrelling down, the music that would come in then would be a tremendous shock, not only from the standpoint of orchestral color, but dynamically; and the greatest contrast that I could think of was an orchestra consisting of percussion. I had about four percussionists, two pianos and a harp."

Steiner provided a similar contrasting color for "King Nine Will Not Return," scored after "A Hundred Yards Over the Rim" but broadcast earlier in September, 1960. Steiner scored a passacaglia for conventional orchestra, consisting of a series of six or eight very slow woodwind notes playing in low registers, which represented the desert. This was balanced with some very high string harmonics. "The score comprises very low sounds as opposed to very high sounds," Steiner said. "The idea was to provide a kind of dreary, bleak color backdrop, rather than any specific dramatic content."

For "The Passersby," an early third-season episode, Steiner scored a lyrical, sentimental melody for strings and harp to accom-

Fred Steiner. Photograph courtesy Fred Steiner.

pany this story of a Civil War soldier who begins to realize that
he and his company are not simply walking home from battle, but
that they are among the dead, marching to the afterlife. "Mute,"
involving a telepathic child, was the first of three hour-long episodes of the show's fourth season that Steiner scored. He provided a mixture of German folksy music (suggesting the girl's
homeland) with a strange string effect, consisting of highly divided violins playing in a very high register, representing the im-
plied thoughts of the telepathic girl. "Miniature" contrasted contemporary modes with an effective passage in one scene, of silent-
movie chase music, playing in a high register to match the image
of a miniature man chased around a dollhouse by a villainous doll.
"By taking out the bass," Steiner recalled, "it sounds like a miniature orchestra playing. The music was in a modern harmonic
idiom so that when the chase took place with this silent-movie music, which was very conventional, you would have a contrast."

     Rene Garriguenc wrote the music to four episodes, including
the effective psychological study of a mob suspecting their neighbors of being invading aliens, "The Monsters Are Due on Maple
Street." Garriguenc, in this score, introduces a homey, Suburban
motif which effectively captures the small-town Americana setting;
the music grows more furtive and dissonant as the power goes
off, the neighbors argue, and little Tommy tells of invaders from

outer space. The latter part of the segment utilizes repetitively descending woodwind progressions over muted brass in a meandering, incidental motif to underly the growing discord of the suspicious suburbanites. Garriguenc also makes use of low brass chords playing off each other as the neighbors hurl accusations, trilling woodwinds as the power returns to Charlie's house, and finally the music grows wild and discordant as lights come on randomly throughout the neighborhood and the mob runs wild and uncontrolled.

The majority of TWILIGHT ZONE episodes that were originally scored featured music composed by Herrmann, Van Cleave, Goldsmith, Steiner or Garriguenc. Other composers provided an episode or two along the way, but few with the frequency of these five.

Jeff Alexander scored "The Trouble with Templeton." Born in Seattle in 1910, Alexander was educated at the Becker Conservatory. He studied with Schillinger and Edmund Ross, and began to score films in 1951. He also worked on many TV scores, including ALFRED HITCHCOCK PRESENTS. His music for "The Trouble with Templeton" consists of a pretty, melancholy piano and string melody which emphasizes the episode's poignancy, but becomes dissonant as Templeton panics in the alley before returning to the present. Alexander uses sharply struck string chords to emphasize the weirdness of the fact that Templeton, a widower, has inexplicably gone back in time to become reunited, temporarily, with his wife.

William Lava, veteran of Universal horror films of the 40's and 50's, provided a delightful score for the "Once Upon a Time" episode, which featured Buster Keaton as a nineteenth-century janitor who toys with a time machine and winds up in 1962. The episode, envisioned as a comedy by its writer, Richard Matheson, featured music only in the 1890 portion, which was filmed in rapid, jerky silent-movie style. Lava wrote a charming honky-tonk silent-film piano score, played by pianist Ray Turner, which was highly appropriate and very nostalgic, matching Keaton's delightful vaudeville performance.

Robert Drasnin, who later worked on LOST IN SPACE and THE TIME TUNNEL as well as a number of made-for-TV movies in the 70's, scored the episode "The Hunt," which told of a hunter and his dog confronting St. Peter after being killed in a hunting accident. Drasnin lent it a homey country theme for harmonica and strummed guitar, later utilizing a woodwind motif. "The Gift" featured a guitar score composed and performed by classical guitarist Laurindo Almeida, who later scored the 1971 TV-movie, DEATH TAKES A HOLIDAY.

Lyn Murray, who had been associated with Nathan Van Cleave

and Fred Steiner in New York before emigrating to Hollywood, provided an interesting score for "A Passage for Trumpet." Other
composers who contributed occasionally to TWILIGHT ZONE include
Tom Morgan (four episodes), Lucien Moraweck (two episodes),
Nathan Scott (two episodes), Wilbur Hatch and Robert Shores
(single episodes).

Most composers were given about ten days in which to compose an original TWILIGHT ZONE score, which was fairly sufficient
for a half-hour episode that rarely needed more than ten or 15
minutes of music. The orchestras which recorded the scores
were typically small, consisting of only about 12 or 14 players,
and sometimes as few as nine. Occasionally there were even less,
as in Tom Morgan's use of only harmonica and guitar in one of his
episodes.

ONE STEP BEYOND got started the same time as THE TWI-
LIGHT ZONE but failed to capture its sense of wonder, and was
cancelled after only two seasons. While based more on scientific
fact than the fanciful TWILIGHT ZONE, ONE STEP BEYOND featured some highly memorable themes composed by Harry Lubin
which were repeatedly tracked throughout the series' episodes.
These included the main title theme, called "Fear," and a quiet
theme entitled "Weird," which accompanied the particularly bizarre
scenes. As one reviewer stated, "Both selections combined string
instruments and electronic effects, backed by a soprano and both
could scare the spit out of you if you happened to be watching
alone in the dark."[7] "Fear," in particular, was a spooky piece,
very much in the league of Miklos Rozsa's theremin theme from
SPELLBOUND. While the series' music has not gained the musical
acclaim that TWILIGHT ZONE scores have, Lubin's fully orchestrated efforts were, nevertheless, quite evocative, providing episode music that was, as the aforementioned reviewer adds, "both
nervewracking and beautiful." Lubin went on to compose cues for
the second season of THE OUTER LIMITS in 1964-65 which was also
largely tracked.

Another early fantasy series noted for its effective use of
music was THRILLER, which debuted in 1960 and ran for two seasons. Pete Rugolo composed the main theme for brass and bongos,
while the episodes were scored by him, Morton Stevens and Jerry
Goldsmith. The budgetary limitations of television were put to
creative use in the THRILLER episodes, which frequently used
chamber ensembles to very good effect. Much of the style of
THRILLER, both aurally and visually, seemed to have been influenced by Hitchcock's PSYCHO, a good example being the music
for the episode, "Pigeons from Hell," which used a predominantly
string orchestra. The episode also featured a striking use of
female voice heard at the end when the apparition appears.

Many of THRILLER's best scores were provided by Jerry

Goldsmith who, as with THE TWILIGHT ZONE, was given the opportunity to compose with a variety of styles. As reviewer John Caps
noted, Goldsmith's "early TV scores for THRILLER continually
tested the borders of atonality to describe various horror scenes."[8]
For the episode, "Hay Fork and Bill Hook," Goldsmith wrote a
pretty Irish folk tune alternately played by woodwind and viola
over rhythmic strings, balanced by atonal, conflicting string figures. As John Caps elsewhere stated: "While the murder mystery
on screen was pedestrian and pedantic, the music immersed us in
the atmosphere of the setting and built up a frightful mood of un-
predictable tension."[9]

"Mr. George" utilized effective, somewhat discordant violin
figures under a pleasant woodwind tune, in a clever chamber variation of a lullaby theme. "Yours Truly, Jack the Ripper" was given
a dirgelike motif for strings in addition to a mellow saxophone theme
for Jack; faint use of accordion was also in evidence from time to
time in the score. For the episode "Terror in Teakwood," Goldsmith composed a virtuoso chromatic piano waltz, which served not
only as a source piece (the episode concerned an obsessed pianist
desecrating the grave of his former rival) but also provided much
of the episode's shivery suspense.

THE OUTER LIMITS, like ONE STEP BEYOND, refrained
from the use of numerous composers called in to score an episode
every so often, as did THRILLER and TWILIGHT ZONE, instead
preferring to stick with a single composer throughout an entire
season. This also necessitated the frequent reuse of material in
succeeding episodes, and so the episodic music for these series
was not as varied as in the others. THE OUTER LIMITS featured
an impressive main title theme composed by Dominic Frontiere, who
was also a production executive on films and TV since the early
50's. Frontiere's opener featured an eerie, electronic buzz over
shimmering harp glissandos and a two-note, see-sawing string motif
culminating in cymbal brushing and a short, four-note brass fanfare. The end title music was an arrangement of these elements,
and often episodes would use these same cues as dramatic cues, as
in the episode "O.B.I.T." Frontiere's main theme was later used,
with virtually no changes at all, in the series THE INVADERS.

The second season of THE OUTER LIMITS was scored by
Harry Lubin, in a somewhat heavy-handed way, providing a main
title theme which opens with a thereminlike electronic wail much
like that of ONE STEP BEYOND; the music fades out for the introductory narration ("WE have control of your television set!"), and
returns to an orchestral fanfare as the title sequence fades out.
Lubin utilized electronic tones in the episodes, as well as conventional atonal instrumentation, predominantly slow chords, vibrato
strings, and blaring horn crescendos.

The various science fiction series created by Irwin Allen

were also noted for their effective use of music, beginning with
VOYAGE TO THE BOTTOM OF THE SEA, which premiered in 1964.
Based on Allen's feature film of 1961, the VOYAGE series utilized
the same main title theme, composed by Paul Sawtell, which was
heard in all 110 episodes except for "Jonah and the Whale." This
second-season opener, broadcast in 1965, made use of an original
title theme composed by Jerry Goldsmith, who scored the entire
episode. Interestingly, Goldsmith's theme foreshadows the basic
harmonic style of brass writing that Goldsmith later used effectively in the main title to LOGAN'S RUN (1976). After this episode,
Sawtell's theme was used until the series' cancellation in 1968.

The episode scores for the first two shows were composed
by Paul Sawtell, after which Hugo Friedhofer joined the composing
roster, frequently sharing assignments with Alexander Courage
(who later became noted for his STAR TREK music). Morton
Stevens also contributed scores to the show's first season, as did
Lionel Newman (who also performed general music supervision on
the series). The subsequent three seasons made use of scores
composed by Courage, Leith Stevens, Lennie Hayton, Herman
Stein, Nelson Riddle, Harry Geller, Irving Gertz and John Williams.

Williams' association with Irwin Allen had been launched when
he scored the pilot episode of LOST IN SPACE, "The Reluctant
Stowaway," in 1965. This relationship later catapulted Williams to
fame with his music for Allen's disaster films of the 70's. Williams
composed a memorable piece for the LOST IN SPACE title theme,
as John Caps has noted: "Williams took a seemingly tragic TV
series title, LOST IN SPACE, and scored a main title theme with
a jaunty, quirky little trumpet line, a computer-like background
and instantly pegged the show for what it was supposed to be, a
half-comic children's adventure. The theme was at once exciting,
promising of excitement, and in itself, funny."[10] Williams composed the music for several episodes, including the pilot.

Herman Stein, a staff composer at Universal in the 50's,
came to television in the early 60's and provided a number of
scores for LOST IN SPACE, as did his compatriot at Universal,
Hans J. Salter. Stein, recalling the manner in which as many as
five composers often contributed to a single film score at Universal,
explained that LOST IN SPACE and other series usually assigned
composers to score entire segments, rather than sections of episodes divided between a team. Composers alternated between episodes, but did not collaborate together on a single segment, except in the manner of library music used to supplement an original score.

Another composer to contribute to LOST IN SPACE was
Gerald Fried, who had gotten his start in feature films of the
50's. Fried came in toward the end of the series and provided

incidental music dominated by futuristic, electronic sounds. Around the same time, Fried also scored episodes of an ill-fated comedy series about cavemen--IT'S ABOUT TIME, which debuted in 1966. Fried composed tongue-in-cheek music suggesting primitive sounds and rattling bones, scored for percussion, bass clarinets and other main instruments.

Once again, Lionel Newman, as the head of Twentieth Century-Fox's television music department, supervised the overall scoring of LOST IN SPACE. Frequently he drew material from earlier Fox films, including many cues from Bernard Herrmann's DAY THE EARTH STOOD STILL and GARDEN OF EVIL. These excerpts were worked in and out of many episodes in the same manner of "tracking" used in TWILIGHT ZONE, along with original cues by Williams, Stein and Fried. This all created a mélange of unrelated musical ideas somehow tied together by the sheer repetition of a few particular motifs for certain characters or incidents.

The second season of LOST IN SPACE, starting on September 14, 1966, opened with a new title theme, also composed by John Williams but replacing the trumpet theme of the first season with a driving motif for french horns. The initial second-season episode, "Blast Off Into Space," was scored by Leith Stevens. Other composers who worked on second-season episodes included Robert Drasnin and Alexander Courage.

Allen's short-lived series, THE TIME TUNNEL, began its single-season run in 1966 with the episode, "Rendezvous with Yesterday." John Williams scored this episode as well as the series' theme, an effective, rapidly paced, up-and-down melody counterpointed against piping flutes, bridged with an adventurous pop-styled melody. Lyn Murray, Paul Sawtell and Leith Stevens also contributed music to individual episodes. Allen's fourth science fiction series, LAND OF THE GIANTS (premiering 1968), supervised again by Lionel Newman, included scores by John Williams, Irving Gertz and others.

A particularly unique sound for televised science fiction was established by Barry Gray, who wrote the music for all of Gerry Anderson's British "Marionation" series beginning with SUPERCAR in 1956 (imported to the U.S. in 1962). Gray, whose background was in popular music as a songwriter, accompanist and arranger, became involved with Anderson in the late 50's while a music director for The Century 21 Organisation in England. Gray brought to juvenile-oriented shows such as STINGRAY, FIREBALL XL-5, THUNDERBIRDS and others a catchy, tuneful melody in addition to a great deal of experimentation with electronic music.

While the Gerry Anderson shows were ultimately directed at a juvenile audience, Gray did not attempt to write a juvenile score. While his thematic material was highly melodic, rhythmic and catchy,

it was not children's music. In particular, the memorable theme
for FIREBALL XL-5 was an adventurous keyboard melody over a
percussionistic rock beat and saxophone rhythm that carried a
great deal of excitement. "It was Gerry's idea not to write kiddie
music for the puppet shows," Gray recalled, "and I should not let
the fact that the shows were done with puppets affect the music
at all. I should write as one would for a film, in a normal way,
and this is what I always did. I never wrote down to children.
I treated the puppets as if they were real people."[11] Series such
as SUPERCAR and STINGRAY, which featured vocal theme songs,
were less dramatic as themes but captured the spirit of the shows.

   Gray provided for UFO a jazzy theme for saxophone and organ, while his harsh, twangy theme for SPACE: 1999 was a return
to more dramatic thematic material through the use of rock orchestration, although Gray's actual involvement with the individual episodes of SPACE: 1999 was slight. "Because of the musical budget," Gray said, "they only recorded the minimum number of sessions for the series as were required by the musicians' union. So
the music editor used to lay music for different episodes either
from music we'd done before for other episodes, or he was allowed
to call on library music when he was short of cues." A unique use
of library tracks on the SPACE: 1999 series was the placement of
classical pieces during outer space scenes, à la 2001: A SPACE
ODYSSEY. Albinoni's moody Adagio, for example, was put to very
good use during a spaceflight scene in the "Dragon's Domain" episode, remarkably capturing the calm of space. The second season
of SPACE: 1999 used a new theme, composed by Derek Wadsworth,
who also scored various episodes.

   The BATMAN TV series featured a rock-and-roll "Batman
Theme" written by pop composer Neal Hefti, otherwise noted for his
catchy themes for Neil Simon films such as THE ODD COUPLE.
The series also utilized mostly rock-styled rhythms and campy
fight music provided by Nelson Riddle and Billy May. May also
composed the blaring pop theme for the GREEN HORNET series.

   The approach to BATMAN and related superhero series of
the 60's was in keeping with the commercial aspects of TV theme
music--a catchy beat and a hummable tune that audiences could
identify. Television music became more and more commercial as
producers and network executives demanded contemporary rock
sounds to attract an audience into the opening moments of their
new shows, up to the point where, in the 70's and 80's, theme music became almost indistinguishable from series to series, seemingly
derived from the same basic ideas. This was especially true for
sitcoms and action series. Fantastic TV shows did not completely
avoid this trend towards pop music, although some notable attempts were made to retain traditional modes of dramatic scoring
in several series, the most notable of the later 60's being STAR
TREK.

Gene Roddenberry, the series' creator, insisted that the musical scores for STAR TREK not consist of sensationalistic electronic effects. It was always his intention to retain a strong degree of characterization in the series, so that the human aspects
of the stories were not lost amid an overabundance of effects and
science fiction. This approach carried over into the music, as
supervised by Robert H. Justman, the series' associate producer
who tended to work with most of the composers. Justman was
very sensitive to music and wanted to do the best job possible in
having the series scored. As George Duning, who scored episodes
during the second and third seasons, said: "So many producers
of those types of films wanted strictly the far-out sounds, the
weird effects, the electronic sounds. My producer on that picture
was Bob Justman, and he said 'I want you to play the story, forget about any crazy electronic sound effects.' He wanted me to
play to the story and not to the fact that it was science fiction."[12]
Fred Steiner, who scored 11 episodes, said of STAR TREK: "The
philosophy, basically, was to write human adventure music. We
did occasionally use some electronic effects--you'd have to in a
show where you had so many varied situations--but the basic underlying philosophy was good old, blood-and-guts, adventure-
romantic movie music. It should have a certain kind of grandeur
to it, because this was a grand, human adventure, going to the
stars for five years in this enormous spaceship."[13] Gerald Fried
added that "we did everything we could to bring dimension and
class and points of view that might not be obvious on the screen
and that could be brought out with music."[14]

The series' pilot episodes (there were two) and the familiar
theme music, were scored by Alexander Courage. Born in New
Jersey, Courage graduated from the Eastman School of Music in
1941 and quickly found work scoring radio programs. He arrived
in Hollywood in 1948 and began working for MGM. In the 60's,
Courage began to work extensively for television, scoring episodes
of VOYAGE TO THE BOTTOM OF THE SEA, LOST IN SPACE and
others. Courage provided a theme for STAR TREK which became
quite popular, opening with an introductory trumpet fanfare that
heralded adventure and discovery, and seguing into a soaring,
tuneful melody for female voice over a rhythmic pop beat. The
fanfare was used frequently in individual episodes, incorporated
by the series' eight composers during scenes of the Enterprise
soaring through space.

Courage's first music was for the original, rejected pilot
episode, "The Cage" (later broadcast as "The Menagerie"), which
was somewhat more electronic in texture than subsequent episodes
once the series was launched. As STAR TREK historian Allan
Asherman said of Courage's debut episode: "Just as Roddenberry
used everyday props in unorthodox ways to suggest an alien or
future type of civilization, Courage took the orchestra's instruments and encouraged them to produce unearthly sounds. In 'The

Cage' even the guitars sound strange. The music that Vina dances to is unearthly and mechanical, and yet beautiful. The combination of strings and percussion that announces the Rigel illusion is gentle and weird at the same time (it is also present when Spock experiences the spores in 'This Side of Paradise'). Whatever Courage's reasons and methods, the end effect is the same; a strange, effective style of music that sounds both a million miles away and emotionally close to home. Courage also used electronic-type sounds in the earliest orchestration of the series' opening theme. Paced quicker than the subsequent version, with very effective echoing sounds, this early rendition was withdrawn before the first ten episodes had been scored."[15]

While Courage's name appears on the credits of more than 20 STAR TREK episodes, he actually composed original music for only four of them (plus the two pilots). As had been the case in THE TWILIGHT ZONE and, in fact, the majority of the television series of the 60's, most of the episodes were tracked with library music originally composed for previous episodes. In the case of STAR TREK, it was up to the three principal music editors, Robert Raff (most of the first season), Jim Henrikson (remainder of first and all of the second season) and Richard Lapham (third season), to decide which scenes could not be scored with existing library music. Producer Robert Justman would then assign a composer to do an original cue for those scenes.

In a vastly informative essay on the scoring practices of STAR TREK, Fred Steiner described the kind of approach taken to score the series: "The music for STAR TREK comprises three types of scores: (1) those which have entirely or mostly new music (note that these sometimes contain a few tracked cues); (2) partial scores, which ... consist of part new and part tracked music; and (3) those made up wholly from track. A survey of the seventy-nine broadcast episodes (counting 'The Menagerie' as two) reveals that, aside from the two pilot films, thirty-one episodes had entire or partial scores created for them. The amounts of new music in these scores ranged anywhere from a few minutes for the partials, up to thirty minutes or more for the entires. In one instance, I was asked to compose only one single piece for an otherwise completely tracked score: 'The Omega Glory' (3/1/68) had a scene which required a short paraphrase of 'The Star Spangled Banner.'"[16] Eight composers provided the original music, with either entire scores or partial ones, during STAR TREK's three-year run: Alexander Courage (both pilots, four episodes, plus library cues for later tracking), Fred Steiner (11 episodes, plus library cues and flag music for "The Omega Glory"), George Duning (five episodes), Gerald Fried (five episodes), Jerry Fielding (two episodes), Sol Kaplan (two episodes), Samuel Matlovsky (one episode) and Joseph Mullendore (one episode, plus library cues, including variations on the main theme).

According to Steiner, the screen credits for the individual
STAR TREK episodes are misleading and don't always reflect the
proper contributions of each composer. Whereas shows like THE
TWILIGHT ZONE usually gave screen credit only to an original
score, nearly all STAR TREK episodes, including those completely
or partially tracked, had a music credit at the end. This invariably led to confusion as to which were original and which were
tracked, and if tracked, who composed what. Tracked scores
were generally assembled from the work of more than one composer, which meant using the simple expedient of crediting only that
composer whose tracked cues totalled 50 percent or more of the
music heard in that episode.

The reasons for using tracked material in lieu of original
scoring were, naturally, predominantly budgetary considerations,
and were under the conditions specified in a contract between De-
silu (the producing company) and the American Federation of Musicians, which governed the practice and reuse of music for television series. One of these conditions prohibited reusing tracked
material from previous seasons or from outside sources. (Steiner
illuminates this in fascinating detail in his essay, and readers desiring further information are referred hither.)[17]

Occasionally an episode utilizing a tracked score would require a special musical treatment unavailable in the library cues.
These scores became what Steiner referred to as partial scores.
What could be scored with tracked material was done in that manner, while scenes necessitating special music were assigned to a
composer who would compose only the cues needed for those
scenes (such as Steiner's flag music in "The Omega Glory"). Other examples, which Steiner cited, include "The City on the Edge
of Forever," for which Steiner wrote about eight minutes of 1930's
period music suitable for this memorable time-travel episode; "The
Corbomite Manuever," which needed six minutes of special music
(composed by Steiner), including a "mechanical yet threatening"
theme for the dangerous Fesarius, and some eerie "baby" music
heard when the monstrous Balok is revealed as only the playful
puppet of a childlike alien; and "What Are Little Girls Made Of,"
which required about five-and-a-half minutes of new music, including a heavy, ominously stalking theme for the giant Ruk, as well
as a light, melodic theme for the attractive female android.

Most of the individual STAR TREK episodes were treated by
their composers as separate entities, with little thematic unity other than in the occasional recurrence of the fanfare. Each episode
would utilize themes composed for the new characters introduced
in that episode, but rarely did the running set of Enterprise crew-
men receive leitmotifs of their own. An exception was in the
"Charlie X" episode, in which Fred Steiner composed a theme for
Captain Kirk which he found useful in later episodes. Gerald
Fried composed a theme for Spock in the "Amok Time" episode which

he was asked to use in subsequent segments. Fried described his Spock Theme as an attempt to describe, musically, the conflicting aspects of emotion and logic within the character: "I wrote it for an instrument that couldn't possibly be romantic, a bass guitar, down in the low register with no resonance. It just thunks out the theme, but I told the player, [jazz guitarist] Barney Kessel, to play as expressively and as warmly as possible. I thought the tension between trying to play espressivo and the impossibility of doing it would be the kind of thing that would be appropriate for Spock." Fried also provided an effective score for "The Paradise Syndrome," composing sensitive melodies suggestive of the alien-yet-familiar nature of the otherworldly Indian community, and the romance between Kirk and Miramanee.

Fred Steiner described his instrumental approach to STAR TREK as being the use of an orchestra without violins. "I set up a musical color in which I used violas and cellos, the low strings, and lots of brass and woodwind, so that we could get as big and as grand a sound as possible from the horns and trombones," he said. Steiner also took trouble to achieve the proper sound during the recording sessions. "I didn't like the recording setup when I went in to record the score at Paramount. I'd worked there before and I'd found that the orchestra was, from my point of view, set up in exactly the wrong way. I persuaded the engineer to try reversing the position of some of the instruments, and I also asked him to put up what I call an overall microphone. That's one of the reasons we got a very good sound, particularly on my scores, because I insisted on this setup." The series also had the advantage of fairly good-sized orchestras, by television standards at least, normally consisting of about 25 musicians.

Steiner, in particular, made a strong use of leitmotifs for individual characters presented during each episode. "There was a theme for Elaan of Troyius," he recalled, "which I treated in a very lyrical way for her, but when the battle started I would treat it in a militaristic way." Steiner also composed a theme for the Romulans, first heard in "Balance of Terror," which was put to good use in later episodes as a leitmotif for various bad guys. Steiner modified the Romulan Theme quite well in the "Mirror, Mirror" episode by simply reversing it. "I was able to turn the theme exactly upside down" he said, "and this was a reflection (no pun intended) of the story."

George Duning's STAR TREK scores, along with other concurrent series such as THE TIME TUNNEL, took each episode singly and avoided a repetition of themes. Allan Asherman referred to Duning's score for the "Return to Tomorrow" episode thusly: "George Duning once again proved himself the best choice to compose the most sensitive scores required for STAR TREK. His melodies for Sargon and Thalassa suggest ancient power coupled with love and desperation."[18]

Another composer who scored two STAR TREK episodes was Sol Kaplan, whose career goes back to the MGM shorts of the early 1940's. Kaplan's music for "The Doomsday Machine" was described by Asherman as "one of the most dramatic and successful scores created for a STAR TREK episode. With the use of brass, strings and percussion (piano), Kaplan's melodies are almost Wagnerian in their ability to express grandeur and tragedy."[19] Respected film and television composer Jerry Fielding, whose untimely death in 1980 deprived the music world of an exceptionally gifted composer, also scored a pair of STAR TREK episodes, including the famous "Trouble with Tribbles."

Most other television series of the later 60's and 70's tended to be scored with predominantly pop motifs. Laurie Johnson came up with an exciting theme for THE AVENGERS (premiering in England in 1961 but not imported to the U.S. until 1966) as did Jerry Goldsmith for THE MAN FROM U.N.C.L.E. (1964), but the bulk of the episodic scoring consisted of stock jazzy, rhythmic pieces that drove the action on but did little else. Gil Mellé provided for NIGHT GALLERY (1970) an oppressive, discordant main theme comprised of jagged, electronic shards of sound, while Eddie Sauter took a similarly atonal approach to the scoring of many individual episodes, as with his eerie, primitive tonalities for the chilling segment, "The Caterpillar." Various other composers also contributed.

Lalo Schifrin provided a catchy theme for the PLANET OF THE APES TV series (1974), as well as scoring several of the episodes. While the series was derived from the popular series of films, Schifrin tried to refrain from being influenced by the music of the feature films. "I did my own theme, and I used my own music," Schifrin said. "It had nothing to do with the films. But, of course, the film dictated some kind of texture, and I think that when you are dealing with apes there are only so many things you can do."[20]

W. Michael Lewis and Laurin Rinder collaborated to provide some varied and evocative music for the speculative documentary series, IN SEARCH OF... (1977). While the title theme was a rather obligatory pop/disco tune for synthesizer over percussion, the background motifs for the individual investigative episodes comprised some effective fantastic scoring, such as the ominous march in the "Vlad Dracula" segment, mixed with thereminlike synthesizer tones and demonically wailing voices; an effective synthesizer and percussion composition for the "Easter Island" program; and a pleasant rock-styled synthesizer theme for an episode on time-travelling. Much of the music is rooted in rock and roll, dominated by electronic keyboards and percussion played by the composers (Lewis is a keyboardist, Rinder a percussionist), and provided an effectively mysterious and evocative backdrop for Leonard Nimoy's explorations into unusual phenomena.

Stu Phillips created a highly effective, adventuresome theme for BATTLESTAR GALACTICA (1978), which owed a great deal to STAR WARS, the series' illegitimate parent, but simultaneous series like WONDER WOMAN and THE SIX MILLION DOLLAR MAN were primarily rhythmic tunes with little original dramatic scoring. A notable exception is Lee Holdridge's score for the period fantasy series, WIZARDS AND WARRIORS (1983). Holdridge provided a lavish, old-fashioned symphonic score in the style of John Williams which lent a prominent class to the farcical series. His main theme was a rhythmic, medieval march with a lot of brass over strings, which lent the rather weak series a strong backdrop of period and adventure. The highly symphonic approach was especially distinctive among so much pop-oriented TV music for other shows, and was in the vein of Holdridge's heroic score for THE BEAST-MASTER the previous year, in terms of its mood. WIZARDS AND WARRIORS was recorded by a 35-piece orchestra, a rare luxury for a TV series.

The DARK SHADOWS series, which debuted in 1966, was the only attempt to mix fantasy and horror elements with a soap opera, and was phenomenally successful at the time. Robert Cobert, a Julliard graduate with much experience in television, provided the music for the series, which eventually amounted to about 20 hours of library cues used where appropriate over the course of the series' 1,000-plus daily episodes. "The music was strange," said Cobert. "It was of a kind a lot of people probably hadn't heard in the afternoon. I made a lot of early use of synthesizers and electronic instruments. I used to use the Ondes Martenot a lot, and other things like that--wild uses of low alto flute and vibes and basses doing things that they shouldn't, and all that sort of stuff. It was fun to write because there was a tremendous amount of really good interesting music that I was able to do."[21]

Cobert provided themes for most of the series' characters, the most popular of which was "Quentin's Theme," which became quite a commercial hit on record. The theme actually originated in a score Cobert wrote for a TV movie, DR. JEKYLL AND MR. HYDE, made by the producer/director of DARK SHADOWS, Dan Curtis. Cobert had written a romantic theme for the female lead, scored for violin with a moving piano background. Later, when Curtis told Cobert he needed a theme for a new DARK SHADOWS character named Quentin, who first appeared through the loudspeaker of an old-fashioned phonograph, Cobert, who was in the midst of several projects, realized that the theme he'd done for JEKYLL & HYDE would work quite nicely. "I took the violin and piano piece to a recording studio," Cobert said, "and took all the highs and lows out of it, filtered it, buzzed it, and made it sound like an old-fashioned record coming out of the phonograph." After its initial appearance, the theme was used in various arrangements in subsequent episodes.

Cobert continued a productive relationship with Dan Curtis, scoring all of his feature films and TV movies. While the first film based on the soap opera, HOUSE OF DARK SHADOWS (1970), contained only stock music from the series, Cobert provided some new material to supplement it for the second feature, NIGHT OF DARK SHADOWS (1971).

Curtis' THE NIGHT STALKER (1972), a highly successful contemporary vampire story set in Las Vegas, was scored with a combination of jazz and modern music. "I wanted a contemporary sound," Cobert recalled. "I went for lots of bass flute and alto flute, vibes, low marimba, bass marimba, a lot of bass clarinet. It was to be a pure, terrifying score with a little bit of jazziness in the background." The theme for Kolchak, the newspaperman who is convinced a series of murders were the work of a modern-day vampire, was a raucus, jazzy theme which emphasized a bass rhythm. "Kolchak was a humorous character," Cobert explained, "so it had that humor in it, and a little rock and a little scariness in it, but when the thing got into high gear, with Kolchak looking around at corpses, I had a lot of alto flutes moaning and stuff like that, which is scary but it's also a little funny. This is a scary movie but you're supposed to laugh, and I think this is the way it came off." The sequel, THE NIGHT STRANGLER (1973), was a continuation of the musical motifs from the first film.

In contrast to the contemporary sound of NIGHT STALKER, Cobert lent a rich, classical flavor to Curtis' TV version of DRACULA (1974). "I think I'm the first person who ever thought of writing a love theme for Dracula," Cobert reflected. "We used a music box very prominently, which played in a sort of Hungarian-ish air that was also quite lovely. I decided when I was doing that to take a chance and actually make it Dracula's love theme, so at the moment when Dracula has the major bite on the girl, up came a hundred violins soaring away!" This approach was highly effective, and in keeping with the film's emphasis on Dracula as a character of depth. John Williams utilized a similar romantic approach in the 1979 feature version of DRACULA.

Cobert provided the scores for more than a dozen TV movies produced and directed by Curtis which involved fantasy and horror subjects during the 70's, and finds he enjoys the challenge of writing such music. "I'm not fond of the horror genre," Cobert admitted. "But I like writing the music for it because you get a closer chance to approximate really serious 'long hair' writing than you do in many other fields." Cobert described his techniques at creating musical horror in such movies: "A lot of the scariness of music depends upon its entrances, depends upon exactly where you use it, how loud or how soft you play it, depends upon the choice of tonalities. There are some instruments that are scary and there are some instruments that aren't. A trumpet is not particularly scary. A bass clarinet is, an alto flute is. Then again, you can use trumpets in combinations with things and they will be scary depending upon your melodic content. There are certain kinds of harmonic devices that conjure up fear in people." Cobert has been quite successful at such conjurings, and Dan Curtis' horror films are noteworthy for the effectively Gothic and moody atmospheres given them by Robert Cobert.

Gil Mellé is another talented composer working frequently in television movies. While first brought to attention with his remarkable electronic score for THE ANDROMEDA STRAIN in 1971, Mellé has worked extensively on television since, providing music for series such as NIGHT GALLERY and THE SIX MILLION DOLLAR MAN, as well as numerous made-for-TV movies, many of which featured imaginative combinations of orchestral and electronic music. (These will be discussed in more detail in Chapter XIII.) Mellé's score for FRANKENSTEIN: THE TRUE STORY (1973) was a completely symphonic score, performed by the London Symphony Orchestra. Mellé consciously tried to avoid writing the kind of monster music that characterized previous Frankenstein films, instead composing a soulful string melody which underlined the inner spirit of the rather tragic monster. Mellé, who often invents electronic instruments to achieve desired sonorities in his synthesizer scores, had a special set of large orchestra bells built for the FRANKENSTEIN score, one of which was an immense bell capable of sounding a low C note, heard during the final Antarctic sequences. "Those bells were enormous," Mellé recalled. "The one that went down to the low C must have been twenty-six feet long, and it took us hours to find the proper recording mode to mike it at and to get the sonorities from the three bells. Until that time the lowest bell ever made was the low E-flat which was made for Richard Strauss' Don Quixote [c. 1898], but mine went down to a low C in the bass clef!"[22]

Mellé scored THE INTRUDER WITHIN (1981), a TV movie about a subterranean horror dredged up by an oil rig, with a mixture of electronics and orchestra. The score opens with a long, low rumbling synthesizer tone over which are added higher notes and a viola motif and, ultimately, shrill high strings as the synthesizer segues to a fast-paced, semi-jazzy motif over percussion. WORLD WAR III (1982) was an effective keyboard-dominated score, performed by Mellé's five-man group, Syren. The music balanced a powerful, throbbing motif for long, sustained synthesizer chords under a rhythmic piano melody with a primary theme consisting of erratic, militaristic snare drum beats over a pulsing synthesizer rhythm. One interesting cue is heard during the climactic battle scene between the Americans and the Russians in the Arctic research facility. "The music for that battle sequence is very linear," Mellé said. "There are no jagged moments, there's no agitato, and it sounds like anything but music for a battle. Most war music is lots of percussion and brass all playing at a breakneck tempo. This was long, flowing, dark philosophical lines. 'War is Insane'

is what the music was saying all through the battle. I was not
scoring what you were looking at, I was scoring the proper mental
attitude of what you were seeing." Mellé's versatile approach to
various types of films, and his unique command of electronic
styles has provided a number of memorable film scores for TV
movies in the fantastic genre.

Billy Goldenberg is also noted for his work on television,
having scored well over 60 TV movies in the 70's and early 80's.
Goldenberg started in television in the late 60's, working under
Stanley Wilson, music supervisor for Universal Television and a
veteran of film and TV. Goldenberg worked on various episodic
series before concentrating on made-for-TV movies, many of which
have been of a fantastic nature. He wrote the modern-styled music for the original NIGHT GALLERY pilot in 1969, and provided a
menacing organ score for RITUAL OF EVIL the following year.
One reviewer wrote of Goldenberg's television music: "He makes
music where other 'composers' are content to keep churning out
noises. Stylistically he is very versatile, yet he excels at providing Herrmann-like chords for television thrillers like Steven Spielberg's excellent DUEL. For this suspenseful tale of a salesman's
terrifying desert encounter with a malevolent oil tanker, Goldenberg
avoided scoring the main title, making the first burst of PSYCHO-
like strings all the more effective."[23] Much of these wild, Herrmannesque swirling strings are buried beneath the roaring engine
sound effects, which isn't Goldenberg's fault, but the music thus
tends to conflict with, rather than accentuate, the overall sound
track. Goldenberg also provides some very apprehensive, ominous
chords during the scene where the salesman sits inside a cafe and
sees the truck parked outside, realizing the driver must be one of
the patrons inside. Another effective cue uses strings and piano
tones to build a tense mood as the truck waits in the tunnel for the
salesman to help the stranded schoolbus.

Goldenberg's score for THE LEGEND OF LIZZIE BORDEN
(1975) mixed a ragtime-styled piano tune under high strings, with
discordant, atonal sounds for the less-savory aspects of Ms. Borden's personality. The murder sequence is a musical tour-de-force
of this kind of music, beginning with mysterious swirling strings
that lead into furtive piano and synthesizer fingering interspersed
with heavy keyboard pounding; this turns into a two-note, up-
down, up-down keyboard motif, growing in length and force, seguing into descending string passages as Lizzie approaches her doomed
mother. Furtive woodwinds emerge, then more use of various suspense passages for a mixture of piano, synthesizer, electric bass,
and strings playing wandering notes as the murder and aftermath
take place.

Laurence Rosenthal provided a number of intriguing scores
for TV movies during the early 70's. Rosenthal, who graduated
from New York's Eastman School of Music and later studied in Paris

with the venerable Nadia Boulanger, gained his apprenticeship in film scoring when he spent several years composing for shorts in the Air Force film unit. In the mid-50's he began to score films in Hollywood and racked up an impressive list of credits, later finding a niche in television during the 70's.

One of his early scores was the psychological thriller, HOW AWFUL ABOUT ALLAN (1970), for which he intentionally played against the horror of the picture through the dominant use of a very classically structured piano theme. "I used some very logical, familiar classical progressions," Rosenthal said of this score, "which have a kind of rationality about them and a clarity and predictability which would play against the madness of Allan."[24] Rosenthal took a similar approach that same year in THE HOUSE THAT WOULD NOT DIE, as well as in SATAN'S SCHOOL FOR GIRLS and THE DEVIL'S DAUGHTER (both 1973). "That's one of the aspects of film scoring that interests me the most," Rosenthal explained. "Even though you can't avoid directly underscoring the action, very often the function of the music can be much more exciting and certainly is unique when the composer can find a musical counterpoint to the action. It's not necessarily directly going against what the visual impressions are, but at least producing a new dimension by way of a kind of psychological or emotional counterpoint." In THE DEVIL'S DAUGHTER, Rosenthal also made prominent use of massed string sounds and dense textures during the scenes where the devil appears.

Rosenthal scored the first two FANTASY ISLAND movies, as well as the first few episodes once it became a series. While the concept classifies as fantasy, the approach to the series was more romantic drama, and so the music played up to that element. "I decided to go completely tongue-in-cheek and write a great big, schmaltzy, tropical paradise opening title with lush, lavish orchestration, and somehow it seemed to work. The rest of the score was rather dramatic and had quite a wide stretch." After Rosenthal left the series, his main theme continued to characterize the mood of the show, although a sappy use of Hawaiian ukelele music tended to dominate the individual episodes. Rosenthal also scored the short-lived LOGAN'S RUN series in 1977, in which he experimented with synthesizers. While avoiding any references to Jerry Goldsmith's music for the original feature film, Rosenthal provided an exciting main theme comprised of a pretty melody over a whirling synthesizer business. "The melody itself is a rather soaring romantic tune with a kind of quick synchopated, pulsating beat under it," Rosenthal recalled, "and over the top was a series of downward slides from a high note, which were made by simply setting the synthesizer in such a way so that all you had to do was strike the note and each one would descend from there. It just kept whipping up the excitement."

Rosenthal provided another contrapuntal approach to THE RE-

VENGE OF THE STEPFORD WIVES (1980). "For the horror of these robot ladies," he said, "I composed a waltz, which can only be described as 'smilingly insipid'. It's pretty, in a kind of predictable, conventional, unfeeling way, with all the beauty and elegance of a mannequin in a store window. Instead of going for horror, I went for its opposite, a kind of painted, artificial beauty." The approach went very well in this story of automatons and plastic, manufactured attractiveness.

Gerald Fried scored a number of TV movies in the late 70's and 80's, providing notable music to otherwise unmemorable films such as CRUISE OF TERROR (1978). For this film, Fried utilized an approach he had favored in some of the horror films he scored during the 50's, paraphrasing from traditional material. "I used voices, mumbling chants," Fried recalled. "One of the lead characters was a minister who would think in terms of Gregorian chants, so I tried to treat it as if it was on a larger dimension than what was actually there."[25] Fried provided another memorable score that same year for MANEATERS ARE LOOSE. As one reviewer commented: "Friedisms too are 'on the loose' in this excellent score, which must be rated among the composer's best efforts. A JAWS-like rhythmic device is used to good effect in the scenes such as where the tigers are on the prowl in the middle of the night. And when one of the tigers is killed by a professional hunter, there is no victorious or inciteful music, but rather a very bittersweet strain enhancing the hunter's regret at being forced to kill the beast."[26]

Fried has said that his responsibility in scoring a film like this, as we have noted before, is basically the same approach on any type of film: "You try to get the audience into the movie to the best of your ability. Credibility is a key word. A fantasy, horror film, or any film isn't worth anything unless people can get into the middle of it. You try to make the people real so that when the tigers start chewing on them, you care more." Fried does point out, however, that one doesn't always have this kind of an opportunity, for a variety of reasons. "Sometimes you go for a cheap shot at scaring somebody, but once again, you get scared only if you believe it, and in order to believe it there have to be real people with whom we can identify to some extent." Fried also provided a jazzy score for THE RETURN OF THE MAN FROM U.N.C.L.E. (1983), in keeping with the approach to the original 1964 series. The Jerry Goldsmith theme music was also used.

Fred Steiner scored an early TV movie in 1966 called HERCULES AND THE PRINCESS OF TROY, providing an effective theme for horn and trombone, as well as several passages scored for solo tympani, an effect Steiner found impressive on the Italian Hercules pictures of the 50's. "I was very struck by some of the musical approaches that the composers had used," Steiner explained. "There were long sequences in which nothing but the tympani were used. Instead of all that busy-busy music with lots of trumpets, just a few carefully placed notes on the tympani. So I used that kind of approach. I wanted to try and see how my music would come out using it."[27] Steiner was pleased with the results, so much so that he later scored a STAR TREK episode in a similar manner. Steiner also scored a TV movie called NIGHT TERROR (1977), setting up an unusual orchestral color through the effective combination of divided strings playing a dissonant, sustained chord mixed with a reverberated solo tuba.

Morton Stevens has scored quite a few TV horror films during the movie-boom of the 70's. Born in New Jersey in 1929 and educated at Juilliard, Stevens worked as an arranger for popular vocalists during the 60's, becoming associated with films and television in the later 60's and 70's. He provided evocative accompaniment for TV movies like POOR DEVIL (1973), a comedy about bungling demons, and THE HORROR AT 37,000 FEET (1973), in which Stevens came up with a slow, melancholy theme for high woodwind melody over lower piping woodwind and keyboard, which created an effectively somber and foreboding atmosphere while remaining nicely symphonic.

A number of other composers have dabbled in televised fantasy with less regularity, and with mixed results. Wladimir Selinsky scored Spielberg's SOMETHING EVIL (1970), an effective haunted-house melodrama, with the random use of synthesizer notes over soft woodwind blares, bell chimes, apprehensive brass tones and slow harp plucks. This discord was balanced with an outdoorsy woodwind theme, with notes ascending and descending evenly over stirring strings and a two-note low brass rhythm, the latter chords echoing forebodingly in effective counterpoint to the secure melody.

Leonard Rosenman scored THE CAT CREATURE (1973) with a highly atonal approach. Irwin Bazelon has spoken at length on this score: "For the opening of THE CAT CREATURE ... Leonard Rosenman sustained a taut chord for an inordinate length of time. The shock of his initial statement jolts the nerves, gradually increasing the tension and suspense by stretching out the musical tones like a rubber band. The chord has a bulldog tenacity, relentless and unrelieved, and the effect creates an aura that helps launch the film on its unearthly course."[28] The use of these eerie strings, punctuated by brass strikes over soft, hollow drumming is unpleasant to listen to, and that is the strength of this passage, which lends an appropriately distressing tone to the events that are about to transpire.

Charles Bernstein scored LOOK WHAT'S HAPPENED TO ROSE-MARY'S BABY (1976) with an approach similar to that of Christopher Komeda in the original feature film of 1968. Bernstein composed a slow lullaby with a slight "poppish" flavor, which is similar to Komeda's but without the haunting quality of the original. Bernstein's theme, sung by female voice over piano, guitar and strings, contrasts with a harsh chant, intoned over celesta with plodding chord progressions. The score thus balanced the innocence of Rosemary with the ritualistic evil of the witches who seek to use her.

Michael Small leans towards an avant-garde approach in his music, which has been highly successful in films such as THE PARALLAX VIEW (1974). Small scored the remarkable PBS TV movie THE LATHE OF HEAVEN (1979) with the sparse use of a repeated, two-note synthesizer melody, almost robotic in movement, slow and mechanical, with just the right touch of oddness about it that fits the strange world George Orr recreates with his dreams. Another PBS production, a mild adaptation of DR. JEKYLL AND MR. HYDE (1981), was scored by David Greenslade solely for synthesizers, an approach which often seemed out of character for the film's setting, because it was somewhat awkward to associate electronic music with Victorian England (the approach has been successful elsewhere, as in Vangelis' CHARIOTS OF FIRE, where the synthesizer represents the inner spirit of the characters rather than the period setting, but Greenslade's electronics never seem to have that connection).

George Duning scored the two-part TV movie GOLIATH AWAITS (1981) with the conventional symphonic approach he favors, with a variety of themes for characters and situations. He specifically tried to avoid bubbling water music and provided as his primary thematic element a "submersion-textured" motif which would lend an atmosphere to the underwater scenes without becoming trite. Duning also wrote a pleasant horn theme, played in both a major and a minor mode, for the captain of the undersea group. Duning also scored a CBS pilot, BEYOND WITCH MOUNTAIN (1983), which was based on the Disney film series, providing (in addition to a pleasant theme for the boy and girl) a notable cue for orchestra and choir which is heard as the old man is taken up to the alien planet, which retains an inspirational spirit along the lines of CLOSE ENCOUNTERS.

Harry Sukman, a former piano soloist with symphony orchestras who began in Hollywood in the 40's on the Paramount music staff, scored the SALEM'S LOT miniseries (1979) with a very atmospheric score dominated by a driving brass theme. The score opens with Herrmannesque pounding brass (somewhat akin to MYSTERIOUS ISLAND) which segues into an effective rapid, low brass arrangement of the Dies Irae which becomes the bass rhythm for a main theme comprised of blaring horn wails and xylophone rolls. Sukman's use of the Dies Irae here is somewhat similar in tempo to that of Gerald Fried's in another vampire movie, THE RETURN OF DRACULA (1958).

Another miniseries, THE MARTIAN CHRONICLES (1980), featured a score composed by Stanley Myers, with a somewhat obligatory pop-styled TV title theme (for synthesizer and horn over a disco drum beat). The dramatic scoring is mostly for a small string group, and is comprised primarily of weaving, rhythmic string strokes over pounding solo drum, based on a repeated two- or three-note motif. This latter piece is quite effective during the sand ship chase. Myers' score was embellished with electronic effects provided by Richard Harvey.

Don Peake composed a most effective atmospheric score for the contemporary vampire movie, I, DESIRE (1982), which is built around an eerie, two-note theme that, unfortunately, is very similar to the one composed by Jerry Goldsmith for the "Back There" episode of TWILIGHT ZONE. Regardless, Peake puts the motif to excellent use, as the growing strings chords over bass synthesizer notes and ominously pounding keyboard conjure up a marvelous mood which far surpasses the rather weak story. This motif is balanced with a pretty Love Theme, alternately arranged for clarinet, woodwind over piano, and piano over bass viol, as well as a pleasant chamber title theme for Victorian-style harpsichord. A number of varied motifs abound, nicely interplaying with each other, but the two-note Vampire Theme always dominates, suitably enough.

Joe Harnell, known for his BIONIC WOMAN and INCREDIBLE HULK TV scores, wrote a fine score for the science fiction miniseries, "V" (1983). Born in New York City in 1924, Harnell was educated at the University of Miami and London's Trinity College. He studied with Copland, Milhaud, Toch and Leonard Bernstein, and later worked as a pianist in dance bands. Harnell was a music director for a variety of vocalists before starting in radio and television in the early 60's.

To provide an undercurrent of tension for "V", Harnell chose to use a four-note motif based on the opening of Beethoven's Fifth Symphony--three short notes followed by a long note. (This, not coincidentally, also happens to be the Morse code signal for the letter "V", and was used effectively as a V-for-victory leitmotif by Maurice Jarre in THE LONGEST DAY.) Harnell's use of the motif, in fast tempo from the string section, accentuates scenes such as the first landing of the aliens' shuttleship, where it maintains a brisk urgency and continuity among the montage of visual shots. "It's a symbol," Harnell said. "The style and undercurrent of the rhythmic device develops throughout the film until it finally appears in its full blown fashion as a Beethoven piece."[29]

Harnell uses a large chorus to sing the fourth movement of the Beethoven work at one point, while elsewhere they whisper passages from the Bible. The Beethoven motif signifies the resistance force among the humans; to underscore the aliens, Harnell provides a variety of strings, contrabass, two synthesizers and choir to achieve an effect often akin to Holst and Bartok. A soft Love Theme is also incorporated to accentuate the script's warmer moments.

As we have seen, despite the inherent limitations imposed on television scoring due to the nature of the medium, quite a few composers have contributed some creative and notable film music to science fiction and horror series and telefilms. Certain series have been especially acclaimed for their frequently excellent music, such as TWILIGHT ZONE and STAR TREK, and many otherwise-forgotten TV movies have been graced by memorable scores. Despite the "sausage factory" commercialism of television, it is to the credit of many composers that so much worthwhile fantastic film music has emerged from the small screen.

Notes

1. Laurence Rosenthal, interview with the author, February 26, 1983

2. Fred Steiner, interview with the author, February 17, 1983

3. John Caps, "Music Makes All the Difference," Soundtrack Collector's Newsletter #11 (August 1977) p. 20

4. Marc Scott Zicree, The Twilight Zone Companion (New York: Bantam Books, 1982) p. 87

5. Jerry Goldsmith quoted by Sam Maronie, "Jerry Goldsmith Interview," Starlog, October 1981

6. Fred Steiner, loc. cit. (and following quotes)

7. Allan Asherman, "Forerunners of THE TWILIGHT ZONE," The Twilight Zone (September 1981) p. 30

8. John Caps, "Serial Music of Jerry Goldsmith," Filmmusic Notebook Vol. 2, #1 (1976) p. 27

9. _____, op. cit. #3, p. 21

10. _____, "John Williams: Scoring the Film Whole," Filmmusic Notebook Vol. 2, #3 (1976) p. 23-24

11. Barry Gray, interview with the author, February 26, 1982 (and following quotes)

12. George Duning, interview with the author, January 8, 1983
     (and following quotes)

13. Fred Steiner, loc. cit. (and following quotes)

14. Gerald Fried, interview with the author, November 29, 1983
     (and following quotes)

15. Allan Asherman, The Star Trek Compendium (New York:
     Wallaby Books, 1981) p. 40-41

16. Fred Steiner, "Keeping Score of the Scores: Music for STAR
     TREK," The Quarterly Journal of the Library of Congress,
     Vol. 40, #1 (Winter 1983) p. 10

17. Also see an expanded version of Steiner essay (ibid.), appear-
     ing in: Wonderful Inventions: Motion Pictures, Broadcast-
     ing, and Recorded Sound at the Library of Congress, edited
     by Irish B. Newsom (Washington, D.C.: Library of Con-
     gress, Fall 1983)

18. Allan Asherman, op. cit., p. 136

19. Ibid., p. 114

20. Lalo Schifrin, interview with the author, October 8, 1982

21. Robert Cobert, interview with the author, January 27, 1983
     (and following quotes)

22. Gil Melle, interview with the author, June 29, 1983 (and fol-
     lowing quotes)

23. Allan Bryce, "TV Music: Intimate Themes," Soundtrack Col-
     lector's Newsletter #13 (March 1978) p. 19

24. Laurence Rosenthal, loc. cit (and following quotes)

25. Gerald Fried, loc. cit.

26. James Marshall and Ronald Bohn, "Gerald Fried," Soundtrack
     Collector's Newsletter #15 (October 1978) p. 4

27. Fred Steiner, loc. cit.

28. Irwin Bazelon, Knowing the Score (New York: Arco Publish-
     ing, Inc., 1981) p. 154

29. Joe Harnell interviewed by David Kraft, "V", CinemaScore
     #11/12 (Winter 1983) p. 8

XII

THE VERSATILITY OF JERRY GOLDSMITH

Jerry Goldsmith's credits include superior work in nearly ev-
every film genre, having been equally distinguished at scoring
Westerns (HOUR OF THE GUN), war films (PATTON), dramas
(LILIES OF THE FIELD), adventures (THE WIND AND THE LION)
and comedies (THE GREAT TRAIN ROBBERY). Goldsmith's sheer
versatility in approaching these diverse subjects keeps him in
great demand. Within the fantastic genre, Goldsmith has likewise
proven to be a highly versatile composer, scoring more than 30 of
them since the mid-60's, not to mention notable television work pre-
viously--and taking almost as many varied approaches as there are
films.

Goldsmith's unique capability to shift gears, to retain a remarkable variety in his musical composition unlike the stylistic similarities that seem to characterize the works of many other composers, is something the composer himself can't even explain. "It
seems like it's me, and that's that," Goldsmith said, thoughtfully.
"Certain composers are doing the same thing over and over again,
which I feel is uninteresting. I don't find that you grow very
much in that way. I like to keep changing, trying to do new
things. Basically, I'm saying the same thing with a little different
twist on it."[1]

Jerry Goldsmith happens to be one of the few film composers
actually born and raised in Los Angeles. Born in 1929, Goldsmith
developed an interest in piano from an early age, and in his teens
he tutored with the distinguished pianist and teacher Jacob Gimpel. Later he studied composition, theory and counterpoint with
Mario Castelnuovo-Tedesco. Goldsmith enrolled in Los Angeles City
College, where he studied music further, and at the same time attended classes on film composition at the University of Southern
California, taught by Miklos Rozsa.

In 1950, Goldsmith found employment as a clerk in the CBS
music department, and was eventually given composition assignments
by Lud Gluskin, CBS's head music director. Radio and television
work followed, including notable scores for fantasy series such as
TWILIGHT ZONE and THRILLER (as we have already discussed in
Chapter XI). Goldsmith's first feature score was composed in 1957,
although it wasn't until the early 60's that this work began to

Jerry Goldsmith. Photograph by Jordon R. Fox. Courtesy J. R.
Fox and Frederick S. Clarke, Cinefantastique.

gather a degree of acclaim. Among these later works was the twelve-tone score for John Huston's FREUD (1962), a moody and straightforward biography with a fantasy dream sequence. As Tony Thomas described, it was "a remarkable composition, stark in character, contemplative in its shifting moods, gentle, sad, eerie, and somehow entirely suitable to this account of the early years of psychiatry."[2]

THE SATAN BUG (1965) was given a fine main theme, introduced by a solo horn fanfare which segues into rhythmic, swaying strings and tympani over a slapping percussion and bass beat, with discordant, aimlessly running xylophone notes on top. This nicely surging motif moves unstoppably onward, dangerously, like the plague virus of the film's title. Goldsmith also makes use of slowly shivering strings under wandering brass notes in some of the suspense sequences, as well as a reverberating electronic device which plays a repeated figure throughout the score.

SECONDS (1966), which told the intriguing story of a middle-aged businessman's frustrations after being transformed into a new identity, was given an effectively contrasting score--piano playing against organ, simple melodies playing against complex, shifting harmonic designs, and moderate tempos playing against slower rhythms. Author/composer Irwin Bazelon has discussed this score most aptly: "The composer uses the piano both as a reflection of Rock Hudson's former life and the new image of his adult youth.... The organ, on the other hand, is employed to emphasize his transformation and the eeriness connected with his rebirth.... The piano music arouses sympathy for Hudson, whereas the organ's ritualistic sound suggests the film's satanic theme. In between, the composer introduces a long, lyric violin line that meanders through the harmonic texture. The theme connects Hudson's old and new identities. In the commuter-train sequence, the violin line is plaintive, but during the sequence in which Hudson travels to California, the muted strings become sentimental, for, despite its horror aspects, the film is in many ways a romantic fantasy."[3]

At the film's conclusion, Goldsmith blends together the piano and organ on their last chord, the two personalities absorbing each other in a tragic, concluding resolution. This score is a particularly fine example of the symbolic use of music, thematically, to underscore what lies behind a film's surface level, and Goldsmith achieves it admirably. As Tony Thomas put it, Goldsmith treated "a disturbing and horrifying visual in a directly opposing manner; and in writing an orderly and almost serene score, somehow came up with a perfect counterpoint."[4]

Goldsmith's next fantastic score is among his best, and remains one of the finest and most talked-about scores of the fantastic genre: PLANET OF THE APES (1968). In the first of what would turn out to be a long-running and increasingly juvenile series

of films, Goldsmith lent a remarkably futuristic/primitive mood to
PLANET OF THE APES wholly through the use of acoustical sound.
This was an especially deft approach in a period when most science fiction films were characterized by the burgeoning electronic
sounds then being developed. "There was a great deal of thought
on my part on how to approach it," Goldsmith recalled. "The obvious way would be to use electronic and all sorts of synthetic
means of reproducing the music, and I feel, without trying to
sound pretentious, that the resources of the orchestra had just
barely begun to be tapped, and I felt it was an exercise for myself to see what I could do to make some strange sounds and yet
try to make them <u>musically</u> rather than effectwise."[5]

For his experiment, Goldsmith gathered an incredible array
of instruments and acoustic sound-producing devices, and carefully orchestrated this seemingly chaotic collection into a cohesive
whole that works perfectly with the film, as more than one reviewer has noted: "The playing was audacious, the rhythms, easily
excitable, and the percussion section of an otherwise standard orchestra was filled with other-worldly hardware such as conch
shells, stainless steel mixing bowls, and Polynesian tools that are
hard even to imagine, much less describe. From the first hand-
stopped piano notes in the low octave, the intervening scratcher
and the bass slide whistle that make up the first four bars of the
score, a whole alien world was outlined. From there and with the
semi-serial melody of the flute, the world of reversed (or is it 'ful-
filled') evolution was drawn orchestrally. Devious pizzicatos and
snorting brass pointed up the absurdities of the proud ape culture
while the mixing bowls, like a whoosh of prehistoric air, helped describe the so-called forbidden zone. There was an arrogant march
for trumpet and high plucked strings. There was a long dramatic
escape sequence full of the low staccato piano playing Goldsmith
had kept in mind from his earliest days...."[6]

"The picture was a huge experiment in itself," Goldsmith
said, "so I thought I would try a few different things on my own.
I like using different types of instruments in my music--whatever
will work and give me the desired sound I'm striving for."[7] Among
these inventive sounds were a gong scraped with a triangle beater,
the use of tuning mixing bowls during the frightening post-scare-
crow sequence, ram's horn, friction drum, bass slide whistle and
a use of avant-garde techniques such as pizzicato, col legno (striking the strings with the wood of the bow), reverberation, and the
clicking sounds of woodwind keys, all combined to increase the
sound scope of the film, as Irwin Bazelon wrote: "The score also
features fast-changing tempos and alternates extremely high, shrill
pitches with low grunts and soft resonances."[8]

Goldsmith has described some of the other unconventional musical effects he achieved for the film: "For that swoosh of air effect in the desert scenes, I used French horns with the mouthpiece

turned around backwards. A Polynesian instrument called Ung-
lungs were used in the cave sequence."[9] All of these varied effects were skillfully integrated into the musical flow of the score,
according to Irwin Bazelon, "as a logical extension of his formal
structure, not as detached effects that attract attention out of pro-
portion to their importance. The music enters the narrative and
supplies that extra dimension of suprareality, in this case of other-
world echoes of sound."[10]

    The score for PLANET OF THE APES was highly successful,
and a similar sound was utilized by Leonard Rosenman when he was
called in to score the sequel, BENEATH THE PLANET OF THE
APES, and the fifth and final movie in the series some years later,
BATTLE FOR THE PLANET OF THE APES. Goldsmith returned to
score the third film, ESCAPE FROM THE PLANET OF THE APES
(1971), in which two of the apes journey to Earth. "Since the
story takes place in a contemporary setting," wrote one reviewer,
"Goldsmith has accordingly scored with a modern sound, lightly
garnished with some of the strange percussion and sonic effects of
his original score. The score is characteristically spare, with the
more sustained (and effective) use of music in the final scenes."[11]
The fourth film in the series, CONQUEST OF THE PLANET OF THE
APES, was scored by Tom Scott, combining electronic effects with
the frenzied percussion, woodwind and horn style originated by
Goldsmith. Scott's music, while at times exciting and effective,
does not have the intensity to enhance the film as the other scores
do.

    The following year Goldsmith provided a less complex but no
less remarkable score for THE ILLUSTRATED MAN (1969). Goldsmith has described this score as one of his personal favorites:
"The style for THE ILLUSTRATED MAN was all my own choice--
serial, but lyrical at the same time. There's a close tie between
impressionism and serialism, so one can slide back and forth."[12]
Goldsmith provided a sad melody, folk-song in quality, which is
first heard as the film opens, sung by a soprano voice over harp
and oboe, eventually joined by a full chamber ensemble. The song
characterizes the melancholy tone of the film and the haunted clairvoyance of the Illustrated Man. As John Caps wrote, "Throughout,
this theme appears with a number of different guises and instruments, at one point done by a synthesizer, a sitar, later a perverted treatment by two violins."[13] Goldsmith uses other instruments to illustrate various elements in the film; a sinister touch
from washboard percussion, a diabolical clarinet motif near the end,
and, as the title character defends his "skin illustrations," the
chamber ensemble of strings and woodwinds rise and fall "in
twelve-tone surges that flow along with the skin illustrations....
Fluttering flute, a regretful guitar and harp piece, angry growling
horns each take a turn. This is music to illustrate the conscience."[14]

    Goldsmith's next effort in the fantastic genre was a TV movie,

THE BROTHERHOOD OF THE BELL, in 1970. This occult thriller
utilized much atonal dissonance, particularly a recurring howling
synthesizer tone, plucked string bass often in a free-form mode,
eerie and birdlike fluttering string chords, balanced with a melodic,
sad theme for solo viola over a semijazzy string bass and brushed
snare drum rhythm, built from a four-note motif.

THE MEPHISTO WALTZ (1971) followed with a similarly diabolical score for this occult chiller. Goldsmith incorporated portions of Liszt's famous classical piece of the same name, played on
piano by his old teacher, Jacob Gimpel, as well as quotations from
the medieval Dies Irae into his score. "His endeavor was to surround," wrote John Caps, "in fact to swamp the piano parts with
one of the most diabolic collections of symphonic sounds, a cauldron
of creaking horns and smoking strings."[15] The mixture of the
classical piano and the atonal effects was highly effective in achieving an unsettling mood of contrasting sensuality and nightmare.
Goldsmith also created a series of loud, thundering quasi-electronic
sound vibrations, during the sequence where the devil comes to kill
the pleading mother's child, which were genuinely frightening.

In contrast to the horrifying music of MEPHISTO WALTZ,
Goldsmith enveloped the psychological spook story, THE OTHER
(1972), with a gorgeous, soaring lyricism, combining his penchant
for Waltonlike outdoorsy music with fluid suspense motifs from
strings, keyboard and harp. As Caps noted, "The concept of
Goldsmith's music was to present first a simple, whistled theme
that could be any child's lullaby except that there was a certain
measure of guilt hidden in the edges of the tune and in the orchestration. As the mystery unravelled so slowly, we were distracted
into the sunny farm country and the theme tune was heard in a
number of shrewdly sunlit variations, each brief and lovely--strings
in unison with a bassoon turning gently underneath while we
watched backlit cottonweed float on the air--piano playing the theme
song while horns set up a repetitive background for a scene in town.
Elsewhere, he wrote a fragile song for the disturbed mother which
was so reluctant and demure that we could hardly hear it, yet it
took the place of pages of script-matter in describing her."[16]

Goldsmith's music for "The Great Game" sequence, where the
boy Niles allows his soul to follow a crow in flight, is a majestic,
Americana version of the main theme, soaring and flawless. Beginning as a furtive motif for strings, harp and faint, tubular bells,
embellished by the caws of the crow on the effects track, the music
gradually takes off in a lyrical melody for woodwind, and eventually for the full string section, as Niles soars high over the Connecticut countryside. But then a discordant counterpoint emerges
in the form of jagged, low octave piano chords as a farmer jabs at
the crow with a pitchfork and Niles drops to the ground, gasping.
This is a marvelous example of musical counterpoint in which a light,
airy motif suddenly takes on a tragic mood, and it works perfectly.

So does Goldsmith's music for the climactic revelatory sequence,
in which we learn the truth about Niles and his brother, Holland.
The music emerges, slowly, for strings and harp as in the crow
sequence (there are also bird cries in the background), with furtive, uncomfortable figures, seguing to a low, shivering cello vibrato as Niles remembers the past; rapid downward harp glissandos
and discordant, frenzied whistle blows follow his remembrance of
Holland's tragic death. Later, Goldsmith utilizes sharp, angular
brass rhythms as Ada discovers the whereabouts of the missing
baby near the film's end, and the fragmentary harmonic chords
mingle with the thunderstorm at the conclusion as Ada resolves
matters herself. The score is a fine mixture of beauty and horror,
as was the film, and it remains one of Goldsmith's finest efforts.

THE REINCARNATION OF PETER PROUD (1975) was given a
melancholy, quasi-lyrical score with a complex orchestration. The
music is dominated with flute and piano over strings, to represent
in somewhat elegaic form the sad inevitability of Proud's life (lives),
mixed with an assortment of synthesized sounds, electric guitar and
electric piano to maintain a subtle undercurrent of eeriness throughout. The theme appears in a variety of guises, as piano solos,
pulsing travel music, and a yearning string movement when Proud
begins to accept the fact of his own reincarnation. Goldsmith also
provides a flowing waltz tune, first for piano and later for lush
strings, to underscore the love interest in the film.

Goldsmith won an Oscar for his music in THE OMEN (1976),
an apocalyptic melodrama concerning the coming of the Antichrist
as prophesied in the Book of Revelation. For this score, Goldsmith
composed a theme for chanting chorus over chimes and organ, which
sounds appropriately like a black mass. Goldsmith devised a series
of simple Latin lyrics ("Versus Cristus, Ave, Ave Satani," etc.),
and utilized the chanting chorus effectively to underscore the story
both symbolically and dramatically. As one reviewer noted: "The
repetition of the 'S' sounds in these ... chantings adds a sneering,
reptilian character to the corrupt doings.... THE OMEN is totally
absorbed with evil as a superior force. Nowhere in the score is
there music of comparable force supporting the side of good to vie
with the 'Ave Satani,' which permeates the film. Even in the closing scenes, when it appears good may overthrow evil, it is not a
heroic support we hear, but the satanic chorus shouting in terror
at possible defeat. Regardless of the evil utterances, they become
a rallying cry for Gregory Peck in a death struggle with the wicked
Mrs. Baylock."[17]

This oppressive Evil Theme is balanced, to some extent, with
a lighter motif for piano, flute and harps, and elsewhere by a full
string section, which accompanies placid scenes and is also used as
a love theme. An icy, pulsating synthesizer effect to illustrate the
lights reflecting in the eyes of the mysterious dog at Damien's birthday party; low, chimelike horns accompany Father Brennan's warn-

ing to the elder Thorne about his son; and woodwinds over plucked strings in a lullaby character as the baby Damien snuggles in his new mother's arms, all subliminally reinforce the apprehension in the story.

For the sequel, DAMIEN: OMEN II (1978), the theme takes on a much more rhythmic quality as the choir is backed with synthesizer strokes and a more dominant use of brass interplaying with strings during breaks in the choral structure.   While several critics have bemoaned the loss of the meditative string writing and innocent piano filigrees of the original, Goldsmith's sequel music is no less effective in maintaining the hellish direction of this second film.

Whereas the first two OMEN pictures emphasized solely the evil nature of the struggle with the dominating "Ave Satani," Goldsmith provides in the third picture, THE FINAL CONFLICT (1981), a beautiful, inspirational string melody which contrasts nicely with the satanic chorale as the two opposing forces of good and evil confront each other openly in the concluding scenes.   The choral theme is not "Ave Satani," but a different motif for melodic female chorus over rhythmic chanted male voice.   The melody rises strikingly up an octave which is very dramatic, while retaining the same driving percussion rhythm that characterized DAMIEN.   Damien's death at the finale is heralded by angelic choir, which segues to mystical strings and female chorus as beams of morning sunlight filter through the Romanesque arches of Damien's abode and victorious verses of biblical scripture appear on the screen; ultimately trumpet accompaniment is added until the music segues into the main chorale theme for the end titles.   This final surge of inspirational music is some of the finest Goldsmith has ever written, and he has said he favors it over the previous OMEN pictures: "It's totally different from the other two OMENs.   The second one was an adaptation of the first one--it was the same music.   This one is totally different, although I do use chorus ... it's a very exciting score."[18]   The music is more dramatic, less oppressive and more optimistic than the first two, because at last here is a ray of hope, and the music culminates gloriously rather than remaining muddled in a hopeless mire of unremitting evil.

Shortly after completing the first OMEN score, Goldsmith provided an interesting electronic composition for LOGAN'S RUN (1976). An approach similar to PLANET OF THE APES was taken, in that the score is primarily atonal, with a variety of tones and textures rather than obvious melodies and harmonies.   Unlike APES, however, which utilized a conventional orchestra to complement the simian and non-technological environment, in LOGAN'S RUN Goldsmith opts for electronic instruments to establish a futuristic and technologically advanced society.   The film concerned a populace living inside a gigantic, domed city, and for the scenes within the dome, Goldsmith provided atonal electronic music, while more symphonic Coplandesque pieces add a warmth to the scenes outside the dome.   Goldsmith also

provided a melodic Love Theme, used sparingly at first but allowed
to open up victoriously at the finale.

For the ominous medical thriller, COMA (1978), Goldsmith composed an effectively symbolical music score. The film told of an or-
ganization devoted to kidnapping comatose hospital patients and
housing them, suspended from wires in a large room, for illicit transplant purposes. Goldsmith's music was dominated by four pianos,
percussion, and a large string section complemented with solo woodwinds. As John Caps has noted, "He made the music itself sound
dangled from tenuous wires by use of half-step chording, strings
out of range or glissing their sound or racing after some monstrously hard to play sforzandos, and by having the pianos play fluttering runs a half step against each other."[19] Goldsmith left the first
half of the film unscored, allowing the orchestra to emerge only
when the doctor begins to discover the truth about those disap-
pearing patients.

THE SWARM (1978) was a lackluster entry into the nature-vs-
mankind cycle of the late 70's, but was scored impressively by
Goldsmith with an action-filled brass-and-strings score. "There
were so many actors that there was not one character you could
really get involved with," Goldsmith said of THE SWARM. He decided instead to concentrate purely on the threat of the bees and
emphasized that aspect in his score. "I used the notes B.E.E. as
a motif and lots of chromatics."[20] This clever in-joke was well-
taken by one reviewer, who reportedly burst out into laughter at
the first few bars of music. Another writer noted the driving
ferocity of much of the music: "The nasty stingers are perfectly
portrayed by the sharp flutter-tongues of the woodwinds, the brassy buzzing of the horns, and the angry, primal screaming of the
whirling strings. Beneath all these furious gyrations lies the basic
power of the bees and the sounding of impending disaster which
echoes throughout the work."[21] Goldsmith does balance all this
with several warmer passages for strings which emphasize the tragic
struggles of the characters.

The futuristic DAMNATION ALLEY (1978) was enriched with
a very pretty, descending melody laced with melancholy and regret,
played by strings (and later solo trumpet) over harp, nicely capturing the unfortunate conditions of the post-holocaust Earth.
CAPRICORN ONE (1978), an effective little thriller about governmental cover-up and the first Mars landing, was given a driving,
repetitious brassy rhythm, alternating with a lyrical string melody,
which played fairly straightforwardly upon the action. THE BOYS
FROM BRAZIL (1978), a clever film about cloned Hitlers being bred
in unsuspecting households, was given a broad score based on a
waltz in three-quarter time with quite a Straussian feel, lending the
film an interesting old-country mood that underlies the desires of
Joseph Mengele to fulfill Hitler's dreams of a master Aryan race.
Goldsmith composed a fine, moody score for MAGIC (1978), a somber

thriller about a demented ventriloquist and a most unusual dummy, emphasizing a slow, dirgelike string passage over piano harmonies with a distinctive low harmonica motif which nicely reinforced the growing menace of the dummy. A Love Theme for strings over piano is also provided, which at one point is very effectively counterpointed with low piano chords going against the rhythm of the piece--as in THE OTHER--which lends a tinge of apprehension to the romantic interludes.

Goldsmith composed an evocative score for the science fiction chiller, ALIEN (1979), which balanced very soft, plaintive motifs with low, extremely brash terror music, again emphasizing a conventional orchestra to achieve very weird sounds. The first theme emphasized the solitude and stillness of space with its slowly swelling pulses and rhythms, creating an almost dreamlike mood of quiet peace. An effective, warbling howl, something like a Bronx cheer, from the brass and woodwinds heralds many of the alien creature's attacks.

For the long-awaited STAR TREK: THE MOTION PICTURE (1979), Goldsmith provided a rousing, dramatic symphonic score suitable to this grand, post-STAR WARS outer space epic. Since John Williams' adventurous STAR WARS music reawakened the moviegoing public--and commercial-minded movie executives with a penchant toward pop scores--to the value of traditional symphonic music, nearly all subsequent science fiction adventures--from lavish productions like STAR TREK to the most low-budget exploiters--tended to follow suit. The producers of STAR TREK: THE MOTION PICTURE reportedly wanted a STAR WARS-styled score, which Goldsmith refused to provide, not wishing to compose a carbon copy of someone else's work. Instead he came up with a rousing, victorious main theme, in a similar heroic mode to STAR WARS but with Goldsmith's own stylistic stamp, which superbly clarified the grand Star Trek adventure. The theme is put to very good use not only over the titles, but in the prolonged sequences where Kirk first sees the revamped Enterprise (the music here sums up the swelling emotion Kirk feels at being reunited with his beloved ship) and again when the Enterprise first departs to rendezvous with the malevolent space cloud. A warm love sonnet is provided for the evolving relationship between Decker and Ilia, and Goldsmith also quietly quotes Alexander Courage's STAR TREK TV theme in two sequences on the Enterprise's bridge, which lends a welcome nostalgic sense of legendry to the film.

The majestic main theme is contrasted with some highly evocative electronic motifs, first used as a leitmotif for the Klingons in the opening scene, and later as a vast musical description of the immense space cloud. The Klingon motif is a rhythmic piece for horn melody over percussion, which lasts only long enough for the deep, twangy electric guitar motif (representing the space cloud) to intrude and overwhelm the Klingon Theme, as the cloud likewise overwhelms the Klingon vessel.

"It was a challenge. It was fun," Goldsmith said of scoring
STAR TREK. "I was able to use a lot of different instruments and
get a variety of effects--especially during the 'space cloud' se-
quences--so overall I was very pleased."[22] Among the electronic
devices Goldsmith put to work in achieving the unusual sounds
heard during the space-cloud scenes was something called a "beam,"
an instrument which resembles an ordinary block of wood, yet emits
a very low frequency vibration when struck.

Goldsmith scored STAR TREK: THE MOTION PICTURE under
a very tedious schedule. Numerous production delays left him with
less and less time in which to compose, orchestrate and record the
score before the film's present premiere date. "They were bringing the film to me for orchestrating in bits and pieces--a sequence
or two at a time," Goldsmith said. "As I recall, I delivered the
music three days before the film opened."[23] In order to finish in
time, Goldsmith called in long-time friend and colleague Fred Steiner (a veteran of many TV series including, coincidentally, STAR
TREK) to assist him, and Steiner wound up composing several sequences for the film. "I ended up writing somewhere between fifteen and twenty minutes of music, all based on his themes," Steiner explained. "It was a typical example of ghostwriting, but using his material."[24]

STAR TREK: THE MOTION PICTURE remains one of Goldsmith's finest efforts, superbly describing the majesty and, in a
sense, the mystique of the whole Star Trek milieu while at the same
time giving us some marvelously effective dramatic underscoring.

Another outer space adventure, OUTLAND (1981), was given
a less adventuresome score, Goldsmith this time opting for an approach similar to that provided in ALIEN. The main theme is a
slow-moving motif for low brass surgings over graceful string
coastings, with a faint typani in the background. Like ALIEN,
this angular motif captures the stillness and solitude of the outer
space mining colony. There is also a rhythmic motif for piping
woodwind over strings and percussion that recalls the style of
STAR TREK's Klingon motif. Here it is used very well to establish
an urgent, suspenseful mood, the low brass rhythm acting as an
anxious heartbeat.

POLTERGEIST (1982), which earned Goldsmith an Oscar
nomination, was given broad, lavish orchestrations similar in scope
to STAR TREK, although maintaining a predominantly darker tone.
POLTERGEIST molds together a diverse variety of thematic material, from very atonal and impressionistic material to the simple,
childlike lullaby. The lullaby is quite effective in counterbalancing
the harsh supernatural horror of the film's more energetic moments,
contrasting an innocent children's tune with the roaring Horror motifs. In this sense, the lullaby works similarly to Lalo Schifrin's lullaby theme from THE AMITYVILLE HORROR (1979), which used the in-

nocence of children as an effective counterpoint against the terrors of the haunted house. Schifrin's theme, however, also suggested a kind of eerie terror of its own, while Goldsmith's, opening into a full arrangement only at the end of the film, signifies a relieved freedom now that the terrors are over. Other themes included a powerful, quasi-religious chorale theme representing the forces within the haunted closet, and a clever quotation from the Dies Irae in one sequence.

Goldsmith had 15 weeks during which to score POLTERGEIST, which was orchestrated by long-time collaborator Arthur Morton and recorded by an 80-piece orchestra supplemented by a chorus of 60. This was followed by another 15 weeks spent writing the music to an exotic animated fantasy, THE SECRET OF NIMH (1982). For Goldsmith, this film was like a small opera, with liberal doses of comedy, romance and adventure. He invested it with a rich, symphonic score for an orchestra and choir of eighty people.

Rather than treating the film as a cartoon, Goldsmith approached it as he would a live-action feature, avoiding any deliberate mickey mousing. Like POLTERGEIST, Goldsmith provided a variety of diverse thematic material from pure romanticism to impressionism, a total of about eight separate leitmotifs, including an impressive choir theme for Nicodemus and the magic amulet. "It's sort of an animated Peter and the Wolf," Goldsmith said, "but it all hangs together cohesively."[25]

This was Goldsmith's first foray into animation, and he had some unusual problems to contend with, including the perplexing fact that much of the animation was incomplete while he was scoring the film. "In animation," Goldsmith said, "the length of the scenes are much shorter than in live action. Things just can't take as long, so it's more difficult to get a flowing line in the music. One can be broader, dramatically, because of the fact that it is all abstract."

After a pair of action films, giving Goldsmith an agreeable relief from the fantasy genre, he returned with a strong score for PSYCHO II (1983). He composed an innocent main theme for a large string section, which represents the inner character of Norman Bates, now that he's supposedly cured of his homicidal tendencies. The theme is also given a slightly eerie quality through an arrangement for synthesized woodwind. This theme is balanced by a series of savage and uncontrollable motifs for orchestra, gongs and synthesizer, representing the harmful Mother personality still embodied within him. Some of these cues include very weird orchestration--even a musician blowing into a drum! As Norman becomes "stranger" during the course of the film, so does the score. The music intentionally avoids referring to Bernard Herrmann's famous music from the original 1960 film, except in the pretitle sequence replaying the famous shower murder. "I tried to get a feeling of innocence and sympathy for Norman," Goldsmith explained. "You're trying to guess who was doing all the naughty work, and you know you want to keep Norman sort of out of it and guessing at everyone else. Also Norman was a victim too.... The shower music was so determinate of the original film. I wanted something horrendous and totally different."[26]

PSYCHO II was followed with an extensive score for TWILIGHT ZONE--THE MOVIE (1983), a big-budget, four-part anthology film in the spirit of Rod Serling's classic TV series. Since there are four separate episodes, Goldsmith took four distinctly different musical approaches for each segment. "What I wanted to do was use all different dramatic developments," said Goldsmith. "They are all different stylistically in music and they're different orchestrally too ... much in the same way I did some of the originals."[27]

Especially evocative is the poignant, soaringly lyrical string music for the Steven Spielberg-directed segment, "Kick the Can," as well as some powerful, thunderous brass and string scoring for the "Nightmare at 20,000 Feet" segment, which reaches a surging climax as Valentine confronts the creature on the plane's wing. Goldsmith composed about an hour's worth of music for the film, including a lengthy end title cue which brings all four musical sections together. Marius Constant's famous TWILIGHT ZONE TV theme is also quoted briefly in the titles, lending a pleasant touch of nostalgia.

Jerry Goldsmith's work for science fiction, fantasy and horror pictures has provided some of the finest scores in the genre. Although he by no means considers himself a genre composer--he's done enough work in other cinematic areas to validate this--and, in fact, claims he's trying to avoid an overabundance of these assignments, his scores for these films have nevertheless constituted some important contributions to fantastic film music; as they have, indeed, to film music in general. Goldsmith's remarkable musical versatility and seemingly endless freshness has served the film industry well, and the fantastic genre has benefited greatly from his work.

Notes

1. Jerry Goldsmith, interview with the author, July 15, 1982

2. Tony Thomas, Film Score (La Jolla: A. S. Barnes & Co., 1979) p. 222

3. Irwin Bazelon, Knowing the Score (New York: Arco Publishing, Inc., 1975) p. 104-105

4. Tony Thomas, Music for the Movies (La Jolla: A. S. Barnes & Co., 1973) p. 211

5. Jerry Goldsmith interviewed by Irwin Bazelon, op. cit., p. 189

6. John Caps, "The Ascent of Jerry Goldsmith," Soundtrack Collector's Newsletter #19 (October 1979) p. 8

7. Jerry Goldsmith interviewed by Sam Maronie, Starlog, October 1981

8. Irwin Bazelon, op. cit., p. 152

9. Jerry Goldsmith interviewed by Dale Winogura, Cinefantastique Vol. 2, #2 (Summer 1972) p. 37

10. Irwin Bazelon, op. cit., p. 152

11. Mark Stevens, "The Score," Cinefantastique Vol. 1, #4 (Fall 1971) p. 42

12. Jerry Goldsmith interviewed by Derek Elley, Films & Filming; quoted by Alexander Strachan, "Two Forgotten Scores-- Jerry Goldsmith in Retrospect," Pro Musica Sana #31 (Summer 1980) p. 14

13. John Caps, "Serial Music of Jerry Goldsmith," Filmmusic Notebook Vol. 2, #1 (1976) p. 30

14. Ibid.

15. _____, "The Ascent of Jerry Goldsmith, Part 2," Sound track Collector's Newsletter #20 (January 1980) p. 4

16. Ibid., p. 4-5

17. William F. Krasnoborski, "Omens and Obsessions," Soundtrack Collector's Newsletter #9 (January 1977) p. 19

18. Jerry Goldsmith interviewed by Allan Bryce, Soundtrack! The Collector's Quarterly #25 (Spring 1981) p. 5

19. John Caps, op. cit. #15, p. 7

20. Jerry Goldsmith quoted by Allan Bryce, "Jerry Goldsmith on 'Star Sound,'" Soundtrack Collector's Newsletter #18 (July 1979) p. 23

21. Tom Underwood, "Buzzing About THE SWARM," CinemaScore #3 (May/June 1979) p. 3

22. Jerry Goldsmith, op. cit. #7

23. Ibid.

24. Fred Steiner, interview with the author, February 27, 1983

25. Jerry Goldsmith, op. cit. #1 (and following quote)

26. _____ quoted by Steven Simak, "Another Pair of Summer Blockbusters from Jerry Goldsmith," CinemaScore #11/12 (Fall 1983) p. 5

27. Ibid.

XIII

ELECTRONICS

With the increase in technology during the 70's and 80's, a corresponding increase was found in the use of music scores achieved solely or complemented through electronic instruments. While this is generally regarded nowadays as synthesizer music, it actually can include three distinct types of music: synthetic musical sounds created by computerized devices such as a synthesizer; electronic amplification of acoustical sounds, such as an electric guitar or electric violin; and the reprocessing of acoustical sounds, such as the enhancement of recorded frog noises sped up and slowed down in Les Baxter's FROGS.

There are many advantages and disadvantages to the use of electronic scoring in motion pictures. Positive aspects include the far-reaching sonic capabilities of synthesizers, as composer Les Baxter has remarked: "Electronic instruments have a limitless range of sound," he said, referring to his score for THE BEAST WITHIN. "They can do things that sound like the spirit souls of animals from another world moaning. These unearthly sounds are something you really can't get any other way."[1] They are also fairly inexpensive for economy-minded producers--instead of paying vast sums for a large orchestra consisting of many musicians, it usually only requires one or two operators to compose and produce a score on synthesizers. (At the same time, they're also putting many musicians out of work.)

Other disadvantages include the fact that, while synthesizers can create remarkable new sounds and very spacey effects, it is nearly impossible to achieve the emotional poignancy or warm coloration of a conventional symphony orchestra. Synthesizer scores have also been tediously abused in recent years, simply because they are so seemingly easy and cheap to produce. Anyone with access to a synthesizer and a recording device can shuffle together an assortment of menacing or atmospheric tonalities and call it a film score. Many have. Les Baxter has also addressed this problem: "In some cases, when the budget is very low, the music is the skimpiest that can be written on the least amount of money, so the music suffers as a result. It's hard to make a sound on a synthesizer, if you work with it long enough, that for a moment or two is not effective; the problem with it is in being too repetitive, or not having enough imagination to have enough variety of sound.

You can make an interesting sound but you can only use it in a
film so many times, and for so long."

Despite the numerous bad examples (which always claim the
highest ratio of anything artistic), electronic film scoring has
achieved some remarkable effects in motion pictures, and especially
in science fiction films. "One thing that has been apparent over
the last twenty years or so," Fred Steiner said recently, "is that
the use of electronic instruments has sort of gone along with the
increase in production of science fiction films. It is one of the
hallmarks of scoring science fiction and fantasy films. In the early days during the 30's, there was a large use of certain kinds of
dissonances, certain chord formations, particularly whole tone tri-
ads, but that music went out of fashion very quickly. The only
thing that was new for this kind of picture was the exploitation
of new sounds."[2]

Some of the earliest uses of electronic film music was in
Miklos Rozsa's deft employment in the 40's of the theremin, which
Rozsa used to create an eerie, haunting sound complementary to
psychological mysteries such as SPELLBOUND (1945). Bernard
Herrmann used electronic accompaniment on many of his science
fiction scores, going back as far as 1951 to THE DAY THE EARTH
STOOD STILL, which balanced a conventional orchestra with theremin, electronic violin, electronic bass and electronic guitar. In
fact, much contemporary style in synthesized horror film music
owes a great deal to Herrmann's music, especially in the use of
slow-moving chord progressions, beginning softly and then quickly
growing in volume and force, only to fade out again.

An effective early electronic score was composed by Manuel
Compinsky for the low-budget alien-invasion movie, KILLERS FROM
SPACE (1954). This intriguing atonal compilation featured a tenuous use of violin and piano in addition to reprocessed sounds and
unusual amplified sound effects. Compinsky also created an unearthly mood through the electronic tones of a Novachord, an instrument which he described as "not unlike an electric organ, but
producing its own unique sound."[3] An effective motif is also provided for eerie, high novachord tones over piano and wildly flailing violin strokes. The novachord had also been used the previous
year by Elmer Bernstein, combined with symphonic instruments in
ROBOT MONSTER and CAT WOMEN OF THE MOON.

The first really notable use of electronics in 1950's science
fiction cinema, and the first feature film to contain nothing but
electronic sounds, was FORBIDDEN PLANET (1956). For this classic outer space thriller, a unique score comprised of "electronic
tonalities" was composed and recorded by Louis and Bebe Barron.
This husband and wife team from New York had been specialists in
electronic music for many years, and at one time were collaborators
with avant-garde composer John Cage. The Barrons had produced

electronic music for a series of experimental films in the early 50's.
They approached MGM's production chief, Dore Schary, hoping to
introduce their unique sounds into feature films. Schary agreed
to hear tapes of their work, and was impressed enough to immediately hire them to score FORBIDDEN PLANET.

The Barron's experimental tapes were played for other MGM
staff composers, who were told that the new music was to be used
in FORBIDDEN PLANET, and it received an enthusiastic response.
With this studio approval, Schary asked the Barrons to transfer
their equipment to the west coast to commence work on the film;
an offer they refused, realizing the impracticality of temporarily
relocating their array of heavy, difficult-to-connect equipment.
Schary worked out a unique arrangement allowing the Barrons to
construct the score in New York and send it, when complete, to
the west coast, the first time MGM had ever contracted for a score
outside of Hollywood.

The Barrons conceived and recorded a great many circuits
which provided the score for the movie, ranging from the hesitating "beta beat" of the Id Monster, to rasping, screeching tonal
swirls as the spacecraft lands on Altair IV, to the bubbly sounds
associated with Robby the Robot. Many of the sounds heard in the
film were compilations of different circuits recorded by the Barrons
and stacked like building blocks (sometimes with as many as seven
components)--the same principle common to the current Moog synthesizer. The score was completely recorded and edited by the
Barrons, who turned in a complete sound track to Schary for use
in the film.

"From the beginning, we discovered that people compared
them with sounds they heard in their dreams," Louis Barron recalled. "When our circuits reached the end of their existence (an
overload point) they would climax in an orgasm of power, and die.
In the film, many of the sounds seem like the last paroxysm of a
living creature."[4]

The score produced by the Barrons--dubbed "electronic
tonalities" due to a potential legal conflict with the Musician's Union, an apt enough designation of the score, which is not really
musical in essence but a careful collage of music effects achieved
electronically--presented a breakthrough in film music, as one
retrospective author noted: "Aside from the unique classical orchestrations of Bernard Herrmann for some early science fiction
films, most of the musical accompaniment associated with the genre
had lacked a degree of originality that was present in the Barrons'
work. All the fantastic elements of FORBIDDEN PLANET, the starship's voyage through deep space, the mystery of Altair IV, the
horror of the Id, are brought more vividly into being because of
the exotic electronic sounds of Louis and Bebe Barron."[5] Another
reviewer described the score as being "dubiously reminiscent of

Karlheinz Stockhausen's work in this field, specifically his 'Kon-
takte.' Nevertheless Robby's coffee-pot plopping theme and the
whooping shriek of the invisible monster as it attacks are superbly used."[6]

A less-enlightened use of electronic music found its way into
the eagerly forgotten pennies-budgeted comedy, INVASION OF THE
STAR CREATURES (1962). Jack Cookerly, somewhat of a pioneer
in electronic sounds who developed many of his own instruments,
collaborated with Elliott Fisher on the score, which was an unfortunately corny compilation of organ and thereminlike noises. Cookerly did much better when he worked with symphonic composer Paul
Dunlap to provide the twangy electronics for Dunlap's DESTINATION
INNER SPACE (1966).

Electronics also found their way into the music of TV's TWI-
LIGHT ZONE. Nathan Van Cleave used amplified violins in several
of his episode scores. Theremin was also used by many episode
composers. Les Baxter experimented with electronics in his scores
for Roger Corman's Poe movies and other films, working wonders
with variable speeds and tape reverb. British composer Barry Gray
also utilized electronic music to great effect in futuristic TV series
such as FIREBALL XL-5 and SUPERCAR. "At the time I was starting to write electronic music for the early Gerry Anderson series,"
Gray recalled, "producing electronic music was a far different ket-
tle of fish than it is today. At that time, one had to rely on tape
manipulation; on using any type of instrument to get a basic sound
from which to work. In those days, I used to use an electric steel
guitar quite a lot, and Hammond organ, and I worked basically on
tape. I also used an audio-sweep oscillator and a ring modulator,
which I had specially built. With all these various instruments I
would get the basic sound onto tape and then I would start working on it. I used to do things like chopping the head off a piano
chord, and then reversing one side of the chord and splicing it
onto itself, so that it would get a very slow-sounding approach
which rose in a crescendo to the top of the chord, and would fade
out again. That's quite a lot of work, and it took a long time to
do even a short section. Of course today, with the advent of
vocorders, synthesizers and what-have-you, there's no problem because one can produce these things very quickly."[7]

In 1971, Gil Mellé created a landmark electronic score for the
taut science fiction thriller, THE ANDROMEDA STRAIN. Mellé, a
self-taught composer who had been a professional jazz musician since
a teenager, had become interested in electronic music in 1959. At
that time, since synthesizers had not yet been developed, Mellé
simply designed and built for himself the electronic instruments
necessary to create the kind of sounds he wanted. In the late
60's Mellé came to Hollywood, and after several unsuccessful years
managed to begin film work with movies-made-for-tv. His first
feature film score was for THE ANDROMEDA STRAIN, for which

<u>Gil Mellé</u>. Photograph by the author.

he composed a purely electronic score which was actually the first
wholly electronic score for a movie. (Mellé rightly discounts FOR-
BIDDEN PLANET, saying that it was not an actual score but a collection of sounds created by electronic circuitry: "The sounds
were generated by ordinary test equipment which you would find
in any television repair station," Mellé said. "They were ordinary
test sign-wave generators, which is <u>not</u> electronic music. AN-
DROMEDA STRAIN was the very first electronic score, as we know
it today. I did a lot of investigation before I made that statement,
but it's true."[8])

      The first challenge Mellé had to meet on THE ANDROMEDA
STRAIN was to compose a score unlike anything else ever heard
before, which is what director Robert Wise demanded. "He wanted
a score with <u>no</u> themes and <u>no</u> recognizable sounds in it," Mellé
recalled. "He didn't want to hear anything that even remotely
sounded like a French horn or a tuba or a drum or anything like
that. In short, what he wanted was a kind of non-score. I don't
think any composer has ever been asked to write music that had no
themes, no chords, no harmonic structure, and with totally new
sonorities! It's certainly the toughest assignment I've ever had."
Mellé met the challenge by creating completely synthesized sounds
and combining them with a great deal of <u>musique concrete</u>--real
life sounds reprocessed through tape recording. Mellé recorded

the sounds of bowling balls striking pins, lumber mills, buzz saws, railway noises, and even Southern California's Jet Propulsion Laboratory. The sounds were then integrated with the synthesized score to achieve an unusual and nightmarish musical texture.

Mellé took over one of the Decca Records recording studios on the Universal lot in order to create the score. He used a variety of electronic instruments including a device called the Percussotron III, one of the first percussion synthesizers, which Mellé had invented especially for the ANDROMEDA STRAIN score. The main title theme is a notably chaotic and frightening composition which starts things off with just the right atmosphere. Comprised of a rapid display of counter rhythms and polymetric flurries, Mellé also employed ten processed pianos in addition to bowling alley sounds used as rhythmic accents.

The film's single repetitive theme is a haunting, rhythmically seething, cricketlike undulation for low-octave electronics and piano chords, which eerily represent the mutating growth and ever-present danger of the andromeda organism. "That was actually a forerunner of the ostinato that was used in JAWS," Mellé said. "The idea was to communicate to the audience that the virus was in the vicinity and posing great danger. We wanted to make the audience aware, and the way to do that was of course to use an ostinato that they would immediately recognize. It was literally a repetitive sound, but not a musical sound in any sense."

Mellé's unique approach on THE ANDROMEDA STRAIN was highly effective, lacing the often frightening picture with an unrelenting undercurrent of aimless microscopic evil. One reviewer wrote that Mellé's score "would be more properly described as a musical use of electronic or synthesized sounds, only occasionally taking on a melodic form. It is in some ways akin to the electronic sounds of MAROONED (not scored by Mellé), but more deliberate in structure and much more effective. It may strike some as a gimmick but the fact is Mellé's unconventional score lends a full measure of support without undermining the documentary flavor Wise has tried to achieve in the film. Mellé backdrops the computer graphics of the main title with a churning vortex of sounds that perfectly sets the tone of the film. The grinding suspense of the final scenes are put across with an almost percussive use of synthesized sounds."[9]

Mellé went on to score many TV movies and low-budget features, including the psychological thriller, YOU'LL LIKE MY MOTHER (1972), for which he provided a combination of 36 musicians and an electronic system of synthesized chords, phrases and tones. A purely electronic score, along the lines of ANDROMEDA STRAIN, was given to a TV movie entitled A COLD NIGHT'S DEATH (1973), which Mellé composed and performed himself in his own studio. While completely electronic, Mellé did rely upon harmonics, melodies, recognizable (if synthesized) sounds and more familiar sonorities.

EMBRYO (1976), a theatrical horror thriller, combined electronic scoring with a small chamber group of ten musicians. THE SENTINEL (1977) used a similar combination of electronic and symphonic orchestration, although instead of the ten musicians of EMBRYO Mellé was able to employ a large orchestra of 80 pieces. Mellé also made memorable use of voices, and invented two instruments especially for the score. One, called the Tubo Continuum, was, according to Mellé, the world's largest stringed instrument (28-feet long), while the other was a digital modulator which enabled Mellé to perform "co-solos" with musicians by reprocessing the acoustical sounds of their instruments as they were channelled through the electronic device.

Mellé considers STARSHIP INVASIONS (1977) a turning point in his film music career, because it allowed him to write all the things he feels he is best at. Whereas his earlier scores were generally either purely symphonic, purely electronic, utilized "jazz fusion" or else contained fairly segregated mixtures of the three, STARSHIP INVASIONS mixed these forms into a tightly integrated whole. "It's risky," Mellé said. "All of a sudden in the middle of a symphonic piece you hear something that's got a pulse with it; a pulsation with the energy of electronics or jazz or both. You're asking for trouble, and yet conceptually I think it's a very valid way to write. I'm good at not just writing an electronic cue or a symphonic cue or a jazz cue, but I feel I'm good at combining them at the same time, integrating them and shifting gears from bar to bar or even within a bar, going from one to the other."

Mellé continued this stylistic trend in his next genre score, BLOOD BEACH (1980), a horror thriller about an underground monster gobbling bathing beauties in the Southern California sand. The score utilized an eclectic mixture of synthesizer and orchestra, including a jazzy romantic theme for piano and horn. There is an effective, repeated theme which readily identified an imminent encounter with the toothsome hungerer. THE LAST CHASE (1980) contained a similar approach at orchestral and electronic fusion in the score. Mellé feels his scores for these three movies represent a maturity of his style as a composer, a crystallization of his musical philosophy. "I started doing that on STARSHIP INVASIONS," he said. "The scores are very dissimilar, but the philosophy is the same: to have a very full orchestral palette and to use all the colors when needed. I'm not talking about musical exhibitionism. I'm talking about having all the colors available and using them if required." Another TV movie, WORLD WAR III (1982), contained a likewise effective mixture of the orchestral and electronic. The score was performed by Mellé's five-man group, Syren, providing a unique blend of musical textures and sonorities, with various touches of jazz.

While noted mostly for his ground-breaking use of electronics
in film music, Mellé remains fairly conservative about an overreliance upon synthesizers. "I feel that to do a picture with merely
electronics is fine if that's what the picture calls for and if that's
what works best. But that may not be the case. I don't feel a
composer should limit himself to that if actually there are moments
that would work much more efficiently with other musical concepts."
Mellé also recognizes the fact that the use of an electronic score is
frequently a purely budgetary consideration on the part of many
filmmakers who find that one musician with a synthesizer is far
more economical than a composer who requires a full orchestra.
"It's a way to eliminate the orchestra and do a score very cheap-
ly," Mellé said, "because the synthesizers are used to simulate and
duplicate the instruments that we've all had in the orchestra for
years. That is a financial consideration. However, aesthetically,
I don't think any greater impact has happened in music in probably
three hundred years than the advent of the synthesizer, because
when it's used as an instrument unto itself and doing what it does
best, which is to create unique musical sonoroties, I think it has
an aesthetic impact on all of music, not just film music."

Whereas both FORBIDDEN PLANET and THE ANDROMEDA
STRAIN utilized electronic sounds atonally, creating otherworldly
atmospheres through ingenious effects, in A CLOCKWORK ORANGE,
synthesizers were used to imitate symphonic instruments, creating
a melodic and classically styled score. CLOCKWORK's director,
Stanley Kubrick, continued his penchant for scoring with familiar
classical music that he had begun with 2001: A SPACE ODYSSEY.
This time, however, he had the classical pieces tinged with a
slightly futuristic tone through effective synthesized adaptations
arranged by Wendy Carlos, then known as Walter. Carlos, long
interested in music and scientific technology, had been involved in
developing electronic music for many years. She collaborated with
engineer Robert Moog to develop a synthesizer on which Carlos created the unique electronic arrangements for her Switched-on Bach
recordings. This experience made her the ideal candidate to trans-
late classical motifs such as Beethoven's Ninth Symphony and the
William Tell Overture into synthesizer adaptations to add a futuristic
and slightly abnormal atmosphere to the audio track, complementing
the film's period and protagonist.

The music in A CLOCKWORK ORANGE is definitely an integral
part of the story, intrinsic to the development of the plot. As one
reviewer noted, "the music provides a key to Alex's mental and emotional makeup.... Throughout the film, Alex never has to say how
he feels about a particular situation; the music says it for him."[10]
Whereas in 2001, Kubrick utilized conventional music orientation,
CLOCKWORK replaced direct correspondence with ironic counterpoint, as in the use of classical music under scenes of perverse violence.

In THE SHINING (1980), Kubrick combined the use of recorded music with original composition, again calling upon the talents of Wendy Carlos and her collaborator, Rachel Elkind. While
the majority of the score consisted of eerie, atonal and nonmelodic
motifs from the repertoire of Ligeti, Bela Bartok and Krzysztof
Penderecki, Carlos and Elkind composed the main title theme and
an introductory motif, both heard in opening scenes as Jack Tor-
rance drives through the Rocky Mountains toward the secluded
Overlook Hotel. Both themes are powerful, heavy synthesized
pieces, with throbbing chords and wailing voices creating a hauntingly ominous aura. The main title is particularly striking, its
tune based on the Dies Irae, providing one of the best arrangements of that time-honored chant to be heard in a horror film.

Carlos and Elkind had initially composed about four and a
half hours of music for THE SHINING, which they submitted to
Kubrick for approval. "The music that we did never quite
grabbed him," Carlos later said. "Rachel's and my tastes and
style had naturally shifted slightly since the days of our CLOCK-
WORK ORANGE work ten years ago. So his fix on why he had
called us in the first place was disturbed, since we were doing
more theatrical, richly textured things than we had done before....
Then he asked us if we knew of any tune or theme that would be
ideal for the movie, a well-known tune that already existed. The
only theme I could think of was the Dies Irae, which traces its
roots back to the Gregorian chants of the Middle Ages."[11] Carlos
recommended Berlioz' Symphonie Fantastique, which uses the theme,
and after hearing it Kubrick became completely hooked on the Berlioz treatment of the motif, so much so that he wouldn't accept anything different. Kubrick turned down all of the orchestral material
that Carlos and Elkind had produced, and only that material imitating the Berlioz style made it into the film. The rest of the score
was dubiously compiled by Kubrick from records, as he had done
in 2001 after rejecting a score composed by Alex North.

Carlos had a better experience scoring Walt Disney's TRON
(1982), a unique combination of live action and computer-generated
animation which took place primarily in a video game world inside
a huge computer. This milieu meant the creation of a particularly
unique score which combined standard orchestral techniques with
electronic music. Carlos decided to "produce a score that has
some areas that are heavy on the electronics and other areas which
are heavy on the orchestra, but which, by and large, will blend
the two most of the time and make the boundaries pretty unclear."[12]
Carlos wrote a score for large orchestra, which was first recorded
by the 105-piece London Philharmonic, and later overdubbed her
synthesizer playing on top of it. Carlos had originally wanted to
record the synthesizer first and record the orchestra playing along
with it, but time shortages resulted in its occurring the other way
around.

Unlike A CLOCKWORK ORANGE and THE SHINING, where Carlos had to derive her music from preexistent works, in TRON she had the opportunity to create thematic material entirely her own. The score balanced two primary themes: a nicely heroic anthem, representing the protagonists; and an effective three-note, ascending motif which basically represents the computer world and its electronic dangers. A Love Theme, a tender blend of synthesizer with violins over chorus, seemed to be a variation upon the anthem. Much of the action music is derived from the video world motif, and it is in some of these sequences that the score's greatest power is evident. The video world scenes are given music in a modern idiom, while the anthem is in a more romantic tradition, providing an interesting sense of grand heroism amid the contemporary style. "The music constantly refers back to the theme," Carlos said. "It's very cyclic. There are places where it's more theme and variation; but it's closer to the spirit of a symphony than any other form."

Carlos believes the synthesizer deserves a permanent place within the conventional orchestral family. "The asset of having a synthesizer as one of the resources within an otherwise orchestral feel is great. It's likely to be one of the most useful members of the orchestra for film scoring because it embraces so many things that suggest dramatic events far more easily than with traditional instruments."

Brian May accomplished a similar mixture of orchestra and electronics in THE SURVIVOR, made in 1979. "I was very happy with the mixing of the synthesizer with the orchestra," May said. "It became an extension of the orchestra rather than the gimmick synthesizer that I think a lot of people are opposed to."[13] Lee Holdridge's THE BEASTMASTER (1982) also used a synthesizer in this manner. "It never really stands out in the orchestration," said Holdridge, "but it's continuously there, either doubling the strings or doubling the low brass, or enhancing the percussion in one form or another. It's very effective because I think it becomes part of the overall texture and you're never really aware of it. Yet somehow the sound of the whole orchestra is a little different, especially in the battle cues or the suspense/mystery cues. It's just constantly lurking around in there."[14] Les Baxter's THE BEAST WITHIN (1982) embellished a predominantly string orchestra with synthesizer to create some unearthly musical effects. Even John Williams, a contemporary paragon of the symphonic score, has employed synthesizers in the midst of a standard orchestra. "I use them more as members of the orchestra, in a way, to supplement effects in winds or in brass," Williams said. "'Fortress of Solitude' from SUPERMAN, for example, has a synthesizer part. There are some in CLOSE ENCOUNTERS, even in THE EMPIRE STRIKES BACK."[15] The Emperor's Theme in Williams' RETURN OF THE JEDI (1983) was an ominous synthesizer motif.

Laurence Rosenthal likewise used subtle synthesizers mixed with orchestra in his score for the disastrous disaster movie, METEOR (1979): "The whole technique was that I wanted an orchestral texture which was completely interlarded, as it were, with synthetic sound," Rosenthal said. He collaborated with synthesist Craig Hundley to produce "certain sounds which would blend with the existing orchestral sound to produce a kind of sound which was neither strictly orchestral nor strictly synthetic."[16] Rosenthal and Hundley also came up with a massive synthesized undulation to convey the immensity of the meteor in space. The final result of the METEOR score, which also used an effective thematic contrast between an orchestral American Theme and a Russian Theme, along the lines of the 1812 Overture, was less effective than it could have been, due in a great part to the reediting of the final scenes by the producers, who suddenly became desperate to hype up the film with more excitement. This resulted in a patching together of various pieces that Rosenthal, who by this time had left the project, scored for other parts of the film. "As a result," Rosenthal explained, "there was just too much music, and too many repetitions--the score ended up being a hodge-podge."

Arthur B. Rubinstein, in BLUE THUNDER (1983), also combined the orchestral and the synthesized to obtain a sound somewhat similar to that of TRON, built around a series of effective action motifs. An interesting effect heard throughout the score are rapid, bass synthesizer chords taking on the droning whirr of a helicopter's rotor. The use of the synthesizer emphasized a strong sense of power and technology, appropriate to this film of futuristic urban weaponry. Rubinstein tried to merge the heroic adventurousness of the RAIDERS OF THE LOST ARK score with the contemporary electronic synthesis called for by the film's subject matter. "It seemed to me that what the film required was, somehow or other, to bring size to the dramatic elements," Rubinstein said. "So the first bit of business for me was to write a theme that had heroics to it, but had a contemporary sensibility. One that could make musical and dramatic sense when played on synthesizers, and yet would also make sense if played by the brasses."[17] In the BLUE THUNDER score, Rubinstein also encountered the problem of composing music that would frequently be inundated by prominent sound effects and helicopter noises, a factor he solved by consciously breaking down the noise and fitting his music in with it, so that the elements would be mutually complementary. "There are stretches where the sound of the synthesizer, and even the sound of synthesizers with a certain amount of brass mixed in, so match (or at least you perceive them as matching) what happens with the helicopters that you're not aware of it." The mixture of electronic and symphonic textures in BLUE THUNDER amounted to a memorable score that accentuated both its technological and heroic aspects, particularly in Rubinstein's interplay of the themes for Murphy, the hero, and his opponent, the impersonal malevolency of the Blue Thunder helicopter. Rubinstein accom-

plished a similar mixture of electronics and symphonics in his score
to WARGAMES (1983), although here the individual styles are kept
fairly segregated until the end, when orchestra and synthesizer
unite in an effective resolution.

While the intermingling of electronics with symphonic music
seems to be the hallmark of the future of synthesized film music,
the employment of synthesizers through the 70's and early 80's was
characterized by scores that were predominantly purely synthesizer.
Many of these efforts were basically atonal and effects-oriented, as
in Carl Zittrer's CHILDREN SHOULDN'T PLAY WITH DEAD THINGS
(1972), a low-low budget and somewhat muddled zombie thriller.
Zittrer gave the film an introductory motif for low synthesizer
tones over FORBIDDEN PLANET-styled electronic burbles, whaps
and whooms. The bulk of the score is comprised primarily of uninteresting zaps and tones, as well as a prolonged use of screaming
howls during the graveyard scenes. Zittrer makes prevalent use
of processed sounds as well, and the score is more a collage of effects than real musical accompaniment. Zittrer continued to provide
synthesizer scores for low-budget horrors, finally teaming with Paul
Zaza in 1979 to provide an effective score for the Sherlock Holmes
thriller, MURDER BY DECREE, as well as the HALLOWEEN-clone,
PROM NIGHT, which made dominant use of disco music in addition
to electronic atmospheres. Zaza later went on to score similar
stalk-and-slash films on his own, including MY BLOODY VALEN-
TINE (1981) and CURTAINS (1983).

Like Zittrer, composer Allen D. Allen scored several micro-
budget horrors of the early 70's, also providing a somewhat random
assortment of electronic tonalities for films such as THE SPECTRE
OF EDGAR ALLAN POE (1972). For THE CLONES (1972), he assembled a sloppy mishmosh of electronic effects, pounding keyboard
chase motifs, and ill-fitting jazz and rock rhythmatics. Some of
the pop pieces are pleasant enough, but don't seem to work with
the pacing of the film.

An effective electronic score was created by Brian Hodgson
and Delia Derbyshire for THE LEGEND OF HELL HOUSE (1973).
This noteworthy British chiller used music very sparsely, but to
shuddery effect, first heard as a kind of rumbling, percussive
semirhythm with low, furtive, synthesized woodwind notes as the
scientific party travels to the haunted Belasco House. Eerie,
ghostly tones represent Belasco House itself, very subtle and atmospheric, with wailing, muted brass sounds interplaying with the
woodwind tones.

SQUIRM (1976), scored by Robert Prince, is a collection of
mostly electronic tones and effects, as in the low, warbling synthesizer rumbles heard during scenes of the worms wriggling, with
strings and plucked harp added for suspense cues. Arlon Ober
provided an effective mixture of electronics and standard orches-

tration for THE INCREDIBLE MELTING MAN (1977). (Ober later scored EATING RAOUL in 1982, with a diverse assemblage of bland, nostalgic, situation-comedy tunes and a great deal of mickey mousing--much of it accomplished through library music.)

The current trend in wholly synthesizer scoring probably got its main boost in 1978 with John Carpenter's innovative score for the phenomenally successful mad-killer film, HALLOWEEN. Carpenter is a talented film director who got his start in 1970 with a pair of highly acclaimed student films made at the University of Southern California. One of these was DARK STAR, a quirky and amusing outer-space farce concerning the adventures of a trio of astronauts gleefully enjoying their assignment to vaporize potentially dangerous, unstable planets. Carpenter co-wrote, produced and directed the small film, which was transformed into a theatrical feature in 1974. He also composed and performed the film's music, a task he continued to undertake on his next half-dozen films.

The idea of a director also being involved in providing a film's music is a rare one, although it had occurred before. In Carpenter's case, it's given him total control over the atmospheric mood of his pictures, both visually and audibly, and this probably has contributed to the overall power of films such as HALLOWEEN. Other filmmakers who scored their own films include Georges Franju (SHADOWMAN, 1975), William Girdler (ASYLUM OF SATAN, 1975), Ted V. Mikels (THE CORPSE GRINDERS, 1972), H. G. Lewis (SHE DEVILS ON WHEELS, 1968; and THE GORE GORE GIRLS, 1971, composing as "Sheldon Seymour"), Harry Bromley Davenport (WHISPERS OF FEAR, 1974, and X-TRO, 1983), Woody Allen (SLEEPER, 1974), Frank LaLoggia (FEAR NO EVIL, 1981, in collaboration with David Spear), Tobe Hooper (THE TEXAS CHAINSAW MASSACRE, 1974, collaborating with Wayne Bell), and producer Ivan Reitman (THEY CAME FROM WITHIN, 1976; and RABID, 1977). It's also worth noting that nearly all of these films were low-budget efforts, which implies that having a score created by the director or producer might also have been a budgetary consideration.

John Carpenter gained his musical background from his father, who was the head of the musical department at the University of Kentucky, as well as a musician performing in recording sessions in Nashville. "I would be at some of these recording sessions," Carpenter explained, "so I got the full spectrum, from classical to rock and roll and country music. It was mainly just osmosis and being exposed to it. I can play just about any keyboard instrument, but I can't read or write a note. Fortunately, I have a good ear."[18]

Carpenter's music for DARK STAR utilized an array of computerized bleeps, whorls, bell-sounds and similar effects, but was particularly effective in its use of the same ominous theme he would

later develop in HALLOWEEN--a moody, chilling group of low-plod-
ding chords beneath a higher, tinkling up-and-down melody (best
heard, in DARK STAR, during the "stuck bomb" sequence near
the end of the film).

Carpenter's next movie, a taut, gripping contemporary thriller called ASSAULT ON PRECINCT 13 (1976), was given a rhythmic,
fast synthesizer beat under a strong five-note bass riff (later repeated in various note sequences), over which a high-pitched, synthesizer wail emerges.   The music is catchy, pulse-pounding, and
drives the claustrophobic action on relentlessly, perfectly matching
the rapid pace sustained in the film's visuals.   "Movies are sound
and image," Carpenter said, and this philosophy is put to prominent use by the director/composer.

The music for HALLOWEEN is based on a pulsating, repetitious melody for a quick, high-pitched, tinkling piano melody over
low, sustained synthesizer chords, occasionally sounding like a
moaning male choir.   The style is somewhat reminiscent of the keyboard opening of Mike Oldfield's 1973 rock symphony, "Tubular
Bells," which had been used that same year in the movie, THE
EXORCIST.   One reviewer wrote of Carpenter's score: "The electronic approach is uniquely tailored for the character of the film.
It not only describes a killer, but an unrelenting, calculating, and
almost mechanical one.   As Jaws was an 'eating machine,' the Shape
is a 'killing machine'--his knife descending as rapidly as a factory
die-cutter ramming up and down as it punches templates in sheet
metal.   The music describes simultaneously the superhuman and the
inhuman aspects of the Shape with its impossible speed and alien
tonality."[19]

In addition to this dominating, pervasive theme, Carpenter
provided a slow-moving, rather dismal theme for Laurie, seemingly
delineating not her personality or liveliness, but only her impending, critical encounter with the Shape.   Also used are a variety of
droning, chilling chords and weird tonalities, including a hair-
raising, raspy percussive "stinger" used for shock sequences.
Carpenter has said he carefully aligns his music, both in composition and placement, where it will most accentuate the overall atmosphere he is directing.   "First of all," Carpenter explained, "the
edited film must work by itself, without any music or sound effects.
It can be rough, but it must tell the story, make sense and have
its own ups and downs.   Then the enhancement of that is the music and the sound effects--everything is brought to life.   So the
first process is editing; then you know what you're dealing with;
you can proceed to enhance it--at least that's my approach."[20]
Carpenter begins formulating the score from the very start as he
initially fleshes out his film.   "Right from the beginning," he continues, "as I'm writing the script, I hear snatches of the score.
Sometimes it changes, depending on how much I think a particular
scene needs, what mood it needs."

While Carpenter did not direct either of the two HALLOWEEN sequels, he did provide the music, along with assistant Alan Howarth. The music for HALLOWEEN II (1981) is an extension of the themes from the first picture, produced through an elaborate system of synthesizers, sequencers, programmers and drum computers. The main HALLOWEEN theme is here given a jangly, rockier beat, and a secondary theme for Laurie presented unchanged. Alan Howarth described Carpenter's intentions for the sequel music: "He wanted to employ the latest available synthesizer techniques to extend and vary some of the themes from the original HALLOWEEN in addition to creating new ones."[21] The new material is mostly utilized during the latter portion of the film, in which wounded Laurie is terrorized by the Shape in a deserted hospital ward, characterized by a series of jangling, high notes wandering over low, percussive synthesizer beats and a deep, droning hum. "The tympani effect produced by the Prophet 10 synthesizer," Howarth continues, "was just the right sound to set the mood for the film's second half and I used it as a connective thread in the Shape's pursuit of Laurie."

Since HALLOWEEN III: SEASON OF THE WITCH (1982) was wholly unrelated except by title to the previous pair, Carpenter's music was logically produced on a different track altogether. Gone are the claustrophobic jangling themes from the first films, replaced with a deep, somber resonance for low synthesizer drone under higher weep-weep-weep noises and an underlying tympanilike percussion rhythm, alternating between slow movements and faster arrangements. "The music style of John Carpenter and myself," Howard said regarding this score, "has further evolved in this film soundtrack by working exclusively with synthesizers to produce our music. This has led us to a certain procedural routine. The film is first transferred to a time coded video tape and synchronized to a 24-track master audio recorder; then, while watching the film we compose the music to these visual images. The entire process goes quite rapidly and has 'instant gratification,' allowing us to evaluate the score in sync to the picture."[22]

After the original HALLOWEEN, Carpenter made a higher-budgeted ghost film entitled THE FOG (1980), investing it with a fine synthesizer and piano score that was especially ethereal and spooky. Carpenter composed the music, which was electronically orchestrated by Dan Wyman. The dominant Terror Theme is comprised of rapid, monotonous metronome bell-like pinging, similar to a motif used during Linda's death in HALLOWEEN. This motif is first heard when Stevie's boy finds the driftwood plaque, when the pinging is embellished with a very evocative, descending high synthesizer melody. The constant ringing acts as a heartthrob with a chillingly visceral quality heralding the ghostly attacks. An atmospheric motif for the fog is comprised of a bass, foghornlike sound, which draws the noise into an awesome, reverberating, unearthly tonal theme. A stinger, as in HALLOWEEN, is used for Mrs. Cobritz's sudden death,

comprised of a shocking, drawn-out synthesizer zap, followed by
an expiring buzzing. As the fog advances on the town, a monotonous synthesizer throbbing is heard under remarkably effective
electronic whaps, punctuating the panicked heartbeat of the doomed
town, highlighted by a high-pitched keyboard tinkling in tempo
with the throbbing rhythm. As the fog lifts, high synthesizer
tones echo a sigh of relief as they eke out a somber melody of aftermath, seguing to a fast-paced version of the Advancing-fog
Theme for high, descending piano and synthesizer notes interplaying over a fast tapping rhythm.

ESCAPE FROM NEW YORK (1981) was Carpenter's first association with synthesist Alan Howarth, who assisted him in realizing the electronic score. Unlike the brooding, mesmerizing music
from HALLOWEEN and THE FOG, this futuristic action film was
scored with a more melodic rock-and-roll theme for synthesizer
over percussion (drums and tambourine) which effectively drives
the story along. The use of the rock beat works in the context of
the film, with its chaotic, underworldly characters and setting, and
the driving, unrelenting purpose of Snake Plisskin.

Carpenter's musical style, while devoid of any orchestral
warmth, has managed to invest these horror films with an oppressive atmosphere of terror--a mood that the synthesizer is highly
equipped to evoke. The rock music base from which his approach
is derived works to his advantage--rather than simply tacking on
a rhythmic beat, as most pure rock scores tend to do, Carpenter
molds the styles of rock to fit the frightening and scary atmosphere
of his films--and the music, however repetitious and droning, works
very well in this type of movie.

HALLOWEEN, perhaps due to its simplicity, its effectiveness,
and its popularity, resulted in a flock of imitators, and in the
next few years horror film audiences were inundated with an onslaught of HALLOWEEN clones, most involving carefree, nubile
young couples interested only in sex, being methodically and creatively murdered by an indestructible psychotic interested only in
killing. Many of these subsequent films borrowed their musical
style from HALLOWEEN as well, and suddenly the synthesizer score
came into vogue. It was inexpensive, simple, and somehow provided a more legitimate way to get elements of rock and roll into
film music. A lot of these scores were written by newcomers, some
of whom were never heard from again. The effectiveness or value
of such scores differ greatly, but many are noticeably derived
from John Carpenter's HALLOWEEN ambience.

One of the first of these was PHANTASM (1979), a film which
didn't happen to mimic the plot of HALLOWEEN. The score featured
a main theme for a high, up-and-down synthesizer repetition over
low, bass synthesizer tones along with choirlike Mellotron chords,
given an underlying rock drum beat. The score was composed

jointly by Fred Myrow and Malcolm Seagrave, both of whom share a background in classical and chamber music. Myrow had been composer-in-residence with the New York Philharmonic, writing a number of film scores including SOYLENT GREEN (1973), while Seagrave was once a college music professor before leaving academia to write an opera. The two have been associated since their graduate school days at USC in 1957. Utilizing a battery of electronic keyboards, piano and percussion instruments, PHANTASM's music does achieve a surreal mood, blending various otherworldly textures in a basic rock rhythm, and providing a fluid mood to the grisly proceedings on screen.

HE KNOWS YOU'RE ALONE (1980), scored by Alexander and Mark Peskanov, was another thing altogether. The film, this time, was very much a HALLOWEEN clone, concerning a psycho who killed only engaged girls because he'd once been jilted on his wedding day. The music utilized a familiar high, tinkling piano melody over lower piano pounds and synthesizer chords, in addition to electrified, PSYCHOlike shrieks during the murder of the bridal store owner. The score also used pop tunes in a number of places.

THE BOOGEY MAN (1980), scored by Tim Krog for Synthe-Sound-Trax Corp., was a much more effective synthesizer score. Krog's main theme is a powerful, plodding, ominous melody, strongly performed by the lower end of the keyboard. It pounds in a weird, ghostlike way, and possesses the sense of awesome power unique to synthesizer music. Krog also provides a tinkling "music box" motif representing the maniac's youthful background, as well as a variety of swirling chords, bell sounds, shock chords, thereminlike wails over deep, oozing, hesitating tones, and other effects which integrate well with the primary themes. Krog's music is along the lines of HALLOWEEN, especially in the tinkling, music box riff, but is more than a simple imitation. Krog provides a strong, omnipresent atmosphere, and a sense of direction, musically, which results in a superior synthesizer score.

MANIAC (1981) represents the other end of the spectrum. Scored by Jay Chattaway, a record arranger and producer who previously worked with composer Gato Barbieri on a 1979 film called FIREPOWER, the music collects an abundance of synthesized tonalities and sound effects which never seem to integrate into a cohesive whole. Chattaway's single pleasant theme is a melodic piece, describing the alienation and psychosis of the maniacal lady-killer, which is a soft woodwind theme over a chiming, harpsichord-like riff. This piece musically suggests the conflicting persona of the killer and contributes an otherwise absent feeling of sympathy to this unlovely character. The remainder of the music consists primarily of monotonous synthesizer tonalities that go nowhere. Like the film's excessive use of gore and graphic violence, Chattaway's score is little more than an overabundance of drones and idle chords that roll around randomly into a directionless muddle.

GRADUATION DAY (1981), another tedious HALLOWEEN clone--this time of high school kids being slaughtered as they prepare for graduation--was given a harsh rock score by Arthur Kempel, comprised mostly of rock-pop melodies as well as predictable and obvious eerie synthesizer motifs. This is hardly dramatic film music, and, unfortunately, seems fairly representative of much recent horror music, often written by newcomers with rock experience but little in the way of a background in musical structure and form. (Rock can work as film music, but only when the idiom is used in a dramatic or programmatic way; simple rhythms, beats or random improvisation rarely will complement the emotional level of a movie). Gary Scott's FINAL EXAM (1981) is another somewhat typical post-HALLOWEEN score for a typical post-HALLOWEEN horror film (now it is coeds being butchered as they dutifully prepare for finals). Scott, who graduated from UCLA with a degree in music, developed his own electronic music studio from which the FINAL EXAM score was generated. The score opens with an impressive introductory passage for piano, string and synthesizer chords but soon evolves into an imitative composition for tinkling piano notes over a low synthesizer drone. This main theme, despite its unoriginality, does manage to remain effective, particularly since Scott reverses the tradition and allows the sustained, heavy bass synthesizer chords to overwhelm the piano tinkling at regular intervals. This motif is balanced by a Wilderness Theme for electric piano and woodwind, which seems to signify the neutrality of the film's mountain setting and the innocence of the heroine while the earlier theme denoted impending doom and meaningless carnage. Enmeshed between these themes are a variety of suspense and incidental pieces, mostly utilizing typical up-and-down rhythms, often by harp, over the low, droning synthesizer chords and often comprising a variation on the main theme. THE SLUMBER PARTY MASSACRE (1982--this time it's a maniac with a huge, phallic electric drill gouging holes in nubile females) didn't use a tinkling high melody over low bass drones, but was given an otherwise routine synthesizer score by Ralph Jones. A graduate of the State University of New York at Buffalo, Jones has worked for more than ten years as a composer and performer of electronic music. His score for SLUMBER PARTY MASSACRE utilizes an effective Horror motif, constructed from rapidly echoed, four-note ascending, somewhat nasal synthesizer notes, which build rapidly on one another and provide a suitably claustrophobic atmosphere of terror. Much of the score, however, uses simple atonal drones and wails, relying solely on synthesizer, cymbals and crystal glasses to achieve effects in place of musical scoring. And, naturally, a HALLOWEEN spoof such as STUDENT BODIES (1982) was given an uninspired (and nonsatirical) score for, yes, tinkling piano over bass synthesizer drones, concocted by Gene Hobson. Most of the other HALLOWEEN clones have followed suit in their music--a few notable exceptions being Dana Kaproff's fine, rich orchestral score for WHEN A STRANGER CALLS (1979), John Mills-Cockell's TERROR TRAIN (1980) and Richard Band's excellent symphonic music for THE HOUSE ON SORORITY ROW (1983).

Other electronic scoring has remained more in the vein of rock music, as in Craig Hundley's scores for ALLIGATOR and SCHIZOID (both 1980), in which he provided a mixture of synthesizer and orchestral music in a fairly pop/rock mode. Hundley, a prolific synthesist, also assisted in the electronic realization of Laurence Rosenthal's METEOR (1979) and Susan Justin's FORBIDDEN WORLD (1982). The later score is an unusually appropriate mixture of New Wave rock stylisms and synthesizer effects--a rare occasion in which a rock-oriented score supports the film's atmosphere and dramatics. Justin, a music graduate of UCLA who also studied in Copenhagen, heads her own New Wave rock band in the Los Angeles area. "I tried to base the soundtrack on my own New Wave songwriting," she said. "I tried to adapt my own style to film."[23] Justin adapts this style nicely--the resultant score is not actually a rock score, except for the instrumental title tune, but instead incorporates a New Wave rock approach in producing a quirky, effective musical score dominated by synthesizer, piano, voice and drums. The main theme, representing the prowling, toothsome alien monster, embodies a repeated three-note motif for synthesizer, piano and voice, embellished by electronic "wind" effects and a semijazzy, high-pitched synthesizer break midway through. A more tender theme for piano over synthesizer is provided to reflect the feelings of the humans struggling to survive. A variety of additional synthesizer effects and quasi-New Wave tunes are used during suspense and attack scenes, and tend to work well in complementing the quirky film's futuristic mood of unearthly, claustrophobic horror.

An especially memorable and effective synthesizer score was composed by Colin Towns for FULL CIRCLE (1976; later rereleased in 1982 as THE HAUNTING OF JULIA). The film was an attractively stylish and very subtle ghost film, and Towns, a former keyboard player with Ian Gillian's pop band, provided a beautiful, stylish blend of vocals, synthesizer and piano. Towns was brought into the project long before shooting started, in order to help sell the project to potential investors by presenting them with a recorded score as well as a script. Towns based his musical impressions, therefore, solely upon reading the script; and by having it conceived ahead of time resulted in its being used as a very foreground element in the film's directorial style. Many scenes are carried by the weight of the music and visuals alone.

The music is simple, but haunting, and very difficult to describe. Its roots are in rock, but it is by no means a rock score. The main theme is an unforgettable melody evocative of both joy and sorrow, played first by melancholy piano and later by a strong, high synthesizer, over shimmering, mid-range synthesizer drones and a slowly repeated up-and-down piano riff. The synthesizer provides a clear-toned and somewhat eerie texture as it carries the tune, particularly in the way it quivers at the end of the sustained notes. A secondary motif for Kate, Julia's ill-fated daughter, is a quiet and introspective melody for piano and synthesizer harmonies over bass synthesizer, which moves fluidly and easily along at a careful pace. There is also a tender Love Theme, first heard by solo flute and later by flute and synthesizer over meandering piano notes, which retains a slightly melancholy character. The music for Julia's reflective walk through the park is a fluid, thoughtful piano theme reminiscent of the style of Erik Satie. There is also a rich vein of dark, brooding bass synthesizer chords under higher, wraithlike tones and warbles during the scene where Julia's husband prowls the cellar.

Towns' musical score mirrors the stylish approach taken by the film itself--it approaches horror indirectly, providing not shocking scenes and terrifying suspense, but a sad, melancholy feeling. The melody captures an essence of joy, but the tempo is tinged with regret, and in many ways FULL CIRCLE is a film exploring regret and resignation. The paradoxical moods evoked by the score perfectly underlie the mood of the film, and the fact that it was composed early on and carefully placed within the overall whole of the film results in an especially powerful marriage of music, sound and image.

Another notable synthesist contributing to electronic film music is Vangelis. Otherwise known as Evangelos Papathanassiou, Vangelis was born in Greece and was a primary member of two European rock bands before venturing on his own into solo electronic music and occasional film scores in Europe. He first came into prominence in the United States when portions of his recorded music were used on the TV series COSMOS, and gained widespread attention with his Oscar-winning score for CHARIOTS OF FIRE (1981). His sole entry thus far into the fantastic genre was for the gritty, futuristic film-noir thriller, BLADE RUNNER (1982), and while not as profound as his CHARIOTS OF FIRE music, it remains an effective synthesizer score. The music is first heard over the main titles, with a slowly ascending, sirenlike synthesizer wail over sustained tones, glissandos and punctuating electronic "drum" whaps, which nicely sets the futuristic scenes. The synthesizer music is nicely blended with a sexy piano-and-saxophone blues ballad for the moody scenes in Deckard's apartment, which offer a nostalgic and relaxed mood to the otherwise urgent proceedings. A number of 40's-ish and period songs were also used in the film to provide the future/nostalgia feeling the director wanted. The end title theme is more in keeping with Vangelis' characteristic style, with a rhythmic, somewhat rocky buzzing synthesizer bass riff under a higher melody. One reviewer wrote of the BLADE RUNNER score: "A fitting counterpart to these awesome sights is Vangelis' soulful score, accented by cooly weaving sax lines, snatches of mournful geisha ballad, and assorted wails. Soaring and eloquent, it is grandeur without pomposity, supplying much feeling."[24]

Vangelis, who resides in England and composed the score in the midst of his vast electronic "laboratory," is a self-taught musician who doesn't read or write music. He composes directly onto tape, orchestrating as he goes, playing different synthesizers at the same time, and wrapping everything up in the dubbing and mixing stages. He is especially keen on the combination of synthesizer and piano, a mixture he employs frequently in his music. "I like changing from one to another," he said. "Each has its own sound and adds its own color. The synthesizer is an extension in musical history the way automobiles were an extension in transportation history. It's a very flexible instrument, and there's nothing faster for scoring a film."[25]

Paul Schrader's sensuous remake of CAT PEOPLE (1982) was given a low-key, rock-oriented synthesizer score by Giorgio Moroder, an Italian-born musician who became interested in electronic music through the pioneering synthesizer rock groups in Germany, such as Kraftwerk, Tangerine Dream and Popol Vuh. Moroder was the object of some controversy in the film music world when he won a seemingly commercial Oscar for his MIDNIGHT EXPRESS score, beating out Williams' SUPERMAN and Goldsmith's THE BOYS FROM BRAZIL.

Moroder remains cautious about how he uses a synthesizer in a score such as CAT PEOPLE. "I hate those sounds which are typical synthesizer," he said. "All that oing-boing that a lot of rock bands use. It's especially harmful to a score. You have to balance the sound so that it's not too much like an obvious synthesizer and not too much like just another instrument. It should be unexaggerated, subtle, and as natural as possible. We spend a lot of time getting that right, adjusting the knobs."[26]

Moroder's synthesizer score, however, was less effective in a fantasy film like CAT PEOPLE than in more contemporary "big city" films such as MIDNIGHT EXPRESS and AMERICAN GIGOLO, as one reviewer noted: Moroder's "para-disco tunes are decidedly out of place in the fantasy film genre. Except for the rather eerie 'Transformation Seduction,' the synthesizer-laden score for CAT PEOPLE makes much of the stylishly photographed film look more like a European fashion commercial than a fantasy."[27] Moroder's music was nice, somber rock and roll but didn't really match the visuals except in maintaining an elegant, sensuous rhythm.

Howard Shore's music for David Cronenberg's SCANNERS (1981) mingled electronics and symphonics for a muddled score which was appropriately "horrendous." The score opens with a dramatic eight-note string motif--somewhat akin to the Dies Irae although the notes are slightly different, as they pound forth in a similar tempo, each note of the same strength. Weird, electronic effects, brass, percussion and repetitious string passages make up the rest of the score. Shore's music for Cronenberg's VIDEO-

DROME (1983) was along similar lines, housing a mixture of slow-
moving strings over synthesizer (for the love scenes between Nicki
and Max) and deep, bass synthesizer chords embellishing Max's
bizarre hallucinations. One reviewer described Shore's music as
a "perceptive, mesmerizing score--fraught with breathing and heartbeat motifs, and blending acoustic and electronic themes as the narrative unites Man with machine."[28]

A harsh and unpleasantly horrific synthesizer score was provided by British composer John Scott for the ALIENlike science fiction horror film, INSEMINOID (1981). Scott, best noted for his
rich, symphonic scores such as THE FINAL COUNTDOWN, decided
to write and perform an entirely electronic film score for INSEM-
INOID. The result is an often rock-oriented, atonal synthesizer
score which won the Best Musical Score award at the 1981 International Festival of Horror and Science Fiction Films in Madrid. Scott
reportedly spent over 300 hours of studio time experimenting with
and recording the soundtrack, which, in some cases, required as
many as ten overdubs and a mixture of nearly 60 separate tracks.
The music is more along the lines of FORBIDDEN PLANET in that
atonal dissonances and electronic effects take the place of thematic
scoring.

More remarkable, however, was John Harrison's richly evocative synthesizer music for George Romero's CREEPSHOW (1982).
Harrison, a long-time friend of Romero who acted as first assistant
director on the film, had an extensive background in rock music
and composition, and offered to provide some short synthesizer
motifs to bridge the assortment of previously recorded library music Romero had originally intended to use for a score, as he had
done on his famous NIGHT OF THE LIVING DEAD (1968). As production commenced, however, it became apparent that a tailor-made
score was needed to match the dynamic visuals, and so Harrison
found himself composing and performing about 75 percent of CREEP-
SHOW's score.

Harrison's score was a mixture of Prophet 5 synthesizer and
piano, with some remarkably effective, ghostly chanting voices
(these were arranged by Michelle Di Bucci) over the titles. This
opening theme establishes something of a lilting quality which contrasts nicely with the dominating horrific aspects of the music.
"Most of the effects I wanted to achieve were ethereal," Harrison
explained. "Ghostlike motifs that would float in and out of the music."[29] Each episode of this five-part anthology film was given a
separate musical identity, although each retained a consistent stylistic texture. "Father's Day" and "The Crate" were scored in the
traditional horror vein: "There's a real traditional Herrmannesque
'sting' and scare when Nate comes out of the grave to get Bedelia,"
Harrison said of the "Father's Day" episode--the sting is also reminiscent of John Carpenter's raspy, surprise stinger from HALLO-
WEEN. "They're Creeping Up On You" contrasts source jazz music

(heard from Pratt's old-fashioned jukebox) with electronic effects when the cockroaches begin to encroach. "When the bugs are creeping around," Harrison said, "I used little electronic statements to hint at each bug. When the bugs finally attack, the whole place goes berserk and I begin a very heavy electronic sound." The "Jordy Verrill" segment is given more of a slapstick approach, much of it involving library music. "Something to Tide You Over" featured some fine solo vocal motifs during the beach scene, in addition to library cues. Working as both the composer and first assistant director gave Harrison a unique insight into the production, which benefited the effectiveness of his score, and the music is a superbly arranged example of dramatic synthesizer scoring at its best.

As we have seen, the evolution of electronic scoring over the past 30 years has made itself known in film music, particularly in the fantastic cinema where it has seen most of its development. One reason, as Les Baxter pointed out earlier, is the remarkable range of sound capable from a synthesizer. As one writer suggested: horror, science fiction and psychological films "deal with subjects removed from reality and subjected to unfamiliar environments. Electronic music is very effective in dealing with these aspects of alienation (alone dealing with the unknown) because it automatically alienates the listener. This is music composed of sounds that the listener has generally not encountered before, so he does not know how to react to them logically. His initial reaction is one of illogical fear, uneasiness, or revulsion--emotions that can easily be exploited by the composer. The important point is that electronic music written in any style is likely to produce the same reaction because of the effects the sounds have upon the subconscious. Thus, electronics is a limited medium for film music (the function of which is to inspire any desired emotion) despite its unlimited capability of sound."[30]

While synthesizer scoring is not limited in its effectiveness to fantastic films--as Vangelis has remarkably demonstrated in his moving score to CHARIOTS OF FIRE--it is limited in the sense that, while retaining an unlimited tonal range, the sounds produced are nevertheless recognizably synthetic, and cannot have the same emotional effect upon the listener as that of a symphony orchestra (one amazing exception would be Colin Towns' FULL CIRCLE).

Another drawback to some synthesizer scores is due to the background many electronic composers have drawn from--the European synthesizer rock groups such as Tangerine Dream, Kraftwerk, Jean-Michel Jarre, Klaus Schulze and so on. Much of the groundbreaking music of these artists has been not-unlikably monotonous, progressing slowly and achieving its effect through patiently developed orchestration, emphasizing mood and ambience over melody and harmony. Much synthesizer scoring carried over this monotony into film music, where it was not always suitable; although some ef-

forts have been made to adapt the synthesizer to more traditional
styles of dramatic film scoring, as with CREEPSHOW and FULL
CIRCLE. Another potential drawback is the prevalence of using
the synthesizer to obtain musical effects instead of real, dramatic
film music, although this has had its place, as in FORBIDDEN
PLANET and THE ANDROMEDA STRAIN. An effort has been made
to avoid both disadvantages through the integrating of a synthesizer with the conventional instruments of the orchestra, as in
TRON, METEOR, BLUE THUNDER and others. Thus, the advantages of the synthesizer are obtained without sacrificing the warmth
and power of a symphony orchestra.

The fantastic cinema has seen the emergence of synthesizer
scoring grow from a clever gimmick into a viable style of film scoring. As with any new style, it has been misused considerably;
but, more importantly, it has provided an often remarkable source
of film music uniquely complementary to the genre, and the efforts
of the Barrons, Gil Mellé, Wendy Carlos, John Carpenter, Arthur
B. Rubinstein, Colin Towns, Vangelis and John Harrison have been
especially noteworthy in the field of film music for fantastic films.

Notes

1. Les Baxter interview with the author, January 9, 1982 (and
   following quotes)

2. Fred Steiner interview with the author, February 17, 1983

3. Manuel Compinsky quoted by Scot W. Holton in letter to the
   author dated December 2, 1980.

4. Louis Barron quoted by Frederick S. Clarke and Steve Rubin,
   "Making of FORBIDDEN PLANET," Cinefantastique Vol. 8,
   #2/3 (1979) p. 43

5. Clarke & Rubin, ibid.

6. John Baxter, Science Fiction in the Cinema (New York: Paperback Library, 1976) p. 113

7. Barry Gray interview with the author, February 26, 1982

8. Gil Melle interview with the author, June 29, 1983 (and following quotes)

9. Mark Stevens, "The Score," Cinefantastique Vol. 1, #3 (Summer 1971) p. 34

10. Tom Haroldson, The Fifth Estate (Detroit). No further details.

11. Wendy Carlos interviewed by Robert Moog, Keyboard, November 1982, p. 59

12. _____ interview with the author, May 20, 1982 (and following quotes)

13. Brian May interviewed by Graeme Flanagan, CinemaScore #11/12, (Fall 1983) p. 24

14. Lee Holdridge interview with the author, October 19, 1982

15. John Williams quoted by Kenneth Terry, "Music Makers," Up Beat Vol. 30, #2 (September 1982) p. 32

16. Laurence Rosenthal interview with the author, May 20, 1982. (and following quotes)

17. Arthur B. Rubinstein interview with the author, May 21, 1983

18. John Carpenter interviewed by Jordon R. Fox, Cinefantastique Vol. 10, #1 (Summer 1980) p. 40

19. Tom Underwood, "HALLOWEEN II," CinemaScore #10 (Fall 1982) p. 25

20. John Carpenter interviewed by Bob Martin, Fangoria #8 (October 1980) p. 25-26

21. Alan Howarth, liner notes to HALLOWEEN II sound-track recording, Varese Sarabande Records, 1981

22. _____, liner notes to HALLOWEEN III--SEASON OF THE WITCH sound-track recording, MCA Records, 1982

23. Susan Justin, liner notes to FORBIDDEN WORLD sound-track recording, WEB Records, 1982

24. Jordon R. Fox, "Film Review," Cinefantastique Vol. 13, #1 (September-October 1982) p. 44

25. Vangelis quoted by Terry Atkinson, "Scoring with Synthesizers," American Film, September 1982, p. 71

26. Giorgio Moroder quoted by Terry Atkinson, ibid., p. 70

27. Jim Doherty, "L.P. Review," Soundtrack! The Collector's Quarterly #2 (June 1982) p. 24

28. Tim Lucas, "VIDEODROME," Cinefantastique, Vol. 13, #4
    (April-May 1983) p. 4

29. John Harrison quoted by Paul Gagne, "The Score: John Har-
    rison's CreepMusic," Cinefantastique, Vol. 13, #2/3 (No-
    vember-December 1982) p. 10 (and following quotes)

30. Tom Underwood, loc. cit.

<u>John Williams</u>. Photograph courtesy San Francisco Symphony.

XIV

DEJA VU
John Williams

The symphonic score, and the use of leitmotifs in the tradition of Max Steiner and Erich Wolfgang Korngold, gradually went out of fashion in the 60's and 70's, with filmmakers favoring pretty melodies that may or may not have been related to specific characters, locales or dramatic situations, and which could also sell records and publicize the movie on radio (often the sole impetus for such scores). The later 70's brought about a profound resurgence of the symphonic tradition of film scoring, much to the relief of many composers, and most prominently through the work of John Williams, whose vast, energetic score for STAR WARS, and his insistence upon utilizing the huge London Symphony Orchestra legitimized once again the proud, romantic tradition of Steiner and Korngold. (Ironically, the distinctly symphonic STAR WARS soundtrack album sold more copies than any other sound track in history!)

While he has not been devoid of criticism, most of which has been directed at his liberal borrowing from classical composers such as Stravinsky and Wagner, his approach is much more intrinsically bound up in a film's whole than a pop score or an atonal score, and has sparked an awareness of the value of film music in the minds of many people. One writer said of Williams: "True, most of his scores are commercially marketable and based on readily identifiable themes, but they contain that emotional commitment and relationship to the film absent for so long. His music is part of the storytelling, as important to the film as scenery."[1]

The son of a tympani player, Williams was born in New York in 1932. He moved with his family to Los Angeles in 1949, and gradually gained an interest in music during high school. While his initial ambition was to become a concert pianist, after studying at UCLA and hearing other students in Rosina Lhevinne's piano class at Juilliard, Williams realized that he may have set his goal too high, and decided he might be better off as a composer. Active as a jazz pianist for many years, he began to play piano in the film orchestras of Columbia and Twentieth Century-Fox during the mid-50's, working with composers such as Alfred Newman, Jerry Goldsmith, Max Steiner and Dimitri Tiomkin. He began to orchestrate for some of these composers, and eventually made the natural transition to writing his own scores, starting out in television.

During the 60's, Williams worked on the Irwin Allen science
fiction shows, scoring episodes of VOYAGE TO THE BOTTOM OF
THE SEA and LAND OF THE GIANTS, as well as contributing
scores and themes to LOST IN SPACE and THE TIME TUNNEL.
Among his first genre films was THE SCREAMING WOMAN, a TV
movie, and Robert Altman's IMAGES, both in 1972. The IMAGES
score was a very mysterious one and served to quietly underline
the psychological aspects of the film's protagonist, lending a
schizophrenic duality to the score that matched that of the character. As John Caps wrote of the IMAGES score: "The writing was
done in two opposite directions, even two different languages:
one a sad, perverse, lullaby for piano later played simply on
celesta, later in a full Brahmsian symphonic movement; the other
was an intricate abstract composition of atonal sounds performed
on units of steel sculpture with remarkable sonic range. Gradually Williams brought these divergent voicings together, not an assimilation of styles but an integration so that they both worked for
the same descriptive purpose, defining the disturbed character...."[2]

The melodic theme was very pretty, treated differently in
varying arrangements, while the abstract motif employed a variety
of percussionistic effects, performed by the acclaimed percussionist, Stomu Yamash'ta, who, for contractual reasons, was also
credited as a cocomposer. In addition to the metallic Baschet instruments, Yamash'ta performed on wind chimes, bells, Inca flute,
Kabuki percussion instruments, and many conventional percussion
instruments including tympani, hand drums, blocks, bells and
marimbas.

Williams' first critical acclaim really began when he happened
to compose a number of films in the disaster cycle of the early 70's:
Irwin Allen's THE POSEIDON ADVENTURE (1972) and THE TOWER-
ING INFERNO (1974), as well as EARTHQUAKE (1974). The score
pleasantly blended moving, symphonic themes with pop tunes identified with various characters. The scores were highly effective, but
nowhere near as whalloping as that for JAWS (1975), the score for
which he won his first Oscar, developing a working relationship with
director Steven Spielberg that would later result in some of the
most memorable marriages of film and music in cinematic history.

A well-directed horror story about a killer shark depleting
the waters off an east-coast beach of numerous bathers, JAWS featured an unforgettable Stravinsky-like ostinato which was used with
terrifying accuracy to signal the imminent appearance of the savage
fish. As with IMAGES, Williams approached the film from two distinct directions, as John Caps noted: "attack and counterattack;
one part fear and one part righteous revenge. The attack section
of course dealt with the Great White Shark himself ... in Williams'
musical design, the shark is Evil personified and he is given a
taunting idée fixe on the basses, their bows sawing back and forth,

a hollow drum and a metallic rapping sound in the background.
This is punctuated by brass notes and a howling Stravinskian tuba
overhead. It all has a frightening primitive irony to it, which Williams then manipulates craftily....

"The counterattack music consists of an almost swashbuckling
fugue used to display the shark chase sequences and giving them
an heroic posture approaching Captain Ahab's similar obsessions of
over a hundred years ago. The determination and optimism of the
music here virtually skims across the water line." [3] Williams alternates and then combines the two motifs throughout the final confrontation scenes, employing the shark ostinato whenever the huge
fin is sighted knifing its way toward the boat, and surging forward
with the Counterattack Theme as the boat manuevers to its occasional advantage. Williams explains more specifically: "To differ-
entiate between what you call the Stravinskian passages and the
swashbuckling fugue, I would say that the former passages have
to do with the attack of the shark specifically, while the fugue
subject, if you examine the film carefully, has to do with the as-
sembly of hardware with which to fight the shark, i.e., the assem-
bly of the cage and demonstrations of Hooper's advanced shark
hunting equipment, etc." [4]

Bill Littman has described a third major motif in the JAWS
score, what he terms a man vs. fish "conflict" theme, a steady,
rhythmical construction centered around a four-note motif which is
often heard as a dramatic counterpoint to the shark ostinato: "Both
shark and 'conflict' themes produce the same overall effect--that
throbbing surge of forward-thrusting energy and determination ...
the 'conflict' theme ... represents the humans' side of the battle.
It's surging and energetic all right, but compared to the shark's
motif it's also weak and indecisive at points. Instead of a fluid,
straight-ahead movement, the 'conflict' theme begins, stops, starts
again, stops, starts once more, doubles back on itself, then repeats. Its lack of consistent strength gives us exactly the feeling
we want, as per the at-odds humans; that is, the shark will be the
more powerful aggressor at all times throughout the picture, musically as well as visually." [5]

As thrilling as the JAWS score was, Williams greatly surpassed
it two years later when he composed the music for George Lucas'
phenomenal STAR WARS (1977). The score is vibrant, full of optimism, heroism and zestful adventure, relating to the wildly romantic and soaring spirits of the characters that people the film. Williams avoids the usage of electronic music to achieve a spacey mood,
instead composing music that corresponds to the film's characters
and spirit and not to its milieu. The score is built around four
major character themes: a rousing and triumphant heroic melody
for Luke Skywalker which becomes the main STAR WARS theme
(Williams said: "I composed a melody that reflected the brassy,
bold, masculine and noble qualities I saw in the character. When

the theme is played softly, I tended towards a softer brass sound.
But I used fanfarish horns for the more heraldic passages."[6]); a
similarly noble and spiritually soaring theme for Luke's mentor,
Obi-Wan Kenobi which also underscores the metaphysical Force he
represents and the Old Republic he remembers ("It has a fairy tale
aspect rather than a futuristic aspect," said Williams. "There is a
lot of English horn ... which is often heard under dialogue. At
other times, the melody becomes the heroic march of the Jedi
Knights."); an ethereal nocture for Princess Leia which also suggests Luke's enchantment with her--like Kenobi's theme it is also
a fairy-tale melody; and finally there is the dark, somber theme
for Darth Vader ("I used a lot of bassoons and muted trombones
and other sorts of low sounds," Williams said.)

In addition to these central themes, shorter motifs are included for various secondary characters and situations: an amusing little Waddling Theme for the Jawas; a short motif for the
Death Star; atonal music for the Tusken Raiders which utilizes
some wild percussion, including tuned logs, steel plates and slap
sticks; a bouncing horn figure for Luke's landspeeder; and the
popular 30's-styled Benny Goodman swing music played by the Cantina Band in the Mos Eisley saloon. For this sequence, Williams
utilized nine jazz musicians performing on trumpet, saxophone,
clarinet, Fender Rhodes piano, percussion and an Arp synthesizer
for the twangy bass line. "I scored it so they sound a little bit
strange," Williams said, "almost familiar but not quite." This tuneful music (there are actually two cues, heard on either side of Obi-
Wan's light-sabre fight with the surly ruffian, although only the
first cue became popular on record) perfectly accented this delightful tour-de-force of alien patrons and lends an appropriate, slightly "abnormal" sound to the recognizable saloon rhythms.

STAR WARS was one of the first films to utilize a full modern
orchestra such as the London Symphony to perform the score. Williams explains why he opted for the larger forces: "It was due to
the outlines of these films that I've been associated with. You
wouldn't do STAR WARS with a ten-piece orchestra. Each picture
seems to suggest a kind of noise that seems appropriate--a weight
that seems right, a breadth, a size that seems to suit it. And really, that's what one tries to do."[7] Williams chose the London Symphony Orchestra because the film was shot in London and because
of Williams' friendship with their principal conductor, Andre Previn.

A criticism leveled at Williams--as well as at Steiner and
Korngold and the other earlier film composers--concerns their liberal drawing upon the work of various serious composers for methods of orchestration and even melodic ideas. STAR WARS is brimming with suggestions or fragments of Holst, Prokofiev, Mahler,
Bruckner, Stravinsky, Debussy and others, as many have pointed
out. One critic reviled Williams for failing to look toward avant-
garde composers like Varese or Cage for futuristic music, but this

reviewer failed to realize that a film such as STAR WARS wasn't
suited to an avant-garde type of score. "A lot of these references
are deliberate," Williams explained. "They're an attempt to evoke
a response in the audience where we want to elicit a certain kind
of reaction. Another thing is that, whenever one is involved in
writing incidental music--where you have specific backgrounds,
specific period, certain kinds of characters and so on--the work is
bound to be derivative in a certain sense. The degree to which
you can experiment, as you can in a concert work, is very limited.
You're fulfilling more of the role of a designer, in the same way
that a set designer would do a design for a period opera." [8] This
may seem to suggest that a futuristic film such as STAR WARS
(which actually takes place in the distant past) should theoretical-
ly be suited to futuristic music more than to late nineteenth- and
early twentieth-century music, but Williams hits closer to the mark
when he points out that films such as STAR WARS cater to an audience's desire for escapism: "In that escapist thing is the whole
romantic idea of getting away, of being transported into another
kind of atmosphere," something his music does exceptionally well.

However it's rationalized, Williams' use of classical music as
a reference point hardly detracts from the effectiveness of his
scores. The music in STAR WARS is intrinsically wedded to not
only the visual images, but to the very characters brought to life
in the film. Its roots are in the romantic tradition, blooming with
leitmotifs, the style first pioneered in films by Steiner and Korngold in scores for KING KONG and THE ADVENTURES OF ROBIN
HOOD in the 30's.

Williams won a second Oscar for his STAR WARS score (interestingly enough, this was the third year in a row that a fantastic film won the music Oscar: JAWS in 1975; Goldsmith's THE
OMEN in 1976; and STAR WARS in 1977), and with the phenomenal
success of the sound-track album (more than 4,000,000 copies sold,
an unheard of figure for normally modest sound track sales) John
Williams nearly became a household word, attaining a status earned
by no other modern composer of the post-1950 period and reserved
until then only for such legendary composers as Rozsa, Herrmann,
Newman, Waxman, and Steiner.

STAR WARS was followed, a scant seven months later, by
another milestone science fiction score, this one for Steven Spielberg's CLOSE ENCOUNTERS OF THE THIRD KIND (1977). Instead
of the profound heroics of George Lucas' space opera, CLOSE EN-
COUNTERS is a more ethereal score of "nearly reverential cosmic
splendor and visionary eloquence," as one reviewer put it. [9] Spielberg gave Williams the opportunity to begin work on the score two
years before the film was completed, allowing the composer to gain
further insight into Spielberg's aims for the picture, although the
music is drawn largely from Williams' own mystic ideas and reflects
the kind of music he prefers to write for himself--he once said that

the CLOSE ENCOUNTERS score is "closer to my own personal idiom." [10]

Williams discussed the genesis of the popular theme from CLOSE ENCOUNTERS in a lecture given at London's National Film Theatre in 1978, as one writer in attendance later reported: "He wrote about 250 five-note combinations before the one actually used was settled upon--more or less randomly, it seems. In other words, the suggestion of some learned critics that he 'stole' the combination from Der Rosenkavalier (or other, more obscure sources) is unfounded. Initially, Williams would have preferred a seven-note combination, but agreed that Spielberg was right in being adamant that the motif be of five notes, since seven would give the start of a melody (something less 'finished' being required)." [11]

The five-note motif referred to is an interesting thematic piece which is not only something of a leitmotif for the friendly aliens, but is used as an integral part of the film's plot and concept. The aliens communicate to the earth scientists not through words or language, but through music--each tone representing some idea or reference point. This five-note motif is the primary message of introduction transmitted by the aliens, heard frequently as source sounds from various scientists and close-encounterers as the UFO investigation progresses, and finally is given a memorable arrangement for synthesizer, tuba and piping woodwind when the alien Mothership lands and converses liberally with the scientists in a heady and fun fugue. The motif is also used orchestrally as a leitmotif during the final scenes of the film. As one reviewer wrote of this theme: "Williams loves contrasts, so for the UFO's signal to earth, he uses a 5-note motif in a descending arc, with a rising fillip on the end. The sheer downward movement is like a shorthand message for 'We're coming down'!" [12]

The majority of the score, however, is built from the same essence of profound wonder that Spielberg developed in his directorial approach. Utilizing, in certain themes, mystical voices and eerie, shimmering violins entwined by harps and flutes, Williams achieves a marvelous sense of awe, joy, and no less than religious anticipation in meeting the benevolent, messianic aliens. A number of choral techniques are used, especially an evocative, two-note ascending figure which lends significance to the frequent mountain visions seen by Roy Neary and Jillian as they are drawn toward their ultimate encounter. A horrific, avant-garde choral composition is used for the rather illogical sequence wherein the "kindly" aliens terrorize Jillian and kidnap her young son. Williams also quotes effectively from the Dies Irae for an action/pursuit motif, the plainsong melody voiced by chanting brass over ethereal strings and lower brass. Williams also interpolates the melody of the song, "When You Wish Upon a Star" (from PINOCCHIO) in the final scene --referring to Spielberg's original placement of the entire song behind the final ascent of the Mothership (an idea he wisely dropped).

The various motifs introduced and reiterated slightly in the earlier portions of the score aren't developed entirely until the film's expansive resolution, in which everything peaks, linked by the orchestral warmth of the Conversation Theme, rising rhapsodically in greater force. "The natural progression here begs for one great crescendo to bring the ecstasy to an end," wrote one reviewer, "but it's to Williams' credit he doesn't give in to this obvious gesture. Instead, he segues into a 'post'-lude, reprising the best of the score for the lengthy end titles, and ends, softly, continually--for the story doesn't end, but goes on, and on, and on, into infinity."[13]

Taking a slight break from heroic and mystical outer-space fictions, Williams scored Brian De Palma's psychic horror film THE FURY (1978) with a darkly evocative score. The slow, waltzlike main theme is quite reminiscent of Bernard Herrmann's VERTIGO theme and utilizes the same sort of quietly building, up-and-down motif, using woodwinds rather than Herrmann's violin, but this grows into Williams's own Terror Theme, dominated by brasses backed by strings, which nicely emphasizes the more horrible aspects of the scenario and retains De Palma's omnipresent mood of surreal gloom.

With JAWS 2 (1978), Williams returned to the memorable mixture of delightful seascapes and low, guttural horror that embellished the Spielberg original. The sequel opens with a gorgeous, four-note ascending theme for intricately plucked harps, over which the familiar shark ostinato from JAWS soon intrudes and eventually overwhelms and devours the delicate harp theme, just as the megalithic shark did to the hapless divers at the film's opening. The score seems broader than that of the original JAWS, attaining a greater sense of lyricism and depth, especially in the various orchestral pieces scored for the various seagoing scenes before the shark and its motif lunges into view.

Williams found himself once again in need of an heroic, adventure score for SUPERMAN (1978), wherein he composed a mighty, brass theme which suitably embodied the Man of Steel, embellished by a fine performance from the London Symphony. The heroic main theme runs throughout the film and maintains a brassy buildup to the action sequences, and is frequently interwoven with other motifs for specific situations. As one reviewer wrote: "The main title overture ... is surely among the most thrilling musical salutations in the history of motion pictures. Yet there is more to Williams' music than simply swashbuckling excitation. There is a deeply felt commitment to his art and to humanity that is evidenced during the moving sequence in which the young Clark Kent realizes that it is time to leave home and find his place in the world.... Williams' music captures both the sadness and the exultation of a growing awareness of the life awaiting him beyond the farm. There are visions of Copland during this musical panorama, echoing a deeply

felt understanding and affection for Americana."[14] Another reviewer wrote that, while the main titles sounded like a disappointing
amalgam of Korngold and Sousa, "Williams' score shines in both the
otherworldly sequences on Krypton and those which make a pretense at dealing with human emotions. When the young Clark Kent
bids farewell to his earthly mother, a warm outpouring of melody
brings to mind the music of Franz Waxman. The farewell of Jor-el
to his infant son and Superman-to-be is equally touching musically,
as well as the encounter between the two later in the ... northern
wastes. The latter features some truly 'chilling' sounds recalling
Vaughan Williams' Scott of the Antarctic (not to mention 'Neptune'
from Holst's 'The Planets'), plus a shimmering quasi-aleatoric passage which spotlights harp, vibraphone, celesta and glockenspiel."[15] Williams also provides an exquisite Love Theme for Superman and Lois Lane, as well as a catchy "March of the Villains"
which, while popularized on the sound-track album, was not actually included in the film.

   John Badham's adaptation of DRACULA (1979), was--outside
of Dan Curtis' 1974 TV version--one of the first to handle its subject matter in a romantic style, sympathizing with the seductive
vampire. Williams' score is in an appropriate nineteenth-century,
Gothic romantic tradition, opening with a swelling, fully symphonic,
sensuous Love Theme which grasps us in its harmonic power in
much the same way that Count Dracula seduces the hapless hero-
ines in his own awesome power. Williams avoids the throbbing,
pulse-pounding, gut-wrenching rhythms that were so effective in
previous DRACULA scores, investing into the film a poignancy and
lyricism that underlies even the dramatic and terrifying moments,
and at the same time embodies the power, passion and horror of
the Dracula figure incarnate in a single musical statement.

   "Williams' scoring of John Badham's vampire film necessitated
stark, brooding music that would convey loneliness as well as terror," wrote one reviewer. "The End Titles perfectly convey the
ageless passion, the lust for life consumed and propagated by a
being too dominant to allow his flow of breath to be stilled. For
this haunted soul Williams has fabricated a desperately romantic
and handsome accompaniment, deeply passionate and filled with
longing."[16] Another reviewer wrote: "The surging and enrap-
tured main theme, with its Wagnerian convolutions, sets the primary scene for the simplistic story line of fatal bloodlust and carnal
damnation. Development of this febrile, Liebestod-like motif is interrupted by set pieces depictive of nocturnal landscapes of the
soul, storm scenes, hairsbreadth escapes and chases, etc. If anything, the music often calls up memories of Berlioz' Faust as filtered
through a twentieth-century imagination. Perhaps at times one is
too much aware of attempts to elicit the desired response in the
auditor, but Williams' work has always borne the imprint of a knowing craftsman rather than of a genius ... his idiosyncratic approach
to film scoring has become so well entrenched that, instead of tick-

ing off the inventive borrowings from the likes of Holst, Korngold, Herrmann and Prokofiev, one is immediately aware of the influence of previous Williams embodiments on his latest effort."[17]

A return to the grand, heroic tradition of STAR WARS was found in Williams' score for the first sequel, THE EMPIRE STRIKES BACK (1980), for which he extended the style and orchestration of the first film into predominantly new material for the second. "I wrote 117 minutes of music for this picture," Williams said. "It opens with the STAR WARS March and it includes the Force theme. With that as a basis I wanted to try to develop material that would wed with the original and sound like part of an organic whole; something different, something new but an extension of what already existed. So, in the creation of new themes and the handling of the original material, the task, both in concept and instrumentation, was one of extending something that I had written three years before. I had to look back while at the same time begin again and extend."[18]

The only thematic material from STAR WARS directly carried over into this sequel were the main Star Wars theme (Luke's motif) and the theme for Obi-Wan Kenobi/the Force, as well as a brief phrase of Leia's Theme used as a Love motif between her and Han Solo. The new themes include a tender and sensitive motif for Yoda, filled with the dignity and sense of wonder befitting this diminutive Jedi Master; and a vast Imperial March which is identified with Darth Vader and the dark side of the Force. This thunderous theme is based on a warlike triplet figure, richly scored in octaves for brass. Various secondary motifs include a sumptuous melody for Bespin, the Cloud City; a stately promenade for the hero's march through Lando's palace; an atmospheric piece for atonal horns, strings and synthesizer, fleshed out with snatches of the Luke and Yoda Themes, for Luke's confrontation with Vader within the magic tree of Dagobah; as well as a rousing variety of virtuoso battle music, some of which required special instrumentation. The battle against the Imperial Walkers on the ice planet Hoth, for example, called for "five piccolos, five oboes, a battery of eight percussion, two grand pianos, two or three harps, in addition to the normal orchestral complement," Williams said. "This was necessary in order to achieve a bizarre mechanical, brutal sound for the sequence showing the Imperial Walkers, which are frightening inventions advancing across a snowscape."[19]

Williams was asked to score SUPERMAN II (1981), but due to prior commitments on another project he had to turn it down. The filmmakers then hired composer Ken Thorne who adapted Williams' thematic material from the first SUPERMAN movie into a score for the sequel. Williams, in the meantime, composed a marvelously energetic score for RAIDERS OF THE LOST ARK (1981), a nonstop action adventure made jointly by George Lucas and Steven Spielberg. Williams composed a vivid, thunderous score which, according to one reviewer, "makes every incident, every stunt not just

dramatic, but epochal."[20] Another reviewer wrote: "If the picture
is to be compared to 1930s and 1940s serials as many have suggested, its score plainly surpasses the music of those early cliffhangers, avoiding for the most part such faults as repetition, crib-
bing from other composers, and a general lack of musical imagination."[21]

The film's major Heroic Theme is a brassy march relating to
the central Indiana Jones character. Like Darth Vader, the villains
of this serial--the Nazis--are depicted with bassoons and low brass;
while the fabled Ark of the Covenant is surrounded with an ominous
chordal progression along the lines of Bernard Herrmann. Williams
also provides a tender and very pretty Love Theme for Indiana and
Marion. These four themes interplay throughout the film as Indiana's quest lures him into encounters with the other three. Other
motifs are highly evocative, especially the profound inspirational
motif for choir and brass heard in the Map Room when the rising
sun's rays illuminate the location of the Ark for Indiana. Williams
scored the opening Peruvian sequence with some superbly atmospheric moods, and provided a clever, scherzolike motif for dancing
strings (later brass) over low, piping woodwinds for Indiana's hectic pursuit of the captured Marion in the basket-filled Cairo streets.
The RAIDERS score, like the music from the SUPERMAN and STAR
WARS films, completed the sense of adventure and excitement maintained by these grand entertainments, propelling the action and underlying their romantic scope (romantic in the full sense of the
word).

Williams took a much different approach when he scored the
quirky, robot comedy, HEARTBEEPS (1981), composing in a more
modern musical idiom and emphasizing electronic instrumentation,
although without losing the pomp for which he has been known.
The score is low-key and quite a contrast to Williams' better-known
orchestral scores, but nonetheless very effective.

The music for Spielberg's E.T.--THE EXTRATERRESTRIAL
(1982) was a marvelously heartwarming score which won Williams his
third Oscar for Best Score. It was not as complex as his earlier
swashbucklers, but combined their excitement and adventure with
a softly intimate and romantic flavor that captured the heart and
wonderment of Spielberg's delightful film. "Williams has made E.T.
a textbook example of the film composer's craft," wrote John Caps.
"not so much the marriage of a specific image with a musical idea,
but the cumulative thrust of a straining, yearning story in tandem
with a rich orchestral score that acts as both narrator and conscience to the movie; a score that sings."[22] The main theme for
E.T. is drawn from similar melodic ground as the STAR WARS
theme--the first three or four notes nearly identical. Both themes
commence with a pronounced two-note ascending phrase followed by
descending notes which form the main melody, but where STAR
WARS goes on to become a heroic, brassy overture, E.T. becomes
a warm, boyish, adventurous theme.

Williams' approach to E.T. was simpler than that taken for the larger outer space movies with their large casts and exotic locales. Because E.T. was the simple story of a growing boy and a lost alien, Williams built the score from the interplay of two separate themes. "There's a theme for the little alien creature and for the little boy, Elliott, who finds and hides him," Williams said. "And that theme is kind of like a love theme. It's not sensual in the way a love theme would be, but it develops as their relationship develops. It starts with a few notes, they look at each other--a little bit uncertain. And it grows and becomes more confident, and more lyrical, as E.T. begins to communicate with the boy. At the end, it's kind of a full-blown sort of operatic aria when E.T. goes away.... In that scene their theme--the Elliott-E.T. Theme--comes back. It's like, in a way, a moment in opera when two lovers are being separated. I build to that kind of musical denouement."[23]

In addition to this thematic intertwining, Williams composed a thunderous, dramatically punctuated motif for brass and percussion which represents the key-jangling authorities who pursue E.T. throughout the picture. This theme also blends with the other two, adding an effective undercurrent of apprehension to the otherwise amusing or warm moments. The rousing orchestrations are in Williams' best form, including an uncharacteristic use of concerto-styled, piano underscoring in several sequences--which becomes especially operatic in the final scene--creating an effective emotional musical punch.

Williams next returned to the STAR WARS milieu to further develop the structural material employed in the first two films for the third picture, and conclusion of the first trilogy, RETURN OF THE JEDI (1983). The JEDI score, again performed by the London Symphony, is almost entirely comprised of the thematic material from the previous pictures, but, like the film's story line, the various musical themes are drawn to a satisfying resolution as the plot developments of the previous films are drawn together and dramatically concluded. The score is a fine summation of the elements introduced in the first two films. Two themes dominate: the Imperial March, representing Darth Vader and the dark side of the Force, and the theme for the Force itself, representing the good side. The interplay, conflict and resolution between these two themes comprise the bulk of the score, just as those elements were the key struggles in the story.

The last phrase from the Vader Theme, interestingly enough, is a nine-note fragment plucked on high solo harp as Vader, turning from the dark side and recapturing the heroic character of his alter ego, Anakin Skywalker, has his mask removed and speaks with Luke just before dying. The profound contrast between this treatment of the theme, and its melodramatic, brassy arrangement used previously, symbolizes the profound change which has come over the man, his soul restored. Luke's Theme (the main STAR WARS fanfare) and Leia's Theme are also in evidence.

New material includes a jaunty theme for the Ewoks (reminiscent of the Jawa theme from STAR WARS), a new Love Theme for Luke and Leia, and a virtuoso piece of tongue-in-cheek excitement for the forest battle on Endor's moon. Williams also provided a set-piece for the scenes in Jabba the Hut's palace, but this strange breed of futuristic New Wave rock, sung to "Huttese" lyrics by a screeching female alien, is hardly in the same calibre as the brilliant "Cantina Band," lacking the delightful charisma of the original piece, and is a very weak element of what was obviously planned as a scene akin to the first film's Cantina sequence.

The score ends with a massive, rhythmic, triumphal chorale chant, sung by the Ewoks supplemented by a large chorus and orchestra, which ends the film on an effectively victorious note. A quick series of jubilant, cheering, downward brass strokes introduces the end titles, which brings in all the themes for a rousing, final refrain, and draws the first STAR WARS trilogy to a very satisfying conclusion.

Although John Williams' output of original film scores took a severe decline after his appointment as regular conductor of the Boston Pops Orchestra, nearly all of the films he has scored have been phenomenally successful, important pictures--and nearly all of them have been science fiction or fantasy. "Williams," Christopher Palmer explained, "almost alone among the new generation of film composers, has developed a sense of the epic: he can write in the grand manner, paint with broad strokes on wide canvas, and do it with conviction. He has acknowledged his need to adopt widely divergent musical styles in order to supply the needs of films widely divergent in character. He has also stated his belief that making the sound of today's films relevant to the films themselves involved borrowing elements, without prejudice, from whatever musical disciplines and traditions suit the purpose."[24]

Williams' unique success--unique in the way it has transcended beyond the film medium more than almost any other film composer-- has earned him the ability to impose his own authority over the amount of time he is given and the size of the orchestra he will use, as well as the opportunity to choose carefully those films on which he will work. Williams' continual association with the films of George Lucas and Steven Spielberg have made his music very much a part of the milestone success of those movies. The music he has composed for them--and others--has had not only a profound effect upon the contemporary development and approach to fantasy and science fiction film scoring, but upon the larger course of film music in general.

Notes

1. Richard Pontzious, "Symphonic Soundtracks Are Making a Comeback," San Francisco Examiner/Chronicle, Sunday November 1, 1981

2. John Caps, "John Williams--Scoring the Film Whole," Filmmusic Notebook Vol. 2, #3, (1976), p. 23

3. Ibid., p. 24

4. John Williams quoted by John Caps, "Keeping in Touch with John Williams," Soundtrack! The Collector's Quarterly #1 (March 1982) p. 6 (also quoted in part in op. cit. #2, p. 24)

5. Bill Littman, "JAWS--Music to Digest By," Gore Creatures #24 (October 1975) p. 34

6. John Williams quoted in liner notes to STAR WARS soundtrack recording (Twentieth Century-Fox Records, 1977) (and following unreferenced quotes)

7. _____ quoted by Kenneth Terry, "Music Makers," Up Beat, Vol. 30, #12 (September 1982) p. 32

8. Ibid., p. 62

9. Steve Vertlieb, "Soundtrack," Cinemacabre #1 (Winter/Spring 1978/79) p. 49

10. Williams, op. cit. #7, p. 62

11. John Wright, "John Williams Lecture," Soundtrack Collector's Newsletter #15 (October 1978) p. 18

12. William F. Krasnoborski, "Close Encounters of the Uncertain Kind," Soundtrack Collector's Newsletter #14 (June 1978) p. 6

13. Ibid., p. 7

14. Steve Vertlieb, "Soundtrack," Cinemacabre #2 (Fall 1979) p. 61

15. Michael Quigley, "L.P. Review," Soundtrack Collector's Newsletter #17 (April 1979) p. 17

16. Steve Vertlieb, loc. cit. #14

17. Paul A. Snook, "Record Review," High Fidelity, November 1979, p. 121

18. John Williams interviewed by Alan Arnold, liner notes to THE EMPIRE STRIKES BACK sound-track recording (RSO Records, 1980)

19. Ibid.

20. Donald C. Willis, Horror and Science Fiction Films II (Metuchen, N.J.: Scarecrow Press, 1982) p. 322

21. Michael Quigley, "L.P. Review," Soundtrack! The Collector's Quarterly #27 (December 1981) p. 28

22. John Caps, "E.T.--The Extra Terrestrial," Soundtrack! The Collector's Quarterly #3 (September 1982) p. 4

23. John Williams interviewed by San Francisco Sunday Chronicle Dateline, 1982. Quoted in CinemaScore #10 (Fall 1982) p. 3

24. Christopher Palmer, "John Williams and His Music," liner notes to THE EMPIRE STRIKES BACK (symphonic suite recording, Chalfont Records, 1980)

XV

RENAISSANCE

The 1970's were a time of great importance to film music.
The traditional, symphonic score was reestablishing its place after
being relegated to near-oblivion during the pop-oriented 60's; electronic scoring was establishing a separate and viable pathway of its
own; and the film scores of this period seemed to suggest--to many
--something of a new Golden Age in movie music. In addition, the
increase in public awareness of film music due to journalism, books,
and best-selling sound-track albums helped to pave the way for an
important period of growth. Veteran composers found traditional
styles of scoring acceptable once more, and promising new faces
managed to emerge and demonstrate a variety of styles both traditional and contemporary. The phenomenal boom in the production
of science fiction, fantasy and horror films that exploded in the
late 70's, resulted in a great variety of genre film music, and of
varying quality and effectiveness.

One composer who has weathered the storm of the 60's is
the talented Elmer Bernstein, whose career began in the 50's with
scores like ROBOT MONSTER. Bernstein has long bemoaned the
imposed commercialism that burdened the film music field during
the 60's and early 70's, although he managed to endure favorably;
he produced some exceptional scores for fantastic films of the 70's.
One of these was SEE NO EVIL (1971), an intriguing film about a
blind woman terrorized by a maniac in a country mansion. Respected composer Andre Previn was originally commissioned to score
the film, and his composition was actually recorded by the London
Symphony, of which he was then resident conductor. However,
the producers disliked Previn's symphonic score and, after a much-
publicized disagreement, rejected the music and hired British composer David Whitaker, whose work apparently didn't satisfy them
either. They finally hired Bernstein to write new music, giving
him only three weeks in which to do it. According to Previn, the
producers had felt his music was "too harsh, too astringent, too
ugly, too rough, and there isn't anything the kids can whistle."[1]

Previn's score was reportedly "a superbly chilling score,
'PSYCHO-like,' with electronic overtones, a synthesizer being employed to stunning effect,"[2] which built up a spooky, shuddery
feeling. Bernstein's score was more romantic in nature, playing

upon the warm, colorful country setting and playing against the suspenseful mood of the picture. It works well enough; in fact, Bernstein's SEE NO EVIL is a profoundly beautiful score in many ways. The music opens with eerie, echoing piano fingering over shimmering strings; this leads into a brass fanfare with rapid drum beats mixed with piano passages and a mild use of electric bass. Frenzied piano, string and brass segments (broken occasionally by a repeated three-note phrase for electric bass) commences, punctuated by jazzy bongo and congo drum beating. The main theme, however, is a lyrical Country Theme--a classical Americana piece for woodwind and muted brass over slow strings. A secondary theme is provided for the blind girl as she takes a horse ride--this is a pretty woodwind melody which builds in power as the horse rides faster and faster, with the mysterious piano-and-string motif from the title threatening to break in from time to time, hinting ominously at unpleasantries to come.

Bernstein's next effort in the genre was for the forgettable science fiction film, SATURN 3 (1980), for which he provided an intense, avant-garde score combining symphonic orchestration with overdubbed electronics, which tend to dominate. A repeated motif is a prominent use of electric bass strums, as well as a low, chanting men's chorus. That same year, Bernstein provided a strong, brassy score for the quasi-fantastic spoof, AIRPLANE!, giving it a broad, symphonic texture with a busy, Alfred Newmanlike Airport Theme and a soaring Love Theme.

Bernstein next composed one of his finest scores for the animated fantasy, HEAVY METAL (1981). The film emphasized a number of rock songs throughout, which had no bearing upon the dramatic action, but Bernstein's score, when heard, was a wondrously rich symphonic score, as one writer noted: "This is a grand, majestic score, glorious and invigorating.... Rarely has Mr. Bernstein achieved such peaks of musical grandeur as he reached with this powerful, symphonic score for the Canadian-made film.... There is a richness and a vitality to Mr. Bernstein's music that is all too rare in film scores these days."[3]

One reviewer described it aptly as Bernstein's STAR WARS: "The score has all the traits of his unmistakable personal idiom: boyish forthrightness, tender modality, syncopated lullabies, bluesy inflections, and an overall rhapsodic exhuberance. This large-scale, copious, well-integrated symphonic tableau contains many captivating ideas that exemplify Bernstein's free-flowing melodic fancy and flair for dramatic evocation. And the strain of whimsicality that runs through the score makes it all the more irresistible."[4]

HEAVY METAL is an anthology, telling five stories in "adult" space opera fashion, and Bernstein's score not only lends continuity to the proceedings but accents the dramatic action superbly in

the way that the rock songs cannot. The "Gremlins" segment utilizes thunderous, epic music highlighting crashing cymbals, trembling strings, pounding brass, chorus and percussion. "Harry
Canyon" is subtly underlined with a moody, big-city jazz flavor.
The "Tarna" segment is embellished with a rich array of sweeping
melody, chorus and bells, particularly in the flying sequence; the
dramatic scoring here is also grandly profound, quite Williamsesque
and stirring, as is the "Den" episode. "How Beautiful" is given a
tender Love Theme for vibrant strings and solo woodwind. The
connecting link between all the separate thematic elements is a
mystical, wordless chorus which heralds the appearance of the evil
Lochnar, a bright-green spherical being which is used as a visual
story-connecting device in the film.

That same year Bernstein wrote an effective, if quite sparse,
score for John Landis' tongue-in-cheek horror show, AN AMERICAN
WEREWOLF IN LONDON. Unfortunately, the bulk of the sound
track used a variety of moon-oriented pop songs which tended to
be more distracting than complementary; their cleverness quickly
wore off and they were poor underscoring for such important
scenes as the main transformation. Bernstein's music was used as
brief connective cues, such as a poignant piano theme, signifying
the friendship between David and Jack, first heard as they hike
toward the foggy Scottish town. A secondary motif is an effective
cue for fast-weaving strings over woodwind and discordant piano
tinkling, which is used during David's dreams while in the hospital. An evocative motif for low, dirgelike brass over weaving
strings creates a notably ominous effect as David's doctor visits
the Scottish inn to discover the truth of his affliction. Bernstein
next scored the futuristic 3-D movie, SPACEHUNTER (1983) with
the kind of grand, majestically heroic theme that he excels at,
balancing it with a variety of eerie orchestral and synthesized
motifs for the bizarre characters and situations depicted in the
film.

In spite of being relegated to scoring a sudden run of rock-
and-roll oriented sound tracks which relied only incidentally on
dramatic scoring, such as AN AMERICAN WEREWOLF IN LONDON
and ANIMAL HOUSE, Bernstein has managed to shine, and compositions such as HEAVY METAL insure his prominence as a foremost film composer whose work remains notable in the fantasy
genre.

David Raksin was back in fine form after a long departure
from genre cinema with WHAT'S THE MATTER WITH HELEN? (1971),
a score he considers among his best. This was a psychological
horror-suspense film which was given a complex structure of harmonic rhythms somewhat rooted in jazz origins. "This score must
not begin like any old horror film score," Raksin explained, "but
ought to add to the element of mystery. The idea was also, to
some extent, to remain a pace behind the revelation of Helen's real

nature; it is <u>not</u> the job of the music to give away the story."[5]
Raksin opens the score with a jolting percussive ostinato that grows
furiously, broken momentarily by a honky-tonk rendition of the
song, "Goody, Goody." This motif is developed throughout the
score, balanced by a melodic main theme, best heard when Adele
describes her troubled past to Linc; as well as soft, murmuring
woodwinds heard when Adele receives malicious telephone calls;
and a memorable motif heard after Helen has murdered the intruder and is disposing of the body with Adele. As film music critic,
Page Cook described it: "as the women drag the body in the
downpour, the turbulence and pathos of Raksin's lengthy disposi-
tion of the thematic material first heard in the titles intensifies the
terrifying scene. Not only because Raksin distorts enharmonically,
but also because he uses consonant double-reeds, adding a disturbing quietude (which Raksin says is 'the characteristic, if anything is, of the score')."[6]

Raksin also approaches the music very symbolically, scoring
not only to the action but investing the score with many passages
suggestive of the mystery which has not yet been solved visually.
One example is the use of a theme Raksin calls "a loser's tune"
which is heard over the relentless jazz rhythms at the start of the
film. Raksin explains: "Seeing the film and hearing the music the
first time around, you are conscious mostly of the energy of the
music. The second time, knowing the story, the appropriateness
of this 'loser's tune' reaches you. Introducing at an early stage
ideas and feelings that belong later in the drama <u>is</u> risky, but it's
quite legitimate to introduce thematic or other material that will
later develop and metamorphose with the story. Not only is this
dramatically and musically sound practice, if you can do it, but if
properly handled it can help to unify the film. For musical <u>forms</u>
per se have integrative power, and music, of course, has the ability to evoke memory. As for the interpolation of 'Goody, Goody,'
it is meant to be a kind of shocker, a seeming irrelevancy, and
therefore challenging--a glimpse of a brief and inexplicable tableau
in a madhouse you may never know more about."[7]

Raksin's capable handling of this complex and intriguing manner of film scoring has resulted in much fine film music, and his
work on WHAT'S THE MATTER WITH HELEN? is an important contribution to genre film music. Raksin also provided an effective
score (incorporating Virgil Thompson's The River as an effective
thematic counterpoint) for Nicholas Meyer's controversial TV movie,
THE DAY AFTER (1983).

Like Raksin's, the film music of Alex North has been unde-
servedly sparse in recent years. North emerged during the 50's
as a respected composer of depth and substance, with a notably
subtle approach to film music. Of Russian heritage, North was
born in Philadelphia and studied at the Curtis Institute of Music,
at Juilliard and later at the Conservatory in Moscow. North even-

tually became associated with composers Ernst Toch and Aaron Copland, whose encouragement assisted his finding work as a dance and theatrical composer, and eventually, scoring documentary and governmental films. In 1951, North was hired to score A STREETCAR NAMED DESIRE, for which he gained an Oscar nomination, and a career in film music quickly followed.

Among North's early genre films was the haunting story of a possessed child, THE BAD SEED (1956). North had scored that picture with an effective contrast, opening the music with a bright, tuneful piano theme heard as the girl is seen practicing. Later, this theme is rapidly devoured by a variety of violent dissonances and chaotic figures, representing the horror of the child's true character. In the 60's, North became noted, something like Miklos Rozsa, as a composer for epic spectacles such as SPARTACUS and CLEOPATRA. This trend seemed to continue when North was hired by Stanley Kubrick, who had directed him on SPARTACUS, to compose a score for his epic outer space film, 2001: A SPACE ODYSSEY (1968). Interestingly enough, Kubrick also hired English composer Frank Cordell to compose a score at the same time, apparently as a precaution. As it was, neither score was used--Kubrick decided instead to employ records of classical and avant-garde music. This piecemeal approach had an interesting effect, but was nevertheless a somewhat arbitrary incorporation of music not intended for such a purpose. As author/composer Irwin Bazelon has indicated: "Kubrick's decision to use selective pieces from the late nineteenth- and twentieth-century concert repertoire--Strauss, Khachaturian and Ligeti--sounds like what it is--a pastiche of odd musical bedfellows. An impressive film like 2001 should have had an important composer and an original score. Having seen a portion of Alex North's music, I am convinced that its use would have enhanced the film; if not North, then perhaps avant-gardist Ligeti from beginning to end."[8]

Composer North recalled his experience on 2001 thusly: "I did half the score. I was very, very frustrated by it all. I really knocked myself out. I wrote fifty minutes of music in three weeks ... I did some very fresh things as far as I myself am concerned.... It was the greatest opportunity to write a score for a film--where there are ... hardly any sound effects."[9] (North eventually intends to work the music he composed for 2001 into his Third Symphony; so it may not be completely lost, musically.)

Incidentally, Alex North wasn't the only composer to suffer, as with the 2001 escapade, beneath a director's musical ignorance. While many composers have had their scores rejected for a variety of reasons, only a few have had the insulting experience of being replaced with arbitrary selections from record albums. THE EXORCIST (1974) was another prime example. Director William Friedkin had initially wanted Bernard Herrmann to score the film. Herrmann had agreed to do it only if he was allowed to record the music in London at the St. Giles Church (for sound purposes), an idea Friedkin felt was impractical. Friedkin then contracted Lalo Schifrin, who composed an accentuated, scary score which Friedkin also disapproved of, feeling it was too frightening and wall-to-wall. "I wanted the music to come and go at strange places and dissolve in and out," Friedkin said in a film studies seminar shortly after the film's release. "No music behind the big scenes. No music ever behind dialogue.... Only music in the montage sequences and the music should be like a cold hand on the back of your neck, like a chill presence that would never assert itself...."[10]

While chilling, Schifrin's score wasn't quiet enough for the director, and wound up being tossed out and replaced with a mélange of motifs culled from record albums--what Friedkin kiddingly called a "Tower Records Score." The resultant score, naturally, sounded like a frayed patchwork and did little to accentuate the story. The most popular theme Friedkin used was a memorable excerpt from Mike Oldfield's intricate rock symphony, "Tubular Bells," which lent a tinkling, impending rhythm to certain themes in a manner not unlike the later HALLOWEEN motif of John Carpenter. Unfortunately, Oldfield's music related to nothing in the picture, nor did its arbitrary fade-ins and fade-outs. The remaining music, consisting of strange, atonal sounds and avant-garde motifs, was likewise sprinkled throughout the film with little regard for dramatic effect.

Friedkin claims he was trying to catch viewers off guard: "The music in that film doesn't telegraph anything. There's no music behind the exorcism at all, no music behind the self-immolation sequence. None. It just comes in, strange little places ... in and out in the middle of a shot, gone, until you can't remember --I mean, then people see credits at the end and they see 17 guys get credit for the music and it's eight bars of this guy and four bars of that guy, and there's some wind harp in there, a couple of hippies took a wind harp up onto a mountain and let the wind play in it and we stuck that in." Such a random stew of unrelated musical fragments was hardly appropriate for a horror film, and what there was, outside of the recognizable "Tubular Bells," tended to either sound invisible or distracting.

Back to Alex North. After the discouraging experience on 2001, North's musical output in Hollywood seemed to diminish drastically. He provided an effectual score for the small terror picture about trained killer rats, WILLARD (1971), as well as for William Castle's SHANKS (1974) and a few others, but it was in his monumental composition for DRAGONSLAYER (1981) that North really hit the mark. This lavish, spectacular medieval adventure fantasy was enriched with a complex, heavy score, proving that North was still in fine command of musical form and orchestration. As one writer announced: "North's now-legendary use of brass in SPARTACUS seems Steineresque compared to its deployment throughout DRAGON-

SLAYER. From the tentative title onwards, the score is a field day of ... low brass and percussion, with strident trumpets cutting through the cacophony; this is the iron-and-steel world of Prokofiev's Second Symphony, devoid of warmth or consolation, a musical portrait of bleak, Dark Ages civilization."[11]

Another writer described the score more specifically: "North conjures illustrative effects in his orchestra with the ease of a supreme magician ... the moorish mists become sliding figures on the violins, the barbarism of the villagers' human sacrificing becomes broken rhythmic percussion charged with growling brass, the chase sequences are scored with a wind/xylophone/piano combination with pumping strings behind. But those are only effects, tricks that get swept up in a score of such complexities of meter, texture, and cadence, even a trained ear would be dazzled. What results is a difficult, bold, and baffling piece of work; North's musical lines are harmonic progressions (vertically stacked) rather than melodic statements. And when the dragon finally rears its snorting, dripping head and breathes fire down over the shield which the squire has fashioned out of fallen dragonscales, North's meters solidify into a running pizzicato figure, his brass roar, and out of the abstract shapes comes a richly detailed storybook woodcut of the dragonslayer's duel."[12]

Among these powerful shapes is a clear, deep solo horn leitmotif for the dragon, Vermithrax Pejorative. This is the theme which opens the film: "Groaning achingly under a pitch-black screen as the movie begins ... the theme is literally belched out by some of the lowest-registered brass heard on a soundtrack since Herrmann went journeying to the center of the earth."[13] The Pejorative Theme is used throughout the score and is a marvelous illustration of the incredibly ancient, monolithic dragon. Another recurring motif is a jaunty marchlike rhythmic piece for woodwind, brass and drumming percussion which gives a lighthearted mood to the film's less brooding and dangerous moments. North also provides a hard-edged oboe theme for the love scene between Galen and Valerian, as well as themes associated with magic, Ulrich's enchanted amulet, and the doomed sacrificial maidens. Another composition summons up, with slowly mystical string, woodwind and percussion ascendings, the tenuous position of the medieval Church as portrayed in the film.

North spent months researching authentic material of DRAGONSLAYER's period and locale in order to capture the spirit of medieval music in the score. "The picture offered me any number of opportunities in a pure dramatic sense that had nothing to do with humanity," North remarked. "Except for the boy-girl thing everything had to be so away from myself.... There was very little compassion in this story. It was not one of those kinds of films where you get thematic ideas in advance, jot them down and rework them later."[14]

DRAGONSLAYER has been described by many as a modern
masterpiece of film scoring--although there were those of a dissenting opinion who felt the music too grim and foreboding ("the
weight of the music drags the film down and makes it seem slow
and pokey when it is actually swift-paced and vigorous ... North's
thudding music is like tossing a lead life ring to a drowning
man..."[15]). But the majority of reviewers tended to agree that
North's effect was an impressive accomplishment and a major entry
into fantastic film music: "The gloom-and-doom heavings emitted
by North's Wagnerian complement of low strings and brasses are
here seasoned with enough sharp modernisms to give the picture
a tang often lacking from script and direction. When an invincibly
American scherzo breaks out at the close, you know that--like it
or not--you have been in the grasp of a commanding composer."[16]

Leonard Rosenman continued to provide many notable scores
during the 60's and 70's, after an impressive debut in the 50's
with EAST OF EDEN (1955). Rosenman scored FANTASTIC VOYAGE
(1966) with an excellent mixture of orchestral and electronic music.
The film's producer initially wanted the movie to be the first "hip"
science fiction film and asked Rosenman to score it with jazz, but
the composer wisely protested. The resultant score lends an appropriately eerie and otherworldly atmosphere to the story of a
miniaturized submarine injected into a dying man's body in order
to destroy a terminal blood clot. In this film, Rosenman experimented with varied counterpoints of klangfarben (tonal colors of
sound), and the score is largely comprised of nonmelodic motifs.
The first part of the film, depicting the attack on the limousine
and the subsequent scenes in the scientific facility, were scored
with sparse electronic sounds. The first real musical passage is
heard as the microscopic Proteus enters the bloodstream and floats
amid large globules of liquid--this is a woodwindy motif over harp,
with a slight, subtle four-note adventuresome melody, suitable for
the start of this "fantastic voyage." Rosenman provides varied
musical textures for the subsequent sequences as the Proteus
makes its way to the brain: long, drawn-out string passages are
used for the journey through the heart; heavy percussion and
woodwind sounds are heard as the crew removes ventricular fibers
from the Proteus's clogged intake valves; high-woodwind warbles
over harp and strings accompany the attack of the antibodies,
while deep, percussionistic rumbles underscore the attack of the
white corpuscles. The score is bound together by a single recurring thematic motif, a four-note melody with the accent on the
third note--this theme reaches its fullest variant during the de-
miniaturization at the successful completion of the mission.

Rosenman scored BENEATH THE PLANET OF THE APES (1970)
with an avant-garde approach in keeping with Jerry Goldsmith's
music of the preceding PLANET OF THE APES. As Tony Thomas
explained, "the picture about the apes has a rather cacophonous
sound, with piercing brass chords over shrill strings, all sugges-

tive of a nightmarish world. At one point Rosenman supplies a
march for a gorilla army, and it is a satiric comment on the moronic, cruel mentality of the animals. He parodies the mutated humans
with mocking distortions of the hymn, 'All Things Bright And
Beautiful.'"[17] Rosenman emphasized similar elements in the final
APES sequel, BATTLE FOR THE PLANET OF THE APES (1973).

THE CAR (1977) was invested with a pounding, ominous
score with a main theme based upon the Dies Irae, which plods
throughout the film and effectively underscores this terror film of
a demonically possessed automobile loose on the rural highways.
The motif is first heard by woodwinds over a very low oboe and
a sliding, appropriately metallic sound; the film is also scored with
a variety of high-pitched string wails, and eerie string and percussion tones.

One of Rosenman's best scores of the 70's was LORD OF THE
RINGS (1978), which embellished this epic undertaking with a
broad symphonic score comprised of fanfares, militaristic rhythms,
meditations, low, chanting chorus and a dominating jaunty, heroic
march. As one reviewer noted: "the composer boldly juxtaposed
ingenious principal themes analogous to earlier epic scoring styles
of Korngold and Alfred Newman with a panoply of primordial avant-
gardisms, structuring an allegorical overview perhaps too subtle to
be widely appreciated in the wake of the STAR WARS euphoria."[18]
Another reviewer wrote: "The score begins more lightly and melodi-
cally, then descends into thicker structures, the sheer violence of
volume, and more angularly related tonalities."[19] Another highly
symphonic score, although much less fully drawn, was provided
for the monster thriller, PROPHECY (1979).

Lalo Schifrin has also had a noticeable hand in the fantastic
films of the 70's. He was born in Argentina, the son of the con-
certmaster of the Buenos Aires Philharmonic, and studied classical
music at the Paris Conservatory while performing jazz in the eve-
nings. Schifrin was also very appreciative of music in films, and
when he arrived in New York to work as an arranger with jazz
performer Dizzy Gillespie, he eventually received the opportunity
to score films. Schifrin has since alternated between making
jazz-pop-oriented recordings and composing for films and television. Among Schifrin's earliest fantastic scores is that for the
speculative documentary, THE HELLSTROM CHRONICLE (1971),
which studied the insect world and its potential for survival over
the human race. Schifrin's remarkable approach to this amazing
film, which emphasized miniature photography and gargantuan
close-ups of minuscule insects, was quite avant-garde, using
aleatory, electronic and serial techniques. What Schifrin tried in
particular to do--and pulled off superbly--was to create the audible world of insects through his music. "We cannot understand
how insects hear," Schifrin said. "Their audio world is impossible
to imagine, so I had to make up their audio sound and augment it.

It's like bringing a microphone or an amplifier and exaggerating
that sound. It was an electro-acoustical score, using acoustic instruments as well as electronics. I did things a little bit crazy.
For instance, during the battle of the ants, I had fifty strings
among the orchestra, and I had them all playing that sequence
with wire brushes, like the drummers have, on the strings, each
one playing his own lines. It was not pizzicato, it was not arco,
not col legno--it was wire brushes! Against that, any time there
was a closeup of the ants, I would bring in the horror with muted
brass and woodwinds. Every sequence of that film was a different
texture, but it was very interesting. It forced me to go almost
to my own limits of the imagination."[20]

The unusual orchestral techniques Schifrin employed in THE
HELLSTROM CHRONICLE really brought this film and its almost
alien world to mind-boggling life, as Irwin Bazelon noted: "During the horror montage where the insects become cannibalistic and
start eating each other, Schifrin's loud electronic sounds, synchronized piano effects, and percussion explosions, together with
the picture, create an atmosphere of physiological turbulence."[21]

Schifrin scored George Lucas' THX 1138 (1971) with a low
key composition dominated by synthesizer, strings and chorus.
The film opens with deep, bass synthesizer tones and high, faint
female chorale wailing over low, somber strings. Throughout, the
music captures the dismal mood of this futuristic society with an
oppressive, melancholy theme, emphasizing powerful, slow-moving
string passages and the chanting chorus which is all but hidden
in places by a harsh organ tone.

An especially haunting score was composed in 1979 for THE
AMITYVILLE HORROR. In this film, Schifrin emphasized the idea
that the haunted Amityville house was itself alive, with a lingering
lullaby sung by three women in a childlike fashion. "An eerie,
haunting nursery rhyme," Schifrin described, "with some of the
'wrong notes' to make it a little bit discordant. It had that innocence of children against high strings, playing very sustained;
and once in a while, low strings and the low orchestra come in,
suggesting the idea of something horrible happening here." The
entire AMITYVILLE score is built around this lullaby; it is given
a variety of orchestrations and several differing motifs are drawn
out of it, but always the lullaby remains the primary element.
Many of Schifrin's bizarre percussives and "scare" motifs, while
somewhat gimmicky on occasion, are genuinely frightening and contribute to the film's otherwise lacking mood. Schifrin was given a
large orchestra of 72 musicians, including the singers, which lent
the film an impressive and memorable sound.

Schifrin scored the prehistoric comedy, CAVEMAN (1981) with
a broad, symphonic score in the best Mack Sennett comedy tradition. The score is a tour-de-force of musical references--every-

thing from the Colonel Bogie March in BRIDGE ON THE RIVER
KWAI to the William Tell Overture and Elgar's Pomp and Circumstance are quoted in various comic sequences, as well as elements
of pure classical, weird sounds (even burping!) and a suggestion
of Strauss' Also Sprach Zarathustra as the cavemen learn to walk
upright. While these amusing references are sprinkled throughout,
the score is held together by Schifrin's catchy main theme, a pop
motif for low horns in harmony with high woodwinds (later by
strings and brass) over loud, hollow-percussion drumming and
rustling. The contemporary motif, played by ancient-sounding instruments, adds a pleasantly zany atmosphere to the proceedings.
Schifrin used primarily a standard symphony orchestra, delving
for weird sounds only in the sequence where the cavemen first in-
vent music. For this scene, Schifrin relied on primitive instruments such as the Amazonian birimbao (the bow from a bow-and-
arrow strummed, with the hand position changing the pitch), and
even rocks cracking against one another.

Schifrin scored Sean Cunningham's A STRANGER IS WATCH-
ING (1971) with an effective motif based on the rhythm of railway
cars. "Because the story took place in the subways of New York,"
Schifrin said, "I used the sound of the railway, transposed to an
orchestra--the rhythm of cars going on the rails--and that was the
hook I took in order to accentuate the horror in that film."

AMITYVILLE II: THE POSSESSION (1982) was given a similar approach to that used in its predecessor, but, because this
film was made by a different production company, Schifrin could
not use the same theme due to copyright reasons. "I used a similar theme," he explained, "but I changed it enough to make another nursery rhyme. In the first score, I used strings, brass,
woodwinds, keyboard (piano and celesta, not synthesizer), percussion, harp and the three voices. In AMITYVILLE II, I kept the
same percussion, I kept the harp, the strings and the voices, but
I didn't use brass or woodwinds. I had three players playing different kinds of keyboards--piano, celesta, and different kinds of
synthesizers; and I used some of the newest kinds of digital synthesizers to give very ethereal and eerie sounds. I also used the
synthesizer to imitate the sound of a medieval horn."

Schifrin's approach to the AMITYVILLE films, that of contrasting a dark, brooding horror with a childlike theme, is a
favorite method of the composer. "What works in THE AMITYVILLE
HORROR is the innocence of children in juxtaposition to the horror.
This is what I really like to do."

John Barry, a popular composer whose career began in England, has occasionally contributed his own style of music to fantastic films. Born in York, England, in 1933, Barry grew up with
an interest in motion pictures (his father operated a string of theaters) and a desire to compose music for films. After a successful

association with big band arrangements in the 50's, Barry became
involved in films when he was asked to assist composer Monty
Norman with the score to the first James Bond movie, DR. NO
(made in 1962). The producers had reportedly been unhappy with
Norman's score, and offered Barry, then an unknown, to rework
it without any screen credit. The popular "James Bond Theme,"
which Barry composed, has since become a staple theme for the
long-running series, and got Barry started on the right track.
He subsequently gained notoriety for scoring nearly all of the succeeding Bond films, establishing a distinctive musical backdrop for
the sexy action thrillers with his flair for rhythm and melody.
In the late 70's, Barry took up residence in Los Angeles, where
he found greater opportunities in scoring Hollywood-made films.

   The James Bond movies maintained a consistent approach to
their music throughout the series, including those scores not written by Barry (LIVE AND LET DIE, George Martin; THE SPY WHO
LOVED ME, Marvin Hamlisch; FOR YOUR EYES ONLY, Bill Conti;
and NEVER SAY NEVER AGAIN, Michel Legrand), in that each film
featured a distinctive theme song whose melody became the primary
theme for that movie (in addition to recurring motifs such as the
omnipresent "James Bond Theme" and the equally representative
007 Theme). While the use of a popular song arose out of the early 60's mania for commercial theme songs, Barry managed to use
the songs as an effective part of his overall score. "With the Bond
movies," Barry said, "it has always been the style to have a title
song, but I integrated it with the dramatic material. The song
has been a complete part of the theme, countermelody, and harmonies of an integrated score, and I think that works."[22]   In addition to the characteristic theme song, Barry scored the Bond films
with a pronounced pop/jazz style, adding an appropriate sense of
gimmickry (without becoming pretentious) to the gadget-laden spy
thrillers. There is also much musical mickey mousing through the
scores, with the music designed in cartoon fashion, wall-to-wall
and often in precise synchronization with visual movements. "The
whole style of the series is Mickeymouse music," Barry said. "It
had to be. Subtlety is not a virtue in a film of that kind of design."[23]

   While DR. NO and FROM RUSSIA WITH LOVE (1963) depended
upon main thematic material of other composers (Monty Norman and
Lionel Bart, respectively), GOLDFINGER (1964) was wholly Barry
and remains perhaps his best Bond score (Barry himself considers
it such). It featured not only a very popular theme song but
some fine dramatic music, especially during the raid on Fort Knox.
One reviewer, speaking of the GOLDFINGER music, offers an interesting view of Barry's overall approach to the Bond films:
"Barry is ostensibly a jazz composer, so he chooses to make extensive use of his brass section. With few exceptions, all sentiment
has been removed from the musical characters. The music doesn't
pine for Jill Materson after she has been painted gold, but instead

lingers with a certain shocked excitement over the surrealism of
the image. No attempt is made here to suggest what Bond is thinking. Instead the piece merely echoes the perversity of Goldfinger's
mind. Whereas many composers would have used strings here to
say 'dead woman,' Barry brilliantly uses metallic percussions to
say, 'golden woman.' The feeling of detachment is imperative."[24]
THUNDERBALL (1965) and YOU ONLY LIVE TWICE (1971) continued this trend, with the latter containing an especially lyrical
love theme for mandolin, harp and strings over percussion, associated with Bond and his Oriental bride. YOU ONLY LIVE TWICE
also introduces the first true science fiction music of the Bond
series--a slowly plodding, heroic theme for brass over pounding
bass keyboard during the outer space scenes. ON HER MAJESTY'S
SECRET SERVICE (1969), DIAMONDS ARE FOREVER (1971) and
THE MAN WITH THE GOLDEN GUN (1975) were similarly effective,
jazzy Bond scores. MOONRAKER (1979) was something of an oddity because, rather than emulating the fast-paced, rock-pop-jazz
of the former 007 movies, Barry chose to embellish the picture with
a slow, lyrical title song and a subtle theme for horns over choir
and rhythmic percussion, which effectively captures the vast stillness of the outer space scenes, yet retaining a driving, James
Bondian movement. Likewise, OCTOPUSSY (1983) emphasized the
lyrical over the driving action, featuring one of Barry's loveliest
theme songs (although the lyrics, like most themes except for
GOLDFINGER, DIAMONDS ARE FOREVER and THE MAN WITH THE
GOLDEN GUN, have little if any relation to the story) and a variety of incidental motifs based upon the familiar Bond and 007
Themes.

Outside of the Bond movies, John Barry is best known for
his mainstream film scores, although in the late 70's he found the
opportunity to score a number of fantasy films, starting with the
ill-fated remake of KING KONG (1976). Barry's score for this
purely commercial endeavor is pleasant enough, although failing to
approach the mystical atmospheres so prevalent in Max Steiner's
original KONG score of 1933. But, then, the 1976 KONG is a far
cry from the classic original, and Barry had attempted to match
the present visuals and not the legendary status of the character.
When an interviewer asked him if he had intentionally avoided any
stylistic similarity to the original KING KONG score, Barry replied:
"No, I didn't go back and listen to it. I only remembered the
original KING KONG from my earlier viewings. Every film has its
own life, its own specifics, its own period of time, so that was
never a problem. What I did was a reaction to what was on the
screen."[25]

The score suffers, perhaps, due to the lack of a cohesive
theme. There is no main title music, and a variety of rhythmic
motifs are used throughout the Skull Island and New York sequences with little interaction or relation. This lack of thematic
continuity may have resulted from the piecemeal manner in which

Barry had to score the picture--due to the race that then existed
between the Dino De Laurentiis company and Universal, which also
planned a KONG film (they later withdrew), Barry was never given
a complete final cut of the film to work from, but instead was required to score the picture reel by reel as it was shot in sequence.
Because of the rush and the lack of anything really worthwhile on
the screen from which to draw from, the music failed to provide
more than a pallid backdrop to this purely exploitative project.
As one reviewer wrote: The Barry score "is not without its merits,
but compared to Steiner's music which nearly defines the genre,
Barry's music is pale and colorless.... A comparison of the two
films is a textbook example of the difference between the triumph
of creative art versus mere mindless technological wizardry. Barry's music, when listened to apart from the film, conjures up none
of the atmosphere and atavistic premonition of Steiner's score,
which is truly a narrative in sound images."[26]

Barry scored somewhat better on THE BLACK HOLE (1979),
although this score, too, tended to be too rhythmic and incidental
where a more dramatic and synchronized action/fantasy score might
have been in order. As well as a John Williamsy, heroic overture
for brass, Barry provides an effective theme for the Black Hole--
a repeated, downward-swirling figure for synthesizer and strings
over lower, swaying strings and impending horn and tympani counterpoint. The motif effectively captures the sense of a whirling
vortex, as the Black Hole is depicted in this film. The remainder
of the score, however, tends to collect various simple colorations
and subtle melodies which inch the film along but don't really let
the story become completely engrossing.

STARCRASH (1979), an Italian STAR WARS offspring, featured a more consistent dramatic score, built around a pretty,
melodic theme for Stella Starr, the film's intrepid space vixen.
This theme is woven through the surging crescendos and weird
musical effects in a flowing, harmonious way, lending the film a
cohesive rhythm and movement, dominated by brass and string
chords over low piano pounding.

After a period of rather routine and mildly interesting activity, Barry emerged in 1980 with a brilliant and compelling score
for the romantic fantasy, SOMEWHERE IN TIME, which is certainly
to be considered one of his finest works. The story told of a contemporary playwright who, after falling in love with the portrait of
an actress who lived 68 years earlier, wills himself back in time to
court her. It was a poignant love story, which Barry invested
with a weepingly lyrical sense of nostalgia and romance. A main
theme for flute and strings embodies the film with an exquisite
sensitivity, which is especially profound during the final scenes
when it characterizes Collier's suffering and loss after being
abruptly thrust back into his own time. The music, swelling powerfully as Collier wanders despondently, is an effective counterpoint

to his mourning as it plays their Love Theme, reinforcing his anguish all the more as it hurtfully recalls the beautiful love he and Elise had shared.

While Barry does not play toward the fantasy aspects of the film, concentrating purely on the emotional depth within the story, his music is related to the fantastic nature of the picture in that it is always related to the past, and Collier's longing to be there with Elise. The titles and opening scene are without music--only when Collier glances down at the watch given him by the old woman (who, we later realize, is Elise), does the music emerge in a short, six-note phrase for piano and strings, which is later heard for violin as Collier arrives at the Grand Hotel and when he spies a photo of the aged Elise in an old magazine. This theme relates to the contemporary Elise, while the main Love Theme, first heard as Collier contemplates the photograph of the youthful Elise, represents the love shared between them in 1912.

Barry's remarkable sense of melody and rhythm have served him well throughout his film career, from the poetic lyricism of SOMEWHERE IN TIME to the catchy gimmicks of the James Bond films. With the possible exception of semilackluster efforts such as KING KONG and portions of THE BLACK HOLE, Barry's genre film music is distinctive and straightforward. He rejects emphatically the idea that film music should be bland or neutral, or simple --as Aaron Copland once put it: "...a small lamp placed beneath the screen to warm it." Barry instead feels that "if music doesn't sing, or dance, or have an interesting harmonic concept, then it shouldn't be there at all. A film score should burn with its own fire, not merely glow in the dark like a pretty charcoal."[27] Barry's occasional work in the fantasy genre has, for the most part, burned nicely.

Laurence Rosenthal wrote a modest yet effective score for THE ISLAND OF DR. MOREAU (1977), which he has described as one of his favorite works: "It really gave me a chance to try to express musically a profound kind of primitivity," he said. "I tried to produce a melodic style that was primitive and struggling, as though to suggest these humanimals were struggling and trying to become human beings; using, for example, a combination of very high bassoon and very high English horn playing in their top registers, producing a strained, agonized sound."[28] Elsewhere the score is straightforward, as in the pretty Love Theme for Braddock and Maria, but overall the music remains furtive, restrained, unresolved. Interestingly enough, the music Rosenthal wrote for the end of the film culminated in a great, tragic cry, which seems ill fitting to the rather sappy, all's-well ending until one realizes that this was not the ending to which Rosenthal composed! Originally, the film was to have finished with the shocking realization that the girl is, in fact, a humanimal and begins to regress into a huge puma in the arms of her rescuer. While this

gave the film a terrific, shocking punch, preview audiences re-
sponded poorly and the ending was reedited to eliminate the reference to the girl's true state. As the budget would not allow for
rerecording, Rosenthal's music was left as is, although it no longer fit the new tone of the denouement.

        Rosenthal suffered a similar fate on METEOR (1980), wherein
his mixture of symphonic and electronic scoring was drastically reedited and hashed about to give more pizzazz to a rapidly crumbling picture (see chapter XIII). He had better luck on CLASH
OF THE TITANS (1981), where he had the opportunity to compose
a broad, sweepingly symphonic score that was perfectly wedded to
the mythological fantasy. Producer Charles Schneer had in mind
a late nineteenth-century romantic, heroic score, something along
the lines of John Williams' style, and Rosenthal agreed that this was
what the picture needed. "I decided to do a great, sweeping adventure in a post-Richard Straussian way. There were certain
moments when I was able to make sounds which were quite different, such as the Medusa sequence, which used a lot of avant-
garde techniques. But it had to be music that wouldn't be too far
away from the general romantic tone of the score." Rosenthal
provided a number of leitmotifs for specific characters and events,
the dominating one being an overall theme of brassy heroism which
represents Perseus. There is, of course, a tender Love Theme for
him and Andromeda; a sympathetic, mournful motif for Calibos; a
comic theme for Bubo, the golden owl; and a quietly soaring theme
for Pegasus. The remarkable fantasy films of Ray Harryhausen
and Charles Schneer, ever since THE 7TH VOYAGE OF SINBAD,
have been noted for their exceptional use of music, and Rosenthal
is a worthy successor. His thematic material is exhilarating, and
his score varied and melodic enough to boost the film's drama and
spectacle to memorable heights.

        A variety of other scores and composers highlighted genre
cinema of the 70's. Gerald Fried, while working primarily in television, composed an effective score for the psychological thriller,
WHATEVER HAPPENED TO AUNT ALICE? (1969), as one writer described: a "fairly electrified ... soundtrack with an array of compositions for cello and double-bass, sometimes brooding, occasionally frenzied, always full of atmosphere."[29] Jaime Mendoza-Nava
started his career in low-budget horror films such as THE WITCH-
MAKER (1969), in which he mingled synthesizer with woodwinds,
electric guitar and subtle female voice. He went on to score a
number of exploitation films during the 70's, including THE LEG-
END OF BOGGY CREEK (1972), which was an evocative, moody
score. Mendoza-Nava also provided the "Topeka" music for A
BOY AND HIS DOG (1975), supplementing Tim McIntyre's score.
Michel Colombier's music for COLOSSUS-THE FORBIN PROJECT
(1970) uses some striking percussion effects in representation of
computer sounds, and a theme utilizing organ and harps. Pat
Williams scored SSSSSSSS (1973, called SSSSSNAKE abroad) with

an icily beautiful piano composition somewhat in the style of Goldsmith's PETER PROUD. Michael Small provided a fine score for
THE STEPFORD WIVES (1975), introducing a pop tune for woodwind and strings over acoustic guitar, electric bass and drums as
the main theme, which represents the homey loneliness of Joanna.
This is contrasted with an eerie motif for piano tinkling under high
string tones, representing the weirdness of Stepford. Small also
offered some weird percussionistic effects during the climactic
revelatory scene where Joanna's friend is revealed to be a robot.
The film ends with a deft muzak tune for piano and organ over
lush strings and brushed drum beat, which is perfect for the
suburban grocery shopping conclusion, capturing the plastic,
"beautiful people" world Stepford has become, before seguing into
the main theme (tinged with melancholy) for the end titles.

Many newcomers arrived in the film music field as the science fiction boom exploded in the late 70's, and almost all of them
took their turn at scoring a fantastic film or two. A number of
them became especially adept, and much of the best genre film music of the 80's was provided by relative newcomers.

One of them was James Horner, who rode the crest of the
symphonic resurgence with a strong hand. While initially accused
of proferring Jerry Goldsmith pastiches with early efforts such as
HUMANOIDS OF THE DEEP and BATTLE BEYOND THE STARS in
1980, Horner eventually gained opportunities to attain his own voice
in scores such as WOLFEN, STAR TREK II and KRULL.

Horner, who studied and ultimately taught music at UCLA, decided to leave the academic field in 1978 to try his hand at scoring
films. After composing music for several independent pictures, he
got his first break through Roger Corman and New World Pictures.
Horner's first genre film was Corman's UP FROM THE DEPTHS
(1979), but he only scored the underwater scenes. The above-
ground sequences utilized distracting stock Filipino rock music.
HUMANOIDS OF THE DEEP (1980) was given an effectually brooding score dominated by strings and percussion which is very much
in a Goldsmithian vein, from the quiet solo trumpet, whispering
strings, harp strums and piano chords that were vaguely reminiscent of the main theme from ALIEN, through the gentle woodwind
melody evocative of portions of A PATCH OF BLUE. Much of this
apparent imitation was a product not only of Horner's admiration
of Goldsmith, but of the filmmakers' desire to have the score sound
like someone else's previous work: "Very often what one is up
against is where a producer has seen the movie and temp-tracked
it with somebody else's music, has fallen in love with that score,
and says this is what we want, period," Horner explained. "You
try and fight against that a bit, but sometimes you can't. I've
been told very amazing things where they say we want exactly
that kind of score, we want that exact kind of cue--just put it
in your language."[30] Despite this ever-present imitative quality,

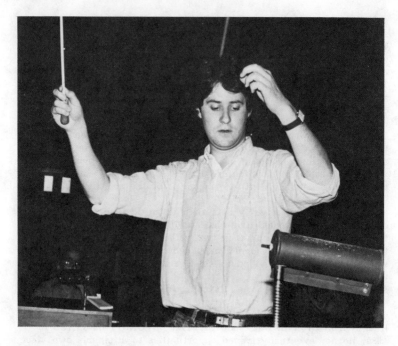

James Horner. Photograph courtesy Gorfaine-Schwartz Agency.

the score retains many evidences of techniques Horner would later
develop with more freedom, such as the echoing string chords that
accompany the prowling sequences.

　　　　BATTLE BEYOND THE STARS (1980) was another film in
which Horner was asked to write a score very much in the vein of
Goldsmith's STAR TREK: THE MOTION PICTURE, but which managed to stand on its own as a fine heroic-adventure score. In
spite of oft-repeated references to ALIEN, PATTON and STAR
TREK, Horner makes the score work marvelously. The music is
quite brassy, in keeping with the contemporary vogue in outer
space movies, and Horner also includes a very pretty Love Theme
for strings as well as deep, rasping electronic tonalities and driving rhythms which recall Goldsmith's space-cloud and Klingon music
from STAR TREK.

　　　　Unlike the rousing brass fanfares of BATTLE BEYOND THE
STARS, in THE HAND (1981) Horner emphasized the string section
to give it an eerie effect, somewhat as he did in HUMANOIDS.
The score opens nicely--explosive percussion leads into heartbeat-
ing brass pumps under swirling strings and low echoing synthesizer chords; this segues into a tinkling piano motif under woodwinds until the theme is taken by the strings, which remain pre-

dominant throughout. DEADLY BLESSING (1981) featured rhythmic, choral chanting to underline the satanic cult, with orchestral punctuation along the lines of Goldsmith's OMEN.

WOLFEN (1981) was a well-orchestrated, broodingly rhythmic score which gave Horner much deserved acclaim. This was a big-budget horror picture with a lot of class; a far cry from the Corman exploiters. It had originally been scored by Craig Safan, who had provided an abstract composition counterpointing wild, chilling high strings with slow, viola chords and various atonal notes, tones, eruptions and so forth, to achieve an unearthly ominous mood somewhat akin to that of Goldsmith's TWILIGHT ZONE episode, "The Invaders," and Morricone's THE THING. The producers disapproved of Safan's score and subsequently rejected it after it had been recorded.

Horner was called in at the last moment and given a frantic twelve days to compose 58 minutes worth of orchestrated music for the film. "I wanted to create a sound world for the Wolfen which was alien, yet which wasn't just a lot of effects," Horner said. "It had to be driving and very primitive. There's no melody--there's a trumpet figure that keeps recurring--but, basically, I wanted to create a very driving type of feeling for the film." Horner's music is mostly made up of low, somber bass string tones punctuated by pizzicato strings and woodwind chirps. During the suspense sequences, an effective use of metal-on-metal pounding creates an alien texture to the sound. Horner also provides a quasi-inspirational motif for high strings over keyboard during the explanatory sequence in the bar between Wilson and the Indians, during which the Wolfen Theme is suggested as one of the Indians remarks, "You have the eyes of the dead." The score is also given a warm Love Theme which contrasts superbly with the driving wolfen music during the scene in Becky's apartment.

One of the score's most striking effects came from the whip-like slashes used to introduce the unique wolfen-point-of-view sequences, which was accomplished electronically. "Half the sound was musical and half was a non-musical effect," Horner said ... "basically a processed gunshot which was enhanced electronically and added to musically." Horner worked closely with sound effects technician Andrew London to achieve this startling, unearthly motif.

STAR TREK II: THE WRATH OF KHAN (1982) provided Horner with a particularly vast challenge. Jerry Goldsmith, to whom Horner had already been stylistically compared, had scored the first STAR TREK feature, and both his music and the memorable television themes were becoming increasingly wedded to the whole Star Trek milieu. In the case of STAR TREK II, however, the producers specifically wanted the music not to sound like Goldsmith's previous score, although they did wish Horner to use Alexander Courage's TV fanfare, which was incorporated very nicely into the score and maintains a nostalgic feeling of legendry and heroic import.

Composed and orchestrated in only four-and-a-half weeks, Horner's music effectively balanced the sweeping scope of the futuristic space adventure with the warm intimacies of the characters, and much of the music retains the "bubbly" brass feel of Horner's earlier BATTLE BEYOND THE STARS. Horner provided a seafaring, nautical sound to the main theme, which represents the starship Enterprise and Captain Kirk. In contrast, the theme for Khan, Kirk's nemesis in this film, is more of an effect-texture than a melody, quietly emphasizing Khan's insanity. The motif works very well when combined with the Enterprise Theme: "You can lay the texture over the theme," Horner explained, "and when it works with the picture it's terrific. It's a very simple device and works very well."

In addition to these two fundamental themes, Horner composed a haunting motif for Spock, one which emphasized his human side through the warm use of conventional instruments rather than unearthly electronics. "By putting a theme over Spock," said Horner, "it warms him and he becomes three-dimensional rather than a collection of schticks."[31] Another theme is heard as the metabolic Genesis Effect transforms the barren planet of Gamma Regula into a lush paradise: "It's not the swelling dawn-of-creation, Stravinsky-violins theme you might expect," Horner said. "It's kind of awe-inspiring. There are large sustained orchestral chords which slowly and almost imperceptibly change."[32] In other moments, Horner approached sequences in the same way as the TV series: "There were certain ways the drama was treated musically on the TV show," he explained. "In certain spots in the film I tried to play upon that. In the sequence where the Ceti eels are put in the helmets ... there you hear a very high, weird lyre. And the strings are doubled with several percussion and electronic instruments. That's a very weird permutation of the STAR TREK love theme from the TV series. It's a strange internal joke on my part. Very few people recognize it, but it's the kind of thing I smile at when I hear it. Maybe I perverted it so much that no one can recognize it now."[33]

Horner replaced French composer Georges Delerue on SOMETHING WICKED THIS WAY COMES (1983), when studio executives revamped the original version submitted by director Jack Clayton. Delerue's approach had been subtle and lyrical, whereas Horner provided an energetic, wall-to-wall score comprising a 61-piece orchestra and female choir. "I wanted to convey a fantasy-adventure mood that wasn't conventional," Horner said. "When a film has a lot of special effects, I think it's a good idea to establish musical themes that are easy to grasp and not weird or strung out. It would have been easy to go very avant-garde, but I wanted to give it a lighter touch."[34] A key scene that needed especially

evocative music was when Mr. Cooger travelled backward on the
magical carousel, regressing into an infant. "What I definitely did
not want to do was play a calliope backwards," Horner explained.
"Instead I combined a full orchestra with this collage of various
calliope pieces. The calliope begins to play 'The Blue Danube
Waltz.' Then the orchestra creeps under that with a haunting
theme and the whole mood begins to shift. We also did layers and
layers of other calliope tunes weaving in and out." [35]

Horner scored the extravagant fantasy, KRULL (1983), with
a rousing mixture of semimedieval themes and the grand, brassy
flourishes of his previous space movie scores. Synthesizers are incorporated with the orchestra to good effect, as are voices--high,
female choir becomes associated with the mystical power of Colwyn
and the glaive, while a deep, male chorus intones darkly to underscore the evil forces of the Beast. It's a very broad score, almost
too broad, in fact, for this muddled and derivative film, which
overall seems too weak for such energetic music.

James Horner is developing into a noteworthy film composer,
and his frequent fine work in the horror and science fiction film
genre have earned him a lasting place as an important contributor
to genre film music.

Australian composer Brian May has also made a name for himself in several fantastic films of the 80's. May was a leading figure
in Australian light music, having conducted the Australian Broadcasting Company's Showband in Melbourne for several years, when
he became associated with filmmaker Richard Franklin. After several nongenre projects, May scored Franklin's psychokinetic thriller,
PATRICK (made in 1977, but not released in the U.S. until 1979).
May's music was a pleasing blend of light melodic themes dominated
by strings, piano and woodwind, with more atonal, sustained string
passages slowly ascending amid woodwind, harp, synthesizer and
percussion. PATRICK was an evocative horror score, suitably eerie
at certain moments, and lightly airy at other times. The score impressed filmmakers George Miller and Byron Kennedy, who hired
May to score their futuristic action thriller, MAD MAX (U.S. 1980).
May's music here emphasized climactic action and battle in its loud,
brassy strokes, building the music around the brutal aspects of the
film's characters. While there is one melodic theme, signifying the
love between Max and his wife, the score is characterized by frenzied orchestration centering around percussion, brass, and pulsating strings. The title music is quite effective here, and the piping
brass figures are matched to the appearance of the first few credits
on the screen. The vaguely jazzy motif quickly becomes a blur of
frantic action, and the music erupts with a brutal violence. "MAD
MAX was a strongly energized score in the violence/action department," May said, "and for that they wanted a totally non-melodic
score. It was very jagged and shearing, and George [Miller] particularly wanted me to antagonize the audience by making them feel

uncomfortable. Sometimes we had jagged notes going against dialog so that the audience would feel frustrated."[36]

Much of the mood of MAD MAX was carried over into Miller's
sequel, THE ROAD WARRIOR (1982; also known as MAD MAX 2),
although the musical violence of MAD MAX is balanced by a rich,
melancholy theme representing the essence of Max, who in this film
has become even more cynical and solitary, though more heroic at
the same time. The music therefore embodies more of his inner
spirit, rather than simply his outer actions as in MAD MAX. The
profound sadness of the theme captures all of the regret, sorrow
and cynicism of Max as he struggles to survive amid the barbaric
wastelands of a post-holocaust Earth. "MAD MAX 2," May said,
"was an optimistic picture, and it was really like a modern revival
of an old western ... I took out all the jaggedness that I'd had in
MAD MAX 1 and thought in terms of soaring French horns. Whereas in MAD MAX 1, I had jagged brass, very atonal and difficult to
play, in MAD MAX 2 I had deep basses, cellos, and lots of short
motifs that were not totally melodic but were just enough to be
unified." Among the motifs for THE ROAD WARRIOR was a series
of repeated, punching brass stabs, which recklessly drove the action forward. May's mixture of profound sorrow and brutal action
was one of the film's most important attributes, and figured greatly
in the film's power.

HARLEQUIN (1980) was scored for a variety of atonal motifs
for strings, piano and percussion, given a thematic unity through
a lush, string Love Theme. This Romantic motif dominates the film,
emerging from the atonal passages and interplaying in the various
action scenes as the film progresses. SNAPSHOT (made in 1978,
released in America in 1981 as THE DAY AFTER HALLOWEEN) featured an evocative four-note, repeatedly ascending piano motif,
which built an atmospheric undercurrent of terror. The SNAPSHOT
score is a richly suspenseful one, which also made an infrequent
use of jazzy rhythm section in some areas. May's music for
THIRST (U.S. 1981) was a noteworthy one for this unusual vampire film, as was his music for THE SURVIVOR (U.S. 1981). This
latter score is reliant primarily upon a two-note, ascending motif
for strings, which is, in effect, the Terror Theme for this ghost
movie. The motif is given a variety of arrangements, often as a
slow-paced, mysterious passage but occasionally sped up to a very
rapid pace for strings, piano and brass. May also makes effective
use of rapid, one-handed fingering on the high end of the piano
and synthesizer, which sends iciclelike shivers down the listener's
back. The use of the synthesizer is notable, emerging sporadical-
ly amid the orchestral score and embellishing the overall texture of
the music.

While May has scored other types of films, the majority of
his recognition has been for horror films. Like most composers,
May is concerned about being typecast as a "horror" composer,

but does find that he enjoys scoring such films. "I love doing them because the composer's got a great opportunity," he said. "Horror and science fiction music tends to be quite forward in a lot of the sequences. It gets to the audience in different ways so that you have a feeling that you're really part of the action in that type of film and you're doing things that are going to tantalize the audience or shock them."

Another composer to emerge from fantastic films of the late 70's is Richard H. Band. Band is the son of producer/director Albert Band, and after discovering an interest in music while growing up in Europe, he spent the next seven years becoming a self-taught musician. Band received formal training in the United States, and eventually became involved with motion-picture scoring when his brother, Charles Band, started to produce films in 1977.

His first score was for the low-budget LASERBLAST (1978), for which he and synthesist Joel Goldsmith (son of Jerry Goldsmith) provided a completely electronic score in only five days. Band's next endeavor, THE DAY TIME ENDED (1979), was a broad symphonic work developed along the lines of a classical symphony. "I am a firm believer in melodic and motific development in film scoring so as to provide a definite sense of continuity," Band explained. "Specifically, the main title motif is developed and expanded throughout the score, culminating in the full melody used for the finale."[37] This approach is particularly striking in the score. Band introduces the main theme briefly during the opening titles, and allows it to reappear in various unresolved instances, so that when it reaches its fullest form in the climactic conclusion it has a marvelous effect, relating not only to the musical resolution but to the fulfillment of the dilemma in the film. This, in addition to the score's overall romantic idiom, really lends a profound effect to an otherwise unremarkable picture. It's all the more remarkable, considering the broad scope and power of the score, to realize that Band accomplished it with an orchestra of only 32 pieces.

Band next scored the horror comedy DR. HECKLE AND MR. HYPE (1980) with what he termed a "bold" approach consisting of a love theme which expanded into a carousel-fairyland atmosphere. "The use of a very serious love theme behind the parts that were comedic in that movie only heightened the sense of the absurdity," Band said. "But at the same time it never made you lose sense of the fact that underneath it all this is a very serious movie and in fact was a tragedy."[38] Band scored PARASITE (1982) in a different manner, choosing to provide a textural effect rather than a thematic backdrop. "I wanted the film to portray emptiness," Band explained. "An after-the-holocaust type of feel, with a thin-ness to the score. Moments that ordinarily might have had music I purposely left silent in order to add to the feeling of desolation, so

as to really heighten the moments when the music did come in."
Band also composed a JAWSlike motif that is used as a structure
to herald the attacks of the alien parasite, which was, according
to Band, "influenced by certain Penderecki techniques, such as
dividing up the string section. Instead of into four or six parts,
I divided the entire string section into close to twenty parts and
had them play certain bowing techniques which created a shrill,
very agitated effect."

Band's score for THE HOUSE ON SORORITY ROW (1983) was
a particularly notable contribution to an otherwise routine mad-
killer-terrorizing-luscious-vixens movie. For this film, Band composed a romantic-styled score based on a number of harmonic,
twelve-tone motifs. "My approach was to get as far away from effect music as I could, and to approach the entire movie from what
the catalyst was for what was going on." An interesting effect
Band accomplished in this score was through the use of a repeated
Music-box motif, playing a variation on the three-note main theme,
which figures prominently in the movie as a trigger for the killer's
actions. The music box, as well as another variation for childlike
voices, emphasizes the mother-child relationship between Mrs.
Slater and her apparently stillborn child, a relationship not clearly
realized until the film's end. "I played with the audience," Band
explained, "in the sense that, what is called a flash forward in
visual terms, I used in musical terms, letting the audience in, on
an emotional level, on what the real story was behind the goings
on."

Band's score, written in three-and-a-half weeks, was recorded by the London Symphony Orchestra, whose services became
increasingly more in demand for film music since John Williams utilized their prowess in STAR WARS. Band's score is enriched by
their playing, although he only employed between 27 and 40 musicians during the recording sessions, and the score provides a fine
fluidity which serves the film well.

Band also scored New World's TIME WALKER (1983) an uneven combination of ancient mummies and marooned aliens which he
scored in only two weeks. Unlike the symbolic thematic approach
to SORORITY ROW, Band chose to score TIME WALKER in a fairly
straightforward manner, utilizing a mixture of orchestra, synthesizer and choir. The score is primarily atonal, opening with an
Egyptian-styled woodwind motif, later developing a variety of
string rustlings, bell-tree tinklings, low synthesizer warbles, and
effective suspense passages for piano, strings and percussion. As
with THE DAY TIME ENDED, the score profoundly opens up at the
climax, where Band, unrestrained, provides a stirring, inspirational
resolution for sustained synthesizer and angelic choir, reminiscent
of CLOSE ENCOUNTERS. Band admits this was his "little tribute
to John Williams!"

Band was given the chance to step up from low-budget horrors when he scored METALSTORM (1983), an expensive outer space adventure filmed in 3-D. Band provided a massive score, contrasting hard-driving "big" music with more mystical and weird textures, which was recorded by a large orchestra of 70 pieces supplemented with a large array of electronics instruments. These were performed live <u>with</u> the orchestra, rather than overdubbed in later. "We brought all the electronics onto the live stage at the Burbank Studios," Band said, "and we had four keyboard players playing close to thirteen different synthesizers and computers along with the orchestra. I don't think anybody's ever attempted this much electronics on a live session with seventy players." Thematically, Band structured the score around a pair of integrated leitmotifs and a third theme-texture which is associated with the villain. "It's very representative of a simple thematic and motific approach, like I've used in previous films, although in a different vein, orchestration-wise. In that sense, it's unlike anything I've done before."

While the majority of Band's film music has been for science fiction and horror films, his music is notable for avoiding clichéd gimmicks. "That's very easy to get caught up in when you're under terrible time restrictions or very limited budgets," he said. "Sometimes you have to fall back on the gimmicks and the tricks of the trade to be able to get it done in time. But if one is to look at scoring films as an art form then one has to look at it from a much broader perspective, and therefore use the tools that are available but not abuse them in the sense of going for the production value of a great gimmick. You have to go for what's behind the reasoning in the script, from a human standpoint. Then if you can use all of those gimmicks as you would tools, their effect will be that much more enhanced." Band's usage of these tools has been quite impressive, and his contributions to recent fantastic film music are important ones.

Another composer noted for his interesting scores for low-budget thrillers is Harry Manfredini, who worked for 20 years as a professional musician (mostly jazz saxophone) before becoming involved in film scoring through an association with composer Arlon Ober. Manfredini's first genre score was the intriguing murder mystery, THE KIRLIAN WITNESS (1978), in which a houseplant is the only "witness" to a murder. To emphasize the investigation, which uses Kirlian photography to extract the plant's impressions of the murder, Manfredini created a suitably intriguing score featuring a variety of evocative sounds, including the use of a double-flanged electronic keyboard and guiro effects (scraping a stick over a notched gourd) run through a harmonizer to change their pitch. THE CHILDREN (1980) was Manfredini's next genre film, which was scored atonally with a variety of ominous string chords and weird piano tones. Much of the score is highly Herrmannesque, such as the PSYCHO-like, stabbing string notes, often given a mutated,

Harry Manfredini. Photograph courtesy Harry Manfredini.

"metallic" feel which coincides with this story of rampaging youths
mutated by nuclear radiation. Bernard Herrmann's PSYCHO score
is also recalled during the driving string chords used in the automobile scenes. "Herrmann's style is, without a doubt, the most
mimicked," Manfredini said. "Every composer since Herrmann has
used his techniques in one way or another. I added a synthesized
sound to the top of the high strings to 'color' it 'metallic.' I think
his 'motif' is often used as an homage. I'm afraid it will be used
in as many ways and variations as there are composers for the rest
of time. It lives in the annals of film music with the JAWS figure
and the 'William Tell Overture.'"[39]

Manfredini's score for FRIDAY THE 13TH (1980) was less
derivative, however, and was an effectual atonal composition for
strings, brass, keyboard and voice. One of the most effective
motifs was the use of echoing vocal gasps which signified the
crazed killer who terrorizes the teenage counselors who are preparing a summer camp. "Mrs. Voorhees was a woman who heard
voices," Manfredini explained. "I got the idea from the extreme
close-up shots of Mrs. Voorhees' mouth in the dissolves where she
says 'Kill her Mommy.' I used the first sound of those words,
'Ki,' 'Ma'. I spoke them into a mike, digitally delayed and echo
repeated them. I also used an optical track instrument called an
Orchestron to get choral voices which I blended into the orchestral
texture. In FRIDAY THE 13TH, PART II, I used a Korg Vocorder
for the same effect."

Manfredini had less than three weeks to score FRIDAY THE
13TH, which was recorded by an orchestra of approximately 24
pieces. The circumstances were the same for the first sequel,
filmed the following year. Both FRIDAY THE 13TH PART II and
PART III (1982) used extensions of the same music composed for
the first film, which creates not only a thematic unity between the
trio but suits the identical plot structures of each film. Most of
PART III, in fact, was made up of music previously recorded for
Parts I and II. Manfredini only wrote new music for the last three
reels, in addition to a heavy and awkward rock/disco title theme.
"In my opinion," Manfredini said, "these pictures are simply commercial attempts that have caught on, and will keep being made
over and over again until they don't make a profit. I jumped on
the commercial bandwagon because I felt the song was in the spirit
of the picture."

SWAMP THING (1982) was given a much lighter musical texture. For this film, based on the popular comic book story of a
scientist mutated into a monstrous, semi-humanoid swamp creature,
Manfredini provided an action/adventure score in a much different
mold than the earlier stalk-and-slash chillers. "Trying to keep
the 'comic book feel,'" Manfredini said, "the score has plenty of
synchornized hits, almost cartoon-like at times." Whereas FRIDAY
THE 13TH allowed Manfredini to experiment with interesting

musical effects, SWAMP THING provided a greater opportunity to
score for character and relationship as well as for action. A driving motif for horn chords and see-sawing strings over percussion
motivate the Swamp Thing's actions, while a poignant, vaguely
Steineresque Love Theme reflects Alec Holland's inner man.

Manfredini's frequent excursions into audible terror have
given him a good handle on composing for the horror genre, and
his work, however unremarkable some of the films may have been,
has made some noteworthy contributions to genre film music. "The
techniques of horror and suspense are varied and change with
each picture and scene," Manfredini said, and then cited some important factors that he takes into account when scoring a horror
movie: "Where the music starts is very important. I try to find
something in the picture to justify and find the start. Often you
do not want the music to be noticed, other times it calls for a
strong hit. Telegraphing what is about to happen is always a con-
cern in the horror genre. Sometimes you want to telegraph, sometimes not. You want to manipulate the audience so they can enjoy
the picture. Part of the fun is being fooled and manipulated.
'Red herrings' are very prevalent in the genre, and are part of
the manipulation techniques of the director. To me, it makes a
difference whether we are leading to a red herring or to a real
scare. I try to score them differently. On the red herring, I
will usually drive very hard and try to create as much tension as
possible, and let the real scares come out of nowhere." Where the
music stops is also an important factor: "Sometimes these are quite
obvious but others require more effort to find. In a suspenseful
situation before a scare, I try to get the music out before the
actual hit. The silence is sometimes more powerful than anything
you can write. I think one of the secrets of the success of FRI-
DAY THE 13TH was the relaxation before the hit."

British composer Trevor Jones has emerged as an important
genre composer with his contributions to a pair of spectacular epic
adventure fantasies, EXCALIBUR (1981) and THE DARK CRYSTAL
(1982). Born in South Africa and raised in an entertainment environment, Jones came to London in 1967 to study at the Royal
Academy of Music, later graduating from York University, where
he helped to establish a four-year course in film scoring. Jones
studied all the aspects of filmmaking at Britain's National Film
School, where, as composer in residence, he wrote the music for
some 22 student projects. While most of EXCALIBUR used operatic
chorale music and medieval chants, Jones provided sporadic synthesizer motifs which seemed to retain more internal continuity than
the seemingly indiscriminate compilation of unevenly matched classical excerpts. THE SENDER (1982) gave Jones a better opportunity for wholly original material (the score mingled a pretty symphonic theme with eerie, rumbling tonalities from synthesizer, percussion and voice). The captivating symphonic score for THE DARK
CRYSTAL gave Jones a grand arena for some remarkable and often
awe-inspiring film music.

Jones was brought into the production early in 1980, two months before the start of principal photography. This allowed him not only to compose the source music performed in the film, such as the elaborate music for the Pod People, but to gain an intimate understanding of the film which would certainly prove valuable in scoring the completed picture. "From the very first in scoring the music for THE DARK CRYSTAL, I set out to find two melodic ideas--one for the Mystics, the other for the Skeksis," Jones said. "These two motifs, when counterpointed, fuse to become one, and in the Great Conjunction at the film's climax they join to become the central theme."[40] In addition to this primary thematic approach, Jones composed a tender Love Theme for Jen and Kira; an intriguing Gelfling song combining voice, flageolet (a baroque flute) and synthesized environmental effects for the relaxing drift down the river; a rhythmic, brassy motif for the gracefully awkward Landstriders; and the festive percussion and pipes music of the Pod People.

Throughout, Jones' orchestration is a remarkable fusion of symphonic, medieval and synthesized instruments, utilizing the symphonic resources of the London Symphony Orchestra embellished with medieval instruments, such as the grumhorn, titin and tabor (used in the Pod Village scene), the double-flageolet, modern okema and synthesizers including the Synclavier and Fairlight computers, and a Prophet 5. "The point was to try and be as inventive as we could but not lose the audience," said Jones. "We started with individual sounds and related those to a symphonic idiom. A film this enormous had to be provided with that sort of symphonic backcloth."[41] Jones' music was sharply felt in the film, and remains a marvelous and important fantasy score.

Another fantasy filmscore along similarly sweeping symphonic lines was Basil Poledouris' CONAN THE BARBARIAN (1982), a highly charged, powerful and exotic score. Poledouris, who studied both music and film at the University of Southern California, managed to combine these contrasting interests when he began to score motion pictures in 1969, eventually gaining recognition with his music to THE BLUE LAGOON in 1980. Poledouris worked with director John Milius on BIG WEDNESDAY (1978) and maintained this working relationship when he was called to score CONAN for the same director. From the start, Milius wanted there to be a lot of music, often referring to the score as "wall-to-wall music," somewhat in the sense of an opera. Milius wanted to minimize the dialog and narration, allowing the visuals and the music to carry most of the action. The first cue in the film, for example, runs nearly 30 minutes--from the fade-in prologue to the conclusion of the Wheel of Pain sequence.

The CONAN score is richly thematic, invested with a number of leitmotifs. "The first theme that I came up with was The Riddle of Steel," Poledouris said, "which in a sense is Conan's theme, but it really represents more the quest that weaves throughout the entire score. It locked down the mythology of the movie. John [Milius] didn't want it to be bright and happy, but more of a ballad." While the visuals serve to set the atmosphere and characterization, Poledouris' theme alone carried the emotional and spiritual romance of Conan's quest--it completes his character. "The Thulsa Doom theme is the other side of the spectrum," the composer explained. "I started looking at a lot of Gregorian chants, and also into some of the Catholic masses. The secondary theme of Thulsa Doom is actually the Dies Irae. Once I had those two themes it was basically a matter of moving them along."[42]

One of the most notable motifs from CONAN is the use of chanted chorus, first heard as Thulsa Doom's raiders thunder through the woods on horseback. The use of the chorale theme is similar to Trevor Jones' arrangement of Carl Orff's Carmina Burana in EXCALIBUR, a similarity not surprising since Milius had originally wanted to use Carmina Burana until he heard it in EXCALIBUR. To retain the same furious, repetitive chanting aspect, Poledouris composed his own theme along similar lines to Orff's piece, but giving it a more Eastern quality. Another notable effect is the chilling, metallic grating sound heard during the Wheel of Pain sequence--accomplished by scraping a triangle across the face of a large gong, called a tam-tam. With CONAN THE BARBARIAN, Basil Poledouris' contribution in creating an environment and providing a profound musical atmosphere is significant. It is among the most evocative fantasy scores of recent years.

A number of other adventurous sword-and-sorcery films followed in the wake of CONAN, among them THE BEASTMASTER (1982), scored by Lee Holdridge, which involved a muscular barbarian with the unlikely power to control animals to aid him in a vengeful quest. Holdridge, a graduate of the Manhattan School of Music, began working in theatre in New York. After much experience arranging for popular recording artists like Neil Diamond, Holdridge became involved in film scoring with JONATHAN LIVINGSTON SEAGULL in 1973. One of his first genre films was a thriller called THE PACK (1977), which concerned a rampaging fellowship of wild, killer dogs, for which he provided a strong score. Although mostly known for his light scores for dramas and romantic films, Holdridge provided a highly melodic, dramatically symphonic score for THE BEASTMASTER. The main theme is a broad, adventurous motif for full orchestra which suitably propels the film along. In addition, Holdridge provides a pleasant flute Love Theme over plucked harp, wind chimes and finger-cymbals; a low tympani motif for the evil, pagan priest; and a synthesizer motif used to reflect the sorcery and power of the Beastmaster. Faint chimes denote Dar's power over the animals, especially the eagle.

Holdridge's basic approach to the film was a mythological one: "You can't tell what period it's set in or where it's set," Holdridge said, "so I decided that it should be mythological in nature, and therefore I opted for what I call a kind of modal approach in symphonic works. I used a lot of percussion and brass in THE BEASTMASTER, and the open sound of the Fourth and Fifth gives a mysterious modal quality to it which makes it sound ancient."[43] Holdridge also wanted very strong themes, the most dominant of which is the central heroic theme that runs throughout the film. This is balanced with a distinctive theme for the eagle, which becomes a symbol for Dar. "The two themes become more and more intertwined as the picture develops," Holdridge explained, "and I find that I was able to work the two together in a nice way, especially in the final moments of the picture when they're all united-- all the themes come together in the very last scene of the movie."

Arthur B. Rubinstein began to make a name for himself in genre film music when he scored both BLUE THUNDER and WAR-GAMES in quick succession. Released during the summer of 1983, both movies were action-packed, high-technology thrillers with rather cynical political overtones. Rubinstein's music accentuated both the heroic and human aspects of the films as well as their technological aspects through a skillful combination of symphonic and electronic musical modes. Rubinstein, who had a background in theatrical play music before moving into TV movies, scored BLUE THUNDER with an effectively heroic, if somewhat bluesy, theme for the protagonist, Murphy, which constantly played off a deeper, four-note theme representing the malevolency inherent within the Blue Thunder helicopter. At the end, when Murphy takes control of the helicopter himself to bring an end to the corrupt parties, the two themes merge in a powerful cry of triumphal heroism. "I recognized that this was not a film that could take a simple, romantic score," Rubinstein said. "There had to be a stranger kind of cohesion to the music, it had to almost have a documentary feeling to it. The thematic material is absolutely simple. What is complicated is the moment-to-moment working-out of rhythms and tempos and sounds that would almost feel at one with the helicopters."[44] The effective blending of the electronics with the symphonic elements, as we have already seen in Chapter XIII, provided a memorable score embodying both the human heroics and the technological spectacle of the film.

Rubinstein's score for WARGAMES likewise summed up the human and electronic elements in a pair of themes for harmonica and synthesizer, respectively. A third motif, for brass and percussion, represents the military. At the end, after the computerized crisis has ended through young David's ingenuity, the human and electronic themes merge for a final recapitulation under the end titles, effectively resolving both story and music. This thematic approach worked itself out as Rubinstein composed the score. What he had initially felt was most important was to determine how he felt about the WOPR, the huge war computer. "I felt that there was something very Faustian about that whole element," said Rubin-

stein. "Something larger than life, somewhat evil, somewhat cynical, but also somewhat sardonic. I decided that the computer is
a malevolent character, and throughout the score whenever the
computer is shown, there is this malevolent-yet-sardonic treatment.
There is a devilish quality to the whole thing, because that's how
I perceived both David and the WOPR. They're both impudent
and impish in their own way. I didn't see David as a charming,
misunderstood kid at all. I saw him as being very much involved
with this impudence." The themes for David and for the WOPR
embody this sense of devilish impudence, although David's theme
does remain somewhat more playful and magical.

Like Richard Band and many other composers gaining acclaim in recent years, Arthur B. Rubinstein has managed to get
deep within the characters of a film, discerning their personalities
and motivations, and portraying those elements musically on the
sound track, underlining almost subliminally those important elements not always made obvious in the visuals.

While sweeping, symphonic scores flourished among science
fiction epics and adventurous heroism abounded in fantasy pictures, horror films tended to be balanced between two camps, as
they were in the 40's. One camp was the melodic, thematic approach in the romantic tradition of Steiner, Salter and Rozsa; the
other was the modern approach of Raksin and Friedhofer. Of
course, there were varying mixtures--but these were the extremes.
Naturally, there was a variable degree of success with each approach, but the romantic style seemed to be easier to control--
more scores emerged in the modern category and many of them
seemed to be little more than clanging noise. The romantic tradition tended to retain more structure, and as a result seemed to
have had a greater effect at seducing an audience into experiencing
the films' terrors more intimately.

Stephen Lawrence embellished ALICE, SWEET ALICE (1978)
with a bittersweet woodwind melody over harpsichord, using voices
quite effectively. An especially frightening mood is achieved at
the start through the use of an extremely rapid, monotonously
whispered reading, by a child, of the Catholic "Hail Mary" over
the woodwind motif during the main titles; this provides not only
a disturbing and spooky opener but relates as well to the evil
child who murdered her sister during a Communion service. Elsewhere, Lawrence effectively writes against the mood of the film,
offering a soft harpsichord melody which serves as a counterpoint
to the film's violence.

Dana Kaproff composed a fine, rich string score for the
well-directed mad-killer film, WHEN A STRANGER CALLS (1979),
filling it with ominous, powerfully fluid and drawn-out string passages which sound clearly, with growing tension, over low keyboard notes. Rick Wilkins scored the Canadian ghost film, THE

CHANGELING (1980), with a haunting, slow piano theme mixed with swirling violins, supplemented by a haunting Music-box motif composed by Howard Blake. British composer Roger Webb scored THE GODSEND (1980) with a pleasing rhythmic, undulating string motif under woodwind chimes and vibraphone or xylophone.

John Cacavas, an American composer who had scored a number of films in England, including Hammer's SATANIC RITES OF DRACULA, wrote the music for the speculative science fiction film, HANGAR 18 (1980). Cacavas lent it a pleasing horn theme, somewhat Steineresque, dominated by a single chord, around which is orchestrated little motifs and brassy punches which always return to the dominant, hard brass note. The score was highly in keeping with the vogue of brassy adventure music that "flourished" after STAR WARS became the prototype for space-movie music.

Director Frank LaLoggia collaborated with composer David Spear (who had also orchestrated Bernstein's HEAVY METAL) to provide the music for his stylish occult thriller, FEAR NO EVIL (1981). The score is built primarily around a driving, eight-note motif, first introduced by plucked strings and piping woodwinds, that immediately inspires a sense of evil import and dramatic confrontation. This motif segues into the second theme, a mellow woodwind tune, although weaving strings maintain an undercurrent of apprehension. Throughout the score, the eight-note Horror motif and the woodwind theme play off each other to very good effect. LaLoggia's use of music was especially notable in this film; in fact he was constantly aware of the role of the score throughout all stages of his production. "I wrote much of the script while actually seated at the piano," LaLoggia said, "concurrently writing and playing the melodies that would eventually become the full orchestrations.... The music helped to inspire the story and vice-versa.... Indeed, while shooting the picture, I was constantly accompanied by my battery-powered cassette recorder so that I could refer to the rough piano renderings of the score to help me with directing and pacing the rhythms of key scenes."[45] LaLoggia elaborated his score and constructed it on a Korg Polyphonic synthesizer, finally bringing in Spear to cocompose and orchestrate his material into a whole, meshing it with acoustical instruments. "The synthesizer tracks," LaLoggia said, "already sounding very classical in tempo ... and intricate counter-rhythms, needed a big, dramatic sound." Spear provided this very effectively--indeed, the score is dominated by its orchestral sound, and resulted in a fine, evocative horror score.

While evocative orchestral richness has not always been felt in atonal and avant-garde horror scores, a distinctive atmosphere of eerie discord and unearthly texture has often been created in such an approach. The 1979 version of INVASION OF THE BODY SNATCHERS was scored by Denny Zeitlin, a jazz composer/pianist from the San Francisco area, who is also a practicing psychiatrist,

whose symphonic modernisms contributed a fine contemporary feel
to this modern horror film. In addition to a variety of wandering
orchestral rhythms and bizarre percussionisms, Zeitlin makes use
of an array of electronic instruments to provide various effects,
although many of them seem somewhat in the realm of gimmickry.
There is no thematic unity in the score, except for a pleasant
Love Theme for a jazzy woodwind and brass melody over piano
and brushed drum rhythm, the bulk of the score being comprised
of atonal musical effects, some of which are quite horrific, such
as the groaning synthesizer wails and deep, percussionistic rumbles which herald the discovery of a new alien seed pod, as well
as grating mandolin and piano effects, and other sounds which
lend an appropriate eeriness to the picture.

More innovative, however, was John Corigliano's music for
ALTERED STATES (1981). For Ken Russell's bizarre, hallucinatory
exploration into metaphysics and the subconscious, Corigliano composed a brilliant, highly acclaimed avant-garde score which has
been favorably compared by many to the Ligeti portions of 2001:
A SPACE ODYSSEY. Corigliano, associate professor of music at
New York City's Lahman College, was a concert hall composer
since the late 50's, was hired by Russell when the director
attended a Los Angeles Philharmonic performance of Corigliano's
Clarinet Concerto. This was Corigliano's first experience on a
feature film (outside of having scored a short documentary in
1974), and he drew primarily from atonality, dissonance, and
unique musical sounds to create the musical backdrop for ALTERED
STATES.

Russell wanted a "far-out" experimental score and Corigliano
aptly supplied it, composing an hour and ten minutes of music in
two-and-a-half months. "What I wanted to get was a feeling of
tension and disorientation and hallucinatory wildness," Corigliano
said. "Hallucinations are not tonal! They're not logical! The
music had to have that quality of constantly becoming something
it wasn't--taking you and turning your head from side to side."[46]

Corigliano wisely chose not to score the many scientific and
academic explanatory sequences, utilizing music, with the exception
of brief emotional dialog scenes, only in the hallucinatory and
transformation scenes where it has the most force. The majority
of the music is orchestral. Corigliano refrained from too much
electronic music, feeling it had become a cliché. The Ape Man
sequence is a good example of this, in which Corigliano opened
with low basses holding a long note, slowly sliding off it and getting thicker and more ominous as the hairy hand first emerges
from the experiment box. "One of my jobs, I felt," Corigliano
said, "was to make the Ape Man scenes more primitive, to make instruments not sound like clarinets and oboes and bassoons like
they do in that inserted janitor scene, but to make them sound
more like unrecognizable sonorities. Some people who saw the film

thought that some of the music in the Ape Man sequence was elec-
tronic--and that's because orchestral instruments can be made to
sound this way."[47]

Among the weird sounds Corigliano achieved orchestrally for
this sequence was a "jet whistle," accomplished by flute and piccolo players buzzing into their instruments as if they were trumpets, as well as unusual string effects such as striking the strings
with the palm, tapping the upper end of the soundboard with
fingertips, tapping the desk with the bow, and playing between
the bridge and tailpiece, all of which created a suitably unusual
and unique sound texture.

Much of the music emerges from the sound effects, as if it
were exuding from the humming machinery before being built up.
The composer explains: "It wasn't unintentional on my part, because a lot of the music is very abstract music. It comes out of
sonority rather than melody of chords, so it was integrated a good
deal with the sound effects." Corigliano's single melodic element
is a love theme, yet this is not simply an obligatory romantic
piece. It is a melancholy theme used very sparsely in the film
which adds a bit of warmth to a primarily sad, one-sided relation-
ship--Jessup being too involved in his experimentation to respond
sensitively to his wife, and the theme echoes this tone effectively
until the end, where it swells triumphantly as Jessup realizes that
the true source he's been seeking is simply--love. Another thematic element that crops up is a quotation from the hymn, "Rock
of Ages," which is used to reflect Jessup's memory of religion
contrasted with his subsequent loss of faith. The phrase is repeated in several scenes, using a clerical organ sonority and given
an atonal harmonic accompaniment.

Among the problems Corigliano encountered on this film was
a startling reshuffling of many scenes and music occurring just
before the film's final release. The distributor, Warner Brothers,
became concerned about some negative response to a preview and
so had the film substantially recut. As a result, many of Corigliano's cues, which were very exact in terms of synchronization,
wound up in different places and in scenes of different timings.
The score is, therefore, not exactly what Corigliano had in mind,
but remains nevertheless vastly effective and one of the most
original fantasy scores of recent years.

Another interesting avant-garde score was for George Romero's MARTIN (1977), a stylish vampire movie told from the creature's point of view. Donald Rubinstein composed a score based
on contemporary jazz, remaining quite melancholy, underscoring
the dismal activities on screen with a variety of discordant harmonics, occasional electronics, and a haunting use of solo female
voice over piano. Rubinstein, a jazz composer and performer from
Boston, applied a variety of unusual percussionistic sounds to

lend an eerie texture to a score held together primarily by woodwinds, keyboard and string quartet. The music aptly describes
the unusual, yet recognizable, world of the contemporary vampire,
remaining suitably somber and sardonic and often quite frightening.

This atonal and motifical approach has been used quite a bit
in recent horror scores to varying effect. Hod David Schudson
scored the low-budget, independent feature, PARTS--THE CLONUS
HORROR (1979) with a mixture of pop and rock motifs, often seeming out of place (as in the extremely distracting rhythmic music
that accompanies the fight scene in the clone donor's house), but
Schudson's main theme really packs a wallop and provides a very
definite sense of omnipresent danger in its use of loud chorale wailing over a dramatic, up-and-down string rhythm. Roger Kellaway
scored THE DARK (1979) with a noisy atonal conglomeration of
weaving strings, tinkling xylophone repetitions, percussive tap-
pings, keyboard mingling with eerie effects and tones, and a gimmicky vocal whispering of the word "daaaaaaaarrrrkkknessssss!"
While it may have emphasized the mood of discomfort and terror,
it seemed more noisy than musical, and indicative of the trend
toward orchestral effects without the musical discipline that Corigliano employed to utilize such effects in a dramatic way.

TERROR TRAIN (1980) was a typical stalk-and-slash mad-
killer movie, and while it avoided the highly imitated synthesizer
scoring of HALLOWEEN, composer John Mills-Cockel provided a primarily atonal, effects-laden score emphasizing horn blares, percussive taps, loud brassy notes and string tones--what has been
termed a "squeaks and groans" score by one composer. Likewise
was Webster Lewis' music for THE HEARSE (1980), which opens
with furtive piano notes and weird percussive sounds joined by
eerie, ascending strings, rising to fade out; which is balanced by
a warmer, innocent melody for high-pitched piano over slow electric bass notes. John Beal scored Tobe Hooper's FUNHOUSE (1981)
with a calliope motif representing the carnival setting, interspersed
with crashing horn, strings and percussion. The calliope motif,
as well as a melancholy theme for solo woodwind, are the only recurring thematic pieces--the majority of the score utilized conventional orchestration (employing a 57-piece orchestra, according to
Hooper) to obtain a variety of suspense and horrific motifs.

Bob Summers' music for THE BOOGENS (1982) opened with a
brassy fanfare that segues to an old-time harmonica tune that effectively accompanies the introductory Gold Rush montage; it ends
with a reflective solo horn over strings. In between, Summers
provides a series of moody, complementary motifs, but seems to
avoid themes and melodies. Jonathan Goldsmith scored VISITING
HOURS (1982), a big-budget stalk-and-slash clone, with a routine
barrage of suspenseful passages and shock gimmicry, although
there is a slow, undulating main theme for a spooky violin melody,
with occasional two-note, echoed piano tapping. INCUBUS (1981),

scored by veteran composer Stanley Myers, has a weird, atonal score dominated by strings, which features an occasional use of low horn moans under plucked strings, and a repeated motif for staccatolike string chords. While Myers' string stabs were not particularly PSYCHO-like, Joe Loduca does employ slashing Herrmannesque strings in EVIL DEAD (1983), although the derivation is effective and Loduca balances it with a memory-waltzlike tune which is associated with the mirrored necklace given one of the characters.

In a sense, atonal scores are associated by many with the horror genre in the same way that spacey electronics are associated with science fiction and soaring, light heroic themes are associated with fantasy. Yet it has been too easy for the atonal approach to descend into simple gimmickry and noise--squeaks and groans. While such motifs do complement the often-directionless horrors depicted on screen, they often fail to provide any underlying structural unity to the score or embellish the characterization or conceptual themes in the film--the traditional objectives of movie music. Of course there have been exceptions, and ALTERED STATES is a choice example of an atonal score which has been put together with a sense of unity, which relates intrinsically to the structure and direction of the film, rather than just banging away in the background. The eerie, fluid string movements of Schifrin and Kaproff tend to approach the horror in terms of contrast and juxtaposition, lending a softer, more haunting and often innocent quality in counterpoint to the horrific elements that atonal scores are more straightforward in embellishing. Horror film music needn't be horrible, or horrifying, music. Whether the idiom is romantic or modernistic, film music has always been at its most effective when approached with imagination and creative experimentation.

Notes

1. Andre Previn quoted in SEE NO EVIL film commentary, FilmFacts, 1971, p. 283

2. Mark Stevens, "The Score," Cinefantastique Vol. 2, #1 (Spring 1972) p. 43

3. Tim A. Willis, "Scoreboard," Nostalgiaphon News & Views Vol. 7, #11 (December 1981) p. 5

4. Paul A. Snook, "Record Review," High Fidelity, January 1982, p. 76

5. David Raksin, letter to Page Cook, Films in Review, October 1971; quoted by Irwin Bazelon: Knowing the Score (New York: Arco Publishing Inc., 1981), p. 100

6. Page Cook, "WHAT'S THE MATTER WITH HELEN?," Films in Review, October 1971; quoted by James Limbacher: Film Music (Metuchen, N.J.: Scarecrow Press, 1974) p. 117

7. David Raksin quoted by Page Cook, ibid., p. 115-116

8. Irwin Bazelon, Knowing the Score (New York: Arco Publishing Inc., 1981) p. 111

9. Alex North interviewed by Irwin Bazelon, ibid., p. 219-220

10. William Friedkin quoted by Elmer Bernstein, "The Annotated Friedkin," Filmmusic Notebook, Winter 1974-75, p. 14

11. Derek Elley, "Film Music," Films and Filming (London, August 1982)

12. John Caps, "Dungeons and Dragons--Three Medieval Scores," Soundtrack! The Collector's Quarterly Vol. 2, #5 (March 1983), p. 4

13. Ken Sutak, "A DRAGONSLAYER Inquiry," Pro Musica Sana #36 (Summer 1982) p. 9

14. Alex North quoted by William H. Rosar, "Notes on DRAGONSLAYER," CinemaScore: The Film Music Journal forthcoming.

15. Bill Warren, "Warren's News & Reviews," Fantasy Newsletter #40 (September 1981) p. 20

16. John Fitzpatrick, "DRAGONSLAYER--Two Views," Pro Musica Sana #34 (Winter 1981-82) p. 3

17. Tony Thomas, Music for the Movies (La Jolla: A. S. Barnes & Co., 1973) p. 206

18. Mike Snell, "Profile--Leonard Rosenman," International Filmusic Journal #2 (U.K. 1980) p. 24

19. John Caps, "The Lord of the Rings," Soundtrack Collector's Newsletter #17 (April 1979) p. 22

20. Lalo Schifrin, interview with the author, October 8, 1982 (and following quotes)

21. Irwin Bazelon, op. cit., p. 85

22. John Barry interviewed by Pat Gray for Irwin Bazelon, op. cit., p. 282

23. Ibid.

24. Paul Harrod, "The Mouse Scores Mickey Never Had," International Filmusic Journal #1 (U.K.: 1979) p. 12

25. John Barry interviewed by Martyn Crosthwaite, International Filmusic Journal #2 (U.K.: 1980) p. 20

26. James Pavelek, "King Kong (1933): The Winner and Still Champion," The Max Steiner Journal #1 (1977) p. 22

27. John Barry quoted by Arthur Knight, "A Chat With the Composer," Saturday Review, July 8, 1972, p. 71

28. Laurence Rosenthal, interview with the author, February 26, 1983 (and following quotes)

29. James Marshall and Ronald Bohn, "Gerald Fried," Soundtrack Collector's Newsletter #15 (October 1978) p. 4

30. James Horner, interview with the author, June 7, 1982 (and following unreferenced quotes)

31. _____ quoted by Kay Anderson, "STAR TREK II: THE WRATH OF KAHN," Cinefantastique Vol. 12, #5/6 (July/ August 1982), p. 72

32. Ibid.

33. _____ quoted by Tom Sciacca, "James Horner--New Melodies for the Starship Enterprise," Starlog #63 (October 1982) p. 22

34. _____ quoted by Stephen Rebello, "SOMETHING WICKED THIS WAY COMES," Cinefantastique Vol. 13, #5 (June-July 1983) p. 48

35. Ibid.

36. Brian May interviewed by Graeme Flanagan, CinemaScore: The Film Music Journal #11/12 (Fall/Winter 1983) p. 23

37. Richard H. Band quoted by Scot W. Holton, liner notes to THE DAY TIME ENDED sound-track recording (Varese Sarabande Records, 1980)

38. _____, interviews with the author, March 1, 1983 and July 26, 1983 (and following quotes)

39. Harry Manfredini, interviews with the author, February, August, and November 1982 (and following quotes)

40. Trevor Jones quoted in liner notes to THE DARK CRYSTAL sound-track recording (Warner Brothers Records, 1982)

41. _____ quoted by Alan Jones, "THE DARK CRYSTAL,"
    Cinefantastique Vol. 13, #4 (April-May 1983) p. 52

42. Basil Poledouris, interview with the author, May 28, 1982

43. Lee Holdridge, interview with the author, October 19, 1982
    (and following quotes)

44. Arthur B. Rubinstein, interview with the author, June 5,
    1983 (and following quotes)

45. Frank LaLoggia, liner notes to FEAR NO EVIL sound-track
    recording (WEB Records, 1981) (and following quote)

46. John Corigliano quoted by Paul Gagne, "The Filming of
    ALTERED STATES," _Cinefantastique_ Vol. 11, #2 (Fall
    1981) p. 37

47. _____ interviewed by David P. James, _Fanfare_ Vol. 5, #4
    (March-April 1982) p. 359 (and following quote)

XVI

CLASSICAL MUSIC

Classical music has always provided a vast repertoire of material which filmmakers have frequently been eager to take advantage of. Classical pieces were often used to accompany early silent
films, performed locally in the individual theaters. At the same
time many original scores were composed for other silent films, and
a number of these were written by popular concert hall composers
of the day. Camille Saint-Saens, for example, composed a score
for strings, piano and harmonium for the 1908 French film, THE
ASSASSINATION OF THE DUC DE GUISE. Mario Castelnuovo-
Tedesco scored the 1945 horror film, THE RETURN OF THE VAM-
PIRE, while famous American composer Ferde Grofé wrote the music
for ROCKETSHIP X-M (1950). Sergei Prokofiev is perhaps the
best-known concert-hall composer who has ventured into cinema,
and his score for ALEXANDER NEVSKY (1938) remains a classic.
Other predominantly classical composers who have occasionally provided an original film score include George Antheil, Victor Herbert,
Arthur Honegger, Darius Milhaud, and Erik Satie.

More frequent, however, is the simple lifting of a traditional
classical piece, now in public domain, and using it as a score.
This was a prevalent practice in the early days of the sound film,
of course, until the strength of original scoring caught on. Many
fantastic films have had classical pieces used as scores. THE
BLACK CAT (1934) featured a score adapted by Heinz Roemheld
from the music of Liszt, Schumann, Beethoven, Schubert and
Tchaikovsky. Of course films such as THE PHANTOM OF THE
OPERA, which require a variety of theatrical source music, have
been brimming with classical pieces. A 1930 rerelease of Lon
Chaney's 1925 PHANTOM provided snatches of Faust on a synchronized sound track, while the 1943 version utilized pastiches
culled from Chopin and Tchaikovsky, in addition to Edward Ward's
original themes. FIRE MAIDENS IN OUTER SPACE (1956) used
the music of Alexander Borodin as a score.

Other fantastic films which have made prominent or complementary use of classical music over the years, include THE TER-
MINAL MAN (1974--Bach's Goldberg Variations No. 25), ZARDOZ
(1974--Beethoven's 7th Symphony, second movement), SLAUGHTER-
HOUSE FIVE (1972--more Bach), and THE GLADIATORS (1971--
Mahler's 3rd Symphony). The flowing and lyrical music played
during Edward G. Robinson's death in SOYLENT GREEN (1973) is

from the first movement of Beethoven's 6th Symphony, seguing into excerpts from Grieg's Peer Gynt. ASYLUM (1972) used music of Mussorgsky in addition to Douglas Gamley's original score. The 1948 fantasy, PORTRAIT OF JENNIE, featured material from Debussy, arranged by Dimitri Tiomkin. THE MEPHISTO WALTZ (1971) utilized Liszt's composition of the same name as well as original music by Jerry Goldsmith. The "Dragon's Domain" episode of SPACE: 1999 used Albinoni's Adagio during a spaceflight scene. Whistled snatches of Grieg's In the Hall of the Mountain King are used as the killer's motif in Fritz Lang's classic M (1931): "Each time the strain is heard the audience knows that something evil is about to occur," wrote one reviewer. "Lang was the first to use this musical device."[1] Although the phrase was actually source music, not underscoring, it achieved a similar effect.

One classical piece used frequently in horror films is Bach's durable Toccata and Fugue in D Minor, an evocative and frightening composition for organ often used as a set piece when one of the malevolent characters is seen playing an organ. Included in its appearances in this manner are Universal's THE BLACK CAT (1934) and THE RAVEN (1935), 20,000 LEAGUES UNDER THE SEA (1954), MYSTERIOUS ISLAND (1961) and OLD DRACULA (1974). It's also been heard as underscoring in Rouben Mamoulian's DR. JEKYLL AND MR. HYDE (1931--as the main title music), FANTASIA (1940), TALES FROM THE CRYPT (1972) and ROLLERBALL (1975).

Another classical piece used frequently by Universal in the 30's was an abbreviated arrangement of the opening scene from Tchaikovsky's Swan Lake. First heard as the main title of DRACULA (1931), the piece was used similarly in MURDERS IN THE RUE MORGUE (1932), THE MUMMY (1933) and MYSTERY OF THE BLUE ROOM (1933). The piece was moody and mysterious, consisting of a melodic progression of tritones (once considered a "dangerous interval" and forbidden in church music, termed diabolus in musica --the devil in music, as William Rosar has pointed out), which makes its use in horror films such as DRACULA quite apropos.

Another oft-quoted motif, which has been mentioned throughout this book, is the Dies Irae (Day of Wrath), a medieval plainsong chant which has been used in a number of classical compositions including: Berlioz's Symphonie Fantastique, Saint-Saens' Danse Macabre, Liszt's Totentanz, Shostakovich's Incidental Music to Hamlet, and Rachmaninoff's Isle of the Dead. Stephen Sondheim also used it in SWEENEY TODD during the segment where the chorus sings "Raise your razor high, Sweeney." Veteran film composer Bernard Herrmann used a variant of it in one of the movements of his Symphony as well as during an episode of THE ALFRED HITCHCOCK HOUR. It's not surprising that many of the classical pieces incorporating the Dies Irae are of a fantastic or macabre nature, since the chant (often associated with its use as a requiem during the Catholic mass for the dead) conjures up images of a dark and foreboding nature.

Films that have quoted the Dies Irae as a major thematic piece include Gerald Fried's THE RETURN OF DRACULA (1957), Ernest Gold's THE SCREAMING SKULL (1958), Leonard Rosenman's THE CAR (1977), Harry Sukman's SALEM'S LOT (1979) and Wendy Carlos' THE SHINING (1980). The motif has also been quoted or paraphrased in portions of countless other scores, including Dimitri Tiomkin's IT'S A WONDERFUL LIFE (1946, near the climax as George Bailey runs back to the bridge, yelling "I want to live!"), Jerry Goldsmith's THE MEPHISTO WALTZ (1971), Douglas Gamley's THE VAULT OF HORROR (1973), John Williams' CLOSE ENCOUNTERS OF THE THIRD KIND (1977; used as an action/chase motif as Roy and Jillian race toward the Devil's Tower), Basil Poledouris' CONAN THE BARBARIAN (1982; adapted as a secondary theme for the Thulsa Doom cult); Goldsmith's POLTERGEIST (1982; two bars are heard during the climactic destruction scene), Ralph Jones' SLUMBER PARTY MASSACRE (1982) and others.

The use of classical music in FANTASIA (1940) was highly unique. In this colorful and entertaining animated feature, eight selections of classical music are used not only as accompaniment but inspirations for eight animated segments, featuring deftly choreographed animated figures from dinosaurs, flying horses, fiery-eyed demons and dancing elephants to Mickey Mouse as a sorcerer's apprentice, cavorting in synchronization with the music. In this case, the music was obviously determined first and the visual concepts molded to fit the sounds--which made the classical score, therefore, much more closely related to the cinematic whole than if classical excerpts had simply been attached to an only vaguely related visual sequence.

The most controversial use of classical music in the fantastic cinema was probably in Stanley Kubrick's 2001: A SPACE ODYSSEY (1968) and A CLOCKWORK ORANGE (1971). The former made striking use of Richard Strauss' dynamic Also Sprach Zarathustra over the beginning and ending (and totally commercializing the piece for the rest of time), as well as Johann Strauss' Blue Danube Waltz, Khachaturian's Gayne Ballet Suite, and a variety of bizarre choral compositions by Gyorgy Ligeti.

While composer Alex North was initially assigned to score 2001, Kubrick was dissatisfied with the composition and decided instead to score the film with a compilation of late nineteenth- and twentieth-century classical recordings. While the eerie atonalities of Ligeti fit the outer space atmospheres nicely, the use of lighter pieces such as the Blue Danube, while unique, prompted mixed reactions from the musical community. Composer Richard H. Band described it neutrally as a "bold" approach: "When they were in space and all of a sudden you heard this waltz, that was a very unique approach to the way one would view space, instead of hearing weird dissonances and high strings and so forth."[2] John Williams has remarked: "Kubrick takes what is the essence of courtly grace,

the waltz, and uses it to accompany these lumbering but weight-
less giants out in space during their kind of sexual coupling ...
the music becomes a work of art that says 'look', that says 'air',
that says 'float' in beautiful orchestral terms."[3]

Jerry Goldsmith, on the other hand, deplored what he considered to be an abominable misuse of music: "I had heard the
music Alex North had written for the film, and which had been
dropped by Kubrick, and I thought what Kubrick used in its
place was idiotic. I am aware of the success of the film but what
North had written would have given the picture a far greater quality. The use of the Blue Danube waltz was amusing for a moment
but quickly became distracting because it was so familiar and unrelated to the visual. North's waltz would have provided a marvelous
effect. He treated it in an original and provocative way. It is a
mistake to force music into a film, and for me 2001 was ruined by
Kubrick's choice of music. His selections had no relationship, and
the pieces could not comment on the film because they were not a
part of it."[4]

Other reviewers tended to analyze Kubrick's choice of music
in more symbolical terms. Author/composer Irwin Bazelon wrote of
the Blue Danube: "Although many composers differ about the use
of this old war horse, and I agree that its evolvement to main-
theme status is idiotic, I am also of the opinion that for this one
episode, Kubrick's choice was a happy one. The waltz is Muzak--
an endless flow of prerecorded, sentimental musical pap, heard in
any air terminal the world over. Kubrick's point is made even
more pronounced when the space traveler arrives at the space station and discovers that Conrad Hilton has living accommodations
sewed up and Howard Johnson has the exclusive franchise for din-
ing facilities."[5]

Orchestrator and author Christopher Palmer has pointed out
how concert music can be built originally and creatively into the
structure of a film, citing as prime examples Kubrick's efforts in
2001 and A CLOCKWORK ORANGE, in which classical pieces were
used both orchestrally and electronically: Also Sprach Zarathustra
"plays a role both functional and symbolic in a most spectacular
manner." In the Dawn of Man sequence, Strauss' Zarathustra is
used "symbolically inasmuch as it represents in its own right the
birth of a superior consciousness ... and functionally in that the
hominoid's actions are cut specifically to the rhythm of the music's
unfolding."[6]

Palmer goes on to point out that "In 2001 there's a rare example of music used purely symbolically and entirely nonfunction-
ally." He cites scenes utilizing the Blue Danube, and explains
that, on the surface level, Kubrick couldn't have chosen a more
ludicrously inappropriate piece of music to accompany these outer

space scenes. "But surely this very fact," Palmer writes, "ought
to suggest that there's more here than meets the ear. The point
here is that in the Blue Danube scenes we are being made aware
all the time of how unfavorably modern man's reactions to the mysterious black monolith contrasts with his hominoid ancestors. These
men of the year 2001 are very different from their ancestors, and
so they get the music of a very different Strauss." Palmer describes this as music used purely symbolically; it does not relate
to what is happening physically on the screen. On the other
hand, Palmer observes, the other music used in the film is purely
functional and nonsymbolic, but in an original way.

Another film that made substantial use of classical music is
EXCALIBUR (1981), which provides a mixture of synthesizer bits
by Trevor Jones with a variety of medieval hymns and chants, as
well as raucus, operatic material by Wagner and Carl Orff. "The
music oscillates spasmodically between early medieval chants," wrote
one reviewer, "later twelfth-century hymns of 'Kyrie Eleison,'
Wagner's Prelude to Parsifal, Tristan and Isolde and Siegfried's
Funeral March, modern Greek dance music with guitars and mandolin ... and music similar to 2001's Zarathustra theme just before
Perceval encounters the Holy Grail. There are also pieces very
like the Gayne Ballet Suite and the choir and whistling wind instruments used for the Stargate sequence in 2001."[7] Orff's Carmina Burana is also used prevalently as a chanting rhythm during
battle scenes, which carries an effective, motivating drive. Another reviewer wrote: "For the most part, John Boorman has drenched
his film in Wagner and Orff, a musical odd couple if there ever was
one. The long-lined Wagner themes tend to be chopped off in mid-
phrase, then repeated ad nauseum. Though the picture is medieval, as film music it belongs to the stone age."[8]

While classical music was used in films out of necessity in
the 30's, recent usage in films such as 2001 and EXCALIBUR seems
a result of artistic inclinations as well as of a director's associating certain scenes with certain pieces of classical music used temporarily for test purposes during production stages. This is what
happened with Kubrick in THE SHINING--in his search for suitable
thematic material, composer Wendy Carlos suggested he listen to
the Dies Irae as used in Berlioz's Symphonie Fantastique, for in-
spiration. As it turned out, Kubrick became so attached to the
Dies Irae as interpreted by Berlioz that he quickly demanded Carlos use it instead of her original material.

Classical music in films remains a subject of mixed feelings
among composers. On the one hand, it would tend to be less effective than music written specifically for the needs of a certain
film or scene, as composer Ernest Gold has pointed out: "I
wouldn't use classical music as a score, I think it interferes. If
you know the music, it draws more attention to itself than it

should.... If you don't know the music, it doesn't support the picture because it wasn't written for the picture."[9] On the other hand, classical music, regardless of the original intentions of its composer, has been used effectively in some films, as composer Les Baxter has said: "I don't believe that concert music has to conjure up, for example, exactly one picture; I believe that a good piece of concert music could be used, let's say, for two vastly different films and would tell very well what was happening. For instance, in FANTASIA, The Rite of Spring was written for a ballet originally and certainly there were no dinosaurs! And yet the Rite of Spring fits beautifully the dinosaur concept in FANTASIA, as did the Beethoven Pastoral Symphony, with the flying horses and all of that. I think that the same music could fit in many different instances."[10]

Classical music will undoubtedly continue to be used in films, for economic, commercial, and artistic reasons; and critical generalities are sometimes difficult to substantiate. Some films have used it effectively, others have not. Despite the apparent disadvantage of its being prerecorded and thus not specifically intended to match certain visuals, classical excerpts have made an impact in the film music of science fiction and fantasy films.

Notes

1. Thomas M. Woolf, "Suspense," VideoPlay Magazine, August/ September 1981, p. 73

2. Richard H. Band, interview with the author, March 1, 1983

3. John Williams, interviewed by Irwin Bazelon, Knowing the Score (New York: Arco Publishing, Inc., 1981) p. 200

4. Jerry Goldsmith, interviewed by Tony Thomas, Film Score (La Jolla: A. S. Barnes & Co., 1979) p. 227-228

5. Irwin Bazelon, op. cit., p. 111

6. Christopher Palmer, "Focus on Films," Filmmusic Notebook, Summer 1975, p. 28-29 (and following quotes)

7. Joseph V. Francarilla, "Film Review," Cinefantastique Vol. 11, #2 (Fall 1981) p. 47

8. John Fitzpatrick, "Current Scores," Pro Musica Sana #33 (Summer 1981) p. 23

9. Ernest Gold, interview with the author, <u>CinemaScore</u> #10 (Fall 1982) p. 19

10. Les Baxter, interview with the author, January 9, 1982

   To attempt to sum up the preceding 16 chapters is a difficult task. This survey of one specialized area of film music (a specialized and neglected field in itself) has turned out to be far more exhaustive than I envisioned when I first began to research it more than eight years ago. At the same time, I became fascinated with the opportunities and accomplishments of film music in the fantastic genre, and my examination of the use of scoring in these kinds of films has heightened my appreciation for film music in general by a great degree.

   We have seen that there are a certain amount of givens in fantastic film music--such as loud, crashing music for horror scenes; weird, spacey music for outer space; airy, wondrous melodies for fantasies; and so forth. Obviously a certain type of story, locale or dramatic situation requires a certain kind of music, and this of course holds true for other types of film as well. The unique thing, in any genre, is what a composer does with that preconceived musical stereotype, in terms of approach; how he or she uses his or her own creativity and artistic concepts to work within (or sometimes against) the expected requirements suggested by the story.

   There are also various instrumental givens--certain instruments conjure up certain emotions better than others. Slow cello chords, low breaths through the bassoon can generate suspense. Squealing strings and sudden blaring horns provide shock. The contrast between high and low musical scales is also essential in the orchestration of a horror or science fiction score; high tones contrasted against normal tones, low against normal, or high against low result in dramatic counterpoint and vividly involving music. Acceleration and deceleration of tempo is another efficient contrast. And of course unusual sounds have also been of particular value in the genre of the unusual.

   We have seen the contrast between musical approaches in fantastic films, which can basically be broken into two extremes: the romantic tradition (characterized by a dominance of melody, harmony and leitmotif) and the more modern musical approach (characterized as being more dissonant and less harmonically lyrical), and we have witnessed the complementary value of both ap-

354

proaches. (These, of course, are not the only musical traditions, but they do seem to demonstrate the most obvious extremes within genre film music. Various mixtures of the two also occur.) We have seen the effectiveness of scoring both for or against specific visuals. We have seen the distinctive approaches taken by films of various countries and how they sometimes differ.

We have studied the unexpected complexity of motion-picture music and realized how much there is under the surface. The symbolic role of music with its leitmotifs and arrangements, and how they relate to the various characters, motivations, and emotions behind the story, is something that goes generally unnoticed by the filmgoing public, felt perhaps only subliminally. It is amazing to discover that in much film music there is so much beyond the simple melody and tempo--how a motif quoted in one passage can alter the whole emotion of a scene, and how a different orchestration of a certain theme can bring a whole new meaning to a relationship as it changes on screen; how various themes relating to various players can interact musically as the characters do. This complexity, of course, is by no means restricted to the fantastic genre, but is intrinsic to film music in general.

We have seen, however, how the fantastic genre has afforded the opportunity for unique and experimental scoring techniques due to the musical freedom given the composer in such films. The music can often be as way-out as the composer wants, because the story itself is usually way-out, and the score needn't always restrain itself to sounding domestic, historical or otherwise rooted in a mundane existence.

Finally, we have seen the simple fact that there has been a lot of fine music composed for films of a fantastic nature. Much of this music has become equally effective on its own when separated from the film, on records or in the concert hall. While many sophisticates look down on the science fiction and fantasy genre as juvenile escapism, comic-book nonsense, or unredeeming garbage (and, let's face it, much of it is--but, then, only a small portion of anything, quantitatively, is really of significant value) they forget one important fact: probably the most significant attraction for many people to the fantastic genre is that here is the great realm of the imagination. In the science fiction, fantasy and horror genre we are free to imagine other worlds, other beings, different histories, amazing and fantastic concepts, and the great "What If's...." The exercise of the imagination, without losing touch with what is real, is always a positive attribute.

This unrestrained imagination seems to have carried over into the music written for these kinds of films. From KING KONG to STAR WARS and beyond, fantasy, horror and science fiction films have inspired a great deal of important, successful, and highly memorable music, as if the imaginative concepts of the genre have

been an influence upon particularly expressive film music. At the
same time the role of this music has been of particular importance
due to the fantastic nature of the genre. In my exploration into
the development, techniques and practice of music in fantastic
films, I have gained an increased insight into the value of music
as an element of film, and have learned much that will add to my
further enjoyment of these films and their music. I hope this survey has likewise served to heighten the reader's awareness of,
and appreciation for, the value and use of music within fantastic
films and, by extension, film music in general.

LANDMARKS

A Selected Chronology

Year	Film	Composer(s)
1931	Frankenstein	Bernhard Kaun
1932	The Mummy	James Dietrich
1932	The Testament of Dr. Mabuse	Hans Erdmann
1933	King Kong	Max Steiner
1934	The Black Cat	Heinz Roemheld (classical)
1935	The Bride of Frankenstein	Franz Waxman
1935	The Werewolf of London	Karl Hajos
1935	The Raven	Clifford Vaughan
1936	Things to Come	Sir Arthur Bliss
1937	Lost Horizon	Dimitri Tiomkin
1939	Son of Frankenstein	Frank Skinner, Hans J. Salter, Charles Previn
1939	The Hunchback of Notre Dame	Alfred Newman
1940	The Thief of Bagdad	Miklos Rozsa
1941	The Wolf Man	Frank Skinner, Hans J. Salter
1942	Cat People	Roy Webb
1942	The Undying Monster	David Raksin, Cyril Mockridge, and Arthur Lange
1942	The Ghost of Frankenstein	Hans J. Salter
1943	The Phantom of the Opera	Edward Ward
1945	The Picture of Dorian Gray	Herbert Stothart
1945	Spellbound	Miklos Rozsa
1946	Beauty and the Beast	Georges Auric
1948	Portrait of Jennie	Dimitri Tiomkin, Bernard Herrmann
1949	Mighty Joe Young	Roy Webb
1950	Destination Moon	Leith Stevens
1950	Rocketship X-M	Ferde Grofé
1951	The Day the Earth Stood Still	Bernard Herrmann
1951	The Thing (From Another World)	Dimitri Tiomkin
1951	When Worlds Collide	Leith Stevens
1951	The Lost Continent	Paul Dunlap
1953	Invaders from Mars	Raoul Kraushaar, Mort Glickman
1953	War of the Worlds	Leith Stevens
1953	It Came from Outer Space	Herman Stein, Irving Gertz, Henry Mancini
1954	Godzilla	Akira Ifukube
1954	The Creature from the Black Lagoon	Herman Stein, Hans J. Salter, Henry Mancini
1954	Them!	Bronislau Kaper
1955	The Night of the Hunter	Walter Schumann

Year	Film	Composer(s)
1956	Forbidden Planet	Louis & Bebe Barron
1956	Curse of the Demon	Clifton Parker
1957	The Amazing Colossal Man	Albert Glasser
1957	The Monolith Monsters	Irving Gertz
1958	The Return of Dracula	Gerald Fried
1958	The Colossus of New York	Nathan Van Cleave, Fred Steiner
1958	The Fly	Paul Sawtell, Bert A. Shefter
1958	Vertigo	Bernard Herrmann
1958	The 7th Voyage of Sinbad	Bernard Herrmann
1958	Horror of Dracula	James Bernard
1959	Journey to the Center of the Earth	Bernard Herrmann
1959-64	The Twilight Zone (TV)	various
1959	The Mummy	Franz Reizenstein
1960	The Time Machine	Russell Garcia
1960	Gorgo	Angelo Francesco Lavagnino
1960	The Curse of the Werewolf	Benjamin Frankel
1960	Psycho	Bernard Herrmann
1960	The Fall of the House of Usher	Les Baxter
1961	Mysterious Island	Bernard Herrmann
1961	The Pit and the Pendulum	Les Baxter
1961	The Innocents	Georges Auric
1963	The Haunted Palace	Ronald Stein
1964	The 7 Faces of Dr. Lao	Leigh Harline
1964	Jason and the Argonauts	Bernard Herrmann
1964	Goldfinger	John Barry
1966	Fantastic Voyage	Leonard Rosenman
1966	Destination Inner Space	Paul Dunlap
1966-71	Dark Shadows (TV)	Robert Cobert
1966-69	Star Trek (TV)	various
1966	One Million Years B.C.	Mario Nascimbene
1968	Planet of the Apes	Jerry Goldsmith
1971	Silent Running	Peter Schickele
1971	The Andromeda Strain	Gil Melle
1971	What's the Matter with Helen?	David Raksin
1971	The Hellstrom Chronicle	Lalo Schifrin
1971	Dr. Jekyll and Sister Hyde	David Whitaker
1972	Asylum	Douglas Gamley
1972	The Other	Jerry Goldsmith
1975	Jaws	John Williams
1976	The Haunting of Julia [Full Circle]	Colin Towns
1976	Carrie	Pino Donaggio
1976	The Omen	Jerry Goldsmith
1977	Starship Invasions	Gil Melle
1977	Orca, the Killer Whale	Ennio Morricone
1977	Star Wars	John Williams
1977	Close Encounters of the Third Kind	John Williams
1978	Halloween	John Carpenter
1978	Superman	John Williams
1979	Star Trek: The Motion Picture	Jerry Goldsmith
1979	Time After Time	Miklos Rozsa

Year	Film	Composer(s)
1979	When a Stranger Calls	Dana Kaproff
1979	The Amityville Horror	Lalo Schifrin
1980	The Final Countdown	John Scott
1980	Friday the 13th	Harry Manfredini
1981	Clash of the Titans	Laurence Rosenthal
1981	Dragonslayer	Alex North
1981	The Final Conflict	Jerry Goldsmith
1981	Wolfen	James Horner
1981	Altered States	John Corigliano
1981	Heavy Metal	Elmer Bernstein
1981	Ghost Story	Philippe Sarde
1982	Conan the Barbarian	Basil Poledouris
1982	Poltergeist	Jerry Goldsmith
1982	The Dark Crystal	Trevor Jones
1982	Quest for Fire	Philippe Sarde
1982	The Beast Within	Les Baxter
1982	Tron	Wendy Carlos
1982	Creepshow	John Harrison
1982	E.T. The Extra-Terrestrial	John Williams
1982	The Road Warrior [Mad Max II]	Brian May
1983	Blue Thunder	Arthur B. Rubinstein
1983	Twilight Zone: The Movie	Jerry Goldsmith
1983	Brainstorm	James Horner
1983	WarGames	Arthur B. Rubinstein
1983	Metalstorm	Richard H. Band
1984	Gremlins	Jerry Goldsmith
1984	Ghostbusters	Elmer Bernstein

Many of the films included in this listing may be considered only marginally fantastic, or merely containing a number of fantastic sequences within the boundaries of a basically mainstream picture. In an attempt to be as complete as possible I have included these borderline films as well, roughly following the example of Walt Lee and Donald C. Willis in determining the criteria for inclusion of films within the genre. Acknowledgement is hereby given to Lee's Reference Guide to Fantastic Films[1] and Willis' Horror and Science Fiction Films[2] for launching my initial research with their invaluable credit listings. (For further details on many of the films listed herein, I would eagerly refer the reader to either of these important reference guides.)

The year date which follows in parentheses each film title (and I have eliminated the 19's from the dates to save space) are those in which the film was released in the United States--not the date in which the film may have been made or released in foreign countries, unless there was no U.S. release. All titles are the American release titles (alternate titles appear in parentheses) unless only the foreign title was available, in which case translations follow, where known. Movies made for television are indicated as "tvm"; television series are noted simply as "tv." "Cart." denotes cartoon or animated short. "Aka" denotes also-known-as (alternate title). The abbreviation "md" following a composer's name or film title indicates that the individual acted only as music director or music supervisor on the title in question, not composer. The actual composer is given, where known. Many films were scored with prerecorded library tracks, or stock music, originally composed for earlier films; where known, these scores are noted as "track," and usually contain works of several composers. For composers working predominantly in a country other than the United States, I have listed the country abbreviation in parentheses following their name. Most musicals or song scores have been omitted.

An asterisk in the left margin opposite a composer's name denotes one who, in my opinion, has made a significant contribution to fantastic film music, as elaborated in the text.

All entries are as complete and accurate as possible, after

cross-checking many sources including credit listings, filmographies, screen credits, ASCAP cue sheets, composer's personal records, and the research of a number of film music scholars. This filmography also includes much uncredited work not noted in many previous composer filmographies, and I am grateful for the assistance of Clifford McCarty, William H. Rosar, Douglass Fake, Herman Stein, Jim Doherty, Greg Shoemaker, Fred Patten, Ronald Stein, Preston Neal Jones, Fred Steiner, and others in compiling these elusive listings.

Notes

1. Walt Lee, <u>Reference Guide to Fantastic Films</u>, Vols. 1-3 (Los Angeles: Chelsea-Lee Books, 1972-74)

2. Donald C. Willis, <u>Horror and Science Fiction Films</u> (Metuchen, N.J.: Scarecrow Press, 1972) and <u>Horror and Science Fiction Films II</u> (Metuchen, N.J.: Scarecrow Press, 1982)

<u>Temple Abady</u> (Br.): MIRANDA (48); THE HORSE'S MOUTH (53; aka THE ORACLE)

<u>Jeffrey Abrams</u>: NIGHTBEAST (82; w/R. Walsh, A. Ober, L. Rogowski)

<u>Anton Garcia Abril</u> (Sp.): UN VAMPIRO PARA DOS (65; A Vampire for Two); ISLAND OF THE DOOMED (66); MISSION STARDUST (68); LAS SIETE VIDAS DEL GATO (70; The Cat's Seven Lives); THE WEREWOLF VS. THE VAMPIRE WOMAN (72); TOMBS OF THE BLIND DEAD (73); DEL TERROR CIEGO (73); DOCTOR JEKYLL AND THE WOLFMAN (74); EL BUGUE MALDITO (74; The Ghost Galleon); THE LORELEI'S GRASP (75; aka WHEN THE SCREAMING STOPS, 80); HORROR OF THE ZOMBIES (76); NIGHT OF THE SEAGULLS (77)

<u>George Acanthus</u> (Fr.): LE FRISSON DES VAMPIRES (70; Vampire Thrills)

<u>Bojan Adamic</u> (Yug.): FANTASTICNA BALADA (58; Fantastic Ballad); HAPPY END (58; cart.); PLES NA KISI (61; Dance in the Rain)

<u>Richard Addinsell</u> (Br.): BLITHE SPIRIT (45); HIGHLY DANGEROUS (50)

<u>John Addison</u> (Br., in US since late 70's): SEVEN DAYS TO NOON (50); HAMLET (70; tv); THE POWER WITHIN (79; tvm); STRANGE INVADERS (83)

<u>A. Agullo</u> (Sp.): MONSTER ISLAND (80)

<u>Yasushi Akutagawa</u> (Ja.): VILLAGE OF THE EIGHT GRAVESTONES (77)

<u>Charles Albertine</u>: FANTASY ISLAND (78, tv; episodes)

<u>Alessandro Alessandroni</u> (It.): LADY FRANKENSTEIN (71); LA PLUS LONGUE NUIT DU DIABLE (71; The Devil's Nightmare)

Alex Alexander (real name Alexander Borisoff): TWO LOST
    WORLDS (50)
Jeff Alexander: ALFRED HITCHCOCK PRESENTS/THE ALFRED
    HITCHCOCK HOUR (55-65, tv; episodes); THE TWILIGHT
    ZONE (60, tv; episodes: The Trouble with Templeton; Come
    Wander with Me); THE WILD WILD WEST REVISITED (79, tvm;
    title theme by R. Markowitz); MORE WILD WILD WEST (80,
    tvm; title theme by R. Markowitz)
Van Alexander: STRAITJACKET (63); I SAW WHAT YOU DID (65);
    TARZAN AND THE VALLEY OF GOLD (66)
Augusto Alguero (Sp.): UNA SENORA LLAMADA ANDRES (70; A
    Lady Called Andrew)
Allen D. Allen: THE SPECTRE OF EDGAR ALLAN POE (72); THE
    CLONES (72)
Billy Allen: THE DEVIL'S MISTRESS (66; w/D. Warren); SHE
    FREAK (66)
Cameron Allen: SUMMER OF SECRETS (76)
Marty Allen: DOCTOR JEKYLL'S DUNGEON OF DEATH (82)
Woody Allen: SLEEPER (74; w/Preservation Hall Jazz Band)
Byron Allred: DON'T ANSWER THE PHONE! (80)
Laurindo Almeida: THE TWILIGHT ZONE (62, tv; episode: The
    Gift); DEATH TAKES A HOLIDAY (71, tvm)
Aminidav Aloni: ONCE (73); UFO TARGET EARTH (74, tvm);
    LOST CITY OF ATLANTIS (78, tvm)
William Alwyn (Br.): THE ROCKINGHORSE WINNER (49); I'LL
    NEVER FORGET YOU (51); THE CRIMSON PIRATE (52); SVEN-
    GALI (54); THE SHIP THAT DIED OF SHAME (55); BURN,
    WITCH, BURN! (61; w/M. Mathieson)
Charles Alzner (Austria): THE FOUNTAIN OF LOVE (69)
Daniele Amfitheatrof: LOST ANGEL (43); SONG OF THE SOUTH
    (46); THE LOST MOMENT (47); BIRD OF PARADISE (51);
    ANGELS IN THE OUTFIELD (51); THE NAKED JUNGLE (54);
    DAY OF TRIUMPH (54). Amfitheatrof's Universal music library
    cues were also re-used in ABBOTT & COSTELLO MEET DR.
    JEKYLL AND MR. HYDE (53), and others.
Gilbert Amy (Fr.): L'ALLIANCE (71; aka THE WEDDING RING)
K. Anandji (India): HARI DARSHAN (72); DARINDA (77)
Michael Anderson: TWELVE TO THE MOON (60); TERRIFIED (62);
    TOWER OF LONDON (62)
Jorge Andreani (Chile): LE DAMA DE LA MUERTE (46; The Lady
    and Death)
George Antheil: REPEAT PERFORMANCE (47); DEMENTIA (53;
    aka DAUGHTER OF HORROR)
Nozumu Aoki (Ja.): GALAXY EXPRESS (80); TOWARD MAGIC
    ISLAND (82); HARMAGEDDON (83; aka EVIL PHANTOM CON-
    FLICT; songs by Keith Emerson)
Hachiro Aoyama (Ja.): BULLET TRAIN BLAST (75)
Louis Applebaum (Can.): THE MASK (61)
Jack Arel (Fr.): LA GRAND CEREMONIAL (68); LE SEVIL DU
    VIDE (71)
Tito Arevalo (Phil.): THE BLOOD DRINKERS (66; md); MAD

DOCTOR OF BLOOD ISLAND (69); DUGO NO VAMPIRA (70;
Blood of the Vampire; lyrics by Robert Arevalo); BEAST OF
BLOOD (70); CURSE OF THE VAMPIRES (70); TWILIGHT PEO-
PLE (71; w/A. Avelino)

Alberto Argudo (Sp.):   EXORCISMO (74)

Rudolfo Arizaga (Arg.):   EL DEMONIO EN LA SANGRE (64; The
Demon in the Blood)

Eduardo Armani (Arg.):   DRINGUE, CASTRITO Y LA LAMPARA DE
ALADINO (54; aka ALADDIN TAKES OFF)

Harry Arnold (Swed.):   48 HOURS TO LIVE (59); INVASION OF
THE ANIMAL PEOPLE (60; w/A. Johannson)

Malcolm Arnold (Br.):   FOUR-SIDED TRIANGLE (53); THE NIGHT
MY NUMBER CAME UP (55); 1984 (55); SUDDENLY LAST SUM-
MER (59; w/B. Orr)

Angel Arteaga (Sp.):   LA CELESTINA (69); EL DIABLO COJUELO
(70; The Lame Devil); FRANKENSTEIN'S BLOODY TERROR
(71); THE HORRIBLE SEXY VAMPIRE (76)

Eduard Artemyer (USSR):   SOLARIS (76); STALKER (79)

Kenny Ascher: MEET MR. KRINGLE (56, tv; aka MIRACLE ON
34TH STREET); THE MUPPET MOVIE (79; w/P. Williams)

Edwin Astley (Br.; aka Edward Astley; aka Ted Astley):   THE
DEVIL GIRL FROM MARS (54); ALIAS JOHN PRESTON (55;
w/A. Elms); JACK THE RIPPER (58; compilation from episodes
of tv series, THE VEIL); THE WOMAN EATER (59); THE GIANT
BEHEMOTH (59; as Ted Astley); THE PHANTOM OF THE OPERA
(62); THE CHAMPIONS (67; Br. tv); KADOYNG (72); DIGBY,
THE BIGGEST DOG IN THE WORLD (74)

Patrick Aulton: STAR MAIDENS (77, tv; theme)

*Georges Auric (Fr.):   THE BLOOD OF A POET (30); L'ETERNEL
RETOUR (43; The Eternal Return); DEAD OF NIGHT (45);
BEAUTY AND THE BEAST (46); THE CHIPS ARE DOWN (47);
CORRIDOR OF MIRRORS (48); PASSPORT TO PIMLICO (49);
THE QUEEN OF SPADES (49); ORPHEUS (49); THE BESPOKE
OVERCOAT (55, short); THE HUNCHBACK OF NOTRE DAME
(56); THE CRUCIBLE (57); TESTAMENT OF ORPHEUS (60);
THE BURNING COURT (61); THE INNOCENTS (61); THE MIND
BENDERS (63)

Ariston Avelino (Phil.):   THE TWILIGHT PEOPLE (72; w/T. Arevalo)

Pepe Avila (Mx.):   FANDO AND LYS (68; aka TAR BABIES)

William Axt: GABRIEL OVER THE WHITE HOUSE (33)

Joe Azarello, et al.:   THE HOLLYWOOD MEATCLEAVER MASSACRE
(77)

Luis Enriquez Bacalov (It.):   PER AMORE ... PER MAGICA (66;
For Love ... For Magic); A WITCH IN LOVE (66); QUESTI
FANTASMI (67; aka GHOSTS ITALIAN STYLE)

Burt Bacharach: THE BLOB (58; title song only; lyrics by Hal
David); CASINO ROYALE (67); LOST HORIZON (72)

Tom Bahler: MARY, MARY, BLOODY MARY (75)

Constantin Bakaleinikoff: Music Director for RKO during 40's; conducted many scores by Paul Sawtell and Roy Webb, others; plus

Constantin Bakaleinikoff (cont.)
  many tracked re-use scores including MEXICAN SPITFIRE SEES
  A GHOST (42), THE FALCON AND THE COEDS (49), others.
Mischa Bakaleinikoff: Music director for Columbia during 40's and
  50's, also composed cues for some films. Credit listings un-
  clear. THE BRIDE OF FRANKENSTEIN (35, md; music F. Wax-
  man); THE SOUL OF A MONSTER (44); CRY OF THE WERE-
  WOLF (44); THE UNKNOWN (46, md; music A. Steinert plus
  track); THE DEVIL'S MASK (46, md; music G. Duning, I.
  Gertz, plus track); MYSTERIOUS INTRUDER (46, md; music
  G. Duning plus track); CRIME DOCTOR'S MANHUNT (46, md);
  THE THIRTEENTH HOUR (47, md; music A. Morton plus track);
  BRICK BRADFORD (47, serial); BRUCE GENTRY (48, serial);
  SUPERMAN (48, serial); THE LOST TRIBE (49); THE ADVEN-
  TURES OF SIR GALAHAD (49, serial); BATMAN AND ROBIN
  (49, serial); PYGMY ISLAND (50, md); MYSTERIOUS ISLAND
  (50, serial); MARK OF THE GORILLA (50, md); FURY OF THE
  CONGO (51); HURRICANE ISLAND (51); THE MAGIC CARPET
  (51); JUNGLE JIM IN THE FORBIDDEN LAND (51); JUNGLE
  MANHUNT (51); CAPTAIN VIDEO (51, serial); BLACKHAWK
  (52, serial); KING OF THE CONGO (52, serial); GOLDTOWN
  GHOST RAIDERS (53); SIREN OF BAGDAD (53); KILLER APE
  (53); THE LOST PLANET (53, serial); JUNGLE MOON MEN (53);
  THE ADVENTURES OF CAPTAIN AFRICA (55, serial); IT CAME
  FROM BENEATH THE SEA (55); CREATURE WITH THE ATOM
  BRAIN (55); EARTH VS. THE FLYING SAUCERS (56); THE
  WEREWOLF (56); ZOMBIES OF MORA TAU (57); TWENTY MIL-
  LION MILES TO EARTH (57); THE 27TH DAY (57); THE GIANT
  CLAW (57); HAVE ROCKET, WILL TRAVEL (59)
Yasuno Bakano (Ja.): XABUNGLE GRAFFITI (83)
Buddy Baker: Composer for Walt Disney Studios: SUMMER MAGIC
  (63); THE MISADVENTURES OF MERLIN JONES (64); A TIGER
  WALKS (64); THE MONKEY'S UNCLE (65); THE GNOME MOBILE
  (67); MILLION DOLLAR DUCK (71); THE DEVIL AND MAX DEV-
  LIN (81; songs by M. Hamlisch)
E. Balsia (USSR): ELGE, QUEEN OF SNAKES (65)
*Richard H. Band: LASERBLAST (78; w/Joel Goldsmith); THE DAY
  TIME ENDED (80); DR. HECKLE & MR. HYPE (80); PARASITE
  (82); THE HOUSE ON SORORITY ROW (83); TIME WALKER (83);
  METALSTORM (83); MUTANT (84); SWORDKILL (84); GHOULIES
  (84); THE MOST DANGEROUS MAN ALIVE (84)
A. Banerjee (India): TARZAN AND KING KONG (65); THE MYS-
  TERY OF LIFE (73)
Anthony Bank (Br.): THE SHOUT (78; w/M. Rutherford)
Don Banks (Br.): NIGHT CREATURE (62; aka CAPTAIN CLEGG);
  NIGHTMARE (64); THE EVIL OF FRANKENSTEIN (64); HYSTERIA
  (64); DIE, MONSTER, DIE! (65); RASPUTIN THE MAD MONK
  (66); THE REPTILE (66); THE MUMMY'S SHROUD (67); TOR-
  TURE GARDEN (67; w/J. Bernard); THE FROZEN DEAD (67)
Kresimir Baranovich (Yug.): THE MAGIC SWORD (49)
Pierre Barbaud (Fr.): LES CREATURES (66)

John Barber: THE INCREDIBLE TWO-HEADED TRANSPLANT (70);
  PINOCCHIO (70)
Warren Barker: BEWITCHED (64-72, tv; episodes); THE GHOST
  AND MRS. MUIR (68, tv; episodes)
Gavin Barns: FREAKS (32; md)
*Louis and Bebe Barron: FORBIDDEN PLANET (56); THE VERY
  EDGE OF THE NIGHT (59); SPACEBOY (72)
*John Barry (Br.): DR. NO (63; Barry composed, uncredited,
  the James Bond Theme; score by M. Norman); FROM RUSSIA
  WITH LOVE (63; title theme by L. Bart); GOLDFINGER (64);
  THUNDERBALL (65); YOU ONLY LIVE TWICE (67); ON HER
  MAJESTY'S SECRET SERVICE (69); DIAMONDS ARE FOREVER
  (71); ALICE'S ADVENTURES IN WONDERLAND (72); ORSON
  WELLES' GREAT MYSTERIES (74, tv; theme); THE MAN WITH
  THE GOLDEN GUN (75); KING KONG (76); MOONRAKER (79);
  THE BLACK HOLE (79); STAR CRASH (79); NIGHT GAMES
  (80); SOMEWHERE IN TIME (80); OCTOPUSSY (83); MURDER
  BY PHONE (82; aka BELLS, 80; aka THE CALLING, HELL'S
  BELLS)
Lionel Bart (Br.): FROM RUSSIA WITH LOVE (63; theme only);
  DR. JEKYLL AND MR. HYDE (73, tvm; w/M. Mandel, Norman
  Sachs)
Jose Bartel (Fr.): SPERMULA (76)
Joss Basselli (Fr.): DOUGAL AND THE BLUE CAT (72; aka POL-
  LUX AND THE BLUE CAT)
R. H. Bassett: SHERLOCK HOLMES (32; w/H. Friedhofer)
George Bassman: THE CANTERVILLE GHOST (44)
Dee Barton: PLAY MISTY FOR ME (71); HIGH PLAINS DRIFTER
  (73)
Julian Bautista (Arg.): CUANDO LE PRIMAVERA SE EQUIVOCA
  (44; When Spring Makes a Mistake)
*Les Baxter: THE BLACK SLEEP (56); PHARAOH'S CURSE (56);
  VOODOO ISLAND (57); THE GUMBY SPECIAL (57, tv); THE
  BRIDE AND THE BEAST (58); GOLIATH AND THE BARBARIANS
  (59; U.S. release only); MACABRE (58); THE INVISIBLE BOY
  (59); GOLIATH AND THE DRAGON (60; U.S. release); ALA-
  KAZAM THE GREAT (60; U.S. release); THE FALL OF THE
  HOUSE OF USHER (60); BLACK SUNDAY (61; U.S. release);
  MASTER OF THE WORLD (61); THE PIT AND THE PENDULUM
  (61); SAMSON AND THE 7 MIRACLES OF THE WORLD (61; U.S.
  release); TALES OF TERROR (61); REPTILICUS (61; U.S. release); DAUGHTER OF THE SUN GOD (62); GOLIATH AND THE
  VAMPIRES (62; aka VAMPIRES; title music only for U.S. release); THE EVIL EYE (62); THE RAVEN (62); PANIC IN THE
  YEAR ZERO (62); THE COMEDY OF TERRORS (63); BATTLE
  BEYOND THE SUN (63); X--THE MAN WITH THE X-RAY EYES
  (63); BLACK SABBATH (64; U.S. release); PAJAMA PARTY
  (64); MUSCLE BEACH PARTY (64); SPACE MONSTER (64, tvm);
  SAMSON AND THE SLAVE QUEEN (64; U.S. release uses Baxter's GOLIATH & THE BARBARIANS music); DR. GOLDFOOT
  AND THE BIKINI MACHINE (65); HOW TO STUFF A WILD

Les Baxter (cont.)
> BIKINI (65); SGT. DEADHEAD AND THE ASTRONAUT (65);
> DR. GOLDFOOT AND THE GIRL BOMBS (66); GHOST IN THE
> INVISIBLE BIKINI (66); THE GLASS SPHINX (68; U.S. re-
> lease); TERROR IN THE JUNGLE (67; w/Stan Hoffman); WILD
> IN THE STREETS (68); THE DUNWICH HORROR (69); EL OGRO
> (70; The Ogre); AN EVENING WITH EDGAR ALLAN POE (70,
> tvm); CRY OF THE BANSHEE (70); FROGS (72); BARON
> BLOOD (72; U.S. release); BLOOD SABBATH (72; aka
> YGALAH; unreleased); BUCK ROGERS IN THE 25TH CENTURY
> (79, tv; episodes); CLIFFHANGERS (79, tv; episodes incl.
> "Curse of Dracula" segment); THE BEAST WITHIN (82)

John Beal: THE FUNHOUSE (81)

Yves Beaudrier (Fr.): L'HOMME QUI REVIENT DE LOIN (50)

Bobby Beausoleil: LUCIFER RISING (81)

Jack Beaver (Br.): SUPERSONIC SAUCER (56, cart.); IT HAP-
PENED HERE (66)

Paul Beaver & Bernard Krause: LAST DAYS OF MAN ON EARTH
(74); Beaver also supplied electronic sounds for AROUND THE
WORLD UNDER THE SEA (66).

Giuseppe Becce (It.): DER MUDE TOD (21; Destiny). Becce's
"Grand Appassionato," a silent film cue, was used as the end
title for FRANKENSTEIN (31)

Joe Beck & Regis Mull: GRIMM'S FAIRY TALES FOR ADULTS (69;
U.S. release)

Simon Bell (Br.): LICENSED TO LOVE AND KILL (79)

Wayne Bell: THE TEXAS CHAINSAW MASSACRE (74; w/T. Hooper); EATEN ALIVE (76; aka DEATH TRAP)

Andrew Belling: THE KILLING KIND (73); WIZARDS (77); END
OF THE WORLD (77); CRASH! (77; aka AKAZA, GOD OF
VENGEANCE); DRACULA'S DOG (78); FAIRY TALES (79)

Carmelo Belona (Sp.): CEMETERY GIRLS (79)

Arthur Benjamin (Br.): THE CLAIRVOYANT (35)

Richard Rodney Bennett (Br.): THE MAN WHO COULD CHEAT
DEATH (59); BILLY LIAR (63); ONE WAY PENDULUM (64);
THE DEVIL'S OWN (66; aka THE WITCHES); BILLION DOLLAR
BRAIN (67); VOICES (73); SHERLOCK HOLMES IN NEW YORK
(76; tvm)

Eddie Benson (Br.): TOWER OF TERROR (41)

Friedel Berlipp: STAR MAIDENS (77, tv; episodes)

F. Berman (It.): WEREWOLF IN A GIRL'S DORMITORY (61)

Carmelo Bernaola (Sp.): THE HUNCHBACK OF THE MORGUE
(75); AQUELLA CASA EN LAS AFUERAS (80; The House in the
Outskirts)

*James Bernard (Br.): THE CREEPING UNKNOWN (55; aka THE
QUATERMASS XPERIMENT); ENEMY FROM SPACE (57; aka
QUATERMASS II); THE CURSE OF FRANKENSTEIN (57); THE
DOOR IN THE WALL (57; short); X THE UNKNOWN (57); HOR-
ROR OF DRACULA (58); THE HOUND OF THE BASKERVILLES
(59); THE STRANGLERS OF BOMBAY (60); THE TERROR OF
THE TONGS (61); KISS OF THE VAMPIRE (63); THE GORGON

(64); DRACULA, PRINCE OF DARKNESS (65); THE PLAGUE OF
THE ZOMBIES (65); SHE (65); THESE ARE THE DAMNED (65);
FRANKENSTEIN CREATED WOMAN (67); TORTURE GARDEN
(67; w/D. Banks); DRACULA HAS RISEN FROM THE GRAVE
(68); THE DEVIL'S BRIDE (68); FRANKENSTEIN MUST BE
DESTROYED (70); TASTE THE BLOOD OF DRACULA (70);
SCARS OF DRACULA (70); THE LEGEND OF THE 7 GOLDEN
VAMPIRES (73; aka THE 7 BROTHERS MEET DRACULA, 79);
FRANKENSTEIN AND THE MONSTER FROM HELL (74); THE
HAMMER HOUSE OF HORROR (80, Br. tv; episodes: Witching
Time, The House That Bled to Death, others)

Lord Berners (Br.): HALFWAY HOUSE (44)

Charles Bernstein: HEX (73); INVASION OF THE BEE GIRLS
(73); LOOK WHAT'S HAPPENED TO ROSEMARY'S BABY (76,
tvm; aka ROSEMARY'S BABY II); LOVE AT FIRST BITE (79);
THE ENTITY (82); CUJO (83); DADDY'S DEADY DARLING (84)

*Elmer Bernstein: ROBOT MONSTER (53); CAT WOMEN OF THE
MOON (53); IT'S A DOG'S LIFE (55); THE TEN COMMAND-
MENTS (56); THE INFORMATION MACHINE (57; animated docu.
short); THE MIRACLE (59); A COMPUTER GLOSSARY (67;
docu. short); SEE NO EVIL (71); THE AMAZING MR. BLUNDEN
(74); SATURN 3 (80); AIRPLANE! (80); HEAVY METAL (81);
AN AMERICAN WEREWOLF IN LONDON (81); AIRPLANE II:
THE SEQUEL (82; adapted by R. Hazard from E.B.'s AIR-
PLANE! score); SPACEHUNTER: ADVENTURES IN THE FOR-
BIDDEN ZONE (83); MICHAEL JACKSON'S THRILLER (83; video
short; score only); GHOSTBUSTERS (84)

Peter Bernstein (son of Elmer): HERE COMES THE BRIDE (73;
aka THE HOUSE THAT CRIED MURDER; aka THE BRIDE);
SILENT RAGE (82; w/M. Goldenberg); NATIONAL LAMPOON'S
CLASS REUNION (82; w/M. Goldenberg)

Robert R. Berry, Jr.: THE MILPITAS MONSTER (76)

Peter Best (Austral.): BARRY McKENZIE HOLDS HIS OWN (74)

Louis Beydts (Fr.): LE BARON FANTOME (42; The Phantom
Baron)

Vijaya Bhaskar (India): MAYA MANUSHYA (76)

Vanraj Bhatia (India): KONDURA (nd); NISHANT (76)

H. Bhoshe (India): JADU TONA (77)

John Bickford: THE BEAST WITH A MILLION EYES (55)

Phillian Bishop: THE SEVERED ARM (73); MESSIAH OF EVIL (75;
aka RETURN OF THE LIVING DEAD; aka DEAD PEOPLE)

Franco Bixio (It.): DRACULA IN THE PROVINCES (75; w/others)

B. Fabricius Bjerre (Denmark; aka Bent Fabric): MED KAERLIG
HILSEN (71; Love Me Darling); PINCHCLIFFE GRAND PRIX (81)

Stanley Black (Br.): THE MONKEY'S PAW (48; md); THE FATAL
NIGHT (48); SHADOW OF THE PAST (50); TONIGHT'S THE
NIGHT (54); THE CRAWLING EYE (58; aka THE TROLLENBERG
TERROR); JACK THE RIPPER (60; Br. release only); MANIA
(60; aka THE FIENDISH GHOULS); THE DAY THE EARTH
CAUGHT FIRE (61; md); HOUSE OF MYSTERY (61); MANIAC
(63); WAR GODS OF THE DEEP (65)

Maurice Blackburn (Can.): PRIMAL FEAR (80)

George Blais: SABRINA, TEENAGE WITCH (71; tv cart.)

Yvette Blais [all tv cartoon series]: STAR TREK (73); SHAZAM!
    (74); ISIS (75); TARZAN, LORD OF THE JUNGLE (76); ARK
    II (76); SPACE ACADEMY (77); SUPER WITCH (77); THE
    YOUNG SENTINELS (77); TARZAN AND THE SUPER SEVEN
    (78); JASON OF STAR COMMAND (79); THE TARZAN AND
    LONE RANGER HOUR (80)

Howard Blake: THE AVENGERS (66/69, tv; episodes); THE
    CHANGELING (80; music box theme only); FLASH GORDON (80;
    incidental music only); THE HUNGER (83; md for classical ex-
    cerpts only); AMITYVILLE 3D (83)

Charles R. Blaker: WARLOCK MOON (74)

*Arthur Bliss (Br.): THINGS TO COME (36); THE CONQUEST OF
    THE AIR (37)

Mike Bloomfield: ANDY WARHOL'S BAD (76)

Harry Bluestone: THE KILLER SHREWS (59; w/Emil Cadkin);
    MARA OF THE WILDERNESS (65)

Martin Boettcher (W. Gm.): THE PHANTOM OF SOHO (63); THE
    MONSTER OF LONDON CITY (64)

Claude Bolling (Fr.): THE HANDS OF ORLAC (64); LUCKY LUKE,
    LA BALLADE DES DALTON (78); THE AWAKENING (80)

F. Bongusto (It.): SEX MACHINE (76; aka CONVIENE FAR BENE
    L'AMORE)

Guy Bonnett (Fr.): SEVEN WOMEN FOR SATAN (74; aka LES
    WEEKENDS MALEFIQUES DU COMTE ZAROFF)

Sean Bonniwell: NIGHT OF THE WITCHES (70)

Tang Boom-Kei (H.K.): THE SPOOKY BUNCH (80)

Lawrence Borden: THE PHOENIX (80)

Perry Botkin, Jr.: QUARK (78, tv); MORK & MINDY (79, tv);
    TARZAN THE APE MAN (81)

Guy Boulanger (Fr.): LE GOULVE (71; aka EROTIC WITCH-
    CRAFT; aka GOLEM'S DAUGHTER); AEROPORT: CHARTER
    2020 (80, Fr. tv)

Anthony Bowles (Br.): RED (76)

Jesus Bracho (Mx.): ENSAYO DE UN CRIMEN (55; Practice of a
    Crime; w/J. Perez)

Scott Bradley: Scored TOM AND JERRY cartoon series and other
    animated shorts, all for producer Fred Quimby; many are overtly
    fantasy: DROOPY (43-57, series); MOUSE TROUBLE (44);
    SCREWBALL SQUIRREL (44); HENPECKED HEROES (46); THE
    CAT CONCERTO (47; md); THE CAT THAT HATED PEOPLE
    (47); DR. JEKYLL AND MR. MOUSE (47); THE INVISIBLE
    MOUSE (47); MOUSE CLEANING (48); PROFESSOR TOM (48);
    THE CAT AND THE MERMOUSE (49); HATCH UP YOUR TROU-
    BLES (49); LITTLE RURAL RIDING HOOD (49); THE YELLOW
    CAB MAN (49, feature)

Philippe Brejean (Fr.): LA NUIT DES TRAQUEES (80; Night of
    Beatings)

Luis Hernandez Breton (Mx.): EL (52; aka THIS STRANGE PAS-
    SION); FACE OF THE SCREAMING WEREWOLF (59); EL VAM-

PIRO SANGRIENTO (63; The Bloody Vampire); LA INVASION
DE LOS VAMPIROS (63; Invasion of the Vampires); DR. SATAN
(67); LA TIA ALEJANDRA (80)
Willem Breuker (Holl): DOODZONDE (79)
Leslie Bricusse (Br.): DR. DOLITTLE (67); WILLY WONKA & THE
CHOCOLATE FACTORY (71; lyrics only)
Britz (Phil.): MEN OF ACTION MEET WOMEN OF DRACULA (69)
J. K. Broady (It.): ASSIGNMENT OUTER SPACE (60)
David Broekman (Musical Director): PHANTOM OF THE OPERA
(25; 1930 "talky" rerelease); FRANKENSTEIN (31; md; music:
B. Kaun); THE OLD DARK HOUSE (32; Main Title only); CON-
DEMNED TO LIVE (35)
Bruce Broughton: BUCK ROGERS (80, tv; episodes: The Satyr,
others); ICE PIRATES (84)
Leo Brouwer (Cuba): UNA PELEA CUBANA CONTRA LOS DEMON-
IOS (72; The Fighting Cuban Against the Demons)
Earl Brown, Jr.: AMERICATHON (79)
Sandro Brugnolini (It.): FANTABULOUS, INC. (67)
Andre S. Brummer: MONSTER FROM THE OCEAN FLOOR (54);
LOVE SLAVES OF THE AMAZON (57; w/H. Stein, S. Wilson,
I. Gertz, et al.)
Jeff Bruner: FOES (77)
Robert Brunner: BLACKBEARD'S GHOST (67); NOW YOU SEE
HIM, NOW YOU DON'T (71); THE STRONGEST MAN IN THE
WORLD (75)
George Bruns: CHRISTOPHER CRUMPET (53, cart.); FUDGET'S
BUDGET (54, cart.); HOW NOW BOING BOING (54, cart.);
EYES IN OUTER SPACE (59, short); ONE HUNDRED AND ONE
DALMATIANS (60); THE ABSENT-MINDED PROFESSOR (61);
BABES IN TOYLAND (61, md; music: V. Herbert); SON OF
FLUBBER (63); THE SWORD IN THE STONE (63); THE MAN
FROM BUTTON WILLOW (65; w/Dale Robertson, Mel Hank); THE
LOVE BUG (68); HERBIE RIDES AGAIN (74)
Aleksanda Bubanovic (Yug.): COWBOY JIM (57; cart.); OSVET-
NIC (58; cart.); TACNO U PONOC (60; Low Midnight; cart.)
Marc Bucci: HUMAN EXPERIMENTS (80)
V. Buchino (Arg.): THE CURIOUS DR. HUMPP (70)
Paul Buckmaster (Br.): MACBETH (71)
Roy Budd (Br.): WELCOME TO BLOOD CITY (77); SINBAD AND
THE EYE OF THE TIGER (77); THE MISSING LINK (80; Fr.);
MAMMA DRACULA (80)
Jose Buenago (Sp.): THE FACE OF TERROR (62)
William Bukovy (Cz.): DO YOU KEEP A LION AT HOME (63); THE
WISHING MACHINE (67)
Chico Buarque: DONA FLOR AND HER 2 HUSBANDS (78)
Geoffrey Burgon (Br.): DR. WHO (78, tv; episodes)
E. F. Burian (Cz.): JOURNEY TO THE BEGINNING OF TIME (67)
Sonny Burke: THE HAND OF DEATH (61)
Val Burton: STRANGER OF THE EVENING (32; aka tv: THE
HIDDEN CORPSE; md); THE INTRUDER (32); TOMBSTONE
CANYON (32; md); A STUDY IN SCARLET (33; md); THE

Val Burton (cont.)
    DELUGE (33; w/E. Kilenyi)
Nicholas Busch (W. Gm.): THE PHANTASMIC WORLD OF MATTHEW
    MADSON (74; w/A. Moore)
Artie Butler: WONDER WOMAN (74, tvm)
David Buttolph: THE GORILLA (39, md); SHOCK (45); THE
    BEAST FROM 20,000 FATHOMS (53); HOUSE OF WAX (53);
    PHANTOM OF THE RUE MORGUE (53)
R. Dale Butts: THE CATMAN OF PARIS (46); CITY THAT NEVER
    SLEEPS (53); PANTHER GIRL OF THE KONGO (55, serial);
    CAROLINA CANNONBALL (54); ALFRED HITCHCOCK PRESENTS
    (55+, tv)
Billy Byers: HAUSER'S MEMORY (70, tvm); MOONCHILD (72; w/
    P. Williams); THE BORROWERS (73, tvm)
Enrico Cabiati (Mx.; aka Henry Caviatti): NEUTRON AGAINST
    THE DEATH ROBOTS (61); NEUTRON & THE BLACK MASK (61);
    THE SNAKE PEOPLE (68; w/A. Uretta); THE INCREDIBLE IN-
    VASION (71; w/A. Uretta)
John Cacavas: HORROR EXPRESS (74); THE SATANIC RITES OF
    DRACULA (74; aka COUNT DRACULA AND HIS VAMPIRE
    BRIDES; aka DRACULA IS DEAD AND WELL AND LIVING IN
    LONDON); THE ABC WEEKEND SPECIAL (77-78; tv; episodes,
    some fantasy); HUMAN FEELINGS (78, tvm); THE TIME MA-
    CHINE (78, tvm); BUCK ROGERS IN THE 25TH CENTURY (79,
    tv; episode: A Dream of Jennifer); ONCE UPON A SPY (80,
    tvm); HANGAR 18 (80; aka tv: INVASION FORCE); MORTU-
    ARY (83)
J. G. Caffi (Sp.): NAZARENO CRUZ Y EL LOBO (74); WHERE
    TIME BEGAN (78; aka FABULOUS JOURNEY TO THE CENTER
    OF THE EARTH)
Steven Cagan: THE CAT AND THE CANARY (79)
Sammy Cahn: JOURNEY BACK TO OZ (71, tv; w/J. Van Heusen)
Christopher Cain: THE FORCE ON THUNDER MOUNTAIN (78, tvm)
James Cairncross (Br.): RING OF TERROR (62)
Darrell Calker: WOODY WOODPECKER (40+, cartoon series); JUKE
    BOX JAMBOREE (42; cart.); THE PIED PIPER OF BASIN
    STREET (44; cart.); POET AND PEASANT (45; cart.); SIG-
    HORN OF POLAROO (45; cart.; md); FORBIDDEN JUNGLE (50);
    THE FLYING SAUCER (50); SUPERMAN AND THE MOLE-MEN
    (51); VOODOO WOMAN (56); FROM HELL IT CAME (57); TER-
    ROR IN THE HAUNTED HOUSE (58); THE AMAZING TRANS-
    PARENT MAN (60); BEYOND THE TIME BARRIER (60)
Gerard Calvi (Fr.): BLUEBEARD (51); ASTERIX THE GAUL (67);
    ASTERIX AND CLEOPATRA (68); THE TWELVE TASKS OF AS-
    TERIX (76; w/Nicolas)
Claudio Calzolari (It.): IL TUNNEL SO HO IL MONDO (68; The
    Tunnel Under the World)
John Cameron (Br.): EVERY HOME SHOULD HAVE ONE (70);
    THE STRANGE VENGEANCE OF ROSALIE (72); PSYCHOMANIA
    (72); THE RULING CLASS (72); NIGHT WATCH (73); WHO?
    (74); THE MAN FROM NOWHERE (76); SPECTRE (77, tvm);

THIEF OF BAGDAD (79, tvm); THE BERMUDA TRIANGLE (78)
Bruno Camfora (It.): THE MAN WHO WAGGED HIS TAIL (57)
Carlo Camilleri and Malcolm Shelby (It./Br.): THE CASTLE OF
   FU MANCHU (68)
Tony Camillo: WELCOME TO ARROW BEACH (74; aka TENDER
   FLESH)
Dimitru Capoianu (Rum.): A SHORT HISTORY (56, cart.); HOMO
   SAPIENS (59, cart.); A BOMB WAS STOLEN (62); PASI SPRE
   LUNA (63); HARAP ALB (64; The White Moor); THE LEGEND
   OF THE SKYLARK (67; ballet short); COMEDIE FANTASTICA
   (75)
Al Capps: SASQUATCH, THE LEGEND OF BIGFOOT (76, tv)
Gerard Carbonara: DR. CYCLOPS (39; w/E. Toch, A. H. Ma-
   lotte); THE MONSTER AND THE GIRL (41, uncredited); HENRY
   ALDRICH HAUNTS A HOUSE (43)
Foster Carling & Earl E. Lawrence: THE INCREDIBLE SHRINKING
   MAN (57; main theme, "The Girl in a Lonely Room," only).
   Theme later reused in MONSTER ON THE CAMPUS, incl. Main
   Title; 58)
Michael Carlos (Austral.): LONG WEEKEND (78)
*Wendy Carlos (formerly Walter Carlos): A CLOCKWORK ORANGE
   (71); THE SHINING (80); TRON (82)
Ralph Carmichael: THE BLOB (58; theme song by B. Bacharach);
   THE 4-D MAN (59); MY MOTHER, THE CAR (65, tv; episodes)
*John Carpenter: DARK STAR (74); ASSAULT ON PRECINCT 13
   (76); HALLOWEEN (78); THE FOG (80); ESCAPE FROM NEW
   YORK (81); HALLOWEEN II (81); HALLOWEEN III: SEASON
   OF THE WITCH (82); CHRISTINE (83). Carpenter also directed.
Pete Carpenter and Mike Post: DR. SCORPION (78, tvm); CAP-
   TAIN AMERICA (79, tvm)
Fiorenzo Carpi (It.): LES AVVENTURES DI PINOCCHIO (75)
Nicolas Carras: FRANKENSTEIN'S DAUGHTER (58); MISSILE TO
   THE MOON (58); SHE DEMONS (58); THE ASTRO-ZOMBIES (69,
   as "Nico Karaski")
*Gustavo Cesar Carrion (Mx.): EL MONSTRUO DE LA SOMBRA
   (56; The Monster of the Shadow); EL ATAUD DEL VAMPIRO
   (57; The Vampire's Coffin); THE CASTLE OF THE MONSTERS
   (75); EL VAMPIRO (58); EL HOMBRE Y EL MONSTRUO (59;
   The Man and the Monster); THE LIVING HAND (59); LOS AS-
   TRONAUTAS (60; The Astronauts); EL MUNDO DE LOS VAM-
   PIROS (60; The World of the Vampires); THE BRAINIAC (60;
   aka EL BARON DEL TERROR); CURSE OF THE CRYING WOMAN
   (61); LA MARCA DEL MUERTO (61; The Mark of Death); THE
   WITCH'S MIRROR (61); FRANKENSTEIN, EL VAMPIRO Y CIA
   (62; Frankenstein, The Vampire, and Co.); CREATURE OF THE
   WALKING DEAD (65); PACTO DIABOLICO (68; Diabolic Pact);
   LOS VAMPIRAS (68; The Vampires); SANTO CONTRA BLUE
   DEMON EN LA ATLANTIS (68; Santo vs the Blue Demon in
   Atlantis); LE VENGANZA DE LAS MUJERES VAMPIRO (69, The
   Vengeance of the Vampire Woman); SANTO Y BLUE DEMON
   CONTRA LOS MONSTRUOS (69; Santo and Blue Demon vs.

*Gustavo Cesar Carrion (cont.)
  the Monsters); LOS CANNALES (69; The Scoundrels); SUICIDE
  MISSION (71); SANTO VS LA HIJADE DE FRANKENSTEIN (72;
  Santo and the Daughter of Frankenstein); SANTO CONTRA LA
  MAGIA NEGRE (72; Santo vs. the Black Magic); SANTO Y
  BLUE DEMON CONTRA DRACULA Y EL HOMBRE LOBO (72;
  Santo and Blue Demon vs. Dracula and the Wolf Man); SUPER-
  ZAN Y EL NINO DEL ESPACIO (72; Superzan and the Space
  Boy); VUELVEN LOS CAMPEONES JUSTICIEROS (72; The
  Champions of Justice Return)
Rafael Carrion (Mx.): CIEN GRITOS DE TERROR (64; One Hun-
  dred Cries of Terror); EL ROBO DE LAS MOMIAS DE GUN-
  JUATO (72; The Theft of the Mummies of Gunjuato)
Benny Carter: NIGHT GALLERY (71, tv; episodes: The Last
  Laurel, A Feast of Blood, They're Tearing Down Tim Riley's
  Bar)
Everett Carter: FRANCIS COVERS THE BIG TOWN (52; w/H.
  Stein, E. Fairchild, and library tracks); REVENGE OF THE
  CREATURE (55; cues, w/M. Rosen, used in addition to H.
  Stein title music and library tracks)
Tristram Cary (Br.): FIVE MILLION YEARS TO EARTH (67; aka
  QUATERMASS AND THE PIT); BLOOD FROM THE MUMMY'S
  TOMB (72)
Charles R. Casey: THE INCREDIBLE HULK (78, tv; episodes);
  CLIFFHANGERS (79, tv; episodes)
D. Castaneda (Mx.): EL SUPERLOCO (36)
Mario Castelnuovo-Tedesco: THE RETURN OF THE VAMPIRE (45);
  THE PICTURE OF DORIAN GRAY (48; uncredited; w/H. Stothart)
Francis Chagrin (Br.): AN INSPECTOR CALLS (54); THE MON-
  STER OF HIGHGATE PONDS (66)
L. Chakraborty(India): RAJDHANI EXPRESS (72)
Chakravarthi (India): DEVATHALARA DEEVINCHANDI (77)
Pan Chao (H.K.): THE GOLDEN HAIRPIN (63)
Charles Chaplin: MODERN TIMES (36; arranged and adapted by
  D. Raksin)
The Charles Austin Group: SCREAM, BABY, SCREAM (69; aka
  MAYHEM)
Hal Chasnoff: THE LOST JUNGLE (34, serial); QUEEN OF THE
  JUNGLE (35, serial; md)
Jay Chattaway: MANIAC (81)
Richard Cherwin (Music director): THE VAMPIRE'S GHOST (45);
  MANHUNT OF MYSTERY ISLAND (45, serial; aka tv: CAPTAIN
  MEPHISTO AND THE TRANSFORMATION MACHINE, 66); VALLEY
  OF THE ZOMBIES (46)
K. Chiahui (H.K.): THE BUTTERFLY MURDERS (79; w/C. Hsun-
  ch'i)
Giancarlo Chiarmello (It.): WHEN WOMEN PLAYED DING DONG (71)
Kiril Chiboulka (Bulgaria): CYCLOPS (76)
Paul Chihara: DEATH RACE 2000 (75); A FIRE IN THE SKY (78,
  tvm); NIGHT CRIES (78, tvm); DEATH MOON (78, tvm); AL-
  MOST HEAVEN (78, tv pilot); DR. STRANGE (78, tvm); THE

DARK SECRET OF HARVEST HOME (78, tvm); THE DARKER
SIDE OF TERROR (79, tvm); MIND OVER MURDER (79, tvm);
BRAVE NEW WORLD (80, tvm); THE HAUNTING PASSION (83,
tvm)
Chitragupta (India): GAYATRI MAHIMA (77)
David Chudnow (Music Director only): DEVIL BAT (41); THE
    MAD MONSTER (42); THE MONSTER MAKER (44, music A. Glas-
    ser); FORBIDDEN JUNGLE (50, music D. Calker)
Suzanne Ciani: THE INCREDIBLE SHRINKING WOMAN (81)
Alessandro Cicognini (It.): FAUST AND THE DEVIL (48); MIRA-
    CLE IN MILAN (51); ULYSSES (54); IL GUIDIZIO UNIVERSALE
    (61; The Last Judgment)
Stelvio Cipriani (It.): LUANA, LA FIGLI A DELLA FORESTA VER-
    GINE (68; Luana, Daughter of the Virgin Forest); NIGHT HAIR
    CHILD (71); BARON BLOOD (72, Ital. release only; aka GLI
    ORRORI DEL CASTELLO DI NORIMBERGA); WHAT THE PEEPER
    SAW (72); TWITCH OF THE DEATH NERVE (73, aka CARNAGE);
    RACCONTI PROIBITI DI NULLA VESTITI (73; aka MASTER OF
    LOVE); PERCE? (75, aka NIGHT CHILD); MAL OCCHIO (75; aka
    THE EVIL EYE); FRANKENSTEIN ITALIAN STYLE (77); TENTA-
    CLES (77); IL TRIANGOLO DELLE BERMUDE (78; Bermuda Tri-
    angle); ENFANTASME (78); THE SHARK'S CAVE (78; aka BER-
    MUDE: LA FOSSA MALEDETTA); THE GREAT ALLIGATOR (81);
    INCUBO SULLA CITTA CONTAMINATA (81); PIRANHA 2 (82)
Dolores Claman: THE MAN WHO WANTED TO LIVE FOREVER (70,
    tvm; aka U.K.: THE ONLY WAY OUT IS DEAD)
James Clark (Br.): VAMPYRES (75)
Richard Clements: HOUSTON, WE'VE GOT A PROBLEM (74, tvm);
    THE INVISIBLE MAN (75, tvm); THE INVISIBLE MAN (75, tv;
    episodes); STRANGE NEW WORLD (75, tvm; w/E. Kaplan)
Rene Cloerec (Fr.): SYLVIA AND THE PHANTOM (45); THE RED
    INN (51); THE CASE OF POISONS (55); MARGUERITE DE LA
    NUIT (55; Marguerita of the Night); THE GREEN MARE (59)
*Robert Cobert: DARK SHADOWS (66-71, tv; theme & episodes);
    THE STRANGE CASE OF DR. JEKYLL AND MR. HYDE (67,
    tvm); HOUSE OF DARK SHADOWS (70); NIGHT OF DARK
    SHADOWS (71); THE NIGHT STALKER (72, tvm); THE NIGHT
    STRANGLER (73, tvm); FRANKENSTEIN (73, tvm); THE NOR-
    LISS TAPES (73, tvm); THE PICTURE OF DORIAN GRAY (73,
    tvm); SCREAM OF THE WOLF (74, tvm); DRACULA (74, tvm);
    TURN OF THE SCREW (74, tvm); TRILOGY OF TERROR (75,
    tvm); BURNT OFFERINGS (76); FALSE FACE (77); CURSE OF
    THE BLACK WIDOW (77, tvm; aka LOVE TRAP); DEAD OF
    NIGHT (77, tvm); SUPERTRAIN (79, tv pilot & series)
S. Coelho (Brzl.): SEDUZIDAS PELO DEMONIO (75)
Stephen Cohn: HEAVEN ON EARTH (79, tv pilot)
Michel Colombier: COLOSSUS, THE FORBIN PROJECT (70)
Albert Colombo: DICK TRACY (37, serial); THE FIGHTING DEVIL
    DOGS (38, serial)
Manuel Compinsky: KILLERS FROM SPACE (54); THE SNOW CREA-
    TURE (54)

Antonio Diaz Conde (Mx.): MI ADORA CLEMENTINA (53; My
     Adored Clementine); THE AZTEC MUMMY (57); THE NEW IN-
     VISIBLE MAN (57); THE ROBOT VERSUS THE AZTEC MUMMY
     (59); SANTA CLAUS (60); THE CURSE OF THE DOLL PEOPLE
     (61); THE CURSE OF THE AZTEC MUMMY (61); SPIRITISM
     (61); DOCTOR OF DOOM (64); THE WRESTLING WOMAN VS.
     THE AZTEC MUMMY (65); HORROR Y SEXO (68; aka NIGHT
     OF THE BLOODY APES)
Joseph Conlan: V--THE FINAL BATTLE (84, tv; w/B. DeVorzon)
Marius Constant: THE TWILIGHT ZONE (59, tv; main theme only)
Bill Conti: STUNT SEVEN (79, tvm); THE RIGHT STUFF (83);
     TWO OF A KIND (83)
Federico Contreras (Sp.): LOS HABITANTES DE LA CASA DES-
     HABITADE (59; The Inhabitants of the Uninhabited House)
Jack Cookerly: THE BLACK SCORPION (57; w/P. Sawtell, B.
     Shefter); INVASION OF THE STAR CREATURES (62; w/E.
     Fisher). Cookerly also assisted P. Dunlap with electronics for
     DESTINATION INNER SPACE (66)
Carmine Coppola: THE PEOPLE (71, tvm)
Frank Cordell (Br.): DEMON (76; theme song by R. Ragland & J.
     Webb)
Carlo Maria Cordio (It.): ATOR (83)
*John Corigliano: ALTERED STATES (81)
Ernesto Cortazar (Mx.): SATANAS DE TODOS LOS HORRORES
     (72; Satan of All Horrors)
Vladimir Cosma (Fr.): DRACULA AND SON (79; aka DRACULA
     PERE ET FILS)
Alec R. Costandinos: WINDS OF CHANGE (78; aka METAMORPHO-
     SIS)
Phil Coulter (Br.): THE WATER BABIES (78)
Alexander Courage: VOYAGE TO THE BOTTOM OF THE SEA (64,
     tv; episodes); LOST IN SPACE (65, tv; episodes); STAR TREK
     (66-69, tv; main theme and episodes: The Cage (aka The
     Menagerie); Where No Man Has Gone Before; The Man Trap;
     The Naked Time; The Enterprise Incident; Plato's Stepchildren.
     Courage's original cues subsequently reused in other episodes,
     including: Court-Martial; Arena; Dagger of the Mind; This
     Side of Paradise; The City on the Edge of Forever; Tomorrow
     Is Yesterday; Miri; The Galileo Seven; The Squire of Gothos;
     The Return of the Archons; A Taste of Armegeddon; The Devil
     in the Dark; Errand of Mercy; Operation: Annihilate; Plato's
     Stepchildren; Wink of an Eye; The Lights of Zetar)
Kerry Crawford: CASTLE ROCK (81, tvm; w/Jonathan Goldsmith)
Bob Crewe: BARBARELLA (67; w/C. Fox)
Carl Crossman and George Potamiamos: APHROUSA (71)
Ernani Cuenco (Phil.): PATAYIN MO SA SINDAK SI BARBARAI
     (74)
Xavier Cugat: WHITE ZOMBIE (32; w/G.B. Williams)
Hoyt Curtin: THE MESA OF LOST WOMEN (52); KISS MEETS THE
     PHANTOM OF THE PARK (78, tvm; fight scene music by F. Kar-
     lin); C.H.O.M.P.S. (79). All following are animated tv series:

THE FLINTSTONES (60); THE BEANIE AND CECIL SHOW (61);
THE JETSONS (62); THE ADVENTURES OF JOHNNY QUEST
(64); THE ATOM ANT-SECRET SQUIRREL SHOW (65); SPACE
GHOST (66); FRANKENSTEIN JR. AND THE IMPOSSIBLES (66);
SPACE KIDDETTES (66); BIRDMAN (67); THE FANTASTIC
FOUR (67); MOBY DICK AND THE MIGHTY MIGHTOR (67);
SAMSON AND GOLIATH (67); SHAZAM! (67); JOSIE AND THE
PUSSYCATS IN OUTER SPACE (72); SEALAB 2020 (72); THE
FLINTSTONES SHOW (72); THE ADDAMS FAMILY (73); GOOBER
& THE GHOST CHASERS (73); JEANNIE (73); KORG: 70,000
B.C. (74); VALLEY OF THE DINOSAURS (74); THE SKATE-
BIRDS (77); BATTLE OF THE PLANETS (78); THE GODZILLA
POWER HOUR (78); BUFORD AND THE GHOST (79); CASPER
AND THE ANGELS (79); FRED & BARNEY MEET THE THING
(79); CAPTAIN CAVEMAN AND THE TEEN ANGELS (80); THE
DRAK PACK (80)
Sidney Cutner: THE FACE BEHIND THE MASK (41; plus track);
  THE LOST WORLD (60; additional cues only, w/H. Jackson;
  main score by P. Sawtell, B. Shefter)
D'Aamarillo (Phil.): DEVIL WOMAN (70)
Philippe d'Aram (Fr.): FASCINATION
Ikuma Dan (Ja.): THE LEGEND OF THE WHITE SERPENT (56;
  aka WHITE MADAM'S STRANGE LOVE); ADVENTURES OF SUN
  WU KUNG (58); THE LAST WAR (61)
Johnny Dankworth (Br.): THE AVENGERS (66-69, tv; episodes)
Ralph Darbo (Belg.): CHROMOPHOBIA (65, cart.)
Castro Dario (Sp.): OSCAR, KINA Y EL LASER (78)
Ajoy Das (India): CHARMURTI (78)
Harry Bromley Davenport (Br.): WHISPERS OF FEAR (74); X-
  TRO (83). Davenport also directed.
William David: THE HORROR (33, md)
Lew Davies: FRIGHT (57)
Peter Maxwell Davies (Br.): THE DEVILS (71; period music by
  D. Munrow)
Ray Davies (Br.): PERCY (71)
Victor Davies: THE PIT (81)
Carl Davis (Br.): UP THE CHASTITY BELT (71); UP POMPEII
  (71); I, MONSTER (72); RENTADICK (72); WHAT BECAME OF
  JACK & JILL (72; w/G. Howe); CATHOLICS (73, tvm); THE
  CANTERVILLE GHOST (74, tvm)
M. de Andrade (Brz.): MACUNAIMA (72)
Guido & Maurizio De Angelis (It.): TORSO (74); PRISONER OF
  THE CANNIBAL GOD (78); KILLER FISH (79; aka AGGUATO
  SUL FONDO); UNO SCERIFFO EXTRATERRESTRE ... POCO
  EXTRA E MOLTO TERRESTRE (79; The Sheriff and the Satel-
  lite Kid); ALIEN 2 (82); YOR (83; w/J. Scott)
George Deaton: THE TOOLBOX MURDERS (77)
Lex De Azevedo: THE SEXORCISTS (74)
Dick De Benedictis: THE FANTASTIC JOURNEY (77, tv; episodes:
  An Act of Love; Dream of Conquest); TABITHA (77, tv);
  EARTHLING (81)

Darrell Deck: RETURN TO BOGGY CREEK (78)
Manuel de Falla (Sp.): EL AMOR BRUJO (67; Evil Love)
Jean-Michel Defaye (Fr.): FIFI LE PLUME (64; Fifi the Feather)
Jami DeFrates: ZAAT (72; w/B. Hodgin); BLOOD WATERS OF
    DR. Z (73; w/B. Hodgin)
Eduardo Sainz de la Maza (Sp.): LA BARCA SIN PESCADOR (64;
    The Boat Without the Fishermen)
Jose de la Vega (Mx.): SE LE PASO DE MANO (52; His Hand
    Slipped); THE PHANTOM OF THE RED HOUSE (54); MISTERIOS
    DE LA MAGIA NEGRA (57; The Mysteries of Black Magic)
Georges Delerue (Fr.): L'IMMORTELLE (62; The Immortal Woman);
    A (64; short) APPEARANCES (64; short); LE DIMANCHE DE LA
    VIE (65; The Sunday Life); OUR MOTHER'S HOUSE (67); THE
    BRAIN (69); MALPERTUIS (72); DAY OF THE DOLPHIN (74);
    FEMMES FATALES (77; aka CALMOS); PHOTO SOUVENIR (78);
    SOMETHING WICKED THIS WAY COMES (83--score recorded but
    not used)
Joseph Delia: THE DRILLER KILLER (79); MS. 45 (81)
Luis de Leon (Mx.): ATTACK OF THE MAYAN MUMMY (63)
Al De Lory: THE DEVIL'S RAIN (75)
Waldo de los Rios (Sp.): THE HOUSE THAT SCREAMED (71);
    THE MURDERS IN THE RUE MORGUE (72); THE CORRUPTION
    OF CHRIS MILLER (75); ISLAND OF THE DAMNED (75; aka
    WOULD YOU KILL A CHILD?)
Pepino DeLuca and Carlos Pes (Br.): SECRET OF DORIAN GRAY
    (70)
Milton DeLugg: SANTA CLAUS CONQUERS THE MARTIANS (64);
    GULLIVER'S TRAVELS BEYOND THE MOON (65; w/Anne De-
    Lugg; U.S. release only)
Eric De Marsan (Fr.): DEMAIN LES MOMES (76)
Andy DeMartino, et al.: SUPER VAN (77)
Marcello De Martino (It.): DEATH ON THE FOUR POSTER (63)
Francesco De Masi (It.; aka Frank Mason): WEAPONS OF VEN-
    GEANCE (63); GOLIATH AND THE SINS OF BABYLON (63);
    LE JENA DE LONDRA (64; The Hyena of London); SAMSON IN
    KING SOLOMON'S MINES (64); THE MURDER CLINIC (66; aka
    LA LAMA NEL CORPO); 087 "MISSIONE APOCALISSE" (66);
    AN ANGEL FOR SATAN (66); LOS ESPIAS MANTONEN SILENCIO
    (66; Spies Kill Silently); WEEKEND MURDERS (72); THE BIG
    GAME (72); BRACULA--THE TERROR OF THE LIVING DEAD
    (72; aka LA ORGIA DE LOS MUERTOS); LO SQUARTATORE DI
    NEW YORK (82; The New York Ripper); THE GHOST (?)
Luis de Pablo (Sp.): THE SPIRIT OF THE BEEHIVE (76; aka
    FRANKENSTEIN)
Francois De Roubaix (Fr.): LES LEVRES ROUGES (72; aka Daughters
    of Darkness)
J.M. de Scarano (Dutch): BLOOD RELATIONS (77; aka LES VAM-
    PIRES EN ONTRAS DE BOL)
Manuel DeSica (It.): CRIMES OF THE BLACK CAT (76); CAGLI-
    OSTRO (77)
Paul Dessau: HOUSE OF FRANKENSTEIN (44; w/F. Skinner; H.

Salter; C. Previn); HOUSE OF DRACULA (45; w/H. Salter; F.
Skinner; W. Lava; P. Sawtell; E. Fairchild; C. Previn; C.
Henderson); THE STRANGE DOOR (51; library tracks used);
MONSTER OF THE CAMPUS (58; library tracks used)

Devarajan (India): SWAMY AIYYAPPAN (75); VANEDEVATHA (76);
VAYANADAN THAMPAN (78)

Frank DeVol: KISS ME DEADLY (55); WHAT EVER HAPPENED TO
BABY JANE? (62); HUSH, HUSH, SWEET CHARLOTTE (64);
THE LEGEND OF LYLAH CARE (68); DOC SAVAGE, THE MAN
OF BRONZE (75); THE GHOSTS OF BUXLEY HALL (80, tvm)

Barry DeVorzon: XANADU (80); LOOKER (81); TATTOO (81);
JEKYLL & HYDE ... TOGETHER AGAIN (82); V--THE FINAL
BATTLE (84, tv; w/J. Conlan)

De Wolfe (Br., Music Library): THE ZOO ROBBERS (73); HOR-
ROR HOSPITAL (75); MONTY PYTHON AND THE HOLY GRAIL
(75; w/N. Innes); SEX EXPRESS (75); JABBERWOCKY (77);
GOLIATHON (80; aka THE MIGHTY PEKING MAN, made 77; w/
C. Yang Yu)

Von Dexter: THE TINGLER (59); HOUSE ON HAUNTED HILL
(59); 13 GHOSTS (60); MR. SARDONICUS (61)

Ted Dicks (Br.): VIRGIN WITCH (70)

Carlos Dierhammer (W. Gm.): SECRET OF DR. MABUSE (64)

James Dietrich: THE MUMMY (33)

Ross DiMaggio: THE MAN WHO TURNED TO STONE (56, track);
THE NIGHT THE WORLD EXPLODED (57, track)

Felice Di Stefano (It.): GLI INVINCIBILI FRATELLI MACISTE
(64; The Invincible Maciste Brothers)

Franz Doelle (Gm.): AMPHYTRION (35)

Robert Emmett Dolan: MURDER, HE SAYS (45); MR. PEABODY
AND THE MERMAID (48). One library track from MR. PEA-
BODY subsequently reused in CREATURE FROM THE BLACK
LAGOON (54)

*Pino Donaggio (It.): DON'T LOOK NOW (74); CARRIE (76);
HAUNTS (76; aka THE VEIL); WHISPERS IN THE DARK (76);
PIRANHA (78); DAMNED IN VENICE (78; aka VENETIAN
BLACK); TOURIST TRAP (79); HOME MOVIES (80); BEYOND
EVIL (80); DRESSED TO KILL (80); THE HOWLING (81); THE
FAN (81); BLOW OUT (81); THE BLACK CAT (82); HERCULES
(83); HERCULES II (84)

Donovan (Br.): THE PIED PIPER (71)

Kiril Dontchev (Brz.): THIRD FROM THE SUN (73)

Jean Dore (Can.): FRENCH WITHOUT DRESSING (65)

J.P. Dorsay (Fr.): BLOOD ROSE (71)

Johnny Douglas (Br.): CRACK IN THE WORLD (65); THE BRIDES
OF FU MANCHU (66)

Sam Douglas: ENTER THE DEVIL (71, tvm)

Luis D'Pablo (Sp.): LOS INVASORES DEL ESPACIO (67; The Invaders from Outer Space)

Carmen Dragon: INVASION OF THE BODY SNATCHERS (56)

Mihai Dragutesco (Br.): ANTI-CLOCK (80)

Oliver Drake: THE MUMMY'S CURSE (44; w/Frank Orth)

Robert Drasnin: THE TWILIGHT ZONE (62, tv; episode: The
Hunt); THE MAN FROM U.N.C.L.E. (64-68, tv; episodes);
LOST IN SPACE (65-68, tv; episodes); THE TIME TUNNEL (66,
tv; episodes); PICTURE MOMMY DEAD (66); DAUGHTER OF
THE MIND (69, tvm); CROWHAVEN FARM (70, tvm); A TASTE
OF EVIL (71, tvm); DR. CROOK'S GARDEN (71, tvm)
Michael Dress (Br.): THE MIND OF MR. SOAMES (69); THE
HOUSE THAT DRIPPED BLOOD (70)
Joseph Dubin: HAUNTED HARBOR (44, serial); THE GHOST GOES
WILD (47, serial)
Antoine Duhammel (Sp.): EL MISTERIO DE LAS NARANJAS
AZULES (65); SINGAPORE, SINGAPORE (69; aka 5 MARINES
PER SINGAPORE); LA MORT EN DIRECT (80; Death Watch)
Roger Dumas (Fr.): THE DEVIL'S HAND (46)
Trevor Duncan (Br.): SCOTLAND YARD DRAGNET (57); QUAT-
ERMASS AND THE PIT (58-59, Br. tv); A FOR ANDROMEDA
(61, tv); LE JETEE (63; The Jetty)
George Duning: SINGIN' IN THE CORN (46, md); THE DEVIL'S
MASK (46; w/I. Gertz, plus track); MYSTERIOUS INTRUDER
(46; plus track); DOWN TO EARTH (47, w/H. Roemheld); THE
GUILT OF JANET AMES (47); HER HUSBAND'S AFFAIRS (47);
THE RETURN OF OCTOBER (48); BELL, BOOK AND CANDLE
(58); 1001 ARABIAN NIGHTS (59); MY BLOOD RUNS COLD (65);
THE TIME TUNNEL (66, tv; episodes); STAR TREK (66, tv;
episodes: Metamorphosis, Return to Tomorrow, And the Chil-
dren Shall Lead, Is There in Truth No Beauty?, The Empath.
Duning's original S.T. music was subsequently re-used in other
episodes, including: Patterns of Time, For the World Is Hollow
and I Have Touched the Sky); THE HOUSE THAT WOULDN'T
DIE (70, tvm; md); BLACK NOON (71, tvm); TERROR IN THE
WAX MUSEUM (73); ARNOLD (73); GOLIATH AWAITS (81,
tvm); BEYOND WITCH MOUNTAIN (81, tv)
*Paul Dunlap: LOST CONTINENT (51); TARGET EARTH! (54); I
WAS A TEENAGE WEREWOLF (57); I WAS A TEENAGE FRANK-
ENSTEIN (57); BLOOD OF DRACULA (57); FRANKENSTEIN
1970 (58); HOW TO MAKE A MONSTER (58); THE FOUR SKULLS
OF JONATHAN DRAKE (59); ANGRY RED PLANET (59); THE
THREE STOOGES MEET HERCULES (61); THE THREE STOOGES
IN ORBIT (62); BLACK ZOO (63); DIMENSION 5 (66); CASTLE
OF EVIL (66); CYBORG 2087 (66); DESTINATION INNER SPACE
(66); THE DESTRUCTORS (67); PANIC IN THE CITY (67)
Rogerio Duprat (Brz.): BRASIL ANO 2000 (69; Brazil Year 2000;
w/Caetana Valeso Capinan & Gilberto Gil); DAUGHTERS OF FIRE
(78)
Arie Dzierlatka (Fr.): LES ANNES LUMIERE (81; Light Years
Away)
Brian Easdale (Br.): PEEPING TOM (60; aka FACE OF FEAR)
Bernard Ebbinghouse (Br.): WE SHALL SEE (64); INVASION (66);
NAKED EVIL (66); GIRLY (66): TALES THAT WITNESS MAD-
NESS (73)
Eric Eericson (Swed.): FORRANDLINGEN (75; Metamorphosis)

Juan Ehlert (Arg.): EL MISTERIOSO TIO SYLAS (47; The Myster-
   ious Uncle Sylas); THE BLACK VAMPIRE (81)
Richard Einhorn: SHOCKWAVES (76; aka DEATH CORPS.); DON'T
   GO IN THE HOUSE (80); EYES OF A STRANGER (81); THE
   PROWLER (81)
Elephant's Memory (group): TAKE OFF (78)
Konrad Elfers (W. Gm.): METROPOLIS (26; jazz score for 60's
   Janus Films release); DR. MABUSE DER SPIELER (27; made 22;
   aka FATAL PASSION OF DR. MABUSE; score for later rere-
   lease)
Danny Elfman (Of Oingo Boingo): FORBIDDEN ZONE (80)
Jonathan Elias: CHILDREN OF THE CORN (84)
Mark Ellinger: THUNDERCRACK (76)
Dean Elliott: RETURN TO THE PLANET OF THE APES (75, tv
   cart.); THE FANTASTIC FOUR (78-79, tv cart.); THUNDARR
   THE BARBARIAN (80, tv cart.)
Jack Elliott: OH, GOD! (77); THE MAGNIFICENT MAGNET OF
   SANTA MESA (77, tvm; w/A. Ferguson); MR. & MRS. DRACULA
   (80, tv)
Peter Elliott: DOCTOR MANIAC (76; aka HOUSE OF THE LIVING
   DEAD)
Don Ellis: RUBY (77); SPIDERMAN (78-79, tv)
Ray Ellis: CAULDRON OF BLOOD (67; U.S. release only); THE
   AMAZING SPIDER MAN (67, tv cart.); THE ABC WEEKEND
   SPECIAL (77-78, tv; episodes; some fantasy); SWEET SIXTEEN
   (83)
Albert Elms (Br.): ALIAS JOHN PRESTON (55; w/E. Astley);
   MANFISH (56); SATELLITE IN THE SKY (56); THE MAN WITH-
   OUT A BODY (57); AMBUSH AT DEVIL'S GAP (66; serial);
   THE CHAMPIONS (67, Br. tv); THE OMEGANS (67, tvm)
Vic Elms (Br.): SPACE: 1999 (75, tv; episodes)
Robert Emenegger: U.F.O.S.: IT HAS BEGUN (76, tv doc.)
Keith Emerson: INFERNO (80); HARMAGEDDON (83; aka EVIL
   PHANTOM CONFLICT; songs only)
Kenyon Emrys-Roberts (Br.): COUNT DRACULA (78, tv)
Ennepitti: DEVIL'S DUE (73)
Brian Eno (Br.): LAND OF THE MINOTAUR (77); JUBILEE (78)
Mr. Erbe & M. Solomon (Can.): THRESHOLD (81)
Hans Erdmann (Gm.): NOSFERATU (22); DAS TESTAMENT DES
   DR. MABUSE (32; aka CRIMES OF DR. MABUSE)
Leo Erdody: DEAD MEN WALK (42); THE FLYING SERPENT (45);
   OUT OF THE NIGHT (45, md; aka STRANGE ILLUSION); WHITE
   PONGO (45, md)
Jose Espeitia (Sp.): ESCALOFRIO DIABOLICO (71; Diabolical
   Shudder)
Manuel Esperon (Mx.): EL QUE MURIO DE AMOR (45; He Who
   Dies of Love); EL CANTO DE LOS SIRENS (48; The Song of
   the Siren); LA MUERTE ENAMORADA (50; Death in Love); EL
   BELLO DURMIENTE (53; The Beautiful Dreamer); THE LIVING
   IDOL (57; w/Rudolfo Halffter); LA MUJER Y LA BESTIA (58;
   The Woman and the Beast); QUE LINDI CHA CHA CHA! (58);

Manuel Esperon (cont.)
   EL FANTASMA DE LA OPERATA (60; The Phantom of the Oper-
   etta)
T. Eyk (Dutch): FLYING WITHOUT WINGS (77)
Brian Fahey (Br.): CURSE OF THE VOODOO (64)
Edgar Fairchild: FRANCIS COVERS THE BIG TOWN (52; E.F.
   scored main title; rest of score by H. Stein, E. Carter & li-
   brary tracks)
Richard Fall: LILIOM (30; w/S. Kaylin)
Bud Fanton: THE CASE OF THE FULL MOON MURDERS (73; aka
   SEX ON THE GROOVE TUBE)
Robert Farrar: DON'T LOOK IN THE BASEMENT (73)
Wes Farrell: GAMMERA THE INVINCIBLE (66; U.S. release only)
Larry Fast & Synergy: THE JUPITER MENACE (83)
Dino Fekaris & Nick Zesses: SUGAR HILL (74; aka VOODOO
   GIRL)
Jack Feldman: UNICORN TALES (77, tv)
Ramon Femeria (Sp.): SOLO UN ATAUD (66; Only a Coffin)
Bernie Fenton (Br.): DEVILS OF DARKNESS (65)
Alan Ferguson: THE DEVIL'S HAND (62)
Allyn Ferguson: THE MAGNIFICENT MAGNET OF SANTA MESA
   (77, tvm; w/J. Elliott)
Ralph Ferraro: THE SHE BEAST (65; aka SISTER OF SATAN);
   FLESH GORDON (74)
Rafel Ferrer (Sp.): EL HOMBRE QUE VINO DEL UMMO (70; The
   Man Who Came from Ummo)
Gianni Ferrio (It.): THE MYSTERIOUS ISLAND OF CAPTAIN
   NEMO (74)
Paul Ferris (Br.): THE SORCERERS (67); THE CONQUEROR
   WORM (68; aka THE WITCHFINDER GENERAL); THE VAMPIRE
   BEAST CRAVES BLOOD (69); THE CREEPING FLESH (73); THE
   TERROR OF SHEBA (75; aka PERSECUTION)
Cy Feuer (Music Director): S.O.S. TIDAL WAVE (39). The fol-
   lowing are serials: THE MYSTERIOUS DR. SATAN (40); KING
   OF THE ROYAL MOUNTED (40); DRUMS OF FU MANCHU (40);
   JUNGLE GIRL (41); ADVENTURES OF CAPTAIN MARVEL (41);
   DICK TRACY VS. CRIME INC. (41)
Nico Fidenco (It.): 2+5 = MISSION HYDRA (66); BANG BANG (68);
   LE ESCLAVO DEL PARISO (68; The Slave of Paradise; w/G.
   del Orso); YPOTRON--FINAL COUNTDOWN (72); KOLOSSAL
   (71); LA REGINA DEL CANIBALE (79)
Brad Fiedel: NIGHT SCHOOL (81); JUST BEFORE DAWN (81)
Jerry Fielding: BEWITCHED (64, tv pilot); TARZAN (66, tv
   pilot); CAPTAIN NICE (67, tv pilot); STAR TREK (67-68, tv:
   episodes: The Trouble with Tribbles, Spectre of the Gun);
   JOHNNY GOT HIS GUN (71); THE NIGHTCOMERS (72); THE
   NIGHT STALKER (74, tv; 8 episodes); THE BIONIC WOMAN
   (76, tv; theme, pilot and 4 episodes); DEMON SEED (77); CRIES
   IN THE NIGHT (81); FUNERAL HOME (82)
Anatoli Filippenko (USSR): DEER-GOLDEN ANTLERS (72)
William Fischer: DARK AUGUST (75)

Lubos Fiser (Cz.): NA KOMETA (70; On the Comet); VALERIE A
TYDEN DIVU (70; Valerie and the Week of Wonders); THE
DEADLY ODOR (70); DINNER FOR ADELE (78)
Elliott Fisher: INVASION OF THE STAR CREATURES (62; w/J.
Cookerly)
Calvin Floyd: IN SEARCH OF DRACULA (75)
David Floyd: WOLFMAN--A LYCANTHROPE (78; w/A. Smith)
Robert Folk: THE SLAYER (82)
Louis Forbes: THE BAT (58); THE MOST DANGEORUS MAN
ALIVE (61)
Romolo Forlai: REINCARNATION OF ISABEL (73; aka THE
GHASTLY ORGIES OF COUNT DRACULA)
Charles Fox: BARBARELLA (67; w/B. Crewe); THE GREEN
SLIME (68; additional music only for U.S. release); PUFNSTUFF
(70); THE STRANGER WITHIN (74, tvm); WONDER WOMAN (75,
tv; theme & episodes); THE NEW, ORIGINAL WONDER WOMAN
(75, tvm); BUG (75); THE NEW, ORIGINAL WONDER WOMAN
(77, tv; theme); OH, GOD! BOOK II (81); ZAPPED! (82)
Carlo Franci (It.; aka Francis Clark): FAME AND THE DEVIL
(50; w/M. Funaro); MEDUSA VS. THE SON OF HERCULES (62;
w/M. Parada); THE BLANCHEVILLE MONSTER (63); HERCULES
AGAINST THE MOON MEN (64); MACISTE E LA REGINA DI
SAMAR (64; Maciste and the Queen of Samar); MACISTE,
GLADIATORE DI SPARTA (64; Maciste, Spartan Gladiator)
Manuel Franco (Phil.): MGA HAGIBIS (70); KAMPON NI SATANAS
(70; Disciple of Satan)
Georges Franju (Fr.): L'HOMME SANS VISAGE (75; The Man
Without a Face; aka SHADOWMAN). Franju also directed.
Benjamin Frankel (Br.): THE MAN IN THE WHITE SUIT (51);
PROJECT M-7 (53); MAD ABOUT MEN (54); THE CURSE OF
THE WEREWOLF (61); THE OLD DARK HOUSE (63)
Siegfried Franz (Gm.): DR. CRIPPEN LEBT (58; Dr. Crippen
Lives)
George Fraser (Br.): GIVE A DOG A BONE (66)
Marc Fredericks: SEEDS OF EVIL (81; made in 1973)
Arnold Freed: THE WEREWOLF OF WASHINGTON (73; aka THE
WHITE HOUSE HORRORS)
Fred Freed (Fr.): ALADIN ET LA LAMPE MERVEILLEUSE (69;
Aladdin and the Wonderful Lamp)
Sam Freed Jr.: MURDER IN THE BLUE ROOM (44, md)
Harry Freedman: THE PYX (73; songs by Karen Black)
*Gerald Fried: THE VAMPIRE (57; aka tv: MARK OF THE VAM-
PIRE); THE RETURN OF DRACULA (58; aka tv: THE CURSE
OF DRACULA); THE LOST MISSILE (58); I BURY THE LIVING
(58); CURSE OF THE FACELESS MAN (58); THE MAN FROM
U.N.C.L.E. (64-68, tv; episodes); STAR TREK (66-69, tv;
episodes: Shore Leave, Catspaw, Friday's Child, Amok Time,
The Paradise Syndrome. Fried's original STAR TREK cues later
reused in other episodes, including Wolf in the Fold, Journey
to Babel); IT'S ABOUT TIME (66-67, tv); MR. TERRIFIC (67,
tv); WHATEVER HAPPENED TO AUNT ALICE (69); SOYLENT

*Gerald Fried (cont.)
   GREEN (73; conducted symphonic music only); THE SPELL (77,
   tvm); CRUISE INTO TERROR (78, tvm); MANEATERS ARE
   LOOSE (78, tvm); THE BEASTS ARE ON THE STREETS (78,
   tvm); THE HARLEM GLOBETROTTERS ON GILLIGAN'S ISLAND
   (81, tvm); RETURN OF THE MAN FROM U.N.C.L.E. (83, tvm)
Hugo Friedhofer: JUST IMAGINE (30); SHERLOCK HOLMES (32;
   w/R.H. Bassett); TOPPER TAKES A TRIP (38; w/E. Powell);
   THE LODGER (43); SO DARK THE NIGHT (46); THE BISHOP'S
   WIFE (47); HOMICIDAL (61); VOYAGE TO THE BOTTOM OF
   THE SEA (64, tv; episodes); PRIVATE PARTS (72); DIE, SIS-
   TER, DIE (78)
Gary William Friedman: SURVIVAL RUN (80)
Fabio Frizzi (It.): HOT DREAMS (74; aka AMORE LIBERO; Free
   Love); DRACULA IN THE PROVINCES (75; w/Bixio, Nebbia,
   Tempera); ZOMBIE (79; aka ZOMBI 2; aka ZOMBIE FLESH EAT-
   ERS; w/G. Tucci); ALDILA (81); PAURA NELLA CITTA' DEI
   MORTI VIVENTI (82; Fear in the City of the Living Dead);
   MANHATTAN BABY (82)
Edgar Froese (W. Gm., member of Tangerine Dream): KAMIKAZE
   1989 (82)
Lou Froman: THE SLIME PEOPLE (61)
Dominic Frontiere: OUTER LIMITS (63-65, tv; theme & 1st Season
   episodes); INCUBUS (65); THE INVADERS (67-68, tv; theme &
   episodes); THE IMMORTAL (69, tvm); THE LOVE WAR (70,
   tvm); A NAME FOR EVIL (70); REVENGE! (71, tvm); HAMMER-
   SMITH IS OUT (71); HAUNTS OF THE VERY RICH (72, tvm);
   SEARCH (72, tvm; aka PROBE); FER-DE-LANCE (74, tvm; aka
   DEATH DIVE); MODERN PROBLEMS (81)
R. Fuentes (Mx.): ORLAK, THE HELL OF FRANKENSTEIN (61);
   LOS FANTASMAS BURLONES (64; The Ghost Jesters)
Wakiko Fukuda (Ja.): MOBILE SUIT GUNDAM (80, tv; w/T. Takai;
   episodes; aka features: GUNDAM I, II, III; 81-82)
Jun Fukumachi (Ja.): PHOENIX (78; theme by M. Legrand)
Wang Fu-Ling (H.K.): THE SNAKE PRINCE (76)
Parmer Fuller: SATURDAY THE 14TH (81)
Mario Funaro (It.): FAME AND THE DEVIL (50; w/C. Franci)
Toru Funaura (Ja.): THE MAGIC BOY (59)
Chan Fun-Kay (H.K.): ENCOUNTER OF THE SPOOKY KIND (81)
Lewis Furey: FANTASTICA (81)
Giovanni Fusco (It.): SANDOKAN THE GREAT (65); AMORE E
   RABBIA (69; Love and Anger)
Tohru Fuyuki (Ja.): ULTRAMAN (67, tv; w/M. Higure, K.
   Mryauchi); ULTRA SEVEN (nd, tv); DOCUMENT OF SOLAR FANG
   DOUGRAM (83)
Edward Gage: INGAGI (30)
Andre Gagnon (Can.): PHOBIA! (80)
Lee Gagnon: SEIZURE (74)
John Gale: DR. PHIBES LIVES AGAIN (72)
Philo Gallo & Clem Vicari: THE REDEEMER ... SON OF SATAN!
   (78); MOTHER'S DAY (80)

*Douglas Gamley (Br.): ONE WISH TOO MANY (56); TOM THUMB (58; w/K. Jones); TARZAN'S GREATEST ADVENTURE (59); HORROR HOTEL (63; jazz by K. Jones); THE HORROR OF IT ALL (64); TALES FROM THE CRYPT (72); THE VAULT OF HORROR (72; aka tv: TALES FROM THE CRYPT II); ASYLUM (72); AND NOW THE SCREAMING STARTS (73); MADHOUSE (74); THE BEAST MUST DIE (74); THE LAND THAT TIME FORGOT (75); FROM BEYOND THE GRAVE (75; aka THE CREATURES, 80); THE MONSTER CLUB (81)

Russell Garcia: RADAR SECRET SERVICE (49; w/R. Hazard); THE TIME MACHINE (60); ATLANTIS, THE LOST CONTINENT (61)

Rene Garriguenc: THE TWILIGHT ZONE (60-63, tv; episodes: The Monsters Are Due on Maple Street; In Praise of Pip; Passage on the Lady Anne; Spur of the Moment)

Mort Garson: SON OF BLOB (71; aka BEWARE! THE BLOB)

Georges Garvarentz (Fr.): TEMPLE OF THE WHITE ELEPHANTS (64); HELENE Y FERNANDA (70); SOMEONE BEHIND THE DOOR (71)

Brian Gasciogne: UNDER MILK WOOD (71); PHASE IV (74; electronic music by D. Vorhaus)

Giorgio Gaslini (It.): LA LUNGA NOTTE DI VERONIQUE (66; The Long Night of Veronica); NIGHT OF THE DEVILS (73); DEEP RED (75; aka PROFUNDO ROSSO; aka THE HATCHET MURDERS; w/Goblin)

Christian Gaubert: THE LITTLE GIRL WHO LIVES DOWN THE LANE (77)

Ron Geesin (Br.): GHOST STORY (73)

Harry Geller: VOYAGE TO THE BOTTOM OF THE SEA (64, tv; episodes); THE CHALLENGE (70, tvm)

Bernard Gerard (Fr.): EL SOLITARIO PASA EL ATAQUE (68; The Solitary Goes to the Attack); MAID FOR PLEASURE (74; w/O. Toussaint)

Yvon Geraud & Francois Tusques (Fr.): LES FEMMES VAMPIRES (67; The Vampire Women); LA VAMPIRE NUE (69; The Nude Vampire)

Don Gere: WEREWOLVES ON WHEELS (71); SWEET SUGAR (72)

Joseph Gershenson: Music Director for Universal Pictures, 1950-1965. (Not a composer). Supervised music department and conducted scores for virtually all Universal's genre films during this period, most of which were scored by H. Stein, H. Salter, F. Skinner, I. Gertz, and H. Mancini.

*Irving Gertz: (Many of these films are collaborative scores in which Gertz's music has appeared--often and where noted as re-used library tracks--along with the work of several other composers): THE DEVIL'S MASK (46; w/G. Duning, plus track); EXPERIMENT ALCATRAZ (50); BANDITS OF CORSICA (53); IT CAME FROM OUTER SPACE (53; w/H. Stein, H. Mancini; 6 cues by Gertz); THE CREATURE WALKS AMONG US (56; w/H. Stein, H. Mancini, H. Salter, H. Roemheld); THE INCREDIBLE SHRINKING MAN (57; w/H. Salter, H. Stein; 9 cues by Gertz; main

*Irving Gertz (cont.)
    theme by F. Carling & E. Lawrence); LOVE SLAVES OF THE
    AMAZON (57; w/H. Stein, et al.); THE MONOLITH MONSTERS
    (57; w/H. Stein, H. Mancini; most of score by Gertz); MON-
    STER ON THE CAMPUS (58; track); THE THING THAT
    COULDN'T DIE (58; track); THE ALLIGATOR PEOPLE (59);
    CURSE OF THE UNDEAD (59); THE LEECH WOMAN (60); THE
    WIZARD OF BAGDAD (61); VOYAGE TO THE BOTTOM OF THE
    SEA (64-68, tv; episodes); LAND OF THE GIANTS (68-70, tv;
    episodes)
Benedetto Ghiglia (It.): SECRET AGENT SUPERDRAGON (66)
Michael Gibbs: MADAME SIN (71, tvm)
David Gibson: SCHLOCK! (72)
Marcello Gigante (It.): THE EMBALMER (65); COMBATE DE
    GIGANTES (66)
G. Gil (Brz.): COPACABANA, MON AMOUR (75)
Herschel Burke Gilbert: PROJECT MOONBASE (53); POOR AL-
    BERT AND LITTLE ANNIE (72, aka I DISMEMBER MAMA, 74);
    THE GEMINI AFFAIR (75); THE WITCH WHO CAME FROM THE
    SEA (76)
Richard Gillis: THE BEES (79); DEMONOID (81)
Jeff Gilman: BIGFOOT--MAN OR BEAST (75, tv); MYSTERIES
    FROM BEYOND THE TRIANGLE (77, tv)
Marcello Giombini (It.): VULCAN, SON OF JUPITER (62); KNIVES
    OF VENGEANCE (65); A TARGET FOR KILLING (66); WAVE OF
    LUST (75); WAR IN SPACE (77); EYES BEHIND THE STARS
    (78); THE EERIE MIDNIGHT HORROR SHOW (78; aka L'OS-
    SESSA--The Obsessed)
Paul Giovani: THE WICKER MAN (74)
William Girdler: ASYLUM OF SATAN (75; Girdler also director)
Claudio Gizzi (It.): ANDY WARHOL'S FRANKENSTEIN (74; aka
    FLESH FOR FRANKENSTEIN); ANDY WARHOL'S DRACULA (74;
    aka BLOOD FOR DRACULA)
Paul Glass: LADY IN A CAGE (64); THE SOLE SURVIVOR (70,
    tvm); FIVE DESPERATE WOMEN (71, tvm); NIGHT GALLERY
    (71, tv; episodes: Lindemann's Catch, The Messiah on Mott
    Street); SANDCASTLES (72, tvm); TO THE DEVIL A DAUGH-
    TER (76)
*Albert Glasser: THE MONSTER MAKER (44); THE GAS HOUSE
    KIDS IN HOLLYWOOD (47); OMOO-OMOO, THE SHARK GOD (49);
    PORT SINISTER (52); THE NEANDERTHAL MAN (52); INVASION
    U.S.A. (52); THE INDESTRUCTIBLE MAN (56); THE AMAZING
    COLOSSAL MAN (57); THE SAGA OF THE VIKING WOMEN AND
    THEIR VOYAGE TO THE WATERS OF THE GREAT SEA SER-
    PENT (57); MONSTER FROM GREEN HELL (57); BEGINNING
    OF THE END (57); ATTACK OF THE PUPPET PEOPLE (58);
    EARTH VS. THE SPIDER (58); GIANT FROM THE UNKNOWN
    (58); TEENAGE CAVEMAN (58); WAR OF THE COLOSSAL
    BEAST (58); TORMENTED (60); THE BOY AND THE PIRATES
    (60); CONFESSIONS OF AN OPIUM EATER (62); THE CREMATORS
    (72). Glasser also scored the TARZAN radio serial during the

30's and 40's.

*Mort Glickman: SPY SMASHER (42, serial; w/A. Schwarzwald, P.
Sawtell; aka SPY SMASHER RETURNS, 66); PERILS OF NYOKA
(42, serial; aka NYOKA AND THE TIGER MAN, 66; aka NYOKA
AND THE LOST SECRETS OF HIPPOCRATES); THE MASKED
MARVEL (43; aka tv: SAKIMA AND THE MASKED MARVEL,
66); SECRET SERVICE IN DARKEST AFRICA (43; aka MAN-
HUNT IN THE AFRICAN JUNGLE; aka tv: THE BARON'S AF-
RICAN WAY, 66); G-MEN VS. THE BLACK DRAGON (43; aka
tv: BLACK DRAGON OF MANZANAR, 66); G-MEN NEVER FOR-
GET (47, md); PREHISTORIC WOMEN (50; ghostwritten for R.
Kraushaar); BRIDE OF THE GORILLA (51; ghostwritten for R.
Kraushaar); UNTAMED WOMEN (52; ghostwritten for R.
Kraushaar); INVADERS FROM MARS (53; ghostwritten for R.
Kraushaar)

Ib Glindemann: JOURNEY TO THE SEVENTH PLANET (61, w/R.
Stein); CRAZY PARADISE (62); NIGHT OF THE LIVING DEAD
(68; Stock library music by Glindeman, et al., used as score)

Goblin (It.; rock group led by filmmaker Dario Argento): PRO-
FUNDO ROSSO (75; Deep Red; aka SUSPIRIA, PART 2--1981
rerelease; w/G. Gaslini); SUSPIRIA (77); DAWN OF THE DEAD
(79); PATRICK (79; Italian release only); CONTAMINATION (80)

Franco Godi (It.): THE SUPER-VIPS (68); THE EXORCIST--
ITALIAN STYLE (75)

Ernest Gold: UNKNOWN WORLD (51); WILLIE THE KID (52; cart.);
THE ASSIGNATION (53; exp. 16mm short); DEMENTIA (53; aka
DAUGHTER OF HORROR; md, score by G. Antheil); GERALD
McBOING BOING ON PLANET MOO (55; cart.); UNIDENTIFIED
FLYING OBJECTS (56, doc.); WINK OF AN EYE (58); THE
SCREAMING SKULL (58); TARZAN'S FIGHT FOR LIFE (58); ON
THE BEACH (59)

Billy Goldenberg: FEAR NO EVIL (69, tvm); NIGHT GALLERY (69,
tvm, pilot); RITUAL OF EVIL (70, tvm); DUEL (71, tvm); PLAY
IT AGAIN, SAM (72); UP THE SANDBOX (72); GHOST STORY
(72, tv); THE LAST OF SHEILA (73); CIRCLE OF FEAR (73,
tv); DON'T BE AFRAID OF THE DARK (73, tvm); THE LEGEND
OF LIZZIE BORDEN (75, tvm); SEARCH FOR THE GODS (75,
tvm); THE U.F.O. INCIDENT (75, tvm); FUTURE COP (76,
tvm); GEMINI MAN (76, tvm; aka CODE NAME: MINUS ONE);
THIS HOUSE POSSESSED (81, tvm)

Mark Goldenberg: SILENT RAGE (82; w/P. Bernstein); NATIONAL
LAMPOON'S CLASS REUNION (82; w/P. Bernstein)

*Jerry Goldsmith: THE TWILIGHT ZONE (59-62, tv; episodes:
The Four of Us Are Dying; The Invaders; The Big Tall Wish;
Back There; Nervous Man in a Four Dollar Room; Nightmare as
a Child; Dust); THRILLER (60-62, tv; episodes: Hay Fork and
Bill Hook; Mr. George; Terror in Teakwood; Yours Truly Jack
the Ripper; others); FREUD (62; w/electronic music by Henk
Badings); VOYAGE TO THE BOTTOM OF THE SEA (64, tv; episode: Jonah and the Whale. Goldsmith's library music used,
uncredited, in other segments); THE MAN FROM U.N.C.L.E.

*Jerry Goldsmith (cont.)

(64-68, tv; theme only; theme later used, arranged by G.
Fried, in RETURN OF THE MAN FROM U.N.C.L.E., tvm, 83);
THE SATAN BUG (65); SECONDS (66); THE GIRL FROM
U.N.C.L.E. (66, tv; theme only); PLANET OF THE APES (68);
THE ILLUSTRATED MAN (69); THE BROTHERHOOD OF THE
BELL (70, tvm); THE MEPHISTO WALTZ (71); ESCAPE FROM
THE PLANET OF THE APES (71); THE OTHER (72); PURSUIT
(72, tvm); THE REINCARNATION OF PETER PROUD (75); THE
OMEN (76); LOGAN'S RUN (76); COMA (78); CAPRICORN ONE
(78); MAGIC (78); THE BOYS FROM BRAZIL (78); DAMNATION
ALLEY (78); THE SWARM (78); DAMIEN: OMEN II (78); ALIEN
(79); STAR TREK: THE MOTION PICTURE (79; assisted by F.
Steiner); THE FINAL CONFLICT (81); OUTLAND (81); POLTER-
GEIST (82); THE SECRET OF NIMH (82); PSYCHO II (83);
TWILIGHT ZONE: THE MOVIE (83); SUPERGIRL (84); GREM-
LINS (84); BABY (84). Goldsmith's library music from TWILIGHT /
ZONE (tv) used in KINGDOM OF THE SPIDERS (73) and ALLIGA-
TOR (80).

Joel Goldsmith (Jerry's son): LASERBLAST (78; w/R. Band);
DOOMSDAY CHRONICLES (79); THE MAN WITH TWO BRAINS
(83). Also assisted with sound effects on STAR TREK: THE
MOTION PICTURE (80); some cues from LASERBLAST reused
as source music in THE HOUSE ON SORORITY ROW (83)

Jonathan Goldsmith: CASTLE ROCK (81; w/K. Crawford); VISIT-
ING HOURS (82)

William Goldstein: TERROR OUT OF THE SKY (78, tvm); THE
ALIENS ARE COMING (80, tvm)

Miles Goodman: THE MAN WHO WASN'T THERE (83)

Gordon Goodwin & Paul Sunston: ATTACK OF THE KILLER TOMA-
TOES (79)

Ron Goodwin (Br.): VILLAGE OF THE DAMNED (60); CHILDREN
OF THE DAMNED (63); THE DAY OF THE TRIFFIDS (63); THE
SELFISH GIANT (71, cart.); FRENZY (72); BEAUTY AND THE
BEAST (76, tvm); UNIDENTIFIED FLYING ODDBALL (79)

Alain Gorageur (Fr.): THE SNAILS (65; cart.); LE CADEAU
D'OSCAR (65; The Gift of Oscar; cart.); FANTASTIC PLANET
(74)

Carlo Gori (It.): SEX PROBITISSIMO (63; Prohibited Sex); HER-
CULES AGAINST THE SONS OF THE SUN (64); COME RUBAM-
MO LE BOMBA ATOMICA (67; How We Stole the Atomic Bomb);
THE LEGEND OF THE WOLF WOMAN (76; aka WEREWOLF WOM-
AN)

Steve Gorn: HUNGRY WIVES (72; aka JACK'S WIFE)

Glenn Gould: SLAUGHTER HOUSE FIVE (72; md; score mostly
Bach)

Ron Grainer (Br.): THE MOUSE ON THE MOON (63); NIGHT
MUST FALL (64); THE PRISONER (68, tv); THE OMEGA MAN
(71); DR. WHO (73, tv; theme & episodes); THE DEVIL WITHIN
HER (76; aka I DON'T WANT TO BE BORN); ROALD DAHL'S
TALES OF THE UNEXPECTED (79, tv)

Clancy B. Grass & Roger Dollarhide: THE VELVET VAMPIRE (71)
Allan Gray (Br.): STAIRWAY TO HEAVEN (46); HER PANELED
    DOOR (50); THE GENIE (53)
*Barry Gray (Br.): SUPERCAR (62, tv); FIREBALL XL-5 (63,
    tv); STINGRAY (65, tv); DR. WHO AND THE DALEKS (65;
    electronic music only); ISLAND OF TERROR (65; electronic
    music only); THUNDERBIRDS ARE GO (66); FAHRENHEIT 451
    (66; electronic music only); CAPTAIN SCARLET AND THE
    MYSTERONS (67, tv); THUNDERBIRDS (68, tv); THUNDER-
    BIRDS SIX (68); JOE 90 (68, tv); THE SECRET SERVICE (69,
    tv); JOURNEY TO THE FAR SIDE OF THE SUN (69; aka DOP-
    PELGANGER); U.F.O. (72, tv); DR. WHO (73, tv; electronic
    music only); SPACE: 1999 (75, tv); INVASION U.F.O. (80;
    feature version of U.F.O. series); THUNDERBIRDS TO THE
    RESCUE (80); REVENGE OF THE MYSTERONS FROM MARS (81)
Don Great: A JOURNEY INTO THE BEYOND (77, U.S. release
    only); CELTIC GHOSTS (80, tv doc.)
George Greeley: MY FAVORITE MARTIAN (63, tv); THE GHOST
    AND MRS. MUIR (68-69, tv)
Bernard Green: EVERYTHING'S DUCKY (61); ZOTZ! (62); THE
    BRASS BOTTLE (64)
Al Greene and Al Jacobs: DEATH CURSE OF TARTU (66)
Walter Greene: WAR OF THE SATELLITES (57); TEENAGE MON-
    STER (57, aka METEOR MONSTER); THE BRAIN FROM PLANET
    AROUS (58); PINK-A-DELLA (68, cart.); TARZAN'S DEADLY
    SILENCE (70; feature from tv series)
Howard Greenfield: BEWITCHED (64, tv; theme; w/J. Keller)
David Greenslade (Br.): DR. JEKYLL AND MR. HYDE (81, tvm)
Johnny Gregory (Br.): BLOOD BEAST FROM OUTER SPACE (65)
Harry Grey (Music Director): UNDERSEA KINGDOM (36, serial;
    aka tv: SHARAD OF ATLANTIS, 61; music: A. Kay, et al.)
Ferde Grofé: ROCKETSHIP X-M (50)
Charles Gross: BLUE SUNSHINE (77); THE GOLD BUG (80, tvm)
Bert Grund (W. Gm.): THE THOUSAND EYES OF DR. MABUSE
    (61)
Dave Grusin: CANDY (68); THE GHOST AND MRS. MUIR (68-69,
    tv; episodes); THE MAD ROOM (69); L.A. 2017 (70, tvm; title
    theme only); THE DEADLY DREAM (71, tvm); A HOWLING IN
    THE WOODS (71, tvm); HEAVEN CAN WAIT (78)
Anthony Guefen: DEADLY EYES (83)
Sergio Guerrero (Mx.): EL SECRETO DE PANCHO VILLA (54; The
    Secret of Pancho Villa); PEPITO Y EL MONSTRUO (57; Pepito
    and the Monster); DOS FANTASMAS Y UNA MUCHACHA (58;
    Two Ghosts and a Girl; as "S. Guerro"); CAPERUCITA Y SUS
    TRES AMIGOS (59; Little Red Riding Hood and Her Three Friends);
    EL SUPERMACHO (60; The Super He-Man); EL TERRIBLE
    GIGANTE DE LAS NIEVES (62; The Terrible Snow Giant); EL
    MUSEO DEL HORROR (63; The Museum of Horror); EL BESO
    DE ULTRATUMBA (64; The Kiss from Beyond the Grave); EL
    AESINO INVISIBLE (64; The Invisible Assassin); AVENTURA
    AL CENTRO DE LA TIERRA (65; The Adventure at the Center

of the Earth); EL VAMPIRO Y EL SEX (68; The Vampire and
Sex); ROOTS OF BLOOD (79)

Christopher Gunning (Br.): GOODBYE GEMINI (70); HANDS OF
THE RIPPER (71)

Alfred Gwynn: THE DEVIL'S MESSENGER (62)

Sven Gyldmark (Swed.): REPTILICUS (62; Swedish release only)

Manos Hadjidakis (Greece): BED OF GRASS (57)

Henry Hadley: THE PHANTOM EMPIRE (35; track w/H. Riesenfeld)

G. Haenstzschel (Gm.): ADVENTURES OF BARON MUNCHAUSEN
(43)

Earle Hagen: PLANET OF THE APES (74, tv; episodes); GHOST
OF A CHANCE (80, tv pilot); FAREWELL TO THE PLANET OF
THE APES (70, tvm compilation of series); TREACHERY AND
GREED ON THE PLANET OF THE APES (80, tvm, from series;
w/L. Schifrin)

Albert Hague: HOW THE GRINCH STOLE CHRISTMAS (66, tv)

*Karl Hajos: SUPERNATURAL (33; w/H. Jackson, M. Roder);
WEREWOLF OF LONDON (35); FOG ISLAND (45). Stock library
tracks by Hajos used in: FLASH GORDON (36, serial); RIDERS
OF THE WHISTLING SKULL (37); DICK TRACY (37, serial);
others.

Chico Hamilton: REPULSION (65)

Marvin Hamlisch: THE WAR BETWEEN MEN AND WOMEN (71); THE
WORLD'S GREATEST ATHLETE (73); THE SPY WHO LOVED ME
(77); THE DEVIL AND MAX DEVLIN (81; songs only)

Hans Hammerschmid (W. Gm.): 2069 A SEX ODYSSEY (78)

Ramzan Hammu (India): THE TWO FACES (75)

Herbie Hancock: THE SPOOK WHO SAT BY THE DOOR (73)

Kentaro Haneda (Ja.): TIME SLIP (80); A TRADITION OF TER-
ROR: "FRANKENSTEIN" (82; Ja. tv); SCIENCE RESCUE PAR-
TY "TECHNOBOYGER" (82; Ja. tv); SPACE CRUISER YAMATO
--FINAL (82; Ja. tv; w/Miyagawa); MACROSS--SUPER TIME
FORTRESS (83; Ja. tv); SPACE COBRA (83; Ja. tv; w/Ohno);
SAYONARA JUPITER (84; songs by Yumi Mathutoya & Jiro
Sugita)

Petr Hapka (Cz.): OPERATION BORORO (73); BEAUTY AND THE
BEAST (79; aka PANNA A NETVOR--The Virgin and the Monster); THE NINTH HEART (80)

*Leigh Harline: BEWARE SPOOKS! (39; main and end titles only;
score tracked); BLONDIE HAS SERVANT TROUBLE (40); THE
BOOGIE MAN WILL GET YOU (41; track; main title by J. Lei-
pelt); WHISPERING GHOSTS (42, w/C. Mockridge; main title by
D. Raksin); ISLE OF THE DEAD (45); THE BRIGHTON
STRANGLER (45; plus track by F. Waxman); THE MIRACLE OF
THE BELLS (48); THE BOY WITH GREEN HAIR (48); IT HAP-
PENS EVERY SPRING (49); MONKEY BUSINESS (52); A VISIT
TO A SMALL PLANET (59); THE WONDERFUL WORLD OF THE
BROTHERS GRIMM (62; score only; songs by B. Merill); THE
SEVEN FACES OF DR. LAO (64)

W. Franke Harling: ONE WAY PASSAGE (32; theme only); Harling's music from the mystery DESTINATION UNKNOWN (33)

was also reused in many Universal horror films of the 30's, including THE RAVEN (35; 20 mins. worth, including main title and auto crash); THE INVISIBLE RAY (36; including Rukh's castle scene).

Joe Harnell: THE BIONIC WOMAN (76-78, tv; theme & episodes); THE INCREDIBLE HULK (77, tvm; 79, tv series; theme & episodes); CLIFFHANGERS (79, tv; theme & episodes); V (83, tvm)

Anthony Harris: SPEEDTRAP (78)

Johnny Harris: THE NEW ADVENTURES OF WONDER WOMAN (77, tv); THE INITIATION OF SARAH (78, tvm); THE EVIL (78); BUCK ROGERS IN THE 25TH CENTURY (79, tv; episodes: Planet of the Slave Girls, Return of the Fighting 69th, Space Rockers, Cosmic Whiz Kid, Ardala Returns)

J.S. Harrison (Br.): THE LEGEND OF SPIDER FOREST (74)

*John Harrison: CREEPSHOW (82)

Ken Harrison: FANTASY ISLAND (78, tv; episodes); MR. MERLIN (81, tv)

Hartl-Kalchauser (Austria): INVISIBLE ADVERSARIES (78)

R. Harvey (Br.): TERRAHAWKS (83, tv)

Bo Harwood & Lance Rubin: HAPPY BIRTHDAY TO ME (81)

Jimmie Haskell: BEWITCHED (64-72, tv; episodes); NIGHT OF THE LEPUS (72); SIGMUND & THE SEA MONSTERS (73, tv); LAND OF THE LOST (74, tv); DOCTOR SHRINKER (76-77, tv); THE KROFFT SUPERSHOW (76-77, tv; segment: Electra Woman and Dyna Girl); DEATH GAME (77)

Wilbur Hatch: THE POWER OF THE WHISTLER (45; Whistler theme, tracked. Score P. Sawtell, plus track); THE TWILIGHT ZONE (59, tv; episode: Still Valley)

Harley Hatcher: THE SOUL HUSTLER (73)

Marvin Hatley: TOPPER (37); TOPPER TAKES A TRIP (39, md; music: E. Powell, H. Friedhofer)

Katsuhisa Hattori (Ja.): INVADERS OF THE SPACE SHIP (59; aka US: PRINCE OF SPACE)

Ryoichi Hattori (Ja.): FUKUSUKE (57; The Top Heavy Frog, cart.)

Johnny Hawksworth (Br.): BANG! (67); THE PENTHOUSE (67); THE NAKED WORLD OF HARRISON MARKS (67); ZETA ONE (69)

Fumio Hayasaka (Ja.): DRUNKEN ANGEL (48); RASHOMON (50); UGETSU (53)

Hiraku Hayashi (Ja.): RIKO NA OYOME-SAN (59); ONIBABA (65); DEATH BY HANGING (68); KURONEKO (68); MOJU (69; The Blind Beast)

Isaac Hayes: MAIDSTONE (71)

Lennie Hayton: VOYAGE TO THE BOTTOM OF THE SEA (64, tv; episodes)

Richard Hazard: RADAR SECRET SERVICE (49; w/R. Garcia); BELA LUGOSI MEETS A BROOKLYN GORILLA (52); SOME CALL IT LOVING (73; "Sleeping Beauty Theme" by B. Harris); TIME EXPRESS (79, tv); AIRPLANE II: THE SEQUEL (82; adapting E. Bernstein score from AIRPLANE!)

Neal Hefti: BATMAN (66-68, tv; theme); OH DAD, POOR DAD,
   MAMA'S HUNG YOU IN THE CLOSET AND I'M FEELING SO SAD
   (67); CONSPIRACY OF TERROR (75, tvm)
Nahum Heiman (Br.): NEITHER THE SEA NOR THE SAND (74)
Gerhard Heinz (Austria): THE SHE-WOLF OF DEVIL'S MOON (78;
   aka DEVIL'S BED)
Jim Helms: NIGHT CREATURE (79, tvm)
Charles Henderson: BLACK FRIDAY (40; w/F. Skinner, H. Salt-
   er, C. Previn); HORROR ISLAND (41; w/F. Skinner, H. Salter,
   C. Previn); THE BLACK CAT (41; w/F. Skinner, H. Salter,
   C. Previn); THE MAD GHOUL (43; w/F. Skinner, H. Salter,
   C. Previn); HOUSE OF DRACULA (45; w/H. Salter, F. Skinner,
   W. Lava, P. Sawtell, E. Fairchild, P. Desau, C. Previn). Some
   of preceding reused library tracks.
David Heneker (Br.): THE TWO FACES OF DR. JEKYLL (60; aka
   HOUSE OF FRIGHT; w/M. Norman)
Michael Hennigan: VOYAGE TO THE BOTTOM OF THE SEA (64,
   tv; episodes)
Joaquin Gutierrez Heras (Mx.): EL RINCON DE LAS VIRGENES
   (72; The Dell of the Virgins)
Frederick Herbert & Arnold Hughes: All following are collabora-
   tive scores utilizing original and tracked material from various
   composers, including Herbert & Hughes: CITY BENEATH THE
   SEA (52); ABBOTT & COSTELLO MEET DR. JEKYLL & MR.
   HYDE (53; track only). Herbert later acted as md on tv's
   ALFRED HITCHCOCK PRESENTS (58 season+) and THE ALFRED
   HITCHCOCK HOUR (62), succeeding S. Wilson.
Juan Hernandez (Sp.): EL CASTILLO DE LAS BOFETADAS (45;
   The Castle of the Slaps in the Face)
Jorge Perez Herrera (Mx.): THE CRIMINAL LIFE OF ARCHIBAL-
   DO DE LA CRUZ (62; made 55; aka ENSAYO DE UN CRIMEN);
   LA HACHA DIABOLICA (64; The Diabolical Axe)
*Bernard Herrmann: THE DEVIL AND DANIEL WEBSTER (40; aka
   ALL THAT MONEY CAN BUY); HANGOVER SQUARE (44); THE
   GHOST AND MRS. MUIR (47); PORTRAIT OF JENNIE (48; song
   only); THE DAY THE EARTH STOOD STILL (51); A CHRIST-
   MAS CAROL (54, tv; lyrics by Maxwell Anderson); VERTIGO
   (58); THE 7TH VOYAGE OF SINBAD (58); A JOURNEY TO THE
   CENTER OF THE EARTH (59); THE TWILIGHT ZONE (59, tv;
   original title theme; episodes with original music: Where Is
   Everybody [debut], Walking Distance, The Lonely, 90 Years
   Without Slumbering, Eye of the BEholder, Little Girl Lost, Liv-
   ing Doll; episodes reusing Herrmann's music from earlier seg-
   ments or other CBS programs: One for the Angels, Mr.
   Denton on Doomsday, Third from the Sun, The Hitch-Hiker,
   The Last Flight, The After Hours, The Howling Man, The Late-
   ness of the Hour, It's a Good Life, Death's Head Revisited,
   The Fugitive, Nightmare at 20,000 Feet, The Last Night of a
   Jockey, The Old Man in the Cave, Night Call, The Seventh Is
   Made Up of Phantoms, Number Twelve Looks Just Like You,
   The Self-Improvement of Salvatore Ross, Queen of the Nile, I

Am the Night--Color Me Black, The Jeopardy Room); PSYCHO
(60); THE THREE WORLDS OF GULLIVER (60); MYSTERIOUS
ISLAND (61); THE ALFRED HITCHCOCK HOUR (62, tv; epi-
sodes: The Life Work of Juan Diaz, The Magregor Affair,
Where the Woodbine Twineth, The Jar); THE BIRDS (63; "sound
consultant," electronic sounds by R. Gassman & O. Sala); JASON
AND THE ARGONAUTS (63); VOYAGE TO THE BOTTOM OF THE
SEA (64, tv; episode "Cave of the Dead" used music from JOUR-
NEY TO THE CENTER OF THE EARTH); LOST IN SPACE (65,
tv; episodes "War of the Robots" and "Fiend Who Walked the
West" reused music from DAY THE EARTH STOOD STILL);
FAHRENHEIT 451 (66; electronic music by B. Gray); THE
BRIDE WORE BLACK (67); COMPANIONS IN NIGHTMARE (68,
tvm); TWISTED NERVE (69); THE NIGHT DIGGER (71); END-
LESS NIGHT (71; aka AGATHA CHRISTIE'S ENDLESS NIGHT);
SISTERS (73); IT'S ALIVE (74); OBSESSION (76); IT'S ALIVE
AGAIN (78; same score as IT'S ALIVE, adapted by L. Johnson)
David Alex Hess: LAST HOUSE ON THE LEFT (72)
Werner R. Heymann: ONE MILLION B.C. (40): TOPPER RETURNS
(41)
Yasuo Higuchi (Ja.): PHOENIX 2772 (80)
Masanubu Higure (Ja.): ULTRAMAN (67, Ja. tv; w/T. Fuyuki, K.
Miyauchi)
Richard Hill: BAFFLED! (73, tvm)
Gustav Hinrichs: PHANTOM OF THE OPERA (25; original '25 re-
lease score, adapted from Gounod's Faust)
Masaaki Hirao & Seiji Yokoyama: SPACE PIRATE CAPTAIN HAR-
LOCK (78, feature & tv series)
Tsuyokuni Hirayoshi (Ja.): AN ANDERSEN FABLE--PRINCESS
MERMAID (75)
Kenjiro Hirose (Ja.): GAMERA VS. VIRAS (68; aka DESTROY
ALL PLANETS)
Hisaishi (Ja.): TECHNOPOLICE 21C (82)
Gene Hobson: STUDENT BODIES (81)
Jonathan Hodge: THE TROUBLE WITH 2B (72); Z.P.G. (72)
Barry Hodgin: ZAAT (72; w/J. DeFrates); BLOOD WATERS OF
DR. Z (73; w/J. DeFrates)
Brian Hodgson & Delia Derbyshire (Br.): THE LEGEND OF HELL
HOUSE (73)
Carl Hoefle: see: J.K. Mayfield
Paul Hoffert (Can.): DR. FRANKENSTEIN ON CAMPUS (70; w/S.
Prokop); THE GROUNDSTAR CONSPIRACY (72); THE SHAPE
OF THINGS TO COME (79)
William Holcombe: PSYCHOMANIA (63)
Lee Holdridge: JONATHAN LIVINGSTON SEAGULL (74; w/Neil
Diamond); THE GEMINI MAN (76, tv; episodes); THE PACK
(77; aka THE LONG HARD NIGHT); THE BEASTMASTER (82);
WIZARDS & WARRIORS (83, tv; theme and all 8 episodes);
SPLASH (84)
Frederick Hollander: LE PROCUREAU HALLERS (30, Fr.); HERE
COMES MR. JORDAN (41); ONCE UPON A TIME (43); ANDRO-

Frederick Hollander (cont.)
CLES AND THE LION (51); THE 5000 FINGERS OF DR. T (53;
w/H. Salter, H. Roemheld); DAS SPUKSCHLOSS IN SPESSART
(60, W. Gm.; The Spook Castle in Spessart)

Victor Hollander: SAMURUN (20)

John Hollingsworth (Br.): Music Director for Hammer Films (not
a composer). Conducted almost all of their horror films 1954-63.

Michael Holm (Br.): MARK OF THE DEVIL (70)

Bill Holmes: THE HORROR OF PARTY BEACH (63); THE CURSE
OF THE LIVING CORPSE (64)

Danny Holmsen (Phil.): MAGIC GUITAR (68); ESCARLATA (69)

Tobe Hooper: THE TEXAS CHAINSAW MASSACRE (74, w/W. Bell).
Hopper also directed.

Antony Hopkins (Br.): THE ANGEL WHO PAWNED HER HARP
(54); CHILD'S PLAY (54)

Stephen Horlick: MADMAN (82)

George Hormel: Library music by Hormel & others reused as score
for NIGHT OF THE LIVING DEAD (68)

*James Horner: UP FROM THE DEPTHS (79); HUMANOIDS FROM
THE DEEP (80); BATTLE BEYOND THE STARS (80); THE HAND
(81); WOLFEN (81); DEADLY BLESSING (81); STAR TREK II:
THE WRATH OF KAHN (82); SOMETHING WICKED THIS WAY
COMES (83); KRULL (83); BRAINSTORM (83); STAR TREK III:
THE SEARCH FOR SPOCK (84)

Joseph Horovitz (Br.): TARZAN'S THREE CHALLENGES (63)

David Horowitz (Fr.): HU-MAN (75)

Horta & Mahana: STAR TREK (73-74, tv; animated series)

Andre Hossein (Fr.): J'AI TUE RASPUTINE (67; I Killed Rasputin; aka THUNDER OVER ST. PETERSBURG)

John Hotchkiss (Br.): CRUCIBLE OF HORROR (71; aka VELVET
HOUSE)

Alan Howarth: THE LOST EMPIRE (84). Howarth also assisted
John Carpenter in creating the electronic scores for HALLOWEEN
II (81); ESCAPE FROM NEW YORK (81); HALLOWEEN III:
SEASON OF THE WITCH (82); CHRISTINE (83)

Erich Hoyt (Br.): THE KEEPER (76)

Don Hulette: TWISTED BRAIN (74, tvm; aka HORROR HIGH)

Daniel Humair: WITCHCRAFT THROUGH THE AGES ('21 original
version; score adapted by J.L. Ponty for '69 English version)

Craig Hundley: ALLIGATOR (80; score also incorporated library
music from TWILIGHT ZONE by J. Goldsmith); SCHIZOID (80;
aka MURDER BY MAIL). Hundley also assisted with electronic
effects on METEOR (79), FORBIDDEN WORLD (82), others.

Gottfried Huppertz (Gm.): DIE NIBELUNGEN (24); METROPOLIS
(26)

Dick Hyman: THE HENDERSON MONSTER (80, tvm)

Harumi Ibe (Ja.): SHINOBI NO MANGI (67, Secret of the Ninja)

*Akira Ifukube (Ja.): GODZILLA, KING OF THE MONSTERS (56);
RODAN (57); SECRET SCROLLS (57); THE MYSTERIANS (59);
THE THREE TREASURES (60); BATTLE IN OUTER SPACE (60);
VARAN THE UNBELIEVABLE (62); THE WHALE GOD (62);

BUDDHA (63); KING KONG VS. GODZILLA (63; Ja. version
only); THE LITTLE PRINCE AND THE EIGHT-HEADED DRAGON
(63); ATRAGON (64); GODZILLA VS. THE THING (64); DOG-
ORA, THE SPACE MONSTER (64); KIGANJO NO BOKEN (65;
Adventures of Takla Makan); GHIDRAH, THE THREE-HEADED
MONSTER (65); MAJIN, THE HIDEOUS IDOL (66); RETURN OF
GIANT MAJIN (67); MAJIN STRIKES AGAIN (67); FRANKEN-
STEIN CONQUERS THE WORLD (66); KAIDEN YUKUJORO (68,
Snow Ghost); KING KONG ESCAPES (68); DESTROY ALL MON-
STERS (69); WAR OF THE GARGANTUAS (70); LATITUDE
ZERO (70); MONSTER ZERO (70); YOG, MONSTER FROM
SPACE (71); GODZILLA VS. GIGAN (76; aka GODZILLA ON
MONSTER ISLAND; U.S. release only, reused themes from
earlier Godzilla films); REVENGE OF MECHA-GODZILLA (77; aka
TERROR OF MECHA-GODZILLA; aka TERROR OF GODZILLA,
78)
Sei Ikeno (Ja.): THE SECRET OF THE TELEGIAN (63); THE
    BRIDE FROM HADES (68)
Shigera Ikeno (Ja.): KAIDAN BOTAN DORO (68), YOKAI DAI-
    SENSO (68; Spook Warfare)
Evzen Illin (Cz.): DEATH OF THE APE MAN (62); KULICKA (63,
    cart.)
Jerrold Immel: THE HOUSE ON SKULL MOUNTAIN (74; songs by
    Ruth Talmadge); LOGAN'S RUN (77, tv; episodes); MEGA-
    FORCE (82)
Neil Innes (Br.): MONTY PYTHON AND THE HOLY GRAIL (75;
    w/D. Wolfe)
Carlo Innocenzi (It.): IL MONSTRUO DELL'ISOLA (73; The Mon-
    ster of the Island); DAVID & GOLIATH (59); GOLIATH
    AGAINST THE GIANTS (60); MILL OF THE STONE WOMEN (60);
    SON OF SAMSON (60); SANSOME (61; Samson); SAMSON & THE
    7 MIRACLES OF THE WORLD (61; Italian release only)
Tommy Irons: THE PSYCHOTRONIC MAN (80)
Lee Irwin: THE PHANTOM OF THE OPERA (25; organ score for
    later tv release)
Kan Ishii (Ja.): GORATH (64)
Taku Izumi (Ja.): THE X FROM OUTER SPACE (67); GE GE GE
    NO KITARO (78)
Martin Jacklin (Br.): THE FACE OF DARKNESS (76)
Howard Jackson: SUPERNATURAL (33; w/K. Hajos, M. Roder);
    THE BODY DISAPPEARS (41; w/additional music by B. Kaun);
    THE MYSTERIOUS DOCTOR (43; w/W. Lava); HOW DOOOO YOU
    DO? (45); TOBOR THE GREAT (54; w/W. Lava); THE SEARCH
    FOR BRIDEY MURPHY (56; additional music only; main score by
    R. Webb); THE LOST WORLD (60; w/S. Cutner, additional mu-
    sic only; main score by P. Sawtell & B. Shefter)
Al Jacobs: STING OF DEATH (66; w/L. Norman); DEATH CURSE
    OF TARTU (66; w/A. Green)
Denny Jaeger & Michel Rubin: THE HUNGER (83)
Mick Jagger (Br.): INVOCATION OF MY DEMON BROTHER (69,
    short)

S. Jagmohan (India): CRIME DOES NOT PAY (72); DARWAZA
(78)
S. Jaikishan (India): JANGAL MEIN MANGAL (72)
Herbert Jarczyk (Yug.): CAVE OF THE LIVING DEAD (65)
Maurice Jarre (Fr.): THE HORROR CHAMBER OF DR.
FAUSTUS (59); BIRD OF PARADISE (62); JUDEX (63); DRAGON SKY
(64); THE EXTRAORDINARY SEAMAN (68); THE ISLAND AT
THE TOP OF THE WORLD (74); MR. SYCAMORE (74); JESUS
OF NAZARETH (77, tvm); MOHAMMAD, MESSENGER OF GOD
(77); MAGICIAN OF LUBLIN (79); WINTER KILLS (79); FIRE-
FOX (82); DREAMSCAPE (84)
Alain Jessua (Fr.): SHOCK TREATMENT (74; aka SHOCK; aka
THE DOCTOR IN THE NUDE; w/R. Koering; Jessua also direc-
tor)
Ward Jewell: CRACKING UP (77)
Antonio Carlos Jobim & Luis Bonfa (Brz.): BLACK ORPHEUS (59)
Max Jocson (Phil.): THE RITES OF MAY (76)
Allan Johannson (Swed.): INVASION OF THE ANIMAL PEOPLE
(58; w/H. Arnold)
J.J. Johnson: BUCK ROGERS IN THE 25TH CENTURY (79, tv;
episodes: Happy Birthday Buck, Olympiad, Escape from
Wedded Bliss, Flight of the War Witch)
Laurie Johnson (Br.): THRILLER (60, tv; episodes); THE
AVENGERS (61, tv; theme & episodes); DR. STRANGELOVE
(63); THE FIRST MEN IN THE MOON (64); SOMEONE AT THE
TOP OF THE STAIRS (73, tvm); CAPTAIN KRONOS: VAM-
PIRE HUNTER (74); KILLER WITH TWO FACES (74, tvm);
ANATOMY OF TERROR (74, tvm); THE DEVIL'S WEB (74, tvm);
ONE DEADLY OWNER (74, tvm); A PLACE TO DIE (74, tvm);
TERROR FROM WITHIN (74, tvm); THE SAVAGE CURSE (74,
tvm); SPELL OF EVIL (74, tvm); IT'S ALIVE AGAIN (78; aka
IT'S ALIVE II; adaptation of IT'S ALIVE score by B. Herr-
mann)
Guy Jones (Br.): THE HUMAN MONSTER (40)
Ken Jones (Br.): TOM THUMB (58; w/D. Gamley); HORROR
HOTEL (60; jazz only; score by D. Gamley); TARZAN THE
MAGNIFICENT (60); TARZAN GOES TO INDIA (62); THE
BRAIN (62); BATTLE BENEATH THE EARTH (67); HORROR
ON SNAPE ISLAND (71)
Kenneth V. Jones (Br.): TOMB OF LIGEIA (64); THE PRO-
JECTED MAN (66); WHOEVER SLEW AUNTIE ROO? (72); PRO-
FESSOR POPPER'S PROBLEMS (74)
Paul Jones: THE BRAIN LEECHES (78)
Quincy Jones: OF MEN AND DEMONS (69, cart.); EGGS (70,
cart.); BROTHER JOHN (71); DIG (72, tv; cart.); THE WIZ
(78); DUNE (84; w/Toto)
Ralph Jones: THE SLUMBER PARTY MASSACRE (82)
Rick Jones: THE FLIPSIDE OF DOMINICK HYDE (80, Br. tv; w/
D. Pierce)
*Trevor Jones (Br.): BLACK ANGEL (81, short); EXCALIBUR
(81); THE SENDER (82); THE DARK CRYSTAL (82)

Wilfred Josephs (Br.): DIE! DIE! MY DARLING (65); THE DEAD-
LY BEES (66); DARK PLACES (74); THE HUNCHBACK OF
NOTRE DAME (76, tvm); THE UNCANNY (77); THE HAMMER
HOUSE OF HORROR (80, tv; episode: Carpathian Eagle)

Paul Jost & George Small: LAST RITES (80; aka DRACULA'S LAST
RITES)

K.J. Joy (India): LIZA (78)

Susan Justin: FORBIDDEN WORLD (82; aka MUTANT)

Bill Justis: DEAR DEAD DELILAH (72)

Hajimi Kabaraji (Ja.): THE BLIND WOMAN'S CURSE (70); A
SCREAM FROM NOWHERE (77; aka THE HIDDEN BEAST)

Dave Kahn: BACK FROM THE DEAD (57; w/R. Kraushaar); THE
UNKNOWN TERROR (57; w/R. Kraushaar)

Berge Kalajian & Gus Pardalis: MISSION MARS (68)

Julius Kalas (Cz.): THE EMPEROR AND THE GOLEM (51)

Bert Kalmar & Harry Ruby: THE BEAUTY & THE BEAST (34;
cart.)

Hiroshi Kamayatsu & Herb Ohta (Ja.): THE WHITE HOUSE ON
THE BEACH (78)

Michael Kamen: VENOM (82); THE DEAD ZONE (83)

Brand Kampka (W. Gm.): GRIMM'S FAIRY TALES FOR ADULTS
(69; German release only)

Artie Kane: THE BAT PEOPLE (74; aka IT LIVES BY NIGHT);
WONDER WOMAN (76, tv; episodes); THE NEW ADVENTURES
OF WONDER WOMAN (77, tv); DEVIL DOG: THE HOUND OF
HELL (78, tvm); EYES OF LAURA MARS (78); WRONG IS
RIGHT (82)

Igo Kantor (Music Director): NIGHTMARE IN WAX (69); KING-
DOM OF THE SPIDERS (77; stock music score); KILL AND
KILL AGAIN (81)

Bronislau Kaper: ALRAUNE (30; aka DAUGHTER OF EVIL);
FINGERS AT THE WINDOW (42); BEWITCHED (45); THREE
WISE FOOLS (46); THEM! (54); FOREVER DARLING (56);
GREEN MANSIONS (59)

Elliot Kaplan: STRANGE NEW WORLD (75, tvm; w/R. Clements);
THE FOOD OF THE GODS (76); FANTASY ISLAND (78, tv;
episodes)

Sol Kaplan: THE TELL-TALE HEART (41, short; as "Sol Kran-
del"); STAR TREK (66-69, tv; episodes: The Enemy Within,
The Doomsday Machine; same music subsequently tracked in
other episodes, including The Deadly Years, Obsession, The
Immunity Syndrome, The Ultimate Computer, The Enterprise
Incident); SHADOW ON THE LAND (68, tvm)

*Dana Kaproff: EXO-MAN (77, tvm); EMPIRE OF THE ANTS (77);
THE AMAZING SPIDERMAN (78-79, tv; episodes); THE LATE
GREAT PLANET EARTH (78); WHEN A STRANGER CALLS (79);
SPIDER-MEN: THE DRAGON'S CHALLENGE (79, tvm); THE
ULTIMATE IMPOSTER (79, tvm); DEATH VALLEY (82); PANDE-
MONIUM (83)

B.V. Karanth (India): THE FERTILITY GOD (76)

Nico Karaski: see Nicholas Carras

Fred Karger: NECROMANCY (72); CHATTERBOX (77)

Fred Karlin: WESTWORLD (73); CHOSEN SURVIVORS (74); BAD
RONALD (74, tvm); FUTUREWORLD (76); LUCAN (77, tvm);
THE TRIAL OF LEE HARVEY OSWALD (77, tvm); THE MAN
FROM ATLANTIS (77, tv); KISS MEETS THE PHANTOM OF THE
PARK (78, tvm; fight scene music only); THE WORLD BEYOND
(78, tvm); SAMURAI (79, tvm); RAVAGERS (79, tvm); VAM-
PIRE (79, tvm)

A. Karzynska (Pol.): WORLD OF HORROR (68; "A Terribly
Strange Bed" segment)

Fred Katz: A BUCKET OF BLOOD (59); THE WASP WOMAN (59);
LITTLE SHOP OF HORRORS (60; reused previous two scores,
not original); THE CREATURE FROM THE HAUNTED SEA (61;
reused score)

Gene Kauer (aka Guenther Kauer): THE ASTOUNDING SHE MON-
STER (58); THE CAPE CANAVERAL MONSTERS (60); MON-
STROSITY (63); DEVIL'S MOUNTAIN (76; md; w/D. Lackey);
CLAWS (77; md; w/D. Lackey); CURSE OF THE MAYAN TEM-
PLE (77, tvm; md; w/D. Lackey)

Serge Kaufman (Fr.): L'ARAIGNEE D'EAU (71; The Water Spider)

*Bernhard Kaun: FRANKENSTEIN (31; main title music only); DR.
X (32); ONE WAY PASSAGE (32; main title only); THE MYSTERY
OF THE WAX MUSEUM (33); DEATH TAKES A HOLIDAY (34;
additional music only; main score by M. Roder, J. Leipold);
RETURN OF THE TERROR (34); THE WALKING DEAD (36); THE
INVISIBLE MENACE (37); THE RETURN OF DR. X (39); THE
BODY DISAPPEARS (41; additional music only; main score by
H. Jackson); THE SMILING GHOST (41; w/W. Lava)

Koban Kawauchi (Ja.): THE MOON MASK RIDER (81, aka THE
MOON KNIGHT)

Arthur Kay (Music Director): ONE FRIGHTENED NIGHT (35); THE
PHANTOM EMPIRE (36; songs by Gene Autry & Smiley Burnette;
score by H. Hadley, H. Riesenfeld); THE UNDERSEA KINGDOM
(36, serial; aka tv: SHARAD OF ATLANTIS, 61); DARKEST
AFRICA (36, serial). Stock library music, credited to Kay, included in DICK TRACY (37); RIDERS OF THE WHISTLING
SKULL (37)

Edward Kay (Music Director): THE APE (40); KING OF THE
ZOMBIES (41); GHOSTS ON THE LOOSE (43); THE APE MAN
(43); REVENGE OF THE ZOMBIES (43); RETURN OF THE APE
MAN (44); THE VOODOO MAN (44); THE SCARLET CLUE (45);
THE JADE MASK (45); THE RED DRAGON (45); SPOOK BUST-
ERS (46); THE STRANGE MR. GREGORY (46); MR. HEX (46);
THE DECOY (46); FACE OF MARBLE (46); BOMBA ON PANTHER
ISLAND (49); MASTER MINDS (49); SNOW DOG (50); GHOST
CHASERS (51); NO HOLDS BARRED (52); HOLD THAT LINE (52)

Buddy Kaye: I DREAM OF JEANNIE (65, tv)

Norman Kaye (Br.): DIAMONDS FOR BREAKFAST (68); JOURNEY
TO THE UNKNOWN (68, tv; episodes)

Samuel Kaylin: LILIOM (30; w/R. Fall); CHARLIE CHAN AT THE
OPERA (36; md); CHARLIE CHAN AT THE OLYMPICS (37);

CHARLIE CHAN AT TREASURE ISLAND (39)
Fred Kaz: THE MONITORS (69); LITTLE MURDERS (71)
Roger Kellaway: THE LEGEND OF HILLBILLY JOHN (72); THE
    DARK (79); THE MAFU CAGE (79); SILENT SCREAM (80);
    EVIL SPEAK (81); SATAN'S MISTRESS (82; aka DARK EYES,
    FURY OF THE SUCCUBUS, DEMON RAGE)
Jack Keller: BEWITCHED (64, tv; theme, w/H. Greenfield)
Arthur Kempel: GRADUATION DAY (81)
Tikon Khrennikov (USSR): ROUSLAND Y LUDMILLA (73)
Shinichi Kikuchi (Ja.): GOLDORAK (79)
Shunsuke Kikuchi (Ja.): WATER CYBORG (66; U.S. tv: 68);
    KONCHO DAISENSO (68; War of the Insects; aka GENOCIDE);
    KYUKETSUKI GOKEMIDORO (68; Goke, Body Snatcher from
    Hell); GAMERA VS. GUIRON (69; aka ATTACK OF THE MON-
    STERS); GAMERA VS. JIGER (70; aka GAMERA VS. MONSTER
    X); GAMERA VS. ZIGRA (71; aka GAMERA VS. LEOMAN);
    HAUNTING (77); PLANETARY ROBOT VANGUARD ACE NAVAL
    BATTLE IN SPACE (78); TARAO BANNAI (78); FIGHTER GEN-
    ERAL DAIMOS (79; short); SUPER MONSTER GAMERA (80);
    DR. SLUMP (82, tv)
Wojciech Kilar (Pol.): UPIOR (68; Vampire; short); LOKIS (70);
    THE KING AND THE MOCKINGBIRD (79)
Edward Kilenyi: THE DELUGE (33; w/V. Burton)
Brian King (Austral.): ALISON'S BIRTHDAY (79)
King Crimson (group): THE DEVIL'S TRIANGLE (73, tv)
Paddy Kingsland (Br.): DR. WHO (83, tv; incidental music)
Gershon Kingsley: SILENT NIGHT, BLOODY NIGHT (72); DEATH-
    HOUSE (81)
Chuji Kinoshita (Ja.): PANDA & THE MAGIC SERPENT (58);
    GAMERA VS. BARUGON (66; aka WAR OF THE MONSTERS);
    CHIBIKKO REMI TO MEIKEN NAPI (70)
Basil Kirchin (Br.): THE SHUTTERED ROOM (66); THE ABOMI-
    NABLE DR. PHIBES (71); THE MUTATIONS (74)
Kitaro (Ja.): QUEEN MILLENIA (82?)
David Klatzkin: FLASH GORDON (36, serial; trumpet fanfare on-
    ly)
Leon Klatzkin: THE ADVENTURES OF SUPERMAN (53, tv; theme);
    THE VEIL (58)
G. Klein: DON'T GO INTO THE WOODS (80)
Klobucar (Yug.): PAUK (69, cart.)
S. Klongvesa (Thai.): PI HUA KAD (80; The Headless Ghost)
Jan Klusak (Cz.): END OF AUGUST AT THE HOTEL OZONE (65)
Peter Knight (Br.): GIVE A DOG A BONE (66; md; music by G.
    Fraser); THE CRIMSON CULT (68)
Akira Kobayashi & Miki Yoshino (Ja.): HOUSE (77)
Charles Koff: THE MAN FROM PLANET X (50); CAPTIVE WOMEN
    (52)
A. Kogan (USSR): LA CAMPANA DE OTONO (79; The Fall of Au-
    tumn)
Sonny Kohl: DEATH BY INVITATION (71)
Ernest Kolz (Switz.): THE DEATH OF THE FLEA CIRCUS DIREC-

Ernest Kolz (cont.)
TOR, OR OTTOCARDO WEISS REFORMS HIS FIRM (72)
Christopher Komeda (aka Krzysztof T. Komeda; Pol.): TWO MEN
AND A WARDROBE (57, cart.); SZANDER (65; The Banner;
cart.); THE FEARLESS VAMPIRE KILLERS (67); ROSEMARY'S
BABY (68)
Frederick Kopp: THE CREEPING TERROR (74, tvm; aka DAN-
GEROUS CHARTER)
Erich Wolfgang Korngold: THE GREEN PASTURES (36; uncredited;
instrumental cues only); BETWEEN TWO WORLDS (44)
Andrzej Korzynsky (W. Gm.): POSSESSION (81)
Yuji Koseki (Ja.): MOTHRA (62)
Joseph Kosma (Fr.): THE DEVIL'S ENVOYS (42; w/M. Thiriet);
LE PETIT SOLDAT (47; The Little Soldier; cart.); JULIETTE
ET LE CLEF DES SONGES (50; Juliet and the Key to Dreams);
DESORDRE (50; Disorder; 16mm short; w/A. Vian, C. Luter);
NOAH'S ARK (50); CURIOUS ADVENTURES OF MR. WONDER-
BIRD (52); TORTICOLO CONTRE FRANKENBURG (52); ALERTE
AU SUD (53; Alert in the South); HUIS CLOS (54; No Exit);
LA CIGALE ET LE FOURMI (55; The Grasshopper and the Ant;
cart.); THE DOCTOR'S HORRIBLE EXPERIMENT (59); PICNIC
ON THE GRASS (59); LA POUPEE (61; The Doll; w/J. Milsch-
berg, B. Parmeggiani); LES HOMMES VEULENT VIVRE! (61;
Man Wants to Live!)
V. Kostic (Yug.): THE TIME OF THE VAMPIRE (70, short)
Taichiro Kosugi (Ja.): CYBORG 009--UNDERGROUND DUEL (67)
Roland Kovac (Gm.): JONATHAN (72)
William Kraft: PSYCHIC KILLER (74); FIRE AND ICE (83)
Martin Kratochrili (Cz.): BLACK SUN (79)
Raoul Kraushaar: (Many of these reportedly ghostwritten by
Mort Glickman): S.O.S. COAST GUARD (37, serial); UN-
KNOWN ISLAND (48; as "Ralph Stanley"); BRIDE OF THE
GORILLA (51; Glickman); UNTAMED WOMEN (52; Glickman);
INVADERS FROM MARS (53; Glickman); THE GOLDEN MISTRESS
(54); CURUCU, BEAST OF THE AMAZON (56); BACK FROM
THE DEAD (57; w/D. Kahn); THE UNKNOWN TERROR (57; w/
D. Kahn); THE THIRTY-FOOT BRIDE OF CANDY ROCK (58);
MR. ED (60-66, tv; episodes); JESSE JAMES MEETS FRANKEN-
STEIN'S DAUGHTER (66); BAMBOO SAUCER (67)
V. Krishnamurthy (India): JAGAN MOHINI (78)
J.A. Kroculick: EVERY SPARROW MUST FALL (64)
Tim Krog (for Synth-Sound-Trax Inc.): THE BOOGEYMAN (80)
Gail Kubik: GERALD McBOING BOING (50; cart.)
H.R. Kugley: ANY BODY ... ANY WAY (80)
Joseph Kumok (Fr.): LE GOLEM (36)
Milan Kymlicka (Can.): THE REINCARNATE (71)
Nick Labuschane: THE DEMON (81)
Doug Lackey: CLAWS (77; w/G. Kauer); CURSE OF THE MAYAN
TEMPLE (77; w/G. Kauer)
Francis Lai (Fr.): LE PETIT POUCET (72; Tom Thumb); THE
FORBIDDEN ROOM (77; aka ANIMA PERSA)

Frank LaLoggia: FEAR NO EVIL (81; w/D. Spear; LaLoggia also
    directed)
Violet Lam (H.K.): THE SECRET (79)
D. Lambert & B. Potter: TUNNELVISION (76)
Phillip Lambro (Sp.): CRYPT OF THE LIVING DEAD (73; aka
    YOUNG HANNAH: QUEEN OF THE VAMPIRES)
Kelly Lammers & John O'Verlin: PLANET OF THE DINOSAURS (80)
Michael Lang: THE SUICIDE CLUB (73; tvm)
Arthur Lange: THE UNDYING MONSTER (42; w/D. Raksin, C.
    Mockridge); THE MAD MAGICIAN (54)
John Lange & Lew Porter: THE INVISIBLE GHOST (41); SPOOKS
    RUN WILD (41); THE CORPSE VANISHES (42); BLACK DRAGONS
    (41)
Bruce Langehorne: IDAHO TRANSFER (75); NIGHT WARNING (83;
    made 79)
Gordon Langford (Br.): THE TROUBLESOME DOUBLE (71, tvm)
Henri Lanoe (Fr.): AN OCCURRENCE AT OWL CREEK BRIDGE
    (62, short; also shown as an episode of tv's TWILIGHT ZONE,
    64)
Andrzej Lapicki (Pol.): WORLD OF HORROR (68; "Lord Arthur
    Savile's Crime" segment)
Richard LaSalle: FLIGHT THAT DISAPPEARED (61); HANDS OF
    A STRANGER (62); THE MERMAIDS OF TIBURON (62); THE
    DAY MARS INVADED EARTH (63); TWICE TOLD TALES (63);
    THE TIME TRAVELERS (64); AQUASEX (66); CITY BENEATH
    THE SEA (71; aka ONE HOUR TO DOOMSDAY); SUPERBEAST
    (72); DAUGHTERS OF SATAN (72); DOCTOR DEATH: SEEKER
    OF SOULS (73); THE NEW ADVENTURES OF WONDER WOMAN
    (77, tv); RETURN OF CAPTAIN NEMO (78, tv); BUCK ROGERS
    IN THE 25TH CENTURY (79, tv; episode: Unchained Women);
    BACK TO THE PLANET OF THE APES (80, tvm; compiled from
    tv series; w/L. Schifrin)
Jacques Lasry & Willy Mattes (W. Gm.): THE HEAD (59)
Teddy Lasry (Fr.): THE SHAME OF THE JUNGLE (79)
Alexander Laszlo: BLACK MAGIC (44); STRANGE IMPERSONATION
    (45, md); SONG OF INDIA (48); TARZAN'S MAGIC FOUNTAIN
    (49); THE SPIRITUALIST (48); THE RENEGADE SATELLITE (54,
    tv); NIGHT OF THE BLOOD BEAST (58); ATTACK OF THE
    GIANT LEECHES (59); THE ATOMIC SUBMARINE (60)
Ken Lauber: MR. AND MRS. DRACULA (80, tv pilot)
Linda Laurie: LAND OF THE LOST (74, tv)
William Lava: HAWK OF THE WILDERNESS (38, serial; aka tv:
    LOST ISLAND OF KIOGA, 66); DAREDEVILS OF THE RED CIR-
    CLE (39, serial); THE SMILING GHOST (41; w/B. Kaun); THE
    MYSTERIOUS DOCTOR (43; w/H. Jackson); THE INVISIBLE
    MAN'S REVENGE (45; w/H. Salter, E. Zeisl); JUNGLE CAPTIVE
    (44; w/P. Sawtell, H. Salter, C. Previn); SHE-WOLF OF LON-
    DON (45); HOUSE OF DRACULA (45; w/H. Salter, F. Skinner,
    C. Previn, P. Sawtell, E. Fairchild, P. Desau, C. Henderson);
    PHANTOM FROM SPACE (52); TOBOR THE GREAT (54; w/H.
    Jackson); REVENGE OF THE CREATURE (55; 4 original cues

William Lava (cont.)
  by Lava; plus title music by H. Stein and library tracks); THE
  DEADLY MANTIS (57); THE TWILIGHT ZONE (61, tv; episode:
  Once Upon a Time); THE PINK PHINK (64, cart.); PINK PIS-
  TONS (66, cart.); CHAMBER OF HORRORS (66); BLOOD OF
  FRANKENSTEIN (71; aka SATAN'S BLOODY FREAKS; aka
  DRACULA VS. FRANKENSTEIN). Lava's Universal library
  tracks were also used in THE STRANGE DOOR (51; incl. main
  title); THE MONOLITH MONSTERS (57; tracks from DEADLY
  MANTIS); MONSTER ON THE CAMPUS (58); THE SWORD OF
  ALI BABA (65)
*Angelo Francesco Lavagnino (It.): STRANO APPUNTAMENTO
  (50; Strange Appointment); CALYPSO (58); THE SIEGE OF
  SYRACUSE (59); WARRIOR EMPRESS (60); THE NIGHT THEY
  KILLED RASPUTIN (60); GORGO (61); ULYSSES AGAINST THE
  SONS OF HERCULES (61); THE WONDERS OF ALADDIN (61);
  THE CORSICAN BROTHERS (61); GOLIATH AND THE VAM-
  PIRES (61; Italian release only); HERCULES, SAMSON & ULYS-
  SES (63); SAMSON & THE SLAVE QUEEN (63; Italian release
  only); SAMSON CONTRO I PARATI (63; Samson vs. the Pir-
  ates); THE CASTLE OF THE LIVING DEAD (64); HERCULES
  AGAINST ROME (64); HERCULES AND THE TYRANTS OF
  BABYLON (64); GLI INVINCIBILI TRE (64; The Invicible Three);
  SNOW DEVILS (65); WAR BETWEEN THE PLANETS (65); WAR
  OF THE PLANETS (65); WILD WILD PLANET (65); GUNGALA,
  LA VIRGINE DELLS GIUNGLA (67; Gungala, the Virgin of the
  Jungle); QUALCOSA STRISCIA NEL BUIO (70; Something Is
  Creeping in the Dark); QUEENS OF EVIL (71; aka IL DELITTO
  DEL DIAVOLO)
Raul Lavista (Mx.): EL FANTASMA DE MEDIANOCHE (39; aka
  EL MISTERIO SE VISTE DE FRAC); DEMONIO Y CARNE (50;
  Devil and Flesh; aka SUSANA); EL HOMBRE SIN ROSTRO (50;
  The Man Without a Face); EL JUVENTUD (53; Return to Youth);
  LA BRUJA (55; The Witch); THE BEAST OF HOLLOW MOUN-
  TAIN (56); PULGARCITI (58; Tom Thumb); EL ESQUELETO
  DE LA SENORA MORALES (59; The Skeleton of Mrs. Morales);
  MACARIO (60); CONQUISTADOR DE LA LUNA (60, Conqueror
  of the Moon); LITTLE RED RIDING HOOD AND THE MONSTER
  (60); SANTO CONTRA LOS ZOMBIES (61; aka INVASION OF
  THE ZOMBIES); SANTO CONTRA LAS MUJERES VAMPIRES (61;
  Samson vs. the Vampire Women); SIMON OF THE DESERT (65);
  LA LOBA (65; The She Wolf; aka HORRORS OF THE BLACK
  FOREST); THE NIGHT OF A THOUSAND CATS (74)
Stephen Lawrence: ALICE, SWEET ALICE (78; aka COMMUNION)
Maury Laws: THE ORIGINAL TV ADVENTURES OF KING KONG
  (66, tv cart.); TOM OF T.H.U.M.B. (66, tv. cart.); THE
  DAYDREAMERS (66; lyrics by Jules Bass); MAD MONSTER
  PARTY (67; lyrics by Bass); THE LAST DINOSAUR (77, tvm;
  w/Bass); THE HOBBITT (77, tvm; w/Bass); THE BERMUDA
  DEPTHS (78, tvm; title song lyrics by Bass); THE RETURN OF
  THE KING (80, tvm; lyrics by Bass)

Imer Leaf: MISS LESLIE'S DOLLS (72)
Mike Leander (Br.): PRIVILEGE (67)
David Lee: THE MASQUE OF THE RED DEATH (64)
Gerald Lee: SATAN'S CHEERLEADERS (77)
Raymond Lefevre (Fr.): LE GENDARME ET LES EXTRA-TERRES-
    TRES (79)
Michel Legrand (Fr.): SEVEN CAPITAL SINS (62; w/S. Distel, P.
    Jansen); L'OR ET LE PLUMB (66; Gold and Lead); THE PLAS-
    TIC DOME OF NORMA JEAN (66); PEAU D'ANE (70; Donkey
    Skin; aka THE MAGIC DONKEY); SMURFS (75); PHOENIX (78;
    Japanese film; theme only); LES FABULEUSES AVENTURES DU
    LEGENDAIRE BARON MICHAUSEN (79); NEVER SAY NEVER
    AGAIN (83); SLAPSTICK (84; score recorded but not used)
Raymond Legrand (Michel's father): LE SEDIQUE AUX DENTS
    ROUGES (71; The Sadist with Red Teeth)
John Leipold: DEATH TAKES A HOLIDAY (34; w/M. Roder; addi-
    tional music by B. Kaun); THE BOOGIE MAN WILL GET YOU
    (41; main title only; score track by L. Harline)
Gary LeMel: THE PSYCHO LOVER (69)
Melvyn Lenard: DAUGHTER OF DR. JEKYLL (57)
Raymond Leppard (Br.): LORD OF THE FLIES (63)
Didier William Le Pauw (Fr.): LEVRES DE SANG (75; Lips of
    Blood); PHANTASMES (76)
Sylvester Levay: AIRWOLF (84, tv)
Joe Levine: TARGET ... EARTH (80, tvm)
Albert Levy (Colombia): KARLA CONTRA LOS JAGUARES (7_;
    Karla VS. the Jaguars); LOS JAGUARES CONTRA EL INVASOR
    MISTERIOSO (7 ; The Jaguars VS. the Mysterious Invader)
Louis Levy (Br., Music Director): THE GHOUL (33)
Shuky Levy: DAWN OF THE MUMMY (81)
Herschell Gordon Lewis: BLOOD FEAST (63); 2000 MANIACS (64;
    w/L. Wellington); SHE-DEVILS ON WHEELS (68; as "Sheldon
    Seymour"; w/Robert Lewis); THE GORE-GORE GIRLS (71; aka
    BLOOD ORGY; as "Sheldon Seymour"); Lewis also directed.
John Lewis: NIGHT GALLERY (71, tv; episode: Since Aunt Ada
    Came to Stay)
Laurie Lewis: THE EVIL TOUCH (73, tvm)
Michael J. Lewis (Br.): THE MAN WHO HAUNTED HIMSELF (70);
    UNMAN, WITTERING AND ZIGO (71); THEATRE OF BLOOD
    (73); THE MEDUSA TOUCH (78); THE LEGACY (78); THE
    LION, THE WITCH AND THE WARDROBE (79, tvm); THE UN-
    SEEN (81); SPHINX (81)
W. Michael Lewis & Laurin Rinder: IN SEARCH OF ... (76, tv);
    SECRETS OF THE BERMUDA TRIANGLE (78); NEW YEAR'S
    EVIL (81); THE NINJA (81)
Webster Lewis: THE HEARSE (80)
Libra (It. group): BEYOND THE DOOR II (79; aka SUSPENSE;
    aka SHOCK)
David Lindup (Br.): JOURNEY TO THE UNKNOWN (68, tv); THE
    SPIRAL STAIRCASE (75); THE HAMMER HOUSE OF HORROR (80,
    tv; episode: Charlie Boy)

*Zdenek Liska (Cz.): POKLAD NA PTACIM OSTROVE (52; The
Treasure of Bird Island; cart.); PAN PROKOUK PRITEL
ZVIRATEK (53, cart.); FLICEK THE BALL (56; The Naughty
Ball; cart.); THE FABULOUS WORLD OF JULES VERNE (58);
DEN ODPLATY (60; The Day of Reckoning; cart.); WHERE THE
DEVIL CANNOT GO (60); BARON MUNCHAUSEN (61); VRAZDA
PO CESKY (66; Murder, Czech Style); BYT (68; The Flat);
THE VALLEY OF BEES (68); OVOCE STROMJ RAJSHYCH JIME
(70); PRIPAD PRO ZACINAJICHO KATA (70; A Castle for a
Young Hangman)

Michael Lloyd: SIGMUND AND THE SEA MONSTERS (73, tv);
LAND OF THE LOST (74, tv); FAR OUT SPACE NUTS (75,
tv); THE LOST SAUCER (75, tv); STRANGER IN OUR HOUSE
(78, tvm)

David Llywelyn (Swiss): BLOODLUST (76)

Malcolm Lockyer (Br.): DR. WHO AND THE DALEKS (65; electronic music by B. Gray); ISLAND OF TERROR (66; electronic
music by B. Gray); ISLAND OF THE BURNING DAMNED (67;
aka ISLAND OF THE BURNING DOOMED); VENGEANCE OF FU
MANCHU (67); THE FACE OF EVE (68); DR. WHO (73, tv; episodes)

Joe LoDuca: EVIL DEAD (82)

William Loose: TARZAN AND THE GREAT RIVER (66); TARZAN
AND THE JUNGLE BOY (68); NIGHT OF THE LIVING DEAD
(68; Capitol library music excerpts by Loose, et al., used as
score); BLACKSNAKE (73; w/A. Teeter); THE LUCIFER COM-
PLEX (78, tvm); THE ALIEN ENCOUNTERS (79, tvm); DEVIL
TIMES FIVE (79; aka THE HORRIBLE HOUSE ON THE HILL);
THE MAN WHO SAW TOMORROW (81; w/J. Tillar)

Fernando M. Lopez (Arg.): LA CUEVA DE ALI BABA (54; The
Cave of Ali Baba)

Mark Lothar (W. Gm.): FAUST (60)

Mundell Lowe: EVERYTHING YOU ALWAYS WANTED TO KNOW
ABOUT SEX (72); TARANTULAS: THE DEADLY CARGO (77,
tvm)

Harry Lubin: ONE STEP BEYOND (62, tv); THE OUTER LIMITS
(63, tv; 2nd season episodes). Lubin's earlier library tracks
used in SON OF ALI BABA (51)

James D. Lumsden: SELF-PORTRAIT IN BRAINS (80)

Elisabeth Lutyens (Br.): THE MALPAS MYSTERY (60); PARA-
NOIAC (63); DR. TERROR'S HOUSE OF HORRORS (64); THE
EARTH DIES SCREAMING (64); THE SKULL (65); THE PSY-
CHOPATH (65); SPACEFLIGHT IC-1 (65); THE TERRORNAUTS
(66); BLOOD FIEND (66; aka THEATRE OF DEATH); MIJN
HACHTEN MET SUSAN OLGA ALBERT JULIE PIET & SANDRA
(75; Dutch)

Tony Macauley: THE BEAST IN THE CELLAR (71); PERCY'S
PROGRESS (79; aka IT'S NOT THE SIZE THAT COUNTS)

John McCabe (Br.): FEAR IN THE NIGHT (72); THE HAMMER
HOUSE OF HORROR (80, tv; episodes: The 13th Reunion,
Growing Pains, Guardian of the Abyss)

W. McCauley: THE NEPTUNE FACTOR (73; w/L. Schifrin)

Teo Macero: THE ORPHAN (79; aka FRIDAY THE 13TH ... THE
     ORPHAN; aka DON'T OPEN THE DOOR: theme song by Janis
     Ian); VIRUS (81; lyrics by J. Ian)

Garry McFarland (Br.): EYE OF THE DEVIL (66)

Don McGinnis: THE FIEND WITH THE ELECTRONIC BRAIN (65,
     tvm; aka PSYCHO A GO-GO; lyrics by Billy Storm); BLOOD
     OF GHASTLY HORROR (71, tvm; aka MAN WITH THE SYN-
     THETIC BRAIN; w/J. Roosa)

Bill McGuffie (Br.): THE GOLDEN RABBIT (62); DALEKS--IN-
     VASION EARTH 2750 A.D. (66); CORRUPTION (67); THE
     ASPHIX (72); DR. WHO (73, tv; episodes)

Tim McIntire: A BOY AND HIS DOG (75; w/J. Mendoza-Nava)

Theo Mackeben (Gm.): DER STUDENTE VON PRAG (35; The Stu-
     dent of Prague)

Rod McKeun: THE BORROWERS (73, tvm)

Robert McMullin: SHADOW OF THE HAWK (76)

Craig McRitchie: THE NIGHT STALKER (74, tv; episodes)

Norio Maeda (Ja.): STAR WOLF (78)

Michel Magne (Fr.): THE DEVIL AND THE TEN COMMANDMENTS
     (62; w/G. Magenta, C. Aznavour); FANTOMAS (64); SHADOW
     OF EVIL (64); OSS 117 MISSION FOR A KILLER (65); FAN-
     TOMAS SE DECHAINE (65; Fantomas Strikes Back); THE EX-
     TERMINATORS (65); A TOUT COEUR A TOKYO POUR OSS 117
     (66; Heart Trump in Tokyo for OSS 117)

George Mahana: MY FAVORITE MARTIANS (73, tv cart.); THE
     NEW ADVENTURES OF MIGHTY MOUSE AND HECKLE & JECKLE
     (79, tv cart.)

Hans-Martin Majewski (W. Gm.): BEYOND THE DARKNESS (74;
     aka MAGDALENA--POSSESSED BY THE DEVIL); DIE ELIXIERE
     DES TEUFELS (77)

J. Maksymiuk (Pol.): WORLD OF HORROR (68; "Canterville
     Ghost" segment)

Luigi Malatesta (It.): SCREAM OF THE DEMON LOVER (70)

Carlos Maleras (Sp.): METAMORFOSIS (71)

Jack Malken & Kim Scholes: THE NESTING (81)

Wil Malone & J. Rose: RAW MEAT (72)

Nikos Mamangates (W. Gm.): DAS GOLDENE DING (71)

Riichiro Manabe (Ja.): THE VAMPIRE DOLL (70); LAKE OF
     DRACULA (72); GODZILLA VS. THE SMOG MONSTER (72);
     GODZILLA VS. MEGALON (73); THE POSSESSED (76; aka THE
     WITCH, YOBA); THE INFERNO (79); THE BLOODTHIRSTY
     ROSES (c.79); THE BLOODTHIRSTY EYES (c.79); TARO OF
     THE DRAGONS (79)

*Henry Mancini: (All of the Universal films of the 50's are colla-
     borative scores in which Mancini's work has appeared, often and
     where noted as reused library tracks, along with the work of
     several other composers): CITY BENEATH THE SEA (52; w/H.
     Stein, M. Rosen, plus track by F. Skinner, H. Salter); AB-
     BOTT & COSTELLO GO TO MARS (53; track); ABBOTT & COS-
     TELLO MEET DR. JEKYLL AND MR. HYDE (53; track); IT

*Henry Mancini (cont.)
CAME FROM OUTER SPACE (53; w/H. Stein, I. Gertz; Mancini
composed ten incidental cues); THE CREATURE FROM THE
BLACK LAGOON (54; w/H. Stein, H. Salter; track by R.E.
Dolan, M. Rosen; Mancini composed six original cues, plus one
cue tracked from EAST OF SUMATRA); REVENGE OF THE
CREATURE (55; track); TARANTULA (55; track, incl. most
of last four reels); THIS ISLAND EARTH (55; w/H. Stein, H.
Salter. Mancini composed 2 cues for final two reels); THE
CREATURE WALKS AMONG US (56; w/H. Stein, H. Roemheld,
H. Salter, I. Gertz. Most of score by Mancini); THE LAND
UNKNOWN (57; w/H. Stein, H. Roemheld, H. Salter; Mancini
composed one cue); THE MONOLITH MONSTERS (57; w/H.
Stein, I. Gertz; Mancini scored second to last reel); MONSTER
ON THE CAMPUS (58; track); THE THING THAT COULDN'T
DIE (58; incl. track); THE SWORD OF ALI BABA (65; track);
WAIT UNTIL DARK (67; excerpts later used [without authoriza-
tion] in THE EYES OF CHARLES SAND, 72, tvm); THE NIGHT
VISITOR (71); FRENZY (72; score written but later rejected;
replaced with R. Goodwin score); THE INVISIBLE MAN (75,
tv); NIGHTWING (79); CONDORMAN (81). Excerpts from Man-
cini's THE WHITE DAWN were re-used in segments of THE
RIGHT STUFF (83).
Johnny Mandel: CODE NAME: HERCULES (76, tvm); ESCAPE TO
WITCH MOUNTAIN (75); FREAKY FRIDAY (77)
*Harry Manfredini: THE KIRLIAN WITNESS (78); THE CHILDREN
(80); FRIDAY THE 13TH (80); FRIDAY THE 13TH, PART II
(81); SWAMP THING (82); FRIDAY THE 13TH, PART III (82);
THE RETURNING (83); THE LAST PICNIC (83)
Detto Mariano (It.): RATATAPLAN (79)
Gino Marinuzzi (It.): HERCULES AND THE CAPTIVE WOMEN (61);
VENUS AGAINST THE SON OF HERCULES (62); I PATRIARCHI
DELLA BIBBIA (63; The Patriarchs of the Bible; w/T. Usuelli);
PLANET OF THE VAMPIRES (65; aka DEMON PLANET); MATCH-
LESS (67; w/P. Piccioni & E. Morricone)
Richard Markowitz: THE MAGIC SWORD (62); THE WILD, WILD
WEST (65-69, tv; theme & episodes; theme later adapted for
THE WILD WILD WEST REVISITED, 79 tvm; MORE WILD WILD
WEST, 80 tvm); THE STRANGER (73, tvm); TALES OF THE
UNEXPECTED (77, tv; episodes); DEATH CAR ON THE FREE-
WAY (79, tvm); BUCK ROGERS IN THE 25TH CENTURY (79,
tv; episode: Cruise Ship to the Stars)
Jan Markowski (Fr.): LES ASTRONAUTES (59; The Astronauts)
Jack Marshall: THE GIANT GILA MONSTER (59); THE MUNSTERS
(64-66, tv); MUNSTER GO HOME! (66)
Philip Martell (Br.): Music Director for Hammer films since 1963;
also music director for Tyburn, 1974-75; other md assignments:
FRANKENSTEIN, THE TRUE STORY (73, tvm)
Augusto Martelli (It.): IL DIO SERPENTE (70; The Serpent God)
Carlo Martelli (Br.): THE CURSE OF THE MUMMY'S TOMB (64);
WITCHCRAFT (64); THE WOMAN WHO WOULDN'T DIE (64);

PREHISTORIC WOMEN (66); IT! (67)

George Martin (Br.): YELLOW SUBMARINE (68; incidental score and md; songs by Lennon & McCartney); LIVE AND LET DIE (73; theme song by P. McCartney)

M. Maruyama (Ja.): A TRADITION IN THE WORLD OF SPIRIT, ACROBUNCH M. (82; w/Yamamoto)

Bill Marx: COUNT YORGA, VAMPIRE (70); THE DEATHMASTER (72); THE RETURN OF COUNT YORGA (71); THE FOLKS AT RED WOLF INN (72; aka TERROR HOUSE, 76); SCREAM, BLACULA, SCREAM (73)

Enzo Masetti (It.): HERCULES (57); HERCULES UNCHAINED (59)

Benedict Mason (Br.): THE TOM MACHINE (81)

Glen Mason (Br.): GO FOR A TAKE (72)

Diego Masson (Fr.): SPIRITS OF THE DEAD (67; "William Wilson" segment)

Muir Mathieson (Br.; Music Director). Conducted scores for: THINGS TO COME (36; music A. Bliss); ELEPHANT BOY (37); CLOUDS OVER EUROPE (39); THE THIEF OF BAGDAD (40; music M. Rozsa); BLITHE SPIRIT (45; music R. Addinsell); VALLEY OF THE EAGLES (51; music N. Rota); SVENGALI (54; music M. Alwyn); THREE CASES OF MURDER (55); CURSE OF THE DEMON (56; music C. Parker); REVENGE OF FRANKENSTEIN (58; music L. Salzedo); TOM THUMB (58; music D. Gamley/K. Jones); THE HEADLESS GHOST (59; music G. Schurmann); NO PLACE LIKE HOMICIDE (61); BURN, WITCH, BURN (61; music W. Alwyn); MR. HORATIO KNIBBLES (71)

Samuel Matlovsky: STAR TREK (67, tv; episode: I Mudd); BIRDS DO IT (66); GAMES (67)

Hachiro Matsui (Ja.): MY FRIEND DEATH (60)

Matsuyama & Watanabe (Ja.): MOBILE SUIT GUNDAM (81, tv; episodes; aka features GUNDAM I, II, III; 81-82)

Peter Matz: THE PRIVATE EYES (80)

Billy May: BATMAN (66, tv; episodes); THE GREEN HORNET (66, tv; theme)

*Brian May (Austral.): PATRICK (79); MAD MAX (80); HARLEQUIN (80); THE DAY AFTER HALLOWEEN (81; aka SNAPSHOT; aka ONE MORE MINUTE); THIRST (81); THE SURVIVOR (81); THE ROAD WARRIOR (82; aka MAD MAX 2)

Hans May (Br.): THE GHOSTS OF BERKELEY SQUARE (47); COUNTERBLAST (48); THE TELL-TALE HEART (53; short)

James K. Mayfield (as "Carl Hoefle"): SCARED TO DEATH (46)

Lincoln Mayorage: BLOOD OF DRACULA'S CASTLE (67)

George Melachrino (Br.): THINGS HAPPEN AT NIGHT (48); HOUSE OF DARKNESS (48); THE GAMMA PEOPLE (55)

*Gil Mellé: THE ANDROMEDA STRAIN (71); NIGHT GALLERY (71, tv; theme & episodes); YOU'LL LIKE MY MOTHER (72); THE ASTRONAUT (72, tvm); THE VICTIM (72, tvm); A COLD NIGHT'S DEATH (73, tvm); THE SIX MILLION DOLLAR MAN (73, tvm); TRAPPED (73, tvm); FRANKENSTEIN: THE TRUE STORY (73, tvm); THE QUESTOR TAPES (74, tvm); KOLCHAK: THE NIGHT STALKER (74, tv); KILLDOZER (74, tvm); THE

*Gil Mellé (cont.)
   ULTIMATE WARRIOR (75); EMBRYO (76); THE SENTINEL (77);
   STARSHIP INVASIONS (77); BLOOD BEACH (80); THE CURSE
   OF KING TUT'S TOMB (80, tvm); THE LAST CHASE (81); THE
   INTRUDER WITHIN (81, tvm); WORLD WAR III (82, tvm)
Mike Melvoin: BUCK ROGERS IN THE 25TH CENTURY (79, tv;
   episode: Planet of the Amazon Women)
Nacho Mendez: DR. TARR'S TORTURE DUNGEON (76; aka HOUSE
   OF MADNESS)
Jaime Mendoza-Nava: EQUINOX (67); THE WITCHMAKER (69);
   THE BROTHERHOOD OF SATAN (71); LEGACY OF BLOOD (71);
   THE LEGEND OF BOGGY CREEK (72); GARDEN OF THE DEAD
   (72; aka TOMB OF THE UNDEAD); BOOTLEGGERS (74); A
   BOY AND HIS DOG (75; w/T. McIntyre); GRAVE OF THE VAM-
   PIRE (75); MYSTERIES FROM BEYOND EARTH (75, tvm);
   CREATURE FROM BLACK LAKE (76); THE SHADOW OF CHI-
   KARA (77); THE TOWN THAT DREADED SUNDOWN (77); VAM-
   PIRE HOOKERS (78); THE EVICTORS (79); PSYCHO FROM
   TEXAS (82)
Gian-Carlo Menotti (It.): THE MEDIUM (51; from Menotti's opera)
Abe Meyer (Music Director): WHITE ZOMBIE (32; music G.B. Wil-
   liams, X. Cugat); THE WHISPERING SHADOW (33); THE
   SPHINX (33); STRANGE PEOPLE (33); THE AVENGER (33);
   TARZAN THE FEARLESS (33, serial); SHRIEK IN THE NIGHT
   (33); THE VAMPIRE BAT (33); THE STAR PACKER (34); THE
   RETURN OF CHANDU (34, serial); A SHOT IN THE DARK (34);
   MYSTERY LINER (34); HOUSE OF MYSTERY (34); GREEN EYES
   (34); THE GHOST WALKS (34); CONDEMNED TO LIVE (35; mu-
   sic incl. D. Broekman); THE ROGUES TAVERN (36); REVOLT
   OF THE ZOMBIES (36); THE MINE WITH THE IRON DOOR (36);
   DEATH FROM A DISTANCE (36); THE NEW ADVENTURES OF
   TARZAN (36, serial); HOUSE OF SECRETS (36)
Franco Micalizzi (It.): BEYOND THE DOOR (75; aka DEVIL WITH-
   IN HER; aka CHI SEI; Italian release only); BATTLE OF THE
   AMAZONS (76; aka KARATE AMAZONS); DIABOLICA (77); IL
   VISITATORE (80, The Visitor; aka STRIDULUM)
Jeff Michael (all tv cartoons): SABRINA, THE TEENAGE WITCH
   (71); STAR TREK (73); SHAZAM! (74); ISIS (75); ARK II (76);
   TARZAN, LORD OF THE JUNGLE (76); SPACE ACADEMY (77);
   SUPERWITCH (77); THE YOUNG SENTINELS (77); TARZAN
   AND THE SUPER SEVEN (78); JASON OF STAR COMMAND (79);
   THE TARZAN & LONE RANGER ADVENTURE HOUR (80)
Michel Michelet (Fr.): THE END OF THE WORLD (30); SIREN OF
   ATLANTIS (48); LURED (47); M (51); CAPTAIN SINBAD (63)
Luciano Michelini (It.): SCREAMERS (81; aka ISLAND OF THE
   FISH-MEN)
Gabriel Migliori (Braz.): O HOMEN LOBO (71; The Wolf Man)
Ted V. Mikels: THE CORPSE GRINDERS (72; Mikels also directed)
John Mills-Cockell: TERROR TRAIN (80); HUMONGOUS (82)
Hiroshi Mima (Ja.): HAUNTED CASTLE (69; aka MYSTERY OF
   THE CAT-WOMAN)

Kohetsu Minami (Ja.): TRITON OF THE SEAS (79)
Paul Misraki (Fr.): SI JEUNNESSE SAVAIT (47; If Youth Only
    Knew); UTOPIA (51, md): ALI BABA & THE FORTY THIEVES
    (54); A DOG, A MOUSE AND A SPUTNIK (58); ATTACK OF
    THE ROBOTS (62); ALPHAVILLE (65); LA BULLE (76; The
    Bubble)
The Missing Link (group): MISTRESS OF THE APES (79)
Hiroshi Miyagawa (Ja.): SPACE CRUISER YAMATO (77, tv; aka
    U.S.: STARBLAZERS); AARIVEDERCI YAMATO (78); GRAND
    PRIX HAWK (78, tv); SPACE CRUISER YAMATO--THE NEW
    VOYAGE (79); BE FOREVER YAMATO (80); YAMATO 3 (80,
    tv); SPACE CRUISER YAMATO--FINAL (82, tv; w/Haneda)
Kunio Miyauchi (Ja.): THE HUMAN VAPOR (64); ULTRAMAN (65,
    tv w/T. Foyoki, M. Higure; later released as feature, 67);
    GODZILLA'S REVENGE (71); GODZILLA VS. GIGAN (76; aka
    GODZILLA ON MONSTER ISLAND; Ja. release only)
H. Miyazaki (Ja.): MIRAI SHONEN KONAN (77)
Vic Mizzy: THE ADDAMS FAMILY (64, tv; theme & episodes);
    THE NIGHT WALKER (64); THE GHOST & MR. CHICKEN (65);
    THE RELUCTANT ASTRONAUT (66); THE SPIRIT IS WILLING
    (66); CAPTAIN NICE (67, tv; theme & episodes); THE PERILS
    OF PAULINE (67, tvm); THE MUNSTERS' REVENGE (81, tvm)
Cyril Mockridge: THE HOUND OF THE BASKERVILLES (39, md);
    WHISPERING GHOSTS (42, w/L. Harline; main title by D. Rak-
    sin); THE UNDYING MONSTER (42; uncredited; w/D. Raksin,
    A. Lange); THE BIG NOISE (44); SENTIMENTAL JOURNEY
    (46); WAKE UP AND DREAM (46); LUCK OF THE IRISH (48);
    LOST IN SPACE (65, tv; episodes)
Mario Molino (It.): GLI ANGELI DEL 2000 (75; The Angels of
    2000)
Henry Mollicone: THE PREMONITION (75; electronics by P.
    Smiley)
Hugo Montenegro: I DREAM OF JEANNIE (65, tv); THE AM-
    BUSHERS (67)
Bruce Montgomery (Br.): THE BRIDES OF FU MANCHU (66)
Hal Mooney: THE HOUND OF THE BASKERVILLES (71, tvm; md);
    NIGHT GALLERY (71, tv; episode: The Tune in Dan's Cafe);
    THE TRIBE (74, tvm)
A. Moore (W. Gm.): THE PHANTASTIC WORLD OF MATTHEW
    MADSON (74; w/N. Busch)
Dudley Moore (Br.): BEDAZZLED (67); THE HOUND OF THE
    BASKERVILLES (77, Br.); Moore also starred.
Gene Moore: CARNIVAL OF SOULS (62)
Spencer Moore: Stock library tracks by Moore, et al., used as
    score for NIGHT OF THE LIVING DEAD (68)
Mike Moran (Br.): TIME BANDITS (81; songs by George Harrison)
Lucien Moraweck: THE TWILIGHT ZONE (60-64, tv; episodes:
    The Purple Testament; Queen of the Nile)
John Morgan: TIMEGATE (uncompleted, 70's); BUCK ROGERS IN
    THE 25TH CENTURY (79, tv; episodes); THE AFTERMATH (80)
Tom Morgan: THE TWILIGHT ZONE (62, tv; episodes: The Last

Tom Morgan (cont.)
    Rites of Jeff Myrtlebank, Hocus-Pocus and Frisby, Mr. Garrity
    and the Graves)
Fernando Garcia Morillo (Sp.): FANTASIA ... 3 (66); EL CASO
    DE LAS DOS BELIEZES (68; The Case of the Two Beauties);
    BESAME, MONSTRUO (68; Kiss Me, Monster)
Ken-Ichiro Morioka (Ja.): MESSAGE FROM SPACE (78)
Angela Morley (formerly Walter Stott): WILL ANY GENTLEMAN...?
    (53; as "Stott"); CAPTAIN NEMO AND THE UNDERWATER CITY
    (69; "Stott"); THE NEW ADVENTURES OF WONDER WOMAN (77,
    tv); WATERSHIP DOWN (78; w/M. Williamson, M. Batt)
Giorgio Moroder: CAT PEOPLE (82); METROPOLIS (26; Moroder
    scored 83 widescreen, Dolby reissue)
Jerome Moross: THE VALLEY OF GWANGI (68)
*Ennio Morricone (It.): LLEGARON LOS MARCIANOS (64; The
    Martians Arrived; aka The Martians Have 12 Hands); NIGHT-
    MARE CASTLE (65); UCCELLACCI E UCCELLINI (65; Hawks and
    Sparrows); AGENT 505 (66); LE STREGHE (67; The Witches;
    w/P. Piccioni); O.K. CONNERY (67; aka OPERATION KID
    BROTHER; w/B. Nicolai); DANGER: DIABOLIK (67); MATCH-
    LESS (67; w/P. Piccioni & G. Marinuzzi); PARTNER (68; aka
    EAT IT); A QUIET PLACE IN THE COUNTRY (68); TEOREMA
    (68); THE BIRD WITH THE CRYSTAL PLUMAGE (70); THE DE-
    CAMERON (72; w/P. Pasolini); YEAR OF THE CANNIBALS (71);
    MADDALENA (71); CAT O'NINE TAILS (71); SCHIZOID (71; aka
    LIZARD IN A WOMAN'S SKIN); COSA AVETTE FATTO A SO-
    LANGE? (72; What Have You Done with Solange?); THE BLACK
    BELLY OF THE TARANTULA (72); FOUR FLIES ON GREY VEL-
    VET (72); CATALEPSIS (72); IL MAESTRO E MARGHERITA (72;
    The Master and Margherite); BLUEBEARD (72); WHEN WOMEN
    HAD TAILS (72); IL DIAVOLO NEL CERVELLO (72; Devil in
    the Brain); VAARWEL (73; aka THE ROMANTIC AGONY);
    SPACE: 1999 (74; Ital. feature compiled from 3 tv episodes);
    SPASMO (74); WHEN WOMEN LOST THEIR TAILS (74); L'ANTI-
    CRISTO (74; Antichrist; aka THE TEMPTER; w/B. Nicolai); LE
    TRIO INFERNAL (74; The Unholy Three); IL SORRISO DEL
    GRANDE TENTATORE (75; aka THE DEVIL IS A WOMAN); PEUR
    SUR LA VILLE (75; aka THE NIGHT CALLER); THE MAGIC MAN
    (76, tv); TODO MONDO (76); ORCA: THE KILLER WHALE (77);
    EXORCIST II: THE HERETIC (77); LEONOR (77); HOLOCAUST
    2000 (77; aka THE CHOSEN); IL MOSTRO (77; The Fiend); THE
    HUMANOID (78); AUTOPSY (79; aka THE VICTIM); BLOODLINE
    (79); THE ISLAND (80); ARABIAN NIGHTS (80; aka IL FIORE
    DELLE MILLE UNA NOTTE); IL PRATO (80; The Meadow); THE
    THING (82); TREASURE OF THE FOUR CROWNS (82); HUNDRA
    (83)
John Morris: YOUNG FRANKENSTEIN (74); DOCTOR FRANKEN
    (80, tvm); HISTORY OF THE WORLD, PART 1 (81); THE ELEC-
    TRIC GRANDMOTHER (82, tvm)
Arthur Morton: IT HAD TO BE YOU (47; w/H. Roemheld); THE
    THIRTEENTH HOUR (47; includes track). Morton is currently

a noted orchestrator, especially for J. Goldsmith.

Marc Moulin (Fr.): TARZOON, LE HONTE DE LA JUNGLE (75;
Tarzoon, the Shame of the Jungle)

Rolf-Sans Mueller (Swed.): VEIL OF BLOOD (78; aka THE
DEVIL'S PLAYTHING)

Joseph Mullendore: THE ADVENTURES OF SUPERMAN (53, tv;
episodes); VOYAGE TO THE BOTTOM OF THE SEA (64, tv;
episodes); LOST IN SPACE (65, tv; episodes); THE TIME
TUNNEL (66, tv; episodes); STAR TREK (66, tv; episode:
The Conscience of the King)

David Munrow (Br.): THE DEVILS (71; period music only);
ZARDOZ (74)

Walter Murphy: THE SAVAGE BEES (76, tvm)

Lyn Murray: ALFRED HITCHCOCK PRESENTS/THE ALFRED
HITCHCOCK HOUR (55-65, tv; episodes); THE TWILIGHT
ZONE (60, tv; episode: A Passage for Trumpet); SNOW
WHITE AND THE THREE STOOGES (61); THE TIME TUNNEL
(66, tv)

Jean Musy: TANYA'S ISLAND (81)

Stanley Myers: TAM LIN (71; aka THE DEVIL'S WIDOW); HOUSE
OF WHIPCORD (74); FRIGHTMARE (75); SCHIZO (76); THE
CONFESSIONAL (77); THE COMEBACK (79; aka THE DAY THE
SCREAMING STOPPED); THE MARTIAN CHRONICLES (80,
tvm); THE WATCHER IN THE WOODS (81); INCUBUS (81)

Fred Myrow: A REFLECTION OF FEAR (73); SOYLENT GREEN
(73); PHANTASM (79; w/M. Seagrave)

I. Nafshun & Al Remington: THE BEAST OF YUCCA FLATS (61)

Sadao Nagase (Ja.): AKUMA NO KESHIN (59; Devil Incarnate,
aka SUPER GIANT #8); DOKUGA OKOKU (59; Kingdom of the
Venomous Moth; aka SUPER GIANT #9)

Ramesh Naidu (India): CHANDANA (74); DEVUDE GELICHADU
(76)

Katsumi Nakamura (Ja.): VAMPIRE DRACULA COMES TO KOBE:
EVIL MAKES WOMEN BEAUTIFUL (79, tvm)

Mahesh Naresh (India): TAME RE CHAMPO NE AME KEL (78)

*Mario Nascimbene (It.): O.K. NERO (53); LAS BACCANTI (60;
The Bacchantes); THE GOLDEN ARROW (62); DICK SMART
2/007 (66); KISS THE GIRLS AND MAKE THEM DIE (66); ONE
MILLION YEARS B.C. (66); THE VENGEANCE OF SHE (67);
DOCTOR FAUSTUS (67); WHEN DINOSAURS RULED THE EARTH
(70); CREATURES THE WORLD FORGOT (71)

Jose Luis Navarro (Sp.): CAULDRON OF BLOOD (67; Spanish
release only)

Franco Nebbia (It.): DRACULA IN THE PROVINCES (75; w/
Bixio, Frizzi, Tempera)

Neiman-Tillar (agency): ALIEN ENCOUNTER (79; probably library
score)

Oliver Nelson: SKULLDUGGERY (70); NIGHT GALLERY (71, tv;
episodes: Midnight Never Ends, Phantom of What Opera?,
The Different Ones, Logoda's Heads, The Sins of the Fathers,
others.); THE SIX MILLION DOLLAR MAN (73, tv)

Michael Nesmith: TIMERIDER (83)

Dan Neufeld: LEMORA, A CHILD'S TALE OF THE SUPERNATURAL
(75; aka LEMORA, THE LADY DRACULA; aka LEGENDARY
CURSE OF LEMORA)

Anthony Newley (Br.): CAN HEIRONYMOUS MERKIN FORGET MER-
CY HUMPPE AND FIND TRUE HAPPINESS? (69; also directed);
WILLY WONKA & THE CHOCOLATE FACTORY (71; lyrics: L.
Bricusse); OLD DRACULA (75; theme song only)

Alfred Newman: THE HUNCHBACK OF NOTRE DAME (39); THE
BLUE BIRD (40); HEAVEN CAN WAIT (43); FOR HEAVEN'S
SAKE (50)

Emil Newman (Music Director): DR. RENAULT'S SECRET (42,
music: D. Raksin); WHISPERING GHOSTS (42; music: D.
Raksin, L. Harline); THE UNDYING MONSTER (42; music:
D. Raksin, C. Mockridge, A. Lange); RENDEZVOUS 24 (46);
THE MAD MAGICIAN (54; music: A. Lange)

Lionel Newman (most as md): IT HAPPENS EVERY SPRING (49;
music: L. Harline); THE ROCKET MAN (53; tracked score);
GORILLA AT LARGE (54); VOYAGE TO THE BOTTOM OF THE
SEA (64, tv); LOST IN SPACE (65, tv); THE TIME TUNNEL
(66, tv); LAND OF THE GIANTS (65, tv); DAUGHTER OF THE
MIND (69, tvm); THE CHALLENGE (70, tvm); WHEN MICHAEL
CALLS (72, tvm); PLANET OF THE APES (74, tv)

Ted Nichols: THE FLINTSTONES (60-70, tv cart.)

*Bruno Nicolai (It.): O.K. CONNERY (67; aka OPERATION KID
BROTHER; w/E. Morricone); EUGENIE ... THE STORY OF HER
JOURNEY INTO PERVERSION (69; aka MARQUIS DE SADE);
COUNT DRACULA (70; aka NIGHTS OF DRACULA); DRACULA
CONTRA EL DR. FRANKENSTEIN (71; w/D. White); EL CRISTO
DEL OCEANO (71; Christ of the Ocean); EXCITE ME (72);
NIGHT OF THE BLOOD MONSTER (72; aka THRONE OF FIRE);
PERCHE QUELLE STRANE GOCCI DE SANGUE SIL CORPE DE
JENNIFER? (72; What Are Those Strange Drops of Blood on the
Body of Jennifer?); TUTTI I COLORI DEL BUIO (72; All the
Colors of Darkness; aka THEY'RE COMING TO GET YOU, 76);
THE NIGHT EVELYN CAME OUT OF THE GRAVE (73); L'ANTI-
CRISTO (74; Antichrist; aka THE TEMPTER; w/E. Morricone);
EYEBALL (78)

Roberto Nicolosi (It.): BLACK SUNDAY (60; Italian release only);
THE EVIL EYE (62; It. release only); WAR OF THE ZOMBIES
(63; aka GODDESS OF ELECTRA); BLACK SABBATH (63; It.
release only); L'OCCHIO NEL LABIRINTO (71; The Eye of the
Labyrinth; aka BLOOD)

Harry Nilsson (Ar.): THE POINT (71); SON OF DRACULA (72);
POPEYE (80)

Noburu Nishiyama (Ja.): KYUKETSU DOKUROSEN (68; The Living Skeleton)

Jack Nitzsche: VILLAGE OF THE GIANTS (65); PERFORMANCE
(70); THE EXORCIST (74; 2 cues used)

Erik Nordgren (Swed.): THE SEVENTH SEAL (56); WILD STRAW-
BERRIES (58); THE MAGICIAN (58); THE VIRGIN SPRING (60)

Lon E. Norman: STING OF DEATH (66; w/A. Jacobs); I EAT
  YOUR SKIN (74)
Monty Norman (Br.): THE TWO FACES OF DR. JEKYLL (60; w/
  D. Heneker; aka HOUSE OF FRIGHT); DR. NO (63; "James
  Bond Theme" by J. Barry)
*Alex North: THE BAD SEED (56); WILLARD (71); SHANKS (74);
  JOURNEY INTO FEAR (76); WISE BLOOD (79); DRAGONSLAYER
  (81). North also composed and recorded an original score for
  2001: A SPACE ODYSSEY (68) which was rejected by director
  Kubrick.
Ed Norton (Music Director): BEYOND ATLANTIS (73; aka SEA
  CREATURES)
Jan Novak (Cz.): CYBERNETIC GRANDMOTHER (62, cart.); A
  JESTER'S TALE (64); THE STOLEN AIRSHIP (69)
Nobuhiko Obayashi (Ja.): MURDER AT AN OLD MANSION (76)
Arlon Ober: THE INCREDIBLE MELTING MAN (77); GALAXINA
  (81; md); X-RAY (81); HAPPY BIRTHDAY (82; aka BLOODY
  BIRTHDAY; aka CREEPS); EATING RAOUL (82); HOSPITAL
  MASSACRE (82); NIGHTBEAST (82; w/R. Walsh, J. Abrams,
  L. Rogowski)
Hiroaki Ogawa (Ja.): THE MANSTER (59)
Yuji Ohno (Ja.): THE INUGAMIS (77); SPACE COBRA (83, tv;
  w/Haneda); ANDROMEDA STORIES (83, tv); LUPIN III (84
  series, tv)
Tom O'Horgan: ALEX IN WONDERLAND (71)
Herb Ohta & Hiroshi Kamayatsu (Ja.): THE WHITE HOUSE ON
  THE BEACH (78)
Tiberiu Olah (Rum.): VLAD TEPES (78; aka VLAD THE IMPALER,
  THE TRUE LIFE OF DRACULA)
Alan Oldfield: DOGS (76)
Mike Oldfield (Br.): THE EXORCIST (74; excerpt from "Tubular
  Bells" recording used); CHARLOTTE (75); THE SPACE MOVIE
  (80, doc.)
A.P. Olea (Sp.): THE BLOOD SPATTERED BRIDE (74); NIGHT-
  MARE HOTEL (73)
Mats Olsson (Swed.): FEAR HAS 1,000 EYES (71)
Sonik-Omi (India): THE SAME NIGHT, THE SAME VOICE (73)
Seitari Omori (Ja.): MONSTER FROM A PREHISTORIC PLANET
  (67; aka GAPPA-TRIPHIBIAN MONSTER); WEIRD TRIP (72)
Ugi Oni (Ja.): HOUSE OF TERROR (76); LUPIN III (78)
The Orphanage (group): CAN ELLEN BE SAVED? (74, tvm)
Cyril Ornadel (Br.): THE FLESH AND BLOOD SHOW (74)
Riz Ortolani (It.): URSUS NELLA VALLE DEL LEONI (61; Ursus
  in the Valley of Lions); HORROR CASTLE (63; aka THE VIR-
  GIN OF NUREMBERG); CASTLE OF BLOOD (64; aka CASTLE
  OF TERROR; aka LA DANZA MACABRA); LA RAGAZZA DEL
  BERSAGLIERE (66; The Bersagliere's Girl); LIGHTNING BOLT
  (66); WEB OF THE SPIDER (71); SEVEN DEAD IN THE CAT'S
  EYES (72); THE DEAD ARE ALIVE (72); THE AMAZONES (73;
  aka THE WAR GODDESS, 74); BEYOND THE DOOR (75; aka
  CHI SEI?; aka DEVIL WITHIN HER; U.S. release only); FAN-

Riz Ortolani (cont.)
    TASMA D'AMORE (81); MADHOUSE (82)
Tony Osborne & Richard Kerr: BEWARE THE BRETHREN (72)
John O'Verlin & Kelly Lammers: PLANET OF DINOSAURS (80)
Pagan & Remirez Angel (Sp.): THE AWFUL DR. ORLOF (61)
Gene Page: BREWSTER McCLOUD (71; songs by J. Phillips);
    BLACULA (72)
Hayes Pagel: THE PHANTOM PLANET (61)
C.N. Pandurangan (India): KATHAVAI THATEEYA MOHNI PAYE
    (75)
Manuel Parada (Sp.): SATANIK (68)
Alan Parker: JAWS 3D (83)
Clifton Parker (Br.): TARZAN AND THE LOST SAFARI (56);
    CURSE OF THE DEMON (56); SCREAM OF FEAR (61)
Bernard Parmeggiani (Fr.): LA POUPEE (61; The Doll; w/J. Kos-
    ma; J. Milschberg); LES JEUX DES ANGES (64, cart.); LE
    DICTIONAIRE DE JOACHIM (65); LE BRULERE DE MILLE
    SOLEILS (65; The Burning of a Thousand Suns; cart.);
    ARAIGNELEPHANT (69; Spider Elephant); LES SOLEILS DE
    L'ILE DE PAQUES (72; The Suns of Easter Island)
Arvo Part (Pol.): TEST PILOT PIRX (79)
Johnny Pate: SATAN'S TRIANGLE (75, tvm); DR. BLACK AND
    MR. HYDE (76); THE WATTS MONSTER (79)
Ivan Patrachich (Hung.): ARENA (69)
Paul Patterson (Br.): THE HAMMER HOUSE OF HORROR (80, tv;
    episodes: Rude Awakening, Children of the Full Moon, The
    Two Faces of Evil, The Mark of Satan)
D. Patucchi (W. Gm.): THE LONG, SWIFT SWORD OF SIEGFRIED
    (71; aka THE EROTIC ADVENTURES OF SIEGFRIED)
Edward Paul: BAMBOO SAUCER (67; md; score R. Kraushaar)
Glen Paxton: THE CLONE MASTER (78, tvm)
Don Peake: THE LEGEND OF BIGFOOT (75); THE HILLS HAVE
    EYES (77); I, DESIRE (82, tvm); THE HOUSE WHERE DEATH
    LIVES (82); KNIGHT RIDER (83, tv)
Kevin Peek: BATTLETRUCK (82; aka WARLORDS OF THE 21ST
    CENTURY)
Gino Peguri (It.): BLOODY PIT OF HORROR (65); SUPERSONIC
    MAN (80)
Ahmad Pejman (Iran): TALL SHADOWS OF THE WIND (78)
I. Pepper: QUEEN KONG (77; arranged by Tony Mimms)
Fondo Jorge Perez (Mx.; aka George Perez): ORLAK, EN LA IN-
    FIERNO DE FRANKENSTEIN (60; Orlak, the Hell of Franken-
    stein); MONSTER DEMOLISHER (60); SANTO ATACA LAS BRU-
    JAS (64; Santo Attacks the Witches)
Jaime Perez (Sp.): EXORCISM'S DAUGHTER (74)
Jose Perez (Mx.): ENSAYO UN CRIMEN (55; Practice of a Crime;
    w/J. Bracho)
Frank Perkins: THE INCREDIBLE MR. LIMPET (63; songs by
    Sammy Fain and Harold Adamson)
Sam Perry: THE HUNCHBACK OF NOTRE DAME (31 reissue of 23
    silent version; w/H. Roemheld)

Alexander and Mark Peskanov: HE KNOWS YOU'RE ALONE (80)
John Petersen: ATRAPADOS (81)
Andrey Petrovic (USSR): THE BLUE BIRD (76)
Emil Petrovics (Hung.): THE PHANTOM ON HORSEBACK (77)
S. Phadke (India): WANTED: SON-IN-LAW SALE (73)
Freddie Phillips (Br.): All cartoons: THE FROG PRINCE (54);
    GALLANT LITTLE TAILOR (54); THE GRASSHOPPER AND THE
    ANT (54, tv); HANSEL AND GRETEL (54, tv); JACK & THE
    BEANSTALK (54); PUSS IN BOOTS (54)
John Phillips: BREWSTER McCLOUD (71; songs only); THE MAN
    WHO FELL TO EARTH (76, md)
Stu Phillips: THE NAME OF THE GAME IS KILL! (68); 2000
    YEARS LATER (68); THE CURIOUS FEMALE (69); SIMON, KING
    OF THE WITCHES (71); THE SIX MILLION DOLLAR MAN (73-79,
    tv; episodes); BATTLESTAR GALACTICA (78, tv; theme & epi-
    sodes); THE AMAZING SPIDERMAN (78-79, tv; episodes);
    SPIDERMAN STRIKES BACK (78, tv); BUCK ROGERS IN THE
    25TH CENTURY (79, tv; theme & episodes: The Plot to Kill a
    City, et al.); GALACTICA 1980 (80, tv; episodes); CONQUEST
    OF THE EARTH (80, tvm); AUTOMAN (83, tv)
Bill Phyx: THE DEVIL'S ECSTASY (77)
Piero Piccioni (It.): DUEL OF THE TITANS (61); IL DEMONIO
    (63; The Demon); IL DISCO VOLANTE (64, the Flying Saucer);
    FROM THE ORIENT WITH FURY (65); THE MAN WHO LAUGHS
    (65); THE TENTH VICTIM (65); MORE THAN A MIRACLE (66);
    MATCHLESS (67; w/G. Marinuzzi & E. Morricone); THE
    WITCHES (67; w/E. Morricone); SCACCO ALLA REGINA (69;
    Check to the Queen); TO', E MORTA LA NONNA! (69; Oh!
    Grandmother's dead); MARTA (71); JACK, EL DESTRUPATOR DE
    LONDRES (71; Jack, the Mangler of London; aka JACK THE
    RIPPER); SISTERS OF SATAN (73); THE MONK (73); IO E
    CATERINA (81); UNA TOMBA APERTIA ... UNA BARA VUOTO
    (82; An Open Grave ... An Empty Coffin)
David Pierce & Rick Jones (Br.): THE FLIPSIDE OF DOMINICK
    HYDE (80, tv)
Alain Pierre (Fr.): DES MORTS (79; Of the Dead)
Tom Pierson: QUINTET (79)
Alda Piga (It.): PLAYGIRLS AND THE VAMPIRE (60); THE VAM-
    PIRES AND THE BALLERINA (62); CURSE OF THE BLOOD-
    GHOULS (62); TARZAK CONTRO GLI UOMINI LEOPARDO (64;
    Tarzak vs. the Leopard Man); Z7 OPERATION REMBRANDT (67)
Juan Pineda (Sp.): BLOOD PIE (71)
Nicola Piovani (It.): IL PROFUMO DELLA SIGNORA IN NERO (74;
    The Perfume of the Woman in Black); L'INVENZIONE DI MOREL
    (74); FLAVIA, PRIESTESS OF VIOLENCE (75)
Franco Pisano (It.): SUPERARGO VS. DIABOLICUS (66); DOREL-
    LIK (67); SUPERARGO AND THE FACELESS GIANTS (67; as
    "Berte Pisano")
Clay Pitts: I DRINK YOUR BLOOD (71)
Eugene Poddany: HOW THE GRINCH STOLE CHRISTMAS (66, tv
    cart.)

Richard A. Podolar: BIGFOOT (72)

Basil Poledouris: TINTORERA (77); CONAN THE BARBARIAN (82);
    AMAZONS (84, tvm); CONAN THE DESTROYER (84)

Jean-Luc Ponty: WITCHCRAFT THROUGH THE AGES (21; 1969
    Br. rerelease; w/D. Humair)

L.J. Ponzak: 2076 OLYMPIAD (77)

Marcel Poot (Belg.): THE EVIL EYE (37)

Ion Popescue-Gopo & Cornel Popescu (Rum.): THE STORY OF
    LOVE (81)

Popol Vuh (W. Gm. group): HEART OF GLASS (76); NOSFERATU
    THE VAMPIRE (79)

Michel Portal (Fr.): SERAIL (76)

Post Associates (firm): STANLEY (72)

Mike Post & Pete Carpenter: DR. SCORPION (78, tvm); CAPTAIN
    AMERICA (79, tvm); THE GREATEST AMERICAN HERO (81, tv;
    Post only)

Edward Powell: TOPPER TAKES A TRIP (39; w/H. Friedhofer)

Reg Powell: FAR OUT SPACE NUTS (75-77, tv; episodes)

Roberto Pregadio (It.): THE GLASS SPHINX (67; Ital. release
    only); EVA, LA VENERE SELVAGGIO (68; Eve, the Savage
    Venus); KING OF KONG ISLAND (68, tv); KRIMINAL (?)

Don Preston: ANDROID (82)

Andre Previn: GOODBYE CHARLIE (64); DEAD RINGER (64);
    ROLLERBALL (75; md and party music)

Charles Previn (Music Director for Universal during the 40's):
    THE MISSING GUEST (38; md); TOWER OF LONDON (39; w/
    F. Skinner, H. Salter); THE INVISIBLE WOMAN (40); BLACK
    FRIDAY (40; w/Skinner, Salter, C. Henderson); THE WOLF
    MAN (42; w/Skinner, Salter); HELLZAPOPPIN (41; md); HOR-
    ROR ISLAND (41; w/Skinner, Salter, Henderson); THE BLACK
    CAT (41; w/Skinner, Salter, Henderson); HOLD THAT GHOST
    (41; w/Skinner, Salter, Henderson); DRUMS OF THE CONGO
    (41; w/Salter); INVISIBLE AGENT (42; w/Salter); THE MUM-
    MY'S TOMB (42; w/Skinner, Salter, H. Roemheld); FRANKEN-
    STEIN MEETS THE WOLF MAN (43; w/Salter, Skinner); SON
    OF DRACULA (42; w/Salter, Skinner); THE MAD GHOUL (43;
    w/Salter, Skinner, Henderson); HOUSE OF FRANKENSTEIN (44;
    w/P. Dessau, Skinner, Salter); JUNGLE CAPTIVE (44; w/P.
    Sawtell, W. Lava, Salter); THE MUMMY's GHOST (44; w/Skin-
    ner, Salter); HOUSE OF DRACULA (45; w/Salter, Skinner,
    Henderson, Dessau, Lava, Sawtell, E. Fairchild). Library
    tracks reused in THE STRANGE DOOR (51)

Henry Price: THE INCREDIBLY STRANGE CREATURES WHO
    STOPPED LIVING AND BECAME MIXED-UP ZOMBIES (64; aka
    TEENAGE PSYCHO MEETS BLOODY MARY; songs by L. Quinn);
    THE THRILL KILLERS (65); SINTHIA THE DEVIL'S DOLL (70;
    aka THE DEVIL'S DOLL)

Frank Primata: MAUSOLEUM (81)

Robert Prince: NIGHT GALLERY (71, tv; episodes: The Dead
    Man, The Little Black Bag, The Funeral, The Nature of the
    Enemy, The Academy, Pamela's Voice, others); GARGOYLES

(72, tvm); CIRCLE OF FEAR (73, tvm); SCREAM, PRETTY
PEGGY (73, tvm); WHERE HAVE ALL THE PEOPLE GONE? (74,
tvm); THE STRANGE AND DEADLY OCCURRENCE (74, tvm);
THE DEAD DON'T DIE (75, tvm); J.D.'S REVENGE (76);
SQUIRM (76); SNOWBEAST (77, tvm); THE NEW ADVENTURES
OF WONDER WOMAN (77, tv); FANTASTIC JOURNEY (77, tv;
theme, pilot and episodes: Atlantium, Beyond the Mountain,
Children of God, Fun House, Innocent Prey, Riddles, Turn-
about); BUCK ROGERS IN THE 25TH CENTURY (79, tv; epi-
sode: Space Vampire)

Jean Prodromides (Fr.): BLOOD AND ROSES (60); SPIRITS OF
THE DEAD (67; "Metzengerstein" segment)

Prohaska (Yug.): LE PEAU DE CHAGRIN (60, cart.)

Skip Prokop: DR. FRANKENSTEIN ON CAMPUS (70; w/P. Hoffert)

S. Pueyo (Sp.): EL EXTRANO CASO DEL DR. FAUSTO (69; The
Strange Case of Dr. Faust)

L. Pyarelal (India): NAGIN (76)

Queen (group): FLASH GORDON (80; incidental music by H.
Blake)

Quintessence (group): MIDNIGHT (82)

Robert O. Ragland: THE THING WITH TWO HEADS (72); ABBY
(74); DEMON (76; aka GOD TOLD ME; w/Janelle Webb; title
song only); GRIZZLY (76); MANSION OF THE DOOMED (76);
Q, THE WINGED SERPENT (82)

*David Raksin: MODERN TIMES (36; arrangements only, adapted
C. Chaplin music); WHISPERING GHOSTS (42; main title music
only; score by L. Harline/C. Mockridge); THE UNDYING MON-
STER (42; w/C. Mockridge, A. Lange); DR. RENAULT'S SE-
CRET (42); THE SECRET LIFE OF WALTER MITTY (47);
WHIRLPOOL (49); THE NEXT VOICE YOU HEAR (50); THE
UNICORN IN THE GARDEN (53, cart.); NIGHT TIDE (61);
WHAT'S THE MATTER WITH HELEN? (71); THE GHOST OF
FLIGHT 401 (78, tvm); THE DAY AFTER (83, tvm)

Ruby Raksin: VALLEY OF THE DRAGONS (61); THE MYSTERIOUS
MONSTERS (75, doc.)

Ron Ramin: THE NEXT STEP BEYOND (78, tv; episodes)

Rosalio Ramirez (Mx.): LAS CINCO ADVERTENCIAS DE SATANAS
(45; Satan's Five Warnings); UN DIA CON EL DIABLO (45; A
Day with the Devil); LA HERENCIA DE LA LLORONA (46; The
Heritage of the Crying Woman); UNA AVENTURA EN LA
NOCHE (47; The Adventure in the Night)

Phil Ramone: THE MIND SNATCHERS (72)

Gyorgy Ranki (Hung.): A BIT OF IMMORTALITY (67); JOURNEY
INSIDE MY BRAIN (71)

Piere Raph (Fr.): REQUIEM POUR UN VAMPIRE (71); LA ROSE
DE FER (73; Rose of Iron); LE DEMONIAQUES (74); LA NUIT
DU CIMETIERE (73)

Joe Raposo: THE POSSESSION OF JOEL DELANEY (71); SAVAGES
(72); RAGGEDY ANN AND ANDY (77)

Alan Rawsthorne (Br.): PANDORA AND THE FLYING DUTCHMAN
(51)

Satyajit Ray (India; also director): GUPI GYNE BAGHA BYNE
     (69); JOI BABA FELUNATH (7 ?; The Elephant God); HIRAK
     RAJAR DESHE (80; The Kingdom of Diamonds)
Coby & Iris Recht: THE APPLE (81)
Ivan Reitman (Can.): THEY CAME FROM WITHIN (76; aka THE
     PARASITE MURDERS; aka SHIVERS; md); RABID (77; also
     producer); THE HOUSE BY THE LAKE (77; aka DEATH WEEK-
     END; also producer)
Franz Reizenstein (Br.): THE MUMMY (79); CIRCUS OF HOR-
     RORS (60)
Joe Renzetti: DEAD AND BURIED (81); THE MYSTERIOUS TWO
     (82, tvm)
Angelo Revello: FAMOUS CLASSIC TALES (73, tv; "Gulliver's
     Travels" segment)
Gianfranco Reverberi & Remolo Forlai (It.): REINCARNATION OF
     ISABEL (73; aka GHASTLY ORGIES OF COUNT DRACULA)
Robert Richards (Br.): THE BLACK TORMENT (64); GONKS GO
     BEAT (65, md); DOCTORS WEAR SCARLET (70); BLOODSUCK-
     ERS (71)
Kim Richmond: IT HAPPENED AT LAKE WOOD MANOR (77, tvm)
Nelson Riddle: VOYAGE TO THE BOTTOM OF THE SEA (64, tv;
     episodes); BATMAN (66-68, tv; episodes)
Hugo Riesenfeld: THE PHANTOM EMPIRE (35, serial; w/H. Had-
     ley); DICK TRACY (37, serial; Riesenfeld's stock library music
     included)
Doug Riley (Can.): CANNIBAL GIRLS (72)
Terry Riley: LIFESPAN (75)
Laurin Rinder & W. Michael Lewis: IN SEARCH OF ... (76, tv);
     SECRETS OF THE BERMUDA TRIANGLE (78); NEW YEAR'S
     EVIL (81); THE NINJA (81)
Walter Rizzati (It.): QUELLA VILLA ACCANTO AL CIMITERO (81,
     House Outside the Cemetery); 1990--THE BRONX WARRIORS (84)
Bruce Roberts: THE CRAZIES (73)
Des Roberts: GUESS WHAT HAPPENED TO COUNT DRACULA? (70)
Eric Robertson: M3: THE GEMINI STRAIN (79; aka PLAGUE)
*Harry Robertson (Br.; aka Harry Robinson): DANNY THE
     DRAGON (66); JOURNEY TO THE UNKNOWN (68-69, tv; theme
     & episodes); THE OBLONG BOX (69); THE VAMPIRE LOVERS
     (70); JUNKET 89 (70); LUST FOR A VAMPIRE (70); TWINS OF
     EVIL (71); BLINKER'S SPY SPOTTER (71, tv); THE JOHNS-
     TOWN MONSTER (71); COUNTESS DRACULA (72); FRIGHT (72);
     DEMONS OF THE MIND (73); THE HOUSE IN NIGHTMARE PARK
     (73); THE BOY WITH TWO HEADS (74); THE FLYING SOR-
     CERER (75); THE GHOUL (75); THE LEGEND OF THE WERE-
     WOLF (75); THE GLITTERBALL (77); A HITCH IN TIME (78);
     SAMMY'S SUPER T-SHIRT (78); ELECTRIC ESKIMO (79); HAWK
     THE SLAYER (81)
Nester Robles: BEAST OF THE YELLOW NIGHT (70); A TASTE OF
     HELL (73)
Milan Roder: SUPERNATURAL (33; w/K. Hajos, H. Jackson);
     DEATH TAKES A HOLIDAY (34; w/J. Leipold; additional music:

B. Kaun)

*Heinz Roemheld: (Many of these films are collaborative scores in
which Roemheld's music has appeared, often, and where noted,
as reused library tracks, along with the work of several other
composers): DRACULA (31; md only); THE HUNCHBACK OF
NOTRE DAME (31 reissue of 23 silent version; w/S. Perry);
MURDERS IN THE RUE MORGUE (31; track: march from WHITE
HELL OF PITZ PALU used as End Title); THE OLD DARK
HOUSE (32; track from WHITE HELL OF PITZ PALU used as
End Title); THE MUMMY (32; track); THE INVISIBLE MAN (33);
THE BLACK CAT (34); DRACULA'S DAUGHTER (36); FLASH
GORDON (36, serial; track); FLASH GORDON'S TRIP TO MARS
(38, serial; track from BLACK CAT, INVISIBLE MAN, DRACULA'S
DAUGHTER used); THE MUMMY'S TOMB (46; w/F. Skinner, H.
Salter, C. Previn); THE FABULOUS JOE (46; md); SIREN OF
ATLANTIS (47; md); IT HAD TO BE YOU (47; w/A. Morton);
DOWN TO EARTH (47; w/G. Duning); WHO KILLED DOC ROB-
BIN (48; md); THE 5000 FINGERS OF DR. T (52; w/H. Salter,
F. Hollander); JACK AND THE BEANSTALK (52); THE CREA-
TURE WALKS AMONG US (56; w/H. Stein, H. Salter, H. Man-
cini, I. Gertz); THE MOLE PEOPLE (56; w/H. Stein, H. Salter);
THE LAND UNKNOWN (57; w/H. Stein, H. Salter, H. Mancini);
THE MONSTER THAT CHALLENGED THE WORLD (57); MON-
STER ON THE CAMPUS (58; track)

Eric Rogers (Br.): MEET MR. LUCIFER (53); QUEST FOR LOVE
(71; theme by Peter Rogers); IN THE DEVIL'S GARDEN (74);
RETURN TO THE PLANET OF THE APES (75; tv cart.)

Shorty Rogers: TARZAN THE APE MAN (59); FOOLS (70);
TABITHA (77, tv); FANTASY ISLAND (78, tv; episodes)

Leonard Rogowski: NIGHTBEAST (82; w/J. Abrams, A. Ober,
R. Walsh)

George Romanis: MANEATER (77, tvm); LIVE AGAIN, DIE AGAIN
(74, tvm); SHARK KILL (76, tvm); BEYOND WESTWORLD (80,
tv)

Sante Romitelli (It.): LOS TRES SUPERMEN EN LA SELVA (71;
The Three Supermen in the Jungle); HATCHET FOR A HONEY-
MOON (74); WONDER WOMEN VS. THE SUPER STOOGES (?;
aka SOTTO A CHI TOCCO!); YETI (77)

Jimmy Roosa & Don McGinnis: BLOOD OF GHASTLY HORROR (71,
tvm; aka MAN WITH THE SYNTHETIC BRAIN)

David Rose: MEN INTO SPACE (60, tv); THE DEVIL AND MISS
SARAH (71, tvm)

Jeremy Rose & Wil Malone: RAW MEAT (72)

Milton Rosen (Many of these films are collaborative scores in which
Rosen's music has appeared, often as reused library tracks,
along with the work of other composers): THE SPIDER WOMAN
STRIKES BACK (45, md); THE TIME OF THEIR LIVES (46);
SLAVE GIRL (47); THE CREEPER (48); SON OF ALI BABA (51;
w/H. Stein; plus track); CITY BENEATH THE SEA (52; w/H.
Stein, H. Mancini; plus track); FRANCIS GOES TO WEST POINT
(52; w/H. Stein, F. Skinner; plus track); ABBOTT & COS-

Milton Rosen (cont.)
     TELLO GO TO MARS (53; track); THE CREATURE FROM THE
     BLACK LAGOON (54; track; original scoring by H. Stein, H.
     Mancini, H. Salter); REVENGE OF THE CREATURE (55; track);
     THE SWORD OF ALI BABA (65; track)
Raimund Rosenberger (W. Gm.): THE TESTAMENT OF DR. MA-
     BUSE (62); THE MAD EXECUTIONERS (63)
*Leonard Rosenman: THE TWILIGHT ZONE (59, tv; episode: And
     When the Sky Was Opened); FANTASTIC VOYAGE (66); COUNT-
     DOWN (67); BENEATH THE PLANET OF THE APES (70); BATTLE
     FOR THE PLANET OF THE APES (73); THE CAT CREATURE (73,
     tvm); JUDGE DEE: THE MONASTERY MURDERS (74, tvm);
     THE PHANTOM OF HOLLYWOOD (74, tvm); RACE WITH THE
     DEVIL (75); THE POSSESSED (77, tvm); THE CAR (77); LORD
     OF THE RINGS (78); PROPHECY (79)
*Laurence Rosenthal: HOW AWFUL ABOUT ALLAN (70, tvm); THE
     HOUSE THAT WOULD NOT DIE (70, tvm); THE LAST CHILD
     (71, tvm); SWEET, SWEET RACHEL (71, tvm); THE DEVIL'S
     DAUGHTER (73, tvm); SATAN'S SCHOOL FOR GIRLS (73, tvm);
     THE ISLAND OF DR. MOREAU (77); LOGAN'S RUN (77, tv;
     episodes); FANTASY ISLAND (77, tvm); RETURN TO FANTASY
     ISLAND (78, tvm); FANTASY ISLAND (78, tv; theme & episodes);
     METEOR (80); THE REVENGE OF THE STEPFORD WIVES (80,
     tvm); CLASH OF THE TITANS (81)
Al Rose: PSYCHOPATH (74)
Renzo Rossellini (It.): THE MACHINE TO KILL BAD PEOPLE (48;
     aka THE CAMERA THAT KILLS BAD GUYS)
Nino Rota (It.): VALLEY OF THE EAGLES (51); IL MONELLO
     DELLA STRADA (51; Street Urchin); THE FACE THAT
     LAUNCHED A THOUSAND SHIPS (54); GHOSTS IN ROME (60);
     BOCCACCIO '70 (62); 8½ (63); JULIET OF THE SPIRITS (65);
     SPIRITS OF THE DEAD (67; "Toby Dammit" segment); SHOOT
     LOUD ... LOUDER, I DON'T UNDERSTAND (67)
Nic Rowley & Marc Wilkinson (Br.): QUATERMASS CONCLUSION
     (80)
M. Roy (India): KAYA HINER KAHINI (73; A Ghost Story)
*Miklos Rozsa: THE THIEF OF BAGDAD (40); THE JUNGLE BOOK
     (42); THE MAN IN HALF MOON STREET (43); SPELLBOUND
     (45); SECRET BEYOND THE DOOR (48); THE STORY OF THREE
     LOVES (53); THE WORLD, THE FLESH AND THE DEVIL (58);
     THE POWER (68); THE PRIVATE LIFE OF SHERLOCK HOLMES
     (70); THE GOLDEN VOYAGE OF SINBAD (74); PROVIDENCE
     (77); THE LAST EMBRACE (79); TIME AFTER TIME (79). [In
     addition, Rozsa's music from Universal films such as A DOUBLE
     LIFE, BRUTE FORCE, THE KILLERS, and others were briefly
     reused in short cues for: THE STRANGE DOOR (51); FRANCIS
     COVERS THE BIG TOWN (52); ABBOTT & COSTELLO MEET
     DR. JEKYLL AND MR. HYDE (53); and others]
Lance Rubin: FANTASY ISLAND (78, tv; episodes); MOTEL HELL
     (80); HAPPY BIRTHDAY TO ME (71; w/B. Harwood)
Michel Rubini & Denny Jaeger: THE HUNGER (83)

*Arthur B. Rubinstein: THE PHOENIX (72, tvm); BLUE THUNDER
     (83); WARGAMES (83)
Donald Rubinstein: MARTIN (78); KNIGHTRIDERS (81)
John Rubinstein: STALK THE WILD CHILD (76, tvm)
Pete Rugolo: THRILLER (60-62, tv; theme & episodes); JACK THE
     RIPPER (60; w/J. McHugh; U.S. release only); DEATH CRUISE
     (74, tvm); THE INVISIBLE MAN (75, tv; episodes)
Gus Russo: BASKET CASE (82)
Carlo Rustichelli (It.): THE DAY THE SKY EXPLODED (58); IL
     LADRO DE BAGDAD (60; The Thief of Bagdad); THE GIANTS
     OF THESSALY (60); THE MINOTAUR (60); MY SON, THE HERO
     (61); L'ATLANTIDE (61; Lost Atlantis); ROGOPAG (62); SAM-
     SON VS. THE GIANT KING (63); WHAT! (63; as "John Murphy");
     CONQUEST OF MYCENE (63); BLOOD AND BLACK LACE (64;
     as "Carlo Rustic"); HERCULES OF THE DESERT (64); I LUNGHI
     CAPELLA DELLA MORTE (64; The Long Hair of Death); SIG-
     NORE E SIGNORI (65; Ladies and Gentleman; aka THE BIRDS,
     THE BEES & THE ITALIANS); KILL BABY KILL (66)
Michael Rutherford (Br.): THE SHOUT (78; w/A. Bank)
Paris Rutherford (Br.): CRUCIBLE OF TERROR (71)
Boris Rychkov (USSR): STAR INSPECTOR (80)
Jan Rychlik (Cz.): THE ANGEL'S COAT (48, cart.); CREATION
     OF THE WORLD (58); BOMBOMANIE (59; Bomb Mania)
Betsumia Sadao (Ja.): ATTACK OF THE MUSHROOM PEOPLE (63;
     aka MATANGO)
Craig Safan: FADE TO BLACK (80); DARK ROOM (81, tv; epi-
     sodes); NIGHTMARES (83); THE LAST STARFIGHTER (84).
     [Also composed and recorded a score for WOLFEN (81) which
     was rejected; replaced with J. Horner score]
Michael Sahl: THE INCREDIBLE TORTURE SHOW (78; aka BLOOD-
     SUCKING FREAKS)
Sabir Said (Malaya): DENDAM PONTIANAK (57; Revenge of the
     Vampire); BAWANG PUTEH, BAWANG MERAH (58; White Onion,
     Red Onion)
Ichiro Saito (Ja.): YOTSUYA KAIDEN-OIWA NO BOREI (69)
Branimir Sakak (Yug.): PICCOLO (59, cart.); SANJAR (61; The
     Dreamer; cart.); DERETI KRUG (61; Ninth Circle); TIFUSARI
     (63, cart.); MASKA CRVENE SMRTI (69; Mask of the Red
     Death)
Sakuma (Ja.): THE SCIENCE NINJA PARTY "GATCHAMAN" (78,
     tv cart.)
Oskar Sala (W. Gm.): THE STRANGLER OF BLACKMOOR CASTLE
     (63)
*Hans J. Salter (Many of these films are collaborative scores in
     which Salter's music, often as reused library tracks, has ap-
     peared along with the work of other composers): TOWER OF
     LONDON (39; uncredited arrangements); THE INVISIBLE MAN
     RETURNS (40; w/F. Skinner); BLACK FRIDAY (40; w/Skinner,
     C. Previn, C. Henderson); THE MUMMY'S HAND (40; w/Skin-
     ner); THE WOLF MAN (41; w/Skinner, Previn); MAN-MADE
     MONSTER (41; w/Skinner, Henderson); HORROR ISLAND (41;

*Hans J. Salter (cont.)
    w/Skinner, Previn, Henderson); HOLD THAT GHOST (41; w/
    Skinner, Previn, Henderson); THE GHOST OF FRANKENSTEIN
    (42); INVISIBLE AGENT (42); THE MAD DOCTOR OF MARKET
    STREET (42); MYSTERY OF MARIE ROGET (42); THE MUMMY'S
    TOMB (42; w/Skinner, Previn, H. Roemheld); NIGHT MONSTER
    (42); THE STRANGE CASE OF DR. RX (42); SHERLOCK
    HOLMES AND THE SECRET WEAPON (42); FRANKENSTEIN MEETS
    THE WOLF MAN (43; w/Skinner, Previn); SON OF DRACULA
    (43; w/Skinner, Previn); THE MAD GHOUL (43; w/Skinner,
    Previn, Henderson); SHERLOCK HOLMES FACES DEATH (43);
    CAPTIVE WILD WOMAN (43); CALLING DR. DEATH (43; w/P.
    Sawtell, Skinner); HOUSE OF FRANKENSTEIN (44; w/Skinner,
    Previn, P. Dessau); THE MUMMY'S GHOST (44; w/Skinner,
    Previn); THE SPIDER WOMAN (44); THE INVISIBLE MAN'S RE-
    VENGE (44; w/W. Lava, E. Zeisl); THE SCARLET CLAW (44);
    WEIRD WOMAN (44; w/P. Sawtell); THE HOUSE OF FEAR (44);
    THE PEARL OF DEATH (44; w/Sawtell); SHERLOCK HOLMES
    VS. THE SPIDER WOMAN (44); JUNGLE CAPTIVE (44; w/P.
    Sawtell [md], W. Lava, C. Previn, D. Tiomkin [track]); JUNGLE
    WOMAN (44; w/Sawtell [md]); HOUSE OF DRACULA (45; track);
    THE FROZEN GHOST (45); THAT'S THE SPIRIT (45); THE
    WOMAN IN GREEN (45); PURSUIT TO ALGIERS (45); HOUSE
    OF HORRORS (46); DRESSED TO KILL (46); TERROR BY NIGHT
    (46); THE BRUTE MAN (46); THE STRANGE DOOR (51; track);
    SON OF ALI BABA (51; track); ABBOTT AND COSTELLO MEET
    THE INVISIBLE MAN (51); YOU NEVER CAN TELL (51); CITY
    BENEATH THE SEA (52; track); FRANCIS COVERS THE BIG
    TOWN (52; track); THE BLACK CASTLE (52); THE 5000 FINGERS
    OF DR. T (52; w/F. Hollander, H. Roemheld); ABBOTT & COS-
    TELLO MEET DR. JEKYLL AND MR. HYDE (53; track); THE
    CREATURE FROM THE BLACK LAGOON (54; Salter provided 7
    cues, including one tracked from GHOST OF FRANKENSTEIN;
    w/H. Stein [main theme], H. Mancini; plus track); REVENGE
    OF THE CREATURE (55; track); THIS ISLAND EARTH (55;
    climax music only); ABBOTT & COSTELLO MEET THE MUMMY
    (55); THE MOLE PEOPLE (56; w/H. Stein, I. Gertz, H. Roem-
    held); THE INCREDIBLE SHRINKING MAN (57; w/H. Stein, I.
    Gertz; main theme by F. Carling/E. Lawrence); THE LAND UN-
    KNOWN (57; w/H. Stein, H. Roemheld, H. Mancini); MONSTER
    ON THE CAMPUS (58; track); THE THING THAT COULDN'T DIE
    (58; track); THE SWORD OF ALI BABA (65, track); LOST IN
    SPACE (65-68, tv; episodes)
Leonardo Salzedo (Br.): THE REVENGE OF FRANKENSTEIN (58);
    THE HAMMER HOUSE OF HORROR (80, tv; episode: The Silent
    Scream)
D.D. Sanches (Brz.): DEVILISH DOLLS (75)
Peter Sandloff (W. Gm.): THE INVISIBLE DR. MABUSE (61); THE
    RETURN OF DR. MABUSE (61)
Blaine Sanford: THE MAGNETIC MONSTER (53)
A. Santisteben (Sp.): NECROPHAGUS (71; aka GRAVEYARD OF

HORROR)

*Philippe Sarde (Fr.): THE TENANT (76); GHOST STORY (81);
QUEST FOR FIRE (82)

Sathyam (India): LADY JAMES BOND (72)

Masahiko Sato (Ja.): BELLADONNA (73)

*Masaru Sato (Ja.): HALF HUMAN (57); GIGANTIS THE FIRE
MONSTER (59); THE H-MAN (59); THRONE OF BLOOD (61);
THE LOST WORLD OF SINBAD (64); SATSUJINYO JUDAI (67;
The Age of Assassins); GODZILLA VS. THE SEA MONSTER (68;
aka EBIRAH, HORROR OF THE DEEP); SON OF GODZILLA (69);
SUBMERSION OF JAPAN (73; aka US: TIDAL WAVE); GOD-
ZILLA VS. MECHA-GODZILLA (76; aka GODZILLA VS. BIONIC
MONSTER, aka GODZILLA VS. COSMIC MONSTER); U.F.O.
BLUE CHRISTMAS (79; aka BLOOD TYPE BLUE); TOWARD THE
TERRA (80)

Eddie Sauter: NIGHT GALLERY (71, tv; episodes: The Caterpil-
lar, The Dark Boy, The Girl with the Hungry Eyes, Little Girl
Lost, The Other Way Out, Hatred Unto Death, How to Cure the
Common Vampire, and others)

Camille Sauvage (Fr.): ORLOFF Y L'HOMME INVISIBLE (70; Orloff and the Invisible Man); LA VIE AMOUREAGE DE L'HOMME
INVISIBLE (72; The Love Life of the Invisible Man)

Buan Savatcho (Thai.): PER, JOM, PHEN (80)

Finn Savery (Denmark): WE ARE ALL DEMONS! (69)

Carlo Savina (It.): TERROR IN THE CRYPT (63); THE SON OF
HERCULES IN THE LAND OF FIRE (63); HERCULES AGAINST
THE BARBARIANS (64); KILLERS ARE CHALLENGED (65);
SECRET AGENT FIREBALL (65); SINGAPORE ZERO HOUR (66);
MALENKA (68); THE YOUNG, THE EVIL AND THE SAVAGE
(68); EL INVENCIBLE HOMBRE INVISIBLE (69; The Invincible
Invisible Man); THE NIGHT OF THE DAMNED (71); LES
AMANTES DEL DIABLO (71; aka THE DIABOLICAL MEETINGS);
HYPNOS (71); LISA AND THE DEVIL (72; aka HOUSE OF EX-
ORCISM, 76)

*Paul Sawtell: SPY SMASHER (42, serial; aka SPY SMASHER RE-
TURNS, 66; w/M. Glickman, A. Schwarzwald); TARZAN TRI-
UMPHS (43); CALLING DR. DEATH (43, md; w/H. Salter, F.
Skinner); TARZAN'S DESERT MYSTERY (43); GILDERSLEEVE'S
GHOST (44); WEIRD WOMAN (44, md; w/Salter); THE PEARL
OF DEATH (44, w/H. Salter); JUNGLE CAPTIVE (44, w/W.
Lava, C. Previn, H. Salterm plus track); JUNGLE WOMAN (44,
w/Salter); THE POWER OF THE WHISTLER (45, plus track.
Whistler theme by W. Hatch); THE MUMMY'S CURSE (45, md);
CRIME DOCTOR'S WARNING (45); GENIUS AT WORK (46, w/R.
Webb); TARZAN AND THE LEOPARD WOMAN (46); THE CAT
CREEPS (46, md); DICK TRACY MEETS GRUESOME (47); TAR-
ZAN AND THE HUNTRESS (47); THE STRANGE DOOR (51; li-
brary tracks used); THE WHIP HAND (51); THE SON OF DR.
JEKYLL (51); TARZAN'S SAVAGE FURY (52); TARZAN AND
THE SHE-DEVIL (53); ABBOTT & COSTELLO MEET DR. JEKYLL
AND MR. HYDE (53; w/H. Stein, plus library tracks); THE

*Paul Sawtell (cont.)

ANIMAL WORLD (55); TARZAN'S HIDDEN JUNGLE (55); THE
BLACK SCORPION (55; w/B. Shefter, J. Cookerly); SHE
DEVIL (57; w/Shefter); KRONOS (57; w/Shefter); THE COSMIC
MAN (58; w/Shefter); THE FLY (58; w/Shefter); IT! THE
TERROR FROM BEYOND SPACE (58; w/Shefter); RETURN OF
THE FLY (59; w/Shefter); GIGANTIS THE FIRE MONSTER (59;
additional cues for U.S. release); THE LOST WORLD (60; w/
Shefter; additional cues by H. Jackson, S. Cutner); VOYAGE
TO THE BOTTOM OF THE SEA (61; w/Shefter); JACK THE
GIANT KILLER (62; w/Shefter); VOYAGE TO THE BOTTOM OF
THE SEA (64, tv; theme & episodes); THE LAST MAN ON
EARTH (64; w/Shefter); MOTOR PSYCHO (65; w/Shefter); THE
TIME TUNNEL (66, tv; episodes); THE BUBBLE (66; aka FAN-
TASTIC INVASION OF THE PLANET EARTH w/Shefter)

Walter Scharf: THE LADY AND THE MONSTER (44); THE WOMAN
WHO CAME BACK (45; md); HANS CHRISTIAN ANDERSEN (52;
songs by Frank Loesser); CINDERFELLA (60); THE NUTTY
PROFESSOR (62); BEN (72); GASP! (77; Yugoslavian film);
SALVAGE-1 (79, tv); MIDNIGHT OFFERINGS (81, tvm).
Scharf's Universal library cues were also reused in FRANCIS
COVERS THE BIG TOWN (52), ABBOTT & COSTELLO MEET DR.
JEKYLL & MR. Hyde (53), and others

Peter Schickele: SILENT RUNNING (71)

Paul Schierbeck (Denmark): DAY OF WRATH (43); ORDET (55;
The Word)

*Lalo Schifrin THE ALFRED HITCHCOCK HOUR (62-65, tv; epi-
sodes); THE MAN FROM U.N.C.L.E. (64-68, tv; episodes);
THE DARK INTRUDER (65, tvm; aka SOMETHING WITH CLAWS);
MURDERER'S ROW (66); WAY ... WAY OUT (66); THE PRESI-
DENT'S ANALYST (67); EYE OF THE CAT (69); THE AQUARI-
ANS (70); IMAGO (70); THE HELLSTROM CHRONICLE (71); THX
1138 (71); EARTH II (71; tvm); THE NEPTUNE FACTOR (73;
w/W. McCauley; aka tv: THE NEPTUNE DISASTER); PLANET
OF THE APES (74, tv; theme & episodes); BRENDA STARR (76,
tvm); GOOD AGAINST EVIL (77, tvm); DAY OF THE ANIMALS
(77); RETURN FROM WITCH MOUNTAIN (78); THE MANITOU
(78); THE CAT FROM OUTER SPACE (78); INSTITUTE FOR RE-
VENGE (79, tvm); THE AMITYVILLE HORROR (79); BACK TO
THE PLANET OF THE APES (80, tvm; from 74 series; w/R.
LaSalle); TREACHERY AND GREED ON THE PLANET OF THE
APES (80, tv; from 74 series; w/E. Hagen); THE NUDE BOMB
(81); WHEN TIME RAN OUT (81); CAVEMAN (81); A STRANGER
IS WATCHING (81); AMITYVILLE II: THE POSSESSION (82);
STARFLIGHT: THE PLANE THAT COULDN'T LAND (83, tvm)

Victor Schlichter (Arg.): MASTER OF HORROR (60)

Willy Schmidt-Gentner (Gm.): FRAU IM MOND (29; Woman in the
Moon)

Kim Scholes & Jack Malken: THE NESTING (81)

Barry Schrader: GALAXY OF TERROR (81; aka PLANET OF HOR-
RORS)

Rudy Schrager: FEAR IN THE NIGHT (47)
Hod David Schudson: GHOSTS THAT STILL WALK (78; w/R.
    Stein, et al.); THE CLONUS HORROR (79); THE ATTIC (81)
Klaus Schulze (W. Gm.): BARRACUDA (78)
Walter Schumann: NIGHT OF THE HUNTER (55). Schumann's
    Universal library tracks were also reused in FRANCIS GOES TO
    WEST POINT (52); ABBOTT & COSTELLO MEET DR. JEKYLL
    AND MR. HYDE (53), and others.
Gerard Schurmann (Br.): THE HEADLESS GHOST (59); HORRORS
    OF THE BLACK MUSEUM (59); KONGA (61); THE LOST CON-
    TINENT (68)
Sherwood Schwartz: IT'S ABOUT TIME (66, tv; episodes)
Milton Schwartzwald: THE CRIME OF DOCTOR CRESPI (35; md);
    ABBOTT AND COSTELLO MEET THE KILLER (49; md)
Score Productions THE STARLOST (73, tv)
Gary Scott: FINAL EXAM (81)
John Scott (Br.; aka Patrick John Scott): A STUDY IN TERROR
    (65); THOSE FANTASTIC FLYING FOOLS (67; aka ROCKET TO
    THE MOON); BERSERK! (68); DOOMWATCH (72); CRAZE (74);
    SYMPTOMS (76; aka THE BLOOD VIRGIN); SATAN'S SLAVE
    (76); THE PEOPLE THAT TIME FORGOT (77); THE FINAL
    COUNTDOWN (80); INSEMINOID (81); HORROR PLANET (82);
    YOR (83; w/G. & M. de Angelis); GREYSTROKE (84)
Nathan Scott: THE TWILIGHT ZONE (60, tv; episodes: A Stop
    at Willoughby, Young Man's Fancy)
Randy Scott: THE JEKYLL AND HYDE PORTFOLIO (72)
Tom Scott: CONQUEST OF THE PLANET OF THE APES (72);
    NINE LIVES OF FRITZ THE CAT (74); AMERICATHON (79)
Bill Scream: CLOSED MONDAYS (74, short)
Malcolm Seagrave: PHANTASM (79; w/F. Myrow)
Walter Sear (It.): DOCTOR BUTCHER, M.D. (82)
Humphrey Searle (Br.): THE ABOMINABLE SNOWMAN OF THE
    HIMALAYAS (57); THE HAUNTING (63)
John Seely (Music Director): THE HIDEOUS SUN DEMON (59; li-
    brary score)
Bernardo Segal: NIGHT SLAVES (70, tvm); MOON OF THE WOLF
    (72, tvm); THE GIRL MOST LIKELY TO ... (73, tvm); MOON
    OF THE WOLF (72, tvm) HOMEBODIES (75)
Gregorio C. Segura (Sp.): SWEET SOUND OF DEATH (65); A
    WITCH WITHOUT A BROOM (66); TRANSPLANT (70); VIVA LA
    AVENTURA (70; Hurrah for Adventure)
Matyas Seiber (Br.): THE ANIMAL FARM (54)
Wladimir Selinsky: SOMETHING EVIL (72, tvm)
Dov Seltzer: THE UPSTATE MURDERS (78)
Renato Serio: ALONE IN THE DARK (82)
Serizawa & Suzuki (Ja.): FUTURE POLICE "URASHIMAN" (82, tv)
L.M. Serra (Arg.): MAS ALLA DE LA AVENTURA (80)
Sheldon Seymour; see H.G. Lewis
Francis Seyrig (Fr.): LAST YEAR AT MARIENBAD (61)
Karl-Heinz Shafer (W. Gm.): THE WHITE GLOVES OF THE DEVIL
    (7?); TENDER DRACULA (75; aka THE CONFESSION OF THE

Karl-Heinz Shafer (cont.)
     BLOOD DRINKER)
Paul Shaffer: MR. MIKE'S MONDO VIDEO (79, md)
John Shakespeare (Br.): THE GIRL FROM STARSHIP VENUS (78;
     aka DIARY OF A SPACE VIRGIN); KILLER'S MOON (78; w/D.
     Warne)
Ravi Shankar: CHARLY (68)
Ray Shanklin & Ed Bogas: FRITZ THE CAT (72); HEAVY TRAF-
     FIC (73)
Ted Shapiro: BLOODEATERS (80; aka FOREST OF FEAR)
Robert Sharples (Br.): THE COSMIC MONSTERS (58)
Christopher Shaw: BETWEEN TWO WORLDS (52)
Roland Shaw (Br.): STRAIGHT ON TILL MORNING (72)
*Bert A. Shefter: M (51; md; music M. Michelet); THE BLACK
     SCORPION (57; uncredited; w/P. Sawtell, J. Cookerly); SHE
     DEVIL (57; w/P. Sawtell); KRONOS (57; w/Sawtell); THE COS-
     MIC MAN (58; w/Sawtell); IT! THE TERROR FROM BEYOND
     SPACE (58; w/Sawtell); THE FLY (58; w/Sawtell); RETURN
     OF THE FLY (59; w/Sawtell); THE LOST WORLD (60; w/Saw-
     tell; additional music by H. Jackson, S. Cutner); JACK THE
     GIANT KILLER (62; w/Sawtell); THE LAST MAN ON EARTH (63;
     w/Sawtell); CURSE OF THE FLY (65); MOTOR PSYCHO (65;
     w/Sawtell); THE BUBBLE (66; aka FANTASTIC INVASION OF
     THE PLANET EARTH; w/Sawtell)
Wong Koy Shin (China): THE STORY OF THE CHINESE GODS
     (76, cart.)
David Shire: NIGHT GALLERY (72/73, tv; alternate theme);
     ISN'T IT SHOCKING? (73, tvm); THE KILLER BEES (74, tvm);
     THE TRIBE (74, tvm); THE BIG BUS (76); TALES OF THE
     UNEXPECTED (77, tv; theme & debut episode); DARK ROOM
     (81, tv); OZ (84)
Osamu Shoji (Ja.): ADIEU GALAXY EXPRESS (81)
Howard Shore: THE BROOD (79); SCANNERS (81); VIDEODROME
     (83)
Richard Shores: THE TWILIGHT ZONE (64, tv; episode: Caesar
     and Me); BILLION DOLLAR THREAT (79, tvm)
Alden Shuman: THE DEVIL IN MISS JONES (73)
Susan Siani: THE INCREDIBLE SHRINKING WOMAN (81)
Stanley Silverman: SIMON (80, md)
Louis Silvers: THE BLACK ROOM (35; md)
Enrico Simonetti: MACUMBA LOVE (60)
N. Simonian (USSR): THE SNOW QUEEN (66)
Tomislav Simovic (Yug.): Most are animated shorts: THE GREAT
     FEAR (58); THE GAME (62); I VIDEL SEM DALJINE MAGLENE
     (64; Far Away I Saw Mist and Mud); CEREMONIJA (65; The
     Ceremony); ZID (65; The Wall); TAMER OF WILD HORSES (66);
     THE SEVENTH CONTINENT (67); OZMEDJO USANI CASE (68;
     Between the Glass and the Lip); MRLJA NA SAVJESTI (68;
     Stain on the Conscience); OPERA CORDIS (68); SCABIES (69);
     THE MAN WHO HAD TO SING (70); PORTRETI (70; Portraits);
     VISITORS FROM THE GALAXY (81)

Dudley Simpson (Br.): MOONBASE 3 (73, tv); DR. WHO (71, tv;
  8th season + episodes); BLAKE'S SEVEN (77, tv; theme)
Frank Sinatra Jr.: THE BEACH GIRLS AND THE MONSTER (65)
Lou Singer: GIGANTOR (66, tv cart.)
Guna Singh (India): BANGALORE BHOOTA (75)
Utam Singh (India): KASTURI (78)
Philippe Sissmann (Fr.): LES RAISONS DE LA MORT (78)
Marlin Skiles: A THOUSAND AND ONE NIGHTS (45); ALADDIN
  AND HIS LAMP (51); FLIGHT TO MARS (51); JALOPY (53);
  LOOSE IN LONDON (53); THE MAZE (53); JUNGLE GENTS (54);
  BOWERY TO BAGDAD (55); CRASHING LAS VEGAS (56); UP
  IN SMOKE (57); THE DISEMBODIED (57); QUEEN OF OUTER
  SPACE (58); THE HYPNOTIC EYE (59); SPACE MONSTER (65);
  THE RESURRECTION OF ZACHARY WHEELER (71)
*Frank Skinner (Most of these films are collaborative scores in
  which Skinner's music has appeared, often as reused library
  tracks, along with the work of other composers): SON OF
  FRANKENSTEIN (39; w/H. Salter, C. Previn); TOWER OF
  LONDON (39); THE PHANTOM CREEPS (39; track); FLASH
  GORDON CONQUERS THE UNIVERSE (40, serial; track from
  SON OF FRANKENSTEIN and TOWER OF LONDON used); THE
  INVISIBLE MAN RETURNS (40; w/Salter); BLACK FRIDAY (40;
  w/Salter, Previn, C. Henderson); THE MUMMY'S HAND (40;
  w/Salter); HELLZAPOPPIN (41); THE WOLF MAN (41; w/Salter,
  Previn); MAN-MADE MONSTER (41; w/Salter, Henderson); HOR-
  ROR ISLAND (41; w/Salter, Previn, Henderson); THE BLACK
  CAT (41; w/Salter, Previn, Henderson); HOLD THAT GHOST
  (41; w/Salter, Previn, H. Roemheld); FRANKENSTEIN MEETS
  THE WOLF MAN (43; w/Salter, Previn); SON OF DRACULA (43;
  w/Salter, Previn); THE MAD GHOUL (43; w/Salter, Previn,
  Henderson); CALLING DR. DEATH (43; w/Salter, P. Sawtell);
  DESTINY (44; w/A. Tansman); HOUSE OF FRANKENSTEIN (44;
  w/Salter, Previn, P. Dessau); THE MUMMY'S GHOST (44; w/
  Salter, Previn); HOUSE OF DRACULA (45; track); PILLOW OF
  DEATH (45; md); STRANGE CONFESSION (45; md); NIGHT IN
  PARADISE (46); ABBOTT & COSTELLO MEET FRANKENSTEIN
  (48); FRANCIS (49); FREE FOR ALL (49); HARVEY (50); SON
  OF ALI BABA (51; track); THE STRANGE DOOR (51; track);
  FRANCIS GOES TO THE RACES (51); IT GROWS ON TREES
  (52); CITY BENEATH THE SEA (52; track); FRANCIS COVERS
  THE BIG TOWN (52; track); FRANCIS GOES TO WEST POINT
  (52; some track); ABBOTT & COSTELLO GO TO MARS (53;
  track); ABBOTT & COSTELLO MEET DR. JEKYLL & MR. HYDE
  (53; track, most from A & C MEET FRANKENSTEIN); REVENGE
  OF THE CREATURE (55; track); FRANCIS IN THE HAUNTED
  HOUSE (56; w/H. Stein, H. Mancini, E. Carter & M. Rosen);
  MAN OF A THOUSAND FACES (57); THE SNOW QUEEN (58;
  U.S. release only); THE SWORD OF ALI BABA (65; track)
Jozef Skrzek (Pol.): WAR OF THE WORLDS: THE NEXT CENTURY
  (81)
Ivor Slaney (Br.): SPACEWAYS (53); PREY (77); TERROR (79);

Ivor Slaney (cont.)
    DEATH SHIP (80)
Franklin Sledge: THE ALIEN DEAD (80)
George Small & Paul Jost: LAST RITES (80; aka DRACULA'S
    LAST RITES)
Michael Small: THE STEPFORD WIVES (75); AUDREY ROSE (77);
    THE LATHE OF HEAVEN (79, tvm)
Bruce Smeaton (Austral.): THE CARS THAT ATE PEOPLE (74;
    aka THE CARS THAT ATE PARIS); PICNIC AT HANGING ROCK
    (75); CIRCLE OF IRON (79; aka THE SILENT FLUTE); THE
    DEVIL'S PLAYGROUND (79); GRENDEL, GRENDEL, GRENDEL
    (81); ICEMAN (84)
Arthur Smith: WOLFMAN--A LYCANTHROPE (78; w/D. Floyd); A
    DAY OF JUDGMENT (80; w/Clay Smith)
Paul J. Smith: DONALD DUCK (34-61; cart. series; w/others);
    20,000 LEAGUES UNDER THE SEA (54); THE SHAGGY DOG (59);
    MOON PILOT (60)
Mark Snow: THE GEMINI MAN (76, tv); THE NEXT STEP BEYOND
    (78, tv; theme)
Sonik-Omi (India): DR. X (72)
Giuliano Sorgini (It.): DON'T OPEN THE WINDOW (76; aka THE
    LIVING DEAD AT MANCHESTER MORGUE; aka LET SLEEPING
    CORPSES LIE)
M. Sorgini (it.): NAKED EXORCISM (75)
Joe Southerland: THE DAY IT CAME TO EARTH (79)
Linda Southworth (Br.): MY SON THE VAMPIRE (52)
David Spear: FEAR NO EVIL (81; w/F. LaLoggia); THE CREATURE
    WASN'T NICE (82)
Eric Spear (Br.): GHOST SHIP (52); IMMEDIATE DISASTER (54);
    THE VULTURE (55)
John Spence: THE AMAZING SPIDERMAN (77, tvm); THE CHI-
    NESE WEB (78, tvm)
Mischa Spoliansky (Br.): THE GHOST GOES WEST (36); THE MAN
    WHO COULD WORK MIRACLES (36)
Philip Springer: WICKED, WICKED (73)
Carl W. Stalling: DAFFY DUCK & THE DINOSAUR (39, cart.);
    PORKY'S ROAD RACE (37, cart.); many other cartoons.
Andrew Stein: DEATHSPORT (78)
*Herman Stein (Most of these films are collaborative scores in which
    Stein's music has appeared, often and where noted as reused li-
    brary tracks, along with the work of other composers): SON
    OF ALI BABA (51; w/M. Rosen, plus track); THE STRANGE
    DOOR (51; Stein arranged Mozart cue "March of the Priests");
    CITY BENEATH THE SEA (52; w/H. Mancini, M. Rosen, plus
    track); FRANCIS COVERS THE BIG TOWN (52; w/E. Fairchild,
    plus track); FRANCIS GOES TO WEST POINT (52; w/F. Skinner,
    M. Rosen, plus track); ABBOTT & COSTELLO GO TO MARS (53;
    incl. track); ABBOTT & COSTELLO MEET DR. JEKYLL AND MR.
    HYDE (53; mostly track); IT CAME FROM OUTER SPACE (53;
    Stein's cues included main title theme; w/I. Gertz, H. Mancini);
    THE CREATURE FROM THE BLACK LAGOON (54; Stein's cues

included main theme; some track; w/Mancini, H. Salter, plus
track from R.E. Dolan, M. Rosen); REVENGE OF THE CREA-
TURE (55; Stein composed original main title; remainder of score
is track); TARANTULA (55; mostly track; Stein on first four
reels, rest H. Mancini); THIS ISLAND EARTH (55; Stein scored
reels 1-7 and most of reel 8; w/H. Mancini and H. Salter on
reels 8-9); THE CREATURE WALKS AMONG US (56; w/H. Roemheld, H. Salter, H. Mancini, I. Gertz); FRANCIS IN THE
HAUNTED HOUSE (56); I'VE LIVED BEFORE (56; Stein scored
all but main theme, by Don Roseland and Ray Cormier); THE
MOLE PEOPLE (56; w/H. Roemheld, H. Salter); THE INCREDIBLE
SHRINKING MAN (57; some track; w/Salter, Gertz; main theme
by F. Carling/E. Lawrence); THE LAND UNKNOWN (57; w/
Roemheld, Salter, Mancini); LOVE SLAVES OF THE AMAZON
(57; w/Gertz, S. Wilson, A. Brummer, H. Vars); THE MONO-
LITH MONSTERS (57; Stein scored all of reel 6 and part of
reel 7; most of score by I. Gertz; w/H. Mancini, plus track
from W. Lava); MONSTER ON THE CAMPUS (58; track); THE
THING THAT COULDN'T DIE (58; track); THE INTRUDER (61);
THE SWORD OF ALI BABA (64; track); VOYAGE TO THE BOT-
TOM OF THE SEA (65-68, tv; episodes); LOST IN SPACE (65-
68, tv; episodes)

Julian Stein: THE FLESH EATERS (64)

*Ronald Stein: THE PHANTOM FROM 10,000 LEAGUES (56); IT
CONQUERED THE WORLD (56); NOT OF THIS EARTH (56);
THE DAY THE WORLD ENDED (56); THE SHE CREATURE (56);
THE UNDEAD (56); ATTACK OF THE CRAB MONSTERS (57);
INVASION OF THE SAUCER MEN (57); THE ATTACK OF THE
50 FOOT WOMAN (58); THE DEVIL'S PARTNER (58); GHOST
OF DRAGSTRIP HOLLOW (59); BATTLE BEYOND THE SUN (59;
track); THE LAST WOMAN ON EARTH (60); DINOSAURUS! (60);
JOURNEY TO THE 7TH PLANET (61; track; plus music by I.
Glindemann); THE PREMATURE BURIAL (62); THE UNDER-
WATER CITY (62); THE TERROR (63; partially tracked); THE
HAUNTED PALACE (63); DEMENTIA 13 (63); VOYAGE TO A
PREHISTORIC PLANET (65; track); PLANET OF BLOOD (65;
aka QUEEN OF BLOOD; track, as "Leonard Morand"); TRACK
OF THE VAMPIRE (65; aka BLOOD PATH; track as "Mark Low-
ry"); PRINCE PLANET (66, tv cart.; 52 episodes, track);
MARS NEEDS WOMEN (66; track); THE EYE CREATURES (68;
track from INV. OF SAUCER MEN); ZONTAR, THE THING
FROM VENUS (68, track); CURSE OF THE SWAMP CREATURE
(68); SPIDER BABY (70); GHOSTS THAT STILL WALK (78,
tv; tracked with new electronics w/H. D. Schudson, et al.);
FRANKENSTEIN'S GREAT AUNT TILLIE (84).

*Fred Steiner: THE COLOSSUS OF NEW YORK (58; uncredited,
w/N. Van Cleave; main theme by Steiner); THE TWILIGHT
ZONE (59-62, tv; episodes: A Hundred Yards Over the Rim,
King Nine Will Not Return, The Passersby, Mute, Miniature, I
Dream of Genie, The Bard); THE BULLWINKLE SHOW (61, tv;
episodes); ROBINSON CRUSOE ON MARS (64; uncredited, w/

*Fred Steiner (cont.)
N. Van Cleave); HERCULES AND THE PRINCESS OF TROY (66,
tvm); STAR TREK (66-69, tv; episodes: Charlie X; Mudd's
Women; The Corbomite Maneuver; Balance of Terror; What Are
Little Girls Made Of?; The City on the Edge of Forever; Who
Mourns for Adonis?; Mirror, Mirror; By Any Other Name; The
Omega Glory (flag music only); Elaan of Troyius; Spock's
Brain.   Steiner's original STAR TREK cues were later tracked
into other episodes, including: The Changeling, The Deadly
Years, The Immunity Syndrome, The Ultimate Computer, The
Tholian Web, The Day of the Dove, That Which Survives, Let
This Be Your Last Battlefield, Whom Gods Destroy, The Mark
of Gideon, The Cloudminders, Requiem for Methuselah, The
Savage Curtain); NIGHT TERROR (77, tvm); STAR TREK: THE
MOTION PICTURE (69, uncredited assistance w/J. Goldsmith;
Steiner composed nine cues, based on Goldsmith's themes)
*Max Steiner: THE MONKEY'S PAW (32); PHANTOM OF CREST-
WOOD (32, md); THE MOST DANGEROUS GAME (32); SECRETS
OF THE FRENCH POLICE (32, md); BIRD OF PARADISE (32);
KING KONG (33); SON OF KONG (33); SHE (35); ARSENIC
AND OLD LACE (44); THE BEAST WITH FIVE FINGERS (47);
TWO ON A GUILLOTINE (64)
Alexander Steinert: STRANGLER OF THE SWAMP (45, md); THE
DEVIL BAT'S DAUGHTER (46); THE UNKNOWN (46; plus track)
Gian Stellari & Guido Robuschi (It.): COLUSSUS & THE HEAD-
HUNTERS (62)
Theodore Stern: THE WORM EATERS (81)
James Stevens (Br.): THEY CAME FROM BEYOND SPACE (67)
*Leith Stevens: THE GREAT RUPERT (50); DESTINATION MOON
(50); WHEN WORLDS COLLIDE (51); SCARED STIFF (53); WAR
OF THE WORLDS (53; music later reused in CRY WOLF, 80);
WORLD WITHOUT END (56); LIZZIE (57); THE TWILIGHT ZONE
(59, tv; episode: Time Enough at Last); VOYAGE TO THE
BOTTOM OF THE SEA (64, tv; episodes); LOST IN SPACE (65-
68, tv; episodes)
Morton Stevens: THRILLER (60, tv; episodes); VOYAGE TO THE
BOTTOM OF THE SEA (64, tv; episodes); WILD WILD WEST (65,
tv; episodes); VISIONS (72, tvm; aka VISIONS OF DEATH);
SHE WAITS (72, tvm); POOR DEVIL (73, tvm); THE HORROR
AT 37,000 FEET (73, tvm); TIME TRAVELERS (76, tvm); THE
STRANGE POSSESSION OF MRS. OLIVER (77, tvm); MANDRAKE
(79, tvm); GREAT WHITE (82); SLAPSTICK (84)
Orville Stoeber: LET'S SCARE JESSICA TO DEATH (71)
Morris W. Stoloff (Music Director): THE SPIDER'S WEB (38, seri-
al); BEWARE SPOOKS! (39; title music by L. Harline, rest
track); THE MAN THEY COULD NOT HANG (39); BEFORE I
HANG (40); LADIES IN RETIREMENT (41; score E. Toch); THE
DEVIL COMMANDS (41); THE FACE BEHIND THE MASK (41;
score S. Cutner, plus track); HERE COMES MR. JORDAN (41;
score F. Hollander); THE BOOGIE MAN WILL GET YOU (41; main
title by J. Leipold; score track by L. Harline); THE RETURN

OF THE VAMPIRE (43; score M. Castelnuovo-Tedesco); ONCE
UPON A TIME (43; score F. Hollander); A THOUSAND AND
ONE NIGHTS (45; score M. Skiles); IT HAD TO BE YOU (47;
score H. Roemheld, A. Morton); DOWN TO EARTH (47; score
G. Duning, H. Roemheld); HER HUSBAND'S AFFAIRS (47;
score G. Duning); THE RETURN OF OCTOBER (48; score G.
Duning); SONG OF INDIA (47; score A. Laszlo); THE SON OF
DR. JEKYLL (51; score P. Sawtell); THE 5000 FINGERS OF DR.
T (53; score F. Hollander, H. Salter, H. Roemheld); 1001
ARABIAN NIGHTS (59; score G. Duning)

Gregory Stone: THE JUNGLE PRINCESS (36)

Herbert Stothart: RASPUTIN AND THE EMPRESS (32); THE
WIZARD OF OZ (39, md); A GUY NAMED JOE (44); THE PIC-
TURE OF DORIAN GRAY (47, w/M. Castelnuovo-Tedesco); BIG
JACK (49)

Walter Stott: see Angela Morley

Ted Stovall: THE BOY WHO CRIED WEREWOLF (73)

Hubert Stuppner (W. Gm.): DIE STIMMEN DER SYLPHIDEN (80,
tv; Voices of the Sylphides)

Jerry Styner: JENNIFER (78; title song by Porter Jordan)

Sparky Sugarman: CINDERELLA 2000 (77)

Koichi Sugiyama (Ja.): BATTLE OF THE PLANETS (77, tv; aka
GATCHAMAN); CYBORG 009 (79, tv); SPACE RUNAWAY IDEON
(80-81, tv); LEGEND OF SYRIUS (81); SPACE RUNAWAY IDEON:
A CONTACT (82); SPACE RUNAWAY IDEON: BE INVOKED (82)

Harry Sukman: RIDERS TO THE STARS (53); GOG (54); SABU
AND THE MAGIC RING (57); AROUND THE WORLD UNDER THE
SEA (66); GENESIS II (73, tvm); PLANET EARTH (74, tvm);
BEYOND THE BERMUDA TRIANGLE (75, tvm); SOMEONE IS
WATCHING ME (78, tvm); SALEM'S LOT (79, tvm)

Bob Summers: BEYOND DEATH'S DOOR (79); LEGEND OF
SLEEPY HOLLOW (79); THE BOOGENS (82); ONE DARK NIGHT
(83)

Paul Sundfor & Gordon Goodwin: ATTACK OF THE KILLER TOMA-
TOES (79)

Karel Svoboda (Cz.): PROHADKS O HONZIKOVI A MARENCE (81;
short)

Ward Swingle (Fr.): AIMEZ-VOUS LES FEMMES? (66; Do You Like
Women?)

Rene Sylviano (Fr.): FRANCIS THE FIRST (47)

Irving Szathmary: GET SMART (65, tv)

Hiroshi Takada (Ja.): BLOOD (74; aka MY BLOOD BELONGS TO
SOMEONE ELSE)

Shin Takada (Ja.): LUSTY TRANSPARENT MAN (78)

Tatsuo Takai (Ja.): MIGHTY ATOM (63-66, tv; theme & episodes);
MOBILE SUIT GUNDAM (80, tv; w/W. Fukuda; episodes; aka
features GUNDAM I, II, III; 81-82)

Toru Takamitsu (Ja.): KWAIDAN (63); WOMAN OF THE DUNES
(64); ILLUSION OF BLOOD (66); EMPIRE OF PASSION (78)

Hiroki Tamaki (Ja.): MYSTERIOUS BIG TACTICS (78; w/N.
Yamamoto)

Shinichi Tanabe (Ja.): HELL ISLAND (77); QUEEN BEE (78);
    HANGING HOUSE ON THE HOSPITAL SLOPE (79)
Tangerine Dream (group): THE KEEP (83); WAVELENGTH (84)
Alexandre Tansman: FLESH AND FANTASY (43); DESTINY (44;
    w/F. Skinner); ABBOTT & COSTELLO GO TO MARS (53; track,
    plus H. Stein, others)
Duane Tatro: THE INVADERS (67, tv; episodes)
Al Teeter: BLACKSNAKE (73; w/W. Loose)
Richard Theiss: THE DAY THE EARTH GOT STONED (80)
Mikis Theodorakis (Grk.): SHADOW OF THE CAT (61); THE LOV-
    ERS OF TERUEL (62); THE DAY THE FISH CAME OUT (67)
Maurice Thiriet (Fr.): THE DEVIL'S ENVOYS (42; w/J. Kosma);
    LE LOUP DES MALVENEURS (42; The Wolf of the Malvenours);
    BERNADETTE OF LOURDES (60)
Lionel Thomas: DRACULA SUCKS (80)
Peter Thomas (W. Gm.): THE INDIAN SCARF (63); THE BLOOD
    DEMON (67); SPACE PATROL (67; tv; aka RAUMPATROULLE);
    CHARIOTS OF THE GODS (69; as "Wilhelm Roggersdorf"); DIE
    WEIBCHEN (70; The Females); HAND OF POWER (72); BOT-
    SCHEFT DER GOETTER (76; Mysteries of the Gods)
Whitley Thomas: MARK OF THE WITCH (70)
Eugen Thomass (W. Gm.): PLUTONIUM (78); MEAT (79); OPERA-
    TION GANYMEDE (80?)
Jean Thome (W. Gm.): THE INVISIBLE TERROR (63)
John Thompson (H.K.): HOUSE OF THE LUTE (79)
Ken Thorne (Br.): THE BED SITTING ROOM (68); ARABIAN AD-
    VENTURE (79); SUPERMAN II (81; adapting J. Williams); THE
    HOUSE WHERE EVIL DWELLS (81); SUPERMAN III (83; adapting
    J. Williams)
H. Kingsley Thurber: DON'T GO INTO THE WOODS ALONE (82)
Reg Tilsley (Br.): HORROR HOUSE (69); INVASION OF THE
    BODY STEALERS (69)
*Dimitri Tiomkin: ALICE IN WONDERLAND (33); MAD LOVE (35);
    LOST HORIZON (36); THE CORSICAN BROTHERS (41); ANGEL
    ON MY SHOULDER (46); IT'S A WONDERFUL LIFE (46); POR-
    TRAIT OF JENNIE (48; song by B. Herrmann); TARZAN AND
    THE MERMAIDS (48); THE THING (FROM ANOTHER WORLD)
    (51). Library tracks reused in JUNGLE CAPTIVE (44)
George Aliceson Tipton: PHANTOM OF THE PARADISE (74; songs
    by Paul Williams); THE DEMON-MURDER CASE (83, tvm)
Ernst Toch: PETER IBBETSON (35); THE GHOST BREAKERS
    (40); DR. CYCLOPS (40; w/G. Carbonara, A.H. Malotte);
    LADIES IN RETIREMENT (41)
Paquito Toledo (Phil.): THE MAGIC SAMURAI (69)
Isao Tomita (Ja.): KIGA KAIKYO (64; Hunger Canal); LEO, THE
    KING OF THE JUNGLE (66-67, tv); NOSTRADAMUS NO DAYO-
    GEN (75; The Great Prophecy of Nostradamus; aka U.S.:
    CATASTROPHE 1999; aka Fr.: THE END OF THE WORLD);
    DEMON POND (80)
*Colin Towns: THE HAUNTING OF JULIA (76; aka FULL CIRCLE)
S.N. Tripathi (India): NAAG CHAMPAG (76)

Armando Trovajoli (It.): UNCLE WAS A VAMPIRE (59; w/R. Ras-
cel); LE PILLOE DI ERCOLE (60; Hercules' Pills); ATOM AGE
VAMPIRE (60); HERCULES AGAINST THE HAUNTED WORLD
(61); MOLE MEN VS. THE SON OF HERCULES (61); PLANETS
AGAINST US (61); THE GIANT OF THE METROPOLIS (62);
LA MONACA DI MONZA (63; The Monk of Monza); THE DEVIL
IN LOVE (66); DOTTOR JEKYLL & GENTILE SIGNORA (79);
PASSIONE D'AMORE (81)
Karel Trow (Fr.): LE TEMPS DE MOURIR (70; The Time to Die)
Christopher Trussell: NIGHT FRIGHT (6?)
Toshiaki Tsushima (Ja.): MAGIC SERPENT (66); GRAND DUEL
IN MAGIC (67); THE GREEN SLIME (68); THE WAR IN SPACE
(78); EARTHQUAKE ISLANDS (79)
Hiroshi Tsutsui (Ja.): VOLTUS V (79); SUPERELECTROMAGNETIC
ROBOT "COMBATLER V" (82)
Giorgio Tucci & Fabbio Frizzi (It.): ZOMBIE (79; aka ZOMBIE
FLESH EATERS; aka ZOMBI 2)
Sahat Tuchinda (Thai.): KUN PI (75)
Jonathan Tunick: AMERICA 2100 (79, tvm)
François Tusques & Yvon Geraud (Fr.): LES FEMMES VAMPIRES
(67; The Vampire Women); LA VAMPIRE NUE (69; The Nude
Vampire)
Ralph Tyrell (Austral.): SHIRLEY THOMPSON VS. THE ALIENS
(72)
Jaroslav Uhlir (Cz.): LONG LIVE GHOSTS! (79)
Umagano (Ja.): BATTLE MECHA-ZANBUNGURL (82, tv)
Piero Umiliani (It.): OMICRON (63); 00-2 AGENTI SUGRETISSIMO
(64; 00-2 Secret Agents); SAMSON & THE MIGHTY CHALLENGE
(64); OPERAZIONE POKER (65); OPERZIONE GOLDSEVEN (66);
UN GOLPE DE MIL MILLIONES (66; A Stroke of a Thousand
Millions); ARGOMAN SUPER-DIABOLICO (66; aka HOW TO
STEAL THE CROWN OF ENGLAND); AGENTE 3S3, MASSACRO
AL SOLE (66; Agent 3S3, Massacre in the Sun); GOLDFACE,
IL FANTASTICO SUPERMAN (67; Goldface, the Fantastic Super-
man); PARANOIA (68); CHINOS Y MINIFALDAS (68; Chinese &
Miniskirts); WITCHCRAFT '70 (69; aka ANGELI BIANCHI, AN-
GELI NERO--White Angel, Black Angel); FIVE DOLLS FOR AN
AUGUST MOON (70); BABA YAGA--THE DEVIL WITCH (73)
Ian Underwood: FUGITIVE FROM THE EMPIRE (81, tvm)
Seiichiro Uno (Ja.): NYOKKORI NYOTON JIMA (67; Great Adven-
tures on Bottle-Gourd Island); JACK AND THE WITCH (67);
FABLES FROM HANS CHRISTIAN ANDERSEN (68); NAGAGUTSU
O HAITA NEKO (69)
Max Urban (Mx.): EL FANTASMA DEL CONVENTO (34; The
Phantom of the Convent); EL MISTERIO DEL RUSTRO PALIDO
(35; The Mystery of the Pallid Face)
Alice Uretta (Mx.): THE FEAR CHAMBER (68); HOUSE OF EVIL
(68); THE SNAKE PEOPLE (70; w/E. Cabiati); THE INCREDIBLE
INVASION (71; w/E. Cabiati)
Remo Usai (Brz.): SIN IN THE VESTRY (75)
Teo Usuelli (It.): I PATRIARCHI DELLA BIBBIA (63; The Patri-

Teo Usuelli (cont.)
  archs of the Bible; w/G. Marinuzzi); THE APE WOMAN (63);
  OPERATION ATLANTIS (65); THE SEVENTH FLOOR (66); IL
  SEME DELL'UOMO (69; The Seed of Man)
Mike Valarde: HORROR OF THE BLOOD MONSTERS (70)
*Nathan Van Cleave: THE CONQUEST OF SPACE (55); THE
  SPACE CHILDREN (57); THE COLOSSUS OF NEW YORK (58;
  w/F. Steiner); THE TWILIGHT ZONE (59-60, tv; episodes:
  Perchance to Dream, What You Need, Elegy, A World of Differ-
  ence, Two, The Midnight Sun, I Sing the Body Electric, Jess-
  Belle, Steel, A Kind of Stopwatch, Black Leather Jackets, From
  Agnes with Love); ROBINSON CRUSOE ON MARS (64; w/F.
  Steiner); PROJECT X (68)
Robert Van Eps: OUTER LIMITS (63, tv; episodes: Tourist At-
  traciton, et al.)
James Van Heusen: JOURNEY BACK TO OZ (71, tvm; w/S. Cahn)
Georges Van Parys (Fr.): MR. PEEK-A-BOO (50); LE GRAND
  MELIES (52; The Great Melies); DIABOLIQUE (55); DOUBLE
  DECEPTION (60)
Melvin Van Peebles: WATERMELON MAN (70; also directed)
Jerry Van Rooyen (W. Gm.): CASTLE OF LUST (68); SUCCUBUS
  (68; w/F. Gulda); THE VAMPIRE HAPPENING (71); KISS ME
  MONSTER (75)
Vangelis (aka Vangelis Papathinassou; Br.): COSMOS (81; tv;
  record music used); BLADE RUNNER (82)
Henry Vars: THE UNEARTHLY (57); LOVE SLAVES OF THE
  AMAZON (57; w/H. Stein, S. Wilson, I. Gertz, et al.); THE
  TWO LITTLE BEARS (61)
Eddy Vartan (Fr.): ELLE CAUSE PLUS ELLE FLINGUE (72)
B. Vasantha (India): RAJA NARTAKIYA RAHASYA (77)
Didier Vasseur (Fr.): CATHY'S CURSE (80)
Clifford Vaughan: THE RAVEN (35); FLASH GORDON (36, serial;
  titles only)
John Veale (Br.): THE INVISIBLE CREATURE (60)
G. K. Venkatesh (India): NAA NINNA BIDENU (78)
Henri Verdun (Fr.): LES DISPARUS DE SAINT-AGIL (38; aka
  BOY'S SCHOOL: aka MYSTERY AT ST. AGIL)
Pablo Vergara (Phil.): TORE NG DIYABLO (69)
Albert Verrechia (It.): DEBORAH (74; aka A BLACK RIBBON
  FOR DEBORAH)
Clem Vicari & Phil Gallo: THE REDEEMER ... SON OF SATAN!
  (78); MOTHER'S DAY (80)
Michael Vickers (Br.): DRACULA A.D. 1972 (72; songs by Stone-
  ground); AT THE EARTH'S CORE (76); WARRIORS OF ATLAN-
  TIS (78)
Gerard Victory (Swd.): VICTOR FRANKENSTEIN (77)
Tommy Vig: TERROR CIRCUS (73)
H. Vileta & M. Versiani (Brz.): THE COLONEL AND THE WOLFMAN
  (78)
Don Vincent: THE NIGHT GOD SCREAMED (71); HAPPY MOTHER'S
  DAY, LOVE GEORGE (73); RUN, STRANGER, RUN (73)

Roland Vincent (Fr.):   L'ETRANGLEUR (72; The Strangler); HOME
SWEET HOME (72)
Carlos Vizziello (Sp.):   SOBRENATURAL: EL REGRESO DE LA
MUERTE (81)
Roman Vlad (It.):   THE BEAUTY AND THE DEVIL (49); THE
DEMON IN ART (50, short); INCANTESIMO TRAGICO (50;
Tragic Spell); DESTINIES (53); THE DEVIL'S COMMANDMENT
(56; w/F. Mannino); CALTIKI, THE IMMORTAL MONSTER (59);
IL MISTERO DEI TREI CONTINENTI (69; The Mystery of Three
Continents); HYPNOSIS (62); THE HORRIBLE DR. HITCHCOCK
(62); THE GHOST (63; w/F. Mannino)
D. Vorhaus: PHASE IV (74; electronic music only; score: B.
Gasciogne)
Derek Wadsworth (Br.):   THE DAY AFTER TOMORROW (75, tv);
SPACE: 1999 SERIES 2 (76, tv; 2nd season episodes)
Roger Wagner: THE OUTER SPACE CONNECTION (75)
Charles Wain (Austral.):   THE LAST WAVE (77)
Adolfo Waitzman (Sp.):   THE BELL OF HELL (73)
Wakakusa (Ja.):   THE UNION OF THE 6 GODS (82; tv)
Rick Wakeman (Br.):   LISZTOMANIA (75); THE BURNING (81)
Charles Walden: THE MIGHTY GORGA (70)
Kenneth Walker: THE ALIEN FACTOR (78)
Oliver Wallace: DONALD DUCK (34-61; cart. series); MURDER
BY TELEVISION (35); PLUTO (40-51; cart. series); ALICE IN
WONDERLAND (51); PETER PAN (53); BEN AND ME (53;
cart.); DARBY O'GILL AND THE LITTLE PEOPLE (58)
Rob Wallace: THE CHILD (77)
Fats Waller: ERASERHEAD (77)
Bryn Walton (Br.):   SECRET RITES (71)
Ken Wannberg: OF UNKNOWN ORIGIN (83)
Edward Ward: THE DEVIL WITH HITLER (42); PRAIRIE CHICKENS
(43); THE PHANTOM OF THE OPERA (43); THE GHOST
CATCHERS (44); THE CLIMAX (44); COBRA WOMAN (44); THE
STRANGE DOOR (51; library tracks used)
Terry Warr (Br.):   THE HOUSE THAT VANISHED (74)
Chumei Watanabe (Ja.):   APPEARANCE OF SUPER GIANT (56; U.S.
compilation of SUPERGIANT #1 and SUPERGIANT #2); ATOMIC
RULERS OF THE WORLD (64; U.S. compilation of SUPERGIANT
#3 and 4); ATTACK FROM SPACE (64; U.S. compilation of
SUPERGIANT #5 and 6; aka INVADERS FROM SPACE); THE
EVIL BRAIN FORM OUTER SPACE (64; U.S. compilation of
SUPERGIANT #7, 8 and 9); 100 MONSTERS (68); HIROKU
KAIBYODEN (69; Haunted Castle); GIANT IRON MAN ONE-
SEVEN--THE AERIAL BATTLESHIP (77); MAZINGER Z (78, tv;
episodes); MOBILE SUIT GUNDAM (81, tv; w/Matsuyama, epi-
sodes; aka feature: GUNDAM I, II, III; 81-82); SPACE DE-
TECTIVE "GYAVAN" (82, tv); SPACE DETECTIVE "SHALIBAN"
(82, tv); ELECTRIC GOD "ARUBEGAS" (83, tv)
Hiroaki Watanabe (Ja.):   ALONG WITH GHOSTS (64)
*Franz Waxman: LILIOM (35); THE BRIDE OF FRANKENSTEIN
(35; later reused in Universal serials: FLASH GORDON, 36--

*Franz Waxman (cont.)
   edited feature version; RADIO PATROL, 37; BUCK ROGERS,
   39); THE GREAT IMPERSONATION (35); TROUBLE FOR TWO
   (36); THE INVISIBLE RAY (36); THE DEVIL DOLL (36); A
   CHRISTMAS CAROL (38); THE PHANTOM CREEPS (39; library
   tracks used); ON BORROWED TIME (39); DR. JEKYLL AND
   MR. HYDE (41); THE HORN BLOWS AT MIDNIGHT (45); THE
   BRIGHTON STRANGLER (45, track; plus L. Harline); NIGHT
   UNTO NIGHT (47); THE TWO MRS. CARROLLS (47); POSSESSED
   (47): ALIAS NICK BEAL (49); THE TWILIGHT ZONE (59, tv;
   episode: The Sixteen-Millimeter Shrine); THE TIME TUNNEL
   (66, tv; episodes); BATMAN (66, tv; episodes)
Sam Wayman: GANJA & HESS (73; aka DOUBLE POSSESSION)
Jimmy Webb: THE LAST UNICORN (82)
Roger Webb (Br.): BURKE AND HARE (71); BEDTIME WITH
   ROSIE (74); THE GODSEND (80); THE HAMMER HOUSE OF
   HORROR (80, tv; theme & episodes)
*Roy Webb: THE SPIRIT OF 1976 (35; short); THE NITWITS (35);
   MUMMY'S BOYS (36); YOU'LL FIND OUT (40); THE CAT PEO-
   PLE (42); I MARRIED A WITCH (42); POWDER TOWN (42, md);
   THE SEVENTH VICTIM (43); PASSPORT TO DESTINY (43);
   THE LEOPARD MAN (43); I WALKED WITH A ZOMBIE (43);
   GHOST SHIP (43); CURSE OF THE CAT PEOPLE (44); EXPERI-
   MENT PERILOUS (44); THE SPIRAL STAIRCASE (45); THE EN-
   CHANTED COTTAGE (45); MAGIC TOWN (45); ZOMBIES ON
   BROADWAY (45); THE BODY SNATCHER (45); BEDLAM (46);
   SINBAD THE SAILOR (46); GENIUS AT WORK (46, w/P. Saw-
   tell); MIGHTY JOE YOUNG (49); THE SEARCH FOR BRIDEY
   MURPHY (56; additional music by H. Jackson)
Larry Wellington: 2000 MANIACS (64, w/H. G. Lewis); THE
   GRUESOME TWOSOME (66, md); HOW TO MAKE A DOLL (67);
   A TASTE OF BLOOD (67; aka THE SECRET OF DR. ALUCARD);
   THE WIZARD OF GORE (71)
Richard Wess: I DREAM OF JEANNIE (65, tv; episodes)
Christopher Whelan (Br.): THE FACE OF FU MANCHU (65)
Burnell Whibley (Br.): VIRGIN WITCH (70); NO BLADE OF
   GRASS (70, md)
*David Whitaker (Br.): SCREAM AND SCREAM AGAIN (70); DR.
   JEKYLL AND SISTER HYDE (71); PSYCHOMANIA (72); VAM-
   PIRE CIRCUS (72); OLD DRACULA (75; theme song by A. New-
   ley); DOMINIQUE (78); THE SWORD AND THE SORCERER (82)
Daniel J. White (Sp.): LA MANO DE UN HOMBRE MUERTO (63;
   The Hand of a Dead Man); THE DIABOLICAL DR. Z (65); KISS
   AND KILL (68; w/G. Wilen); RIO 70 (70); EL DR. MABUSE (71);
   DRACULA CONTRA EL DR. FRANKENSTEIN (71; w/B. Nicolai);
   LOS AMANTES DE LA ISLA DEL DIABLO (?); LA COMTESSE
   AUX SEINS NUS (75; The Bare-Breasted Countess)
Reid Whitelaw: NOCTURNA (79)
Carson Whitsett: WONDER WOMEN (73)
Jean Winer (Fr.): LE GOLEM (66)
Rolf Wilhelm (W. Gm.): SIEGFRIED (67; aka WHOM THE GODS

WISH TO DESTROY; aka DIE NIBELUNGEN)

Rick Wilkins: THE CHANGELING (80)

Marc Wilkinson (Br.): IF ... (68); BLOOD ON SATAN'S CLAW
(71); THE MAN AND THE SNAKE (72); THE RETURN (73);
THE HAMMER HOUSE OF HORROR (80, tv; episode: A Visitor
from the Grave); THE FIENDISH PLOT OF DR. FU MANCHU
(80); THE QUATERMASS CONCLUSION (80; w/N. Rowley)

Charles Williams (Br.): THE NIGHT HAS EYES (42; aka TERROR
HOUSE, 43)

Edward Williams (Br.): UNEARTHLY STRANGER (63)

Guy Bevier Williams: WHITE ZOMBIE (32; w/X. Cugat; source
music only)

*John Williams: VOYAGE TO THE BOTTOM OF THE SEA (64, tv;
episodes); LOST IN SPACE (65, tv; theme & episodes); THE
TIME TUNNEL (66, tv; theme & episodes); LAND OF THE GI-
ANTS (68, tv); IMAGES (72); THE SCREAMING WOMAN (72,
tvm); EARTHQUAKE (74); JAWS (75); STAR WARS (77);
CLOSE ENCOUNTERS OF THE THIRD KIND (77); JAWS 2 (78);
THE FURY (78); SUPERMAN (78; score later adapted by K.
Thorne for SUPERMAN II, 81; and SUPERMAN III, 83);
DRACULA (79); THE EMPIRE STRIKES BACK (80); HEART-
BEEPS (81); RAIDERS OF THE LOST ARK (81); E.T. THE
EXTRATERRESTRIAL (82); RETURN OF THE JEDI (83); INDI-
ANA JONES AND THE TEMPLE OF DOOM (84); WINDSOR Mc-
KAY'S NEMO (84)

Patrick Williams: THE FAILING OF RAYMOND (71, tvm); MOON-
CHILD (72; w/B. Byers); SSSSSSS (73); HEX (75); STOW-
AWAY TO THE MOON (75, tvm); GOOD HEAVENS (76, tv);
THE MAN WITH THE POWER (77, tvm); CHARLIE CHAN AND
THE CURSE OF THE DRAGON QUEEN (81)

Paul Williams: THE PHANTOM OF THE PARADISE (74; songs only); THE BOY IN THE PLASTIC BUBBLE (76); THE MUPPET
MOVIE (79; w/K. Asher)

Pip Williams: TRAIN RIDE TO HOLLYWOOD (75)

Malcolm Williamson (Br.): THE BRIDES OF DRACULA (60); THE
HORROR OF FRANKENSTEIN (70); CRESCENDO (72); NOTHING
BUT THE NIGHT (75); WATERSHIP DOWN (78; w/A. Morley;
M. Batt)

Mortimer Wilson: THE THIEF OF BAGDAD (24)

Ross Wilson: 20TH CENTURY OZ (78)

Stanley Wilson: RADAR PATROL VS. SPY KING (49-50; serial);
KING OF THE ROCKET MEN (49, serial; aka LOST PLANET
AIRMEN, 51); THE INVISIBLE MONSTER (50, serial); RADAR
MEN OF THE MOON (51, serial; aka tv: RETIK THE MOON
MENACE, 66); ZOMBIES OF THE STRATOSPHERE (52, serial);
ALFRED HITCHCOCK PRESENTS/THE ALFRED HITCHCOCK
HOUR (55-65, tv; md); LOVE SLAVES OF THE AMAZON (57;
w/H. Stein, I. Gertz, et al.); THE DARK INTRUDER (65, tvm;
md; score L. Schifrin); COLOSSUS THE FORBIN PROJECT (70,
md; score M. Colombier)

Stefan Wohl (Brz.): THE GHOST HUNTER (75)

Herbert Woods: BUCK ROGERS IN THE 25TH CENTURY (79, tv; episode: Twiki Is Missing)

Frank Worth: BRIDE OF THE MONSTER (56)

Paul Woznicki: FIEND (81)

Gary Wright: ENDANGERED SPECIES (82)

George Wyle: IT'S ABOUT TIME (66, tv; episodes)

Dan Wyman: WITHOUT WARNING (80); THE RETURN (80); HELL NIGHT (81). Wyman also orchestrated THE FOG (music: J. Carpenter)

Richard Wynkoop: THE RESURRECTION OF EVE (73)

Maso Yagi (Ja.): LEGEND OF DINOSAURS AND MONSTER BIRDS (77)

Tadashi Yamaguchi (Ja.): GAMMERA, THE INVINCIBLE (66; Ja. release only); THE RETURN OF THE GIANT MONSTERS (67; aka GAMERA VS. GAOS)

Masayuki Yamamoto (Ja.): GALAXY CYLONE BRYGER (81-82, tv); A TRADITION IN THE WORLD OF SPIRIT, ACROBUNCH (82, tv; w/M. Maruyama; aka ACROBUNCH: LEGENDARY HAUNTS OF WICKED MEN); MISSION IN OUTER SPACE, SRUNGLE (82); J9II GALAXY WHIRLWIND BAXINGER (82-83, tv); J9III GALAXY TORNADO SASRYGER (83, tv; aka JJ9 GALAXY WHIRLWIND SASURAIGER)

Naozumi Yamamoto (Ja.): THE SPACE GIANTS (70, tv); COMPUTER FREE FOR ALL (69); MYSTERIOUS BIG TACTICS (78; w/H. Tamaki)

Stomu Yamash'ta: IMAGES (72; percussion arrangements; score: J. Williams); THE MAN WHO FELL TO EARTH (76; w/J. Phillips)

Wong Tse Yan (H.K.): AILILIA (75)

Yano (Ja.): PSYCHO ARMOR "GOVARIAN" (83, tv)

Gabriel Yared: MALEVIL (81)

Wong Chu Yen (H.K.): MAGIC CURSE (7?)

Toshiaki Yokota (Ja.): GHOST FESTIVAL AT SAINT'S VILLAGE (79, tv)

Seiji Yokoyama (Ja.): SPACE FANTASY EMERALDUS (78); SPACE PIRATE CAPTAIN HARLOCK (78, tv & feature; w/M. Hirao); TOMB OF DRACULA (80); FUTURE WAR 198X (82)

Miki Yoshino & Akira Kobayashi (Ja.): HOUSE (77)

Chris Young: PRANKS (82); THE POWER (83)

Victor Young: THE GLADIATOR (38, md); GULLIVER'S TRAVELS (39); THE MAD DOCTOR (40); THE REMARKABLE ANDREW (41); THE UNINVITED (44); GOLDEN EARRING (47); NIGHT HAS A THOUSAND EYES (48); A CONNECTICUT YANKEE IN KING ARTHUR'S COURT (48)

Joij Yuassa (Ja.): FUNERAL PARADE OF ROSES (70); AKURUO-TO (81; Island of the Evil Spirit)

Chen Yung-yu (H.K.): THE SUPER INFRAMAN (77, md); BLACK MAGIC 2 (77); GOLIATHON (80; aka THE MIGHTY PEKING MAN, made 77; w/ De Wolfe)

Gordon Zahler (Music Director): PLAN 9 FROM OUTER SPACE (56); FIRST SPACESHIP ON VENUS (59; U.S. release only); SHOCK

CORRIDOR (63); THE HUMAN DUPLICATORS (64); MUTINY IN
OUTER SPACE (65); THE NAVY VS. THE NIGHT MONSTERS
(66); JOURNEY TO THE CENTER OF THE EARTH (67, tv
cart.); FANTASTIC VOYAGE (68, tv cart.)

Lee Zahler (Most are serials): KING OF THE KONGO (29, sound
version); KING OF THE WILD (31, md); THE LIGHTNING WAR-
RIOR (31); THE PHANTOM OF THE WEST (31); THE MONSTER
WALKS (32); SAVAGE GIRL (32); HURRICANE EXPRESS (32);
THE LOST CITY (35); THE AMAZING EXPLOITS OF THE
CLUTCHING HAND (36); MANDRAKE THE MAGICIAN (39); THE
SHADOW (40); THE SPIDER RETURNS (41); THE GREEN ARCH-
ER (41); THE IRON CLAW (41); CAPTAIN MIDNIGHT (42);
THE SECRET CODE (42); THE PHANTOM (43-44); THE BATMAN
(43); TIGER FANGS (43); THE DESERT HAWK (44); THE MON-
STER AND THE APE (45); WHO'S GUILTY (45, md); HOP HAR-
RIGAN (46); THE WHITE GORILLA (47); JACK ARMSTRONG
(47)

Christian Zanesi, Pierre Tardy & Françoise Burgoin (Fr.): TIME
MASTERS (82)

Paul Zaza: MURDER BY DECREE (79; w/C. Zittrer); PROM
NIGHT (80; w/Zittrer); MY BLOODY VALENTINE (81); CUR-
TAINS (83)

Eric Zeisl: THE INVISIBLE MAN'S REVENGE (44; w/H. Stein,
W. Lava); FRANCIS GOES TO THE RACES (51; w/others);
ABBOTT & COSTELLO MEET DR. JEKYLL AND MR. HYDE
(53; library tracks used)

Denny Zeitlin: INVASION OF THE BODY SNATCHERS (78)

Wolfgang Zeller (Gm.): L'ATLANTIDE (32; Lost Atlantis); VAM-
PYR (32); WAJAN (34; Son of a Witch); DIE UNJEIMLICHEN
WUNSCHE (39; The Unholy Wish)

Nick Zesses & Dino Fekaris: SUGAR HILL (74; aka VOODOO
GIRL)

Josef Zimanich: MAN BEAST (55, md); SPACE MASTER X7 (58)

Don Zimmers: SCREAMS OF A WINTER NIGHT (79)

Peter Zinner: KING KONG VS. GODZILLA (62; U.S. release only;
Zinner also edited U.S. version)

B. Zirkovic (Yug.): THE REDEEMER (77)

Carl Zittrer: CHILDREN SHOULDN'T PLAY WITH DEAD THINGS
(72); BLOOD ORGY OF THE SHE DEVILS (73); DERANGED (74);
DEATH DREAM (74; aka DEAD OF NIGHT; aka THE NIGHT
ANDY CAME HOME); BLACK CHRISTMAS (75; aka SILENT
NIGHT, EVIL NIGHT; aka tv: STRANGER IN THE HOUSE);
MURDER BY DECREE (79; w/P. Zaza); PROM NIGHT (80, w/
P. Zaza)

An International Checklist of Recorded Music

Sound-track recordings of film scores are the boon of the film music enthusiast, for it gives one the opportunity to listen to a film's music without the distractions of dialog, sound effects and poor theatrical speakers. It's one of the paradoxes of film music that the music, while intrinsically a part of the whole audiovisual creation that is a motion picture, can often stand on its own, apart from the film, as a serious--or at the very least, enjoyable--composition of music.

Commercial sound-track records have been around for nearly five decades, and a listing of them all would be nearly endless, especially in view of the glut during the last decade. Actually, though, sound-track albums are issued for very few films, because in comparison with the commercial types of music like rock, country or even classical, movie sound tracks have traditionally maintained very poor sales, being pressed and sold in fractions of the quantities of rock albums. One unsurprising exception is the sound track to STAR WARS, an album which did much to legitimize symphonic film music on record: more than 4 million copies of John Williams' two-record sound track were sold, more than any other movie sound track. But it's very expensive to produce a movie sound-track album, and most companies are hesitant to undertake this gamble in view of bleak sales potentials. In the United States, musicians' union contracts require that a record company pay each of the musicians their original fee again when the music is recorded for an album, which is often more than a record producer can afford in initial overhead--one reason why small ensemble and synthesizer scores (as well as foreign-recorded scores, where such rules don't apply) have been quite prevalent recently.

Regardless of the drawbacks, a great deal of music from science fiction, fantasy and horror films has been preserved on vinyl over the years. It has been said that the earliest recording for such a film was a set of discs released by Polyphone in Germany to accompany showings of the 1929 silent film, DIE FRAU IM MOND (Woman in the Moon). A limited pressing of four themes from KING KONG was made during the 30's as well, but the earliest commercial sound-track recording was a set of 78-rpm discs, released in England by Decca, of Arthur Bliss' THINGS TO COME

score. The first American sound-track recording was a set of 78's
released by RCA from Miklos Rozsa's JUNGLE BOOK in 1942. It's
perhaps interesting that both of these landmark sound-track records were for fantastic films.

What follows is a carefully researched checklist of recorded
music from fantastic films. I am particularly indebted to G. Roger
Hammonds for his generous assistance in allowing me to use the
format and discography in his limited-edition 1982 book, Recorded
Music for the Science Fiction, Fantasy and Horror Film (published
in similar form to what follows by Sound Track Album Retailers,
Quarryville, PA), which I have combined with my own material
and format to arrive at the following listing. In addition, I want
to acknowledge with thanks the valuable assistance over the years
of Jim Doherty, Marc Weilage, Jim Wnoroski, Luc Van De Ven,
Rodney L. Sims, Greg Shoemaker and Gary Dorst who contributed
in one way or another to the compilation which follows.

Each film is listed as follows:

U.S. release title (composer, year of U.S. release)
    Alternate or foreign title, if applicable
    Country Abbrev. rpm label and # (title, where known, if
        collection, along with any additional information about the
        recording; year of record, if other than film release date,
        where known.)

All albums listed are considered to contain a full sound
track, unless noted as only "theme," "suite" or "excerpt," or if
the listing is for a 45-rpm single. The number following the country denotes 33-rpm lp, 45-rpm single, or 78-rpm set. The music
should be considered to be an original sound-track recording unless
noted as nst (not sound track), in which case the conductor/ar-
ranger, where known, will be included.

After the main alphabetical listing, I have included a supple-
mentary list of collections of film music from fantastic films. These
collections are broken down in the main list, but have been included by themselves as well.

Abbreviations used:

    Country of origin:
    AU - Australia
    CA - Canada
    FR - France
    GB - Great Britain
    GE - Germany
    HO - Holland
    IT - Italy
    JA - Japan

NZ - New Zealand
SP - Spain
US - United States

nst: not original sound track, rerecorded score
r/r: rerecorded by (conductor's name)
p/r: private release; not regular commercial release, but a
        legally licensed recording
b/r: bootleg recording (unlawful private release, pirate re-
        cording)
2/lp: 2-record set (also 3/lp, and so on)
ep: extended play 45-rpm single (more than one band per
        side)
w/d: with dialog (there are dialog excerpts or narration in ad-
        dition to the music)
w/fx: 'with sound effects but no dialog
10":   ten-inch lp record, as opposed to common twelve-inch
        record
nfd: no further details were available on this recording

A for Andromeda (Trevor Duncan, 1961, tv)
    GB   33   BBC REH 324 (1 band on BBC Space Themes, 1979)

Abby (Robert O. Ragland, 1974)
    US   ep   American International Records 12154 (5 bands, promo
                ep)

Abominable Dr. Phibes, The (Basil Kirchin, 1971)
    US   33   American International A 1040 (3 original themes and
                8 bands of source music)

Absent Minded Professor, The (George Bruns, 1960)
    US   33   Disneyland ST-1911 (w/d, 1960)
    US   33   Disneyland DQ 1323 (w/d; reissue of ST-1911, backed
                with THE SHAGGY DOG, 1967)

Addams Family, The (Vic Mizzy, 1964, tv)
    US   33   RCA LPM-3421/LSP-3421 (w/d)
    US   33   Epic LN 24125/26125 (Theme on Music for Monsters,
                Munsters, Mummies and Other TV Fiends/Milton De-
                Lugg Orch.) nst
    US   33   ABC (S)513 (theme only/nfd)
    US   33   Audio Fidelity 2146/6146 (theme only/nfd)
    US   33   Dot 3616/25616 (theme, r/r Lawrence Welk) nst
    US   45   Dot 45-16697 (theme, r/r Lawrence Welk) nst

Adieu Galaxy Express (Osamu Shoji, 1981)
    JA   33   Columbia DB 7114/5 (2/lp; Columbia Symph. & Japan
                Choral Soc.)
    JA   33   Columbia CX-7042 (Digital Trip)

Adventures of Pinocchio, The (Fiorenzo Carpi, 1974)
    Le Avventura Di Pinocchio
    IT   33   Cam 9038
    IT   45   Cam AMP-206

Adventures of Superman, The (Leon Klatzkin, 1953, tv)
    US   33   Artco ART 10 1206 (1 band on Space Hits/Star Phase
                Orch.) nst
    US   33   GNP Crescendo GNPS 2133 (1 band on Greatest Sci-
                ence Fiction Hits II/Neil Norman Orch., 1981) nst
    US   33   Springboard SPB 4114 (1 band on Super Disco from
                the Movie Superman/Festival '79 Orch.) nst
    US   33   Wonderland WLP-301 (Theme on Theme from Star
                Trek/Jeff Wayne Space Shuttle) nst

Aladdin's Lamp (Godeigo & Tubono, 1982)
    JA   33   Columbia CZ 7169 (w/d)

Alakazam the Great (Les Baxter, 1961)
    US   33   Veejay LP 6000

Albator, Le Corsaire de l'Espace (Charden, 1980, tv)
    FR   45   Pathe Marconi/EMI 2C 008 63526

L'Aldila (Fabio Frizzi, 1981)
    IT   33   Beat LPF 052

Alfred Hitchcock Presents (Gounod; arr. by Stanley Wilson, 1955,
           tv)
    US   33   Imperial LP 12005 (theme on Music to Be Murdered
                By/Jeff Alexander Orch.) nst
    US   33   DRG SL 5183 (reissue of LP 12005; 1981)
    US   333   Tops L-1661 (theme on TV Themes/Richard Gleason
                Orch.)
    US   33   Epic LN-24125 (theme on Music for Monsters, Mun-
                sters, Mummies & Other TV Fiends/Milton DeLugg
                Orch.) nst

Alice's Adventures in Wonderland (John Barry, 1973)
    US   33   Warner Bros BS 2671
    US   ep   Rainbow PRO-543 (promo ep)
    GB   33   Warner Bros K56009

Alien (Jerry Goldsmith, 1979)
    US   33   20th Century Fox T-593 (note: not all music really
                from film)
    FR   33   RCA/20th Century-Fox T-593
    GB   33   20th Century-Fox T-593
    IT   33   20th Century-Fox 6370-295
    JA   33   20th Century-Fox FML 120
    US   33   GNP Crescendo GNPS 2128 (1 band on Greatest S.F.

                    Hits/Neil Norman Orch.) nst
US   33   Philips 411 185-1 (1 band on Out of This World/John
            Williams & Boston Pops, 1983) nst

Alien Contamination (Goblin, 1981)
    Contamination
    IT   33   Cinevox MDF 33/142
    FR   33   Polydor Cinevox 2393 327 (Excerpts on Les Meilleures
                Musiques de Films Fantastiques)
    IT   33   Cinevox CIA 5014 (1 band on Squalo-Exorcista e Altri
                Film Della Paura)

Allegro Non Troppo (classical, 1978)
    US   33   DG 25-36-400
    GB   33   DG Privilege 2535400

Altered States (John Corigliano, 1981)
    Au Dela Du Reel
    US   33   RCA ABL1 3983
    FR   33   RCA BL 13983
    US   33   RCA XRL1 4020 (1 band on Film Classics, r/r Chris-
                topher Keene, 1981) nst

Amazing Colossal Man, The (Albert Glasser, 1957)
    US   33   Starlog SR-1001 (9½ min. suite on The Fantastic Film
                Music of Albert Glasser, 1978)

Ambushers, The (Hugo Montenegro, 1967)
    US   45   A&M 893

American Werewolf in London, An (Elmer Bernstein, 1981)
    US   33   Casablanca NBLP 7260 (music "inspired by" film, writ-
                ten and performed by Meco) nst
    US   45   Casablanca 2339 (same as above) nst
    GB   33   Casablanca 6480 065 (same as above) nst
    SP   33   Fonogram Casablanca 6480 065 (same as above) nst

Americathon (Tom Scott & rock songs, 1979)
    US   33   Lorimar JS 36174
    JA   33   CBS/Sony 25 AP 1719

Amityville Horror, The (Lalo Schifrin, 1979)
    Amityville, La Maison de Diable
    US   33   AIR/Casablanca AILP 3003
    FR   33   Vogue PIP 571 060
    IT   33   Casablanca CALP 6047

Andromeda Stories (Yuji Ohno, 1983, tv)
    JS   33   VAP 30055 23 (w/d)

Andromeda Strain, The (Gil Mellé, 1971)
    US   33   Kapp KRS 5513 (first pressing released with hexa-

gonal-shaped disc)
FR   33   Arabella MCA 204880 (1 band on 12 Terrifiantes
          Bandes Originales de Films)
JA   33   Mu Land LZ 7016M (1 band on SF Fact Vol. 1/Electoru
          Polyphonic Orch., 1979) nst

Andy Warhol's Dracula (Claudio Gizzi, 1974)
   Blood for Dracula
   US   33   Varese Sarabande STV 81156 (1982)

Andy Warhol's Frankenstein (Claudio Gizzi, 1974)
   Flesh for Frankenstein
   US   33   Varese Sarabande STV-81157 (1982)

Angels of the Year 2000 (Mario Molino, 1969)
   Gli Angeli Del 2,000
   IT   33   Cam SAG-9020

Angry Red Planet (Paul Dunlap, 1959)
   US   33   GNP Crescendo GNPS 2163 (1 band on Greatest S.F.
             Hits III/Neil Norman, 1983) nst

Apple, The (Coby Recht & Iris Recht, 1981)
   US   33   Cannon 1001 (p/r)

Around the World Under the Sea (Harry Sukman, 1966)
   US   33   Monument 18050
   US   45   Monument 45-959

Arrivederci Yamato (Hiroshi Miyagawa, 1980)
   JA   33   Columbia CS 7077/78 (2/lp, w/d)
   JA   33   Columbia CQ 7011 (Combatants of Love)

Arsenic and Old Lace (Max Steiner, 1944)
   US   33   Tony Thomas TT-MS-17 (excerpt on Max Steiner:
             Memories, p/r, 1981)

Assault on Precinct 13 (John Carpenter, 1976)
   UK   45   Pye 7N 46064 (2 bands; side 1 has overdubbed vocal
             not from film)

Astro Boy (uncredited, 1963, tv)
   US   33   Cosmo M-31 (The Story of 3 Magicians, w/d)

Ator (Carlo Maria Cordio, 1983)
   US   33   Citadel CT-7032

Atragon (Akira Ifukube, 1963)
   Atoragon
   JA   33   Toho AX 8108 (8 bands on Fantasy World of Japanese
             Pictures, Part 3, 1978)

JA   33   StarChild K22G 7111 (excerpts on Science Fiction
            Film Themes, Vol. 1, 1983)
JA   33   King K22G 7046 (3 bands on Akira Ifukube Movie
            Themes, v. 4, 1982)

Attack of the Killer Tomatoes (Gordon Goodwin, 1979)
    US   45   4 Square Prods. KT-100 (promo release)

Attack of the Monsters (Shunsuke Kikuchi, 1969)
    Gamera Tai Guiron/Gamera vs. Guiron
    JA   33   Toho AX 8120 (3 bands on Gamera, 1978)
    JA   33   Daiei KKS-4026 (excerpts on Gamera, w/d; diff. from
                Toho lp)

Attack of the Mushroom People (Betsumia Sadao, 1963)
    Matango
    JA   33   Toho AX 8107 (2 bands on Fantasy World of Japanese
                Pictures part 2, 1978)
    JA   33   StarChild K22G 7114 (excerpt on Science Fiction Film
                Themes, vol. 4, 1983)

Audrey Rose (Michael Small, 1977)
    IT   45   Philips SFL 2194 (theme, r/r Chris Carpenter Orch.)
                nst

Autopsy (Ennio Morricone, 1976)
    The Victim
    JA   45   Seven Seas/Cam FMS 9 (2 bands)
    IT   33   Seven Seas K18P 4105 (1 band on Horror Movie Spe-
                cial, 1983)

Avengers, The (Laurie Johnson, 1966-69, tv)
    US   33   Hanna Barbera HST 9506 (1 theme & 11 bands source
                music)
    US   33   Starlog/Varese Sarabande ASV 95003 (1 side only,
                1982)
    US   ep   Evatone EV-1111814AXT (promo ep)
    GB   33   Unicorn/Kanchana KPM 7009 (1 album side, same as
                ASV 95003; 1982)
    GB   45   Unicorn/Kanchana C 15 (theme)
    US   45   Warner Bros. 5814 (theme, r/r The Marketts) nst
    US   45   Columbia 444000 (theme, r/r Jerry Murad's Harmoni-
                cats) nst

Awakening, The (Claude Bolling, 1980)
    US   33   Entr'acte ERS 6520

Babes in Toyland (Victor Herbert, 1934)
    US   33   Mark 56-577 (w/d)

Babes in Toyland (Victor Herbert, 1961)
    US   33   Disneyland DQ-1219

Bad Seed, The (Alex North, 1956)
US 33   RCA LPM-1395
US ep   RCA EPA-4010
IT 33   Cinevox 33/25 (reissue of LPM-1395)
US 33   Citadel CT-6023 (1 band on Film Music of Alex North,
         p/r, 1977)

Barbarella (Bob Crewe & Charles Fox, 1968)
US 33   Dynavoice DY-31908
US 45   Dynavoice DY-927
IT 33   Dot 533D-003
US 33   Cinema LP-8005 (theme on Destination Moon and Oth-
         er Themes, b/r, 1974)
US 45   Command RS 45-4125B (theme r/r Doc Severinsen)
         nst
JA 33   Mu-Land LZ-7016-M (theme on S.F. Fact, Vol. 1/
         Electoru Polyphonic Orch. 1979) nst
GB 33   MFP 50355 (theme on Star Wars & Other Space Themes/
         Geoff Love Orch.) nst

Bat, The (Louis Forbes, 1959)
US 45   Capitol 4239 (nfd)

Batman (Nelson Riddle, Neal Hefti, et al., 1966-68, tv)
US 33   20th Century-Fox S-3180/4180 (w/d)
US 33   RCA (S) 3573
US 33   Wonderland WLP-301 (Theme on Theme from Star Trek/
         Jeff Wayne Space Shuttle) nst
US 33   Leo CH-1023 (Theme on The Amazing TV Themes/nfd)
US 33   Decca (7)4754 (theme only/nfd)
US 33   Metro (S)564 (theme only/nfd)
US 33   Reprise (S)6210 (theme only/nfd)
US 33   Warners (S)1642 (theme only/nfd)
US 45   Warner Bros. 5096 (theme, r/r Neal Hefti) nst

Battle Beyond the Stars (James Horner, 1980)
US 33   Rhino NSP 300

Battle in Outer Space (Akira Ifukube, 1960)
Uchu Dai Sensoh
JA 33   Toho DX 4007
JA 33   Toho AX 9106 (1 band on Fantasy World of Japanese
         Pictures, Part 1, 1978)
JA 33   StarChild K22G 7113 (excerpt on Science Fiction Film
         Themes, Vol. 3, 1983)
JA 33   King K22G 7045 (3 bands on Akira Ifukube Movie
         Themes, Vol. 3, 1982)

Battle Mecha-Zanbungurl (Umagano, 1982)
Battle Mecha "Xabungle"
JA 33   StarChild K22G 7082
JA 33   StarChild K22G 7100 ("Vol. 2")

Battle of the Amazons (Franco Micalizzi, 1976)
   Karate Amazones
   JA   33   Tam YX-8023
   JA   33   Tam YX-7004 (1 band on Soundtrack Best Collection)

Battle of the Planets (Koichi Sugiyama, 1977, tv)
   Gatchaman
   JA   33   Columbia CS 7042
   JA   33   Columbia CS 7095 (Hit Songs of...)
   JA   33   Columbia CQ 7009 (Symphonic Suite)

Battlestar Galactica (Stu Phillips, 1978)
   Galactica, La Battaile de l'Espace/Kampfstern Galactica
   US   33   MCA 3051
   US   33   MCA 37079 (reissue of 3051)
   US   33   MCA 3078 (The Saga of B.G., w/d)
   CA   33   MCA 3051
   FR   33   CPF Barclay/MCA 110 101
   GE   33   MCA 3051 0062.118
   IT   33   MCA 4037
   JA   33   MCA VIM 7234
   US   ep   Starlog EV-101804 (1 band on promo ep)
   US   33   Casablanca NBLP 7126 (disco version, r/r Giorgio
           Moroder) nst
   US   33   Crescendo GNPS 2128 (theme on Greatest S.F. Hits/
           Neil Norman Orch. 1979) nst
   US   33   Philips 411 185-1 (Theme on Out of This World/John
           Williams & Boston Pops, 1983) nst
   FR   33   Arabella MLA 204880 (1 band on 12 Terrifiantes Bandes
           Originales de Films)

Battletruck (Kevin Peek, 1982)
   JA   33   Nexus K28P 4099
   JA   45   Nexus K07S 8010 (vocal only)

Be Forever Yamato (Hiroshi Miyagawa, 1981)
   JA   33   Columbia CQ 7051 (Volume 1)
   JA   33   Columbia CQ 7052 (Volume 2)
   JA   33   Columbia CZ 7061/62 (2/lp, w/d)
   JA   33   Columbia CB 7099/01 (3/lp, w/d)

Beach Blanket Bingo (Les Baxter, Jerry Styner, et al., 1965)
   US   33   Capitol ST-2323

Beast from 20,000 Fathoms, The (David Buttolph, 1953)
   Il Risveglio Del Dinosauro
   IT   33   Blu BLRL 15001 (Excerpt, w/d, on Fantascienza) p/r

Beast with Five Fingers, The (Max Steiner, 1946)
   US   33   London CS 6866 (nfd; Bach Chaconne, arranged by
           Steiner for film, performed by Alice De Larrocha) nst

Beastmaster, The (Lee Holdridge, 1982)
　　US　33　Varese Sarabande STV-81174

Beauty and the Beast (Ron Goodwin, 1976)
　　GB　33　Chandos ABRD 1014 (1 band on Drake 400/Ron Good-
　　　　　　win Orch. 1980) nst

Bedazzled (Dudley Moore, 1967)
　　US　33　London MS 82009
　　US　45　Parrot 3016
　　GB　33　Decca LK-4923

Bedknobs and Broomsticks (R. and R. Sherman, 1972)
　　US　33　Buena Vista BS-5003 (songs)

Beginning of the End (Albert Glasser, 1957)
　　US　33　Starlog SR-1001 (1 band on Fantastic Film Music of Al-
　　　　　　bert Glasser, 1978)

Bell, Book and Candle (George Duning, 1959)
　　US　33　Colpix SCP-502 (1959)
　　US　33　Citadel 6006 (reissue of SCP-502; 1977)
　　US　33　Citadel 7006 (remastered reissue of 6006; 1980)
　　US　45　Colpix CP-103 (theme, r/r Morris Stoloff) nst

Belladonna (Masahiko Sato, 1973)
　　IT　33　Cinevox MDF 33/90

Ben (Walter Scharf, 1972)
　　US　45　Motown 1207 (song)
　　US　45　Columbia 45731 (nst)

Beneath the Planet of the Apes (Leonard Rosenman, 1970)
　　US　33　Amos AAS-8001

Bermuda Triangle, The (Stelvio Cipriani, 1978)
　　Il Triangolo Delle Bermude
　　IT　45　Beat BTF 108

Between Two Worlds (Erich Wolfgang Korngold, 1944)
　　US　33　Citadel CT 7010 (suite on Film Music for Piano) nst
　　US　33　RCA LSC-3330 (2 bands on The Sea Hawk: Classic
　　　　　　Film Scores of Erich Wolfgang Korngold/r/r C. Ger-
　　　　　　hardt 1972) nst

Bewitched (Warren Barker, Jimmy Haskell, 1964, tv)
　　US　33　ABC s513 (Theme on Theme from Peyton Place and
　　　　　　Other TV Themes/Frank De Vol Orch.) nst
　　US　33　Epic LN 24125 (Theme on Music for Monsters, Mun-
　　　　　　sters, Mummies & Other TV Fiends/Milton DeLugg
　　　　　　Orch.) nst

US   33   Dot 3616/25616 (theme, r/r Lawrence Welk) <u>nst</u>
US   33   Audio Fidelity 2146/6146 (theme only/nfd)

Beyond the Door (It. release: Franco Micalizzi, 1975)
   Chi Sei/Devil Within Her/Diabolica/Le Demon Aux Tripes
   FR   33   Barclay 90028
   FR   45   EMI/Pathe C004 14207
   IT   33   Cam 9062
   JA   33   Tam YX-8031
   IT   33   RCA TVC1 1142 (2 bands on <u>Le Colonne Sonore Di</u>
                  <u>Franco Micalizzi</u>, 1975)

Beyond the Door II (Libra, 1979)
   Schock
   IT   33   Cinevox MDG 113
   JA   33   Seven Seas FML 118 (different cover)
   IT   33   Cinevox CIA 5014 (1 band on <u>Squalo-Exorcista e Altri</u>
                  <u>Film Della Paura</u>)
   JA   33   Seven Seas K18P 4105 (1 band on <u>Horror Movie Spe-</u>
                  <u>cial</u>, 1983)

Beyond the Moon (uncredited, 1954)
   US   33   Cinema LP 8005 (1 band on <u>Destination Moon and Oth-</u>
                  <u>er Themes</u>, b/r, 1974)

Big Game, The (Francesco De Masi, 1972)
   IT   33   Beat LPF 019 S

Billion Dollar Brain (Richard Rodney Bennett, 1967)
   US   33   United Artists UAS-5174

Bionic Woman, The (Jerry Fielding, 1976, tv)
   US   33   Pickwick SPC-3566 (1 band on <u>TV Hits</u>/Birchwood
                  Pops Orch.) <u>nst</u>
   US   33   Wonderland WLP 313 (1 band on <u>Theme from Star</u>
                  <u>Wars</u>/Wonderland Space Shuttle) <u>nst</u>
   GB   33   MFP 50439 (1 band on <u>Themes for Superheroes</u>/Geoff
                  Love Orch.) <u>nst</u>

Bird of Paradise (Max Steiner, 1932)
   US   33   Medallion ML 305/306 (p/r, 2/lp, w/d, complete sound
                  track, 1980)
   US   33   Medallion 309 (suite on <u>The Film Music of Max Steiner</u>,
                  p/r, 1980)

Bird of Paradise (Maurice Jarre, 1962)
   L'Oiseau du Paradis
   FR   ep   Phillips 432.823

Bird with the Crystal Plumage, The (Ennio Morricone, 1970)
   L'Ucello Dalle Piume Cristallo

US	33	Capitol ST-642 (rerecorded score) nst
IT	33	Cinevox MDF 33/31 (original version)
IT	33	Cinevox CIA 5036 (reissue of MDF 33/31, 1983)
US	33	Cereberus CEM S 0108 (reissue of MDF 33/31; diff. cover)
FR	33	Barclay 930 022 (1 band on Cinemusic, vol. 1, 1977)
IT	33	Cinevox CIA 5009 (2 bands on I Films di Dario Argento, 1980)
IT	33	RCA TPL2 1174 (1 band on I Film Della Violenza, 2/lp, 1975)
IT	33	Cinevox MDF 33/74-75 (1 band on Fotogramma Per Fotogramma, 2/lp, 1976)
IT	33	Cinevox CIA 5014 (1 band on Squalo-Exorcista e Altri Film Della Paura)
FR	33	Barclay 930.014/15 (1 band on Il Etait Une Fois ... La Revolution, et 22 Musiques de Films de Ennio Morricone, 2/lp, 1976)
JA	33	Seven Seas K18P 4105 (1 band on Horror Movie Special, 1983)

Excerpts also on other Ennio Morricone collections (nfd)

Birds, The (Remi Gassman & Oscar Sala, 1963)

US	45	Decca 31477 (1 band, "inspired by film," r/r the Surf Riders)

Bishop's Wife, The (Hugo Friedhofer, 1947)

US	45	Capitol 1627 (nst)

Black Belly of the Tarantula, The (Ennio Morricone, 1972)
La Tarantola Dal Ventre Nero

US	33	Cerberus CEM-S-0116 (1 side only, 1982)
JA	45	Canyon Y-38
FR	33	Cam 6901 (1 band on Inedit)
IT	33	Cam CML 022 (1 band on Giallo N.1; p/r)
IT	33	Cam CML 023 (1 band, different, on Giallo N.2; p/r)
IT	33	RCA TPL2 1174 (1 band on I Film Della Violenza, 2/lp, 1975)

Excerpts on other Ennio Morricone collections.

Black Friday (Hans J. Salter, 1940)

US	33	Citadel CT-6026 (excerpts incorporated into "Horror Rhapsody" on Music for Frankenstein, Dracula, The Mummy, The Wolf Man and Other Old Friends; p/r, 1978)
US	33	Citadel CT 7012 (reissue of CT-6026 as Horror Rhapsody, 1979)
FR	33	Decca 900 411 (reissue of CT-6026 as Horror Rhapsody/Malpertuis, 1979)

Black Hole, The (John Barry, 1979)
Le Trou Noir

US   33   Buena Vista 5008 (digital release)
US   33   Disneyland 3821 (w/d; The Story of The Black Hole)
FR   33   Ades Disneyland VS 5008F
GB   33   Pickwick Intl. SHM 3017
JA   33   Disneyland GX 7007
JA   33   Disneyland BX 7038 (w/d)
US   33   Casablanca NBLP 7196 (1 side only, r/r Meco Monardo)
       nst

Black Orpheus (Antonio Carlos Jobim & Luis Bonfa, 1959)
US   33   Epic LN-3672
US   33   Fontana 67520e (reissue of LN-3672)
JA   33   Phillips FDX 289
US   33   MGM (S)E-4491 (Theme on Cinema Legrand/Michel
       Legrand Orch.) nst
US   33   London SP-44020 (1 band on Hit Themes from Foreign
       Films)
US   33   London SP-44078 (Theme on Film Spectacular Vol. III/
       Stanley Black & London Festival Orch.) nst
US   33   Warner Bros W-1548 (Theme on International Film
       Festival/Werner Mueller Orch.) nst
US   33   Capitol SP-8603 (Theme on Music from Great French
       Motion Pictures/Frank Pourcel Orch.) nst
US   33   Longines SYS-5312-5317 (1 band on Somewhere My
       Love and Other Romantic Movie Melodies/Longines
       Symphonette Society, 6/lp) nst
US   33   MGM SE-4185 (Theme on Twilight of Honor and Other
       Great Motion Picture Themes)

Black Sabbath (Les Baxter, 1964)
I Tre Volti Della Paura
US   33   Tony Thomas/BAX LB-100 (p/r, 1981)
IT   33   RCA 10394 (1 band; nfd)

Black Sunday (Les Baxter, 1961)
US   33   Capitol ST-1537 (1 band on Jewels of the Sea/Les
       Baxter Orch.) nst

Black Zoo (Paul Dunlap, 1963)
US   45   Chancellor C-1137 (r/r) nst

Blackbeard's Ghost (Richard Brunner, 1967)
US   33   Disneyland DQ-1305

Blacula (Gene Page, 1972)
US   33   RCA LSP-4806

Blade Runner (Vangelis, 1982)
US   33   Full Moon-Warner Bros. 23748-1 (r/r New American
       Orch.) nst
FR   33   WEA Full Moon 250002-1 (same as above) nst

```
GB   33   WEA K 99262 (same) nst
GE   33   Ariola 205091 (same) nst
SP   33   WEA K 99262 (same) nst
FR   45   WEA Full Moon 259994-7 (same) nst
US   33   GNP Crescendo GNPS 2163 (1 band on Greatest S.F.
          Hits III/Neil Norman Orch., 1983) nst
```

Blake's Seven (Dudley Simpson, 1977, tv)
```
GB   45   BBC RESL 58 (1979)
GB   33   BBC REH 324 (Theme on BBC Space Themes, 1979)
GB   33   BBC REH 365 (Theme on Top BBC TV Themes, Vol.
          2, 1979)
GB   33   MFP 50439 (Theme on Themes for Superheroes/Geoff
          Love Orch.) nst
```

Blithe Spirit (Richard Addinsell, 1945)
```
US   33   Camden CAL-233 (1 band on Themes of Great Women
          in Films/Clebanoff Strings and Symphonic Orch.) nst
US   33   Mercury/Wing SRW 16399 (1 band on Film Music/Cos-
          mopolitan Orch.) nst
US   45   Camden CAE-103 (r/r) nst
US   78   Columbia 7441-M (r/r) nst
```

Blithe Spirit (Noel Coward, tv; nfd)
```
US   33   Beastly Hun NOCO 1100 (p/r, nfd)
US   33   Sandpiper 1 (p/r, nfd)
```

Blob, The (Burt Bacharach, 1958)
```
US   45   Columbia 4-41250 (song, sung by The Five Blobs,
          1960)
US   33   Poo LP 104 (same song on Great S.F. Film Music, b/r,
          1978)
```

Blood and Black Lace (Carlo Rustichelli, 1964)
     Sei Donne Per L'Assassino
```
IT   45   Cam CA-2559
```

Blood and Roses (Jean Prodromides, 1961)
     Et Mourir de Plaisir
```
FR   33   Fontana 460.713 (excerpt, r/r, nfd) nst
```

Blood Feast (Herschel Gordon Lewis, 1963)
```
US   33   Rhino RNSP 305 (1 side of The Amazing Film Scores
          of Herschell Gordon Lewis, 1984)
```

Bloodline (Ennio Morricone, 1980)
```
US   33   Varese Sarabande STV 81131
```

Blue Thunder (Arthur B. Rubinstein, 1983)
     Tuono Blu
```
US   33   MCA 6122
```

GB   33   MCA MCF 3183
IT   33   Ricordi MCA 4197
JA   33   MCA VIM 7291
US   33   MCA 13966 (Dance Version, r/r The Beepers, 12"
          single)

Bluebeard (Ennio Morricone, 1971)
   Barbablu/Barbe Bleue
US   33   Cerberus CEMS 0105 (1980)
FR   33   Philips 6325 402
IT   33   General Music ZSLGE 55122
FR   33   WEA General Music 803009 (1 band on Ennio Morricone:
          Bandes Originales des Films, 1980)

Bluebird, The (Alfred Newman, 1940)
US   33   Decca 8123 (1 band on Serenade to the Stars of Hol-
          lywood/Alfred Newman Orch.) nst
US   33   Vocalation VL 3749 (1 band on Holiday for Strings/
          Alfred Newman Orch.) nst

Bluebird, The (Andrey Petrovic, 1976)
JA   ep   Columbia YK-62-MK (4 bands, w/d)

Boccaccio '70 (Nino Rota, 1962)
FR   33   RCA 430389
IT   33   RCA PML 10308
US   33   RCA FOC FSO 5 (episode #3: The Temptation of Dr.
          Antonio)
FR   33   RCA 430 389 (3 bands; episode #3)
IT   33   RCA S 5 (3 bands; episode #3)
JA   33   CBS Sony 2302 (3 bands, nonfantasy episode Il Lavoro)

Body Snatcher from Hell (Shunsuki Kikucki, 1968)
JA   33   Toho AX 8124 (1 band on Fantasy World of Japanese
          Pictures, Part 5, 1978)

Boogey Man, The (Tim Krog, 1981)
US   33   Synthe-Sound-Trax ARM 8027 (p/r)

Borrowers, The (Rod McKuen, 1973, tvm)
US   33   Stanyon SRQ 4014

Boy and the Pirates, The (Albert Glasser, 1960)
US   33   Starlog SR 1001 (18 min suite on The Fantastic Film
          Music of Albert Glasser, 1978)

Boy in the Plastic Bubble, The (Paul Williams, 1976)
US   45   Midland MB-11206

Boys from Brazil, The (Jerry Goldsmith, 1978)
   Ces Garçons Qui Venaient du Bresil

US   33   A&M SP 4731
FR   33   Sonopresse 2S008 62850
GB   33   A&M AMLH 64731

Brain, The (George Delerue, 1969)
 Le Cerveau
 FR   ep   Philips 370.806
 US   45   Acta 837

Brain Leeches, The (Paul Jones, 1978)
 US   45   SPI 86-41

Brainstorm (James Horner, 1983)
 US   33   Varese Sarabande STV-81197
 GB   33   That's Entertainment TER 1074

Brewster McCloud (John Phillips, Gene Page, 1971)
 US   33   MGM 1SE28

Bride of Frankenstein, The (Franz Waxman, 1935)
 US   33   RCA ARL1-0708 (1 band on Sunset Boulevard: The
            Classic Film Scores of Franz Waxman/r/r Charles
            Gerhardt, 1974) nst
 US   33   RCA AGL1-3783 (reissue of ARL1-0708)

Bride Wore Black, The (Bernard Herrmann, 1967)
 La Mariée Etait en Noir
 FR   ep   United Artists 36.112 (4 bands)
 US   33   Cinema LP 8006 (same 4 bands on The Film Music of
            B.H.; b/r, 1975)

Brides of Dracula (Malcolm Williamson, 1960)
 US   45   Coral (nfd; "Dracula Cha-Cha-Cha" by Rod McKuen,
            "inspired by" film)

Brigadoon (Lerner & Lowe, 1954)
 US   33   MGM E-3135 (musical; songs)

Brigadoon (Lerner & Lowe, tv special/nfd)
 US   33   Columbia CSM 385

Buck Rogers in the 25th Century (Stu Phillips, 1969)
 US   33   MCA 3097
 US   33   MCA 37087 (reissue of 3097)
 GB   33   MCA MCF 3013
 US   33   GNP Crescendo GNPS 2133 (theme on Greatest S.F.
            Hits II/Neil Norman Orch., 1981) nst
 FR   33   Arabella MCA 204880 (1 band on 12 Terrifiantes
            Bandes Originales de Films)

Bullet Train Blast (Hachiro Aoyama, 1975)
 JA   45   RCA JRT-1448

Burke and Hare (Roger Webb, 1971)
    GB   33   EMI TWO 349 (1 band on Music of the Movies/Roger
            Webb Orch.) nst

Burning, The (Rick Wakeman, 1981)
    Carnage
    US   33   Varese Sarabande STV-81162
    GB   33   Charisma CLASS 12
    JA   33   Eastworld WTP 90107 (different cover)
    FR   33   Charisma 6-302-176 (as Carnage)

Cabin in the Sky (Joseph Shrank, Vernon Duke, 1942)
    US   33   Columbia CSP CCL 2792 (songs)
    US   33   Hollywood Sound 5003 (p/r)

Cabinet of Caligari (Gerald Fried, 1962)
    US   33   London 3347 (1 band on Best of the New Film Themes/
            Frank Chacksfield Orch.) nst

Can Hieronymous Merkin Forget Mercy Humppe and Find True
               Happiness? (Anthony Newley, 1969)
    US   33   Kapp KS-5509

Candy (Dave Grusin, 1968)
    Candy e Il Suo Pazzo Mondo
    US   33   ABC SOC-9
    IT   33   Cam SAG 9029

Capricorn One (Jerry Goldsmith, 1978)
    US   33   Warner Bros. BSK 3201
    IT   33   WEA/Warner Bros. 56523
    JA   33   Seven Seas FML 85 (different cover)
    JA   45   Seven Seas FMS 50
    US   33   GNP Crescendo GNPS 2163 (1 band on Greatest SF
            Hits III/Neil Norman, 1983) nst

Captain Kronos, Vampire Hunter (Laurie Johnson, 1972)
    US   33   Starlog/Varese Sarabande SV 95002 (2 bands on First
            Men in the Moon, r/r Laurie Johnson, 1981) nst
    GB   33   Unicorn/Kanchana DKP 9001 (same as SV 95002)

Captain Nemo and the Underwater City (Walter Stott, 1969)
    US   33   Longines Symphonette SYS-5312/6 (1 band on Some-
            where My Love and Other Movie Melodies, r/r Walter
            Stott) nst

Captain Scarlet and the Mysterons (Barry Gray, 1967)
    GB   33   Hallmark HMA 227 (6 bands)
    GB   33   PRT DOW 3 (theme on No Strings Attached/Barry
            Gray Orch., 1981) nst
    GB   33   Contour 2870 185 (theme on Children's TV Themes/
            Cy Payne Orch., 1972) nst

Captain Video (uncredited, 1949-56, tv)
  US   45   RCA VY-2008

Carrie (Pino Donaggio, 1976)
  US   33   United Artists UA LA 716 H
  FR   33   United Artists UA US 30033
  IT   33   United Artists UA 24015
  JA   33   United Artists FML 73

Case of the Ancient Astronauts (Peter Howell, tv)
  GB   33   BBC REH 324 (1 band on BBC Space Themes, 1979)

Casino Royale (Burt Bacharach, 1967)
  US   33   Colgems S 5005
  US   33   London 514
  US   33   A&M S 844 (theme, r/r Herb Alpert & Tijuana Brass)
               nst
  GB   33   Sunset 5184 (theme, r/r) nst
  GE   33   Philips 600260 (theme, r/r) nst
  US   33   Musicor 3133 (theme, r/r) nst

Cat O'Nine Tails (Ennio Morricone, 1971)
  Il Gatto a Nove Code/Die Neunschwanzige Katz/Le Chat a Neuf
               Queus
  IT   45   General Music ZGE 50167
  GE   45   BASF 051-90263
  IT   33   General Music ZSLGE 55064 (1 band on Colori)
  IT   33   Cinevox CIA 5009 (2 bands on I Films Di Dario Ar-
               gento, 1980)
  IT   33   RCA DPSL 10599 (1 band on Un Film, Una Musica, 2/
               lp, 1973)

Cat People (Giorgio Moroder, 1982)
  La Feline
  US   33   Backstreet BSR 6107
  FR   33   Ariola MCA 204 634
  GB   33   MCA MCF 3138
  GE   33   Ariola 204634
  IT   33   Ricordi Backstreet MCA 4159
  JA   33   Backstreet VIM 7282
  SP   33   Ariola MCA I 204634
  US   45   Backstreet BSR 52024

Catalepsis (Ennio Morricone, 1972)
  La Corta Notte della Bambole di Vetro
  HO   33   RCA NL 31498 (1 band on Ennio Morricone: Portrait
               in Music)
  IT   33   RCA TPL-2 1174 (1 band on I Film Della Violenza, 2/
               lp, 1975)
  IT   33   General Music 33/01-3/01-4 (1 band on Musiche Di
               Ennio Morricone, vol. 2, p/r, 2/lp)

Catastrophe 1999 (Isao Tomita, 1974)
    Nosutoradamusu No Dai-Yogen
    JA   33   Tam AX 8012
    JA   33   Toho AX 8804 (reissue of 8012, different cover)
    JA   45   Toho AT-1069
    JA   33   Toho AX 8123 (1 band on Fantasy World of Japanese
                  Pictures, part 4, 1978)
    JA   33   Tam YX-7004 (1 band on Soundtrack Best Collection)
    JA   33   StarChild K22G 7120 (Excerpt on S.F. Film Themes,
                  vol. 10, 1983)

Champions, The (Edwin Astley, 1967, tv)
    GB   33   Marble Arch S-1179 (1 band on Top TV Themes/Tony
                  Hatch and Cyril Stapleton Orch.) nst

Chariots of the Gods (Peter Thomas, 1974)
    US   33   Polydor FD-6504

Charly (Ravi Shankar, 1968)
    US   33   World Pacific S-21454

Children of the Corn (Jonathan Elias, 1984)
    US   33   Varese Sarabande STV 81203

Children of the Damned (Ron Goodwin, 1963)
    US   33   Poo LP 106 (1 band on Great Fantasy Film Music, b/r,
                  1979)

Chitty Chitty Bang Bang (R. & R. Sherman, 1968)
    US   33   United Artists UAS 5188 (songs)
    JA   33   United Artists GXH 6028 (songs)
    US   33   United Artists UA 101 (promo lp, title song done in
                  eight different languages)

Chosen, The (Ennio Morricone, 1978)
    Holocaust 2000
    US   33   Cerberus CEMS 0103
    FR   33   Vogue LDA 20 346
    IT   33   Beat LPF 040 (different cover)
    JA   33   Polydor MPF 1264 (different cover)
    US   33   Poo LP 106 (1 band on Great Fantasy Film Music, b/r,
                  1979)

Christine (various, 1983)
    US   33   Motown 6086ML (1 original cue by John Carpenter and
                  Alan Howarth, plus 10 "oldies" rock & roll songs)

Christmas Carol, A (Bernard Herrmann, 1954, tv)
    US   33   Unicorn RHS 850 (p/r)

Christmas That Almost Wasn't, The (Ray Carter & Paul Tripp,
                1966)
  US   33   RCA Camden CAL 1086 (songs only, w/d)

Circus of Horrors (Franz Reizenstein, 1960)
  US   33   Imperial 59132
  AU   33   Imperial AUSLP 1010 (1982 reissue of 59132)
  US   45   Imperial IM-2662 (song, sung by Gary Miles)
  US   45   Liberty F-55261 (song, sung by Gary Miles)
  US   33   Poo LP 106 (song, sung by Gary Miles, on Great Fan-
                tasy Film Music, b/r, 1979)
  US   45   Dot 45-1610 (theme, r/r Billy Vaughan) nst

Clash of the Titans (Laurence Rosenthal, 1981)
    Kampf Der Titanen/Le Choc Des Titans
  US   33   Columbia JS 37386
  FR   33   CBS 70 206
  GE   33   CBS 70206
  GB   33   Columbia 73588
  HO   33   CBS 70206
  JA   33   CBS/Sony 25AP 2114
  GB   33   CBS 73634 (1 band on Film '81)

Clockwork Orange, A (Walter [Wendy] Carlos & classical, 1971)
  US   33   Warner Bros. BS-2573
  JA   33   Warner/Pioneer P8209W
  US   33   Columbia KC-31480 (classical only) nst
  GB   33   CBS/Harmony 30052 (1 band on Great Classic Hits
                from the Movies) nst
  GB   33   Warner Bros. K56089 (1 band on Soundtrack!, 1974)
  JA   33   Mu-Land LZ 7016-M (1 band on S.F. Fact Vol. 1/
                Electoru Polyphonic Orch., 1979) nst

Close Encounters of the Third Kind (John Williams, 1977)
    Rencontres du Troisieme Type/Incontri Ravvicinati del Terzo
                Tipo
  US   33   Arista AL-9500 (including promo 45 single AS 9500,
                nst)
  US   45   Arista ASO-300
  FR   33   Pathe Marconi/Arista 2C 068 60391
  GB   33   Arista DLART 2001
  GE   33   Arista 1C 064-60 391
  IT   33   Arista 064 60
  IT   45   Arista 006 6039
  JA   33   Arista 1ES 81010
  JA   45   Arista 1ER 20389
  US   33   Pickwick SPC 3616 (r/r Pickwick Studio Orch.) nst
  US   33   RCA ARL1-2698 (5 theme suite, r/r Charles Gerhardt,
                includes music not on Arista 9500; 1978) nst
  US   33   MCA 6114 (Excerpts on Themes from E.T. and More/
                Walter Murphy)

US   33   London ZM 1001 (12 min. suite, r/r Zubin Mehta) <u>nst</u>
US   33   Arista ABM 2005 (1 band on <u>Soundtrack Memories</u>)
US   33   RCA AQLI-3650 (reissue of ARL1-2698)
US   33   Philips 9500 921 (10 min. suite on <u>Pops in Space</u> in-
          cludes new music for THE SPECIAL EDITION, r/r
          J. Williams) <u>nst</u>
US   33   Sine Qua Non SQN 7808 (1 band on <u>Galactic Hits</u>/The
          Odyssey Orch., 1980) <u>nst</u>
GB   33   RCA RL 12698 (same as ARL1-2698; 1978) <u>nst</u>
GB   33   MFP 50375 (Excerpts on <u>Close Encounters and Other</u>
          <u>Galactic Themes</u>/Geoff Love Orch.) <u>nst</u>
GB   33   Ronco RTD 2036 (1 band on <u>Cinema & Broadway Gold</u>,
          2/lp, 1979) <u>nst</u>
GB   33   Decca SXL 6885 (same as ZM 1001) <u>nst</u>
IT   33   RCA NL 12698 (same as ARL1-2698; 1978) <u>nst</u>

<u>Coma</u> (Jerry Goldsmith, 1978)
US   33   MGM MG-1-5403
GB   33   MGM Super 2315 400
JA   33   MGM MMF 1019

<u>Conan the Barbarian</u> (Basil Poledouris, 1982)
US   33   MCA 6108
FR   33   RCA PL 37666
IT   33   RCA BL 31637
JA   33   MCA VIM 7283

<u>Conquest of Space</u> (Nathan Van Cleave, 1955)
US   33   Margery 2400 (1 band on <u>Music by Manson</u>/Eddy Man-
          son Orch.) <u>nst</u>

<u>Cosmos</u> (various, all previously released music; 1981, tv)
US   33   RCA ABL1-4003
GB   33   RCA RCALP 5032
JA   33   RCA RPL 8063

<u>Crack in the World</u> (Johnny Douglas, 1965)
US   33   RCA Camden CAS-926 (1 band on <u>The Sweetheart</u>
          <u>Tree and Other Film Favorites</u>/nfd) <u>nst</u>

<u>Creature from the Black Lagoon</u> (Herman Stein, Hans Salter, et al.,
          1954)
     L'etrange Creature de Lac Noir (note: only Salter credited on
          lp)
US   33   Coral CRL 757240 (1 band on <u>Themes from Horror</u>
          <u>Movies</u>/Dick Jacobs Orch.; w/d between bands) <u>nst</u>
US   33   Varese Sarabande VC 81077 (1978 reissue of CRL
          757240 remastered without narration, different cover)
          <u>nst</u>
FR   33   MCA 410.064 (reissue of VC 81077 as <u>Les Grands</u>
          <u>Themes du Cinema et Fantastique et de Science Fic-</u>

                    tion) nst
JA   33   MCA VIM 7264 (reissue of VC 81077, different cover)
            nst
US   33   Citadel TT-HS-4 (15 min. suite on Classic Horror Mu-
            sic of Hans Salter, 1980)

Creature Walks Among Us, The (Henry Mancini, et al., 1956)
      La Creature Est Parmi Nous
JA   33   Coral CRL 757240 (1 band on Themes from Horror
            Movies/Dick Jacobs Orch.) nst
US   33   Varese Sarabande VC 81077 (reissue of CRL 757240)
            nst
FR   33   MCA 410.064 (reissue of VC 81077) nst
JA   33   MCA VIM 7264 (reissue of VC 81077, different cover)
            nst

Creepshow (John Harrison, 1982)
US   33   Varese Sarabande STV 81160
FR   33   Milan A207

Cristo Del Oceano, El (Bruno Nicolai, 1971)
IT   33   Gemelli CS 3002
JA   33   Seven Seas 765 (w/d)
JA   33   Seven Seas GXH 4 (1 band on Screen Gold Disk: Im-
            mortal Themes)

Cry of the Banshee (Les Baxter, 1970)
US   33   Citadel CTV 7013 (20 min. suite, 1980)

Cyborg 009--Underground Duel (Taichiro Kosugi, 1967)
      Cyborg 009--Kaiji Senso
JA   33   Columbia CS 7047
JA   33   Columbia CAK 639 (w/d)
JA   45   Columbia SCS 467

Cyborg 009 (Koichi Sugiyama, 1979, tv)
JA   33   Columbia CQ 7018 (Symphonic Suite)
JA   33   Columbia CX 7005

Cyclops, The (Albert Glasser, 1957)
US   33   Starlog SR-1001 (1 band on Fantastic Film Music of A.
            Glasser, 1978)

Damien: Omen II (Jerry Goldsmith, 1978)
US   33   20th Century-Fox T 563
JA   33   20th Century-Fox FML 109

Damn Yankees (Richard Adler & Jerry Ross, 1958)
US   33   RCA LOC-1047 (songs)

Damnation Alley (Jerry Goldsmith, 1977)
  US   33   Poo LP 104 (1 band on Great Science Fiction Film Mu-
            sic, b/r, 1978)
  JA   33   Mu-Land LZ 7016-M (1 band on S.F. Fact, Vol. 1/
            Electoru Polyphonic Orch., 1979) nst

Damned in Venice (Pino Donaggio, 1978)
  Nero Veneziano/Venetian Black
  IT   33   Ariston 1233

Danger: Diabolik (Ennio Morricone, 1968)
  Diabolik
  IT   45   Parade PRC 5052 (song)
  US   33   Poo LP 104 (same song as Great S.F. Film Music, b/r,
            1978)

Darby O'Gill and the Little People (Oliver Wallace, 1965)
  US   33   Disneyland ST-1901 (w/d)

Dark Crystal, The (Trevor Jones, 1982)
  US   33   Warner Bros. 23749-1
  FR   33   CBS 70233
  GB   33   CBS 70233
  IT   33   CBS 70233
  SP   33   CBA 70233

Dark Shadows (Robert Cobert, 1966, tv)
  US   33   Philips 600-314
  US   45   Roulette R-7082 (contains 2 bands not on Philips lp)
  US   45   Epic 5-10440 (r/r The First Theremin Era) nst

Dark Star (John Carpenter, 1974)
  US   33   Citadel CT 7022 (w/d)
  US   33   GNP Crescendo GNPS 2133 (5 min. suite on Greatest
            Science Fiction Hits II/Neil Norman Orch., 1981) nst

Daughters of Darkness (Francois De Roubaix, 1970)
  Les Levres Rouges
  FR   33   Philips EPS-4029
  US   33   Poo LP 106 (1 band on Great Fantasy Film Music, b/r,
            1979)

Dawn of the Dead (Goblin, 1978)
  Zombi
  US   33   Varese Sarabande VC 81106
  IT   33   Cinevox MDF 33/121 (different cover)
  IT   33   Cinevox CIA 5035 (reissue, 1983)
  JA   33   Seven Seas FML 113
  FR   33   Polycor 813254-1
  JA   33   Seven Seas K18P 4105 (1 band on Horror Movie Spe-
            cial, 1983)

FR   33   Polydor Cinevox 2393 327 (excerpts on <u>Les Meilleures</u>
                  <u>Musiques de Films Fantastiques</u>)
IT   33   Cinevox MDF 33/124 (1 band on <u>Films in Musica, Vol.</u>
                  <u>4</u>)
IT   33   Cinevox CIA 5014 (1 band on <u>Squalo-Exorcista e Altri</u>
                  <u>Film Della Paura</u>)

Day After Halloween, The (Brian May, 1981)
   Snapshop/One More Minute
   US   33   Citadel CTV-7020
   FR   33   Milan A-120-157 (1 band on <u>Horror and Science Fic-</u>
                  <u>tion</u>), 1982)

Day of the Animals (Lalo Schifrin, 1977)
   US   33   CTI 5003 (1 band on <u>Towering Toccata</u>/Lalo Schifrin
                  Orch., 1977) <u>nst</u>

Day of the Dolphin (Georges Delerue, 1973)
   US   33   Avco Embassy AV-11014
   JA   33   H&L VIP 7230 (different cover)

Day the Earth Stood Still, The (Bernard Herrmann, 1951)
   US   33   London SP 44207 (suite on <u>Fantasy Film World of</u>
                  <u>Bernard Herrmann</u>/r/r B. Herrmann, 1974) <u>nst</u>
   US   33   London STCO 95534 (different suite on <u>Great Movie</u>
                  <u>Themes Vol. 1</u>/nfd) <u>nst</u>
   US   33   London CSL 1001 (suite on <u>Great Science Fiction Film</u>
                  <u>Music</u>, p/r edition of SP 44207 for S.F. Book Club)
                  <u>nst</u>
   US   ep   Starlog EV-101804 (1 band on promo ep)
   US   33   GNP Crescendo GNPS 2128 (1 band on <u>Greatest Sci-</u>
                  <u>ence Fiction Hits</u>/Neil Norman Orch., 1979) <u>nst</u>
   JA   33   Mu-Land LZ-7017-M (1 band on <u>S.F. Fact Vol. 2</u>/
                  Electoru Polyphonic Orch., 1979) <u>nst</u>

Day the Fish Came Out, The (Mikis Theodorakis, 1967)
   US   33   20th Century-Fox S-4194

Day Time Ended, The (Richard Band, 1980)
   US   33   Varese Sarabande STV-81140 (digital recording)
   FR   33   Milan A 120 157 (1 band on <u>Horror and Science Fic-</u>
                  <u>tion</u>, 1982)

Daydreamer, The (Maury Laws, 1966)
   US   33   Columbia OS-1940

Deadly Mantis, The (William Lava, 1957)
   La Chose Surgie des Tenebres
   US   33   Coral CRL 757240 (1 band on <u>Themes from Horror</u>
                  <u>Movies</u>/Dick Jacobs Orch.) <u>nst</u>
   US   33   Varese Sarabande VC 81077 (remastered 1978 reissue

of CRL 757240) nst
FR   33   MCA 410.064 (reissue of VC 81077 as Les Grands
             Thèmes du Cinema et Fantastique et de Science Fic-
             tion) nst
JA   33   MCA VIM 7264 (reissue of VC 81077, different cover)

Deathwatch (Antoine Duhamel, 1981)
   La Mort en Direct
FR   33   Vogue Pip OJM 503 001

Deep Red (Giorgio Gaslini, Goblin, 1975)
   Profondo Rosso/Suspiria, Part II
IT   33   Cinevox MDF 33/85
IT   33   Cinevox CAI 5004 (reissue of MDF 33/85; 1980)
IT   33   Orizzonte ORL-8063 (reissue of MDF 33/85)
JA   33   EMI EOS-8407 (as Suspiria, Part II, different cover,
             1981)
IT   33   Cinevox CIA 5009 (2 bands on I Films di Dario Ar-
             gento, 1980)
IT   33   Cinevox MDF 33/97 (1 band on Films in Musica, vol.
             2)
FR   33   Polydor Cinevox 2393 327 (Excerpts on Les Meilleures
             Musiques de Films Fantastiques)

Deep Throat (various, 1972)
   US   33   DT Music 1001 (b/r)
   US   33   Sandy Hook SH 2036 (p/r, w/d)
   US   45   Bell 45,339 (theme, r/r Baja Marimba Band) nst
   IT   45   Durium Marche Estere DE.2847 (nfd)

Demain les Momes (Eric Demarsan, 1976)
   FR   45   RCA 42-141

Demon (Robert O. Ragland, 1977)
   Gold Told Me To
   US   45   Tru Luv SMA 119 (theme song, sung by George G.
                Griffin)

Demon, The (Piero Piccioni, 1963)
   Il Demonio
   IT   ep   Cam CEP 45 103

Destination Moon (Leith Stevens, 1950)
   US   10"   Columbia CL-6151 (1950)
   US   33   Omega OSL-3 (r/r Sandauer, 1959)
   US   10"   Capitol CAS 3080 (w/d, 1950)
   US   33   Cinema LP-8005 (side 1 only; b/r reissue of OSL-3,
                1974)
   US   33   Varese Sarabande STV-81130 (reissue of OSL-3, 1980)

Destroy All Monsters (Akira Ifukube, 1968)
  JA   33   Toho AX 8100 (1 band on Godzilla, 1978)
  JA   33   Toho AX 8112 (2 bands on Godzilla, vol. 2, 1979)
  JA   33   Toho AX 8147 (2 bands on Godzilla, vol. 3, 1980)
  JA   33   StarChild K22G 7117 (excerpts on Science Fiction Film
              Themes vol. 7, 1983)
  JA   33   King K22G 7051 (3 bands on Akira Ifukube Movie
              Themes, vol. 9, 1982)

Destroy All Planets (Kenjiro Hirose, 1968)
  Gamera Tai Uchi Kaiju Bairusu/Gamera vs. Virus
  JA   33   Toho AX 8120 (2 bands on Gamera)
  JA   33   Daiei KKS-4026 (excerpts, w/d, on Gamera)
  JA   33   Daiei KKS-4031 (excerpts, w/d, on Gamera II)

Devil and Daniel Webster, The (Bernard Herrmann, 1941)
  All That Money Can Buy
  US   33   London Phase-4 SP 44144 (suite on Music from the
              Great Film Classics, r/r Bernard Herrmann, 1972)
              nst
  GB   33   Pye Virtuoso 13010 (5 bands on Welles Raises Kane,
              r/r B. Herrmann) nst
  GB   33   Unicorn UNS 237 (1975 reissue of 13010) nst
  GB   33   Unicorn UN1 72008 (remastered 1979 reissue of 13010)
              nst

Devil and Max Devlin, The (Marvin Hamlisch, 1981)
  US   33   A&M PRO-1 (promo release)
  US   33   DLP 105 (Song on The Great Movie Themes, Vol. 1;
              b/r, 1984)

Devil in Love, The (Armando Trovajoli, 1966)
  IT   33   Parade FPR(S) 314

Devil in Miss Jones, The (Alden Shuman, 1973)
  US   33   Janus JLS-3059

Devil in the Brain (Ennio Morricone, 1972)
  Il Diavolo Nel Cervello
  IT   33   General Music ZSLGE 55076
  IT   33   RCA TPL2-1077 (1 band on I Film Della Violenza, 2/
              lp, 1975)
  FR   33   WEA/General Music 803 009 (1 band on Ennio Morri-
              cone: Bandes Originales des Films, 1980)

Devil Is a Woman, The (Ennio Morricone 1975)
  Il Sorriso Del Grande Tentatore
  IT   33   LPF 026
  IT   33   General Music 34/01-3/01-4 (1 band on Musiche di
              Ennio Morricone, vol. 2, p/r, 2/lp)

Devil's Bride (James Bernard, 1968)
   The Devil Rides Out
   GB   45   Spark SRL-1012 (rock song, "inspired by film," per-
              formed by Icarus) nst

Devil's Commandment, The (Martini & Brighetti, 1956)
   Tempi Duri Per I Vampiri
   US   33   RCA FSO-4 (1 band on Original Soundtracks Recorded
              in Italy)

Devil's Eye, The (Domenico Scarlatti, 1961)
   Djavulns Oga
   US   33   Proprius 7809 (1 band on Music from the Films of
              Ingmar Bergman/ r/r Kabi Lareti) nst

Devil's Hand, The (Alan Ferguson, 1962)
   US   45   Chess 1795

Diamonds Are Forever (John Barry, 1971)
   US   33   United Artists UAS 5220
   GB   33   United Artists UA 29216
   JA   33   United Artists GXH 6017
   GB   33   United Artists UAD-6002718 (theme on The James
              Bond Collection)
   GB   33   Polydor 2383462 (jazz rock version of theme on The
              Very Best of John Barry) nst
   Theme also on various r/r James Bond collections (nfd)

Do You Like Women? (Ward Swingle, 1966)
   Aimez-vous Les Femmes?
   FR   45   Philips 434.902
   FR   33   Philips P-77.233 L (1 band on Cinema Sans Image)

Dr. Dolittle (Leslie Bricusse, 1967)
   US   33   20th Century-Fox DS 5101

Dr. Faustus (Mario Nascimbene, 1968)
   GB   33   CBS 63189

Dr. Goldfoot and the Bikini Machine (Jerry Styner, et al., 1966)
   US   45   Dee Gee 3010 (theme song, r/r The Supremes) nst

Dr. Goldfoot and the Girl Bombs (Les Baxter, et al.)
   US   33   Tower DT-5053 (includes songs)

Dr. Jekyll and Mr. Hyde (Franz Waxman, 1941)
   GB   33   Decca PFS 4432 (10 min. suite on Satan Superstar/
              Stanley Black and Nat. Philharmonic, 1978) nst
   JA   33   London GP 9051 (same as PFS 4432)

Dr. Jekyll and Sister Hyde (David Whitaker, 1972)

US   33   Capitol 11340 (suite on Hammer Presents Dracula/
          Philip Martell, 1974) nst
GB   33   EMI TWOA 5001 (same as above)

Dr. No (Monty Norman & John Barry, 1963)

US   33   UAS 5108
US   33   United Artists Ascot US-16504 (half side only)
GB   33   United Artists UAS 5108
GB   33   Sunset SLS 50395 (reissue of UAS 5108)
IT   33   EMI 1C 054 82922 (reissue of UAS 5108)
JA   33   United Artists GXH 6015
US   33   Columbia CS-9293 (theme on The Great Movie Sounds
          of John Barry)
GB   33   Ember NR 5025 (excerpts on John Barry Plays 007)
          nst
GB   33   United Artists UAD 6002718 (excerpts on The James
          Bond Collection)
GB   33   CBS 22014 (James Bond Theme on The Music of John
          Barry, 2/lp)
Theme(s) also on various other r/r James Bond collections.

Dr. Slump (Shunsuke Kikuchi, 1982)

JA   33   Columbia CX 7060

Dr. Strangelove (Laurie Johnson, 1964)

US   33   Starlog/Varese Sarabande SV-95002 (1 band on First
          Men in the Moon, r/r Laurie Johnson, 1981) nst
GB   33   Unicorn/Kanchana DKP 9001 (same as SV-95002)
US   33   Colpix CP-464 (1 band on Dr. Strangelove and Other
          Great Themes/nfd)
US   33   London PS-434 (1 band on Marches from the Movies/
          Band of the Grenadier Guards) nst

Doctor Who (Ron Grainer, 1963+, tv)

US   33   DRG DS 15108 (theme of Exciting Television Music on
          R.G.)
GB   33   BBC REH 462 (Dr. Who--the Music, 1983)
GB   33   BBC REH 324 (theme of BBC Space Themes, 1979)
GB   33   BBC REH 316 (excerpts on 22 Sounds from Time and
          Space, 1979)
GB   33   BBC REH 442 (theme on Space Invaded, 1982)
GB   33   Contour 2870 185 (theme on Children's TV Themes/Cy
          Payne Orch., 1972) nst
GB   33   MFP 50439 (theme on Themes for Superheroes/Geoff
          Love Orch.) nst
GB   33   R.K. RKLB-1003 (theme on Roald Dahl's Tales of the
          Unexpected and Other Themes/Ron Grainer, 1980)
GB   33   STET OS-15016 (theme/nfd)
GB   33   Century 21 LA-6 (theme on Favourite TV Themes/Barry
          Gray) nst

GB   33   MFP 50355 (Theme on Star Wars & Other Space
            Themes/Geoff Love Orch.) nst
GB   33   Argo ZSW 564 (Dr. Who & The Pescatons, spin-off
            story, includes theme, w/d)
GB   33   BBC REH 364 (Genesis of the Daleks, spin-off story,
            includes theme, w/d)

Dogora, the Space Monster (Akira Ifukube, 1964)
    Uchu Daikaiju Dogora
JA   33   Toho AX 8107 (3 bands on Fantasy World of Japanese
            Pictures, Part 2, 1978)
JA   33   Starchild K22G 7113 (excerpts on Science Fiction Film
            Themes, vol. 3, 1983)
JA   33   King K22G 7047 (2 bands on Akira Ifukube Movie
            Themes, v. 5, 1982)

Dona Flor and Her 2 Husbands (Chico Buraque, 1978)
US   33   Peters Int'l 1011

Donkey Skin (Michel Legrand, 1970)
    Peau D'ane
FR   33   Paramount 2C 062 91975

Don't Look Now (Pino Donaggio, 1973)
    A Venezia Un Dicembre Rosso Shocking
GB   33   Enterprise 3003
GB   33   That's Entertainment TER 1007 B (remastered 1981 re-
            issue of 3003, different cover)
IT   33   Carosello CLN 25030 (includes some music not on oth-
            ers)

Don't Open the Window (Giuliano Sorgini, 1974)
    The Living Dead and Manchester Morgue/Let Sleeping Corpses
            Lie
GB   33   Beat LPF 028
JA   33   Tam YX-8033 (w/d, diff. cover, incl. some music not
            on LPF 028)

Doodzonde (William Breuker, 1979)
HO   33   Bvhaast 021

Dottor Jekill & Gentil Signora (Armando Trovajoli, 1980)
IT   45   CBS 7932

Dougal and the Blue Cat (Joss Basselli, 1972)
GB   33   MFP 50017 (w/d)

Dracula (John Williams, 1979)
US   33   MCA 3166
FR   33   Arabella Eurodisc MCA 201 275
GB   33   MCA 3018

IT   33   MCA 4058
JA   33   Victor VIM 7257
FR   33   Arabella MCA 204880 (1 band on 12 Terrifiantes Bandes
           Originales de Films)

Dracula and Son (Vladimir Cosma, 1979)
   Dracula Père et Fils
FR   45   Vogue V 140 142

Dracula Has Risen from the Grave (James Bernard, 1968)
   Dracula et Les Femmes
FR   33   MFP 2M 046 96966 (1 band, w/fx, on Musique de Films
           d'Horreur et de Catastrophes/Geoff Love Orch.) nst
US   33   Poo LP 104 (same band on Great S.F. Film Music, b/r,
           1978) nst

Dracula in the Provinces (Bixio-Nebbia-Frizzi-Tempera, 1975)
   Il Cavalieri Costante Nicosin Demoniaco Ovvero Dracula in Bri-
           anza
IT   45   Cinevox MDF 082 (song "Vampiro Spa")

Dragonslayer (Alex North, 1981)
US   45/lp   Label X/Southern Cross LXSE-2-001 (2/lp mastered
             at 45-rpm, full score, boxed edition, p/r, 1983)

Dreams of a Rarebit Fiend (unlisted, 1903)
US   33   Folkways 3886-87

Dressed to Kill (Pino Donaggio, 1980)
   Pulsions
US   33   Varese Sarabande STV-81148
FR   33   Disc AZ az/2 357
JA   33   Trip AW 1058

Dunwich Horror, The (Les Baxter, 1970)
US   33   American International ST-A-1028 (1970)
US   33   Varese Sarabande VC 81103 (1979 reissue of ST-A-
           1028, diff. cover)
US   33   Poo LP 106 (1 band on Great Fantasy Film Music, b/r,
           1979)

E.T. the Extra-Terrestrial (John Williams, 1982)
US   33   MCA 6109
US   33   MCA 6113 (picture disc edition)
US   33   MCA 16014 (audiophile pressing, digital recording on
           "virgin vinyl")
AU   33   MCA 6109
FR   33   Arabella MCA 204889
GB   33   MCA MCF 3160
GE   33   Ariola 204889
IT   33   Ricordi MCA 4161

IT	33	Ricordi MCA MCF-3160 (picture disc edition)
JA	33	MCA VIM 7285
SP	33	Ariola MCA I 204889
US	45	MCA 52072
FR	45	Arabella MCA 104797
US	33	Philips 6514 328 (1 band on Aisle Seat--Great Film Music/John Williams & Boston Pops, 1982) nst
US	33	EMI 32109 (Symphonic Suite/Frank Barber Orch.) nst
US	33	MCA 7000 (The Story of E.T., w/d, boxed edition)
US	33	Angel RL 32109 (1 band on John Williams' Symphonic Suites/Frank Barber Orch.) nst
US	33	Philips 411 185-1 (1 band on Out of This World/John Williams & Boston Pops, 1983) nst
US	33	GNP Crescendo GNPS 2163 (1 band on Greatest S.F. Hits III/ Neil Norman Orch., 1983) nst
US	45	GNP Crescendo GNP 828 (1 band/Neil Norman Orch.) nst
US	33	MCA 6114 (Excerpts on Themes from E.T. and More/ Walter Murphy)
FR	33	Arabella Eurodisc MCA 205715 (Theme on 12 Celebres B.O. de Films, Vol. 2, 1983)
GE	33	Europa 111579 (Theme on Beliebte Titelmelodien/Studio Orch.) nst
GE	ep	Buena Vista 36511 (w/d in German)
GB	33	MCA 7000 (The Story of E.T., w/d, boxed edition)
GB	33	MFP 5594 (same as Angel RL 32109)
JA	33	Philips 28PC 67 (Excerpts on The Flying Theme/John Williams & Boston Pops--same as Philips 6514 328)
JA	33	Victor VIP 7321 (Excerpts on E.T. and Star Wars--The Best 12 Arts of John Williams/Film Studio Orch.) nst

Earthquake (John Williams, 1974)

US	33	MCA 2081
FR	33	Arabella MCA 204880 (1 band on 12 Terrifiantes Bandes Originales de Films)

Eating Raoul (Arlon Ober, 1982)

US	33	Varese Sarabande STV 81164

8½ (Nino Rota, 1963)
Otto e Mezzo

US	33	RCA OLS-6
FR	33	RCA NL 33210
IT	33	RCA FSO 6
IT	33	Cam MAG 10004 (reissue of FSO 6)
JA	33	Seven Seas/Cam GXH 6037 (reissue of FSO 6)
SP	33	RCA SNL1 7229
US	33	Capitol P-8608 (1 band on Music from Great Italian Motion Pictures/Pino Calvi Orch.) nst
US	33	United Artists UAL-3360 (1 band on Themes from Great Films Made in Rome/Riz Ortolani Orch.) nst

US 33   Warner Bros. W-1548 (1 band on International Film
          Festival/Werner Mueller Orch.) nst
IT 33   Cam SAG 9053 (1 band on Tutti i Film di Fellini, 1973)
IT 33   WEA/General Music 803030 (1 band on Nino Rota In-
          edits, 1982)

Eight Man (uncredited, 1982)
   JA 33   King K22G 7003

Electric God "Arubegas" (Chumei Watanabe, 1983, tv)
   JA 33   Columbia CQ 7082

Empire of Passion (Toru Takemitsu, 1978)
   JA 33   Victor KVX 1064 (excerpts on Film Music of Toru
             Takemitsu, vol. 3, 1980)

Empire Strikes Back, The (John Williams, 1980)
   L'empire Contre'Attaque
   US 33   RSO RS-2-4201 (2/lp)
   FR 33   Polydor RSO 2479 261 (2/lp)
   GB 33   RSO Super RSS 23 (1/lp)
   IT 33   RSO 2394257 (2/lp)
   JA 33   RSO MWZ 8113/14 (2/lp)
   US 33   Chalfont SDQ 313 (digital suite/Charles Gerhardt) nst
   US 33   RSO RPO-4201 (single lp, promo release)
   US 33   RSO RS-1-3081 (The Adventures of Luke Skywalker,
             w/d)
   GB 33   RSO 2479 257 (w/d; same as RS-1-3081)
   JA 33   Polydor MWF 1068 (w/d; same as RS-1-3081)
   FR 33   Andes ST 3894F (w/d, 1983)
   FR 45   Andes LLP 458F (w/d, 1983)
   US 33   Buena Vista 62102 (Story of, w/d)
   GB 33   Disneyland D 62102 (Story of, w/d)
   US 33   Philips 9500 921 (digital suite on Pops in Space/John
             Williams & Boston Pops) nst
   JA 33   Philips 28 PC 1 (same as 9500 921)
   US 33   GNP Crescendo GNPS 2133 (8 min. suite on Greatest
             S.F. Hits II/Neil Norman Orch.) nst
   US 33   RSO RS-1-3085 (Empire Jazz, r/r Ron Carter) nst
   US 33   RSO RS-1-3079 (electronic version, r/r Boris Midney)
             nst
   US 10"   RSO RO-1-3086 (r/r Meco Monardo) nst
   US 33   Peter Pan 1116 (4 bands, r/r Now Sound Orch.) nst
   US 33   Sine Qua Non SQN 7808 (3 bands on Galactic Hits/
             The Odyssey Orch., 1980) nst
   US 33   Varese Sarabande 704.210 (4 bands on The Star Wars
             Trilogy/Varujan Kojin, 1983) nst
   US 45   RSO RS-1038 (r/r Meco Monardo) nst

Enchanted Cottage, The (Roy Webb, 1945)
   US 33   Entr'acte ERM 6092 (suite/nfd)

Enfantasme (Stelvio Cipriani, 1978)
    IT   33   Beat LPF 044 (7 bands/nfd)

Eraserhead (Peter Ivers, Fats Waller, 1977)
    US   33   IRS Records SP 70027 (w/d)

Escape from New York (John Carpenter, 1981)
    New York 1997/1997 Fuga da New York/Die Klappershlange
    US   33   Varese Sarabande STV 81134
    FR   33   SPI Milan A 120 137
    GB   33   That's Entertainment TER 1011
    GE   33   Celine 0004
    GE   45   Celine 0003
    IT   33   Mess. Mus. VIP 20285
    FR   33   Milan A 120 157 (2 bands on Horror and Science Fic-
                tion, 1982)

Escape from the Planet of the Apes (Jerry Goldsmith, 1971)
    US sound track announced by Columbia but cancelled prior to
        pressing

Escape to Witch Mountain (Johnny Mandel, 1974)
    US   33   Disneyland 3809 (w/d)

Espy (Masaaki Hirao, 1974)
    Esupai
    JA   33   Toho AX 8123 (1 band on Fantasy World of Japanese
                Pictures, part 4, 1978)

Eugenie ... the Story of Her Journey Into Perversion (Bruno Nicolai,
        1969)
    Marquis De Sade's Philosophy in the Boudoir
    IT   33   Gemelli GG-10.024 (p/r)

Evening with Edgar Allen Poe, An (Les Baxter, 1970, tv)
    US   33   Citadel CTV 7013 (1 side only; 24 min. suite, 1980)

Evil Dead (Joe LoDuca, 1983)
    US   33   Varese Sarabande STV 81199 (1984)

Evil Eye, The (Stelvio Cipriani, 1975)
    Malocchio
    IT   45   Cinevox MDF 065

Excalibur (Trevor Jones & classical, 1981)
    US   33   Warner Bros. BSK 3574 (announced but never re-
                leased)
    US   45   Warner Bros. WBS 49734 (side A: classical/side B:
                "Death of Uhrvens," Trevor Jones sound-track
                theme)
    FR   45   Island 6010412 (same as WBS 49734?)

GB 45   Island WIP 6729 (same as WBS 49734?)
US 33   Angel S-37841 (4 bands on Classics from Excalibur
         and Other Great Films/classical only)
US ep   Angel SPRO 9654 (1 band on promo ep/classical)
US 33   RCA XRL 1 4316 (2 bands on Film Classics Take 2/
         classical, 1982) nst
FR 33   Island 6313 216 (4 bands on Musiques Figurant Dans
         Le Film "Excalibur"/same as S-37841)
GB 33   Island ILPS 9682
GB 33   Island 12WIP 6729 (12" single)
HO 33   Ariola 203947-302
IT 33   Ricordi ILPS 19682
IT 33   EMI OB 78063
SP 33   Island/Ariola 203947
Note: all above recordings are classical selections except side
         B of WBS 49734)

Exorcist, The (various, 1973)
US 33   Warner Bros. W 2774
JA 33   Warner/Pioneer P 8464W
GB 33   Music for Pleasure MFP-50248 (1 band on Big Terror
         Movie Themes/Geoff Love Orch.) nst

Exorcist II: The Heretic (Ennio Morricone, 1977)
    Esorcista 2: L'eretico/L'heretique/Der Ketzer
US 33   Warner Bros. BS 3068
FR 33   Warner Bros. BS 3039
GB 33   Warner Bros. K 56397
IT 33   Warner Bros. 56397
JA 33   Warner Bros. P 10324
SP 33   Warner Bros. HWBS 321 123
US 45   Warner Bros. PRO 677 (promo release)
JA 45   Warner Bros. P 177W
GB 33   Decca PFS 4432 (1 band on Satan Superstar/Stanley
         Black, 1978) nst
JA 33   London GP 9051 (same as PFS 4432)
IT 33   General Music GM 33/01-3/01-4 (2 bands on Musiche
         di Ennio Morricone, Vol. 2, p/r 2/lp)

Eyes of Laura Mars, The (Artie Kane, 1978)
US 33   Columbia JS 35487
GB 33   CBS 70163
GE 33   CBS 83007
IT 33   CBS 83007
JA 33   CBS/Sony 25 AP 1108
GE 45   CBS 6657

Fahrenheit 451 (Bernard Herrmann, 1967)
US 33   London SP 44207 (5 bands on Fantasy Film World of
         Bernard Herrmann r/r B. Herrmann, 1974) nst
US 33   London CSL 1001 (same as SP 44207; p/r edition

for S.F. Book Club, 1974) nst
US   33   London SPC 2117 (same 5 bands on Bernard Herrmann
          Conducts) nst

Fantasia (classical, 1940)
  US   33   Disneyland SWDS 101e (3/lp, conducted by L. Stow-
            kowski)
  US   33   Disneyland SDWX 101 (reissue of above)
  US   33   Buena Vista 104 (new digital version for 1983 rere-
            lease, conducted by Irwin Kostal, 2/lp)
  JA   33   Columbia CS 7217/8 (2/lp, Kostal version)
  IT   33   Buena Vista 25015 (Kostal version)

Fantastic Planet (Alain Gorageur, 1973)
  La Planete Sauvage
  FR   33   EMI 2C 066-12698

Fantastica (Lewis Furey, 1981)
  FR   33   RCA/Saravah RSL 1085
  FR   45   RCA/Saravah RSB 495

Fantomas Strikes Back (Michel Magne, 1966)
  Fantomas Se Dechaine
  FR   ep   Barclay 70916 (5 bands)

Fear in the Night (John McCabe, 1972)
  US   33   Capitol 11340 (1 band on Hammer Presents Dracula/
            Philip Martel Orch., 1974) nst
  GB   33   EMI TWOA 5001 (same as Capitol 11340, 1974) nst

Fear No Evil (Frank LaLoggia & David Spear, 1981)
  US   33   WEB ST 106 (p/r)

Fellini Satyricon (Nino Rota, 1970)
  US   33   United Artists UAS 5208
  GB   33   United Artists UAS 29118
  JA   33   United Artists SU 30
  IT   33   Cam SAG 9053 (1 band on Tutti i Film di Fellini,
            1973)

Femmes Fatales (Georges Delerue, 1977)
  Calmos
  FR   33   Black and Blue 33.400

Fiend, The (Ennio Morricone, 1977)
  Il Mostro
  IT   45   Beat BTF 102

The Final Conflict (Jerry Goldsmith, 1981)
  US   33   DLP 105 (Finale on The Great Movie Themes, vol. 1;
            b/r, 1984)

Flash Gordon (Queen, 1980)
   US   33   Elektra 5E-518 (w/d)
   US   45   Elektra E-4792 (slight different from lp version)
   GM 33   EMI EMC 3351
   JA   33   Warner/Pioneer P 10960E
   US   33   GNP Crescendo GNPS 2163 (1 band on Greatest S.F.
              Hits III/Neil Norman Orch., 1983) nst

Flash Gordon's Trip to Mars (various)
   US   33   Pelican LP 2006 (w/d mostly)

Flavia, Priestess of Violence (Nicola Piovani, 1975)
   Flavia La Monaca Musulmana
   IT   33   Cinevox MDF 33/73

Flesh and Fantasy (Alexandre Tansman, 1943)
   US   33   Camden CAL-205 (1 band on Film Music/Janssen Sym-
              phony of Los Angeles) nst
   US   33   Camden CAL-233 (1 band on Film Music/Harlan Ramsey
              & Cosmopolitan Orch.) nst

Flesh Gordon (Paul Ferraro, 1973)
   US   33   privately released special pressing, no label or num-
              ber

Flying Saucer, The (Piero Piccioni, 1964)
   Il Disco Volante
   IT   45   Style STMS 602

Fog, The (John Carpenter, 1980)
   US   33   Varese Sarabande STV 81191 (1984)

For Love ... For Magic (Luis E. Bacalov, 1966)
   Per Amore ... Per Magia
   IT   33   RCA S28 (conducted by E. Morricone)

For Your Eyes Only (Bill Conti, 1981)
   Solo per i Tuoi Occhi
   US   33   Liberty L00-1109
   GB   33   Liberty LBG 30337
   GE   33   EMI 064 400023
   IT   33   EMI 064 57003
   JA   33   United Artists K 28 4030

Forbidden Planet (Louis and Bebe Barron, 1956)
   Il Pianeta Proibito
   US   33   Planet Records PR-001 (p/r, 1976)
   US   78   MGM 12243 (10" 78-rpm single, "inspired by film," r/r
              David Rose) nst
   US   33   MGM E-3397 (same band, r/r David Rose, on Music
              from Motion Pictures) nst

US   33   Cinema LP 1005 (same band as on 12243 on Destination
           Moon and Other Themes, b/r, 1974)
IT   33   Blu BLRL 1500 (1 band on Fantascienza, p/r, nfd)

Forbidden World (Susan Justin, 1982)
US   33   WEB 107 (p/r)

Forbidden Zone (Danny Elfman, 1980)
US   33   Varese Sarabande STV 81170 (1983)

Forever Darling (Bronislau Kaper, 1956)
US   45   MGM 12144
US   45   MGM 12478

Four Flies on Grey Velvet (Ennio Morricone, 1972)
Quattro Mosche di Velluto Grigio/Quatre Mouches de Velours
           Gris
IT   45   Cinevox MDF 031
IT   33   Cinevox CIA 5009 (2 bands on I Films di Dario Ar-
           gento, 1980)
IT   33   Cinevox MDF 33/74-75 (2 bands on Fotogramma Per
           Fotogramma, 2/lp, 1976)
IT   33   RCA TPL2 1174 (1 band on I Film Della Violenza, 2/
           lp, 1975)
FR   33   Barclay 930.014/15 (2 bands on Il Etait Une Fois
           ... La Revolution, et 22 de Films de E. Morricone,
           2/lp, 1976)
FR   33   Barclay 930023 (excerpt on Cinemusic, vol. 2, 1977)

Frankenstein Conquers the World (Akira Ifukube, 1964)
Fuharankenshutain Tai Barugon
JA   33   Toho AX 8108 (4 bands on Fantasy World of Japanese
           Pictures, part 3, 1978)
JA   33   StarChild K66G 7118 (excerpts on Science Fiction
           Film Themes, vol. 8, 1983)
JA   33   King K22G 7048 (2 bands on Akira Ifukube Movie
           Themes, vol. 6, 1982)

Frau Im Mond, Die (uncredited, 1929)
GE   78   Polyphone UTA 504J (p/r 78 rpm set for theatres
           showing film)

Freaky Friday (Kasha & Hirschorn, 1976)
US   45   Disney 566 (song)

Frenzy (Ron Goodwin, 1972)
US   33   Centurion CLP 1210 (1 band on Filmusic, vol. 2, b/r)
GB   33   EMI Studio 2 TWOX 1007 (1 band on Spellbound/Ron
           Goodwin Orch.) nst
GB   33   EMI TWOSP 108 (1 band on First 25 Years/Ron
           Goodwin Orch., 2/lp) nst

GB 33 HMV 3739 (1 band on British Music for Films and TV/
        Marcus Dods Orch., 1979) nst
GB 33 Music for Pleasure MFP 50035 (1 band on Big Sus-
        pense Movie Themes/Geoff Love Orch.) nst
NZ 33 EMI SLZ-8582 (same as TWOX 1007)

Friday the 13th (Harry Manfredini, 1980)
    Weekend di Terror
    US 33 Gramavision GR 1030 (includes music from Parts 1, 2
            and 3; 1983)
    GB 33 That's Entertainment TER-1045 (same as GR 1030)
    IT 33 Carosello CIX 49 (same as GR 1030)
    SP 33 Serdisco ME 34132 ("maxi-single," theme from Part
            3, r/r Michael Zager Band, 1983)
    GE 33 Milan A 212 (Muertres En 3 Dimensionsm 1984)

Fritz the Cat (Ray Shanklin & Ed Bogas, 1972)
    US 33 Fantasy M-89406

From Russia with Love (John Barry, 1963)
    US 33 United Artists UAS 5114
    GB 33 United Artists SULP 1052
    US 33 Capitol ST-2075 (Theme on From Russia with Love/
            Jimmie Haskell Orch.) nst
    US 33 Polydor 184023 (Theme on Film Themes/Henry Logues
            Orch.) nst
    GB 33 Ember NR 5025 (Themes on John Barry Plays 007)
            nst
    GB 33 United Artists UAD 6002718 (Theme on James Bond
            Collection)
    GB 33 CBS 22014 (Theme on The Music of John Barry, 2/lp)
            nst
    Theme also on various r/r James Bond collections (nfd)

Fury, The (John Williams, 1977)
    US 33 Arista AB-4175
    GB 33 Arista SPART 1056
    IT 33 EMI 064 61934

Future Police "Urashiman" (Seriwaxa & Suzuki, 1982, tv)
    JA 33 Columbia CX 7089

Future War 198X (Seiji Yokoyama, 1982)
    JA 33 Columbia CS 7070

Galaxy Cyclone Bryger (Masayuki Yamamoto, 1981-82, tv)
    JA 33 StarChild K22G-7067 (lyrics: Yamamoto & Tsutomi
            Kikuchi)

Galaxy Tornado Sasryger (Masayuki Yamamoto, 1983, tv)
    JA 33 StarChild K22G-7135

JA   33   StarChild K22G 7157 (Sasuraiger JJ9)

Galaxy Whirlwind Baxinger (Masayuki Yamamoto, 1982-83, tv)
JA   33   StarChild K22G-7097

Galaxy Express 999 (Nozumi Aoki, 1979)
JA   33   Columbia CQ 7014 (Symphonic Suite)
JA   33   Columbia SC 7022 (w/d in English)
JA   33   Columbia CS 7096 (Hit Themes from...)
JA   33   Columbia CQ 7025 (Symphonic Poem Galaxy Express)
JA   33   Columbia CQ 7023 (Suite for 2 Pianos, 1 side only)
JA   33   Columbia CQ 7032 (Chorus Suite, 1 side only)
JA   33   Columbia CS 7136/7 (2/lp, w/d in Japanese)
JA   33   Columbia CW 7247/50 (All About Galaxy Express, 4/
           lp boxed w/d)
JA   33   Columbia CB 7114/5 (Symphonic Poem, 2/lp)
JA   33   Victor JBX 200
JA   45   Columbia CK 537
IT   33   RCA BL 31665

Gamera vs. Monster X (Shunsuke Kikuchi, 1970)
    Gamera Tai Daimaju Jaiga/Gamera vs. Jiger
JA   33   Toho AX 8120 (1 band on Gamera, 1978)
JA   33   Daiei KKS-4031 (excerpts on Gamera II, w/d)

Gamera vs. Zigra (Shunsuke Kikuchi, 1971)
    Gamera Tai Shinkai Kaiju Jigura/Gamera vs. Leoman
JA   33   Toho AX 8120 (1 band on Gamera, 1978)
JA   33   Daiei KKS-4031 (excerpts on Gamera II, w/d)

Games (Samual Matlovsky, 1967)
US   33   Mercury 61149 (1 band, nfd) nst

Gammera the Invincible (Tadashi Yamaguchi, Japanese release,
           1966)
JA   33   Toho AX 8120 (3 bands on Gamera, 1978)
JA   33   Daiei KKS-4026 (excerpts on Gamera, w/d)

Gammera the Invincible (Wes Farrell, U.S. release, 1966)
US   45   Date 2-1545 (r/r song performed by The Moons)

Gas-s-s-s (Barry Melton, 1970)
UA   33   American Int'l A-1038

Ge Ge Ge No Kitaro (Taku Izumi, 1978)
JA   33   Columbia SKK 2122

Get Smart (Irving Szathmary, tv, 1965)
US   33   GNP Crescendo GNPS 2166 (1 band on Secret Agent
           File/ Various, 1984) nst

Ghidrah, the 3 Headed Monster (Akira Ifukube, 1965)
  Ghidorah, Sandai Kaiju Chikyu Saidai No Kessen
  JA   33   Toho AX 8100 (2 bands on Godzilla, 1978)
  JA   33   Toho AX 8112 (1 band on Godzilla, vol. 2, 1979)
  JA   33   Columbia CS-7190 (suite on Monster King Godzilla,
        1980)
  JA   33   StarChild K22G 7114 (Excerpts on S.F. Film Themes,
        vol. 4, 1983)
  JA   33   King K22G 7048 (3 bands on Akira Ifukube Movie
        Themes, vol. 6, 1982)

Ghost, The (Francesco De Masi, nfd)
  Lo Spettro
  IT   33   Disco Edimerc EC 0113 (Gli Aspetti del Dramma, p/r)

Ghost and Mrs. Muir, The (Bernard Herrmann, 1947)
  US   33   FMC 4 (complete score, r/r Elmer Bernstein, p/r)
        nst
  GB   33   Unicorn 400-4 (4 bands, r/r B. Herrmann; nfd)

Ghost of Dragstrip Hollow, The (Ronald Stein, 1959)
  US   45   American Int'l A-45-537 (song from film by Nick
        Venet, sung by The Renegades)

Ghost of Frankenstein, The (Hans J. Salter, 1942)
  US   33   Tony Thomas TT-HS-3 (p/r, 1980)
  US   33   Tony Thomas TFHS 1/2 (25 min. suite on Film Music
        of Hans J. Salter, p/4, 1979)

Ghost Squad (Philip Green, tv; nfd)
  US   33   Phillips PHS 600 027 (1 band on TV Thriller Themes/
        James Gregory Orch.) nst
  US   45   London 45-10505 (1 band, r/r Tony Hatch)

Ghost Story (uncredited, 1972, tv)
  US   33   Peter Pan S-8114 (r/r) NOTE: Although presented
        as an original sound track, this lp contains none of
        the original scoring

Ghost Story (Philippe Sarde, 1981)
  US   33   MCA 5287

Ghosts in Rome (Nino Rota, 1961)
  Fantasmi a Roma
  IT   ep   RCA EPA 30398
  US   33   RCA FSO-4 (1 band on Original Soundtracks Recorded
        in Italy)

Gigantis the Fire Monster (Masaru Sato, 1959)
  Gojira No Gyakushu/Godzilla Raids Again

JA   33   Columbia CX-7020 (Excerpts on Godzilla Original
            Background Music vol. 1, 1982)

Glass Slipper, The (Bronislau Kaper, 1955)
  US   33   Delos 25421 (1 band on Film Themes of Bronislau
              Kaper; r/r for solo piano by B. Kaper) nst
  US   33   MGM E 3694 (1 band on On the Hollywood Sound
              Stage/John Green Orch.) nst

Godzilla, King of the Monsters (Akira Ifukube, 1956)
  Gojira
  JA   33   Toho AX 8082 (2 bands on Works of Akira Ifukube,
              1978)
  JA   33   Toho AX 8100 (3 bands on Godzilla, 1978)
  JA   33   Toho AX 8112 (6 bands on Godzilla, vol. 2, 1979)
  JA   33   Toho AX 8147 (1 band on Godzilla, vol. 3, 1980)
  JA   33   StarChild K22G 7111 (Excerpts on S.F. Film Themes,
              vol. 1, 1983)
  JA   33   King K22G 7043 (4 bands on Akira Ifukube Movie
              Themes, vol. 1, 1982)
  JA   33   Columbia CX-7020 (Excerpts on Godzilla Original
              Background Music, vol. 1, 1982)
  JA   33   Columbia CX-7021 (Excerpts on Godzilla Original
              Background Music, vol. 2, 1982)
  JA   33   Seven Seas K16P-4033 (Excerpt on S.F. & Spectacle
              Themes) nst
  JA   33   Toho DR-1001 (Excerpt w/d on Monster Themes)
  IT   45   Cinevox MDF 111
  US   33   Poo LP 104 (1 band on Great S.F. Film Music, b/r)
  US   33   GNP Crescendo GNPS 2128 (1 band on Greatest Sci-
              ence Fiction Hits/Neil Norman Orch., 1979) nst
  IT   33   Cinevox CIA 5014 (1 band on Squalo-Exorcista e Altri
              Film Della Paura)

Godzilla on Monster Island (Japanese release: Kunio Miyauchi,
              1971)
  Gojira Tai Giagan/Godzilla vs. Gigan
  JA   33   Toho AX 8147 (1 band on Godzilla, Part 3, 1980)
  JA   33   Toho DR-1001 (Excerpts on Monster Themes; nfd)

Godzilla vs. the Cosmic Monster (Masaru Sato, 1976)
  Meka-Gojira No Gyakushu/Godzilla vs. Mecha-Godzilla/G. vs.
              Bionic Monster
  JA   33   Toho AX 8100 (1 band on Godzilla, 1979)
  JA   33   Toho AX 8147 (5 bands on Godzilla, vol. 3, 1980)
  JA   33   Columbia CS 7190 (suite, w/d, on Monster King God-
              zilla, 1980)
  JA   33   StarChild K22G 7119 (Excerpts on S.F. Film Themes,
              vol. 9, 1983)
  JA   33   Toho DX-1009 (Excerpts on Movie & TV Themes lp/
              nfd)
  JA   45   Toho DT-1014

Godzilla vs. Megalon (Riichiro Manabe, 1976)
    Gojira Tai Megallo
    JA   33   Toho AX 8097 (1 band on Film Music of Riichiro
                  Manabe, 1978)
    JA   33   Toho AX 8147 (2 bands and 1 nst band on Godzilla,
                  vol. 3, 1980)
    JA   33   Columbia CZ 7096 (excerpts on Godzilla, vol. 5, 1982)
    JA   33   StarChild K22G 7118 (Excerpts on S.F. Film Themes,
                  vol. 8, 1983)
    JA   45   Toho DT-1006

Godzilla vs. the Sea Monster (Masaru Sato, 1966)
    Nankai No Dai Ketto/Ebirah, Horror of the Deep
    JA   33   Toho AX 8112 (1 band on Godzilla, vol. 2, 1979)
    JA   33   Toho AX 8147 (1 band on Godzilla, vol. 3, 1980)

Godzilla vs. the Smog Monster (Riichiro Manabe, 1971)
    Gojira Tai Hedora
    JA   33   Toho AX 8112 (1 band on Godzilla, vol. 2, 1979)
    JA   33   Toho AX 8147 (1 band on Godzilla, vol. 3, 1980)
    JA   33   Columbia CZ 7068 (Excerpts on Godzilla, vol. 4, 1982)
    JA   33   Toho DR-1001 (Excerpts, w/d on Monster Themes)
    JA   45   Toho DC-1003 (w/d, 7" 33-rpm single)

Godzilla vs. the Thing (Akira Ifukube, 1965)
    Mosura Tai Gojira
    JA   33   Toho AX 8100 (3 bands on Godzilla, 1978)
    JA   33   Toho AX 8112 (4 bands on Godzilla, vol. 2, 1979)
    JA   33   Columbia CS 7190 (suite, w/d, on Monster King God-
                  zilla, 1980)
    JA   33   Toho DR-1001 (Excerpts, w/d, on Monster Themes)
    JA   33   StarChild K22G 7113 (Excerpts on S.F. Film Themes,
                  vol. 3, 1983)
    JA   33   Columbia CX-7020 (Excerpts on Godzilla Original Back-
                  ground Music, vol. 1, 1982)
    JA   33   King K22G 7047 (5 bands on Akira Ifukube Movies
                  Themes, vol. 5, 1982)

Godzilla's Revenge (Kunio Miyauchi, 1971)
    US   45   Crown Records (unnumbered promo, March of the
                  Monsters)
    JA   33   StarChild K22G 7111 (Excerpts on S.F. Film Themes,
                  vol. 1, 1983)

Gog (Harry Sukman, 1954)
    US   33   Decca DL-8060 (1 band on Hollywood Rhapsodies/Vic-
                  tor Young Orch.) nst

Golden Earrings (Victor Young, 1947)
    US   33   Decca DL-8008 (10" lp, 6 bands, 1950)
    US   33   Decca DL-8481 (reissue of DL-8008, 1957)
    US   33   Varese Saraband STV-81117 (reissue of DL-8008, 1982)

Golden Voyage of Sinbad, The (Miklos Rozsa, 1973)
   US   33   United Artists UA-LA 308-G
   GB   33   United Artists UAS 29567
   JA   33   Mu-Land LZ-7017-M (Theme on S.F. Fact, vol. 2/
               Electoru Polyphonic Orch., 1979) nst

Goldfinger (John Barry, 1964)
   US   33   United Artists UAS-4117
   GB   33   United Artists UA-1076
   SP   33   Belter 46
   US   33   Columbia CS-9293 (Theme on The Great Movie Sounds
               of John Barry)
   US   33   United Artists UAS 3424 (themes on John Barry Plays
               Goldfinger) nst
   US   33   United Artists S-21010 (theme on The Incredible World
               of James Bond)
   US   33   United Artists SP3 (special issue of S-21010)
   US   33   London SP-44078 (theme on Film Spectacular vol. III/
               Stanley Black & London Festival Orch.) nst
   GB   33   Ember NR-5025 (theme on John Barry Plays 007) nst
   GB   33   United Artists UAD 6002718 (theme on James Bond
               Collection)
   GB   33   CBS 22014 (theme on The Music of John Barry, 2/lp)
   FR   33   Sonopresse UASF 5117 (1979)

Goldorak (Shinichi Kikuchi, 1979)
   CA   33   HS/CBS PRC 90561

Goliath and the Barbarians (Les Baxter, 1959)
   US   33   American Int'l 1001S (1960)
   US   33   Varese Sarabande VC 81078 (reissue of 1001S, differ-
               ent cover, 1979)

Goliath and the Sins of Babylon (Francesco de Masi, 1963)
   IT   33   Cam 30.094

Goliath II (George Bruns, 1960)
   US   33   Disneyland ST-1902 (w/d)

Goodbye Charlie (Andre Previn, 1964)
   US   33   20th Century-Fox 4165

Goodbye Gemini (Christopher Gunning, 1970)
   GB   33   DJM Records DHLP-408

Gorath (Kan Ishii, 1962)
Yosei Gorasu
   JA   33   Toho AX 8106 (4 bands on Fantasy World of Japanese
               Pictures, part 1, 1978)
   JA   33   StarChild K22G 7115 (Excerpt on S.F. Film Themes,
               vol. 5, 1983)

Grand Prix Hawk (Hiroshi Miyagawa, 1978)
  JA   33   Columbia CX 7107
  JA   33   Columbia CS-7051 (w/d in Japanese)
  JA   33   Columbia CZ-7009 (w/d in English)

Great Muppet Caper, The (Joe Raposo, 1981)
  US   33   Atlantic SD 16047 (songs)
  US   45   Atlantic 3829

Greatest American Hero, The (Mike Post, tv, 1981)
  US   45   Elektra E-47147 (theme, r/r Mike Post) nst
  US   33   Elektra E1-600028Y (theme on Television Theme Songs/
                Mike Post Orch., 1982) nst

Green Hornet, The (Billy May, 1966, tv)
  US   33   20th Century-Fox S-3186 (w/d)
  US   33   Leo CH-1023 (Theme on The Amazing TV Themes/
                nfd)

Green Mare, The (Rene Cloerec, 1959)
  La Jument Verte
  FR   ep   RCA 76.365 (4 bands)

Green Slime, The (U.S. release: Charles Fox, 1969)
  US   45   MGM/Verve K/14052 (promo; theme song, sung by
                The Green Slimes)
  US   33   Poo LP 104 (same song on Great S.F. Film Music,
                b/r, 1978)

Grip of the Spider (Riz Ortolani, 1971)
  Nella Stretta Morsedel Ragno
  IT   33   RCA SP-8037

Grizzly (Robert O. Ragland, 1976)
  US   33   Truluv HWR 301
  JA   33   Seven Seas FML 59 (includes some music not on HWR
                301)

Gulliver's Travels (Victor Young, 1939)
  US   78   Decca DA-100

Gulliver's Travels Beyond the Moon (Milton DeLugg, 1966)
  US   33   Mainstream S/4001

H-Man, The (Masaru Sato, 1958)
  Bijyo To Ekitainingen
  JA   33   Toho AX 8106 (4 bands on Fantasy World of Japanese
                Pictures, part 2, 1978)

H2S (Ennio Morricone, 1969)
  US   33   Poo LP 105 (1 band on Hornet's Nest, b/r, 1978)

Halloween (John Carpenter, 1978)
```
US   33   Varese Sarabande STV 81176 (1983)
JA   33   Columbia SX 7013 (w/d, r/r "Bowling Green Philhar-
               monic," 1979) nst
GE   33   Celine CL 008 (same as STV 81176, 1983)
```

Halloween II (John Carpenter & Alan Howarth, 1981)
```
US   33   Varese Sarabande STV 81152
FR   33   SPI Milan A 120/60
```

Halloween III: Season of the Witch (John Carpenter & Alan
               Howarth, 1982)
```
US   33   MCA 6115
```

Hammer House of Horror, The (Roger Webb, 1981, tv)
```
GB   45   Chips CHI 104
```

Hands of Orlac, The (Claude Bolling, 1959)
Les Mains D'Orlac
```
FR   ep   Philips/Medium 432.524 (5 bands)
```

Hanging House on the Hospital Slope (Shinichi Tanabe, 1979)
```
JA   33   Toho AX 5032
```

Hangover Square (Bernard Herrmann, 1945)
```
US   33   Camden CAL 205 (suite on Film Music/Janssen Sym-
               phony of Los Angeles) nst
US   33   Camden CAL 233 (1 band on Film Music/Cosmopolitan
               Orch.) nst
US   33   Cinema LP 8006 (piano concerto on The Film Music of
               Bernard Herrmann, b/r, 1975) nst
US   33   RCA ARL1-0707 (concerto on Citizen Kane:  The
               Classic Film Music of Bernard Herrmann, r/r Charles
               Gerhardt, 1975) nst
```

Hans Christian Andersen (songs: Frank Loesser, 1952)
```
US   10"  Decca DL-5433
US   33   Decca DL-8479 (1 side only)
```

Harlequin (Brian May, 1980)
```
FR   33   Movie Music MM-2002
```

Haunting, The (Humphrey Searle, 1963)
```
US   45   MGM K13163 (1 band, "inspired by film," composed
               by Lalo Schifrin) nst
US   33   MGM SE 4185 ST (same band on Twilight of Honor &
               Other Great Themes, 1963) nst
US   33   MGM SE 4192 (same band on The Prize, 1963) nst
US   33   MGM SE 4742 (same band on Medical Center & Other
               Great Themes/Lalo Schifrin Orch.) nst
```

Haunting of Julia, The (Colin Towns, 1976)
   Full Circle
   FR   33   Polydor 2933.740
   GB   33   Virgin V 2093
   FR   45   Polydor 2 097 945 (1978)

Have Rocket Will Travel (uncredited, 1959)
   US   45   Colpix 120 (theme arranged or conducted by George
            Duning)

Hawk the Slayer (Harry Robertson, 1981)
   GB   33   Chips CHLP 1

Hawks and Sparrow (Ennio Morricone, 1966)
   IT   33   RCA DPSL 10599 (1 band on Un Film, Una Musica,
            2/lp, 1973)

Heart of Glass (Popul Vuh, 1976)
   GE   33   Brain 0060.079
   GE   33   Egg 900.536

Heaven Can Wait (Dave Grusin, 1978)
   US   33   RCA AQL1 3052 (1 band on Theme Scene/Henry Man-
            cini Orch.) nst

Heavy Metal (Elmer Bernstein & rock songs, 1981)
   US   33   Asylum 5E-547 (score)
   US   33   Full Moon/Asylum 90004 (rock songs, 2/lp)
   HO   33   Epic 88558 (score)
   HO   33   2 Epic EPC 88558 (rock songs, 2/lp)
   SP   33   Epic EPC 88 558 (score)
   US   45   Full Moon/Asylum 47204 (rock songs)
   US   45   Elektra/Asylum 47204 (rock songs)

Heavy Traffic (Ray Shanklin & Ed Bogas, 1973)
   US   33   Fantasy 9436

Hell Island (Shinichi Tanabe, 1977)
   Gokumon Toh
   JA   33   Toho AX 5013
   JA   45   Toho AT 4054

Hercules (Enzo Masetti, 1957)
   US   33   LBY 1036 (w/d & narration by Conrad Nagel)

Hercules (Pino Donaggio, 1983)
   US   33   Varese Sarabande STV 81187

Hobbit, The (Maury Laws, 1977, tv)
   US   33   Buena Vista BV 103 (complete sound track, w/d, w/
            fx, 2/lp, boxed set)

US   33   Disneyland 3819 (songs only, condensed from BV 103)

Home Movies (Pino Donaggio, 1980)
US   33   Varese Sarabande STV 81139

Horror Castle (Riz Ortolani, 1965)
Le Vergine Di Norimberga/The Virgin of Nuremberg
IT   33   Cam 30.119

Horror Chamber of Dr. Faustus, The (Maurice Jarre, 1959)
Les Yeux Sans Visage
FR   ep   Vega V 45 P 20 (4 bands)

Horror Express (John Cacavas, 1974)
US   33   Citadel CT 6026 (10 bands, 1 side only, on Music for
          Frankenstein, Dracula, The Mummy, The Wolf Man
          and Other Old Friends, 1978)
US   33   Citadel CT 7012 (reissue of CT 6025 as Horror Rhap-
          sody, 1979)

Horror High (Don Hulette, 1973)
Twisted Brain (tv title)
US   45   unnumbered promo (credits Jerry Coward, song)

Horror of Dracula (James Bernard, 1958)
Le Cauchemar de Dracula
US   33   Coral CRL 757240 (2 bands on Themes from Horror
          Movies/Dick Jacobs Orch.) nst
US   33   Varese Sarabande VC 81077 (remastered 1978 reissue
          of CRL 757240 as Themes from Classic S.F., Fantasy
          & Horror Films) nst
FR   33   MCA 410.064 (reissue of VC 81077) nst
JA   33   MCA VIM 7264 (reissue of VC 81077) nst

House (Akira Kobayashi & others, 1978)
JA   33   Columbia YX 7177

House of Frankenstein (Hans Salter & others, 1944)
La Maison de Frankenstein
US   33   Coral CRL 757240 (1 band on Themes from Horror
          Movies/Dick Jacobs Orch.) nst
US   33   Varese Sarabande VC 81077 (remastered 1978 reissue
          of CRL 757240 as Themes from Classic S.F., Fantasy
          & Horror Films) nst
FR   33   MCA 410.064 (reissue of VC 81077) nst
JA   33   MCA VIM 7264 (reissue of VC 81077) nst

House of Terror (Ugi Ono, 1976)
Inugnami Ichizoku
JA   33   JVC Victor SJV 1282
JA   45   JVC Victor KV 54t

House on Haunted Hill (Von Dexter, 1958)
 US 45 Columbia 4-41366 (1 band, r/r Frank De Vol)
 US 45 Orbit 533 (1 band, or song, credited to Kayne &
     Loring)

House Outside the Cemetery (Walter Rizzati, 1981)
 Quella Villa Accanto Al Cimitero
 IT 33 Beat LPF 061 (Excerpts on I Film Della "Paura")

How the Grinch Stole Christmas (Albert Hague, 1966, tv)
 US 33 MGM/Leo LES 901 (w/d narration)

How to Steal the Crown of England (Piero Umiliani, 1966)
 Come Rubare la Carona di Inghilterra/Argoman Superdiabolico
 IT 33 Beat LP 001 (1 band on I Sogni Della Musica n. 1)
 IT 33 Beat LP 003 (2 bands on I Sogni Della Musica n. 2,
     1972)

How We Stole the Atomic Bomb (Lallo Gori, 1967)
 Come Rubammo la Bomba Atomica
 IT 45 Beat BTF 027

Howling, The (Pino Donaggio, 1981)
 US 33 Varese Sarabande STV 81150
 JA 33 Victor VIP 28033
 FR 33 Milan A-120-157 (1 band on Horror and Science Fic-
     tion, 1982)

Human Vapor, The (Kunio Miyauchi, 1960)
 Gasu-Ningen Dai Ichi-Go
 JA 33 Toho AX 8107 (3 bands on Fantasy World of Japanese
     Pictures, part 2, 1978)

Humanoid, The (Ennio Morricone, 1979)
 L'humanoide
 IT 33 RCA BL 31432
 IT 33 General Music GM 33/01-3/01-4 (2 bands on Musiche
     di Ennio Morricone, Vol. 2, p/r, 2/lp)
 FR 33 RCA CL 31559 (Excerpts on Ennio Morricone Master-
     pieces, 2/lp)

The Hunchback of Notre Dame (Alfred Newman, 1939)
 The cue heard when Phoebus chases Quasimodo to rescue Es-
     meralda was reused by Newman in the 1953 film The
     Robe, and appears as the latter half of the cue,
     "The Rescue of Demetrius," on its sound-track album
     (US 33 Decca DL 79012; and earlier versions)

Hunger, The (Rubini & Jaeger, 1983)
 Predateurs
 US 33 Varese Sarabande STV 81184

FR   33   Milan ACH 005

Hunger Canal (Isao Tomita, 1964)
    Kiga Kaikyo
    JA   33   King SKD(M) 370-1 (1 band on Famous Japanese
                Films, 2/lp)

Hush, Hush Sweet Charlotte (Frank De Vol, 1964)
    US   45   Capitol 5341 (title song, sung by Al Martino)
    US   45   Columbia 4-43251 (title song, sung by Patti Page)
                nst
    US   33   Camden CAS 926 (1 band on The Sweetheart Tree
                and Other Film Favorites/Johnny Douglas Orch.)
                nst
    GB   33   EMI EMA 778 (1 band on Miss Bette Davis/nfd) nst

I Bury the Living (Gerald Fried, 1958)
    US   33   Poo LP 104 (1 band on Great S.F. Film Music, b/r,
                1978)

I Saw What You Did (Van Alexander, 1965)
    US   45   Decca 31787 (Theme, r/r The Tell Tales) nst

Iceman (Bruce Smeaton, 1984)
    US   33   Southern Cross SCRS 1006

Ideon II (uncredited, nfd)
    JA   33   King K22G 7007

Images (John Williams, 1972)
    US   33   Classic Int'l Filmusic CIF-1002 (b/r, 1975)

In Search of... (W. Michael Lewis & Laurin Rinder, 1977, tv)
    US   33   AVI Records AVL-6008

Incredible Hulk, The (Joe Harnell, 1978, tv)
    US   45   MCA 40953 (2 bands, theme and love theme)
    GB   45   EMI (same as MCA 40953, nfd)
    US   45   Epic 8-505 (theme, r/r Billy Sherill Orch.) nst
    US   33   Victor PB 11916 (theme on Dallas and Other TV
                Themes/Floyd Cramer, 1980) nst
    GB   33   MFP 50439 (Theme on Themes for Superheroes/Geoff
                Love Orch.) nst

Incredible Mr. Limpet, The (Sammy Fain & Harold Adamson, 1963)
    US   45   Warner Bros. 5431 (song only)

Incredible Shrinking Man, The (Hans Salter & others, 1957)
    L'homme Qui Retrecit
    UA   33   Tony Thomas TT-HS-4 (16 min. suite on Classic Hor-
                ror Music of Hans J. Salter, p/r, 1980)

US 33   Coral CRL 757240 (Theme on Themes from Horror
         Films/Dick Jacobs Orch.) nst
US 33   Varese Sarabande VC 81077 (1978 reissue of CRL
         757240 as Themes from Classic S.F., Fantasy & Hor-
         ror Films) nst
FR 33   MCA 410.064 (reissue of VC 81077) nst
JA 33   MCA VIM 7264 (reissue of VC 81077) nst
US 45   Capitol F3676 (theme, r/r Ray Anthony) nst
US 33   Poo LP 104 (Theme, r/r Ray Anthony, on Great S.F.
         Film Music, b/r, 1978)

Incredibly Strange Creatures Who Stopped Living and Became
                Mixed Up Zombies (Libby Quinn & Henry Price, 1963)
Teenage Psycho Meets Bloody Mary (reissue title)
US 45   Rel # R-105 (promo)

Incubo Sulla Citta Contaminata (Stelvio Cipriani, 1981)
IT 33   Cinevox TI 8005

Inferno (Keith Emerson, 1980)
IT 33   Cinevox MDF 33/138
IT 33   Cinevox CIA 5022 (reissue of MDF 33/138)
JA 33   28MM-0008 (different cover)

Inseminoid (John Scott, 1982)
US 33   Citadel CT 7028
FR 33   Milan A-120-157 (1 band on Horror and Science Fic-
         tion, 1982)

Invaders, The (Dominic Frontiere; tv, 1967)
US 33   GNP Crescendo GNPS 2163 (Theme on Greatest S.F.
         Hits III/Neil Norman, 1983) nst

Invaders from Mars (Raoul Kraushaar/Mort Glickman, 1953)
JA 33   Mu Land LZ 7019 M (1 band on Space Adventure
         Vol. 2/Electoru Polyphonic Orch.) nst

Invaders from Space (Chumei Watanabe, 1958)
Super Giant 5/6 / Attack from Space / Jinko Eisen To Jinrui
         No Hametsu
JA 33   Toho AX 8124 (1 band on Fantasy World of Japanese
         Pictures part 5, 1978)

Invasion of the Body Snatchers (Denny Zeitlin, 1978)
L'invasion des Profanateurs
US 33   United Artists UALA 940
FR 33   Sonopresse/UA 2S068 62618
JA 33   United Artists FML 114

Invisible Boy, The (Les Baxter, 1957)
US 45   Capitol F3842 (r/r, nfd) nst

Island, The (Ennio Morricone, 1980)
    US   33   Varese Sarabande STV-81147

Island of Dr. Moreau (Laurence Rosenthal, 1977)
    US   33   Wells HG-4000 (b/r)
    US   33   Varese Sarabande VC 81086 (unreleased)
    JA   33   Mu Land LZ 7017 M (1 band on S.F. Fact Vol. 2/
                  Electoru Polyphonic Orch., 1979) nst

Island of the Evil Spirit (Joij Yuassa, songs by Paul McCartney,
               1981)
    JA   33   East World WTP 90108

It Came from Outer Space (Herman Stein, 1953)
    La Meteor de la Nuit
    US   33   Coral CRL 757240 (1 band on Themes from Horror
                  Movies/Dick Jacobs Orch.) nst
    US   33   Varese Sarabande VC 81077 (1978 reissue of CRL
                  757240 as Themes from Classic S.F., Fantasy and
                  Horror Films) nst
    FR   33   MCA 410.064 (reissue of VC 81077)
    JA   33   MCA VIM 7264 (reissue of VC 81077)

It's About Time (Gerald Fried, 1966, tv)
    US   33   Leo CH-1023 (Theme on The Amazing TV Themes/nfd)

It's Alive 2 (Bernard Herrmann & Laurie Johnson, 1978)
    US   33   Starlog SR-1002

Jack and the Beanstalk (Jerry Livingston & Helen Deutsch, mid-
               50's, tv)
    US   45   Unique Records 363 (song "I'll Go Along with You,"
                  performed by The Petticoats and Joe Healy Orch.)

Jack the Giant Killer (Paul Sawtell & Bert Shefter, 1962)
    US   33   Poo LP 104 (1 band on Great S.F. Film Music, b/r,
               1978)

Jack the Ripper (jimmy McHugh & Pete Rugolo, U.S. release, 1960)
    US   33   RCA 2119
    US   45   RCA 47-7694

Jack the Ripper (Stanley Black, GB release, 1960)
    US   33   RCA Camden CAL 596

Jason and the Argonauts (Bernard Herrmann, 1963)
    US   33   London Phase-4 SPC 21137 (4 bands on The Mysteri-
               ous Film World of Bernard Herrmann, r/r B.
               Herrmann, 1975) nst

Jaws (John Williams, 1975)
    Les Dents de la Mer/Der Weiss Hai

US	33	MCA 2087
FR	33	MCA 414003
GB	33	MCA MCF 2716
GE	33	MCA MAPS 7999
JA	33	MCA MCS 8082
JA	33	MCA VIM 7274 (1981 reissue of MCS 8082)
US	45	MCA 40439
JA	45	MCA VIM 1024
US	33	MCA 6114 (Theme on Themes from E.T. and More/ Walter Murphy Orch.) nst
US	33	RCA APL1-1379 (Theme on Henry Mancini Conducts the London Symphony Orchestra in a Concert of Film Music) nst
FR	33	Arabella MCA 204880 (1 band on 12 Terrifiantes Bandes Originales de Films)
GB	33	Ronco RTD 2036 (1 band on Cinema and Broadway Gold, 2/lp, 1979) nst
GB	33	Music for Pleasure MFP-50248 (Theme on Big Terror Movie Themes/Geoff Love Orch.) nst
IT	33	Cinevox CIA 5014 (1 band on Squalo-Exorcista e Altri Film Della Paura)

Jaws 2 (John Williams, 1978)
Les Dents de la Mer II/Der Weiss Hai II

US	33	MCA 3045
FR	33	Barclay/MCA 511 004
GB	33	MCA MCF 2847
JA	33	MCA VIM 7232
JA	33	MCA VIM 7286 (reissue of VIM 7232)
FR	33	Arabella MCA 204880 (1 band on 12 Terrifiantes Bandes Originales de Films)

Jaws 3D (Alan Parker, 1983)

US	33	MCA 6124
GB	33	MCA MCF 3194
IT	33	Ricordi MCA 4193
JA	33	MCA VIM 7293

Jetsons, The (Hoyt Curtin, 1962, tv)

US	33	Hanna-Barbera 2037
US	33	Columbia COL 13903 (Jetsons--First Family on the Moon, w/d)

Joe 90 (Barry Gray, 1968, tv)

GB	33	Contour 2870 185 (Theme on Children's TV Themes/ Cy Payne Orch., 1973) nst
GB	33	PRT DOW 3 (Theme on No Strings Attached/Barry Gray Orch., 1981) nst
GB	33	RK RKLB 1003 (1 band on Roald Dahl's Tales of the Unexpected and Other Themes/Ron Grainer Orch., 1980) nst

GB   45   PRT 7P 216 (Theme, r/r Barry Gray Orch.) nst

Jonathan Livingston Seagull (Neil Diamond & Lee Holdridge, 1974)
  US   33   Columbia KS 32550
  JA   33   CBS SOPO-1
  US   33   Varese Sarabande VC 81081 (suite on Film Music/Lee
            Holdridge, 1979) nst

Journey Back to Oz (S. Cahn, J. Van Heusen, 1971)
  Return to Oz
  US   33   R.F.O. 101 (b/r)
  US   45   Filmation FM 017
  US   33   Texize S 7243 (w/d; promo release)

Journey to the Center of the Earth, A (Bernard Herrmann, songs
            by Van Heusen, 1959)
  US   33   London Phase-4 SP 44107 (7 bands on The Fantasy
            Film World of Bernard Herrmann, r/r B. Herrmann,
            1974) nst
  US   33   London CSL 1001 (promo release of SP 44107, 1974)
  US   33   Bearsville BR 6965 (1 band on Ra/Utopia; rock ver-
            sion) nst
  US   45   Dot 16006 (song)
  US   ep   Dot 1091 (3 songs)

Journey to the Far Side of the Sun (Barry Gray, 1969)
  Doppelganger
  GB   33   United Artists UAG 30281 (suite, r/r B. Gray, on
            Musical Highlights from Filmharmonic '79, 1980) nst

Jubilee (Brian Eno & others, 1978)
  US   33   Antilles AN 7070 (1 band on Music for Films/Brian
            Eno)
  GB   33   Polydor Deluxe 2302 079

Juliet of the Spirits (Nino Rota, 1965)
  Giulietta Degli Spiriti
  US   33   Mainstream S/56062
  US   33   Lumiere L 1000 (p/r reissue of S/56062)
  FR   33   Pema Music/Cam FMC 500.001 (reissue of S/56062
            with extra music)
  IT   33   Cam CDR 33-2
  IT   33   Cam SAG 9053 (1 band on Tutti i Film di Fellini,
            1973)
  IT   33   RCA NL-33204 (1 band on La Dolce Vita and Other
            Celebrated Films by Fellini)
  US   33   Mainstream S/56063 (1 band on Great Original Sound-
            tracks and Movie Themes)

Jungle Book, The (Miklos Rozsa, 1942)
  US   78   RCA DM-905 (3/lp)

US   33   RCA LM 2118 (w/d, 1 side only, 1957)
US   33   Sound/Stage SS-2308 (same version as LM 2118 on
          Side 1 of The Film World of Miklos Rozsa, b/r, 1975)
US   33   RCA ARL1 0911 (1 band on Spellbound: The Classic
          Film Scores of Miklos Rozsa, r/d Charles Gerhardt,
          1975) nst
US   33   Entr'Acte ERM 6002 (suite, r/r Victory Symphony
          Orch., w/d)

Jupiter Menace, The (Larry Fast & Synergy, 1982)
   US   33   Passport PB 6014

Kamikaze 1989 (Edgar Froese, 1982)
   GB   33   Virgin V2255
   IT   33   Virgin VIL 12255

Killer Fish (Guido & Maurizio De Angelis, 1979)
   Agguata Sul Fondo
   IT   33   Ricordi ATV ATVL 2501

King Kong (Max Steiner, 1933)
   US   78   Allied Artists 1001 (limited release)
   US   33   Decca DL-79079 (suite on 50 Years of Movie Music from
             Flickers to Widescreen/Jack Shaindlin, 1960's) nst
   US   33   MSMS Del/F 25410 (1 band on Max Steiner: The
             RKO Years 1932-1935, p/r)
   US   33   United Artists UALA 373 G (r/r Leroy Holmes, 1975)
             nst
   US   33   Entr'acte ERS 6504 (r/r Fred Steiner, 1976) nst
   US   33   RCA ARL1-0136 (8 min. suite on Now Voyager: The
             Film Scores of Max Steiner, r/r Charles Gerhardt,
             1973) nst
   FR   33   MFP 2M 046-96966 (1 band on Musiques de Films
             d'Horreur et de Catastrophes/Geoff Love Orch.)
             nst

King Kong (John Barry, 1976)
   US   33   Reprise MS 2260
   GB   33   Reprise REP 54090
   IT   33   Reprise W 54090
   JA   33   Tam YX 7032 (has 1 extra band not on other lp's)
   JA   45   Tam YT 4010
   US   45   MCA 40669 (theme, r/r Roger Williams) nst

King Kong Escapes (Akira Ifukube, 1967)
   Kingu Kongu No Gyakushu
   JA   33   Toho AX 8123 (4 bands on Fantasy World of Japanese
             Pictures, part 4, 1978)
   JA   33   StarChild K22G 7116 (Excerpts on S.F. Film Themes,
             Vol. 6, 1983)
   JA   33   King K22G 7051 (3 bands on Akira Ifukube Movie
             Themes, vol. 9, 1982)

King Kong Vs. Godzilla (Akira Ifukube, 1963)
   Kingu Kongu Tai Gojira
   JA   33   Toho AX 8100 (4 bands on Godzilla, 1978)
   JA   33   Toho AX 8112 (3 bands on Godzilla, vol. 2, 1979)
   JA   33   Toho AX 8147 (1 band on Godzilla, vol. 3, 1980)
   JA   33   Toho AX 8082 (1 band on Works of Akira Ifukube,
            1978)
   JA   33   StarChild K22G 7112 (Excerpts on S.F. Film Themes,
            Vol. 2, 1983)
   JA   33   King K22G 7046 (3 bands on Akira Ifukube Movie
            Themes, vol. 4, 1982)

Kingdom of the Spiders (various library music used, 1977)
   US   33   Poo LP 106 (1 band, originally scored for The Twi-
            light Zone tv episode "Back There" by Jerry Gold-
            smith, on Great Fantasy Film Music, b/r, 1979)

Kiss Me Deadly (Frank De Vol, 1955)
   US   45   Capitol 3136 (nfd) nst

Kiss of the Vampire (James Bernard, 1963)
   Kiss of Evil
   US   33   Poo LP 104 (1 band on Great S.F. Film Music, w/fx,
            b/r, 1978) nst
   FR   33   MFP 2M 046-96966 (same band on Musiques de Films
            d'Horreur et de Catastrophe/Geoff Love Orch., w/
            fx) nst

Kiss the Girls and Make Them Die (Mario Nascimbene, 1967)
   Operazione Paradiso
   IT   45   Parade PRC 5013

Kolossal (Nico Fidenco, 1977)
   IT   45   Beat BTF 101

Kriminal (R. Pregadio, nfd)
   IT   45   Beat 45-BT-024

Kronos (Paul Sawtell & Bert Shefter, 1957)
   US   33   Poo LP 104 (1 band on Great S.F. Film Music, b/r,
            1978)

Krull (James Horner)
   US   33   Southern Cross SCRS 1004
   JA   33   Victor VIP 28079

Kwaidan (Toru Takemitsu, 1964)
   JA   33   JVC Victor SJX 7504 (1 album side on Works of Toru
            Takemitsu)
   JA   33   Victor VIP 1062 (1 band on Film Music of Toru Take-
            mitsu, vol. 1, 1980)
   JA   33   Victor KVX 1002 (reissue of VIP 1062)

Land of the Giants (John Williams, tv, 1968)
   US   33   GNP Crescendo GNPS 2163 (Theme on Greatest S.F.
             Hits III/Neil Norman, 1983) nst

Land of the Minotaur (Brian Eno, 1976)
   US   33   Antilles AN-7070 (4 bands on Music for Films/Brian
             Eno)
   GB   33   Polydor 2310-623 (same as AN-7070)

Last Dinosaur, The (Maury Laws, 1977)
   JA   45   Capitol ECR 20311

Last Judgement, The (Alessandro Cicognini, 1961)
   Il Giudizio Universale
   US   33   RCA FSO-4 (1 band on Original Soundtracks Re-
             corded in Italy)

Last War, The (Ikuma Dan, 1960)
   Dai Sanji Sekai Taisen - Yonju - Ichi Jikan No Kyofu
   JA   33   Toho AX 8123 (5 bands on Fantasy World of Japanese
             Pictures, part 4, 1978)

Last Year at Marienbad (Francis Seyrig, 1961)
   L'année Dernière à Marienbad
   FR   ep   Philips 432.700 (5 bands)
   US   33   Warner Bros. W-1548 (1 band on International Film
             Festival/Werner Mueller Orch.) nst

Latitude Zero (Akira Ifukube, 1969)
   Ido Zero Daisakusen
   JA   33   Toho AX 8108 (2 bands on Fantasy World of Japanese
             Pictures, part 3, 1948)
   JA   33   King K22G 7050 (4 bands on Akira Ifukube Movie
             Themes, vol. 8, 1982)

Legend of Cyrius (Uncredited, 1981)
   JA   33   Warner Bros. L-12501

Legend of Dinosaurs and Monster Birds (Masao Yagi, 1977)
   Kyoryu--Kaicho No Densetsu
   JA   33   Bourbon BMA-1001

Legend of Lylah Care, The (Frank DeVol, 1968)
   US   45   MGM K-13990

Legend of the White Serpent (Ikuma Dan, 1956)
   Byakufujin No Yoren
   JA   33   Toho AX 8123 (3 bands on Fantasy World of Japanese
             Pictures, part 4, 1978)

Leo, the King of the Jungle (Isao Tomita, 1966, tv)
   JA   33   Columbia CS 7015

Leonor (Ennio Morricone, 1977)
   FR   33   General Music 803 009 (1 band/nfd)

Lifespan (Terry Riley, 1973)
   FR   33   Stop Records ST 1011

Liquid Sky (S. Tsukerman, B. Hutchinson, C. Smith, 1983)
   US   33   Varese Sarabande STV 81181

Lisa and the Devil (Carlo Savina, 1975)
   La Casa Dell'exorcismo/House of Exorcism
   IT   33   Philips L6444 504

Lisztomania (Rick Wakeman, 1975)
   US   33   A&M 4546

Little Girl Who Lives Down the Lane, The (Christian Gaubert,
        1977)
   JA   33   Polydor MPF 1087
   JA   45   Philips SFL 2170 (2 bands not on the lp)

Little Mermaid, The (Ron Goodwin, 1966)
   CA   33   Capitol SQ 6417

Little Norse Prince, The (uncredited, 1969)
   Adventures of Hols, Prince of the Sun
   JA   33   Columbia CA 7020-21 (2/lp, w/d)

Little Prince, The (Lerner & Lowe, 1973)
   US   33   ABC 854

Little Prince and the Eight-Headed Dragon, The (Akira Ifukube,
        1963)
   Wanpaku Oji No Orochitaiji
   JA   33   Toho AX 8124 (19 bands on Fantasy World of Japanese
        Pictures, part 5, 1978)

Little Shop of Horrors (Fred Katz, 1960)
   US   33   Rhino RNSP-304 (1984)

Littlest Angel, The (Liam O'Kun, 1967, tv)
   US   33   Mercury SRM 1603

Live and Let Die (George Martin, 1973)
   US   33   United Artists UA-LMAS-100
   US   45   Paramount PAA-0230 (theme, r/r Frank Pourcel
        Orch.) nst
   GB   33   Ronco RTD 2036 (1 band on Cinema & Broadway Gold,
        2/lp, 1979) nst
   Foreign additions also (nfd)

Locke the Superman III (various, 1982)
    JA   33   Columbia CX 7059
    JA   33   Columbia CX 7084

Logan's Run (Jerry Goldsmith, 1976)
    US   33   MGM MG1-5302
    JA   33   MGM MMF 1006
    US   45   MGM M1 4848
    JA   45   MGM DMQ 6001

Logan's Run (Laurence Rosenthal, 1977, tv)
    GB   33   MFP 50375 (1 band/nfd)

Long Hair of Death, The (Carlo Rustichelli, 1964)
    I Lunghi Capelli Della Morte
    IT   45   Cam CDR 45.14

Looker (Barry De Vorzon, 1981)
    US   45   Warner Bros. WBS 49851

Lord of the Flies (Raymond Leppard, 1963)
    US   33   Ava AS 30 (2 bands on Lord of the Flies and Other
                Themes/Elmer Bernstein & Eliot Lawrence Orch.,
                1963) nst
    US   33   London PS 347 (1 band on Best of the New Film
                Themes/Frank Chacksfield Orch.) nst
    US   33   MGM SE-4192 (1 band on The Prize/Eliot Lawrence
                Orch., 1963) nst

Lord of the Rings (Leonard Rosenman, 1978)
    Il Signore Degli Anelli
    US   33   Fantasy LOR-1 (2/lp)
    CA   33   Fantasy 2160 1111 (2/lp)
    IT   33   Fonit Cetra LPD 1001 (2/lp)
    JA   33   Victor VIP 9561-62 (w/lp)
    US   33   Fantasy LOR-PD2 (2/lp, picture disc version)

Lost Horizon (Dimitri Tiomkin, 1937)
    US   10" Decca DL 5154 (w/d Ronald Coleman narration)
    US   33   RCA ARL1-1669 (16 bands on Lost Horizon: The
                Classic Film Scores of Dimitri Tiomkin, r/r Charles
                Gerhardt, 1976) nst
    US   33   Coral CRL 57006 (Theme on Movie Themes from Hol-
                lywood/Dimitri Tiomkin Orch.) nst
    GB   33   RCA RL 42317 (same as ARL1-1669; 1977) nst

Lost Horizon (Burt Bacharach, 1973)
    US   33   Bell 1300
    US   33   Colgems LH-1 (has alternate first track; blue vinyl
                pressing)

Lost in Space (John Williams, 1965, tv)
    US   33   GNP Crescendo GNPS 2163 (2 themes on Greatest S.F.
                    Hits III/Neil Norman Orch., 1983) nst
    US   45   GNP Crescendo GNP 828 (1 band/Neil Norman Orch.,
                    1983) nst

Love at First Bite (Charles Bernstein, plus disco songs, 1979)
    Amore al Primo Morso/Le Vampire de Ces Dames
    US   33   Parachute RRLP 9016
    FR   33   Vogue PIP PC 51010
    GB   33   Parachute RRL 2008
    JA   33   Parachute FML 128

Lovers of Teruel, The (Mikis Theodorakis, 1962)
    Les Amants de Teruel
    FR   ep   Philips 432.790 (5 bands)

Lucifer Rising (Bobby Beausoleil, 1982)
    US   33   Lethal Records (private release, nfd)

Lucky Luke (Claude Bolling, 1971)
    FR   33   United Artists 29290

Lucky Luke, La Ballade des Dalton (Claude Bolling, 1978)
    FR   33   RCA PL 37195

Lupin III (Ugi Ono, 1977)
    JA   33   Satril YP-7071 (LP 1)
    JA   33   Satril YP-7072 (LP 2)
    JA   33   Satril YP-7073 (LP 3)
    JA   45   Satril YK-95
    JA   33   Columbia CX 7013 (Volume 2)
    JA   33   Columbia CX 7026 (Music only, 2nd series)
    JA   33   Columbia CX 7079 (w/d)
    JA   33   Columbia CX 7074 (The Castle of Kariosutoro, w/d)
    JA   33   Columbia CX 7090 (The Castle of Kariosutoro, music
                    only)
    JA   33   Columbia CZ 7153/4 (Castle of Kariosutoro, 2/lp, w/d)

Lust for a Vampire (Harry Robinson, 1970)
    GB   45   (Love Theme, "Strange Love," on 45-rpm single,
                    nfd)

MacBeth (Paul Buckmaster, 1971)
    GB   33   EMI SHSP 4019 (performed by The Third Ear Band)

Macross--Super Time Fortress (Kentaro Haneda, 1983, tv)
    JA   33   Victor JBX 25008
    JA   33   Victor JBX 25013 (Vol. 2)
    JA   33   Columbia CX 7098 (Synthesizer Fantasy Macross)
    JA   33   Victor 45004/5 (Vol. 5/Rhapsody in Love, 2/lp, one
                    disc is w/d)

Mad Max (Brian May, 1980)
```
US  33  Varese Sarabande STV 81144
FR  33  SPI Milan A 120 143
JA  45  Blow Up LK 123 (r/r Yasumori) nst
FR  33  Milan A-120-157 (3 bands on Horror and Science Fic-
            tion, 1982)
```

Maddalena (Ennio Morricone, 1971)
```
IT  33  General Music ZSLGE 55063
IT  45  General Music ZGE-50243
IT  33  RCA DPSL 10599 (1 band on Un Film, Una Musica, 2/
            lp, 1973)
IT  45  ZT 7013
HO  45  Negram 207
FR  45  Pathe MC 052.994 63
FR  45  Negram 99463
GB  45  PVT 148
GE  45  Ariola 101141-100
IT  33  Ricordi SMRL 6098 (vocal version of theme, "Chi
            Mai" on Dedicato a Milva)
IT  33  General Music GML 10011 (1 band/nfd)
IT  33  General Music ZSLGE 55064 (2 bands on Colori)
IT  33  RCA NL 33079 (1 band/nfd)
```

Madeline ... Anatomia di Un Incubo (Maurizio Vandelli, 1974)
```
IT  33  Ariston 12124
```

Magic Christian, The (Ken Thorne & others)
```
US  33  Commonwealth United 6004 (w/d)
```

Magic Flute, The (Classical--Mozart, 1976)
```
US  33  A&M SP-4577
```

Magic Man, The (Ennio Morricone, 1972, tv)
L'Uomo e La Magia/Mysticae
```
IT  33  Cometa CMT-1 (p/r, 1976)
IT  33  Cometa CMT 1003/11 (1 band on I Per Tetto Un Cielo
            di Stelle, 1979)
IT  33  General Music GMS 0014 (1 band/nfd)
IT  45  General Music FMS-004 (song version, sung by Rocky
            Roberts)
```

Magic Pony, The (Tom Ed Williams, 1977)
```
US  33  West End WE 102
```

Majin, Monster of Terror (Akira Ifukube, 1966)
Daimajin/Majin, The Hideous Idol
```
JA  33  Columbia CX 7019
JA  33  Toho AX 8082 (1 band on Works of Akira Ifukube,
            1978)
JA  33  Toho AX 8125 (9 bands on Fantasy World of Japanese
```

Pictures, part 6, 1979)
JA   33   King K22G 7050 (3 bands on Akira Ifukube Movie
                 Themes, vol. 8, 1982)

Majin Strikes Again (Akira Ifukube, 1966)
  Daimajin Gyakushu
JA   33   Toho AX 8125 (4 bands on Fantasy World of Japanese
                 Pictures, part 6, 1979)
JA   33   King K22G 7050 (2 bands on Akira Ifukube Movie
                 Themes, vol. 8, 1982)

Malevil (Gabriel Yared, 1981)
FR   33   RCA PSL 1089

Malpertuis (George Delerue, 1972)
FR   33   Sofrason Decca 900 411 (1 side only, p/r, 1979)

Mama Dracula (Roy Budd, 1981)
FR   33   WEA 58251

Man Called Flintstone, A (Ted Nichols & John McCarthy, 1966)
US   33   Hanna-Barbara HLP 2055

Man from U.N.C.L.E., The (Jerry Goldsmith, Gerald Fried, Robert
                 Drasnin, Walter Scharf, Lalo Schifrin, Morton Stev-
                 ens, tv, 1964)
US   33   RCA LPM/LSP 3475
GB   33   RCA RD 7758 (same as LPM/LSP 3475)
US   33   RCA LPM/LSP 3574 (More Music from...)
GB   33   RCA RD 7832 (same as LPM/LSP 3574)
US   33   GNP Crescendo GNPS 2166 (Theme on Secret Agent
                 File/Various, 1984) nst
US   33   Leo CH-1023 (Theme on The Amazing TV Themes/nfd)
US   33   Audio Fidelity 2146/6146 (theme only/nfd)
US   33   Camden (S)927 (theme only/nfd)
US   33   London 44077 (theme only/nfd)
US   33   Metro (S) 544 (theme only/nfd)
US   33   Metro (S)565 (theme only/nfd)
US   33   Verve (6)8624 (theme only/nfd)

Man in the White Suit, The (Benjamin Frankel, 1951)
US   33   Citadel CT-OFI-1 (1 band on The Golden Age of
                 British Film Music, p/r)

Man-Made Monster (Hans J. Salter, 1941)
US   33   Citadel CT 6026 (Excerpts incorporated into "Horror
                 Rhapsody" on Music for Frankenstein, Dracula, The
                 Mummy, The Wolf Man and Other Old Friends, p/r,
                 1978)
US   33   Citadel CT 7012 (reissue of CT 6026 as Horror Rhap-
                 sody, 1979)

FR   33   Decca 900 411 (reissue of CT 6026 as Horror Rhap-
          sody/Malpertuis, 1979)

Man of a Thousand Faces (Frank Skinner, 1957)
US   33   Decca DL-8623 (1957)
US   33   Varese Sarabande STV-81121 (1981 reissue)
US   45   Decca 9-30433 (theme, r/r Bill Snyder)

Man with the Golden Gun, The (John Barry, 1975)
US   33   United Artists UA-LA358-G
Foreign pressings also (nfd)

Maniac (Jay Chattaway, 1981)
US   33   Varese Sarabande STV 81143
FR   33   Milan A-120-151
IT   33   Cinevox MDF 33/143
FR   33   Milan A-120-157 (2 bands on Horror and Science Fic-
          tion, 1982)

Marnie (Bernard Herrmann, 1964)
US   33   Sound/Stage 2306 (b/r, red vinyl edition, 1974)
US   33   Crimson CR-101 (contains music not on 2306; b/r,
          1979)
US   33   London Phase-4 SP-44126 (suite on Music for the
          Great Movie Thrillers, r/r B. Herrmann, 1973) nst
US   45   Capitol 5219 (nst)
JA   33   London K28P 4002 (1980 reissue of SP-44126) nst

Martin (Donald Rubinstein, 1976)
US   33   Varese Sarabande VC 81127

Master and Margarita, The (Ennio Morricone 1971)
Le Maitre et Margurite/Il Maestro e Margherita/The Teacher and
          Margaret
FR   45   RCA OC 27
IT   45   RCA 4-1142
IT   33   RCA DPSL 10599 (1 band on Un Film, Una Musica, 2/
          lp, 1973)
FR   33   RCA 461011 (1 band on Les Bandes Sonores de Ses
          Films, vol. 2)
FR   33   RCA LPK 10564 (1 band/nfd)
FR   33   RCA PL-31279 (1 band on Coffret, 1977)
FR   33   RCA CL 31559 (Excerpts on Ennio Morricone Master-
          pieces, 2/lp)

Master of the World (Les Baxter, 1961)
US   33   VeeJay LP 4000
US   33   Varese Sarabande VC 81070 (reissue of LP 4000)
US   33   Cinema LP 8005 (1 band on Destination Moon and Oth-
          er Themes, b/r, 1974)

Matchless (Ennio Morricone, Piero Piccioni & Gino Marinuzzi, 1967)
      IT   33   Cometa 1015/20 (p/r)

Mazinger Z (William Saylor, C. Watanabe, 1978, tv)
      JA   33   Columbia CS 7056
      JA   33   Columbia CZ 7005 (w/d in English, boxed edition)
      JA   33   Columbia CS 7097 (Hit Themes, songs only)
      JA   33   Animex 7133 (music only--Watanabe, 1983)

Medium, The (Gian-Carlo Menotti, 1951)
      US   33   Mercury MGL-7 (w/d, 2/lp; opera)

Megaforce (Jerrold Immel, 1982)
      US   45   Boardwalk NB7 11 146 (r/r by "707") nst
      JA   45   Boardwalk 07SP 636 (r/r by "707") nst

Men Into Space (David Rose, 1959, tv)
      US   33   RCA LPM 2180 (theme on Double Impact/Buddy Mor-
                   row Orch.) nst

Message from Space (Ken-Ichiro Morioka, 1978)
      JA   33   Columbia CQ 7004 (Symphonic Suite)
      JA   45   Columbia CK 510
      US   33   Poo LP 106 (1 band on Great Fantasy Film Music, b/
                   r, 1979)

Meteor (Laurence Rosenthal, 1979)
      JS   33   Seven Seas FML 122
      JA   33   Seven Seas FML 129 (reissue of FML 122)
      JA   33   Seven Seas FML 131 (1 band on Soundtrack 1980)
      JA   33   Seven Seas GXC 6161 (1 band on All About Newest
                   Screen Themes)
      JA   33   Seven Seas K16P 4033 (1 band on S.F. and Spectacle
                   Themes)
      US   33   CBA IM 35876 (1 band on Music from the Galaxies/
                   Ettore Stratta) nst

Midnight (Quintessence, 1982)
      US   33   Traq TR-114

Milpitas Monster, The (Robert Berry, 1976)
      US   45   Janel 3876A (p/r; theme songs)

Miracle, The (Elmer Bernstein, 1959)
      US   33   FMC 2 (8 bands on The Miracle/Toccata for Toy
                   Trains, r/r E. Bernstein, 1974) nst

Miracle on 34th Street (Ken Ascher, 1956)
      Meet Mr. Kringle
      US   45   Columbia 4-41532 (1 band)

Mission in Outer Space, "Srungle" (Masayuki Yamamoto, 1982)
    JA   33   Victor JBX 25015

Mister Ed (uncredited, 1962, tv)
    US   33   Colpix CP-209 (w/d)

Mighty Atom (score: T. Takai; effects: Matsuo Ohno, 1963-66,
                tv)
    Iron Arms Atom
    JA   33   Teichiku BH 3016
    JA   33   Victor SJX 2183 (Mighty Atom--Roots of Electronic
                Sound; effects only)

Mighty Atom (various, 1980-81, tv)
    JA   33   For Life 25K 1 (songs only)

Mr. Sycamore (Maurice Jarre, 1974)
    US   45   PFW 92575 (promo release)
    US   33   Centurion CLP 1600 (1 band on Filmusic, b/r, 1978)

Mobile Suit Gundam (tv; Wakiko Fukuda & Tetsuo Takai, 1980 epi-
                sodes; Chumei Watanabe & Matsuyama, 1981 episodes;
                aka feature: Gundam I, II, III; 1981-82)
    JA   33   King SKD 2005
    JA   33   King K25G 7001 (Symphonic Poem Gundam)
    JA   33   King K25G 7017 (Gundam Original Suite, vol. 1)
    JA   33   King K25G 7018 (Gundam Original Suite, vol. 2)
    JA   33   King K20G 7019/20 (Gundam Drama, w/d, 2/lp)
    JA   33   King K25G 7029 (pop instr. and songs)
    JA   33   Columbia CX-7077 (Piano Suite Gundam/Yamato) nst
    JA   33   King K25G 7090 (Best of Gundam)
    JA   33   Columbia CX-7076 (Digital Trip Mobile Suit Gundam)
    JA   33   King SKD 2015 (Gundam at Battlefield)
    JA   33   King K25G 7029 (Gundam II)
    JA   33   King K20G 7030/31 (Gundam II, w/d, 2/lp)
    JA   33   King K25G-7071 (Gundam III)
    JA   33   King K20G 7072/73 (Gundam III, w/d, 2/lp)
    JA   33   King SKK 2136/7 (Gundam III, 2/lp)
    JA   45   King TV(SH) 57

Moby Dick (Philip Sainton, 1956)
    JA   33   RCA LPM 1247
    US   33   Movie Music MM-5146 (reissue of LPM 1247, p/r)

Modern Problems (Dominic Frontiere, 1981)
    US   45   Capitol 5091

Modern Times (Charles Chaplin, 1936)
    US   33   United Artists 4049 (stereo: 5049e; 1959)
    US   33   United Artists UAS-5222 (reissue of 4049)

The Mole People (Hans J. Salter, and others, 1956)
    Le Peuple de L'enfer
    US   33   Coral CRL 757240 (1 band on Themes from Horror
                    Movies/Dick Jacobs Orch.) nst
    US   33   Varese Sarabande VC 81077 (remastered 1978 reissue
                    of CRL 757240 as Themes from Classic S.F., Fantasy
                    & Horror Films) nst
    FR   33   MCA 410.064 (reissue of VC 81077)
    FR   33   MCA VIM 7264 (reissue of VC 81077)

The Monster Club (various, 1981)
    GB   33   Chips CHILP 2

Monster from a Prehistoric Planet (Seitaro Omori, 1967)
    Daikaiju Gappa/Gappa, Triphibian Monster
    JA   33   Toho AX 8124 (1 band on Fantasy World of Japanese
                    Pictures, part 5, 1978)

Monster Zero (Akira Ifukube, 1965)
    Kaiju Daisenso
    JA   33   Toho AX 8100 (2 bands on Godzilla, 1978)
    JA   33   Toho AX 8112 (2 bands on Godzilla, vol. 2, 1979)
    JA   33   StarChild K22G 7115 (Excerpts on S.F. Film Themes,
                    vol. 5, 1983)
    JA   33   Columbia CX 7020 (Excerpts on Godzilla Original Back-
                    ground Music, vol. 1, 1982)
    JA   33   King K22G 7049 (3 bands on Akira Ifukube Movie
                    Themes, vol. 7, 1982)

Moonbase 3 (Dudley Simpson, 1973, tv)
    GB   33   BBC REH 188 (1 band on Original Music from Great
                    BBC TV Shows)
    GB   33   BBC REH 324 (1 band on BBC Space Themes, 1979)

Moon Pilot (Paul Smith, 1962)
    US   45   Vista 392

Moonraker (John Barry, 1979)
    US   33   United Artists UALA 971-1
    FR   33   Sonopresse/UA 2S 068 82696
    GB   33   United Artists UAG 302247
    IT   33   EMI 054 82696
    JA   33   United Artists FML 125
    US   33   CBS IM 35876 (1 band on Music from the Galaxies/
                    Ettore Stratta, 1980) nst
    US   33   GNP Crescendo GNPS 2166 (1 band on Secret Agent
                    File/Various, 1984) nst
    JA   33   Seven Seas FML 131 (1 band on Soundtrack 1980)
    JA   33   Warner Bros. P13002 W (same as IM 35876) nst

More Than a Miracle (Piero Piccioni, 1966)
    C'era Una Volta/Once Upon a Time

US   33   MGM SE 4515 ST
IT   33   WEA T 60834 (3 bands, 1 of which not on SE 4515
          ST, on Le Musiche di Piero Piccioni Per I Film di
          Francesco Rosi)

Mothra (Yuji Koseki, 1961)
  Mosura
  JA   33   Toho AX 8123 (3 bands on Fantasy World of Japanese
            Pictures, Part 4, 1978)
  JA   33   StarChild K22G 7112 (Excerpts on S.F. Film Themes,
            vol. 2, 1983)
  JA   33   Toho DR 1001 (Excerpts on Monster Themes, w/d)
  JA   45   King TV 41 (Aelinas' song, adapted by Akira Ifukube,
            1978) nst
  US   33   Poo LP 104 (song, different version, on Great S.F.
            Film Music, b/r, 1978)

The Mummy (Franz Reizenstein, 1959)
  US   45   Coral Q72-378 (music "inspired by film," performed
            by Bob McFadden) nst

The Mummy's Hand (Hans J. Salter & others, 1940)
  US   33   Citadel CT 6026 (Excerpts incorporated into "Horror
            Rhapsody" on Music for Frankenstein, Dracula, The
            Mummy, The Wolf Man and Other Old Friends, p/r,
            1978)
  US   33   Citadel CT 7012 (reissue of CT 6026 as Horror Rhap-
            sody, 1979)
  FR   33   Decca 900 411 (reissue of CT 6026 as Horror Rhap-
            sody/Malpertuis, 1979)

Munsters, The (Jack Marshall, 1964, tv)
  US   45   Coral 62436
  US   33   Golden LP 139 (w/d)

Muppet Movie, The (Paul Williams, 1979)
  US   33   Atlantic SD 16001
  GB   33   CBS 70170 (different cover)
  US   45   Atlantic 3610

Murder Clinic, The (Francesco De Masi as "Frank Mason," 1966)
  La Lama Nel Corpo
  IT   33   Cam CDR 33/18
  IT   45   Cam CDR 45 32

My Favorite Martian (George Greeley, 1963, tv)
  US   33   Warner Bros. 1529 (theme on Top TV Themes of 1964/
            Carl Brandt & Warner Bros. Orch.) nst

My Mother the Car (Paul Hampton, 1965, tv)
  US   33   Columbia 4-43585

My Son the Vampire (Linda Southworth, 1952)
  US   45   Warner Bros. 5419 (r/r Allan Sherman; song)

Mysterians, The (Akira Ifukube, 1957)
  JA   33   Toho AX 8106 (4 bands on Fantasy World of Japanese
                Pictures, part 1, 1978)
  JA   33   Toho AX 8082 (1 band on Works of Akira Ifukube,
                1978)
  JA   33   StarChild K22G 7120 (Excerpts on S.F. Film Themes,
                vol. 10, 1983)
  JA   33   King K22G 7044 (3 bands on Akira Ifukube Movie
                Themes, vol. 2, 1982)

Mysterious Big Tactics (Naozumi Yamamoto & Hiroki Tamai, 1978)
  JA   33   King SKK 2124 (w/d)

Mysterious Island (Bernard Herrmann, 1961)
  US   33   London Phase-4 SPC 21137 (5 bands on The Mysteri-
                ous Film World of Bernard Herrmann, r/r B. Herr-
                mann, 1975) nst

Mysterious Island of Captain Nemo (Gianni Ferrio, 1974)
    L'ile Mysterieuse e Capitaine Nemo/Isola Misteriosa e Capitano
                Nemo
  FR   33   RCA 461.013
  IT   33   Cinevox MDF 33/62

Necromancy (Fred Karger, 1972)
  US   45   Lunar 500 (1 band)

Never Say Never Again (Michel Legrand, 1983)
  US   45   A&M AM-2596 (theme song, sung by Lani Hall)
  JA   33   Seven Seas K28P 4122
  JA   45   A&M AMP 787
  GB   45   A&M AM 159

New Avengers, The (Laurie Johnson, 1978, tv)
  GB   33   Unicorn/Kanchana KPM 7009 (4 bands on The Aveng-
                ers, 1980)
  US   33   Starlog/Varese Sarabande ASV 95003 (same as KPM
                7009, 1982)
  GB   45   Unicorn/Kanchana C 15 (1980)
  GB   45   EMI 2562 (w/d)
  US   33   K-Tel BU 4780 (1 band on 20 Great TV Themes/
                Sounds Orch.) nst

Night Caller, The (Ennio Morricone, 1975)
    Peur Sur La Ville/El Poliziotto Della Brigata Criminale
  FR   33   Warner Bros. WP-56135
  FR   45   Warner Bros. 16549
  IT   45   CBS 3262

FR 33 General Music GML 10011 (1 band/nfd)
FR 33 WEA/General Music GM 803009 (1 band on Ennio Mor-
            ricone: Bandes Originales des Films, 1979)
FR 33 WEA/General Music 803004 (1 band on Ennio Morricone:
            Disque d'Or, 1979)

Night Child (Stelvio Cipriani, 1976)
    Perche!?
    IT 33 Cinevox MDF 074

Night Digger, The (Bernard Herrmann, 1971)
    US 33 Cinema LP 8015 (14 min. suite, r/r Hans Rossback,
                b/r, 1975)

Night Evelyn Came Out of the Grave, The (Bruno Nicolai, 1971)
    La Notte Che Evelyn Usca Dalla Tomba
    IT 33 Cam CMO 022 (2 bands on Giallo N.1/Ambiente-
                Movimento) p/r

Night Gallery--Episode: The Tune in Dan's Cafe (Hal Mooney,
                1971)
    US 45 Decca 32989

Night of the Blood Monster (Bruno Nicolai, 1972)
    Il Trono dei Fuoco/The Throne of Fire
    IT 33 Cinevox MDF 33/32

Night of the Hunter (Walter Schumann, 1955)
    US 33 RCA LPM-1136 (w/d, narration by Charles Laughton)
    AU 33 RCA LPM 1136 (reissue of above, 1983)

Night of the Living Dead (various, 1968)
    US 33 Varese Sarabande STV 81151 (1982)

Night Visitor, The (Henry Mancini, 1971)
    US 33 Citadel CT 6015 (16 min. suite, 1 side only, p/r,
                1977)

Night Walker, The (Vic Mizzy, 1964)
    US 45 Decca 31738 (theme, r/r Sammy Kaye)

Night Watch (John Cameron, 1973)
    US 45 Brut BR 807 (credits George Barrie)

Nightcomers, The (Jerry Fielding, 1971)
    US 33 Citadel CT-JF-1 (p/r)

Nightmare Castle (Ennio Morricone, 1965)
    Gli Amanti d'Oltre Tomba
    IT 33 RCA SP 10004 (4 bands on Drammatica e Musiche di
                Tensione Psicologica #1, p/r)

Nine Lives of Fritz the Cat, The (Tom Scott, 1974)
US   45   Ode 66048

1990--I Guerrieri del Bronx (Walter Rizzati, 1982)
IT   33   Beat LPF 062 (1983)

No Blade of Grass (Burnell Whibley, 1970)
US   45   Mark 276 (nst/nfd)
US   33   MGM SE 4761 (1 band, credited to Nelius/Carroll, on
Sweet Gingerbread Man/Mike Curb Congregation)
nst
JA   33   Mu-Land LZ 7016 M (1 band, credited by Nelius/Car-
roll, on S.F. Fact Vol. 1/Electoru Polyphonic Orch.,
1979) nst

Nocturna (Norman Bergen & Reid Whitelaw, 1979)
US   33   RCA PD 11442 (2/lp)

Nosferatu, The Vampire (Popol Vuh, 1979)
Nosferatu, Fantome de la Nuit/Bruder des Schattens-Sohne des
Lichts
FR   33   Egg 900 573 (40 mins. music in 10 bands)
IT   33   EMI PDY 7005 (34 mins. music in 4 bands, different
cover)
GE   33   Brain 0060.167 (different music and cover/nfd)

Nutcracker Fantasy (Tchaikovsky, 1979)
JA   33   Sanrio MQF 6001 (adapted by Wakatsuki & Haneda;
Kazuhiro Koizumi conducting New Nipon Philhar-
monic Orch.)

Obsession (Bernard Herrmann, 1976)
US   33   London Phase-4 SPC 21160
US   45   London 5N-90021-DJ (promo release)
JA   45   London FMS 45

Octopussy (John Barry, 1983)
US   33   A&M SP 4967
FR   33   A&M AMLX 64967
GB   33   A&M AMLX 64967
GE   33   A&M 64967
IT   33   A&M AMLX 64967
JA   33   A&M AMLX 64967
SP   33   Epic AM AMLX 64967
FR   45   CBS A&M AMS 9713 (incl. instrumental main theme not
on lp)
US   33   GNP Crescendo GNPS 2166 (1 band on Secret Agent
File/vairous, 1984) nst

Oh, Dad, Poor Dad, Mama's Hung You in the Closet and I'm Feeling So Sad (Neal Hefti)
US   33   RCA LPM 3750

Oh, God! (Jack Elliott, 1977)
   US   33   Springboard SPB 4093 (1 band on The Movie Hits,
            vol. 2/Film Festival Orch.) nst
   US   33   United Artists UA LA 908 H (1 band on You Light
            Up My Life/Ferrante & Teicher) nst

Olympus-7000 (Adler, tv, nfd)
   US   33   Command CS-07-SD

Omega Man, The (Ron Grainer, 1971)
   US   33   Poo LP 104 (1 band on Great S.F. Film Music, b/r,
            1978)
   GB   33   MFP 50375 (1 band on Close Encounters and Other
            Galactic Themes/Geoff Love Orch.)

The Omen (Jerry Goldsmith, 1975)
   US   33   Tattoo BJL1-1888
   GB   33   Tattoo 1-1888
   JA   33   RCA RVP 6097
   US   45   Tattoo JH 10741
   JA   45   RCA SS-3039
   GB   33   Decca PFS 4432 (11 min. suite on Satan Superstar/
            Stanley Black, 1978) nst
   JA   33   London GP 9051 (same as PFS 4432) nst
   IT   45   Philips SFL-2194 (theme, r/r Chris Carpenter) nst

Omicron (Piero Umiliani, 1963)
   IT   ep   Cam CEP 45 104 (6 bands)

On a Clear Day You Can See Forever (Burton Lane, 1970)
   US   33   Columbia S-30086 (songs)

On Her Majesty's Secret Service (John Barry, 1969)
   US   33   United Artists UAS 5204
   GB   33   United Artists 29040
   GB   33   United Artists 6002718 (Themes on The James Bond
            Collection)
   GB   33   CBS 22014 (Theme on The Music of John Barry, 2/lp)
   (Themes also on various r/r James Bond collections; other for-
            eign editions of full sound track, nfd)

On the Beach (Ernest Gold, 1960)
   US   33   Roulette SR 25098
   JA   33   Nippon Columbia GES 3670 (reissue of SR 25098)
   JA   33   Roulette SU 1016 (p/r reissue of SR 25098, 1980)
   US   33   London PS 320 (1 band on Film Themes of Ernest
            Gold/Gold conducts the London Symphony) nst
   US   33   London LL3320 (same as PS 320)
   US   45   Top Rack RA-2030 (Theme, r/r Ernest Masim) nst

1001 Arabian Nights (George Duning, 1960)
   US   33   Colpix SCP 410

US   33   Varese Sarabande VC 81138 (reissue of SCP 410)

One Step Beyond (Harry Lubin, 1959, tv)
    US   33   Decca DL 78970
    US   33   Varese Sarabande STV 81120 (reissue of DL 78970)
    US   45   Decca 31070

Onibaba (Hikaru Hayashi, 1965)
    The Hole
    JA   33   King SKD(M) 370-1 (1 band on Famous Japanese
                    Movies, 2/lp, 1976)
    JA   33   Toho AX 8065 (1 band on Works of Hikaru Hayashi,
                    1978)

Open Grave ... An Empty Coffin, An (Piero Picconi, 1982)
    Una Tomba Aperta ... Una Bara Vuota
    IT   33   Beat LPF 061 (1 band on I Film Della Paura, 1982)

Operation Kid Brother (Ennio Morricone & Bruni Nicolai, 1967)
    O.K. Connery
    IT   45   Parade PRC 5042

Orca, the Killer Whale (Ennio Morricone, 1978)
    JA   33   Tam YM-7036
    JA   45   Tam YT-4028
    FR   45   Philips 6172077
    JA   33   Seven Seas K16P-4033 (1 band on S.F. & Spectacle
                    Themes)

Original TV Adventures of King Kong, The (Maury Laws, 1966,
                    tv)
    US   33   Epic BN-26231e
    US   33   Epic LN-24125 (Theme on Music for Monsters, Mun-
                    sters, Mummies and Other TV Fiends/Milton DeLugg
                    Orch.) nst
    US   33   Leo CH-1023 (Theme on The Amazing TV Themes/nfd)

Orpheus (Georges Auric, 1949)
    Orphee
    FR   33   Vega C 30-A-98 (1 band on 25 Ans de Musique de
                    Cinema)

Orson Welles' Great Mysteries (John Barry, 1973, tv)
    GB   33   Polydor 2383 300 (Theme on Play It Again/John Barry
                    Orch.) nst
    JA   45   Polydor DPQ 6069

Our Mother's House (Georges Delerue, 1967)
    CA   33   MGM 4495
    CA   33   Polydor SE 4495 (1978 reissue)
    US   33   MGM 4495 (b/r reissue)

Outer Limits, The (Dominic Frontiere, 1963, tv)
   US   33   Epic LN-24125 (Theme on Music for Monsters, Mun-
               sters, Mummies and Other TV Fiends/Milton DeLugg
               Orch.) nst
   US   33   GNP Crescendo GNPS 2128 (Theme on Greatest S.F.
               Hits/Neil Norman Orch., 1979) nst

Outland (Jerry Goldsmith, 1981)
   US   33   Warner Bros. HS 3551
   GB   33   Warner Bros. K 5691
   GE   33   WEA 56921

Pajama Party (uncredited, 1964)
   US   33   Buena Vista BV-3325

Pandora and the Flying Dutchman (Alan Hawthorne, 1951)
   US   78   MGM 30352 (1 band, credited to Hubert Clifford, on
               78 single)

Partner (Ennio Morricone, 1974)
   Il Sosia/Le Partenaire
   IT   33   Cam SAG 9010 (5 bands/nfd)
   IT   45   Cam AMP 50

Patrick (U.S. release: Brian May, 1979)
   US   33   Varese Sarabande VC 81107
   FR   33   Milan A-120-157 (1 band on Horror and Science Fic-
               tion, 1982)

Patrick (IT. release: Goblin, 1979)
   IT   33   Cinevox MDF 33/133
   IT   33   Cinevox CIA 5014 (1 band on Squalo--Exorcista e Al-
               tri Film Della Paura)
   IT   33   Cinevox MDF 33/134 (1 band on Films in Musica, vol.
               5)
   FR   33   Polydor Cinevox 2393 327 (Excerpts on Les Meilleures
               Musiques de Films Fantastiques)

Paura Nella Citta' Dei Morti Viventi (Fabio Frizzi, 1982)
   Fear in the City of the Living Dead
   IT   33   Beat CR-11

Percy (Raymond Davies, 1971)
   GB   33   Pye NSPL 18365

Perfume of the Lady in Black, The (Nicola Piovani, 1977)
   IT   45   Beat BTF 087

Phantasm (Fred Myrow & Malcolm Seagrave, 1979)
   US   33   Varese Sarabande VC 81105
   GB   33   Gem GEMLP 102

JA   33   Seven Seas FML 127
FR   33   Milan A-120-157 (3 bands on <u>Horror and Science Fiction</u>, 1982)
JA   33   Seven Seas K18P4105 (1 band on <u>Horror Movie Special</u>, 1983)

Phantom of the Opera (uncredited, 1925)
US   33   Angel S-36073 (suite on <u>Sounds of Silents: Music for Silent Film</u>/Lee Erwin) <u>nst</u>
US   33   New World NW 227 (suite on <u>Mighty Wurlitzer--Music for Palace Organ</u>) <u>nst</u>

Phantom of the Opera (Edward Ward, 1943)
US   33   STK 114/2 (2/lp, w/d, complete soundtrack, 1980)
US   45   London 6015 ("Lullaby of the Bells," r/r, nfd) <u>nst</u>
US   78   London LA-7 (#121) ("Lullaby of the Bells" on <u>Music from the Films</u>/Mantovani, 1948) <u>nst</u>

Phantom of the Opera (Edwin Astley, 1962)
US   45   Coral CRL-62334 (film's operatic aria, sung by Heather Sears)

Phantom of the Paradise, The (Paul Williams, 1974)
US   33   A&M SP 3653
US   33   A&M SP 3176 (reissue of SP 3653)
IT   33   Slam 63653
US   45   A&M 1664

Phoenix (Jun Kukamachi; theme by Michel Legrand, 1978)
Hinotori/Firebird
JA   33   Alfa ALR-6008

Phoenix 2772 (Yasuo Higuchi, 1978)
Hinotori 2772--Ai No Cosmozone/Space Firebird
JA   33   Columbia CS-7042
JA   33   Columbia CS 7175/6 (2/lp, w/d)

Picnic at Hanging Rock (Bruce Smeaton & Gheorghe Zamfir, 1975)
          1975)
US   33   DRG 8202 (Excerpt on <u>Music from Great Australian Films</u>, 1982)
AU   33   Festival L37789 (2 bands on <u>Music from the Best of Australia's Films</u>, 1982)

Piranha (Pino Donaggio, 1978)
US   33   Varese Sarabande STV 81126

Piranha 2 (Stelvio Cipriani, 1982)
Piranha Paura/Piranha Fear
IT   33   Polydor 2060 261
IT   33   Polydor 2448-133
FR   33   General Music 803 040 (as "Steve Powder")

Pit and the Pendulum, The (Les Baxter, 1961)
   US 45   American Int'l AIP 609 (promo, w/d)

Plan 9 from Outer Space (Gordon Zahler, 1956)
   US 33   PLAN 9 (p/r, w/d 1983)

Planet of the Apes (Jerry Goldsmith, 1968)
   US 33   Project 3 PR5023SD
   JA 33   Mu-Land LZ 7017-M (1 band on S.F. Fact Vol. 2/
             Electoru Polyphonic Orch., 1979) nst
   JA 33   Seven Seas K16P-4033 (1 band on S.F. & Spectacle
             Themes) nst

Planet of the Apes (Lalo Schifrin, 1974, tv)
   US 45   20th Century-Fox TC 2150 (Theme, "Ape Shuffle,"
             r/r L. Schifrin) nst
   US 33   Wonderland WLP 301 ("Ape Shuffle" on Themes from
             Star Trek and Planet of the Apes/The Jeff Wayne
             Space Shuttle) nst

Point, The (Harry Nilsson, 1971)
   US 33   RCA LSPX 1003
   US 33   RCA AYL1 3811 (reissue of LSPX 1003)
   GB 33   MCA MCF 2826

Poltergeist (Jerry Goldsmith, 1982)
   US 33   MG-1-5408
   GB 33   MGM 2315 439
   IT 33   Polydor 2315 439
   JA 33   MGM 28MM 0182
   US 33   MCA 6114 (1 band on Themes from E.T. and More/
             Walter Murphy Orch.) nst

Popeye (Harry Nilsson, 1980)
   US 33   Boardwalk S 36880

Portrait of Jennie (score: D. Tiomkin; song: B. Herrmann, 1948)
   US 33   Columbia CL 612 (song on Soundstage: Hi-Fi Music
             from Hollywood/Paul Weston Orch.) nst

Power, The (Miklos Rozsa, 1968)
   US 33   Citadel CT-MR-1 (10 bands on Film Music: Miklos
             Rozsa, p/r, 1978)

Power, The (Chris Young, 1984)
   US 33   Cerberus CST 0211

Pranks (Chris Young, 1982)
   US 33   Citadel CT 7031

Prato, Il (Ennio Morricone, 1979)
   Le Prateria/The Meadow

IT   33   Cam SAG 9100
IT   33   Cam RSAG 9102 (1 band on <u>Ciak</u>)

President's Analyst, The (Lalo Schifrin, 1967)
  US   45   Dunhill 4116 (song, by Barry McGuire)

Prisoner, The (Ron Grainer, 1968, tv)
  US   33   GNP Crescendo 2163 (1 band on <u>Greatest S.F. Hits</u>
            <u>III</u>/Neil Norman Orch., 1983) <u>nst</u>
  US   33   GNP Crescendo GNPS 2166 (1 band on <u>Secret Agent</u>
            <u>File</u>/Various, 1984) <u>nst</u>

Prisoner of the Cannibal God (Guido & Maurizio De Angelis, 1978)
  La Montagna del Dio Cannibale/Slave of the Cannibal God
  IT   33   Cometa CMT 1007/19 (1 side only, 9 bands) p/r

Private Life of Sherlock Holmes (Miklos Rozsa, 1970)
  GB   33   Polydor Super 238440 (1 band on <u>Rozsa Conducts</u>
            <u>Rozsa</u>, r/r M. Rozsa, 1977) <u>nst</u>

Private Parts (Hugo Friedhofer, 1972)
  US   33   Delos DEL 25420 (15 min. suite on <u>Von Richtofen and</u>
            <u>Brown</u>/Private Parts, 1981)

Privilege (Mike Leander, 1967)
  US   33   Universal 73005

Prom Night (Carl Zittrer & Paul Zaza, 1980)
  JA   33   RPL 8089 (all disco songs)

Providence (Miklos Rozsa, 1977)
  FR   33   EMI 2C 066-14406
  FR   33   Pema 900.057 (reissue of 2C 066-14406)
  JA   33   Seven Seas FML 117
  US   33   DRG/STET SL 9502 (reissue of 2C 066-14406, 1981)
  US   33   Citadel CT 7004 (1 band on <u>Rozsa: Solo Works</u>)

Psycho (Bernard Herrmann, 1960)
  GB   33   Unicorn RHS 336 (r/r B. Herrmann, 1975) <u>nst</u>
  GB   33   Unicorn UN1-75001 (remastered reissue of <u>RHS</u> 336)
            <u>nst</u>
  IT   33   RCA NL 33224 (remastered reissue of RHS 336, 1981)
            <u>nst</u>
  US   33   London Phase-4 SP 44126 (suite on <u>Music from the</u>
            <u>Great Movie Thrillers</u>, r/r B. Herrmann, 1973) <u>nst</u>
  JA   33   London K28P 4002 (reissue of SP 44126, 1980) <u>nst</u>
  GB   33   Unicorn UN1-72015 (6 bands, partial reissue of UN1-
            75001)
  GB   33   Music for Pleasure MFP-50248 (1 band on <u>Big Terror</u>
            <u>Movie Themes</u>/Geoff Love Orch.) <u>nst</u>
  US   33   London SPC 21151 (Excerpts on <u>Herrmann Conducts</u>
            <u>Psycho and Others</u>, 1976)

Psycho Armor "Govarian" (Yano; tv, 1983)
   JA   33   StarChild K22G 7144
   JA   33   StarChild K22G 7173 (Vol. 2)

Psycho II (Jerry Goldsmith, 1983)
   US   33   MCA 6119
   GB   33   MCA MCF 3174
   IT   33   Ricordi MCA 4189
   JA   33   MCA VIM 7292

Pufnstuf (Charles Fox, 1970)
   US   33   Capitol SW-542

Q: The Winged Serpent (Robert O. Ragland, 1983)
   US   33   Ceberus CST-0206

Quatermass Experiment, The (various, incl. classical, 1979, tv)
   GB   33   BBC REH 324 (1 band on BBC Space Themes, 1979)
   GB   33   Decca SPA 580 (1 band on Classic TV Themes, 1980)
   GB   33   MFP 50355 (1 band on Star Wars and Other Space
                Themes/Geoff Love Orch.)
   Note: theme music used is Holst's The Planets ("Mars")

Queen Bee (Shinichi Tanabe, 1978)
   Joobachi
   JS   33   Toho AX 5018
   JA   45   Toho AT 4067

Queen Kong (I. Pepper, 1978)
   IT   45   Cam AMP 189

Queen Millenia (Kitaro, 1982)
   JA   33   Canyon C28G0124
   JA   33   Canyon 38G0135 (w/d)
   JA   33   Canyon C28G-0091 (Symphonic Suite)

Queens of Evil (A.F. Lavagnino, 1971)
   Le Regine/Il Delitto del Diavolo
   JA   33   Seven Seas SR 634
   JA   33   Seven Seas GXH 6032 (7 bands/nfd)

Quest for Fire (Philippe Sarde, 1982)
   La Guerre du Feu
   US   33   RCA ABL1-4724
   GB   33   RCA LP 6034
   FR   33   RCA PL 37581
   IT   33   RCA BL 37581
   JA   33   RCA RPL 8133

Quiet Place in the Country, A (Ennio Morricone, 1969)
   Un Tranquillo Posto di Campagna

IT   33   General Music GM 33/01-1/01-2 (1 band on <u>Musiche</u>
                <u>di Ennio Morricone</u>, 2/lp, p/r)

Raiders of the Lost Ark (John Williams, 1981)
Les Aventuriers de l'Arche Perdue
US   33   Columbia JS 37373
GB   33   CBS 70205
FR   33   CBS 70205
IT   33   CBS 70205
JA   33   CBS Sony 25AP 2093
US   33   CBS JS 37696 (<u>The Movie on Record</u>, w/d)
JA   33   Sony 28AP2255 (<u>The Movie on Record</u>, w/d)
US   33   Buena Vista 452 (7" 33-rpm children's single, story
                & music)
US   33   Phillips 6514 328 (1 band on <u>Aisle Seat--Great Film</u>
                <u>Music</u>/John Williams and Boston Pops, 1982) <u>nst</u>
US   33   MCA 6114 (1 band on <u>Themes from E.T. and More</u>/
                Walter Murphy) <u>nst</u>
US   33   GNP Crescendo 2163 (1 band on <u>Greatest S.F. Hits</u>
                <u>III</u>/Neil Norman Orch., 1983) <u>nst</u>

Rainbow Corps Robin (uncredited, nfd)
JA   33   Columbia CS 7073

Rashomon (Fumio Hayasaka, 1951)
JA   33   Victor KVX-1045 (1 side only, 1978) <u>nst</u>
US   33   Varese Sarabande STV 81142 (1 side only, 1984)
US   33   Reader's Digest RD4-141 (1 band on <u>Reader's Digest</u>/
                nfd)

Reincarnation of Peter Proud, The (Jerry Goldsmith, 1975)
Il Misterioso Caso di Peter Proud
IT   45   Cinevox MDF 089 (1 band, r/r Leon Herbert) <u>nst</u>
JA   45   RCA VIP 2215 (same as MDF 089, different cover)
US   33   Centurion CLP 1600 (same band on <u>Filmusic</u>, b/r,
                1978)

Repulsion (Chico Hamilton, 1965)
IT   33   Cam 1 (4 bands on <u>Repulsion/Notte di Terrore</u>)

Return of Dracula (Gerald Fried, 1958)
Curse of Dracula
US   33   Poo LP 104 (1 band on <u>Great S.F. Film Music</u>, b/r,
                1978)

Return of Majin (Akira Ifukube, 1966)
Daimajin Ikaru
JA   33   Toho AX 8125 (4 bands on <u>Fantasy World of Japanese</u>
                <u>Pictures, part 6</u>, 1979)

Return of the Giant Monsters (Tadashi Yamaguchi, 1967)
Gamera Tai Gaos/Gamera vs. Gaos
JA   33   Toho AX 8120 (3 bands on <u>Gamera</u>, 1978)
JA   33   Daiei KKS-4026 (Excerpts on <u>Gamera</u>, w/d, music &
                songs)

Return of the Jedi (John Williams, 1983)
Le Retour du Jedi

US   33   RSO 811 767-1 Y-1
FR   33   Polydor RSO 8117671
GB   33   RSO RSD-5023
GE   33   Polygram 8117671
JA   33   RSO 28MW 0031
NZ   33   RSO 811-767-1
SP   33   Polydor RSQ 811767 1
US   33   Buena Vista 63155 (picture disc edition)
US   33   Buena Vista 62103 (Story of.., w/d)
GB   33   Buena Vista S62103 (Story of..., w/d)
FR   33   Adés ST 3895F (w/d)
FR   45   Adés LLP 469 F (w/d)
US   33   RCA CRC1-4748 (digital version, r/r C. Gerhardt)
          nst
US   33   RCA XRL1-4867 (1 band, r/r C. Gerhardt, on Film
          Classics--Take 3, 1983) nst
US   33   Varese Sarabande 704.210 (6 bands on The Star Wars
          Trilogy/Varujan Kojin, 1983) nst
US   33   Philips 411 185-1 (4 bands on Out of This World/John
          Williams & Boston Pops, 1983) nst
US   33   GNP Crescendo GNPS 2163 (1 band on Greatest S.F.
          Hits III/Neil Norman Orch., 1983) nst
GE   33   Delta AS 19020 (1 band on Die Grossten Science Fic-
          tion Hits/Neil Norman, 2/lp, 1984) nst
JA   45   Warner Bros. P1791 (Theme, and "Lapti Nek" vocal)

Return of the King (Maury Laws, 1980, tv)
     Hibbito No Boken/The Hobbit II
     US   33   Disneyland 3822 (w/d)
     US   ep   Disneyland 382

Return of Ultraman (Fuyuki, 1982)
     JA   33   Columbia CZ 7142

Revenge of the Creature (Herman Stein, 1955)
     La Vengeance de la Creature
     US   33   Coral CRL 757240 (1 band on Themes from Horror
               Movies/Dick Jacobs Orch.) nst
     US   33   Varese Sarabande VC 81077 (remastered 1978 reissue
               of CRL 757240 as Themes from Classic S.F., Fantasy
               and Horror Films) nst
     FR   33   MCA 410.064 (reissue of VC 81077)
     JA   33   MCA VIM 7264 (reissue of VC 81077)

Ripper of New York, The (Francesco De Masi, 1982)
     Squartatore di New York
     IT   33   Beat LPD 055
     IT   33   Beat LPF 061 (Excerpts on I Filma Della "Paura",
               1982)

Road Warrior, The (Brian May, 1982)
     Mad Max II/Interceptor: K Guerriero della Strada

```
US   33   Varese Sarabande STV 81155
FR   33   SPI Milan A 120 163
GB   33   That's Entertainment TER 1016
IT   33   Beat LPF 059
JA   33   Warner/Pioneer P 11142
```

Roald Dahl's Tales of the Unexpected (Ron Grainer, 1979, tv)
```
US   33   DRG DS 15018 (1 band on The Exciting Television
               Music of R.G., 1980)
GB   33   STET DS 15018 (same as above)
GB   33   RK RKLB 1003 (Theme on Roald Dahl's Tales of the
               Unexpected and Other Themes/Ron Grainer, 1980)
               nst
```

Robert Rider (nfd)
```
JA   33   King K22G 7004
JA   33   King K22G 7015
```

Rocketship X-M (Ferde Grofe, 1950)
```
US   33   Starlog SR 1000 (1977)
JA   33   Mu-Land LZ 7017-M (1 band on S.F. Fact, vol. 2/
               Electoru Polyphonic Orch., 1979) nst
```

Rocky Horror Picture Show, The (Richard O'Brien, 1976)
```
US   33   Ode 77332
US   33   Ode 21653 (reissue of 77332)
CA   33   Ode SP 77031
GB   33   Ode 78332
US   33   Ode OPD 91653 (picture disc edition)
US   33   R.H.P.S. (no number, complete soundtrack, b/r)
```

Rodan (Akira Ifukube, 1958)
Radon
```
JA   33   Toho AX 8082 (1 band on Works of Akira Ifukube,
               1978)
JA   33   Toho AX 8107 (4 bands on Fantasy World of Japanese
               Pictures, part 2, 1978)
JA   33   StarChild K22G 7112 (Excerpts on S.F. Film Themes,
               vol. 2, 1983)
JA   33   King K22G 7044 (3 bands on Akira Ifukube Movie
               Themes, vol. 2, 1982)
```

Ro Go Pag (Carlo Rustichelli, 1962)
Lavimoci Il Cervello
```
IT   ep   Cam CEP 45.90 (4 bands)
```

Rollerball (Andre Previn & classical, 1975)
```
US   33   United Artists UA LA 470-G
IT   33   EMI 054 83183
GB   33   Music for Pleasure MFP-50248 (1 band on Big Terror
               Movie Themes/Geoff Love Orch.) nst
```

JA   33   United Artists GXH2 (1 band on <u>Screen Gold Disk:</u>
            <u>Action Film Themes</u>/nfd)

<u>Rosemary's Baby</u> (Christopher Komeda, 1968)
  US   33   Dot DLP 25875
  US   45   Dot 45-1712-6 (Lullaby theme, sung by Mia Farrow)
  FR   45   Atlantic 650 123 (Lullaby theme, r/r Arif Mardin)
                      <u>nst</u>
  FR   45   Rivera 121 200 (Lullaby theme, r/r Helene Montheral)
                      <u>nst</u>
  GB   33   Decca PFS 4432 (1 band on <u>Satan Superstar</u>/Stanley
                      Black, 1978) <u>nst</u>
  JA   33   London GP 9051 (same as PFS 4432)

<u>Ruby</u> (Don Ellis, 1977)
  US   45   Prodigal 0634F (theme, sung by Don Dunn)

<u>Samson vs. the Giant King</u> (Carlo Rustichelli, 1963)
  Maciste Alla Corte Dello Zar
  IT   45   Cam CA-2562

<u>Santa Claus Conquers the Martians</u> (Milton De Lugg, 1964)
  US   45   Four Corner FC 4-114

<u>Scars of Dracula</u> (James Bernard, 1970)
  US   33   Poo LP 106 (1 band on <u>Great Fantasy Film Music</u>, b/r,
                      1979)

<u>Schizoid</u> (Ennio Morricone, 1972)
  Una Lucertola Con la Pelle di Donna/Lizard in a Woman's Skin
  IT   33   General Music ZSLGE 55064 (2 bands on <u>Colori</u>)

<u>Science Ninja Party "Gatchaman," The</u> (Sukuma, 1978, tv)
  Kagaku Ninjatai Gatchaman/The Gatchaman Force
  JA   33   Columbia CX 7024

<u>Science Rescue Party "Technoboyger"</u> (Kentaro Haneda, 1982, tv)
  JA   33   Columbia CX 7057

<u>Science Team--Tanser Five</u> (uncredited, 1978, tv)
  JA   45   CBS/Sony 05SH542

<u>Screamers</u> (Luciano Michelini, 1981)
  L'isola Degli Uomini Pesce/Island of the Fish-Men
  US   33   WEB Records ST 101 (p/r, has 2 bands not on 1009)
  IT   33   Cometa CMT-1009.21 (has 4 bands not on ST 101)

<u>Secret Agent Superdragon</u> (Benedetto Ghiglia, 1966)
  New York Chiama Superdrago
  IT   33   Cam 33.16

Secret of Dorian Gray (Carlo Pes & Peppino De Luca, 1970)
    Il Dio Chimavano Dorian
    IT   33   Cam PRE 9 (1 side only; promo release)

Secret of NIMH, The (Jerry Goldsmith, 1982)
    Mrs. Brisby--Das Geheimnis von NIMH
    US   33   Varese Sarabande STV 81169 (1983)
    GB   33   That's Entertainment TER-1026
    GE   33   Metronome 50023

Secret of the Telegian, The (Sei Ikeno, 1960)
    Senso Ningen
    JA   33   Toho AX 8107 (2 bands on Fantasy World of Japanese
                    Pictures, part 2, 1978)

Selfish Giant, The (Ron Goodwin, 1971)
    CA   33   Capitol SQ 6401
    GB   33   Studio 2 TWOSP 108 (song, "Building a Wall" on The
                    Ron Goodwin Story--The First 25 Years)

Serpent God, The (Augusto Martelli, 1970)
    Il Dio Serpente
    IT   33   Cinevox MDF 33/40
    IT   33   Cinevox CIA 5002 (reissue of MDF 33/40, different
                    cover)
    IT   45   Cinevox MDG 40
    IT   33   Cinevox MDF 33/49 (1 band on Films in Musica Vol. 1)
    IT   33   Cinevox CIA 5010 (1 band on Cinemaerotico)

Seven Brothers Meet Dracula, The (James Bernard, 1974)
    The Legend of the 7 Golden Vampires
    GB   33   Warner Bros. K 56085 (w/d, narrated by Peter Cush-
                    ing, 1975)

Seven Faces of Dr. Lao, The (Leigh Harline, 1964)
    US   33   Centurion CLP 1210 (1 band on Filmusic Vol. 2, r/r
                    Lalo Schifrin, b/r, 1979)
    US   33   Poo LP 106 (same band on Great Fantasy Film Music,
                    b/r, 1979)

Seventh Victim, The (Roy Webb, 1943)
    GB   33   Decca PFS 4432 (6 min. suite in Satan Superstar/
                    Stanley Black, 1978)
    JA   33   London GP 9051 (same as PFS 4432)

7th Voyage of Sinbad, The (Bernard Herrmann, 1958)
    US   33   Colpix CP 504 (mono, 1959)
    US   33   Reissued by Request LP 1300 (different cover, b/r
                    reissue, 1974)
    US   33   Varese Sarabande STV 81135 (reissue of CP 504, true
                    stereo, 1980)

GB 33   United Artists UAS 29763 (reissue of CP 504, mono,
            1975)
JA 33   20th Century-Fox GXH 6046 (reissue of CP 504/nfd)
US 33   London SP 44207 (3 bands on The Fantasy Film World
            of Bernard Herrmann, r/r B. Herrmann, 1974) nst
US 45   Capitol F3980 (1 band, r/r Nelson Riddle) nst
JA 33   Mu-Land LZ 7017-M (1 band on S.F. Fact, Vol. 2/
            Electoru Polyphonic Orch., 1979) nst

Shaggy Dog, The (various, 1959)
    US 33   Disneyland WDL 3044 (1 side only, 1959)
    US 33   Disneyland WDL 1044 (reissue of 3044, 1962)
    US 33   Disneyland DQ-1323 (reissue of 3044, 1967)

Shame of the Jungle, The (Teddy Lasry, 1979)
    Tarzoon Le Vergogna Della Giungla
    IT 33   Cam AMP 168

She (Max Steiner, 1935)
    US 33   Cinema LP 8004 (b/r, 1974)

She (James Bernard, 1964)
    US 33   Capitol 11340 (1 band on Hammer Presents Dracula,
               r/r Philip Martell Orch., 1975)
    GB 33   EMI TWOA 5001 (same as 11340, 1974)

Sheriff and the Satellite Kid (Guido & Maurizio de Angelis, 1980)
    Uno Sceriffo Extraterrestre ... Poco Extra e Molto Terrestre/
               Der Grosse Mit Seinem Ausseridischen Kelinin
    GE 33   Polydor 2374 152
    IT 45   Kangaroo KTRN 3904

Shining, The (Wendy Carlos & classical, 1980)
    US 33   Warner Bros. HS 3449
    FR 33   Warner Bros. 56 827
    HO 33   Warner Bros. 56827
    JA 33   Warner Bros. P 1089 4
    US 45   Mercury 6038-047

Shock! (Rene Koering & Alain Jessua, 1974)
    Traitment de Choc/L'uomo Che Uccideva a Sangue Freddo
    IT 33   Cam SAG 9049
    JA 33   CineDisc M-5008 (different cover)

Shock Treatment (Richard O'Brien, 1981)
    US 33   Ode LLA-3615 (1981)

Shoot Loud ... Louder, I Don't Understand (Nino Rota, 1967)
    Spara Forte ... Piu Forte, Non Capisco
    FR 33   General Music 803030 (3 bands/nfd)
    FR 45   WEA/General Music 801013 (1 band)
    IT 45   Parade PRC 5014 (1 band)

Siegfried (Rolf Wilhelm, 1966)
   Die Nibelungen/Whom the Gods Wish to Destroy
   GE   33   Limelight 0011 (1980)

Siegfried, Part 2 (Rolf Wilhelm, 1966)
   Die Nibelungen 2 (Teil. "Krimhilds Rache")/Whom the Gods
         Wish to Destroy
   GE   33   Celine CL-0002 (1 side only on Via Mala/Die Nibe-
         lungen, 1981)

Sigmund and the Sea Monster (Janssen & Hart, 1973, tv)
   US   33   Chelsea BCL1-0332 (album title: Friends/Johnnie
         Whittaker)

Silent Running (Peter Schickele, 1971)
   US   33   Decca DL-7-9188 (1971)
   US   33   Varese Sarabande VC 81072 (reissue of DL-7-9188,
         green vinyl, 1978)
   US   45   Decca 32890 (song, sung by Joan Baez)
   IT   45   MCA 32890 (same song, here titled 2002: La Seconda
         Odissen)

Sinbad and the Eye of the Tiger (Roy Budd, 1977)
   US   33   Poo LP 106 (1 band on Great Fantasy Film Music,
         b/r, 1979)
   US   33   GNP Crescendo GNPS 2133 (1 band on Greatest S.F.
         Hits II/Neil Norman Orch., 1981) nst

Sisters (Bernard Herrmann, 1973)
   US   33   Entr'acte ERQ 7001-ST (quadraphonic stereo, 1975)

Six Million Dollar Man, The (Oliver Nelson, 1973, tv)
   US   33   Mercury SRM1 1089 (1 band on TV's Greatest Detec-
         tive Themes/John Gregory Orch.) nst
   GB   33   Philips 6308 255 (same as SRM1 1089)

Skeleton Dance (Carl W. Stalling, 1929)
   US   33   Disneyland 4021

Sky at Night, The (classical, 1958, tv)
   GB   33   BBC REH 324 (1 band on BBC Space Themes, 1979)
   GB   33   BBC REH 442 (1 band on Space Invaded, 1982)
   GB   33   Decca SPA 580 (1 band on Classic TV Themes, 1980)
   Note: music used is Sibelius, Pelleas and Melisande, 1st movement)

Slapstick (Stevens & Legrand, 1984)
   US   33   Varese Sarabande STV-81163 (includes 1 side with
         Stevens score/1 side with rejected Legrand score)
   FR   33   Milan A 201

Slaughterhouse Five (Mozart, arranged by Glen Gould, 1972)
   US   33   Columbia S 3133

Sleeper (Woody Allen, 1973)
  US 33 Pickwick SPC 3375 (1 band on Movie Themes/Pickwick
          Orch.) nst

Slipper and the Rose, The (R. & R. Sherman, 1976)
  Love Story of Cinderella
  US 33 MCA 2097
  GB 33 EMI EMC 3116 (has 4 bands not on US version)
  JA 33 EMI EMS 80755

Slumber Party Massacre (Ralph Jones, 1982)
  US 33 WEB ST-109 (1982)

Smurfs (Michel Legrand, 1975)
  La Flute a Sex Schtroumpfs
  CA 33 Polydor 2417 317

Snow Devils (A. F. Lavagnino, 1965)
  US 33 Poo LP 106 (1 band on Great Fantasy Film Music, b/
          r, 1979)

Snow Queen, The (Frank Skinner, 1959)
  US 33 Decca DL-78977 (w/d, 1960)

Snow White and the 3 Stooges (Lyn Murray, 1961)
  US 33 RCA CS-8450 (w/d, 1961)
  US 45 Carlton 553
  US 45 20th Century-Fox 249 (theme, credited to Harry Har-
          ris, r/r Harry Simeone Orch. & The Bluebells, 1961)

Solaris (Eduard Artemiev & Bach, 1972)
  JA 33 Columbia/Melodia YX 7212 MK
  US 33 Poo LP 106 (1 band on Great Fantasy Film Music, b/r,
          1979)
  US 33 RCA ARL1-2616 (1 band on Kosmos/Isao Tomita) nst
  JA 33 Mu-Land LZ 7017-M (1 band on S.F. Fact, Vol. 2/
          Electoru Polyphonic Orch., 1979) nst

Something Creeping in the Dark (A.F. Lavagnino, 1977)
  Qualcosa Striscia Nel Buio
  IT 33 Cam CML 023 (1 band on Giallo N.2 (Suspence Dram-
          matico), p/r)

Somewhere in Time (John Barry, 1980)
  US 33 MCA 5154
  JA 33 Victor VIM 7270

Son of Blob (Mort Garson, 1971)
  Beware the Blob!
  US 45 MGM PK-1006 (1972)
  US 33 Poo LP 106 (theme on Great Fantasy Film Music, b/r,
          1979)

Son of Dracula (Hans J. Salter, 1943)
    Le Fils de Dracula
    US   33   Coral CRL 757240 (1 band on Themes from Horror
                Movies/Dick Jacobs Orch.) nst
    US   33   Varese Sarabande VC 81077 (remastered reissue of
                CRL 757240 as Themes from Classic S.F., Fantasy
                and Horror Films, 1978) nst
    FR   33   MCA 410.064 (reissue of VC 81077)
    JA   33   MCA VIM 7264 (reissue of VC 81077)

Son of Dracula (Harry Nilsson, 1972)
    US   33   Rapple ABL1-0220

Son of Frankenstein (Frank Skinner, 1939)
    US   33   Citadel 6026 (Excerpts incorporated into "Horror
                Rhapsody" on Music for Frankenstein, Dracula, The
                Mummy, The Wolfman and Other Old Friends, p/r,
                1978)
    US   33   Citadel CT 7012 (reissue of CT 6026 as Horror Rhap-
                sody, 1979)
    FR   33   Decca 900 411 (reissue of CT 6026 as Horror Rhap-
                sody/Malpertuis, 1979)

Son of Godzilla (Masaru Sato, 1969)
    Gojira No Musuko
    JA   33   Toho AX 8100 (1 band on Godzilla, 1978)
    JA   33   Toho AX 8112 (2 bands on Godzilla, vol. 2, 1979)
    JA   33   Toho AX 8147 (1 band on Godzilla, vol. 3, 1980)
    JA   33   Columbia CX 7020 (Excerpts on Godzilla Original
                Background Music, vol. 1)

Soul Hustler, The (Harley Hatcher, 1973)
    US   33   MGM SE-4943

Space Cobra (Yuji Ohno & Kentaro Haneda, 1983)
    JA   33   Columbia CX 7074

Space Cruiser Yamato (Hiroshi Miyagawa, 1977)
    Uchi Senigan Yamato/Star Blazers (US, tv)
    JA   33   Columbia CZ 7001 (Symphonic Suite Yamato)
    JA   33   Columbia CS 7004 (w/d in English, boxed set w/book)
    JA   33   Columbia CQ 7006 (Recorded Live) nst?
    JA   33   Columbia CS 7007/8 (2/lp, w/d)
    JA   33   Columbia CZ 7111/2 (Part 3, 2/lp, w/d)
    JA   33   Columbia CX 7015 (Symphonic Suite, Part 3)
    JA   33   Columbia CQ 7031 (Space Cruiser Yamato--Chorus
                Suite)
    JA   33   Columbia CS 7033 (SOS Yamato, w/d in Japanese)
    JA   33   Columbia CX 7035 (Original Background Music)
    JA   33   Columbia CX 7049 (Mellow Guitar Yamato) nst
    JA   33   Columbia CQ 7058 (Songs of Yamato) nst

JA 33 Columbia CX 7061 (Rhapsody for Piano)
JA 33 Columbia CX 7064 (Romantic Violin Yamato) nst
JA 33 Columbia CB 7068/80 (13/lp set w/d, with hardbound
        book, complete 26 episode sound track)
JA 33 Columbia CQ 7072 (Choral Suite)
JA 33 Columbia CX 7075 (Synthesizer Fantasy Yamato) nst
JA 33 Columbia CX 7077 (Piano Suite--Yamato/Gundam)
JA 33 Columbia CS 7090 (Excerpts on World of Reiji Mat-
        sumoto) nst
JA 33 Seven Seas K16P 4033 (Excerpts on S.F. & Spectacle
        Themes) nst
JA 33 Polydor MR 3162 (Yamato--I Adore the Eternity of
        Love/disco version) nst
JA 45 Columbia SCS 241

Space Cruiser Yamato--Final (Hiroshi Miyagawa & Kentaro Haneda,
        1982, tv)
JA 33 Columbia CX 7055 (Overture to Final)
JA 33 Columbia CX 7081 (Volume 1)
JA 33 Columbia CX 7095 (Volume 2)
JA 33 Columbia CX 7114 (Volume 3)
JA 33 Columbia CX 7102 (Final Yamato--Synthesizer Fantasy)
        nst
JA 33 Columbia CS 7256/8 (3/lp, w/d)
JA 33 Animage ANL 1001 (r/r) nst
JA 33 Animage ANL 1004 (Part Two, r/r) nst

Space Cruiser Yamato--The New Voyage (Hiroshi Miyagawa, 1979,
        tv)
JA 33 Columbia CQ 7029
JA 33 Columbia CS 7144/5 (2/lp, w/d)

Space Detective "Gyavan" (Chumei Watanabe, 1982, tv)
JA 33 Columbia CX 7072

Space Detective "Shaliban" (Chumei Watanabe, 1982, tv)
JA 33 Columbia CQ 7081

Space Fantasy Emeraldus (Seiji Yokoyama, 1978)
JA 33 Columbia CQ 7002 (w/d)

Space Fantasy Emeraldus 2 (Seiji Yokoyama, 1978?)
JA 33 Columbia CQ 7021

Space: 1999 (Barry Gray & Derek Wadsworth, 1975-77, tv)
JA 33 RCA ABL1-1422 (Gray's themes only)
JA 33 GNP Crescendo GNPS 2128 (Gray's theme on Greatest
        S.F. Hits/Neil Norman Orch., 1979) nst
GB 33 MFP 50355 (Gray's theme on Star Wars and Other
        Space Themes/Geoff Love Orch.) nst
JA 33 GNP Crescendo GNPS 2163 (Wadsworth's theme on
        Greatest S.F. Hits III/Neil Norman Orch., 1983) nst

Space Patrol (Peter Thomas, 1967, tv)
Raumpatrouille
GE   33   Fontana 6434.261

Space Pirate Captain Harlock (Seiji Yokoyama & Masaaki Hirao,
          1978, tv)
Uchi Kaizoku Kyaputen Harokku
JA   33   Columbia CQ 7005 (Symphonic Suite)
JA   33   Columbia CS 7070 (w/d in Japanese)
JA   33   Columbia CZ 7023 (Suite for 2 Pianos, 1 side only)
JA   33   Columbia CQ 7032 (Chorus Suite, 1 side only)
JA   33   Columbia CX 7051 (Original Back Ground Music)
JA   33   Columbia CX 7097 (Synthesizer Fantasy) nst

Space Runaway Ideon (Koiji Sugiyama, 1980-81, tv; feature: 1982)
JA   33   StarChild K25G 7083 (A Contact)
JA   33   StarChild K25G 7084 (Be Invoked)
JA   33   StarChild K18G 7085/87 (A Contact/Be Invoked, 3/lp,
          w/d)
JA   33   StarChild K20G 7076/77 (Space Runaway Ideon III,
          2/lp)
JA   33   Columbia CX 7101 (Synthesizer Fantasy)

Space Shuttle (Wasserman, 1981, tv)
GE   45   CBS A 1688
GB   33   BBC REH 442 (1 band on Space Invaded, 1982)

Space Soldier Valdius (nfd)
JA   33   King K22G 7002

Spasm (Ennio Morricone, 1974)
Spasmo
IT   45   RCA TBBO 1018 (1974)
IT   33   RCA TPL2 1174 (1 band on I Film Della Violenza, 2/
          lp, 1975)
HO   33   RCA NL 31498 (1 band/nfd)

Spellbound (Miklos Rozsa, 1945)
US   78   ARA A-2
US   10"   REM LP-1 (1950)
US   33   Warner Bros. WS-1213 (r/r Ray Heindorf, 1958) nst
US   33   Stanyan SRQ-4021 (1975 reissue of WS 1213) nst
AU   33   Powerworks POW 4025 (1984 reissue/nfd)
US   33   Decca DL-79079 (Theme on 50 Years of Movie Music
          from Flickers to Widescreen/Jack Shaindlin, 1960's)
          nst
US   33   Camden CAL-233 (Theme on Film Music/Harlan Ramsey
          & Cosmopolitan Orch.) nst
US   33   Somerset/Alshire P-7000 (1 band on Award Winning
          Scores from the Silver Screen/101 Strings) nst
US   33   Capitol P-456 (Spellbound Concerto, r/r Miklos Rozsa)

nst
US   33   Delos DEL-F25419 (Theme on Classic Film Themes for
           Organ/Gaylord Carter) nst
US   33   RCA LSP-2410 (Theme on La Dolce Vita and Other
           Great Motion Picture Themes/Ray Ellis Orch.) nst
US   33   Columbia Entre AL-3029 (Theme on Music for Films/
           Queen's Hall Light Orch.) nst
US   33   MGM E-3172 (Theme on Lush Themes from Motion
           Pictures/Leroy Holmes Orch.) nst
US   33   Craftsmen C-8002 (Theme on Movie Themes/John
           Carlton and The Craftsmen All-Stars) nst
US   33   London SP-44031 (Theme on Film Spectacular, Vol. II/
           Stanley Black & London Festival Orch.) nst
US   33   Galaxy 2DP723 (Theme on The Hollywood Strings
           Double Feature Film Hit Spectacular, 2/lp) nst
US   33   Rondo-lette SA-160 (Theme on Immortal Film Music/
           Ross Case Orch.) nst
US   33   Columbia CL-794 (Theme on Love Music from Holly-
           wood/Paul Weston Orch.) nst
US   33   RCA LPT-1008 (Theme on Theme Music from Great
           Motion Pictures/Al Goodman Orch.) nst
US   33   Capitol SP-8634 (Theme on Whittemore & Lowe Play
           for the Late Late Show) nst
US   33   Mercury SRW-16399 (Theme on Music of Great Women
           of Film/Clebanoff Strings) nst
US   33   Reader's Digest RD4-141 (Theme on Reader's Digest/
           nfd) nst
US   33   RCA ARL1 0911 (2 bands on Spellbound: The Clas-
           sic Film Scores of Miklos Rozsa, r/r C. Gerhardt,
           1975) nst
GB   33   Music for Pleasure MFP 5232 (2 bands on Miklos Rozsa
           Movie Themes, 1963) nst
GB   33   EMI Studio Two TWOX-1007 (Spellbound Concerto on
           Spellbound/Ron Goodwin Orch., 1973) nst
GB   33   Saga XID-5018 (Theme on Music from the Films/Lon-
           don Variety Theatre Orch.) nst

Spermula (Jose Bartel, 1977)
   FR   33   WEA 56275 (1976)

Spiderman (Don Ellis, 1978, tv)
   JA   33   Columbia CQ 7010
   GB   33   MFP 50439 (Theme on Themes for Super Heroes/Geoff
           Love Orch.) nst

Spirits of the Dead (episode 3: "Toby Dammit"; Nino Rota, 1969)
Histoires Extra-Ordinaires
   IT   33   Cam SAG 9053 (1 band on Tutti i Film di Fellini,
           1973)
   FR   33   Polydor 2393.084 (1 band on Rota/Fellini)

Spy Who Loved Me, The (Marvin Hamlisch, 1977)
   L'Espion qui m'Aimait/007 La Spia che mi Amara
   US 33   United Artists UA-LA-774-H
   US 45   United Artists XW 1064
   FR 33   United Artists UAG 30098
   GB 33   United Artists UAS 30098
   IT 33   United Artists UA 24060
   JA 33   United Artists FML 80
   GB 33   Ronco RTD 2036 (1 band on Cinema & Broadway Gold,
            1979)

Stairway to Heaven (Allan Gray, 1946)
   GB 33   Columbia Entre RL-3029 (1 band on Music for Films/
            Charles Williams & Sidney Torch and Queen's Hall
            Light Orch.) nst

Star Crash (John Barry, 1979)
   Sterne Im Duell/Scontri Stellari
   GE 33   Polydor 2374 138
   IT 33   Durium 30314

Star Trek (Alexander Courage, 1966, tv)
   US 45   MCA 40578 (nfd, probably same as 105 354)
   US 45   Columbia 3-10448 (r/r The Inside Star Trek Orch.)
            nst
   US 45   Dot 17038 (Theme, r/r Charles Green, on B side of
            Leonard Nimoy 45)
   FR 45   MCA 105 354 (r/r Ramin) nst
   US 33   Wonderland WLP 301 (Theme on Themes from Star
            Trek and Planet of the Apes/The Jeff Wayne Space
            Shuttle) nst
   US 33   MCA 6114 (Theme on Themes from E.T. and More/
            Walter Murphy Orch.) nst
   US 33   Sine Qua Non SQN 7808 (Theme on Galactic Hits/
            The Odyssey Orch., 1980) nst
   US 33   Dot DLP 25794 (Theme on Mr. Spock's Music from Out-
            er Space, r/r--Charles Green?) nst
   US 33   GNP Crescendo GNPS 2128 (Theme on Greatest S.F.
            Hits/Neil Norman Orch., 1979) nst
   US 33   Philips 411 185-1 (Theme on Out of This World/John
            Williams & Boston Pops, 1983) nst
   GB 33   Contour 2870 185 (Theme on Children's TV Themes/
            Cy Payne Orch., 1972) nst
   GB 33   Philips 6382-069 (Theme on Great TV Themes/Tony
            Osborne Orch.) nst
   GB 33   MFP 50355 (1 band on Star Wars and Other Space
            Themes/Geoff Love Orch.) nst
   US 33   GNP Crescendo GNPS 2163 ("Vena's Dance," from
            episode: "The Cage," on Greatest S.F. Hits III/
            Neil Norman, 1983) nst

Star Trek--The Motion Picture (Jerry Goldsmith, 1979)
US	33	Columbia JS 36334
CA	33	Columbia JS 36334
FR	33	CBA 70 174
GB	33	CBS 70174
JA	33	CBS/Sony 25AP 1752

US 33   GNP Crescendo GNPS 2133 (1 band on Greatest S.F.
         Hits II/Neil Norman Orch., 1981) nst
US 33   Philips 411 185-1 (1 band on Out of This World/John
         Williams & Boston Pops, 1983) nst
US 33   Casablanca NBLP 7196 (1 side only, r/r Meco Monar-
         do) nst
JA 33   Seven Seas K16P 4033 (1 band on S.F. and Spectacle
         Themes) nst
US 45   Warner Bros./Curb WBS 49154 (song, vocal by Shaun
         Cassidy)

Star Trek II: The Wrath of Khan (James Horner, 1982)
La Colere de Khan
US	33	Atlantic 19363
FR	33	Atlantic ATLK 50905
GB	33	Atlantic K50905
GE	33	WEA 50905
IT	33	Atlantic W 50905 (1983)
JA	33	Atlantic P 11301

Star Wars (John Williams, 1977)
Guerre Stellari/La Guerre des Etoiles/Kreig der Sterner
US	33	20th Century-Fox 2T 541 (2/lp)
FR	33	20th Century-Fox AZ STEC 264/65 (2/lp)
GB	33	20th Century-Fox BTD 541 (2/lp)
GE	33	20th Century-Fox 6641 699 (2/lp, different cover)
IT	33	20th Century-Fox 6641707 (2/lp)
JA	33	20th Century-Fox FMW 37/38 (2/lp)
JA	33	20th Century-Fox 35MW 0032/3 (reissue)
FR	45	20th Century-Fox AZSG 651
IT	45	C.T.I. 307
FR	45	Ades LLP 455 F (w/d, 1983)
FR	33	Ades ST 3893 F (w/d, 1983)
GB	33	Disneyland Storyteller D 62101 (w/d)

US 33   20th Century-Fox T550 (The Story of Star Wars, w/d)
US 33   20th Century-Fox PR 103 (picture disc version of
         T550)
US 33   Stereo Gold Award SGA-1001 (7 bands on Star Wars--
         A Stereo Space Odyssey/Colin Frechter) nst
US 33   London ZM 1001 (6 band suite in Zubin Mehta Con-
         ducts Suites from Star Wars and Close Encounters of
         the Third Kind) nst
US 33   RCA ARL1-2698 (6 band suite on Music from John
         Williams' CE3K and Star Wars/Charles Gerhardt, 1978)
         nst

US   33   RCA ARL1-2792 (1 band on The Spectacular World of
          Classic Film Scores/Charles Gerhardt, 1978) nst
US   33   RCA AQL1-3650 (reissue of ARL1-2698)
US   33   Phillips 9500 921 (2 bands on Pops in Space/John
          Williams and Boston Pops, 1980) nst
US   33   Varese Sarabande VCDM 100 20 (1 band on Digital
          Space/Morton Gould, 1980) nst
US   33   Millenium MNLP 8001 (9 band suite on Star Wars and
          Other Galactic Funk/Meco Mondardo) nst
US   33   Musicor MUS 8801 (6 bands on Music from Star Wars/
          Electric Moog Orch.) nst
US   33   GNP Crescendo GNPS 2128 (1 band on Greatest S.F.
          Hits/Neil Norman Orch., 1979) nst
US   33   Varese Sarabande 704.210 (3 bands on The Star Wars
          Trilogy/Varujan Kojin, 1983)
US   33   Sine Qua Non SQN 7808 (2 bands on Galactic Hits/
          The Odyssey Orch., 1980) nst
US   33   Angel RL 32109 (Suite in John Williams' Symphonic
          Suites/Frank Barber Orch.) nst
GB   33   RCA RL 12698 (same as ARL1-2698, 1978) nst
GB   33   MFP 5594 (same as RL 32109) nst
GB   33   Decca SXL 6885 (same as ZM 1001) nst
GB   33   MFP 503555 (Excerpts on Star Wars and Other Space
          Themes/Geoff Love Orch.) nst
GB   33   Ronco RTD 2036 (1 band on Cinema and Broadway
          Gold, 2/lp, 1979) nst
GB   33   Decca SXL 6880 (suite on Star Wars/2001, r/r Zubin
          Mehta) nst
GE   33   Europa 111579 (Theme on Beliebte Titelmelodien/Studio
          Orch.) nst
IT   33   RCA NL 12698 (same as ARL1-2698, 1978) nst
IT   33   Cinevox CIA 5021 (1 band on Kolossal, 1981)
JA   33   Victor VIP 7321 (Excerpts on E.T. and Star Wars--
          The Best 12 Arts of John Williams/Film Studio Orch.)
          nst
JA   33   RSO 35MW0032/33 (reissue of FMW 37/38, 2/lp, 1983)
JA   33   Seven Seas K16P 4033 (1 band on S.F. & Spectacle
          Themes) nst
JA   45   RSO 7DW 0030 (1983)

Star Wolf (Norio Maeda, 1978)
     JA   33   Columbia CQ 7007

Starzinger (nfd, 1978)
     JA   33   Columbia CS 7076

Stingray (Barry Gray, 1965, tv)
     GB   33   Contour 2870 185 (1 band on Children's TV Themes/
               Cy Payne Orch., 1972) nst
     GB   33   Century 21 LA-6 (2 bands on Favourite TV Themes/
               Barry Gray Orch.) nst

GB 33   P.R.T. DOW-3 (1 band on No Strings Attached/Barry
         Gray Orch., 1981) nst

The Story of Three Loves (Miklos Rozsa, 1953)
   US   33   London PS-112 (1 band on Music from the Films/
             Mantovani Orch.) nst
   GB   33   Saga XID-5018 (1 band on Music from the Films/Lon-
             don Variety Theatre Orch.) nst
   GB   33   Polydor SUPER 2383 327 (1 band on Miklos Rozsa Con-
             ducts His Great Film Music/Royal Philharmonic Orch.)
             nst

Straight On 'Till Morning (Roland Shaw, 1972)
   GB   45   Columbia BS-8912 (theme song, sung by Annie Ross)

Study in Terror, A (John Scott, 1965)
   Notte di Terrore
   US   33   Roulette SR-801 (1967)
   IT   33   Cam 1 (1.5 album sides)

Sugar Hill (Nick Zesses & Dino Fekaris, 1974)
   Voodoo Girl
   US   45   Motown (nfd)

Supercar (Barry Gray, 1962, tv)
   US   33   Peter Pan 8008
   US   33   Capitol ST 1869 (Theme on More Hit TV Themes/Nel-
             son Riddle Orch.) nst
   GB   33   Century 21 LA-6 (Theme on Favourite TV Themes/
             Barry Gray Orch., 1966) nst

Super Electromagnetic Robot "Combatler V" (Hiroshi Tsutsui, 1977)
   Chodenji Robo Konbatora "V"
   JA   33   Columbia CX 7010 (1982)

Superfuzz (La Bionda, 1981)
   Poliziotto Superpiu
   IT   33   Durium DAI 30 365

Super Jetter (nfd)
   JA   33   King K22G 7008

Superman (John Williams, 1978)
   US   33   Warner Bros. 2BSK 3257 (2/lp)
   FR   33   WEA/Warner Bros. 66084 (2/lp)
   GB   33   Warner Bros. K66084 (2/lp)
   IT   33   Warner Bros. 66084 (2/lp)
   JA   33   Warner Bros. P 5557/58 (2/lp)
   US   45   Warner Bros. WBS 8729
   FR   45   WEA/Warner Bros. 17 292
   US   33   Phillips 9500 921 (1 band on Pops in Space/John

Williams and Boston Pops, 1980) <u>nst</u>
US	33	CBS IM 35876 (1 band on <u>Music from the Galaxies</u>/ Ettore Stratta, 1980) <u>nst</u>
US	33	MCA 6114 (1 band on <u>Themes from E.T. and More</u>/ Walter Murphy) <u>nst</u>
US	33	Sine Qua Non SQN 7808 (Theme on <u>Galactic Hits</u>/ The Odyssey Orch., 1980) <u>nst</u>
JA	33	Warner Bros. P 13002 W (same as IM 35876) <u>nst</u>

Superman II (Ken Thorne, from Williams, 1981)
US	33	Warner Bros. HS 3505 (laser etched disc)
FR	33	WEA/Warner Bros. 56 892
GB	33	Warner Bros. K56892
IT	33	WEA 56892
JA	33	Warner Bros. P 10975 (different cover)
GB	45	Warner Bros. K17778

Superman III (Ken Thorne, from Williams, 1983)
US	33	Warner Bros. WB-23879
GB	33	Warner Bros. 92 38791
GE	33	WEA 923879-1
IT	33	Warner Bros. 92 38791
JA	33	Warner Bros. P-11375
NZ	33	Warner Bros. 23889-1
SP	33	WEA 923879 1
JA	45	Warner Bros. P1774

Super-Vips, The (Franco Godi, 1968)
Vip Mio Fratello Superuomo
| IT | 33 | Cam SAG 90009 |

Survival Run (Gary William Friedman, 1980)
| US | 33 | (no label or #, b/r release, 1982) |

Survivor, The (Brian May, 1981)
| FR | 33 | Disco Shop DSD 1 |

Suspiria (Goblin, 1977)
CA	33	Attic LAT 1042
GB	33	EMI EMC 3222 (different cover)
IT	33	Cinevox MDF 33/108 (different cover)
IT	33	Cinevox CIA 5005 (reissue of MDF 33/108, 1980)
JA	33	Odeon EOS 80845 (different cover)
JA	45	Odeon EOR 20264
FR	33	Polydor Cinevox 2393 327 (Excerpts on <u>Les Meilleures Musiques de Films Fantastiques</u>)
IT	33	Cinevox CIA 5009 (3 bands on <u>I Films di Dario Argento</u>, 1980)
IT	33	Cinevox MDF 33/111 (1 band on <u>Films in Musica Vol. 3</u>)

Swamp Thing (Harry Manfredini, 1982)
   US   33   Varese Sarabande STV 81154

Swarm, The (Jerry Goldsmith, 1978)
   US   33   Warner Bros. 3208
   GB   33   Warner Bros. K 56541
   JA   33   Warners/Pioneer 10537
   JA   33   Warners/Pioneer P 6437 (1 band on Great Warner
             Brothers Spectaculars, 1979)
   GB   33   Warner Bros. K 26121 (same as P 6437)

Sweet Sixteen (Ray Ellis, 1983)
   US   33   Regency RI-8505

Sword and the Sorcerer, The (David Whitaker, 1982)
   Talon, im Kampfgegen das Imperium/L'Epee Sauvage
   US   33   Varese Sarabande STV 81158
   FR   33   Milan A 184
   GE   33   Celine 010
   GB   33   That's Entertainment TER 1023

Tarantula (Henry Mancini, and others, 1955)
   US   33   Coral CRL 757240 (1 band on Themes from Horror
             Movies/Dick Jacobs Orch.) nst
   US   33   Varese Sarabande VC 81077 (remastered 1978 reissue
             of CRL 757240 as Themes from Classic S.F., Fantasy
             and Horror Films) nst
   FR   33   MCA 410.064 (reissue of VC 81077) nst
   JA   33   MCA VIM 7264 (reissue of VC 81077) nst

Tarzan (Sidney Lee, 1966, tv)
   US   33   MGM LES 902
   US   33   Leo CH-1023 (Theme on The Amazing TV Themes/nfd)

Tarzan the Ape Man (Shorty Rogers, 1960)
   US   33   MGM SE-3798

Technopolice 21C (Hisaishi, 1982?)
   JS   33   Victor JBS 25006 (1982)

Tempter, The (Enno Morricone & Bruno Nicolai, 1978)
   L'anticristo/Antichrist
   IT   45   Beat BTF 089
   JA   45   Seven Seas FM 1094
   JA   45   Seven Seas FM 1099
   JA   33   Seven Seas GXH 6 (1 band on Screen Gold Disk:
             Panic and Spectacle Themes; longer version)
   JA   33   Seven Seas K18P 4105 (1 band on Horror Movie Special,
             1983)

Tender Dracula (Karl Heinz Shafer, 1975)
La Grande Trouille ou Tendre Dracula
FR   33   Eden Roc ER 62503

Tenebrae (Simonetti, Pignatelli & Morante, 1983)
Tenebre/Tenebres/Darkness
FR   33   Polydor Cinevox 8106931
GB   33   That's Entertainment TER 1064
IT   33   Cinevox MDF 33/157
JA   33   Nexus K28P 365
JA   33   Seven Seas K18P 4105 (1 band on Horror Movie Special, 1983)

Tentacles (Stelvio Cipriani, 1977)
FR   33   Barclay 900.5353
IT   33   Cam SAG 9079
JA   33   Polydor MPF 1065 (different cover)
JA   45   Polydor DPQ 6052

10th Victim, The (Piero Piccioni, 1965)
US   33   Mainstream S/6071 (1966)
US   33   Mainstream S/6079 (1 band on Detectives and Agents and Great Suspense Motion Picture Themes)

Teorema (Ennio Morricone, 1968)
Theoreme/Theorem/Teorema: Geometrie der Liebe
FR   33   Barclay 920 083
FR   33   Barclay 80128
IT   33   Ariete ARLP 2002 (same as 80128, different cover)
JA   33   Barclay L25B 5002 (1983 reissue of 80128)
IT   45   Ariete AR 8005
JA   33   HIT 1679 (2 bands/nfd)
FR   33   Barclay 85010-11 (1 band/nfd)
FR   33   Barclat 930024 (1 band/nfd)
IT   33   General Music 33/01-1/01-2 (1 band on Musiche di Ennio Morricone, 2/lp, p/4)

Terrahawks (R. Harvey, 1983, tv)
GB   33   Anderburt HX 100

Terror House (Charles Williams, 1943)
The Night Has Eyes
GB   33   Saga XID 5018 (1 band on Music from the Films/Gilbert Victor & London Variety Theatre Orch.) nst

Terror in the Woods (Ennio Morricone, 1972)
Cosa Avete Fatto a Solange?/What Have You Done to Solange?/ Das Geheimnis der grunen Stecknadel/The Secret of the Green Pins
IT   33   RCA DPSL 10599 (1 band on Un Film, Una Musica, 2/ lp, 1973)

IT   33   SRS 582 (1 band/nfd)
GB   33   RCA Starcall HY 1007 (1 band on Film Favourites, 2/
            lp, 1973)
HO   33   RCA NL 31498 (1 band/nfd)

Terror of Mecha-Godzilla, The (Akira Ifukube, 1978)
    Meka-Gojira No Gyakushi/Revenge of Mecha-Godzilla
JA   33   Toho AX 8100 (2 bands on Godzilla, vol. 2, 1979)
JA   33   StarChild K22G 7119 (Excerpts on S.F. Film Themes,
            vol. 9, 1983)
JA   33   King K22G 7052 (1 band on Akira Ifukube Movie
            Themes, vol. 10, 1982)

Testament of Orpheus, The (Georges Auric, 1960)
    Le Testament D'Orphee
FR   33   Columbia 1075

Theatre of Blood (Michael J. Lewis, 1973)
    US   33   Poo LP 104 (1 band on Great S.F. Film Music, b/r,
            1978) nst
    FR   33   MFP 2M 046 96966 (1 band on Musiques de Films
            D'horreur et de Catastrophe/Geoff Love Orch.) nst

Them! (Bronislau Kaper, 1954)
    Assalto Alla Terra
IT   33   Blu BLRL 15001 (Excerpt, w/d, on Fantascienza, p/r)

They're Coming to Get You (Bruno Nicolai, 1976)
    Tutti i Colori del Buio/All the Colors of Darkness
IT   33   Gemelli GG-ST 10.014 (p/r)

Thief of Bagdad, The (uncredited, 1924)
    US   33   Pelican LP 2011 (suite on Sounds from the Silent
            Screen/Gaylord Carter) nst

Thief of Bagdad, The (Miklos Rozsa, 1940)
    US   33   RCA LM-2118 (1 side only, w/d, 1957)
    US   33   Film Music Collection FMC 8 (r/r Elmer Bernstein,
            p/r, 1977) nst
    US   33   Warner Bros. 3183 (1978 reissue of FMC 8, 1978) nst
    GB   33   Polydor Super 2383 327 (suite on Miklos Rozsa Con-
            ducts His Great Film Music, r/r M. Rozsa, 1975)
            nst
    US   33   RCA ARL1 0911 (1 band on Spellbound: The Classic
            Film Scores of Miklos Rozsa, r/r Charles Gerhardt,
            1975) nst

Thing, The (Ennio Morricone, 1982)
    Das Ding
    US   33   MCA 6111
    FR   33   Arabella MCA 205091

```
GB  33    MCA MCF 3148
GE  33    Ariola 205091
IT  33    Ricordi MCA 4164
```

Thing (from Another World), The (Dimitri Tiomkin, 1951)
   La Cosa da Un Altro Mondo
   US 33   RCA ARL1-2792 (suite on Spectacular World of Classic
             Film Scores, r/r Charles Gerhardt, 1978) nst
   US 33   GNP Crescendo GNPS 2163 (1 band on Greatest S.F.
             Hits III/Neil Norman, 1983) nst
   GB 33   RCA RL 42005 (same as ARL1-2792) nst
   IT 33   Blu BLRL 15001 (Excerpt, w/d, on Fantascienza, p/r)

Thing with Two Heads, The (Robert O. Ragland, 1972)
   US 33   Pride PRD 0005ST (pop songs, "inspired by film")
             nst

Things to Come (Sir Arthur Bliss, 1936)
   GB 78   Decca K810/K811/K817
   GB 33   EMI ASD 3416 (8 bands on Things to Come/Colour
             Symphony, r/r Arthur Bliss) nst
   US 33   London STS 15112 (suite, r/r Arthur Bliss) nst
   GB 33   Chalfont C 77.001 (1 band on Music of England/
             Bournemouth Symphony Orch.) nst
   GB 33   EMI Studio Two TWOX-1007 (1 band, "March," on
             Spellbound/Ron Goodwin Orch., 1973) nst
   GB 33   EMI TWOX 1064 ("March" on The Very Best of Ron
             Goodwin, 1977) nst
   US 33   London Phase-4 SPC 21149 (suite on Great British
             Film Scores, r/r Bernard Herrmann, 1976) nst
   US 33   Varese Sarabande VCDM 1000 20 (suite on Digital
             Space/ Morton Gould & London Symphony, 1980)
             nst
   GB 33   MFP 50355 (1 band on Star Wars and Other Space
             Themes/Geoff Love Orch.)
   GB 33   Decca PFS 4363 (same as SPC 21149)

Thirst (Brian May, 1979)
   US 33   Varese Sarabande VC 81141 (unreleased)

This Island Earth (Herman Stein, and others, 1955)
   Les Survivants de L'infini
   US 33   Coral CRL 757240 (2 bands on Themes from Horror
             Movies/Dick Jacobs Orch.) nst
   US 33   Varese Sarabande VC 81077 (remastered reissue of
             CRL 757240 as Themes from Classic S.F., Fantasy
             & Horror Films) nst
   FR 33   MCA 410.064 (reissue of VC 81077)
   JA 33   MCA VIM 7264 (reissue of VC 81077)
```
```

Those Fantastic Flying Fools (John Scott, 1967)
   Rocket to the Moon
   GB 33   Polydor 583.013

Three Treasures, The (Akira Ifukube, 1958)
   Nippon Tanjo/The Birth of Japan
   JA 33   Toho AX 8106 (8 bands on Fantasy World of Japanese
              Pictures, part 1, 1978)
   JA 33   Toho AX 8086 (1 band on Works of Akira Ifukube,
              1978)
   JA 33   King K22G 7045 (4 bands on Akira Ifukube Movie
              Themes, vol. 3, 1982)

3 Worlds of Gulliver, The (Bernard Herrmann, 1960)
   US 33   Colpix CP 414 (w/d, 1960)
   US 33   Citadel CT 7018 (1981 reissue of CP 414, w/d)
   US 33   London Phase-4 SPC 21137 (13 bands on Mysterious
              Film World of Bernard Herrmann, r/r B. Herrmann,
              1975) nst

Thriller (Pete Rugolo, 1960, tv)
   US 33   Time S-2034 (1961)

Thrilling (Ennio Morricone & Luis E. Bacalov, 1965)
   La Regola del Giuoco/The Rules of the Game
   IT 45   RCA ARC AN 4068 (1 band, vocal)
   IT 33   Cam CML 023 (1 band, different, on Giallo N.2--
              Suspence--Dramatico, p/r)

Thunder Over St. Petersburg (Andre Hossein, 1967)
   J'ai Tue Raspoutine/I Killed Rasputin
   IT 33   Curci SPLP 903

Thunderball (John Barry, 1965)
   US 33   United Artists UAS 5132
   GB 33   United Artists SULP 1110
   GB 33   Sunset SLS 50396 (reissue of SULP 1110)
   GB 33   EMI Imports IC 054 82923 (reissue of SULP 1110)
   US 33   United Artists S-21010 (themes on The Incredible
              World of James Bond)
   US 33   United Artists SP 3 (Special issue of S-21010)
   GB 33   Ember NR 5025 (themes on John Barry Plays 007)
              nst
   GB 33   CBA 22014 (1 band on The Music of John Barry,
              2/lp) nst
   GB 33   United Artists UAD 6002718 (themes on The James
              Bond Collection)
   US 33   GNP Crescendo GNPS 2166 (1 band on Secret Agent
              File/Various, 1984) nst
   US 33   London SP-44078 (theme on Film Spectacular Vol. III/
              Stanley Black & London Festival Orch.) nst

US   33   Columbia CS-9293 (theme on The Great Movie Sounds
            of John Barry)
US   45   Parrot 45-9801 (theme song, sung by Tom Jones)
US   45   Kapp K-723 (theme song, r/r Jimmy Sedlar)
US   45   RCA 47-723 (theme song, sung by Ann-Margret)
Themes also on various other r/r James Bond collections (nfd)

Thunderbirds (Barry Gray, 1968, tv)
   GB   33   Hallmark HMA 227 (1 side only, with Thunderbirds
               Are Go)
   GB   33   Century 21 LA-6 (Theme on Favourite TV Themes/
               Barry Gray Orch.) nst
   GB   33   Contour 2870 185 (Theme on Children's TV Themes/
               Cy Payne Orch., 1972) nst
   GB   33   MFP 50355 (Theme on Star Wars and Other Space
               Themes/Geoff Love Orch., 1977) nst
   GB   33   PRT DOW 3 (Theme on No Strings Attached/Barry
               Gray Orch., 1981) nst
   GB   33   United Artists UAG 30281 (Excerpts incorporated into
               suite, "Pinewood in Space," r/r Barry Gray, on
               Musical Highlights from Filmharmonic '79) nst
   GB   45   EMI/Col. SEG 8510 (vocal by Cliff Richard and the
               Shadows) nst
   GB   45   PRT 7P 216 (theme, r/r Barry Gray) nst

Thunderbirds Are Go (Barry Gray, 1966)
   GB   33   Hallmark HMA 227 (1 side only, with Thunderbirds)

Thunderbirds Six (Barry Gray, 1968)
   GB   33   United Artists UAG 30281 (see listing under Thunder-
               birds above)

Tidal Wave (Masaru Sato, 1976)
   Nippon Chinbotsu/Submersion of Japan
   JA   45   Toho AT 1051 (1973)
   JA   33   Toho AX 6079 (1 band on Works of Masaru Sato, 1978)
   JA   33   Toho AX 8123 (1 band on Fantasy World of Japanese
               Pictures, part 4, 1978)
   JA   33   Tam YX 7004 (1 band on Soundtrack Best Collection)

Time After Time (Miklos Rozsa, 1979)
   US   33   Entr'acte ERS 6517

Time Machine, The (Russell Garcia, 1960)
   US   45   Verve 10217
   US   33   Cinema LP 8005 (1 band on Destination Moon and Oth-
               er Themes, b/r, 1974)
   US   33   Poo LP 104 (1 band on Great S.F. Film Music, b/r,
               1978)
   US   33   Poo LP 106 (different band on Great Fantasy Film Mu-
               sic, b/r, 1979)

GB   33   MFP 50375 (1 band on Close Encounters and Other
          Galactic Themes/Geoff Love Orch.) nst

Time Tunnel, The (John Williams, 1966, tv)
 US   33   GNP Crescendo GNPS 2133 (Theme on Greatest S.F.
     Hits II/Neil Norman Orch., 1981) nst
 JA   33   Mu-Land LZ 7017 M (Theme on S.F. Fact Vol. 2/
     Electoru Polyphonic Orch., 1979) nst

Tom Thumb (Gamley & Jones; songs: Peggy Lee, 1958)
 US   33   Lion L 70084 (w/d, 1959)
 US   33   MGM CH 104 (w/d)
 US   45   Metro K20012 (song sung by Russ Tamblyn)

Tom Thumb (Francis Lai, 1972)
 Le Petit Poucet
 FR   33   Gamma 165 Disques 23-TT-015

Tomb of Dracula (Seiji Yokoyama, 1980)
 JA   33   Columbia CQ 7057

Tomorrow's World (John Dankworth, tv/nfd)
 GB   33   BBC REH 324 (1 band on BBC Space Themes, 1979)
 GB   33   BBC REH 344 (1 band on Space Invaded, 1982)

Topper Takes a Trip (T. Marvin Hatley, music director, 1939)
 US   33   Music Box TMH-4305 (2 bands on Music for Laurel &
     Hardy (and Friends), p/r, 1982)

Torso (Guido & Maurizio De Angelis, 1975)
 I Corpi Delle Vittime Presentano Tracce di Violenza Carnale
 IT   33   RCA NL 33006 (1 band on Le Colonne Sonore di Guido
     & Maurizio De Angelis, 1976)

Tourist Trap (Pino Donaggio, 1979)
 US   33   Varese Sarabande VC 81102
 FR   33   Milan A-120-157 (1 band on Horror and Science Fic-
     tion, 1982)

Toward Magic Island (Nozumi Aoki, 1982)
 Unico
 JA   33   Japan JAL 2510

Toward the Terra (Masaru Sato, 1980)
 Terra He
 JA   33   Columbia CQ 7041 (Symphonic Suite)
 JA   33   Columbia CS 7186/87 (2/lp, w/d)

Tradition in the World of Spirit, "Acrobunch," A (M. Maruyama
    & Masayuki Yamamoto, 1982, tv)
 Acrobunch: Legendary Haunts of Wicked Men

JA   33   StarChild K22G 7093 (Vol. 1)
JA   33   StarChild K22G 7122 (Vol. 2)

Tradition of Terror: "Frankenstein," A (Kentaro Haneda, 1982,
            tv)
JA   33   Columbia CX 7031

Treasure of the Four Crowns, The (Ennio Morricone, 1982)
Le Tresor des Quatre Couronnes
FR   33   General Music 803 053 (1983)

Trio Infernal, Le (Ennio Morricone, 1974)
Il Trio Infernale/The Infernal Trio/Unholy Three
FR   33   Yuki 873.001
FR   45   Yuki 871.001
JA   45   Seven Seas FM 1099
FR   33   General Music 806.039 (Excerpts on Ennio Morricone,
            3/lp)
FR   33   WEA/General Music 803 007 (2 bands on Ennio Mor-
            ricone: Disque D'Or, Vol. 2, 1979)
FR   33   WEA/General Music 803 009 (1 band on Ennio Morri-
            cone: Bandes Originales des Films, 1979)

Triton of the Seas (Kohsetsu Minami, 1979)
Umi No Toriton
JA   33   Columbia CS 7044
JA   33   Columbia CQ 7027 (Themes from...)
JA   45   Crown MW 1002

Tron (Wendy Carlos, 1982)
US   33   CBS SM 37782
GB   33   CBS 70223
FR   33   CBA 73665
IT   33   Columbia 73665
JA   33   CBS/Sony 25AP 2384
SP   33   CBS 73665
US   33   Disneyland 2517 (Story of Tron, w/d)
IT   33   Disneyland STP 2517 (Story of Tron, w/d, 1983)

Tunnelvision (D. Lambert & B. Potter, 1976)
UT   ep   ABC R-375 (7" 33.3-rpm ep, promo release)

20th Century Oz (Ross Wilson, 1978)
US   33   Celestial OZ-4001
US   33   "Oz" OZS-1001 (promo release)

20,000 Leagues Under the Sea (Paul Smith & songs, 1954)
US   33   Disneyland DQ-1314
US   78   RCA Y-4004 (w/d, r/r Norman Leydon) nst
US   33   Coral CRL 57061 (1 band on Main Title/Dick Jacobs
            and George Cates Orch's.) nst

Twilight Zone, The (various, 1959-65, tv)
US   33   RCA LSP 2180 (Marius Constant's theme on Double
          Impact/Buddy Morrow Orch.) nst
US   33   Coral CL 1586 (Constant's theme, plus 10 bands of
          source music on The Twilight Zone/Marty Manning
          Orch.) nst
US   33   GNP Crescendo GNPS 2133 (Constant's theme on
          Greatest S.F. Hits II/Neil Norman Orch., 1981)
US   33   Philips 411 185-1 (Constant's theme on Out of This
          World/John Williams & Boston Pops, 1983) nst
US   33   Poo LP-106 (Excerpts from Jerry Goldsmith's "Back
          There" episode included as "Kingdom of the Spiders,"
          and Bernard Herrmann's "Walking Distance" episode
          included as "Convulsions Love Theme" on Great Fan-
          tasy Film Music, b/r, 1979)
US   33   Varese Sarabande STV 81171 (Volume 1, 1983; in-
          cludes Constant's main and end titles, episodes:
          The Invaders [Goldsmith], Perchance to Dream [Van
          Cleave], Walking Distance [Herrmann], The 16 Milli-
          meter Shrine [Waxman])
US   33   Varese Sarabande STV 81178 (Volume 2, 1983; in-
          cludes Herrmann's main & end titles, episodes:
          Where Is Everybody? [Herrmann], 100 Yards Over
          the Rim [Steiner], The Big Tall Wish [Goldsmith],
          A Stop at Willoughby [Scott])
US   33   Varese Sarabande STV 81185 (Volume 3, 1983; in-
          cludes alternate main & end titles by Constant, epi-
          sodes: The Lonely [Herrmann], Back There
          [Goldsmith], And When the Sky Was Opened [Rosen-
          man], A World of Difference [Van Cleave])
US   33   Varese Sarabande STV 81192 (Volume 4, 1984; in-
          cludes alternate main & end titles by Herrmann,
          stock jazz themes by Goldsmith and Garriguenc, epi-
          sodes: Nervous Man in a Four-Dollar Room [Gold-
          smith], Elegy [Van Cleave], King Nine Will Not Re-
          turn [Steiner], Two [Van Cleave]
US   33   Varese Sarabande--forthcoming/planned--(Volumes 5
          and 6, 1984): to include episodes: What You Need
          [Van Cleave], The Passersby [Steiner], Dust [Gold-
          smith], I Sing the Body Electric [Van Cleave], The
          Trouble with Templeton [Alexander], Young Man's
          Fancy [Scott], The Bard [Steiner], Passage on the
          Lady Anne [Garriguenc])

Twilight Zone--The Movie (Jerry Goldsmith, 1983)
US   33   Warner Bros. WB-23887
GE   33   WEA 923887-1
GB   33   Warner Bros. K9238871
JA   33   Warner Pioneer P 11415
SP   33   WEA 9238871
JA   45   Warner Bros. P1794

<u>Twins of Evil</u> (Harry Robinson, 1975)
  GB   45   DJM DJS-254 (Song, with lyrics not used in film, r/r
             Essjay)

<u>Twisted Nerve</u> (Bernard Herrmann, 1968)
  FR   ep   Polydor 583.728 (8 bands)
  US   33   Cinema LP 8006 (same 8 bands on <u>Film Music of</u>
             <u>Bernard Herrmann</u>, 1 side only, b/r, 1975)

<u>200 Motels</u> (Frank Zappa, 1971)
  US   33   United Artists UA 9956-2 (songs; 2/lp)

<u>Two Mrs. Carrolls, The</u> (Franz Waxman, 1947)
  US   33   RCA ARL1-0422 (Suite in <u>Casablanca: Classic Film</u>
             <u>Scores for Humphrey Bogart</u>, r/r Charles Gerhardt,
             1974)

<u>Two on a Guillotine</u> (Max Steiner, 1965)
  US   45   MGM 31734 (nst/nfd)
  US   33   RCA LSP 4205 (1 band on <u>Love Trip</u>/Peter Nero
             Orch.) <u>nst</u>

<u>2001: A Space Odyssey</u> (Classical, 1969)
  US   33   MGM S1E 13ST (<u>Volume 1</u>)
  US   33   MGM SE 4722 (<u>Volume 2</u>)
  GE   33   MGM 665096
  JA   33   MGM MMF 1010 (Volume 1, 1977 reissue)
  JA   33   MGM MMF 1028 (<u>Volume 2</u>, 1977 reissue)
  US   33   Columbia MS 7176 (r/r Eugene Ormandy) <u>nst</u>
  US   33   Sine Qua Non SQN-7808 (1 band on <u>Galactic Hits</u>/
             <u>The Odyssey Orch.</u>, 1980) <u>nst</u>
  US   33   Philips 411 185-1 (1 band on <u>Out of This World</u>/John
             Williams & Boston Pops, 1983) <u>nst</u>
  US   33   London SP-44173 (1 band on <u>Film Spectacular Vol. IV</u>/
             Stanley Black & London Festival Orch.) <u>nst</u>
  US   33   Reader's Digest RD4-141 (1 band on <u>Reader's Digest</u>/
             nfd)
  GB   33   Decca SXL 6880 (Orchestral suite on <u>Star Wars</u>/2001/
             Zubin Mehta Orch., 1977) <u>nst</u>
  GB   33   Music for Pleasure MFP-50355 (1 band on <u>Star Wars</u>
             <u>and Other Space Themes</u>/Geoff Love Orch.) <u>nst</u>
  GB   33   Music for Pleasure MFG-50035 (1 band on <u>Big Sus-</u>
             <u>pense Movie Themes</u>/Geoff Love Orch.) <u>nst</u>
  JA   33   Mu-Land LZ 7017-M (1 band on <u>S.F. Fact Vol. 2</u>/
             Electoru Polyphonic Orch., 1979) <u>nst</u>

<u>2000 Maniacs</u> (H.G. Lewis & Larry Wellington, 1964)
  US   33   Rhino RNSP 305 (1 side of <u>The Amazing Film Scores</u>
             <u>of Herschell Gordon Lewis</u>, 1984)

<u>2000 Years Later</u> (Stu Phillips, 1969)
  US   45   Warner Bros./7 Arts 7266

U.F.O. (Barry Gray, 1972, tv)
  GB 33 Contour 2870 185 (Theme on Children's TV Themes/
             Cy Payne Orch., 1972)
  GB 33 MFP 50355 (Theme on Star Wars and Other Space
             Themes/Geoff Love Orch.) nst
  US 33 GNP Crescendo GNPS 2163 (Theme on Greatest S.F.
             Hits III/Neil Norman Orch., 1983)

U.F.O. Blue Christmas (Masaru Sato, 1980)
  Buru Kurisumasu/Blood Type: Blue
  JA 33 Toho Cinedisc DX-4 (10 bands on 7" lp)

U.F.O. Robot "Grendiser" (Shunsuke Kikuchi, 1982)
  JA 33 Columbia CX 7099

Ultraman (Tohru Fuyuki, Masanubu Higure, Kunio Miyauchi, 1965,
        tv)
  JA 33 Toshiba TC-6324
  JA 33 Columbia CQ 7020
  JA 33 King SKK 2102 (An Encyclopedia of Ultra Man, w/d)
  JA 33 King SKK 2121 (Sound Ultraman, w/d)
  JA 33 King SKK 2126 (Sound Ultraman 2, w/d)
  JA 33 King SKK 2127 (Ultraman/Ultra Q, w/d)
  JA 33 King SKK 2129 (Ultraman Returned, w/d; Fuyuki)
  JA 33 King SKK 2130 (Ultraman Ace, w/d; Fuyuki)
  JA 33 King SKK 2131 (Ultraman Taro, w/d; Higure)
  JA 33 King SKK 2132 (Ultraman Leo, w/d; Fuyuki)
  JA 33 King SKD 2007 (All of Ultraman)
  JA 33 King SKA 254 (Symphonic Suite Ultraman)
  JA 33 King SKM 2311-2315 (The Completed Works of Ultra-
             man, 5/lp)
  JA 33 Polydor MQY 2501 (The World of Ultraman, Miyauchi)
  JA 33 Toho DX 4008 (Complete Work of Ultraman)
  JA 33 Victor JBX 190 (An Encyclopedia of Ultraman)
  JA 33 Victor SJX 2167 (Big Marches of Ultraman)
  JA 33 Columbia CZ 7140 (reissue of Polydor MQY 2501)
  JA 33 Columbia CZ 7142 (reissue of King SKK 2129)
  JA 33 Columbia CZ 7143 (reissue of King SKK 2130)
  JA 33 Columbia CZ 7144 (reissue of King SKK 2131)
  JA 33 Columbia CZ 7145 (reissue of King SKK 2132)
  JA 33 Columbia CZ 7146 (The Ultra Man, Miyauchi, reissue)
  JA 33 Columbia CZ 7147 (Ultraman '80, Fuyuki)
  Earlier King SKK lp's also reissued on Columbia CS-7101, 7102,
             7103, 7104, 7105 and 7106 (nfd). All King and
             Columbia lp's issued between 1977-1982

Ultra Seven (Tohru Fuyuki, tv/nfd)
  JA 33 Columbia CZ 7024
  JA 33 Columbia CZ 7141 (World of Ultra Seven)
  JA 33 King SKK 2128
  JA 33 Victor JBX 190

Unicorn in the Garden (David Raksin, 1954)
   US   33   Classic Editions 1055 (lp-length suite)

Unidentified Flying Oddball (Ron Goodwin, 1979)
   The Spaceman and King Arthur
   GB   33   Chandos ABRD 1014 (1 band on Drake 400/Ron Good-
           win Orch.) nst

Uninvited, The (Victor Young, 1944)
   US   33   Decca DL 8056 (1 band on Pearls on Velvet/Victor
           Young Orch.) nst
   US   33   Decca DL 8798 (1 band on Forever Young/Victor
           Young Orch.) nst
   US   33   Delos DEL F-25419 (1 band on Classic Film Themes
           for Organ/Gaylord Carter) nst

Union of the 6 Gods, "God Mars," The (Wakakusa, 1982, tv)
   JA   33   StarChild K22G 7068 (Vol. 1)
   JA   33   StarChild K22G 7089 (Vol. 2)
   JA   33   StarChild K25G 7104 (God Mars Back Ground Music)
   JA   33   StarChild K20G 7107/08 (Story of..., 2/lp, w/d)
   JA   33   StarChild K22G 7096 (Highlights of, w/d)
   JA   33   StarChild K25G 7137 (The Memory of Godmars; new
           themes based on film)

Unknown, The (Mischa Bakaleinikoff, music director, 1946)
   US   33   Sonodor MO-SON 105 (1 band on Lolita and Other
           Film Hits/Orchestra Del Oro) nst

Up the Sandbox (Billy Goldenberg, 1972)
   US   45   Columbia 45780
   US   33   Centurion CLP 1600 (1 band on Filmusic, b/r, 1978)
   US   33   Centurion CLP 1601 (1 band on The Film and Tele-
           vision Music of Billy Goldenberg, b/r)

Vampire, The (1957, Gerald Fried)
   Mark of the Vampire
   US   45   RKO Unique 410 (nfd)

Vampire Lovers, The (Harry Robinson, 1971)
   US   33   Capitol 11340 (suite on Hammer Presents Dracula/
           Philip Martell, 1974)
   GB   33   EMI TWOA 5001 (same as 11340)

Varan the Unbelievable (Akira Ifukube, 1958)
   Daikaiju Baran
   JA   33   Toho AX 8107 (4 bands on Fantasy World of Japanese
           Pictures, part 2, 1978)
   JA   33   StarChild K22G 7115 (Excerpts on S.F. Film Themes,
           vol. 5, 1983)
   JA   33   King K22G 7045 (3 bands on Akira Ifukube Movie

Themes, vol. 3, 1982)
US 33 Poo LP 106 (1 band on Great Fantasy Film Music, b/r,
        1979)

Vertigo (Bernard Herrmann, 1958)
US 33 Mercury MG 20384 (1958)
US 33 Sound/Stage SS-2301 (b/r reissue, 1974, different
        cover)
JA 33 Mercury FDX 282 (reissue, 1977)
HO 33 Mercury SRI 75117 (reissue, 1978)
US 45 Mercury 71325X45 (theme, r/r Billy Ecksteine) nst
US 33 London Phase-4 SP 44126 (Suite on Music for the
        Great Movie Thrillers, r/r B. Herrmann, 1973) nst
JA 33 London K28P 4002 (1980 reissue of SP 44126) nst

Village of the Damned (Ron Goodwin, 1960)
  Il Villaggio dei Dannati
IT 33 Blu BLRL 15001 (Excerpt, w/d, on Fantascienza, p/r)

Village of the 8 Gravestones (Yasushi Akutagawa, 1977)
  Yatsuhaka Mura
US 33 Varese Sarabande VC 81084 (1979)
JA 33 Victor KVX 1001 (1977)
JA 45 Victor KV 1001

Virus (Teo Macero, 1980)
JA 33 Columbia YX 5027 AX
JA 33 Columbia YX 7247 (Symphonic Suite Virus)

Visitor, The (Franco Micalizzi, 1979)
  Stridulum
IT 33 RCA BL 31433

Voltus Five (Hiroshi Tsutsui, 1979)
JA 33 Columbia CZ 7027 (1980)

Voyage to the Bottom of the Sea (Paul Sawtell & Bert Shefter,
        1961)
US 45 Chancellor 1081 (song, by Russel Faith, sung by
        Frankie Avalon)

Voyage to the Bottom of the Sea (Paul Sawtell, 1964)
US 33 Audio Fidelity AFSD 6146 (Theme on TV Potpourri/
        Dick Dia Orch.) nst
US 33 GNP Crescendo GNPS 2133 (Theme on Greatest S.F.
        Hits II/Neil Norman Orch., 1981) nst

Wait Until Dark (Henry Mancini, 1967)
US 33 Decca (7) 4956
US 45 RCA 9340
US 33 Project 3 PR-5013-SD (1 band on Film Fame. Marvelous

Movie Themes /Enoch Light & the Light Brigade) nst
US   33   Longines SYS-5312-5317 (1 band on Somewhere My
Love and Other Romantic Movie Melodies /Longines
Symphonette Society, 6 /lp) nst

Wargames (Arthur B. Rubinstein, 1983)
US   33   Polydor 815 005-1 Y-1 (w /d)
GB   33   Polydor POLD 5124 (w /d)
JA   33   Polydor 28MM 0314 (w /d)
US   33   Buena Vista 2105 (The Story of Wargames, w /d)
FR   33   Polydor 8150051 (w /d)

War Goddess, The (Riz Ortolani, 1974)
JA   33   Cine-Disc 5010

War in Space, The (Toshiaki Tsushima, 1978)
JA   33   Toho DX 4005
JA   33   Toho AX 8123 (1 band on Fantasy World of Japanese
Pictures, part 4, 1978)

War of the Gargantuas, The (Akira Ifukube, 1967)
Sanda Tai Gaila
JA   33   Toho AX 8108 (5 bands on Fantasy World of Japanese
Pictures, part 3, 1978)

War of the Insects (Shunsuke Kikuchi, 1968)
Konchu Daisenso /Genocide
JA   33   Toho AX 8124 (1 band on Fantasy World of Japanese
Pictures, part 5, 1978)

War of the Monsters (Chuji Kinoshita, 1968)
Gamera Tai Barugon /Gamera vs. Barugon
JA   33   Toho AX 8120 (3 bands on Gamera, 1978)
JA   33   Daiei KKS-4026 (Excerpts, w /d, on Gamera, music &
songs)

War of the Satellites (Danny Hamilton, 1958)
US   33   GNP Crescendo GNPS 2133 (1 band on Greatest S.F.
Hits II /Neil Norman Orch., 1981) nst

War of the Worlds (Leith Stevens, 1953)
La Guerra dei Mondi
US   33   Poo LP 104 (1 band on Great S.F. Film Music, b /r,
1978)
US   33   GNP Crescendo GNPS 2163 (1 band on Greatest S.F.
Hits III /Neil Norman Orch., 1983) nst
US   45   GNP Crescendo GNPS 828 (1 band /Neil Norman Orch.,
1983) nst
IT   33   Blu BLRL 15001 (Excerpt, w /d, on Fantascienza,
p /r)

Warlords of Atlantis (Michael Vickers, 1978)
  7 Cities to Atlantis
  JA   33   Mu-Land LZ 7017-M (1 band on S.F. Fact Vol. 2/
              Electoru Polyphonic Orch., 1979) nst

Water Babies (Phil Coulter & Bill Martin, 1979)
  GB   33   Ariola ARLB 5030
  GB   33   MFP 50503 (reissue)

Watermelon Man (Melvin Van Peebles, 1970)
  US   33   Beverly Hills BHS 26

Watership Down (A. Morley, M. Williamson, M. Batt, 1978)
  US   33   Columbia 35707
  GB   33   CBS 70161
  IT   33   CBS 70161
  JA   33   CBS/Sony 25 3P 125
  US   45   Columbia 18-02627
  IT   45   CBS 6947

Wavelength (Tangerine Dream, 1984)
  US   33   Varese Sarabande STV-81207

Way Way Out (Lalo Schifrin, 1966)
  US   45   20th Century-Fox 45 6651
  US   33   20th Century-Fox 3192 (1 band on Fabulous Film
              Themes/Harry Betts Orch.) nst

Werewolf in a Girl's Dormitory (F. Berman, 1961)
  US   45   Cub Records (nfd/theme song, "The Ghoul in
              School," 1963)

Westworld (Fred Karlin, 1973)
  US   33   MGM 1SE 47st
  JA   33   Mu-Land LZ 7016-M (1 band on S.F. Fact Vol. 1/
              Electoru Polyphonic Orch., 1979) nst

Whale God, The (Akira Ifukube, 1962)
  Kujira Gami
  JA   33   Toho AX-8082 (1 band on Works of Akira Ifukube,
              1978)
  JA   33   King K22G-7047 (3 bands on Akira Ifukube Movie
              Themes, Vol. 5, 1982)

What! (Carlo Rustichelli)
  La Frusta e Il Corpo
  IT   33   Cam CMS 30.132

Whatever Happened to Baby Jane? (Frank De Vol, 1962)
  US   45   MGM 13107 (Theme song, sung by Bette Davis &
              Dabbie Burton)

US 45   Radiant 1514 (Theme, r/r Bob Bain) <u>nst</u>

<u>What's the Matter with Helen?</u> (David Raksin, 1971)
    US 33   Dynamation DY-1200 (p/r)

<u>When Women Had Tails</u> (Ennio Morricone, 1970)
    Quando le Donne Avevano la Coda/Les Femmes Avaient Une
        Queu
    IT 33   Cam SAG 9032 (1970)
    US 33   E.M. 1002 (b/r reissue of SAG 9032, 1974)
    FR 33   Carrere 67066 (1 band on <u>Sonny</u>, 1975)
    FR 33   MFP 2M 026 13330 (reissue of 67066, 1977)
    CA 33   RCA CAM 6901 (1 band/nfd)

<u>When Worlds Collide</u> (Leith Stevens, 1951)
    GB 33   MFP 50355 (1 band on <u>Star Wars and Other Space</u>
        <u>Themes</u>/Geoff Love Orch.)

<u>Whisper in the Night, A</u> (Pino Donaggio, 1977)
    Un Sussurro nel Buio/Whispers in the Dark
    IT 45   Produttori Associati PA/NP 3262

<u>White Gloves of the Devil, The</u> (Karl-Heinz Shafer/nfd)
    FR 33   nfd

<u>White House on the Beach, The</u> (Herb Ohta & Hiroshi Kamayatsu,
        1978)
    Nagisa No Shiroi Ie
    JA 33   King SKA 240

<u>Wild in the Streets</u> (Les Baxter, 1968)
    US 33   Tower SKAO 5099
    CA 33   Capitol SKAO 6284

<u>Willi Wonka & the Chocolate Factory</u> (Newley & Bricusse, 1971)
    US 33   Paramount PAS-6012

<u>Witchcraft '70</u> (Piero Umiliani, 1969)
    Angeli Bianchi ... Angeli Nero/White Angel ... Black Angel
    IT 33   Omicron LPS-0017

<u>Witches, The</u> (Ennio Morricone & Piero Piccioni, 1967)
    La Streghe/Les Socieres
    IT 45   United Artists 35785
    IT 45   United Artists 3113
    US 33   Poo LP 106 (1 band on <u>Great Fantasy Film Music</u>, b/r,
        1979)

<u>Winds of Change</u> (Alec R. Costandino, 1979)
    US 33   Casablanca NBLT 6167

Wiz, The (Quincy Jones, 1978)
  US   33   MCA 2-14000 (2/lp)
  FR   33   MCA 410104-05 (2/lp)
  IT   33   AM-AMCAL 24038 (2/lp)
  JA   33   MCA VIM 9515-16 (2/lp)

Wizard of Baghdad (Irving Gertz, 1961)
  US   45   20th Century-Fox 234 (1 band, credited to Lamper-
               Farrow-Saxon, on 1960 single, r/r Dick Shawn)

Wizard of Oz, The (Harold Arlen & Herbert Stothart, 1939)
  US   33   MGM E-3464 (w/d, mono only, 1956)
  US   33   MGM SE-3996 (stereo reissue of E-3464, 1962)
  JA   33   Polydor MMF 1023 (reissue of SE-3996)
  US   33   Philips 6514 (1 band on Aisle Seat--Great Film Music/
               John Williams & Boston Pops, 1982) nst

Woman of the Dunes (Toru Takemitsu, 1964)
  Suna No Onna
  JA   33   King SKD(M) 370-1 (1 band on Famous Japanese
               Movies, 2/lp, 1976)
  JA   33   Victor KVX 1070 (1 band on Film Music of Toru Take-
               mitsu, vol. 9, 1982)

Wonder Woman (Charles Fox, 1976, tv)
  US   45   Shady Brook 003 (promo release, 1977)
  GB   33   MFP 50439 (Theme on Themes for Superheroes/Geoff
               Love Orch.) nst

Wonder Women vs. the Super Stooges (Sante Romitelli/nfd)
  Sotto a Chi Tocca!
  IT   45   Cam AMP-100

Wonderful World of the Brothers Grimm, The (Merrill & Harline,
               1962)
  US   33   MGM S1E 3ST (boxed edition, w/d)
  FR   33   Metro 2355.016 (different cover)
  US   33   Kapp KL-1289 (1 band on More Sounds of Hollywood/
               Emmanuel Vardi Orch.) nst
  FR   45   London RE-10-148M (Theme, r/r Lawrence Welk)
  FR   45   United Artists 3603M (Theme, r/r Al Caiola)

World, The Flesh and The Devil, The (Miklos Rozsa, 1959)
  US   45   RCA 47-7550 (Excerpt of source music, by Nemeroff,
               only)

Wuthering Heights (Alfred Newman, 1939)
  US   33   Capricorn CP-1286 (1 band on Film Themes by Alfred
               Newman)
  US   33   Mercury MG 20037 (1 band on Motion Picture Music/
               Alfred Newman Orch.) nst

US   33   Decca DL-8123 (1 band on A. Newman themes lp/nfd)
          nst
US   33   Columbia CL-794 (1 band on Love Music from Holly-
          wood/Paul Weston Orch.) nst

Wuthering Heights (Michel Legrand, 1970)
     US   33   American Int'l A-1039

X from Outer Space, The (Taku Izumi, 1967)
     Uchu Daikaiju Guilala
     JA   33   Toho AX 8124 (1 band on Fantasy World of Japanese
               Pictures, part 5, 1978)

X-tro (Harry Bromley Davenport, 1983)
     GB   33   That's Entertainment TER-1052

Xanadu (John Farrar & Jeff Lynne, songs, 1980)
     US   33   MCA 6100
     HO   33   Jet LX 526
     JA   33   CBS/Sony 25AP 1900
     US   45   MCA 41246 (song: Electric Light Orch.)
     US   45   MCA 41247 (song: Olivia Newton-John)
     US   45   MCA 51007 (song: Electric Light Orch.)

Year at the Top, A (Hegel & George, 1977, tv)
     US   33   Casablanca NBLP 7068

Year of the Cannibals (Ennio Morricone, 1970)
     I Cannibali/Les Cannibales
     US   33   Cerberus CEMS 0111 (1 side only on Sonny & Jed/
               The Cannibals, 1982)
     IT   45   Cam AMP 077 (song)
     FR   33   Carrere 67066 (song on Sonny)
     FR   33   MFP 2M026 13330 (reissue of 67066)
     IT   33   REM NAVY 67066 (1 band/nfd)
     IT   33   Cam CML 023 (1 band/nfd)

Yellow Submarine, The (George Martin & The Beatles, 1968)
     US   33   Capitol SW-153
     US   33   Apple SE-153
     Foreign editions also (nfd)

Yog, Monster from Space (Akira Ifukube, 1970)
     Nankai No Daikaiju/Space Amoeba
     JA   33   Toho AX 8108 (2 bands on Fantasy World of Japanese
               Pictures, part 3, 1978)
     JA   33   King K22G 7050 (2 bands on Akira Ifukube Movie
               Themes, vol. 8, 1982)

Yor (John Scott, Guido & Maurizio De Angelis, 1983)
     US   33   Southern Cross SCRS 1005
     FR   33   Polydor 815393 7 (1 side only; De Angelis only)

You Only Live Twice (John Barry, 1967)
US   33   United Artists UAS 5155
GB   33   United Artists SULP 1171
JA   33   United Artists GXH 6016
US   33   GNP Crescendo GNPS 2166 (1 band on Secret Agent
          File/Various, 1984) nst
GB   33   United Artists UAD 6002718 (Excerpts on The James
          Bond Collection)
GB   33   CBS 22014 (Theme on The Music of John Barry, 2/lp)
          nst
Themes also on various other r/r James Bond collections (nfd)

Young Frankenstein (John Morris, 1974)
US   33   ABC ABCD 870 (w/d)
US   45   ABC 12063
US   33   Asylum 5E-501 (2 bands on Mel Brooks' Greatest Hits)

Zardoz (David Munrow & classical, 1974)
FR   45   Polydor 2058.446 (1 band, r/r Zzebra) nst
JA   33   Mu-Land LZ 7017-M (1 band on S.F. Fact, Vol. 2/
          Electoru Polyphonic Orch., 1979) nst
GB   33   CBS/Harmony 30052 (1 band on Great Classic Hits
          from the Films)

Zero Population Growth (Jonathan Hodge, 1972)
Z.P.G.
JA   33   Mu-Land LZ 7017-m (1 band on S.F. Fact Vol. 2/
          Electoru Polyphonic Orch., 1979) nst

Zombie (Fabio Frizzi & Giorgio Tucci, 1980)
Sanguelia/Zombi 2/Zombie Flesh Eaters
JA   33   East World WTP 80146 (1 band on The Elephant
          Man/Mystery's Shadow) nst

Recorded Music from Fantastic Films (collections)

Akira Ifukube Movie Themes
(10-record set, individually packaged, all mono. Issued 1982.
Also called Akira Ifukube: Complete Work of Movie Themes.
Original sound-track excerpts)
        Vol. 1 (JA   33   King K22G 7043)
             Godzilla (4 bands) (plus 10 nongenre films)

        Vol. 2 (JA   33   King K22G 7044)
             Rodan (3), The Mysterians (3), (plus 7 nongenre films)

<u>Vol. 3</u> (JA   33   King K22G 7045)
    Varan the Unbelievable (4), Battle in Outer Space (3),
    The Three Treasures (3) (plus 4 nongenre films)

<u>Vol. 4</u> (JA   33   King K22G 7046)
    King Kong vs. Godzilla (3), Atragon (3), (plus 5 non-
    genre films)

<u>Vol. 5</u> (JA   33   King K22G 7047)
    Godzilla vs. the Thing (3), Dogora the Space Monster
    (2) (plus 5 nongenre films)

<u>Vol. 6</u> (JA   33   King K22G 7048)
    Ghidrah (3), Frankenstein Conquers the World (2) (4
    nongenre)

<u>Vol. 7</u> (JA   33   King K22G 7049)
    Monster Zero (3) (plus 7 nongenre films)

<u>Vol. 8</u> (JA   33   King K22G 7050)
    Majin (3), Yog--Monster from Space (2), Latitude Zero
    (4), Majin Strikes Again (2) (plus 4 nongenre films)

<u>Vol. 9</u> (JA   33   King K22G 7051)
    Destroy All Monsters (3), King Kong Escapes (3) (6
    nongenre)

<u>Vol. 10</u> (JA   33   King K22G 7052)
    Terror of Mecha-Godzilla (1), War of the Gargantuas (3)
    (3 nongenre)

<u>BBC Space Themes</u>
    (GB   33   BBC REH 324) Issued 1979. Original themes from
British tv shows.
    Blake's Seven (Simpson)
    A for Andromeda (Duncan)
    Case of the Ancient Astronauts (Howell)
    Dr. Who (Grainer)
    Moonbase 3 (Simpson)
    Quatermass Experiment (classical--Holst)
    The Sky at Night (classical--Wasserman)
    Tomorrow's World (Dankworth)
    (and other bands)

<u>Big Terror Movie Themes</u>/Geoff Love Orchestra
    (GB   33   MFP 50248)
    Rollerball
    (others/nfd)

<u>Children's TV Themes</u>/Cy Payne Orchestra
    (GB   33   Contour 2870-185, issued 1972)

Dr. Who (Grainer)
Thunderbirds Are Go (Gray)
Fireball XL-5 (Gray)
Stingray (Gray)
Star Trek (Courage)
Joe 90 (Gray)
Captain Scarlet and the Mysterons (Gray)
U.F.O. (Gray)
(plus 4 nongenre tv themes)

The Classic Horror Music of Hans J. Salter
(US   33   Tony Thomas TT-HS-4, p/r, 1980) Original sound-
track excerpts, actually composed by Salter and others (see
comp. list)
    The Creature from the Black Lagoon (15 min. suite)
    The Incredible Shrinking Man (16 min. suite)

Close Encounters and Other Galactic Themes/Geoff Love Orchestra
(GB   33   MFP 50375)
    Close Encounters of the Third Kind (Williams)
    The Omega Man (Grainer)
    The Time Machine (Garcia)
    (others/nfd)

Destination Moon and Other Themes
(US   33   Cinema LP 8005, b/r, 1974.) Although jacket reads
"Performed by the Hollywood Cinema Orchestra," bands are
compiled from previously released foreign and out-of-print American records and 45's.
    Destination Moon (full score, from 1959 Omega OSL-3
    record)
    Forbidden Planet (Barron)
    The Time Machine (Garcia)
    Barbarella (Crewe & Fox)
    Beyond the Moon (uncredited/nfd)
    Forbidden Island (Laszlo--nongenre)
    Moonraker (uncredited/nfd; not the 007 film)
    Master of the World (Baxter)
    The Lost Continent (Lavagnino--nongenre)

E.T. and Star Wars--The Best 12 Arts of John Williams/Film Studio Orch.
(JA   33   Victor VIP 7321)
    Star Wars
    E.T.
    (others/nfd)

Fantascienza
(IT   33   Blu BLRL 15001, p/r) Original soundtrack excerpts,
w/d.
    The Beast from 20,000 Fathoms (Buttolph)

Forbidden Planet (Barron)
Them! (Kaper)
The Thing (Tiomkin)
Village of the Damned (Goodwin)
War of the Worlds (Stevens)

The Fantastic Film Music of Albert Glasser, vol. 1
    (US 33   Starlog SR-1001, 1978) Original sound-track excerpts.
    The Amazing Colossal Man (9 min. suite)
    Beginning of the End (1 band)
    The Cyclops (1 band)
    The Boy and the Pirates (18 min. suite)
    (plus 4 nongenre films)

The Fantasy Film World of Bernard Herrmann
    (US 33   London Phase-4 SP-44207) Issued 1974. Special
    pressing for Science Fiction Book Club as Great Science Fiction
    Film Music, London CSL-1001. Bernard Herrmann conducts the
    Royal Philharmonic Orchestra.
    Journey to the Center of the Earth (15 min. suite)
    The 7th Voyage of Sinbad (8 min. suite--3 bands)
    The Day the Earth Stood Still (11 min. suite)
    Fahrenheit 451 (11 min. suite)

The Fantasy World of Japanese Pictures
    (6-record set, individually packaged, issued 1978-79) Original
    excerpts.
    Part 1 (JA   33   Toho AX-8106)
        Battle in Outer Space (Ifukube--1), Gorath (Ishii--4),
        The Mysterians (Ifukube--4), The Three Treasures
        (Ifukube--8)

    Part 2 (JA   33   Toho AX-8107)
        Dogora, the Space Monster (Ifukube--3), Varan the Un-
        believable (Ifukube--4), Rodan (Ifukube--4), The H-
        Man (Sato--2), Secret of the Telegian (Ikeno--2), At-
        tack of the Mushroom People (Sadao--2), The Human
        Vapor (Miyauchi--3)

    Part 3 (JA   33   Toho AX-8108) (all Ifukube)
        Atragon (2), Latitude Zero (8), Frankenstein Conquers
        the World (4), War of the Gargantuas (5), Yog, Mon-
        ster from Space (2)

    Part 4 (JA   33   Toho AX-8123)
        Mothra (Koseki--3), Legend of the White Serpent (Dan--
        3), The Last War (Dan--5), King Kong Escapes
        (Ifukube--4), Submersion of Japan (Sato--1), Catas-
        trophe 1999 (Tomita--1), Espy (Hirao--1), The War in
        Space (Tsushima--1)

Part 5 (JA   33   Toho AX-8124)
　　The Little Prince and the 8-Headed Dragon (Ifukube--
　　19), Invaders from Space (Watanabe--1), The X from
　　Outer Space (Izumi--1), Body Snatcher from Hell
　　(Kikuchi--1), War of the Insects (Kikuchi, 1), Monster
　　from a Prehistoric Planet (Omori--1)

Part 6 (JA   33   Toho AX-8125) (all Ifukube)
　　Majin, the Hideous Idol (8), The Return of Majin (4),
　　Majin Strikes Again (4)

I Film Della "Paura" (Films of Fear)
　　(IT   33   Beat LPF 061) Original sound-track excerpts.
　　Manhattan Baby (Frizzi)
　　E Tu Virrau Nel Terrore ... L'Aldila (Frizzi)
　　House Outside the Cemetery (Rizzati)
　　The Ripper of New York (De Masi)
　　An Open Grave ... An Empty Coffin (Piccioni)

Film Music of Bernard Herrmann
　　(US   33   Cinema LP-8000, b/r, 1975) Although jacket reads
　　"Performed by the Hollywood Cinema Orchestra," bands actually
　　compiled from foreign and out-of-print domestic records.
　　The Twisted Nerve (8 bands)
　　The Bride Wore Black (4 bands @ 45-rpm)
　　Hangover Square (piano concerto)

I Films di Dario Argento
　　(IT   33   Cinevox CIA 5009) Issued 1980. Original sound-
　　track excerpts.
　　The Bird with the Crystal Plumage (Morricone--2)
　　Cat O'Nine Tails (Morricone--2)
　　Deep Red (Goblin--2)
　　Four Flies on Grey Velvet (Morricone--2)
　　Suspiria (Goblin--3)

First Men in the Moon, and others
　　(GB   33   Unicorn/Kanchana DKP 9001; US   33   Starlog/
　　Varese SV-95002) Issued 1981. Laurie Johnson conducts the
　　London Studio Symphony Orchestra in excerpts of his scores.
　　First Men in the Moon (8 bands)
　　Dr. Strangelove (1 band)
　　Captain Kronos, Vampire Hunter (2 bands)
　　Hedda (8 bands, nongenre)

Galactic Hits/The Odyssey Orchestra
　　(US   33   Sine Qua Non SQN 7808, 1980)
　　The Empire Strikes Back (Williams--3 bands)
　　Close Encounters of the Third Kind (Williams--1)
　　Star Wars (Williams--2)
　　2001: A Space Odyssey (classical--1)

     Star Trek (Courage, tv--1)
     Superman (Williams--1)

Gamera
   (JA   33   Daiei KKS-4026) Issued early 70's.   Excerpts, w/d,
music and songs.
    Gammera the Invincible (Yamaguchi)
    Gamera vs. Barugon (Kinoshita)
    Gamera vs. Gaos (Yamaguchi)
    Gamera vs. Guiron (Kikuchi)
    Gamera vs. Viras (Hirose)

Gamera II
   (JA   33   Daiei KKS-4031) Issued early 70's.   Excerpts, w/d,
music and songs.
    Gamera vs. Viras (Hirose)
    Gamera vs. Monster X (Kikuchi)
    Gamera vs. Zigra (Kikuchi)

Gamera
   (JA   33   Toho AX 8120) Issued 1978.   Original sound-track
excerpts.
    Gammera the Invincible (Yamaguchi--3 bands)
    Gamera vs. Barugon (Konoshita--3)
    Gamera vs. Gaos (Yamaguchi--3)
    Gamera vs. Virus (Hirose--2)
    Gamera vs. Guiron (Kikuchi--3)
    Gamera vs. Monster X (Kikuchi--1)
    Gamera vs. Zigra (Kikuchi--1)

Godzilla!
   (JA   33   Toho AX 8100) Issued 1978.   Original sound-track
excerpts.
    Godzilla (Ifukube--3 bands)
    Ghidrah the Three-Headed Monster (Ifukube--2)
    King Kong vs. Godzilla (Ifukube--4)
    Destroy All Monsters (Ifukube--1)
    Terror of Mecha-Godzilla (Ifukube--2)
    Son of Godzilla (Sato--1)
    Godzilla vs. Cosmic Monster (Sato--1)
    Godzilla vs. The Thing (Ifukube--3)
    Monster Zero (Ifukube--2)

Godzilla! Vol. 2
   (JA   33   Toho AX 8112) Issued 1979.   Reissued 1983 on JA
   33   Columbia CZ-7057.   Original sound-track excerpts.
    Godzilla (Ifukube--6)
    King Kong vs. Godzilla (Ifukube--3)
    Godzilla vs. The Thing (Ifukube--4)
    Ghidrah, the Three-Headed Monster (Ifukube--1)
    Monster Zero (Ifukube--2)

Godzilla vs. the Sea Monster (Sato--1)
Son of Godzilla (Sato--2)
Destroy All Monsters (Ifukube--2)
Godzilla vs. the Smog Monster (Manabe--1)

Godzilla! Vol. 3
(JA   33   Toho AX-8147) Issued 1980.   Reissued 1983 on JA
33   Columbia CZ-7058.   Original sound-track excerpts.
Godzilla (Ifukube--2)
Destroy All Monsters (Ifukube--2)
Godzilla vs. the Smog Monster (Manabe--1)
Godzilla vs. Megalon (Manabe--3)
Son of Godzilla (Sato--1)
Godzilla vs. Cosmic Monster (Sato--6)
Monster Zero (Ifukube--1)
Godzilla vs. the Sea Monster (Sato--1)
King Kong vs. Godzilla (Ifukube--1)
Godzilla on Monster Island (Miyauchi--2)

Godzilla! Vol. 4
(JA   33   Columbia CZ 7068) Issued 1983.   Original sound-
track excerpts.
Godzilla vs. the Smog Monster (Manabe)
(others/nfd)

Godzilla! Vol. 5
(JA   33   Columbia CZ-7069) Issued 1983.   Original sound-
track excerpts.
Godzilla vs. Megalon (Manabe)
(others/nfd)

Godzilla Original Background Music, vol. 1
(JA   33   Columbia CX 7020) Issued 1982.   Original sound-
track excerpts.
Godzilla (Ifukube)
Gigantis, the Fire Monster (Sato)
Godzilla vs. The Thing (Ifukube)
Monster Zero (Ifukube)
Son of Godzilla (Sato)

Godzilla Original Background Music, vol. 2
(JA   33   Columbia CX 7021) Issued 1982.   Original sound-
track excerpts.
(nfd)

Godzilla Tradition (aka Godzilla Densetsu)
(JA   33   StarChild K28G 7110) nst: 12 themes from Godzilla films newly arranged for synthesizer by Makoto Inoue.
(nfd)

Godzilla collections--various; issued early 70's. Many nst.
JA   33   Toho DX 1004 (collection of themes/nfd)
JA   33   Toho DC-1001 (7" lp; collection of themes/nfd)
JA   33   Toho DX-1009 (Movie and TV Themes lp includes
            Godzilla vs. Cosmic Monster/nfd)
JA   45   Toho AS-1027 (Godzilla Christmas song, r/r Kenbo
            Kaminarimon)
JA   45   Toho DU-1001 (Godzilla Hit, r/r themes/nfd)
JA   45   Toho DU-1003 (themes, r/r same person as DU-1001/
            nfd)
JA   45   Toho DS-1004 (Godzilla rock & roll/nfd)

Great Fantasy Film Music
    (US   33   Poo LP 106, b/r, 1979) Original and r/r themes.
        The Time Machine (Garcia)
        Sinbad and the Eye of the Tiger (Budd)
        The Dunwich Horror (Baxter)
        Solaris (Artimiev)
        Daughters of Darkness (De Roubiax)
        Varan the Unbelievable (Ifukube)
        The Witches (Morricone/Piccioni)
        The Scars of Dracula (Bernard)
        Son of Blob (Garson)
        Circus of Horrors (song only)
        Dead Ringer (Previn--nongenre)
        Twilight Zone (episode "Walking Distance" [Herrmann] as
            "Convulsions Love Theme" and episode "Back There"
            [Goldsmith] as "Kingdom of the Spiders")
        Children of the Damned (Goodwin)
        Snow Devils (Lavagnino)
        The Chosen [Holocaust 2000] (Morricone)
        Message from Space (Morioka)
        The 7 Faces of Dr. Lao (Harline, r/r L. Schifrin)

Great Science Fiction Film Music
    (US   33   Poo LP 104, b/r, 1978) Original and r/r themes.
        Jack the Giant Killer (Sawtell & Shefter)
        Kiss of the Vampire (Bernard, w/fx)
        Godzilla (Ifukube)
        Theatre of Blood (Lewis)
        Danger: Diabolik (Morricone)
        Return of Dracula [Curse of Dracula] (Fried)
        The Omega Man (Grainer)
        The Time Machine (Garcia, different excerpt from LP-106)
        The Green Slime (Tsushima)
        The First Men in the Moon (Johnson)
        The Blob (Bacharach)
        Damnation Alley (Goldsmith)
        The Mysterians (Ifukube)
        Dracula Has Risen from the Grave (Bernard, w/fx)
        War of the Worlds (Stevens)

Kronos (Sawtell & Shefter)
I Bury the Living (Fried)
Mothra (Koseki, adapted by Ifukube)
The List of Adrian Messenger (Goldsmith--nongenre)
The Incredible Shrinking Man (Carling & Lawrence, r/r Ray
    Anthony)

Greatest Science Fiction Hits/Neil Norman & His Cosmic Orchestra
    (US   33   GNP Crescendo GNPS 2128) Issued 1979. Pop ar-
rangements by Norman and Les Baxter.
    Moonraker (Barry--theme)
    Alien (Goldsmith--1 band)
    Star Trek (Courage--theme)
    Battlestar Galactica (Phillips--theme)
    The Outer Limits (Frontiere--theme)
    Close Encounters of the Third Kind (Williams--1 band)
    Superman (Williams--2 bands)
    Star Wars (Williams--theme)
    Space: 1999 (Gray--theme)
    The Day the Earth Stood Still (Herrmann--1 band [Radar])
    Godzilla (Ifukube--1 band)
    2001: A Space Odyssey (classical--1 band)
    One Step Beyond (Lubin--theme)
    The Black Hole (Barry--1 band)
    (plus 3 original compositions by Norman [1] and Les Bax-
        ter [2])

Greatest Science Fiction Hits II/Neil Norman & His Cosmic Orchestra
    (US   33   GNP Crescendo GNPS 2133) Issued 1981. Pop ar-
rangements by Norman and Les Baxter.
    Star Wars/The Empire Strikes Back (Williams--7 min. suite)
    Voyage to the Bottom of the Sea (Sawtell--theme)
    Sinbad and the Eye of the Tiger (Budd--1 band)
    The Time Tunnel (Williams--theme)
    The Twilight Zone (Herrmann & Constant themes)
    Star Trek: The Motion Picture (Goldsmith--theme)
    Buck Rogers in the 25th Century (Larson--theme)
    War of the Satellites (Hamilton--1 band)
    Dr. Who (Grainer--theme)
    The Adventures of Superman (Klatzkin--theme)
    Dark Star (Carpenter--5 min. suite)
    (plus 3 original compositions by Norman [1] and Les Bax-
        ter [2])

Greatest Science Fiction Hits III/Neil Norman
    (US   33   GNP Crescendo GNPS 2163) Issued 1983. Pop ar-
rangements by Norman and Hall Daniels.
    Lost in Space (Williams--2 themes)
    Land of the Giants (Williams--theme)
    The Prisoner (Grainer--theme)

The Thing (Tiomkin--1 band)
War of the Worlds (Stevens--1 band)
Angry Red Planet (Dunlap--1 band)
Space: 1999 (Wadsworth--2nd season theme)
Capricorn One (Goldsmith--1 band)
Blade Runner (Vangelis--1 band)
The Invaders (Frontiere--theme)
E.T. (Williams--1 band)
Flash Gordon (Queen--1 band)
Star Trek: episode "The Cage" (Courage--"Vena's [sic]
    Dance")
Return of the Jedi (Williams--suite)
U.F.O. (Gray--theme)
Raiders of the Lost Ark (Williams--1 band)
(Plus 2 original compositions by Norman)

Die Grössten Science Fiction Hits
    GE   33   Delta AS 19020; compiles 23 themes from preceding
    three Neil Norman lp's into one 2/lp set, 1983

Hammer Presents Dracula/Philip Martell conducting the Hammer
City Orch.
    (GB   Studio 2 TWOA 5001; also on US   33   Capitol 11340)
    Issued 1974. Side 1 contains music from HORROR OF DRACULA
    and other Hammer Dracula films beneath an original story nar-
    rated by Christopher Lee. Side 2 contains suites, arranged
    and conducted by Hammer's music director, Philip Martell.
        Fear in the Night (McCabe)
        She (Bernard)
        The Vampire Lovers (Robinson)
        Dr. Jekyll and Sister Hyde (Whitaker)

Horror and Science Fiction Box Office
    (FR   33   Milan A-120-157) Issued 1982. Original excerpts.
        Inseminoid (Scott--1)
        Escape from New York (Carpenter--2)
        Phantasm (Myrow & Seagrave--3)
        Mad Max (May--3)
        The Howling (Donaggio--1)
        Patrick (May--1)
        Maniac (Chattaway--2)
        The Day After Halloween (May--1)
        Tourist Trap (Donaggio--1)
        The Day Time Ended (Band--1)

Horror Movie Special see: Screen Super Special '83

Horror Rhapsody
    (US   33   Citadel CT-6026, p/r, 1978, as Music for Franken-
    stein, Dracula, The Mummy, The Wolf Man and Other Old
    Friends; remastered reissue on Citadel CT 7012, 1979, as

Horror Rhapsody. Also on FR   33   Decca 900.411, 1979, as
Horror Rhapsody/Malpertuis.) On the Citadel lp's, side 1 contains music from HORROR EXPRESS (John Cacavas); on the
Decca lp it contains George Delerue's Malpertuis score. Side 2
contains "Horror Rhapsody," a 24-minute suite comprised of
original themes composed by Hans J. Salter (and others) for
1940's Universal horror films. According to G. Roger Hammonds, the sequence is as follows: "The first half of the suite
is comprised of themes from the last half of MAN MADE MON-
STER with brief themes from SON OF FRANKENSTEIN. These
are followed by BLACK FRIDAY which segues into THE MUM-
MY'S HAND and the "Lament" from SON OF FRANKENSTEIN.
The last five minutes of themes with their air of patriotism and
slapstick are as yet unidentified."

Les Meilleures Musiques de Films Fantastiques/Goblin
    (JA   33   Polydor/Cinevox 2393 327)   Original sound-track
    excerpts.
        Alien Contamination
        Dawn of the Dead
        Deep Red
        Patrick
        Suspiria

Monster King Godzilla (also called Godzilla, vol. 1)
    (JA   33   Columbia CS 7190) Issued 1980. Original sound-
    track excerpts, w/d, w/fx.
        Ghidrah, the Three-Headed Monster (Ifukube)
        Godzilla vs. The Thing (Ifukube)
        Godzilla vs. Cosmic Monster (Sato)
        (others nfd)

Monster Themes
    (JA   33   DR 1001) Issued early 70's. Original excerpts,
    w/d.
        Godzilla (Ifukube)
        Godzilla vs. the Smog Monster (Manabe)
        Godzilla vs. The Thing (Ifukube)
        Mothra (Koseki)
        Godzilla on Monster Island (Miyauchi)

Music for Frankenstein, Dracula, The Mummy, The Wolf Man and
Other Old Friends see: Horror Rhapsody

Music for Monsters, Munsters, Mummies and Other TV Fiends/
Milton DeLugg
    (US   33   Epic LN 24125/LS 26125) r/r themes
        The Addams Family (Mizzy)
        Alfred Hitchcock Presents (Gounod, arranged S. Wilson)
        Bewitched (Berker & Haskell)
        The Original TV Adventures of King Kong (Laws)

    The Outer Limits (Frontiere)
    (plus non-film themes by DeLugg)

Music for the Great Movie Thrillers/Bernard Herrmann and L.P.O.
    (US   33   London Phase-4 SP 44126; 1973. Reissued 1980 on
    JA   33   London K28P 4002 as Music from the Great Hitchcock
    Thrillers.) Suites and excerpts from Hitchcock film scores;
    composer Herrmann conducts the London Philharmonic Orches-
    tra.
        Psycho (14 min. suite)
        Marnie (10 min. suite)
        North by Northwest (overture, nongenre)
        Vertigo (10 min. suite)
        The Trouble with Harry (8 min. suite, nongenre)

Music from the Galaxies/Ettore Stratta and L.S.O.
    (US   33   CBS IM 35876; 1980. Also on JA   33   Warner Bros.
    P 13002 W). R/r themes; Stratta conducts London Symphony
    Orchestra. Digital Recording. (Reissued nondigital 1982 on
    US   33   CBS FM 37266)
        Meteor (Rosenthal)
        Superman (Williams)
        Moonraker (Barry)
        Star Wars (Williams)
        Alien (Goldsmith)
        The Black Hole (Barry)
        Battlestar Galactica (Phillips)
        Star Trek (Goldsmith)

Musiques de Films D'Horreur et de Catastrophes/Geoff Love
Orchestra
    (FR   33   MFP MFP2M 046-96966) r/r excerpts, w/fx.
        Kiss of the Vampire (Bernard)
        Dracula Has Risen from the Grave (Bernard)
        King Kong (Steiner)
        Theatre of Blood (Lewis)
        (others/nfd)

The Mysterious Film World of Bernard Herrmann/B. Herrmann and
N.P.O.
    (US   33   London Phase-4 SPC 21137) Issued 1975. Herrmann
    conducts the National Philharmonic Orchestra.
        Mysterious Island (5 bands)
        Jason and the Argonauts (4 bands)
        The Three Worlds of Gulliver (13 bands)

No Strings Attached/Barry Gray Orchestra
    (GB   33   PRT DOW-3; 10" lp) Issued 1981. Gray conducts
    his themes.
        Thunderbirds
        Joe 90

Stingray
Captain Scarlet and the Mysterons

Pops in Space/John Williams and the Boston Pops Orchestra
    (US   33   Philips 9500 921; also on JA   33   Philips 28 PC 1)
    Issued 1980. Williams conducts his film music.
        Star Wars (2 bands)
        Close Encounters of the Third Kind (10 min. suite, in-
            cludes music from The Special Edition)
        Superman (2 bands)
        The Empire Strikes Back (3 bands)

S.F. and Spectacle Themes
    (JA   33   Seven Seas K16P 4033) Issued 1981. Excerpts,
    some r/r.
        Space Cruiser Yamato (Miyagawa)
        Godzilla (Ifukube)
        Planet of the Apes (Goldsmith)
        Meteor (Rosenthal)
        Orca: The Killer Whale (Morricone)
        Star Trek: The Motion Picture (Goldsmith)
        Star Wars (Williams)

S.F. Fact Vol. 1/Electoru Polyphonic Orchestra
    (JA   33   Mu-Land LZ 7016-M) Issued 1979. Pop arrange-
    ments of themes.
        No Blade of Grass (Nelius-Carroll)
        Zero Population Growth (Hodge)
        Fahrenheit 451 (Herrmann)
        A Clockwork Orange (Carlos & Elkind)
        Westworld (Karlin)
        The Day the Fish Came Out (Theodorakis)
        The Andromeda Strain (Melle)
        Barbarella (Crew & Fox)
        Close Encounters of the Third Kind (Williams)
        Damnation Alley (aka Survival Run; Goldsmith)

S.F. Fact Vol. 2/Electoru Polyphonic Orchestra
    (JA   33   Mu-Land LZ 7017-M) Issued 1979. Pop arrange-
    ments.
        The Time Tunnel (Williams)
        Zardoz (Munrow)
        The Day the Earth Stood Still (Herrmann)
        2001: A Space Odyssey (classical)
        Solaris (classical excerpt)
        Planet of the Apes (Goldsmith)
        The Golden Voyage of Sinbad (Rozsa)
        The 7th Voyage of Sinbad (Herrmann)
        Rocketship X-M (Grofe)
        Forbidden Planet (Barron)
        The Island of Dr. Moreau (Rosenthal)
        7 Cities to Atlantis [Warlords of Atlantis] (Vickers)

Satan Superstar/Stanley Black and N.P.O.
  (GB   33   Decca PFS 4432; also on JA   33   London GP 9051)
  Issued 1978. Suites and excerpts; Stanley Black conducts National Philharmonic.
      Dr. Jekyll and Mr. Hyde (Waxman, 10 min. suite)
      Rosemary's Baby (Komeda--1 band)
      Exorcist II: The Heretic (Morricone--1 band)
      The Omen (Goldsmith--1 band)
      (other epic & suspense films)

Science Fiction Film Music Evening--Symphonic Fantasia #1 Through #3
      JS   33   StarChild K20G 7169/0 Issued 1983. (Themes from
              Akira Ifukube's science fiction films, r/r Tokyo
              Symphony Orchestra/nfd) nst

Science Fiction Film Themes (issued 1983)
      Volume 1 (JA   33   StarChild K22G 7111)   28 bands
          Godzilla (Ifukube)
          Godzilla's Revenge (Miyauchi)
          Atragon (Ifukube)

      Volume 2 (JA   33   StarChild K22G 7112)   21 bands
          King Kong vs. Godzilla (Ifukube)
          Mothra (Koseki)
          Rodan (Ifukube)

      Volume 3 (JA   33   StarChild K22G 7113)   16 bands
          Godzilla vs. The Thing (Ifukube)
          Dogora, the Space Monster (Ifukube)
          Battle in Outer Space (Ifukube)

      Volume 4 (JA   33   StarChild K22G 7114)   27 bands
          Ghidrah, the Three-Headed Monster (Ifukube)
          Attack of the Mushroom People (Sadao)

      Volume 5 (JA   33   StarChild K22G 7115)   16 bands
          Monster Zero (Ifukube)
          Varan the Unbelievable (Ifukube)
          Gorath (Ifukube)

      Volume 6 (JA   33   StarChild K22G 7116)   16 bands
          King Kong Escapes (Ifukube)
          (others)

      Volume 7 (JA   33   StarChild K22G 7117)   14 bands
          Destroy All Monsters (Ifukube)
          (others)

      Volume 8 (JA   33   StarChild K22G 7118)   18 bands
          Frankenstein Conquers the World (Ifukube)
          Godzilla vs. Megalon (Manabe)

Volume 9 (JA   33   StarChild K22G 7119)   20 bands
   Godzilla vs. Cosmic Monster (Sato)
   Terror of Mecha-Godzilla (Ifukube)
   (others)

Volume 10 (JA   33   StarChild K22G 7120)   23 bands
   The Mysterians (Ifukube)
   Catastrophe 1999 (Tomita)
   (others)

Volume 11 (JA   33   StarChild K22G 7147)   13 bands from 4
"Gamera" films; Yamaguchi, Konoshita/nfd

Volume 12 (JA   33   StarChild K22G 7148)   11 bands from 4
s.f. films; Ifukube/nfd

Volume 13 (JA   33   StarChild K22G 7149)   20 bands from 5
s.f. films; Ifukube, Sato/nfd

Volume 14 (JA   33   StarChild K22G 7150)   11 bands from 11
s.f./monster films; Sato, etc./nfd

Screen Super Special '83:   Best S.F. Screen Themes
   (JA   33   Seven Seas K18P4101) Issued 1983.   2 original excerpts, 16 r/r themes.
      (nfd)

Screen Super Special '83:   Horror Movie Special
   (JA   33   Seven Seas K18P 4105) Issued 1983.   11 original
   excerpts, 5 r/r themes.
      Dawn of the Dead [Zombi] (Goblin)
      Beyond the Door II [Shock] (Libra)
      L'Anticristo (Morricone & Nicolai)
      Autopsy [The Victim] (Morricone)
      Phantasm (Myrow & Seagrave)
      Bird with the Crystal Plumage (Morricone)
      Tenabre (Simonetti, Pignatelli & Morante)
      (others)

Space Adventure Vol. 1/Electoru Polyphonic Orchestra
   (JA   33   Mu-Land LZ 7018-M) Issued 1983.   Pop arrangements.
      (nfd)

Space Adventure Vol. 2/Electoru Polyphonic Orchestra
   (JA   33   Mu-Land LZ 7019-M) Issued 1983.   Pop arrangements.
      Invaders from Mars (Kraushaar)
      (others/nfd)

Space Invaded--BBC Space Themes
    (GB   33   BBC REH 442) Issued 1982. British tv themes.
       Tomorrow's World (Dankworth)
       K9 and Co. (nfd)
       Dr. Who (Grainer)
       The Sky at Night (Classical)
       Space Shuttle (Wasserman)
       The Comet Is Coming (nfd)

Squalo--Exorcista e Altri Film Della Paura (Films of Fear)
    (IT   33   Cinevox CIA 5014)
       Godzilla (Ifukube)
       Alien Contamination (Goblin)
       Bird with the Crystal Plumage (Morricone)
       Dawn of the Dead [Zombi] (Goblin)
       Patrick (Goblin--Italian release)
       Beyond the Door 2 [Shock] (Libra)
       Jaws (Williams)
       7 Note in Nero (nfd)

Star Wars and Other Space Themes/Geoff Love Orchestra
    (GB   33   MFP 50355) r/r themes.
       Star Wars (Williams)
       U.F.O. (Gray)
       Star Trek (Courage)
       Barbarella (Crewe & Fox)
       Space: 1999 (Gray)
       2001: A Space Odyssey (classical)
       Things to Come (Bliss)
       Thunderbirds (Gray)
       Dr. Who (Grainer)
       When Worlds Collide (Stevens)
       The Quatermass Experiment (tv; classical--Holst)

The Star Wars Trilogy/Varujan Kojin
    (US   33   Varese Sarabande 704.210; GB   33   That's Enter-
    tainment TER 1067) Issued 1983. Digital recording, symphonic
    suites.
       Star Wars (3 bands)
       The Empire Strikes Back (4 bands)
       Return of the Jedi (6 bands, all of side 2; includes 2 bands
          not on sound-track lp)

Theme from Star Trek and Planet of the Apes/Jeff Wayne Space
Shuttle
    (US   33   Wonderland WLP-301) r/r themes
       Star Trek (Courage)
       Planet of the Apes (tv, Schifrin)
       Batman (Hefti)
       Adventures of Superman (Klatzkin)

Theme from Star Wars/Wonderland Space Shuttle
   (US   33   Wonderland WLP 313) r/r themes.
      Star Wars (Williams)
      The Bionic Woman (Fielding)
      (others/nfd)

Themes for Superheroes/Geoff Love Orchestra
   (GB   33   MFP 50439) r/r themes.
      Bionic Woman (Fielding)
      Blake's Seven (Simpson)
      Dr. Who (Grainer)
      The Incredible Hulk (Harnell)
      Spiderman (Ellis)
      Wonder Woman (Fox)

Themes from E.T. and More/Walter Murphy Orchestra
   (US   33   MCA 6114) Issued 1982. r/r themes.
      E.T. (Williams)
      Close Encounters of the Third Kind (Williams)
      Jaws (Williams)
      Star Trek (Courage)
      Raiders of the Lost Ark (Williams)
      Superman (Williams)
      Poltergeist (Goldsmith)

Themes from Horror Movies/Dick Jacobs Orchestra
   (US   33   Coral CRL 57240) Issued c.1970. r/r excerpts,
   with sound effects and narration between bands. Remastered
   reissue, without effects and narration, issued 1978 on Varese
   Sarabande VC 81077 as Themes from Classic Science Fiction,
   Fantasy and Horror Films. Also on JA   33   MCA VIM 7264,
   and on FR   33   MCA/Barclay 410.064 as Les Grands Themes
   du Cinema et Fantastique et de Science Fiction.
      Son of Dracula (Salter)
      The Incredible Shrinking Man (Carling & Lawrence)
      This Island Earth (Stein)
      The Mole People (Salter)
      The House of Frankenstein (Salter & Dessau)
      The Horror of Dracula (Bernard--2 bands)
      The Creature from the Black Lagoon (Salter & Stein)
      It Came from Outer Space (Stein)
      The Creature Walks Among Us (Mancini)
      The Deadly Mantis (Lava)
      Tarantula (Mancini)
      Revenge of the Creature (Stein)

Themes from Star Trek and Planet of the Apes/Jeff Wayne Space
Shuttle
   (US   33   Wonderland WLP-301) r/r themes
      Star Trek (Courage)
      Planet of the Apes (tv, Schifrin)

12 Terrifiantes Bandes Originales de Films
   (FR   33   Arabella MCA 204880) nfd
      Earthquake (Williams)
      Jaws (Williams)
      Airport (Newman--nongenre)
      Krakatoa East of Java (De Vol--nongenre)
      Rollercoaster (Schifrin--nongenre)
      Jaws 2 (Williams)
      The Deadly Mantis (Lava)
      Sorcerer (Tangerine Dream--nongenre)
      Dracula (Williams)
      The Andromeda Strain (Melle)
      Buck Rogers in the 25th Century (Larson)
      Battlestar Galactica (Phillips)

Works of Akira Ifukube
   (JA   33   Toho AX 8086) Issued 1978. Original sound-track
   excerpts.
      Godzilla (2 bands)
      Rodan (1)
      King Kong vs. Godzilla (1)
      The Three Treasures (1)
      Majin (1)
      The Mysterians (1)
      (plus 7 nongenre films)

Further Resources

For further information, the following regular publications contain material of interest to the film music researcher and enthusiast:

Soundtrack! The Collector's Quarterly
Editor: Luc Van De Ven
Astridlaan 171, 2800 Mechelen, Belgium.
U.S. orders: P.O. Box 3599, Hollywood, CA 90078.
(The magazine is written in English)

CinemaScore: The Film Music Journal
Editor: Randall D. Larson
P.O. Box 70868, Sunnyvale, Ca. 94086

Score
Editor: Julius Wolthuis
Cinemusica, Postbus 406, 8200 AK Lelystad, Holland.
(The magazine is written in Dutch)

Pro Musica Sana
(The Journal of the Miklos Rozsa Society)
Editor: John Fitzpatrick
319 Avenue C., No. 11-H, New York, NY 10009

The New Zealand Film Music Bulletin
Editor: Colin A. Adamson
35 Jenkin Street, Invercargill, New Zealand.

In addition to these and more specialized society newsletters
and journals, the following magazines feature a regular column on
film music:

Cinefantastique (P.O. Box 270, Oak Park, IL 60303; interview
    column)
Films in Review (209 East 66th St., #4C, New York, NY 10021;
    opinion column)
Cinemacabre (P.O. Box 10005, Baltimore, MD 21204; review
    column)
Midnight Marquee (5910 Glen Falls Av., Baltimore, MD 21206;
    regular essays)

Filmography

John Barry: CLASH OF THE TITANS (81; score rejected; replaced
    by L. Rosenthal); THE RIGHT STUFF (83; score rejected; re-
    placed by B. Conti)
Malcolm Clarke (Br.): DR. WHO (71-82, tv; episodes: Dr. Who
    and the Sea Devils, Earthshock, others)
Klaus Doldinger (W. Gm.): THE NEVERENDING STORY (84; w/G.
    Moroder)
Johnny Douglas (Br.): DAY OF THE TRIFFIDS (63; additional mu-
    sic, uncredited; main score: R. Goodwin)
Murphy Dunne: SPACE RAIDERS (83)
Ron Goodwin (Br.): THE DAY OF THE TRIFFIDS (63; includes
    additional music, uncredited, by J. Douglas); UNIDENTIFIED
    FLYING ODDBALL (79; is aka THE SPACEMAN AND KING
    ARTHUR)
Peter Howell (Br.): DR. WHO (80-83, tv; episodes: Meglos, The
    Leisure Hive, Warrior's Gate, Kinda, Snakedance, others)
Shinshiro Ikebe (Ja.): CONAN, THE BOY IN THE FUTURE (84,
    tv)
Roger Limb (Br.): DR. WHO (81-83, tv; episodes: The Keeper
    of Traken, Four to Doomsday, Arc of Infinity, others)
D. Maas (W. Gm.): ASCENSEUR (84; The Lift)
Dennis McCarthy: V--THE FINAL BATTLE (84, tv; 2nd and 3rd
    segments, w/B. DeVorzon & J. Conlan)
Giorgio Moroder: THE NEVERENDING STORY (84; w/K. Doldinger)
Edward Powell: THE OUTER LIMITS (63-65, tv; episodes, un-
    credited, w/D. Frontiere)
Tangerine Dream (group): FIRESTARTER (84)
Toto (group): DUNE (84; w/Q. Jones)

Discography

Alien (Jerry Goldsmith, 1979)
    US   33   CBS IM 35876 (1 band on Music from the Galaxies/Et-
        tore Stratta, 1980) nst

Altered States (John Corigliano, 1981)
    US   33   RCA AGL1-5066 (reissue of ABL1-3983)

Battle Mecha-Zanbungurl (Umagano, 1982)
　　JA　33　StarChild K22G 7168 (new themes, 1984)

Battlestar Galactica (Stu Phillips, 1978)
　　US　33　CBS IM 35876 (1 band on Music from the Galaxies/Ettore Stratta, 1980) nst

Black Hole, The (John Barry, 1979)
　　US　33　CBS IM 35876 (1 band on Music from the Galaxies/Ettore Stratta, 1980) nst

Blue Thunder (Arthur B. Rubinstein, 1983)
　　US　45　MCA 52217 (7" reissue of 13966)

Brainstorm (James Horner, 1983)
　　FR　33　RCA Milan A 230
　　JA　33　Victor VIP 28084 (1984)
　　SP　33　Vinilo VSO 1002 (1984)

Conan, the Boy in the Future (Shinshiro Ikebe, 1984, tv)
　　JA　33　Canyon C25G 0194

Creatures the World Forgot (Mario Nascimbene, 1970)
　　La Lotta Del Sesso Sei Milioni di Anna Fa
　　IT　33　Kangaroo Team ZPLKT 34209(3) (1 band on Mario Nascimbene--L'Impronta del Suono, 3/lp boxed set, 1984)

Dr. Faustus (Mario Nascimbene, 1968)
　　IT　33　Kangaroo Team ZPLKT 34209(3) (1 band on Mario Nascimbene--L'Impronta del Suono, 3/lp boxed set, 1984)

Doctor Who (Ron Grainer & others, 1966+, tv)
　　GB　33　BBC 22462 (Dr. Who--The Music; same as REH 462; includes Grainer theme, episode music by M. Clarke, P. Howell, R. Limb, 1983)

Escape from New York (John Carpenter, 1981)
　　IT　33　Ricordi VIP 20285 (1984 reissue)

Final Countdown, The (John Scott, 1980)
　　US　33　Casablanca NGLP232
　　JA　33　EMI EWS 81306 (diff. cover and sequence)

Final Exam (Gary Scott, 1981)
　　US　33　AEI 3105

Finian's Rainbow (Burton Lane, 1968)
　　US　33　Warner Bros. BS 2550

Fireball XL-5 (Barry Gray, 1963, tv)
　　GB　33　Contour 2870 185 (theme on Children's TV Themes/Cy

Payne Orch., 1972) <u>nst</u>
GB   33   Century 21 LA-6 (theme on <u>Favourite TV Themes</u>/Barry Gray Orch.) <u>nst</u>
Theme reportedly released on US and GB 45 single (nfd)

<u>Firestarter</u> (Tangerine Dream, 1984)
US   33   MCA 6131

<u>First Men in the Moon, The</u> (Laurie Johnson, 1964)
US   33   Starlog/Varese Sarabande SV-95002 (1 side only, r/r
L. Johnson, 1981) <u>nst</u>
GB   33   Unicorn/Kanchana DKP 9001 (same as SV-95002) <u>nst</u>
GB   33   CS-8104 (1 band on a themes lp, nfd)
US   33   Poo LP 104 (1 band on <u>Great Science Fiction Film Music</u>, b/r, 1978)

<u>Ghostbusters</u> (Elmer Bernstein, 1984)
US   33   Arista AL8-8246 (2 Bernstein cues, 8 rock songs)

<u>Gog</u> (Harry Sukman, 1954)
US   33   Decca DL-8060 (1 band on <u>Hollywood Rhapsodies</u>/Victor Young Orch.) <u>nst</u>

<u>Gremlins</u> (Jerry Goldsmith, 1984)
US   33   Geffen GHSP 24044 Y ("mini-lp", 4 Goldsmith cues, 3 rock songs)

<u>Greystoke</u> (John Scott, 1984)
US   33   Warner Bros. 25120-1

<u>House Outside the Cemetery, The</u> (Walter Rizzatti, 1981)
Quella Villa Accanto Al Cimitero
IT   33   Beat LPF 056 (1984)

<u>Indiana Jones and the Temple of Doom</u> (John Williams, 1984)
US   33   Polydor 8215 921

<u>Island at the Top of the World, The</u> (Maurice Jarre, 1974)
US   33   Disneyland 3814 (w/d)

<u>King Kong</u> (John Barry, 1976)
SP   33   Hispavox Reprise HRES 291 88
US   45   CBS 3 10471 (song, r/r Andy Williams) <u>nst</u>
IT   45   CBS 5019 (same as 3 10471)
GB   45   Philips 6042 245 (song, r/r Demis Roussos)

<u>Krull</u> (James Horner, 1983)
FR   33   Ades Danubus 2108 (6 tracks)
GE   33   Cine Disc 205 984 (6 tracks)
(US lp has 8 tracks)

Lift, The (D. Maas, 1984)
  Ascenseur
  GE   33   Milan A 242

Locke the Superman III (various, 1982)
  JA   33   Animex CX 7142 (1984)

Lupin III (Ugi Ono, 1977, tv)
  JA   33   VAP 30140 25 (1984)

Macross--Super Time Fortress (Kentaro Haneda, 1983, tv)
  JA   33   JBX 25039 (Extra 1/Rhapsody in Love, w/d, w/fx,
     1984)
  JA   33   JBS 25040 (Extra 2/Macross in Love, w/d, w/fx, 1984)

Man with the Golden Gun, The (John Barry, 1975)
  GB   33   United Artists UAS 29671
  IT   33   United Artists UAS 29671
  JA   33   Seven Seas FML 36

Mobile Suit Gundam (various, 1980, tv)
  JA   33   StarChild K22G 7164 (Vol. 1, new themes, 1984)
  JA   33   StarChild K22G 7165 (Vol. 2, new themes, 1984)

Mysterians, The (Akira Ifukube, 1957)
  US   33   Poo LP 104 (1 band on Great Science Fiction Film Mu-
     sic, b/r, 1978)

One Million Years B.C. (Mario Nascimbene, 1966)
  Un Milione Di Anna Fa
  IT   33   Kangaroo Team ZPLKT 34209(3) (1 band on Mario
     Nascimbene--L'Impronta del Suono; 3/lp boxed set, 1984)

Psycho II (Jerry Goldsmith, 1983)
  GE   33   MCA 205 637-320

Queen Millenia (Kitaro, 1982)
  JA   33   Canyon C20G 0337 (The Best of Queen Millenia, 1984)

Reincarnation of Peter Proud, The (Jerry Goldsmith, 1975)
  US   33   Monogram JG-7711 (1 side only, original soundtrack,
     b/r, 1984)

Sisters (Bernard Herrmann, 1973)
  US   33   Entr'acte ERQ 7001-ST (quadraphonic stereo, 1975)
  US   33   Southern Cross SCAR 5004 (audiophile reissue of
     above, 1984)

Space Runaway Ideon (Koichi Sugiyama, 1980-81, tv)
  JA   33   StarChild K22G 7166 (new themes, 1984)

Splash (Lee Holdridge, 1984)
    US   33   Cherry Lane 00301

Star Trek: The Motion Picture (Jerry Goldsmith, 1979)
    US   33   CBS IM 35876 (1 band on Music from the Galaxies/Et-
    tore Stratta, 1980) nst

Star Trek III--The Search for Spock (James Horner, 1984)
    US   33   Capitol SKBK 12360
    US   45   Capitol B-5365

Star Wars (John Williams, 1977)
    US   33   CBS IM 35876 (1 band on Music from the Galaxies/Et-
    tore Stratta, 1980) nst
    GE   33   RSO 817997-1 (Star Wars Komplett; 4/lp, 1984)

Starcrash (John Barry, 1979)
    FR   33   Carrere 67333

Twilight Zone--The Movie (Jerry Goldsmith, 1983)
    IT   33   WEA 238871

Union of the 6 Gods, "God Mars", The (Wakakusa, 1982, tv)
    JA   33   StarChild K22G 7167 (new themes, 1984)

Vengeance of She, The (Mario Nascimbene, 1967)
    La Donna Venuta Dal Passato
    IT   33   Kangaroo Team KPLKT 34209(3) (1 band on Mario
    Nascimbene--L'Impronta del Suono; 3/lp boxed set, 1984)

Underscores refer to photographs